1991

Jerome Beaty
Emory University

THE NORTON INTRODUCTION TO FICTION

Second Edition

W · W · NORTON & COMPANY · NEW YORK · LONDON

Published simultaneously in Canada by George J. McLeod Limited, Toronto.
Printed in the United States of America

First Edition

W. W. Norton & Company, Inc. 500 Fifth Avenue, New York, N.Y. 10110
W. W. Norton & Company Ltd. 25 New Street Square, London EC4A 3NT

ISBN 0 393 95156-1

1 2 3 4 5 6 7 8 9 0

D. H. Lawrence: "The Rocking Horse Winner" from *The Complete Short Stories, Vol. I*, copyright © 1962 by Angelo Ravagli and C. M. Weekley, Executors of the Estate of Frieda Lawrence Ravagli. "Odour of Chrysanthemums," copyright © 1962 by Angelo Ravagli and C. M. Weekley, Executors of the Estate of Frieda Lawrence Ravagli, and "Horse Dealer's Daughter," copyright 1922 by Thomas Seltzer, Inc., renewed 1950 by Frieda Lawrence, from *The Complete Short Stories of D. H. Lawrence, Vol. II*. Reprinted by permission of Viking Penguin Inc. Excerpts from *Selected Literary Criticism*, edited by Anthony Beal, copyright © 1956 by Frieda Lawrence. Selections from *Phoenix I*, edited by Edward O. McDonald, copyright © 1936 by Frieda Lawrence, © renewed 1964 by the Estate of the late Frieda Lawrence Ravagli. Reprinted by permission of Viking Penguin, Inc.

Ursula K. Le Guin: "The Ones Who Walk Away from Omelas," copyright 1973 by Ursula K. Le Guin. Reprinted by permission of the author and the author's agent, Virginia Kidd.

Doris Lessing: "Our Friend Judith" from *A Man and Two Women*, copyright 1958, 1962, 1963 by Doris Lessing. Reprinted by permission of Simon & Schuster, a Division of Gulf and Western, and Curtis Brown Ltd. "The Temptation of Jack Orkney" from *Stories* by Doris Lessing Copyright © 1972 by Doris Lessing. Reprinted by permission of Alfred A. Knopf, Inc. and Curtis Brown Ltd.

Katherine Mansfield: "Her First Ball," copyright 1922 by Alfred A. Knopf, Inc., and renewed 1950 by John Middleton Murry. Reprinted from *The Short Stories of Katherine Mansfield* by permission of Alfred A. Knopf, Inc.

N. Scott Momaday: from *The Way to Rainy Mountain* © 1969 by the University of New Mexico Press. Reprinted by permission.

Alice Munro: "Boys and Girls" from *The Dance of the Happy Shades* by Alice Munro. Copyright © Alice Munro, 1968. Reprinted by permission of McGraw-Hill Ryerson Limited, Toronto.

Albert Murray: "Train Whistle Guitar" is reprinted by permission of the author, Albert Murray, and his agent, James Brown Associates, Inc. Copyright © 1953 by Albert Murray.

Joyce Carol Oates: "The Lady With the Pet Dog" from *Marriages and Infidelities* by Joyce Carol Oates by permission of the publisher, Vanguard Press, Inc. Copyright © 1968, 1969, 1970, 1971, 1972 by Joyce Carol Oates.

Flannery O'Connor: "The Artificial Nigger," copyright © 1955 by Flannery O'Connor. Reprinted from her volume *A Good Man Is Hard to Find and Other Stories* by permission of Harcourt Brace Jovanovich, Inc.

Tillie Olsen: "O Yes" excerpted from the book *Tell Me A Riddle* by Tillie Olsen. Copyright © 1960, 1961 by Tillie Olsen. Reprinted by permission of Delacorte Press/Seymour Lawrence.

Grace Paley: "A Conversation With My Father" from *Enormous Changes at the Last Minute* by Grace Paley. Copyright © 1972, 1974 by Grace Paley. Reprinted with the permission of Farrar, Straus & Giroux, Inc.

Mordecai Richler: "The Summer My Grandmother Was Supposed to Die" from *The Street* by Mordecai Richler. Copyright © 1975 by Mordecai Richler. Reprinted by permission of Monica McCall, International Creative Management and The Canadian Publishers McClelland and Stewart Limited, Toronto.

Isaac Bashevis Singer: "Tanhum" from *Old Love* by Isaac Bashevis Singer. Copyright © 1966, 1975, 1976, 1977, 1978, 1979 by Isaac Bashevis Singer. Reprinted by permission of Farrar, Straus and Giroux, Inc.

Chuang Tzu: "The Brigand and the Sage" and "King Mu and the Wizard" from *Three Ways of Thought in Ancient China* by Arthur Waley. Reprinted by permission of George Allen & Unwin (Publishers) Ltd.

Contents

Foreword to the Second Edition xxi
Acknowledgments xxiii

SPENCER HOLST • The Zebra Storyteller 3

A Preface to Fiction 4

ELEMENTS 7

1 Plot 7

EDGAR ALLAN POE • The Cask of Amontillado 12
RICHARD CONNELL • The Most Dangerous Game 17
ERNEST HEMINGWAY • The Short Happy Life of Francis Macomber 32

2 Focus and Voice 55

AMBROSE BIERCE • An Occurrence at Owl Creek Bridge 59
SHIRLEY JACKSON • The Lottery 66
MORDECAI RICHLER • The Summer My Grandmother Was Supposed to Die 72

3 Characterization 83

SHERWOOD ANDERSON • The Egg 88
TONI CADE BAMBARA • My Man Bovanne 95
DORIS LESSING • Our Friend Judith 100

4 Symbols 113

NATHANIEL HAWTHORNE • Young Goodman Brown 117
FLANNERY O'CONNOR • The Artificial Nigger 127

5 Theme 142

KATHERINE MANSFIELD • Her First Ball 146
ANTON CHEKHOV • The Lady with the Dog 151

KINDS AND MODES 163

6 A Kind: Initiation 163

JAMES JOYCE • Araby 165
ALICE MUNRO • Boys and Girls 169
TILLIE OLSEN • O Yes 180
WILLIAM FAULKNER • The Old People 191

7 A Mode: Fantasy 204

ARTHUR C. CLARKE • Hide and Seek 207
JORGE LUIS BORGES • The Garden of Forking Paths 215
HAL BENNETT • Dotson Gerber Resurrected 223
GABRIEL GARCIA MARQUEZ • A Very Old Man with Enormous Wings 234

8 The Short Story and Other Narratives 239

CORNPLANTER • The Great Mosquito 242
OHAYOHOK • A Human Kayak 243
AFRICAN FOLK TALE • What a Little Thing Did 246
CHUANG TZU • The Brigand and the Sage 250
CHUANG TZU • King Mu and the Wizard 254
N. SCOTT MOMADAY • *from* The Way to Rainy Mountain 256
from The Thousand Nights and a Night 260

CONTEXTS 269

9 The Author's Work 269

D. H. LAWRENCE • Odour of Chrysanthemums 274
D. H. LAWRENCE • The Horse Dealer's Daughter 284
D. H. LAWRENCE • The Rocking-Horse Winner 301
D. H. LAWRENCE • Passages from Essays and Letters 312

10 Tradition 318

AUGUSTUS BALDWIN LONGSTREET • The Horse-Swap 320
SAMUEL CLEMENS • The Celebrated Jumping Frog of Calaveras County 326
WILLIAM FAULKNER • Spotted Horses 330

11 Setting 344

KATE CHOPIN • Beyond the Bayou 346
F. SCOTT FITZGERALD • Babylon Revisited 350
JAMES BALDWIN • Sonny's Blues 366

STORIES FOR FURTHER READING 389

GEORGE WASHINGTON HARRIS • Mrs. Yardley's Quilting 389
HERMAN MELVILLE • Bartleby, the Scrivener 395
HENRY JAMES • The Tree of Knowledge 422
SIR ARTHUR CONAN DOYLE • The Adventure of the Speckled Band 432
FRANZ KAFKA • A Hunger Artist 451
ISAAC BASHEVIS SINGER • Tanhum 457
JOHN CHEEVER • The Country Husband 466
ALBERT MURRAY • Train Whistle Guitar 484
GRACE PALEY • A Conversation with My Father 497
URSULA K. LE GUIN • The Ones Who Walk Away from Omelas 501
WOODY ALLEN • The Kugelmass Episode 506
JOYCE CAROL OATES • The Lady with the Pet Dog 515

THE NOVEL 529

A Preface to the Novel 529

JOSEPH CONRAD • Heart of Darkness 537
DORIS LESSING • The Temptation of Jack Orkney 600

FOREWORD TO THE SECOND EDITION

The Norton Introduction to Fiction is both an anthology and a textbook—a "teaching anthology"—for the indispensable course in which college student and college teacher begin to read fiction seriously together. In revising for this, the Second Edition, I have tried to freshen the *anthology* with new selections that, like those they join, are both enjoyable to read and profitable to learn about, and I have tried to strengthen the *textbook* by reorganizing chapters and writing new chapter introductions, so that readers might hold, within a single volume, not merely fiction worth studying but also assistance in developing the critical tools needed for that study.

For this edition, I have chosen 44 stories, 7 short narratives that follow non-Western traditions, and 2 short novels. Of these, all the narratives, one of the short novels, and fully 30 of the stories are new. Among the additions are both deservedly familiar stories and stories that I hope will provide the quickening thrill of discovery. I have added stories by Spencer Holst, Edgar Allan Poe, Ambrose Bierce, Mordecai Richler, Toni Cade Bambara, Doris Lessing, James Joyce, Alice Munro, Arthur C. Clarke, Gabriel García Márquez, Augustus Baldwin Longstreet, Samuel Clemens, Kate Chopin, F. Scott Fitzgerald, George Washington Harris, Grace Paley, Ursula K. LeGuin, Woody Allen, and Joyce Carol Oates, added a second Faulkner story, and substituted one story by Jorge Luis Borges for earlier selections. Also new to this edition are short narratives from the American Indians and Eskimos, and from Africa, China, and the Middle East, and Doris Lessing's masterful short novel, *The Temptation of Jack Orkney*.

As before, however, *The Norton Introduction to Fiction* is meant to be more than a grab-bag of good things to read. The works are not only selected but are arranged in order to introduce a reader to the serious study of literature. Stories are first analyzed by questions of craft, the so-called elements of fiction, such as plot, characterization, and theme. Then stories are grouped by kind (initiation stories) and mode (fantasy stories), and, to show that even kinds and modes are variations within a single genre, I have added a sample of narratives other than the short story. Finally, stories are placed in broader contexts: an author's oeuvre, a particular literary tradition, and historical or cultural setting. (A fourth section of stories is left simply for further reading, as a reservoir of additional examples, for independent study or a different approach.) The first two sections are intended to support the close-reading and/or generic approach that has been familiar in literature classrooms for many years; the third section is intended to supplement and augment that approach, to suggest some ways of seeing a work of literature within its temporal and cultural frameworks. All in all, the book's arrangement seeks to facilitate the reader's movement from narrower to broader questions, mirroring the way people read—wanting to learn more as they experience more.

In or out of the classroom, the study of the short story leads almost inevitably to the study of the novel. Two short novels have been included here—*Heart of Darkness* and *The Temptation of Jack Orkney* —preceded by "A Preface to the Novel" which attempts to suggest the difference between reading a short story and a novel, and to offer a very, very brief history of the novel as a context for reading these selections—and other novels.

In this Second Edition I have reshaped my own editorial helps, striving in these revisions for ever clearer explanation, ever more straightforward organization. Each chapter is now introduced by a discussion of basic concepts necessary for talking or writing about fiction. "Plot," for example, includes definitions and discussion of the terms generally used in analyzing the narrative structure of a story, but I have tried not to get in the way of an individual instructor adding other terms and definitions or, indeed, approaching the stories in the chapter from a different direction than plot. In preparing these pedagogical aids, I have avoided overexplaining or dictating the readers' responses in advance (and some readers will want to use the book, as indeed it can be used, as a quarry for their own discoveries).

Certain editorial procedures that proved their usefulness in the First Edition have been retained. First of all, the works are annotated, as is customary in Norton anthologies; the notes are informational and not interpretative, for the aim is to help readers understand and appreciate the story, not to dictate a meaning or a response. To offer the texts in the form most immediately available to their particular audience, I have normalized spelling according to modern American usage. In order to avoid giving the impression that all literature was written at the same time, I have noted for each selection the date of first book publication (or, when preceded by a *p*, first periodical publication).

In all my work on this edition, I have been guided by teachers in other English departments and in my own, by my partners in the editing of *The Norton Introduction to Literature*, by Norton editors Barry Wade and John Benedict and their staffs, by students who wrote me as the author of the textbook they were using, and by those who were able to approach me after class as their teacher: I hope that I have been able with such help to offer you a solid and stimulating introduction to the experience of fiction.

J.B.

ACKNOWLEDGMENTS

If you are old enough to edit a textbook, you are indebted to literally hundreds of people—family, colleagues, teachers, and students. I am. If you cannot thank them wittily, it is more important anyway to thank them sincerely. I do.

I would first of all like to thank the editor of the *Norton Introduction to Poetry*, and my co-editor on the *Norton Introduction to Literature*, J. Paul Hunter of the University of Rochester. Alas, I cannot thank the late Carl E. Bain, editor of the *Norton Introduction to Drama* and also co-editor of the *Norton Introduction to Literature*, but I wish at least to acknowledge his essential assistance. The three of us together conceived the general scheme common to our volumes.

I would also like to thank my colleagues, many of whom have taught this book and evaluated my efforts, for their constant encouragement and enlightenment. Of my colleagues at Emory University, I would like especially to thank Michaelyn Burnett, Lee Pederson, Harry Rusche, Ronald Schuchard, and Floyd C. Watkins. And I thank also T. E. Blom (University of British Columbia); Frank W. Childrey (Northwest Mississippi Junior College); Randy R. Conine (El Centro College); Michael P. Dean (University of Mississippi); Stephen F. Evans (University of Kansas); Norman Feltes (York University); John M. Foley (University of Missouri); Frederick Goldberg (Clayton Junior College); Larry Gray (Southeastern Louisiana University); Christopher Hudgins (University of Nevada); Kristin Hunter (University of Pennsylvania); William Morgan (Illinois State University); Douglas Peterson (Michigan State University); Nils Peterson (San Jose State University); Ronald Schleifer (University of Oklahoma); Patricia Vicari (Scarborough College of the University of Toronto); Melissa Walker (Mercer University); and Dorothy A. Winsor (Wayne State University).

Special thanks are due to Shawn Beaty for many hours of capable assistance and to Mrs. Trudy Kretchman for her cheerful cooperation.

On several occasions during the preparation of this work a retreat from everyday was needed. The Ossabaw Island Project provided it, and I wish to thank the Ossabaw Island Foundation and particularly Eleanor West for the provision and for the grace with which it was offered.

I would also like to thank my friends at W.W. Norton & Company, especially John Benedict, Karen Fischer, Josepha Gutelius, Diane O'Connor, and Barry Wade.

The assistance, encouragement, and constructive criticism of my wife, V. Elaine Beaty, has been invaluable. Editing this book has taken many hours away from my time at home; she and the children have accepted this necessity cheerfully—but not, I trust, *too* cheerfully.

THE NORTON INTRODUCTION TO FICTION

Second Edition

SPENCER HOLST

The Zebra Storyteller

Once upon a time there was a Siamese cat who pretended to be a lion and spoke inappropriate Zebraic.

That language is whinnied by the race of striped horses in Africa.

Here now: An innocent zebra is walking in a jungle and approaching from another direction is the little cat; they meet.

"Hello there!" says the Siamese cat in perfectly pronounced Zebraic. "It certainly is a pleasant day, isn't it? The sun is shining, the birds are singing, isn't the world a lovely place to live today!"

The zebra is so astonished at hearing a Siamese cat speaking like a zebra, why—he's just fit to be tied.

So the little cat quickly ties him up, kills him, and drags the better parts of the carcass back to his den.

The cat successfully hunted zebras many months in this manner, dining on filet mignon of zebra every night, and from the better hides he made bow neckties and wide belts after the fashion of the decadent princes of the Old Siamese court.

He began boasting to his friends he was a lion, and he gave them as proof the fact that he hunted zebras.

The delicate noses of the zebras told them there was really no lion in the neighborhood. The zebra deaths caused many to avoid the region. Superstitious, they decided the woods were haunted by the ghost of a lion.

One day the storyteller of the zebras was ambling, and through his mind ran plots for stories to amuse the other zebras, when suddenly his eyes brightened, and he said, "That's it! I'll tell a story about a Siamese cat who learns to speak our language! What an idea! That'll make 'em laugh!"

Just then the Siamese cat appeared before him, and said, "Hello there! Pleasant day today, isn't it!"

The zebra storyteller wasn't fit to be tied at hearing a cat speaking his language, because he'd been thinking about that very thing.

He took a good look at the cat, and he didn't know why, but there was something about his looks he didn't like, so he kicked him with a hoof and killed him.

That is the function of the storyteller.

1971

A PREFACE TO FICTION

The Zebra Storyteller seems to suggest that the purpose of stories is to prepare us for the unexpected. Though the storyteller thinks he is just spinning stories out of his own imagination, in order to amuse, his stories prove to be practical. When the extraordinary, the unheard-of occurs—like a Siamese cat speaking Zebraic—he is prepared because he has already imagined it, and he alone is able to protect his tribe against the unusual.

Other storytellers make the function of fiction less direct and less extraordinary. According to them, fiction prevents readers from projecting false hopes and fears (such as the zebras' superstitious belief that they are being preyed on by the ghost of a lion and so are helpless) and shows them what they can actually expect in their everyday lives, so that they can protect themselves. Hetty Sorrel, in George Eliot's novel *Adam Bede,* is being paid admiring attention by the young squire (who, by the way, eventually seduces her), and she dreams of marriage, elopement, and all sorts of vague pleasures. Her imagination has not been trained by narrative to project possible "stories": "Hetty had never read a novel," George Eliot tells us, "[so] how could she find a shape for her expectations?"

We are all storytellers, then, of one stripe or another. Whenever we plan the future or ponder a decision, we are telling stories, projecting expectations through narrative. Even scientists tell stories that begin with a fiction called a hypothesis ("What if . . .") and travel mentally through the unknown toward invention. Whenever we tell stories or read them, we are educating our imaginations, either extending our mental experience in the actual, as Hetty might have done by reading novels, or peparing ourselves for the extraordinary and unexpected, like the Zebra storyteller.

The actual and the extraordinary suggest what two different kinds of readers or a reader in two different moods looks for in fiction. Some readers like fiction, they say, because they enjoy reading about people like themselves, or about places, things, experiences, and ideas that are familiar and agreeable. Most of us initially prefer American literature and twentieth-century literature to literature remote in time or place. Indeed, stories must somehow be related to our own lives before we can find them intellectually or emotionally meaningful. Similarity of fictional characters, times, and places to those we know is only the most direct and obvious form of this relationship. No matter what our literary experience and taste, most of us relate in a special way to stories about people like us, experiences like our own, and especially to a story that mentions our home town or our neighborhood or the name of the street that we used to walk along on our way to school. (I got particular enjoyment, for example, in annotating the name of the station called out by the train conductor in *The Artificial Nigger.*) Whether we call this reading for identification or for relevance, no one would deny that one of the many things that fiction may be "for" is learning about ourselves and the world around us.

However, there are probably many readers—or all readers in certain moods—who would say that the last things they want in a story are people like themselves, experiences like those of their everyday lives, and places and times like here and now. They want to (or are accused of wanting to) escape. The desire to escape through literature, like the desire to identify, defines what is in fact one basic motive in reading fiction. If fiction must be relevant enough to relate meaningfully to us, it must also be "irrelevant," different, other, strange—as strange, perhaps, as a Siamese cat speaking Zebraic. That is, it must take us out of ourselves, out of the confining vision of our own eyes, conditioned by our own background and experience. It must show us that there are ways of looking at the world other than our own, other human and limited but also viable ways of looking at reality. So this collection includes a sprinkling of stories written in the last century, a few written in vastly different cultures, and a fair number written about worlds that have not existed or do not (yet) exist, as well as many stories about approximately our own time and place.

What a story shows us or teaches us many readers at first call a story's **message**—an objective, universal truth that they were unaware of before reading the story. We gradually become aware, however, that stories tell us not so much what life means as what it's like. They deal with perceptions rather than abstract or "objective" truths. These perceptions may be translated into messages, but we soon discover that the messages boil down to things like "There's good and bad in everybody," "Hurting people is wrong," and "Everything is not what it seems"—messages that Western Union, much less Western literature, might not find too urgent or startlingly illuminating. Indeed, it may not even be the truth of the perception embodied in a story (truth in the sense of our agreement or conversion) that is at the heart of the reading experience so much as the human or subjective truth: are we convinced that if we had those eyes rather than our own and were there rather than here, this is what we might see, or how we might see? Whenever we can say yes, we have expanded our consciousness: we have been able to escape or transcend the limitations of our own vision, our own past and conditions, and we are able to see, to a greater or lesser extent, a new world, or the world in a new way. Even more important, perhaps, is to recognize through apprehension of another's "distortion" of reality that objects do not in fact exist for us in themselves, as they are supposed to, but as they are perceived by us—a discovery that may awaken us to actively looking at things for ourselves rather than accepting them at conventional face value. For example, we "know" a table top is rectangular, but in a story we are told it is diamond-shaped. We understand that if we were to look at the table top from a certain angle it would look diamond-shaped. But doesn't that imply that the table top is rectangular only when we look from a certain angle? And are we looking at it from that angle? We look again, and we recognize that though we've always known it's a rectangle, we've never really *seen* it as one. The story has not only allowed us to see reality from another angle, but it has helped us to sharpen our own vision.

Stories, then, educate our perceptions—of others and of ourselves—as well as educating our expectations—of the ordinary and the extraordinary.

Elements

1 PLOT

If you have not yet read the very brief story that precedes the Preface, Spencer Holst's *The Zebra Storyteller,* you may want to glance at it now, for you can see in the arrangement of the action there the skeleton of the typical short story **plot** or **plot structure.** Plot simply means the arrangement of the action. The **action** refers to an imagined event or happening or to a series of such events. These events have a kind of imagined reality of their own, almost, we feel, separate from the words of the story and the plot or arrangement. The **arrangement,** on the other hand, suggests not a real or imagined world but manipulation by someone: the author. We shall refer to that imaginary world and the events in it as the story's **history,** and to all kinds of manipulation or arrangement, including plot, language, point of view, and many other fictional devices, as the **structure** of the story.

The action of a story usually involves **conflict** (a struggle between opposing forces), and it often falls into something like the same five parts that we can see in a typical play. The conflict in this little tale is between the Siamese cat and the zebras, especially the zebra storyteller. The first part of the action, called the **exposition,** introduces characters, situation, and, usually, time and place. The exposition here is achieved in three sentences: the time is "once upon a," the place Africa, the characters a Siamese cat who speaks Zebraic and an innocent zebra, and the situation (which includes the cat's linguistic prowess) their meeting. From that point on we are in the second part of the plot, the **rising action:** events that complicate the situation and intensify or multiply the conflict or conflicts. The first conflict here is over in a hurry—the zebra who is "fit to be tied" is tied up and eaten. Complications build with the cat's continuing success in killing zebras, and the zebras' growing fears and consequent superstitious belief that the ghost of a lion haunts the region, preying on zebras. The **turning point** (or **climax**) of the action is the third part of the story, the appearance of the zebra storyteller. From this point on the complications that grew in the first part of the story are untangled—the zebra storyteller, for example, is not surprised when he meets a Siamese cat speaking Zebraic. This is the fourth part of the story, the **falling action.** The story ends at the fifth part, the **conclusion** or **catastrophe:** the point at which the situation that was destabilized at the beginning of the story (when the Zebraic-speaking cat appears) becomes stable once more: Africa is once again free of cats speaking the language of zebras.

Before the parts of the action can be arranged, of course, they must be selected. The opening passages of the first two stories in this chapter may show some of the things involved in selection.

"The thousand injuries of Fortunato I had borne as I best could, but when he ventured upon insult I vowed revenge." So begins Edgar Allan Poe's *The Cask of Amontillado*. What kinds of injuries? Were there actually that many? Were they real injuries or imaginary? What was the insult? Why was the insult worse than all the injuries? Poe could have invented answers for these questions, but he chose not to.

The first scene of Richard Connell's *The Most Dangerous Game* provides some information—the general location of the yacht, the superstition about the island, the fact that Rainsford is an expert hunter—but it is a rather full scene for one that, on first reading at least, seems to have no essential connection with the exciting events that follow. And Whitney, who appears to be a major character here, we see no more. Why does Connell include this scene and this character?

Authors leave out some things that seem to be important to the story and include some things that do not seem very important. Selection of events is a significant element of storytelling.

But what do we mean when we say an author selects events? Selects from where? It's not as if these events exist somewhere, as, say, historical events do. Like scientists with their hypotheses and philosophers with their premises, many of us who talk or write about fiction begin with a fiction: we speak as if the people and places exist and the events of a story take place in a world of the author's imagination, a world from which he or she chooses the story elements, a world we can understand and almost re-create, in terms of our own; a world I've already called the history behind the story, as opposed to the structure (which is anything that we can assume a storyteller has done to that imaginary world).

This chapter is concerned with one specific kind of structure, that which has to do with the selection, connection, and ordering of the events: the structure known as plot.

Once events have been selected, they must be connected. In the history, events take place in simple chronological sequence: "The king died and then the queen died," to use one critic's example. This sequential narrative of events, the critic says, is not a plot. But if we connect the events, if we structure the history—"The king died and then the queen died of grief"—then we have a plot.

Many of us are used to thinking of cause-and-effect as a natural part of an event, as somehow *in* the event, rather than as an interpretation of a relationship between two events. Often authors, bent on "telling the truth by lying" (as some have described the function of fiction) and getting us to accept the fiction as a kind of truth, try to exploit this misperception on our part. They try to hide their structuring of that history from us. Sometimes they will put the causes of events inside the fiction itself: Montresor's scheme of revenge against Fortunato in *The Cask of Amontillado* is not the author's plot, Poe seems to tell us, but Montresor's; it is he, not the author, who interprets Fortunato's insult as cause for revenge and generates the events that follow. Sometimes, when the characters do not make the connections, the author makes the reader do it. Hemingway is very reluctant to structure his stories by connecting events or other details. He just puts down one after another, as if they came into the story that way directly from the history. He uses few connectives, and most of these are "neutral," noninterpretive *ands*. In the eleventh paragraph of *The Short Happy Life of Francis Macomber*, for example, an *and* appears where many of us would expect (and perhaps silently insert) a *so*: Macomber is waiting for his wife to enter their tent: "She did not speak to him when she came in *and* he left the tent at once. . . ." Consider the *and* in this sentence: "He was dressed in the same sort of safari clothes that Wilson wore except that his were new, he was thirty-five years old, kept himself very fit, was good at court games, had a number of big-game fishing records, and had just shown himself, very publicly, to be a coward." Wouldn't *but* seem more natural here? And how about the odd selection and collection of details in this sentence? What relationship is there between Macomber's just having revealed his cowardice and his dress, age, physical condition, fishing ability? Why, without interpretation, reasons, connection, lay out these details in a sentence whose major purpose seems to be to tell us of the recent act of cowardice? Despite their innocent appearance, the selection and connection are not part of an unmediated factual report of the history: they are elements of a carefully contrived plot structure. Poe puts the causal connection on a character; Hemingway puts it on the reader. The hand of the author in the structuring is obscured, if not invisible.

In the history, events exist in chronological sequence, and they can be reported that way in the story: "The king died and then the queen died." But the story can be ordered differently without changing or concealing the order in the history. "The queen died after the king died" recounts the same history, but the sequence in the sentence is not the sequence of events in the history. The history has been structured. The reader of the first sentence focuses on the king first, the reader of the second sentence on the queen. The difference in emphasis can be significant.

In some stories, such as *The Most Dangerous Game*, the events of the history are not reordered in the telling but seem to come unstructured from the history: Rainsford speaks with Whitney aboard the yacht; Whitney goes below; Rainsford falls overboard. The events are presented one after another in the same sequence as in the history. The reader reads along finding out what happens next. In a good many stories, however, the sequence in the story is not the sequence in which the supposed events occurred. In a detective story, for example, the major action (the crime) has taken place before the story begins, and the forward action of the story is the detective's attempt to re-create the past and figure out what happened. The reader does not ask *What will happen?* but *What has happened?* In such stories it is obvious that the author is creating a plot, ordering the events in a sequence different from that of the history.

Though the sequence of events in the detective story is reordered in terms of the reader's knowledge of the events—we learn who done it in the past only long after the story begins—the past is not usually replayed. We do not see the crime reenacted before us (although the detective may describe the crime when he gives his solution). The story simply begins in the middle of the history—after the crime—and moves forward as the detective figures out what happened. In *The Short Happy Life of Francis Macomber*, however, there is a replay or **flashback.** As in a detective story, *Macomber* begins in the middle of the history. The history is made up essentially of two hunting episodes. The story begins not with the first but between the two. The first sentence of the story ends, "pretending that nothing had happened," clearly suggesting that, as in the detective story, something significant *had* happened. The reader asks what it was, with curiosity and interest aroused. There are some clues in the first few pages, but neither a detective nor the reader has to reconstruct the past episode from clues. That episode is brought forward into the fictional present and re-presented. About six pages into the story we are told, "It had started the night before," and the following paragraph begins a scene that took place before the first hunt (the lion hunt)—before the time of the opening of the story. Our curiosity is satisfied, but the events of the hunt are so exciting that we shift into suspense, wondering what will happen next.

One reason for structuring the history into plot is to engage, intensify, and keep the reader's attention, to make the reader read on. The story of a crime can be written chronologically, so that we know who done it from the beginning and are just reading on to discover if, when, how the criminal is caught; Dostoevsky tells the story of *Crime and Punishment* this way. Such stories are not, strictly speaking, detective stories. They play on suspense, but not quite so much on curiosity. It is the sheer power of curiosity that keeps us reading intensely when we know as little as Watson or Sherlock Holmes himself at the beginning. Nor is it only the detective story that plays upon our curiosity. We have already seen how the phrase "pretending that nothing had happened" at the end of the first sentence of *Macomber* sets us to wondering just what had happened; by the time we find out, six pages later, we are already deep into the characters and situation—we're hooked. Even titles, such as *The Artificial Nigger* and *A Very Old Man with Enormous Wings*, can make us pick up a story; after that, it's up to the story to keep us engaged.

As strong as, perhaps stronger than curiosity—the desire to know what is happening or has happened—is suspense, the expectation of and doubt about what is *going* to happen next, as in the lion hunt in *Macomber*. Some of the stories in this volume have titles which promise suspense: *The Most Dangerous Game, The Lottery, Hide and Seek*. The first of these may be the best in which to examine how plot can arouse, modify, and satisfy our expectations, in which to watch not only the story but our own minds as we read the story.

What *is* the most dangerous game? Russian roulette, perhaps? Within the first fifty words we run across such terms as *mystery, suggestive, curious dread, superstition,* and we may begin to think of the supernatural (but what kind of "game" does that suggest?). In the same passage is *Ship-Trap*, and another possible meaning for game, another direction for our anticipation, opens up: hunting and trapping game. This is reinforced in the next twenty-five lines by the talk of hunting. The game must be some exceedingly fierce animal. All sorts of expectations build: supernatural animals, monsters, prehistoric animals, cannibals, Satan himself—worse! By the time Whitney says good night and we come to the first break on the page, our expectations are at a pretty high pitch. There's a good deal of suspense, and our minds are actively scanning four, five, maybe six possibilities of what kinds of things might happen next.

Try reading another couple of pages—say, down to Rainsford's introducing himself ("I'm Sanger Rainsford of New York")—watching yourself anticipate and put together details or clues. What kind of reinforcement do those early references to mystery and superstition get from the unexpected, mirage-like appearance of a palatial château, a tall spiked iron gate, a gargoyle on the door knocker, and a gigantic man opening the door? Don't you find yourself trying to fit these things into a pattern? Sooner or later some possibilities are eliminated and one pattern dominates; the story may at some point simply tell you what possibility will be pursued. It is not too long before you learn for sure what the game is. But by that time there are new reasons for suspense—how will it come out? You get to another layer of suspense following Rainsford through a **serial ordeal,** a series of dangerous episodes.

Stories are not all fun and games, no matter how dangerous. Many of them seek to give you new insights into human perception, experience, meaning. They strive to tell truths—new, subjective truths, but truths—even though they "lie" about the actuality of the people and events represented. But first they have to get your attention, and one way is by arousing your curiosity and exciting your anticipation; that's what plot is primarily for. In order to keep you engaged and alert, a story must make you ask questions about what will happen or what will be revealed next. To fully respond to a story you must be alert to the signals and guess along with the author. For at least in one aspect, fiction is a guessing game. Like all guessing games, from quiz shows to philosophy, the plot game in fiction has certain guidelines. A good (well structured) plot will play fair with you, offering at appropriate points all the necessary indicators or clues to what will happen next, not just springing new and essential information on you at the last minute ("Meanwhile, unknown to our hero, the Marines were just on the other side of the hill . . ."). It is this playing fair that makes the ending of a well-structured story satisfying or, when you look back on it, inevitable. Most stories also offer a number of reasonable but false signals (red herrings) to get you off the scent, so that in a well-structured story the ending, though inevitable, is also surprising. And though there is usually an overarching action from beginning to end, in many stories there are layers of expectation or suspense, so that as soon as one question is answered another comes forth to replace it, keeping you in doubt and suspense as to the final outcome.

Unlike most guessing games, however, the reward is not for the right guess—anticipating the outcome before the final paragraph—but for the number of guesses, right *and* wrong, that you make, the number of signals you respond to. If you are misled by none of the false signals in the early pages of *The Most Dangerous Game,* you may be closer to being "right," but you've missed a good deal of both the experience and the implication of the story. How do you react, in *The Cask of Amontillado,* to Montresor's concern for Fortunato's coughing? What do you anticipate? What is it that you later discover? Alertness to signals, anticipating what is to come next, remembering what has been said and signaled earlier, are essential to fully appreciating and understanding stories. By the time you finish the Connell story, you should be able to figure out why he structured it so, why the first scene was there. You might have some idea—though not necessarily a firm and simple answer—as to why, in addition to arousing suspense, Hemingway wanted *The Short Happy Life of Francis Macomber* to begin in the middle of the history and later flash back to the beginning. You may know why insult is more important to Montresor than injury; you may even be able to suggest why Poe did not recount the thousand injuries or the fatal insult.

EDGAR ALLAN POE

The Cask of Amontillado

The thousand injuries of Fortunato I had borne as I best could, but when he ventured upon insult I vowed revenge. You, who so well know the nature of my soul, will not suppose, however, that I gave utterance to a threat. *At length* I would be avenged; this was a point definitely settled—but the very definitiveness with which it was resolved precluded the idea of risk. I must not only punish but punish with impunity. A wrong is unredressed when retribution overtakes its redresser. It is equally unredressed when the avenger fails to make himself felt as such to him who has done the wrong.

It must be understood that neither by word nor deed had I given Fortunato cause to doubt my good will. I continued, as was my wont, to smile in his face, and he did not perceive that my smile *now* was at the thought of his immolation.

He had a weak point—this Fortunato—although in other regards he was a man to be respected and even feared. He prided himself on his connoisseurship in wine. Few Italians have the true virtuoso spirit. For the most part their enthusiasm is adopted to suit the time and opportunity, to practice imposture upon the British and Austrian millionaires. In painting and gemmary, Fortunato, like his countrymen, was a quack, but in the matter of old wines he was sincere. In this respect I did not differ from him materially;—I was skilful in the Italian vintages myself, and bought largely whenever I could.

It was about dusk, one evening during the supreme madness of the carnival season, that I encountered my friend. He accosted me with excessive warmth, for he had been drinking much. The man wore motley. He had on a tight-fitting parti-striped dress, and his head was surmounted by the conical cap and bells. I was so pleased to see him that I thought I should never have done wringing his hand.

I said to him—"My dear Fortunato, you are luckily met. How remarkably well you are looking to-day. But I have received a pipe[1] of what passes for Amontillado, and I have my doubts."

"How?" said he. "Amontillado? A pipe? Impossible! And in the middle of the carnival!"

"I have my doubts," I replied; "and I was silly enough to pay the full Amontillado price without consulting you in the matter. You were not to be found, and I was fearful of losing a bargain."

"Amontillado!"

"I have my doubts."

"Amontillado!"

"And I must satisfy them."

"Amontillado!"

"As you are engaged, I am on my way to Luchresi. If any one has a critical turn, it is he. He will tell me——"

"Luchresi cannot tell Amontillado from Sherry."

"And yet some fools will have it that his taste is a match for your own."

"Come, let us go."

"Whither?"

"To your vaults."

"My friend, no; I will not impose upon your good nature. I perceive you have an engagement. Luchresi——"

"I have no engagement;—come."

"My friend, no. It is not the engagement, but the severe cold with which I perceive you are afflicted. The vaults are insufferably damp. They are encrusted with niter."

"Let us go, nevertheless. The cold is merely nothing. Amontillado! You have been imposed upon. And as for Luchresi, he cannot distinguish Sherry from Amontillado."

Thus speaking, Fortunato possessed himself of my arm; and putting on a mask of black silk and drawing a *roquelaire*[2] closely about my person, I suffered him to hurry me to my palazzo.

There were no attendants at home; they had absconded to make merry in honor of the time. I had told them that I should not return until the morning, and had given them explicit orders not to stir from the house. These orders were sufficient, I well knew, to insure their immediate disappearance, one and all, as soon as my back was turned.

I took from their sconces two flambeaux, and giving one to Fortunato, bowed him through several suites of rooms to the archway that led into the vaults. I passed down a long and winding staircase, requesting him to be cautious as he followed. We came at length to the foot of the descent, and stood together on the damp ground of the catacombs of the Montresors.

The gait of my friend was unsteady, and the bells upon his cap jingled as he strode.

"The pipe?" said he.

"It is farther on," said I; "but observe the white web-work which

1. A cask holding 126 gallons.
2. Roquelaure, man's heavy, knee-length cloak, usually trimmed in fur and silk-lined, 18th century.

gleams from these cavern walls."

He turned towards me, and looked into my eyes with two filmy orbs that distilled the rheum of intoxication.

"Niter?" he asked, at length.

"Niter," I replied. "How long have you had that cough?"

"Ugh! ugh! ugh!—ugh! ugh! ugh!—ugh! ugh! ugh! ugh! ugh! ugh!—ugh! ugh! ugh!"

My poor friend found it impossible to reply for many minutes.

"It is nothing," he said, at last.

"Come," I said, with decision, "we will go back; your health is precious. You are rich, respected, admired, beloved; you are happy, as once I was. You are a man to be missed. For me it is no matter. We will go back; you will be ill, and I cannot be responsible. Besides, there is Luchresi——"

"Enough," he said; "the cough is a mere nothing; it will not kill me. I shall not die of a cough."

"True—true," I replied; "and, indeed, I had no intention of alarming you unnecessarily—but you should use all proper caution. A draft of this Medoc will defend us from the damps."

Here I knocked off the neck of a bottle which I drew from a long row of its fellows that lay upon the mold.

"Drink," I said, presenting him the wine.

He raised it to his lips with a leer. He paused and nodded to me familiarly, while his bells jingled.

"I drink," he said, "to the buried that repose around us."

"And I to your long life."

He again took my arm, and we proceeded.

"These vaults," he said, "are extensive."

"The Montresors," I replied, "were a great and numerous family."

"I forget your arms."

"A huge human foot d'or,[3] in a field azure; the foot crushes a serpent rampant whose fangs are imbedded in the heel."

"And the motto?"

"*Nemo me impune lacessit.*"[4]

"Good!" he said.

The wine sparkled in his eyes and the bells jingled. My own fancy grew warm with the Medoc. We had passed through long walls of piled skeletons, with casks and puncheons intermingling, into the inmost recesses of the catacombs. I paused again, and this time I made bold to seize Fortunato by an arm above the elbow.

"The niter!" I said; "see, it increases. It hangs like moss upon the vaults. We are below the river's bed. The drops of moisture trickle among the bones. Come, we will go back ere it is too late. Your cough——"

"It is nothing," he said; "let us go on. But first, another draft of the Medoc."

I broke and reached him a flagon of De Grâve.[5] He emptied it at a breath. His eyes flashed with a fierce light. He laughed and threw the

3. Of gold.
4. No one provokes me with impunity.
5. Like Médoc, a French wine.

bottle upward with a gesticulation I did not understand.

I looked at him in surprise. He repeated the movement—a grotesque one.

"You do not comprehend?" he said.

"Not I," I replied.

"Then you are not of the brotherhood."

"How?"

"You are not of the masons."[6]

"Yes, yes," I said; "yes, yes."

"You? Impossible! A mason?"

"A mason," I replied.

"A sign," he said, "a sign."

"It is this," I answered, producing from beneath the folds of my *roquelaire* a trowel.

"You jest," he exclaimed, recoiling a few paces. "But let us proceed to the Amontillado."

"Be it so," I said, replacing the tool beneath the cloak and again offering him my arm. He leaned upon it heavily. We continued our route in search of the Amontillado. We passed through a range of low arches, descended, passed on, and descending again, arrived at a deep crypt, in which the foulness of the air caused our flambeaux rather to glow than flame.

At the most remote end of the crypt there appeared another less spacious. Its walls had been lined with human remains, piled to the vault overhead, in the fashion of the great catacombs of Paris. Three sides of this interior crypt were still ornamented in this manner. From the fourth the bones had been thrown down, and lay promiscuously upon the earth, forming at one point a mound of some size. Within the wall thus exposed by the displacing of the bones, we perceived a still interior crypt or recess, in depth about four feet, in width three, in height six or seven. It seemed to have been constructed for no especial use within itself, but formed merely the interval between two of the colossal supports of the roof of the catacombs, and was backed by one of their circumscribing walls of solid granite.

It was in vain that Fortunato, uplifting his dull torch, endeavored to pry into the depth of the recess. Its termination the feeble light did not enable us to see.

"Proceed," I said; "herein is the Amontillado. As for Luchresi——"

"He is an ignoramus," interrupted my friend, as he stepped unsteadily forward, while I followed immediately at his heels. In an instant he had reached the extremity of the niche, and finding his progress arrested by the rock, stood stupidly bewildered. A moment more and I had fettered him to the granite. In its surface were two iron staples, distant from each other about two feet, horizontally. From one of these depended a short chain, from the other a padlock. Throwing the links about his waist, it was but the work of a few seconds to secure it. He was too much astounded to resist. Withdrawing the key I stepped back from the recess.

6. Masons or Freemasons, an international secret society condemned by the Catholic church. Montresor means by mason one who builds with stone, brick, etc.

"Pass your hand," I said, "over the wall; you cannot help feeling the niter. Indeed it is *very* damp. Once more let me *implore* you to return. No? Then I must positively leave you. But I must first render you all the little attentions in my power."

"The Amontillado!" ejaculated my friend, not yet recovered from his astonishment.

"True," I replied; "the Amontillado."

As I said these words I busied myself among the pile of bones of which I have before spoken. Throwing them aside, I soon uncovered a quantity of building stone and mortar. With these materials and with the aid of my trowel, I began vigorously to wall up the entrance of the niche.

I had scarcely laid the first tier of the masonry when I discovered that the intoxication of Fortunato had in a great measure worn off. The earliest indication I had of this was a low moaning cry from the depth of the recess. It was *not* the cry of a drunken man. There was then a long and obstinate silence. I laid the second tier, and the third, and the fouth; and then I heard the furious vibrations of the chain. The noise lasted for several minutes, during which, that I might hearken to it with the more satisfaction, I ceased my labors and sat down upon the bones. When at last the clanking subsided, I resumed the trowel, and finished without interruption the fifth, the sixth, and the seventh tier. The wall was now nearly upon a level with my breast. I again paused, and holding the flambeaux over the mason-work, threw a few feeble rays upon the figure within.

A succession of loud and shrill screams, bursting suddenly from the throat of the chained form, seemed to thrust me violently back. For a brief moment I hesitated, I trembled. Unsheathing my rapier, I began to grope with it about the recess; but the thought of an instant reassured me. I placed my hand upon the solid fabric of the catacombs, and felt satisfied. I reapproached the wall. I replied to the yells of him who clamored. I reechoed, I aided, I surpassed them in volume and in strength. I did this, and the clamorer grew still.

It was now midnight, and my task was drawing to a close. I had completed the eighth, the ninth and the tenth tier. I had finished a portion of the last and the eleventh; there remained but a single stone to be fitted and plastered in. I struggled with its weight; I placed it partially in its destined position. But now there came from out the niche a low laugh that erected the hairs upon my head. It was succeeded by a sad voice, which I had difficulty in recognizing as that of the noble Fortunato. The voice said—

"Ha! ha! ha!—he! he! he!—a very good joke, indeed—an excellent jest. We will have many a rich laugh about it at the palazzo[7]—he! he! he!—over our wine—he! he! he!"

"The Amontillado!" I said.

"He! he! he!—he! he! he!—yes, the Amontillado. But is it not getting late? Will not they be awaiting us at the palazzo, the Lady Fortunato and the rest? Let us be gone."

"Yes," I said, "let us be gone."

7. Palace.

"*For the love of God, Montresor!*"

"Yes," I said, "for the love of God!"

But to these words I hearkened in vain for a reply. I grew impatient. I called aloud—

"Fortunato!"

No answer. I called again—

"Fortunato!"

No answer still. I thrust a torch through the remaining aperture and let it fall within. There came forth in return only a jingling of the bells. My heart grew sick; it was the dampness of the catacombs that made it so. I hastened to make an end of my labor. I forced the last stone into its position; I plastered it up. Against the new masonry I re-erected the old rampart of bones. For the half of a century no mortal has disturbed them. *In pace requiescat!*[8]

p. 1846

RICHARD CONNELL

The Most Dangerous Game

"Off there to the right—somewhere—is a large island," said Whitney. "It's rather a mystery—"

"What island is it?" Rainsford asked.

"The old charts call it 'Ship-Trap Island,'" Whitney replied. "A suggestive name, isn't it? Sailors have a curious dread of the place. I don't know why. Some superstition—"

"Can't see it," remarked Rainsford, trying to peer through the dank tropical night that was palpable as it pressed its thick warm blackness in upon the yacht.

"You've good eyes," said Whitney, with a laugh, "and I've seen you pick off a moose moving in the brown fall bush at four hundred yards, but even you can't see four miles or so through a moonless Caribbean night."

"Nor four yards," admitted Rainsford. "Ugh! It's like moist black velvet."

"It will be light in Rio," promised Whitney. "We should make it in a few days. I hope the jaguar guns have come from Purdey's. We should have some good hunting up the Amazon. Great sport, hunting."

"The best sport in the world," agreed Rainsford.

"For the hunter," amended Whitney. "Not for the jaguar."

"Don't talk rot, Whitney," said Rainsford. "You're a big-game hunter, not a philosopher. Who cares how a jaguar feels?"

"Perhaps the jaguar does," observed Whitney.

"Bah! They've no understanding."

"Even so, I rather think they understand one thing—fear. The fear of pain and the fear of death."

8. May he rest in peace.

"Nonsense," laughed Rainsford. "This hot weather is making you soft, Whitney. Be a realist. The world is made up of two classes—the hunters and the huntees. Luckily, you and I are hunters. Do you think we've passed that island yet?"

"I can't tell in the dark. I hope so."

"Why?" asked Rainsford.

"The place has a reputation—a bad one."

"Cannibals?" suggested Rainsford.

"Hardly. Even cannibals wouldn't live in such a God-forsaken place. But it's gotten into sailor lore, somehow. Didn't you notice that the crew's nerves seemed a bit jumpy today?"

"They were a bit strange, now you mention it. Even Captain Nielsen—"

"Yes, even that tough-minded old Swede, who'd go up to the devil himself and ask him for a light. Those fishy blue eyes held a look I never saw there before. All I could get out of him was: 'This place has an evil name among sea-faring men, sir.' Then he said to me, very gravely: 'Don't you feel anything?'—as if the air about us was actually poisonous. Now, you mustn't laugh when I tell you this—I did feel something like a sudden chill.

"There was no breeze. The sea was as flat as a plate-glass window. We were drawing near the island then. What I felt was a—a mental chill; a sort of sudden dread."

"Pure imagination," said Rainsford. "One superstitious sailor can taint the whole ship's company with his fear."

"Maybe. But sometimes I think sailors have an extra sense that tells them when they are in danger. Sometimes I think evil is a tangible thing—with wave lengths, just as sound and light have. An evil place can, so to speak, broadcast vibrations of evil. Anyhow, I'm glad we're getting out of this zone. Well, I think I'll turn in now, Rainsford."

"I'm not sleepy," said Rainsford. "I'm going to smoke another pipe up on the after deck."

"Good night, then, Rainsford. See you at breakfast."

"Right. Good night, Whitney."

There was no sound in the night as Rainsford sat there, but the muffled throb of the engine that drove the yacht swiftly through the darkness, and the swish and ripple of the wash of the propeller.

Rainsford, reclining in a steamer chair, indolently puffed on his favorite brier. The sensuous drowsiness of the night was on him. "It's so dark," he thought, "that I could sleep without closing my eyes; the night would be my eyelids—"

An abrupt sound startled him. Off to the right he heard it, and his ears, expert in such matters, could not be mistaken. Again he heard the sound, and again. Somewhere, off in the blackness, some one had fired a gun three times.

Rainsford sprang up and moved quickly to the rail, mystified. He strained his eyes in the direction from which the reports had come, but it was like trying to see through a blanket. He leaped upon the rail and balanced himself there, to get greater elevation; his pipe, striking a rope, was knocked from his mouth. He lunged for it; a short, hoarse cry came from his lips as he realized he had reached too far and had lost his balance. The cry was pinched off short as the blood-warm waters of the Caribbean Sea closed over his head.

He struggled up to the surface and tried to cry out, but the wash from the speeding yacht slapped him in the face and the salt water in his open mouth made him gag and strangle. Desperately he struck out with strong strokes after the receding lights of the yacht, but he stopped before he had swum fifty feet. A certain cool-headedness had come to him; it was not the first time he had been in a tight place. There was a chance that his cries could be heard by some one aboard the yacht, but that chance was slender, and grew more slender as the yacht raced on. He wrestled himself out of his clothes, and shouted with all his power. The lights of the yacht became faint and ever-vanishing fireflies; then they were blotted out entirely by the night.

Rainsford remembered the shots. They had come from the right, and doggedly he swam in that direction, swimming with slow, deliberate strokes, conserving his strength. For a seemingly endless time he fought the sea. He began to count his strokes; he could do possibly a hundred more and then—

Rainsford heard a sound. It came out of the darkness, a high screaming sound, the sound of an animal in an extremity of anguish and terror.

He did not recognize the animal that made the sound; he did not try to; with fresh vitality he swam toward the sound. He heard it again; then it was cut short by another noise, crisp, staccato.

"Pistol shot," muttered Rainsford, swimming on.

Ten minutes of determined effort brought another sound to his ears —the most welcome he had ever heard—the muttering and growling of the sea breaking on a rocky shore. He was almost on the rocks before he saw them; on a night less calm he would have been shattered against them. With his remaining strength he dragged himself from the swirling waters. Jagged crags appeared to jut into the opaqueness; he forced himself upward, hand over hand. Gasping, his hands raw, he reached a flat place at the top. Dense jungle came down to the very edge of the cliffs. What perils that tangle of trees and underbrush might hold for him did not concern Rainsford just then. All he knew was that he was safe from his enemy, the sea, and that utter weariness was on him. He flung himself down at the jungle edge and tumbled headlong into the deepest sleep of his life.

When he opened his eyes he knew from the position of the sun that it was late in the afternoon. Sleep had given him new vigor; a sharp hunger was picking at thim. He looked about him, almost cheerfully.

"Where there are pistol shots, there are men. Where there are men, there is food," he thought. But what kind of men, he wondered, in so forbidding a place? An unbroken front of snarled and ragged jungle fringed the shore.

He saw no sign of a trail through the closely knit web of weeds and trees; it was easier to go along the shore, and Rainsford floundered along by the water. Not far from where he had landed, he stopped.

Some wounded thing, by the evidence a large animal, had thrashed about in the underbrush; the jungle weeds were crushed down and the moss was lacerated; one patch of weeds was stained crimson. A small, glittering object not far away caught Rainsford's eye and he picked it up. It was an empty cartridge.

"A twenty-two," he remarked. "That's odd. It must have been a fairly large animal too. The hunter had his nerve with him to tackle it with a light gun. It's clear that the brute put up a fight. I suppose the first three shots I heard was when the hunter flushed his quarry and wounded it. The last shot was when he trailed it here and finished it."

He examined the ground closely and found what he had hoped to find—the print of hunting boots. They pointed along the cliff in the direction he had been going. Eagerly he hurried along, now slipping on a rotten log or a loose stone, but making headway; night was beginning to settle down on the island.

Bleak darkness was blacking out the sea and jungle when Rainsford sighted the lights. He came upon them as he turned a crook in the coast line, and his first thought was that he had come upon a village, for there were many lights. But as he forged along he saw to his great astonishment that all the lights were in one enormous building—a lofty structure with pointed towers plunging upward into the gloom. His eyes made out the shadowy outlines of a palatial château; it was set on a high bluff, and on three sides of it cliffs dived down to where the sea licked greedy lips in the shadows.

"Mirage," thought Rainsford. But it was no mirage, he found, when he opened the tall spiked iron gate. The stone steps were real enough; the massive door with a leering gargoyle for a knocker was real enough; yet about it all hung an air of unreality.

He lifted the knocker, and it creaked up stiffly, as if it had never before been used. He let it fall, and it startled him with its booming loudness. He thought he heard steps within; the door remained closed. Again Rainsford lifted the heavy knocker, and let it fall. The door opened then, opened as suddenly as if it were on a spring, and Rainsford stood blinking in the river of glaring gold light that poured out. The first thing Rainsford's eyes discerned was the largest man Rainsford had ever seen—a gigantic creature, solidly made and black-bearded to the waist. In his hand the man held a long-barreled revolver, and he was pointing it straight at Rainsford's heart.

Out of the snarl of beard two small eyes regarded Rainsford.

"Don't be alarmed," said Rainsford, with a smile which he hoped was disarming. "I'm no robber. I fell off a yacht. My name is Sanger Rainsford of New York City."

The menacing look in the eyes did not change. The revolver pointed as rigidly as if the giant were a statue. He gave no sign that he understood Rainsford's words, or that he had even heard them. He was dressed in uniform, a black uniform trimmed with gray astrakhan.

"I'm Sanger Rainsford of New York," Rainsford began again. "I fell off a yacht. I am hungry."

The man's only answer was to raise with his thumb the hammer of his revolver. Then Rainsford saw the man's free hand go to his forehead in a military salute, and he saw him click his heels together and stand at attention. Another man was coming down the broad marble steps, an erect, slender man in evening clothes. He advanced to Rainsford and held out his hand.

In a cultivated voice marked by a slight accent that gave it added precision and deliberateness, he said: "It is a very great pleasure and honor to welcome Mr. Sanger Rainsford, the celebrated hunter, to my home."

Automatically Rainsford shook the man's hand.

"I've read your book about hunting snow leopards[1] in Tibet, you see," explained the man. "I am General Zaroff."

Rainsford's first impression was that the man was singularly handsome; his second was that there was an original, almost bizarre quality about the general's face. He was a tall man past middle age, for his hair was a vivid white; but his thick eyebrows and pointed military mustache were as black as the night from which Rainsford had come. His eyes, too, were black and very bright. He had high cheek bones, a sharp-cut nose, a spare, dark face, the face of a man used to giving orders, the face of an aristocrat. Turning to the giant in uniform; the general made a sign. The giant put away his pistol, saluted, withdrew.

"Ivan is an incredibly strong fellow," remarked the general, "but he has the misfortune to be deaf and dumb. A simple fellow, but, I'm afraid, like all his race, a bit of a savage."

"Is he Russian?"

"He is a Cossack,"[2] said the general, and his smile showed red lips and pointed teeth. "So am I."

"Come," he said, "we shouldn't be chatting here. We can talk later. Now you want clothes, food, rest. You shall have them. This is a most restful spot."

Ivan had reappeared, and the general spoke to him with lips that moved but gave forth no sound.

"Follow Ivan, if you please, Mr. Rainsford," said the general. "I was about to have my dinner when you came. I'll wait for you. You'll find that my clothes will fit you, I think."

It was to a huge, beam-ceilinged bedroom with a canopied bed big enough for six men that Rainsford followed the silent giant. Ivan laid out an evening suit, and Rainsford, as he put it on, noticed that it came from a London tailor who ordinarily cut and sewed for none below the rank of duke.

The dining room to which Ivan conducted him was in many ways remarkable. There was a medieval magnificence about it; it suggested a baronial hall of feudal times with its oaken panels, its high ceiling, its vast refectory table where twoscore men could sit down to eat. About the hall were the mounted heads of many animals—lions, tigers, elephants, moose, bears; larger or more perfect specimens Rainsford had never seen. At the great table the general was sitting, alone.

"You'll have a cocktail, Mr. Rainsford," he suggested. The cocktail was surpassingly good; and, Rainsford noted, the table appointments were of the finest—the linen, the crystal, the silver, the china.

They were eating *borsch*, the rich, red soup with whipped cream so dear to Russian palates. Half apologetically General Zaroff said: "We do our best to preserve the amenities of civilization here. Please forgive any lapses. We are well off the beaten track, you know. Do

1. The ounce, native to the Himalayas, and quite rare.

2. From the southern part of European Russia, the Cossacks were known as exceptionally fine horsemen and light cavalrymen and, under the Czars, were feared for their ruthless raids.

you think the champagne has suffered from its long ocean trip?"

"Not in the least," declared Rainsford. He was finding the general a most thoughtful and affable host, a true cosmopolite. But there was one small trait of the general's that made Rainsford uncomfortable. Whenever he looked up from his plate he found the general studying him, appraising him narrowly.

"Perhaps," said General Zaroff, "you were surprised that I recognized your name. You see, I read all books on hunting published in English, French, and Russian. I have but one passion in my life, Mr. Rainsford, and it is the hunt."

"You have some wonderful heads here," said Rainsford as he ate a particularly well cooked filet mignon. "That Cape buffalo[3] is the largest I ever saw."

"Oh, that fellow. Yes, he was a monster."

"Did he charge you?"

"Hurled me against a tree," said the general. "Fractured my skull. But I got the brute."

"I've always thought," said Rainsford, "that the Cape buffalo is the most dangerous of all big game."

For a moment the general did not reply; he was smiling his curious red-lipped smile. Then he said slowly: "No. You are wrong, sir. The Cape buffalo is not the most dangerous big game." He sipped his wine. "Here in my preserve on this island," he said in the same slow tone, "I hunt more dangerous game."

Rainsford expressed his surprise. "Is there big game on this island?"

The general nodded. "The biggest."

"Really?"

"Oh, it isn't here naturally, of course. I have to stock the island."

"What have you imported, general?" Rainsford asked. "Tigers?"

The general smiled. "No," he said. "Hunting tigers ceased to interest me some years ago. I exhausted their possibilities, you see. No thrill left in tigers, no real danger. I live for danger, Mr. Rainsford."

The general took from his pocket a gold cigarette case and offered his guest a long black cigarette with a silver tip; it was perfumed and gave off a smell like incense.

"We will have some capital hunting, you and I," said the general. "I shall be most glad to have your society."

"But what game—" began Rainsford.

"I'll tell you," said the general. "You will be amused, I know. I think I may say, in all modesty, that I have done a rare thing. I have invented a new sensation. May I pour you another glass of port, Mr. Rainsford?"

"Thank you, general."

The general filled both glasses, and said: "God makes some men poets. Some He makes kings, some beggars. Me He made a hunter. My hand was made for the trigger, my father said. He was a very rich man with a quarter of a million acres in the Crimea, and he was an ardent sportsman. When I was only five years old he gave me a little gun, specially made in Moscow for me, to shoot sparrows with. When I shot some of his prize turkeys with it, he did not punish me; he

3. Big, quick, intelligent, when separated from the herd ("rogue"), one of the most dangerous of African game animals.

complimented me on my marksmanship. I killed my first bear in the Caucasus when I was ten. My whole life has been one prolonged hunt. I went into the army—it was expected of noblemen's sons—and for a time commanded a division of Cossack cavalry, but my real interest was always the hunt. I have hunted every kind of game in every land. It would be impossible for me to tell you how many animals I have killed."

The general puffed at his cigarette.

"After the debacle in Russia[4] I left the country, for it was imprudent for an officer of the Czar to stay there. Many noble Russians lost everything. I, luckily, had invested heavily in American securities, so I shall never have to open a tea room in Monte Carlo or drive a taxi in Paris. Naturally, I continued to hunt—grizzlies in your Rockies, crocodiles in the Ganges, rhinoceroses in East Africa. It was in Africa that the Cape buffalo hit me and laid me up for six months. As soon as I recovered I started for the Amazon to hunt jaguars, for I had heard they were unusually cunning. They weren't." The Cossack sighed. "They were no match at all for a hunter with his wits about him, and a high-powered rifle. I was bitterly disappointed. I was lying in my tent with a splitting headache one night when a terrible thought pushed its way into my mind. Hunting was beginning to bore me! And hunting, remember, had been my life. I have heard that in America business men often go to pieces when they give up the business that has been their life."

"Yes, that's so," said Rainsford.

The general smiled. "I had no wish to go to pieces," he said. "I must do something. Now, mine is an analytical mind, Mr. Rainsford. Doubtless that is why I enjoy the problems of the chase."

"No doubt, General Zaroff."

"So," continued the general, "I asked myself why the hunt no longer fascinated me. You are much younger than I am, Mr. Rainsford, and have not hunted as much, but you perhaps can guess the answer."

"What was it?"

"Simply this: hunting had ceased to be what you call 'a sporting proposition.' It had become too easy. I always got my quarry. Always. There is no greater bore than perfection."

The general lit a fresh cigarette.

"No animal had a chance with me any more. That is no boast; it is a mathematical certainty. The animal had nothing but his legs and his instinct. Instinct is no match for reason. When I thought of this it was a tragic moment for me, I can tell you."

Rainsford leaned across the table, absorbed in what his host was saying.

"It came to me as an inspiration what I must do," the general went on.

"And that was?"

The general smiled the quiet smile of one who had faced an obstacle and surmounted it with success. "I had to invent a new animal to hunt," he said.

"A new animal? You're joking."

4. The Revolution of 1917 which overthrew the Czar and prepared the way for Communist rule.

"Not at all," said the general. "I never joke about hunting. I needed a new animal. I found one. So I bought this island, built this house, and here I do my hunting. The island is perfect for my purposes—there are jungles with a maze of trails in them, hills, swamps—"

"But the animal, General Zaroff?"

"Oh," said the general, "it supplies me with the most exciting hunting in the world. No other hunting compares with it for an instant. Every day I hunt, and I never grow bored now, for I have a quarry with which I can match my wits."

Rainsford's bewilderment showed in his face.

"I wanted the ideal animal to hunt," explained the general. "So I said: 'What are the attributes of an ideal quarry?' And the answer was, of course: 'It must have courage, cunning, and, above all, it must be able to reason.'"

"But no animal can reason," objected Rainsford.

"My dear fellow," said the general, "there is one that can."

"But you can't mean—" gasped Rainsford.

"And why not?"

"I can't believe you are serious, General Zaroff. This is a grisly joke."

"Why should I not be serious? I am speaking of hunting."

"Hunting? Good God, General Zaroff, what you speak of is murder."

The general laughed with entire good nature. He regarded Rainsford quizzically. "I refuse to believe that so modern and civilized a young man as you seem to be harbors romantic ideas about the value of human life. Surely your experiences in the war—"

"Did not make me condone cold-blooded murder," finished Rainsford stiffly.

Laughter shook the general. "How extraordinarily droll you are!" he said. "One does not expect nowadays to find a young man of the educated class, even in America, with such a naïve, and, if I may say so, mid-Victorian point of view. It's like finding a snuff-box in a limousine. Ah, well, doubtless you had Puritan ancestors. So many Americans appear to have had. I'll wager you'll forget your notions when you go hunting with me. You've a genuine new thrill in store for you, Mr. Rainsford."

"Thank you, I'm a hunter, not a murderer."

"Dear me," said the general, quite unruffled, "again that unpleasant word. But I think I can show you that your scruples are quite ill founded."

"Yes?"

"Life is for the strong, to be lived by the strong, and, if need be, taken by the strong. The weak of the world were put here to give the strong pleasure. I am strong. Why should I not use my gift? If I wish to hunt, why should I not? I hunt the scum of the earth—sailors from tramp ships—lascars, blacks, Chinese, whites, mongrels—a thoroughbred horse or hound is worth more than a score of them."

"But they are men," said Rainsford hotly.

"Precisely," said the general. "That is why I use them. It gives me pleasure. They can reason, after a fashion. So they are dangerous."

"But where do you get them?"

The general's left eyelid fluttered down in a wink. "This island is called Ship-Trap," he answered. "Sometimes an angry god of the high seas sends them to me. Sometimes, when Providence is not so kind, I help Providence a bit. Come to the window with me."

Rainsford went to the window and looked out toward the sea.

"Watch! Out there!" exclaimed the general, pointing into the night. Rainsford's eyes saw only blackness, and then, as the general pressed a button, far out to sea Rainsford saw the flash of lights.

The general chuckled. "They indicate a channel," he said, "where there's none: giant rocks with razor edges crouch like a sea monster with wide-open jaws. They can crush a ship as easily as I crush this nut." He dropped a walnut on the hardwood floor and brought his heel grinding down on it. "Oh, yes," he said, casually, as if in answer to a question, "I have electricity. We try to be civilized here."

"Civilized? And you shoot down men?"

A trace of anger was in the general's black eyes, but it was there for but a second, and he said, in his most pleasant manner: "Dear me, what a righteous young man you are! I assure you I do not do the thing you suggest. That would be barbarous. I treat these visitors with every consideration. They get plenty of good food and exercise. They get into splendid physical condition. You shall see for yourself tomorrow."

"What do you mean?"

"We'll visit my training school," smiled the general. "It's in the cellar. I have about a dozen pupils down there now. They're from the Spanish bark San Lucar that had the bad luck to go on the rocks out there. A very inferior lot, I regret to say. Poor specimens and more accustomed to the deck than to the jungle."

He raised his hand, and Ivan, who served as waiter, brought thick Turkish coffee. Rainsford, with an effort, held his tongue in check.

"It's a game, you see, pursued the general blandly. "I suggest to one of them that we go hunting. I give him a supply of food and an excellent hunting knife. I give him three hours' start. I am to follow, armed only with a pistol of the smallest caliber and range. If my quarry eludes me for three whole days, he wins the game. If I find him"—the general smiled—"he loses."

"Suppose he refuses to be hunted?"

"Oh," said the general, "I give him his option, of course. He need not play that game if he doesn't wish to. If he does not wish to hunt, I turn him over to Ivan. Ivan once had the honor of serving as official knouter[5] to the Great White Czar,[6] and he has his own ideas of sport. Invariably, Mr. Rainsford, invariably they choose the hunt."

"And if they win?"

The smile on the general's face widened. "To date I have not lost," he said.

Then he added, hastily: "I don't wish you to think me a braggart, Mr. Rainsford. Many of them afford only the most elementary sort of problem. Occasionally I strike a tartar. One almost did win. I eventually had to use the dogs."

"The dogs?"

5. In Czarist Russia the official flogger of criminals.

6. Probably Nicholas II (1868–1918) who was overthrown by the Revolution and executed; "White" designates those opposed to the Communists, or "Reds."

"This way, please. I'll show you."

The general steered Rainsford to a window. The lights from the windows sent a flickering illumination that made grotesque patterns on the courtyard below, and Rainsford could see moving about there a dozen or so huge black shapes; as they turned toward him, their eyes glittered greenly.

"A rather good lot, I think," observed the general. "They are let out at seven every night. If anyone should try to get into my house—or out of it—something extremely regrettable would occur to him." He hummed a snatch of song from the Folies Bergère.[7]

"And now," said the general, "I want to show you my new collection of heads. Will you come with me to the library?"

"I hope," said Rainsford, "that you will excuse me tonight, General Zaroff. I'm really not feeling at all well."

"Ah, indeed?" the general inquired solicitously. "Well, I suppose that's only natural, after your long swim. You need a good, restful night's sleep. Tomorrow you'll feel like a new man, I'll wager. Then we'll hunt, eh? I've one rather promising prospect—"

Rainsford was hurrying from the room.

"Sorry you can't go with me tonight," called the general. "I expect rather fair sport—a big, strong black. He looks resourceful—Well, good night, Mr. Rainsford; I hope you have a good night's rest."

The bed was good, and the pajamas of the softest silk, and he was tired in every fiber of his being, but nevertheless Rainsford could not quiet his brain with the opiate of sleep. He lay, eyes wide open. Once he thought he heard stealthy steps in the corridor outside his room. He sought to throw open the door; it would not open. He went to the window and looked out. His room was high up in one of the towers. The lights of the château were out now; and it was dark and silent, but there was a fragment of sallow moon, and by its wan light he could see, dimly, the courtyard; there, weaving in and out in the pattern of shadow, were black, noiseless forms; the hounds heard him at the window and looked up, expectantly, with their green eyes. Rainsford went back to bed and lay down. By many methods he tried to put himself to sleep. He had achieved a doze when, just as morning began to come, he heard, far off in the jungle, the faint report of a pistol.

General Zaroff did not appear until luncheon. He was dressed faultlessly in the tweeds of a country squire. He was solicitous about the state of Rainsford's health.

"As for me," sighed the general, "I do not feel so well. I am worried, Mr. Rainsford. Last night I detected traces of my old complaint."

To Rainsford's questioning glance the general said: "Ennui. Boredom."

Then, taking a second helping of *crêpes suzette*, the general explained: "The hunting was not good last night. The fellow lost his head. He made a straight trail that offered no problems at all. That's the trouble with these sailors; they have dull brains to begin with, and they do not know how to get about in the woods. They do excessively stupid and obvious things. It's most annoying. Will you have another

7. Paris theater and music hall which in 1918 reestablished itself as the scene for revues, spectaculars, etc.

glass of Chablis, Mr. Rainsford?"

"General," said Rainsford firmly, "I wish to leave this island at once."

The general raised his thickets of eyebrows; he seemed hurt. "But, my dear fellow," the general protested, "you've only just come. You've had no hunting—"

"I wish to go today," said Rainsford. He saw the dead black eyes of the general on him, studying him. General Zaroff's face suddenly brightened.

He filled Rainsford's glass with venerable Chablis from a dusty bottle.

"Tonight," said the general, "we will hunt—you and I."

Rainsford shook his head. "No, general," he said, "I will not hunt."

The general shrugged his shoulders and delicately ate a hothouse grape. "As you wish, my friend," he said. "The choice rests entirely with you. But may I not venture to suggest that you will find my idea of sport more diverting than Ivan's?"

He nodded toward the corner to where the giant stood, scowling, his thick arms crossed on his hogshead of a chest.

"You don't mean—" cried Rainsford.

"My dear fellow," said the general, "have I not told you I always mean what I say about hunting? This is really an inspiration. I drink to a foeman worthy of my steel—at last."

The general raised his glass, but Rainsford sat staring at him.

"You'll find this game worth playing," the general said enthusiastically. "Your brain against mine. Your woodcraft against mine. Your strength and stamina against mine. Outdoor chess! And the stake is not without value, eh?"

"And if I win—" began Rainsford huskily.

"I'll cheerfully acknowledge myself defeated if I do not find you by midnight of the third day," said General Zaroff. "My sloop will place you on the mainland near a town."

The general read what Rainsford was thinking.

"Oh, you can trust me," said the Cossack. "I will give you my word as a gentleman and a sportsman. Of course you, in turn, must agree to say nothing of your visit here."

"I'll agree to nothing of the kind," said Rainsford.

"Oh," said the general, "in that case—But why discuss that now? Three days hence we can discuss it over a bottle of Veuve Cliquot,[8] unless—"

The general sipped his wine.

Then a businesslike air animated him. "Ivan," he said to Rainsford, "will supply you with hunting clothes, food, a knife. I suggest you wear moccasins; they leave a poorer trail. I suggest too that you avoid the big swamp in the southeast corner of the island. We call it Death Swamp. There's quicksand there. One foolish fellow tried it. The deplorable part of it was that Lazarus followed him. You can imagine my feelings, Mr. Rainsford. I loved Lazarus; he was the finest hound in my pack. Well, I must beg you to excuse me now. I always take a siesta after lunch. You'll hardly have time for a nap, I fear. You'll want to start, no doubt. I shall not follow till dusk. Hunting at night is so

8. A fine champagne; Chablis, above, is a very dry white Burgundy table wine; Chambertin, later, is a highly esteemed red Burgundy wine.

much more exciting than by day, don't you think? Au revoir, Mr. Rainsford, au revoir."

General Zaroff, with a deep, courtly bow, strolled from the room.

From another door came Ivan. Under one arm he carried khaki hunting clothes, a haversack of food, a leather sheath containing a long-bladed hunting knife; his right hand rested on a cocked revolver thrust in the crimson sash about his waist. . . .

Rainsford had fought his way through the bush for two hours. "I must keep my nerve. I must keep my nerve," he said through tight teeth.

He had not been entirely clear-headed when the château gates snapped shut behind him. His whole idea at first was to put distance between himself and General Zaroff, and, to this end, he had plunged along, spurred on by the sharp rowels of something very like panic. Now he had got a grip on himself, had stopped, and was taking stock of himself and the situation.

He saw that straight flight was futile; inevitably it would bring him face to face with the sea. He was in a picture with a frame of water, and his operations, clearly, must take place within that frame.

"I'll give him a trail to follow," muttered Rainsford, and he struck off from the rude paths he had been following into the trackless wilderness. He executed a series of intricate loops; he doubled on his trail again and again, recalling all the lore of the fox hunt, and all the dodges of the fox. Night found him leg-weary, with hands and face lashed by the branches, on a thickly wooded ridge. He knew it would be insane to blunder on through the dark, even if he had the strength. His need for rest was imperative and he thought: "I have played the fox, now I must play the cat of the fable."[9] A big tree with a thick trunk and outspread branches was nearby, and, taking care to leave not the slightest mark, he climbed up into the crotch, and stretching out on one of the broad limbs, after a fashion, rested. Rest brought him new confidence and almost a feeling of security. Even so zealous a hunter as General Zaroff could not trace him there, he told himself; only the devil himself could follow that complicated trail through the jungle after dark. But, perhaps, the general was a devil—

An apprehensive night crawled slowly by like a wounded snake, and sleep did not visit Rainsford, although the silence of a dead world was on the jungle. Toward morning when a dingy gray was varnishing the sky, the cry of some startled bird focused Rainsford's attention in that direction. Something was coming through the bush, coming slowly, carefully, coming by the same winding way Rainsford had come. He flattened himself down on the limb, and through a screen of leaves almost as thick as tapestry, he watched. The thing that was approaching was a man.

It was General Zaroff. He made his way along with his eyes fixed in utmost concentration on the ground before him. He paused, almost beneath the tree, dropped to his knees and studied the ground. Rainsford's impulse was to hurl himself down like a panther, but he saw

9. The fox boasts of his many tricks to elude the hounds; the cat responds he knows only one—to climb the nearest tree—but that this is worth more than all the fox's tricks.

that the general's right hand held something metallic—a small automatic pistol.

The hunter shook his head several times, as if he were puzzled. Then he straightened up and took from his case one of his black cigarettes; its pungent incense-like smoke floated up to Rainsford's nostrils.

Rainsford held his breath. The general's eyes had left the ground and were traveling inch by inch up the tree. Rainsford froze there, every muscle tensed for a spring. But the sharp eyes of the hunter stopped before they reached the limb where Rainsford lay; a smile spread over his brown face. Very deliberately he blew a smoke ring into the air; then he turned his back on the tree and walked carelessly away, back along the trail he had come. The swish of the underbrush against his hunting boots grew fainter and fainter.

The pent-up air burst hotly from Rainsford's lungs. His first thought made him feel sick and numb. The general could follow a trail through the woods at night; he could follow an extremely difficult trail; he must have uncanny powers; only by the merest chance had the Cossack failed to see his quarry.

Rainsford's second thought was even more terrible. It sent a shudder of cold horror through his whole being. Why had the general smiled? Why had he turned back?

Rainsford did not want to believe what his reason told him was true, but the truth was as evident as the sun that had by now pushed through the morning mists. The general was playing with him! The general was saving him for another day's sport! The Cossack was the cat; he was the mouse.[1] Then it was that Rainsford knew the full meaning of terror.

"I will not lose my nerve. I will not."

He slid down from the tree, and struck off again into the woods. His face was set and he forced the machinery of his mind to function. Three hundred yards from his hiding place he stopped where a huge dead tree leaned precariously on a smaller, living one. Throwing off his sack of food, Rainsford took his knife from its sheath and began to work with all his energy.

The job was finished at last, and he threw himself down behind a fallen log a hundred feet away. He did not have to wait long. The cat was coming again to play with the mouse.

Following the trail with the sureness of a bloodhound, came General Zaroff. Nothing escaped those searching black eyes, no crushed blade of grass, no bent twig, no mark, no matter how faint, in the moss. So intent was the Cossack on his stalking that he was upon the thing Rainsford had made before he saw it. His foot touched the protruding bough that was the trigger. Even as he touched it, the general sensed his danger and leaped back with the agility of an ape. But he was not quite quick enough; the dead tree, delicately adjusted to rest on the cut living one, crashed down and struck the general a glacing blow on the shoulder as it fell; but for his alertness, he must have been smashed beneath it. He staggered, but he did not fall; nor did he drop his revolver. He stood there, rubbing his injured shoulder, and Rainsford,

1. A cat, sure of his prey, plays with a mouse before killing him.

with fear again gripping his heart, heard the general's mocking laugh ring through the jungle.

"Rainsford," called the general, "if you are within sound of my voice, as I suppose you are, let me congratulate you. Not many men know how to make a Malay man-catcher. Luckily, for me, I too have hunted in Malacca. You are proving interesting, Mr. Rainsford. I am going now to have my wound dressed; it's only a slight one. But I shall be back. I shall be back."

When the general, nursing his bruised shoulder, had gone, Rainsford took up his flight again. It was flight now, a desperate, hopeless flight, that carried him on for some hours. Dusk came, then darkness, and still he pressed on. The ground grew softer under his moccasins; the vegetation grew ranker, denser; insects bit him savagely. Then, as he stepped forward, his foot sank into the ooze. He tried to wrench it back, but the muck sucked viciously at his foot as if it were a giant leech. With a violent effort, he tore his foot loose. He knew where he was now. Death Swamp and its quicksand.

His hands were tight closed as if his nerve were something tangible that someone in the darkness was trying to tear from his grip. The softness of the earth had given him an idea. He stepped back from the quicksand a dozen feet or so and, like some huge prehistoric beaver, he began to dig.

Rainsford had dug himself in in France[2] when a second's delay meant death. That had been a placid pastime compared to his digging now. The pit grew deeper; when it was above his shoulders, he climbed out and from some hard saplings cut stakes and sharpened them to a fine point. These stakes he planted in the bottom of the pit with the points sticking up. With flying fingers he wove a rough carpet of weeds and branches and with it he covered the mouth of the pit. Then, wet with sweat and aching with tiredness, he crouched behind the stump of a lightning-charred tree.

He knew his pursuer was coming; he heard the padding sound of feet on the soft earth, and the night breeze brought him the perfume of the general's cigarette. It seemed to Rainsford that the general was coming with unusual swiftness; he was not feeling his way along, foot by foot. Rainsford, crouching there, could not see the general, nor could he see the pit. He lived a year in a minute. Then he felt an impulse to cry aloud with joy, for he heard the sharp crackle of the breaking branches as the cover of the pit gave way; he heard the sharp scream of pain as the pointed stakes found their mark. He leaped up from his place of concealment. Then he cowered back. Three feet from the pit a man was standing, with an electric torch in his hand.

"You've done well, Rainsford," the voice of the general called. "Your Burmese tiger pit has claimed one of my best dogs. Again you score. I think, Mr. Rainsford, I'll see what you can do against my whole pack. I'm going home for a rest now. Thank you for a most amusing evening."

At daybreak Rainsford, lying near the swamp, was awakened by a sound that made him know that he had new things to learn about

2. During World War I he had quickly dug a hole or trench to shelter himself from exploding shells, bullets, etc.

fear. It was a distant sound, faint and wavering, but he knew it. It was the baying of a pack of hounds.

Rainsford knew he could do one of two things. He could stay where he was and wait. That was suicide. He could flee. That was postponing the inevitable. For a moment he stood there, thinking. An idea that held a wild chance came to him, and, tightening his belt, he headed away from the swamp.

The baying of the hounds drew nearer, then still nearer, nearer, ever nearer. On a ridge Rainsford climbed a tree. Down a watercourse, not a quarter of a mile away, he could see the bush moving. Straining his eyes, he saw the lean figure of General Zaroff; just ahead of him Rainsford made out another figure whose wide shoulders surged through the tall jungle weeds; it was the giant Ivan, and he seemed pulled forward by some unseen force; Rainsford knew that Ivan must be holding the pack in leash.

They would be on him any minute now. His mind worked frantically. He thought of a native trick he had learned in Uganda. He slid down the tree. He caught hold of a springy young sapling and to it he fastened his hunting knife, with the blade pointing down the trail; with a bit of wild grapevine he tied back the sapling. Then he ran for his life. The hounds raised their voices as they hit the fresh scent. Rainsford knew now how an animal at bay feels.

He had to stop to get his breath. The baying of the hounds stopped abruptly, and Rainsford's heart stopped too. They must have reached the knife.

He shinned excitedly up a tree and looked back. His pursuers had stopped. But the hope that was in Rainsford's brain when he climbed died, for he saw in the shallow valley that General Zaroff was still on his feet. But Ivan was not. The knife, driven by the recoil of the springing tree, had not wholly failed.

Rainsford had hardly tumbled to the ground when the pack took up the cry again.

"Nerve, nerve, nerve!" he panted, as he dashed along. A blue gap showed between the trees dead ahead. Ever nearer drew the hounds. Rainsford forced himself on toward that gap. He reached it. It was the shore of the sea. Across a cove he could see the gloomy gray stone of the château. Twenty feet below him the sea rumbled and hissed. Rainsford hesitated. He heard the hounds. Then he leaped far out into the sea. . . .

When the general and his pack reached the place by the sea, the Cossack stopped. For some minutes he stood regarding the blue-green expanse of water. He shrugged his shoulders. Then he sat down, took a drink of brandy from a silver flask, lit a perfumed cigarette, and hummed a bit from "Madame Butterfly."

General Zaroff had an exceedingly good dinner in his great paneled dining hall that evening. With it he had a bottle of Pol Roger and half a bottle of Chambertin. Two slight annoyances kept him from perfect enjoyment. One was the thought that it would be difficult to replace Ivan; the other was that his quarry had escaped him; of course the American hadn't played the game—so thought the general as he tasted his after-dinner liqueur. In his library he read, to soothe himself, from the works of Marcus Aurelius.[3] At ten he went up to his bedroom. He was deliciously tired, he said to himself, as he locked himself in. There was a little moonlight, so, before turning on his light, he went to the window and looked down at the courtyard. He could see the great hounds, and he called: "Better luck another time," to them. Then he switched on the light.

A man, who had been hiding in the curtains of the bed, was standing there.

"Rainsford!" screamed the general. "How in God's name did you get here?"

"Swam," said Rainsford. "I found it quicker than walking through the jungle."

The general sucked in his breath and smiled. "I congratulate you," he said. "You have won the game."

Rainsford did not smile. "I am still a beast at bay," he said, in a low, hoarse voice. "Get ready, General Zaroff."

The general made one of his deepest bows. "I see," he said. "Splendid! One of us is to furnish a repast for the hounds. The other will sleep in this very excellent bed. On guard, Rainsford. . . ."

He had never slept in a better bed, Rainsford decided.

1924

ERNEST HEMINGWAY

The Short Happy Life of Francis Macomber

It was now lunch time and they were all sitting under the double green fly of the dining tent pretending that nothing had happened.

"Will you have lime juice or lemon squash?" Macomber asked.

"I'll have a gimlet,"[1] Robert Wilson told him.

"I'll have a gimlet too. I need something," Macomber's wife said.

"I suppose it's the thing to do," Macomber agreed. "Tell him to make three gimlets."

The mess boy had started them already, lifting the bottles out of the canvas cooling bags that sweated wet in the wind that blew through the trees that shaded the tents.

"What had I ought to give them?" Macomber asked.

"A quid[2] would be plenty," Wilson told him. "You don't want to spoil them."

"Will the headman distribute it?"

"Absolutely."

3. Roman Emperor (A.D. 161–180), Stoic philosopher, writer, and humanitarian, who, though good to the poor and opposed to the cruelty of gladiatorial shows, persecuted early Christians.

1. Drink of lime juice, gin, and soda or water.

2. Slang for a British pound.

Francis Macomber had, half an hour before, been carried to his tent from the edge of the camp in triumph on the arms and shoulders of the cook, the personal boys, the skinner and the porters. The gun-bearers had taken no part in the demonstration. When the native boys put him down at the door of his tent, he had shaken all their hands, received their congratulations, and then gone into the tent and sat on the bed until his wife came in. She did not speak to him when she came in and he left the tent at once to wash his face and hands in the portable wash basin outside and go over to the dining tent to sit in a comfortable canvas chair in the breeze and the shade.

"You've got your lion," Robert Wilson said to him, "and a damned fine one too."

Mrs. Macomber looked at Wilson quickly. She was an extremely handsome and well-kept woman of the beauty and social position which had, five years before, commanded five thousand dollars as the price of endorsing, with photographs, a beauty product which she had never used. She had been married to Francis Macomber for eleven years.

"He is a good lion, isn't he?" Macomber said. His wife looked at him now. She looked at both these men as though she had never seen them before.

One, Wilson, the white hunter, she knew she had never truly seen before. He was about middle height with sandy hair, a stubby mustache, a very red face and extremely cold blue eyes with faint white wrinkles at the corners that grooved merrily when he smiled. He smiled at her now and she looked away from his face at the way his shoulders sloped in the loose tunic he wore with the four big cartridges held in loops where the left breast pocket should have been, at his big brown hands, his old slacks, his very dirty boots and back to his red face again. She noticed where the baked red of his face stopped in a white line that marked the circle left by his Stetson hat[3] that hung now from one of the pegs of the tent pole.

"Well, here's to the lion," Robert Wilson said. He smiled at her again and, not smiling, she looked curiously at her husband.

Francis Macomber was very tall, very well built if you did not mind that length of bone, dark, his hair cropped like an oarsman, rather thin-lipped, and was considered handsome. He was dressed in the same sort of safari clothes that Wilson wore except that his were new, he was thirty-five years old, kept himself very fit, was good at court games, had a number of big-game fishing records, and had just shown himself, very publicly, to be a coward.

"Here's to the lion," he said. "I can't ever thank you for what you did."

Margaret, his wife, looked away from him and back to Wilson.

"Let's not talk about the lion," she said.

Wilson looked over at her without smiling and now she smiled at him.

"It's been a very strange day," she said. "Hadn't you ought to

3. Cowboy-type hat.

put your hat on even under the canvas at noon? You told me that, you know."

"Might put it on," said Wilson.

"You know you have a very red face, Mr. Wilson," she told him and smiled again.

"Drink," said Wilson.

"I don't think so," she said. "Francis drinks a great deal, but his face is never red."

"It's red today," Macomber tried a joke.

"No," said Margaret. "It's mine that's red today. But Mr. Wilson's is always red."

"Must be racial," said Wilson. "I say, you wouldn't like to drop my beauty as a topic, would you?"

"I've just started on it."

"Let's chuck it," said Wilson.

"Conversation is going to be so difficult," Margaret said.

"Don't be silly, Margot," her husband said.

"No difficulty," Wilson said. "Got a damn fine lion."

Margot looked at them both and they both saw that she was going to cry. Wilson had seen it coming for a long time and he dreaded it. Macomber was past dreading it.

"I wish it hadn't happened. Oh, I wish it hadn't happened," she said and started for her tent. She made no noise of crying but they could see that her shoulders were shaking under the rose-colored, sun-proofed shirt she wore.

"Women upset," said Wilson to the tall man. "Amounts to nothing. Strain on the nerves and one thing'n another."

"No," said Macomber. "I suppose that I rate that for the rest of my life now."

"Nonsense. Let's have a spot of the giant killer," said Wilson. "Forget the whole thing. Nothing to it anyway."

"We might try," said Macomber. "I won't forget what you did for me though."

"Nothing," said Wilson. "All nonsense."

So they sat there in the shade where the camp was pitched under some wide-topped acacia trees with a boulder-strewn cliff behind them, and a stretch of grass that ran to the bank of a boulder-filled stream in front with forest beyond it, and drank their just-cool lime drinks and avoided one another's eyes while the boys set the table for lunch. Wilson could tell that the boys all knew about it now and when he saw Macomber's personal boy looking curiously at his master while he was putting dishes on the table he snapped at him in Swahili. The boy turned away with his face blank.

"What were you telling him?" Macomber asked.

"Nothing. Told him to look alive or I'd see he got about fifteen of the best."

"What's that? Lashes?"

"It's quite illegal," Wilson said. "You're supposed to fine them."

"Do you still have them whipped?"

"Oh, yes. They could raise a row if they chose to complain. But they don't. They prefer it to the fines."

"How strange!" said Macomber.

"Not strange, really," Wilson said. "Which would you rather do? Take a good birching or lose your pay?"

Then he felt embarrassed at asking it and before Macomber could answer he went on, "We all take a beating every day, you know, one way or another."

This was no better. "Good God," he thought. "I am a diplomat, aren't I?"

"Yes, we take a beating," said Macomber, still not looking at him. "I'm awfully sorry about that lion business. It doesn't have to go any further, does it? I mean no one will hear about it, will they?"

"You mean will I tell it at the Mathaiga Club?" Wilson looked at him now coldly. He had not expected this. So he's a bloody four-letter man as well as a bloody coward, he thought. I rather liked him too until today. But how is one to know about an American?

"No," said Wilson. "I'm a professional hunter. We never talk about our clients. You can be quite easy on that. It's supposed to be bad form to ask us not to talk though."

He had decided now that to break would be much easier. He would eat, then, by himself and could read a book with his meals. They would eat by themselves. He would see them through the safari on a very formal basis—what was it the French called it? Distinguished consideration[4]—and it would be a damn sight easier than having to go through this emotional trash. He'd insult him and make a good clean break. Then he could read a book with his meals and he'd still be drinking their whisky. That was the phrase for it when a safari went bad. You ran into another white hunter and you asked, "How is everything going?" and he answered, "Oh, I'm still drinking their whisky," and you knew everything had gone to pot.

"I'm sorry," Macomber said and looked at him with his American face that would stay adolescent until it became middle-aged, and Wilson noted his crew-cropped hair, fine eyes only faintly shifty, good nose, thin lips and handsome jaw. "I'm sorry I didn't realize that. There are lots of things I don't know."

So what could he do, Wilson thought. He was all ready to break it off quickly and neatly and here the beggar was apologizing after he had just insulted him. He made one more attempt. "Don't worry about me talking," he said. "I have a living to make. You know in Africa no woman ever misses her lion and no white man ever bolts."

"I bolted like a rabbit," Macomber said.

Now what in hell were you going to do about a man who talked like that, Wilson wondered.

Wilson looked at Macomber with his flat, blue, machine-gunner's eyes and the other smiled back at him. He had a pleasant smile if you did not notice how his eyes showed when he was hurt.

"Maybe I can fix it up on buffalo," he said. "We're after them next, aren't we?"

"In the morning if you like," Wilson told him. Perhaps he had been wrong. This was certainly the way to take it. You most cer-

4. Highest regard.

tainly could not tell a damned thing about an American. He was all for Macomber again. If you could forget the morning. But, of course, you couldn't. The morning had been about as bad as they come.

"Here comes the Memsahib," he said. She was walking over from her tent looking refreshed and cheerful and quite lovely. She had a very perfect oval face, so perfect that you expected her to be stupid. But she wasn't stupid, Wilson thought, no, not stupid.

"How is the beautiful red-faced Mr. Wilson? Are you feeling better, Francis, my pearl?"

"Oh, much," said Macomber.

"I've dropped the whole thing," she said, sitting down at the table. "What importance is there to whether Francis is any good at killing lions? That's not his trade. That's Mr. Wilson's trade. Mr. Wilson is really very impressive killing anything. You do kill anything, don't you?"

"Oh, anything," said Wilson. "Simply anything." They are, he thought, the hardest in the world; the hardest, the cruelest, the most predatory and the most attractive and their men have softened or gone to pieces nervously as they have hardened. Or is it that they pick men they can handle? They can't know that much at the age they marry, he thought. He was grateful that he had gone through his education on American women before now because this was a very attractive one.

"We're going after buff in the morning," he told her.

"I'm coming," she said.

"No, you're not."

"Oh, yes, I am. Mayn't I, Francis?"

"Why not stay in camp?"

"Not for anything," she said. "I wouldn't miss something like today for anything."

When she left, Wilson was thinking, when she went off to cry, she seemed a hell of a fine woman. She seemed to understand, to realize, to be hurt for him and for herself and to know how things really stood. She is away for twenty minutes and now she is back, simply enamelled in that American female cruelty. They are the damnedest women. Really the damnedest.

"We'll put on another show for you tomorrow," Francis Macomber said.

"You're not coming," Wilson said.

"You're very mistaken," she told him. "And I want *so* to see you perform again. You were lovely this morning. That is if blowing things' heads off is lovely."

"Here's the lunch," said Wilson. "You're very merry, aren't you?"

"Why not? I didn't come out here to be dull."

"Well, it hasn't been dull," Wilson said. He could see the boulders in the river and the high bank beyond with the trees and he remembered the morning.

"Oh, no," she said. "It's been charming. And tomorrow. You don't know how I look forward to tomorrow."

"That's eland he's offering you," Wilson said.

"They're the big cowy things that jump like hares, aren't they?"

"I suppose that describes them," Wilson said.

"It's very good meat," Macomber said.

"Didn't you shoot it, Francis?" she asked.

"Yes."

"They're not dangerous, are they?"

"Only if they fall on you," Wilson told her.

"I'm so glad."

"Why not let up on the bitchery just a little, Margot," Macomber said, cutting the eland steak and putting some mashed potato, gravy and carrot on the down-turned fork that tined through the piece of meat.

"I suppose I could," she said, "since you put it so prettily."

"Tonight we'll have champagne for the lion," Wilson said. "It's a bit too hot at noon."

"Oh, the lion," Margot said. "I'd forgotten the lion!"

So, Robert Wilson thought to himself, she *is* giving him a ride, isn't she? Or do you suppose that's her idea of putting up a good show? How should a woman act when she discovers her husband is a bloody coward? She's damn cruel but they're all cruel. They govern, of course, and to govern one has to be cruel sometimes. Still, I've seen enough of their damn terrorism.

"Have some more eland," he said to her politely.

That afternoon, late, Wilson and Macomber went out in the motor car with the native driver and the two gun-bearers. Mrs. Macomber stayed in the camp. It was too hot to go out, she said, and she was going with them in the early morning. As they drove off Wilson saw her standing under the big tree, looking pretty rather than beautiful in her faintly rosy khaki, her dark hair drawn back off her forehead and gathered in a knot low on her neck, her face as fresh, he thought, as though she were in England. She waved to them as the car went off through the swale of high grass and curved around through the trees into the small hills of orchard bush.

In the orchard bush they found a herd of impala,[5] and leaving the car they stalked one old ram with long, wide-spread horns and Macomber killed it with a very creditable shot that knocked the buck down at a good two hundred yards and sent the herd off bounding wildly and leaping over one another's backs in long, leg-drawn-up leaps as unbelievable and as floating as those one makes sometimes in dreams.

"That was a good shot," Wilson said. "They're a small target."

"Is it a worthwhile head?" Macomber asked.

"It's excellent," Wilson told him. "You shoot like that and you'll have no trouble."

"Do you think we'll find buffalo tomorrow?"

"There's a good chance of it. They feed out early in the morning and with luck we may catch them in the open."

"I'd like to clear away that lion business," Macomber said. "It's not very pleasant to have your wife see you do something like that."

5. Antelope of bush country of east and south Africa with lyre-shaped horns.

I should think it would be even more unpleasant to do it, Wilson thought, wife or no wife, or to talk about it having done it. But he said, "I wouldn't think about that any more. Anyone could be upset by his first lion. That's all over."

But that night after dinner and a whisky and soda by the fire before going to bed, as Francis Macomber lay on his cot with the mosquito bar over him and listened to the night noises, it was not all over. It was neither all over nor was it beginning. It was there exactly as it happened with some parts of it indelibly emphasized and he was miserably ashamed at it. But more than shame he felt cold, hollow fear in him. The fear was still there like a cold slimy hollow in all the emptiness where once his confidence had been and it made him feel sick. It was still there with him now.

It had started the night before when he had wakened and heard the lion roaring somewhere up along the river. It was a deep sound and at the end there were sort of coughing grunts that made him seem just outside the tent, and when Francis Macomber woke in the night to hear it he was afraid. He could hear his wife breathing quietly, asleep. There was no one to tell he was afraid, nor to be afraid with him, and, lying alone, he did not know the Somali proverb that says a brave man is always frightened three times by a lion; when he first sees his track, when he first hears him roar and when he first confronts him. Then while they were eating breakfast by lantern light out in the dining tent, before the sun was up, the lion roared again and Francis thought he was just at the edge of camp.

"Sounds like an old-timer," Robert Wilson said, looking up from his kippers and coffee. "Listen to him cough."

"Is he very close?"

"A mile or so up the stream."

"Will we see him?"

"We'll have a look."

"Does his roaring carry that far? It sounds as though he were right in camp."

"Carries a hell of a long way," said Robert Wilson. "It's strange the way it carries. Hope he's a shootable cat. The boys said there was a very big one about here."

"If I get a shot, where should I hit him," Macomber asked, "to stop him?"

"In the shoulders," Wilson said. "In the neck if you can make it. Shoot for bone. Break him down."

"I hope I can place it properly," Macomber said.

"You shoot very well," Wilson told him. "Take your time. Make sure of him. The first one in is the one that counts."

"What range will it be?"

"Can't tell. Lion has something to say about that. Won't shoot unless it's close enough so you can make sure."

"At under a hundred yards?" Macomber asked.

Wilson looked at him quickly.

"Hundred's about right. Might have to take him a bit under. Shouldn't chance a shot at much over that. A hundred's a decent range. You can hit him wherever you want at that. Here comes the Memsahib."

"Good morning," she said. "Are we going after that lion?"

"As soon as you deal with your breakfast," Wilson said. "How are you feeling?"

"Marvellous," she said. "I'm very excited."

"I'll just go and see that everything is ready," Wilson went off. As he left the lion roared again.

"Noisy beggar," Wilson said. "We'll put a stop to that."

"What's the matter, Francis?" his wife asked him.

"Nothing," Macomber said.

"Yes, there is," she said. "What are you upset about?"

"Nothing," he said.

"Tell me," she looked at him. "Don't you feel well?"

"It's that damned roaring," he said. "It's been going on all night, you know."

"Why didn't you wake me," she said. "I'd love to have heard it."

"I've got to kill the damned thing," Macomber said, miserably.

"Well, that's what you're out here for, isn't it?"

"Yes. But I'm nervous. Hearing the thing roar gets on my nerves."

"Well then, as Wilson said, kill him and stop his roaring."

"Yes, darling," said Francis Macomber. "It sounds easy, doesn't it?"

"You're not afraid, are you?"

"Of course not. But I'm nervous from hearing him roar all night."

"You'll kill him marvellously," she said. "I know you will. I'm awfully anxious to see it."

"Finish your breakfast and we'll be starting."

"It's not light yet," she said. "This is a ridiculous hour."

Just then the lion roared in a deep-chested moaning, suddenly guttural, ascending vibration that seemed to shake the air and ended in a sigh and a heavy, deep-chested grunt.

"He sounds almost here," Macomber's wife said.

"My God," said Macomber. "I hate that damned noise."

"It's very impressive."

"Impressive. It's frightful."

Robert Wilson came up then carrying his short, ugly, shockingly big-bored .505 Gibbs and grinning.

"Come on," he said. "Your gun-bearer has your Springfield and the big gun. Everything's in the car. Have you solids?"[6]

"Yes."

"I'm ready," Mrs. Macomber said.

"Must make him stop that racket," Wilson said. "You get in front. The Memsahib can sit back here with me."

They climbed into the motor car and, in the gray first daylight, moved off up the river through the trees. Macomber opened the breech of his rifle and saw he had metal-cased bullets, shut the bolt and put the rifle on safety. He saw his hand was trembling. He felt in his pocket for more cartridges and moved his fingers over the cartridges in the loops of his tunic front. He turned back to where

6. They are using jacketed bullets for quick, clean kill; the Springfield is a thirty-caliber rifle as opposed to Wilson's fifty-caliber Gibbs.

Wilson sat in the rear seat of the doorless, box-bodied motor car beside his wife, them both grinning with excitement, and Wilson leaned forward and whispered,

"See the birds dropping. Means the old boy has left his kill."

On the far bank of the stream Macomber could see, above the trees, vultures circling and plummeting down.

"Chances are he'll come to drink along here," Wilson whispered. "Before he goes to lay up. Keep an eye out."

They were driving slowly along the high bank of the stream which here cut deeply to its boulder-filled bed, and they wound in and out through big trees as they drove. Macomber was watching the opposite bank when he felt Wilson take hold of his arm. The car stopped.

"There he is," he heard the whisper. "Ahead and to the right. Get out and take him. He's a marvellous lion."

Macomber saw the lion now. He was standing almost broadside, his great head up and turned toward them. The early morning breeze that blew toward them was just stirring his dark mane, and the lion looked huge, silhouetted on the rise of bank in the gray morning light, his shoulders heavy, his barrel of a body bulking smoothly.

"How far is he?" asked Macomber, raising his rifle.

"About seventy-five. Get out and take him."

"Why not shoot from where I am?"

"You don't shoot them from cars," he heard Wilson saying in his ear. "Get out. He's not going to stay there all day."

Macomber stepped out of the curved opening at the side of the front seat, onto the step and down onto the ground. The lion still stood looking majestically and coolly toward this object that his eyes only showed in silhouette, bulking like some super-rhino. There was no man smell carried toward him and he watched the object, moving his great head a little from side to side. Then watching the object, not afraid, but hesitating before going down the bank to drink with such a thing opposite him, he saw a man figure detach itself from it and he turned his heavy head and swung away toward the cover of the trees as he heard a cracking crash and felt the slam of a .30–06 220-grain solid bullet that bit his flank and ripped in sudden hot scalding nausea through his stomach. He trotted, heavy, big-footed, swinging wounded full-bellied, through the trees toward the tall grass and cover, and the crash came again to go past him ripping the air apart. Then it crashed again and he felt the blow as it hit his lower ribs and ripped on through, blood sudden hot and frothy in his mouth, and he galloped toward the high grass where he could crouch and not be seen and make them bring the crashing thing close enough so he could make a rush and get the man that held it.

Macomber had not thought how the lion felt as he got out of the car. He only knew his hands were shaking and as he walked away from the car it was almost impossible for him to make his legs move. They were stiff in the thighs, but he could feel the muscles fluttering. He raised the rifle, sighted on the junction of the lion's head and shoulders and pulled the trigger. Nothing happened though he pulled until he thought his finger would break. Then he knew he had the safety on and as he lowered the rifle to move the safety over he moved another frozen pace forward, and the lion seeing his silhouette now clear of the silhouette of the car, turned and started off at a trot, and, as Macomber fired, he heard a whunk that meant that the bullet was home; but the lion kept on going. Macomber shot again and everyone saw the bullet throw a spout of dirt beyond the trotting lion. He shot again, remembering to lower his aim, and they all heard the bullet hit, and the lion went into a gallop and was in the tall grass before he had the bolt pushed forward.

Macomber stood there feeling sick at his stomach, his hands that held the Springfield still cocked, shaking, and his wife and Robert Wilson were standing by him. Beside him too were the two gun-bearers chattering in Wakamba.[7]

"I hit him," Macomber said. "I hit him twice."

"You gut-shot him and you hit him somewhere forward," Wilson said without enthusiasm. The gun-bearers looked very grave. They were silent now.

"You may have killed him," Wilson went on. "We'll have to wait a while before we go in to find out."

"What do you mean?"

"Let him get sick before we follow him up."

"Oh," said Macomber.

"He's a hell of a fine lion," Wilson said cheerfully. "He's gotten into a bad place though."

"Why is it bad?"

"Can't see him until you're on him."

"Oh," said Macomber.

"Come on," said Wilson. "The Memsahib can stay here in the car. We'll go to have a look at the blood spoor."

"Stay here, Margot," Macomber said to his wife. His mouth was very dry and it was hard for him to talk.

"Why?" she asked.

"Wilson says to."

"We're going to have a look," Wilson said. "You stay here. You can see even better from here."

"All right."

Wilson spoke in Swahili to the driver. He nodded and said, "Yes, Bwana."

Then they went down the steep bank and across the stream, climbing over and around the boulders and up the other bank, pulling up by some projecting roots, and along it until they found where the lion had been trotting when Macomber first shot. There was dark blood on the short grass that the gun-bearers pointed out with grass stems, and that ran away behind the river bank trees.

"What do we do?" asked Macomber.

"Not much choice," said Wilson. "We can't bring the car over. Bank's too steep. We'll let him stiffen up a bit and then you and

7. A Bantu dialect spoken in Kenya.

I'll go in and have a look for him."

"Can't we set the grass on fire?" Macomber asked.

"Too green."

"Can't we send beaters?"

Wilson looked at him appraisingly. "Of course we can," he said. "But it's just a touch murderous. You see we know the lion's wounded. You can drive an unwounded lion—he'll move on ahead of a noise—but a wounded lion's going to charge. You can't see him until you're right on him. He'll make himself perfectly flat in cover you wouldn't think would hide a hare. You can't very well send boys in there to that sort of a show. Somebody bound to get mauled."

"What about the gun-bearers?"

"Oh, they'll go with us. It's their *shauri*.[8] You see, they signed on for it. They don't look too happy though, do they?"

"I don't want to go in there," said Macomber. It was out before he knew he'd said it.

"Neither do I," said Wilson very cheerily. "Really no choice though." Then, as an afterthought, he glanced at Macomber and saw suddenly how he was trembling and the pitiful look on his face.

"You don't have to go in, of course," he said. "That's what I'm hired for, you know. That's why I'm so expensive."

"You mean you'd go in by yourself? Why not leave him there?"

Robert Wilson, whose entire occupation had been with the lion and the problem he presented, and who had not been thinking about Macomber except to note that he was rather windy, suddenly felt as though he had opened the wrong door in a hotel and seen something shameful.

"What do you mean?"

"Why not just leave him?"

"You mean pretend to ourselves he hasn't been hit?"

"No. Just drop it."

"It isn't done."

"Why not?"

"For one thing, he's certain to be suffering. For another, some one else might run onto him."

"I see."

"But you don't have to have anything to do with it."

"I'd like to," Macomber said. "I'm just scared, you know."

"I'll go ahead when we go in," Wilson said, "with Kongoni tracking. You keep behind me and a little to one side. Chances are we'll hear him growl. If we see him we'll both shoot. Don't worry about anything. I'll keep you backed up. As a matter of fact, you know, perhaps you'd better not go. It might be much better. Why don't you go over and join the Memsahib while I just get it over with?"

"No, I want to go."

"All right," said Wilson. "But don't go in if you don't want to. This is my *shauri* now, you know."

"I want to go," said Macomber.

They sat under a tree and smoked.

8. Problem (a Swahili word).

"Want to go back and speak to the Memsahib while we're waiting?" Wilson asked.

"No."

"I'll just step back and tell her to be patient."

"Good," said Macomber. He sat there, sweating under his arms, his mouth dry, his stomach hollow feeling, wanting to find courage to tell Wilson to go on and finish off the lion without him. He could not know that Wilson was furious because he had not noticed the state he was in earlier and sent him back to his wife. While he sat there Wilson came up. "I have your big gun," he said. "Take it. We've given him time, I think. Come on."

Macomber took the big gun and Wilson said:

"Keep behind me and about five yards to the right and do exactly as I tell you." Then he spoke in Swahili to the two gun-bearers, who looked the picture of gloom.

"Let's go," he said.

"Could I have a drink of water?" Macomber asked. Wilson spoke to the older gun-bearer, who wore a canteen on his belt, and the man unbuckled it, unscrewed the top and handed it to Macomber, who took it noticing how heavy it seemed and how hairy and shoddy the felt covering was in his hand. He raised it to drink and looked ahead at the high grass with the flat-topped trees behind it. A breeze was blowing toward them and the grass rippled gently in the wind. He looked at the gun-bearer and he could see the gun-bearer was suffering too with fear.

Thirty-five yards into the grass the big lion lay flattened out along the ground. His ears were back and his only movement was a slight twitching up and down of his long, black-tufted tail. He had turned at bay as soon as he had reached this cover and he was sick with the wound through his full belly, and weakening with the wound through his lungs that brought a thin foamy red to his mouth each time he breathed. His flanks were wet and hot and flies were on the little openings the solid bullets had made in his tawny hide, and his big yellow eyes, narrowed with hate, looked straight ahead, only blinking when the pain came as he breathed, and his claws dug in the soft baked earth. All of him, pain, sickness, hatred and all of his remaining strength, was tightening into an absolute concentration for a rush. He could hear the men talking and he waited, gathering all of himself into this preparation for a charge as soon as the men would come into the grass. As he heard their voices his tail stiffened to twitch up and down, and, as they came into the edge of the grass, he made a coughing grunt and charged.

Kongoni, the old gun-bearer, in the lead watching the blood spoor, Wilson watching the grass for any movement, his big gun ready, the second gun-bearer looking ahead and listening, Macomber close to Wilson, his rifle cocked, they had just moved into the grass when Macomber heard the blood-choked coughing grunt, and saw the swishing rush in the grass. The next thing he knew he was running; running wildly, in panic in the open, running toward the stream.

He heard the *ca-ra-wong!* of Wilson's big rifle, and again in a second crashing *carawong!* and turning saw the lion, horrible-looking now, with half his head seeming to be gone, crawling toward Wilson in the edge of the tall grass while the red-faced man worked the bolt on the short ugly rifle and aimed carefully as another blasting *carawong!* came from the muzzle, and the crawling, heavy, yellow bulk of the lion stiffened and the huge, mutilated head slid forward and Macomber, standing by himself in the clearing where he had run, holding a loaded rifle, while two black men and a white man looked back at him in contempt, knew the lion was dead. He came toward Wilson, his tallness all seeming a naked reproach, and Wilson looked at him and said:

"Want to take pictures?"

"No," he said.

That was all any one had said until they reached the motor car. Then Wilson had said:

"Hell of a fine lion. Boys will skin him out. We might as well stay here in the shade."

Macomber's wife had not looked at him nor he at her and he had sat by her in the back seat with Wilson sitting in the front seat. Once he had reached over and taken his wife's hand without looking at her and she had removed her hand from his. Looking across the stream to where the gun-bearers were skinning out the lion he could see that she had been able to see the whole thing. While they sat there his wife had reached forward and put her hand on Wilson's shoulder. He turned and she had leaned forward over the low seat and kissed him on the mouth.

"Oh, I say," said Wilson, going redder than his natural baked color.

"Mr. Robert Wilson," she said. "The beautiful red-faced Mr. Robert Wilson."

Then she sat down beside Macomber again and looked away across the stream to where the lion lay, with uplifted, white-muscled, tendon-marked naked forearms, and white bloating belly, as the black men fleshed away the skin. Finally the gun-bearers brought the skin over, wet and heavy, and climbed in behind with it, rolling it up before they got in, and the motor car started. No one had said anything more until they were back in camp.

That was the story of the lion. Macomber did not know how the lion had felt before he started his rush, nor during it when the unbelievable smash of the .505 with a muzzle velocity of two tons had hit him in the mouth, nor what kept him coming after that, when the second ripping crash had smashed his hind quarters and he had come crawling on toward the crashing, blasting thing that had destroyed him. Wilson knew something about it and only expressed it by saying, "Damned fine lion," but Macomber did not know how Wilson felt about things either. He did not know how his wife felt except that she was through with him.

His wife had been through with him before but it never lasted. He was very wealthy, and would be much wealthier, and he knew she would not leave him ever now. That was one of the few things that he really knew. He knew about that, about motorcycles—that was earliest—about motor cars, about duck-shooting, about fishing, trout, salmon and big-sea, about sex in books, many books, too many books, about all court games, about dogs, not much about horses, about hanging on to his money, about most of the other things his world dealt in, and about his wife not leaving him. His wife had been a great beauty and she was still a great beauty in Africa, but she was not a great enough beauty any more at home to be able to leave him and better herself and she knew it and he knew it. She had missed the chance to leave him and he knew it. If he had been better with women she would probably have started to worry about him getting another new, beautiful wife; but she knew too much about him to worry about him either. Also, he had always had a great tolerance which seemed the nicest thing about him if it were not the most sinister.

All in all they were known as a comparatively happily married couple, one of those whose disruption is often rumored but never occurs, and as the society columnist put it, they were adding more than a spice of *adventure* to their much envied and ever-enduring *Romance* by a *Safari* in what was known as *Darkest Africa* until the Martin Johnsons lighted it on so many silver screens where they were pursuing *Old Simba* the lion, the buffalo, *Tembo* the elephant and as well collecting specimens for the Museum of Natural History.[9] This same columnist had reported them *on the verge* as least three times in the past and they had been. But they always made it up. They had a sound basis of union. Margot was too beautiful for Macomber to divorce her and Macomber had too much money for Margot ever to leave him.

It was now about three o'clock in the morning and Francis Macomber, who had been asleep a little while after he had stopped thinking about the lion, wakened and then slept again, woke suddenly, frightened in a dream of the bloody-headed lion standing over him, and listening while his heart pounded, he realized that his wife was not in the other cot in the tent. He lay awake with that knowledge for two hours.

At the end of that time his wife came into the tent, lifted her mosquito bar and crawled cozily into bed.

"Where have you been?" Macomber asked in the darkness.

"Hello," she said. "Are you awake?"

"Where have you been?"

"I just went out to get a breath of air."

"You did, like hell."

"What do you want me to say, darling?"

"Where have you been?"

"Out to get a breath of air."

"That's a new name for it. You *are* a bitch."

"Well, you're a coward."

"All right," he said. "What of it?"

"Nothing as far as I'm concerned. But please let's not talk, darling, because I'm very sleepy."

"You think that I'll take anything."

9. Martin and Osa Johnson from 1921 to 1936 made nature films in Africa.

"I know you will, sweet."

"Well, I won't."

"Please, darling, let's not talk. I'm so very sleepy."

"There wasn't going to be any of that. You promised there wouldn't be."

"Well, there is now," she said sweetly.

"You said if we made this trip that there would be none of that. You promised."

"Yes, darling. That's the way I meant it to be. But the trip was spoiled yesterday. We don't have to talk about it, do we?"

"You don't wait long when you have an advantage, do you?"

"Please let's not talk. I'm so sleepy, darling."

"I'm going to talk."

"Don't mind me then, because I'm going to sleep." And she did.

At breakfast they were all three at the table before daylight and Francis Macomber found that, of all the many men that he had hated, he hated Robert Wilson the most.

"Sleep well?" Wilson asked in his throaty voice, filling a pipe.

"Did you?"

"Topping," the white hunter told him.

You bastard, thought Macomber, you insolent bastard.

So she woke him when she came in, Wilson thought, looking at them both with his flat, cold eyes. Well, why doesn't he keep his wife where she belongs? What does he think I am, a bloody plaster saint? Let him keep her where she belongs. It's his own fault.

"Do you think we'll find buffalo?" Margot asked, pushing away a dish of apricots.

"Chance of it," Wilson said and smiled at her. "Why don't you stay in camp?"

"Not for anything," she told him.

"Why not order her to stay in camp?" Wilson said to Macomber.

"You order her," said Macomber coldly.

"Let's not have any ordering, nor," turning to Macomber, "any silliness, Francis," Margot said quite pleasantly.

"Are you ready to start?" Macomber asked.

"Any time," Wilson told him. "Do you want the Memsahib to go?"

"Does it make any difference whether I do or not?"

The hell with it, thought Robert Wilson. The utter complete hell with it. So this is what it's going to be like. Well, this is what it's going to be like, then.

"Makes no difference," he said.

"You're sure you wouldn't like to stay in camp with her yourself and let me go out and hunt the buffalo?" Macomber asked.

"Can't do that," said Wilson. "Wouldn't talk rot if I were you."

"I'm not talking rot. I'm disgusted."

"Bad word, disgusted."

"Francis, will you please try to speak sensibly?" his wife said.

"I speak too damned sensibly," Macomber said. "Did you ever eat such filthy food?"

"Something wrong with the food?" asked Wilson quietly.

"No more than with everything else."

"I'd pull yourself together, laddybuck," Wilson said very quietly. "There's a boy waits at table that understands a little English."

"The hell with him."

Wilson stood up and puffing on his pipe strolled away, speaking a few words in Swahili to one of the gun-bearers who was standing waiting for him. Macomber and his wife sat on at the table. He was staring at his coffee cup.

"If you make a scene I'll leave you, darling," Margot said quietly.

"No, you won't."

"You can try it and see."

"You won't leave me."

"No," she said. "I won't leave you and you'll behave yourself."

"Behave myself? That's a way to talk. Behave myself."

"Yes. Behave yourself."

"Why don't *you* try behaving?"

"I've tried it so long. So very long."

"I hate that red-faced swine," Macomber said. "I loathe the sight of him."

"He's really *very* nice."

"Oh, *shut up,*" Macomber almost shouted. Just then the car came up and stopped in front of the dining tent and the driver and the two gun-bearers got out. Wilson walked over and looked at the husband and wife sitting there at the table.

"Going shooting?" he asked.

"Yes," said Macomber, standing up. "Yes."

"Better bring a woolly. It will be cool in the car," Wilson said.

"I'll get my leather jacket," Margot said.

"The boy has it," Wilson told her. He climbed into the front with the driver and Francis Macomber and his wife sat, not speaking, in the back seat.

Hope the silly beggar doesn't take a notion to blow the back of my head off, Wilson thought to himself. Women *are* a nuisance on safari.

The car was grinding down to cross the river at a pebbly ford in the gray daylight and then climbed, angling up the steep bank, where Wilson had ordered a way shovelled out the day before so they could reach the parklike wooded rolling country on the far side.

It was a good morning, Wilson thought. There was a heavy dew and as the wheels went through the grass and low bushes he could smell the odor of the crushed fronds. It was an odor like verbena and he liked this early morning smell of the dew, the crushed bracken and the look of the tree trunks showing black through the early morning mist, as the car made its way through the untracked, parklike country. He had put the two in the back seat out of his mind now and was thinking about buffalo. The buffalo that he was after stayed in the daytime in a thick swamp where it was impossible to get a shot, but in the night they fed out into an open stretch of country and if he could come between them and their swamp with the car, Macomber would have a good chance at them in the open. He did not want to hunt buff with Macomber in thick cover. He did not want to hunt buff or anything else with Macomber at all, but he was a professional hunter and he had hunted with some rare ones in his time. If they got buff today there would only be rhino to come and the poor man would have gone through his dangerous game and things might pick up. He'd have nothing more to do with the woman and Macomber would get over that too. He must have gone through plenty of that before by the look of things. Poor beggar. He must have a way of getting over it. Well, it was the poor sod's[1] own bloody fault.

He, Robert Wilson, carried a double size cot on safari to accommodate any windfalls he might receive. He had hunted for a certain clientele, the international, fast, sporting set, where the women did not feel they were getting their money's worth unless they had shared that cot with the white hunter. He despised them when he was away from them although he liked some of them well enough at the time, but he made his living by them; and their standards were his standards as long as they were hiring him.

They were his standards in all except the shooting. He had his own standards about the killing and they could live up to them or get some one else to hunt them. He knew, too, that they all respected him for this. This Macomber was an odd one though. Damned if he wasn't. Now the wife. Well, the wife. Yes, the wife. Hm, the wife. Well he'd dropped all that. He looked around at them. Macomber sat grim and furious. Margot smiled at him. She looked younger today, more innocent and fresher and not so professionally beautiful. What's in her heart God knows, Wilson thought. She hadn't talked much last night. At that it was a pleasure to see her.

The motor car climbed up a slight rise and went on through the trees and then out into a grassy prairie-like opening and kept in the shelter of the trees along the edge, the driver going slowly and Wilson looking carefully out across the prairie and all along its far side. He stopped the car and studied the opening with his field glasses. Then he motioned to the driver to go on and the car moved slowly along, the driver avoiding wart-hog holes and driving around the mud castles ants had built. Then, looking across the opening, Wilson suddenly turned and said,

"By God, there they are!"

And looking where he pointed, while the car jumped forward and Wilson spoke in rapid Swahili to the driver, Macomber saw three huge, black animals looking almost cylindrical in their long heaviness, like big black tank cars, moving at a gallop across the far edge of the open prairie. They moved at a stiff-necked, stiff bodied gallop and he could see the upswept wide black horns on their heads as they galloped heads out; the heads not moving.

"They're three old bulls," Wilson said. "We'll cut them off before they get to the swamp."

The car was going a wild forty-five miles an hour across the open and as Macomber watched, the buffalo got bigger and bigger until he could see the gray, hairless, scabby look of one huge bull and how his neck was a part of his shoulders and the shiny black of his

1. Chap or fellow, now nonpejorative but originally "sodomite" (cp. "bugger").

horns as he galloped a little behind the others that were strung out in that steady plunging gait; and then, the car swaying as though it had just jumped a road, they drew up close and he could see the plunging hugeness of the bull, and the dust in his sparsely haired hide, the side boss of horn and his outstretched, wide-nostrilled muzzle, and he was raising his rifle when Wilson shouted, "Not from the car, you fool!" and he had no fear, only hatred of Wilson, while the brakes clamped on and the car skidded, plowing sideways to an almost stop and Wilson was out on one side and he on the other, stumbling as his feet hit the still speeding-by of the earth, and then he was shooting at the bull as he moved away, hearing the bullets whunk into him, emptying his rifle at him as he moved steadily away, finally remembering to get his shots forward into the shoulder, and as he fumbled to re-load, he saw the bull was down. Down on his knees, his big head tossing, and seeing the other two still galloping he shot at the leader and hit him. He shot again and missed and he heard the *carawonging* roar as Wilson shot and saw the leading bull slide forward onto his nose.

"Get that other," Wilson said. "Now you're shooting!"

But the other bull was moving steadily at the same gallop and he missed, throwing a spout of dirt, and Wilson missed and the dust rose in a cloud and Wilson shouted, "Come on. He's too far!" and grabbed his arm and they were in the car again, Macomber and Wilson hanging on the sides and rocketing swayingly over the uneven ground, drawing up on the steady, plunging, heavy-necked, straight-moving gallop of the bull.

They were behind him and Macomber was filling his rifle, dropping shells onto the ground, jamming it, clearing the jam, then they were almost up with the bull when Wilson yelled "Stop," and the car skidded so that it almost swung over and Macomber fell forward onto his feet, slammed his bolt forward and fired as far forward as he could aim into the galloping, rounded black back, aimed and shot again, then again, then again, and the bullets, all of them hitting, had no effect on the buffalo that he could see. Then Wilson shot, the roar deafening him, and he could see the bull stagger. Macomber shot again, aiming carefully, and down he came, onto his knees.

"All right," Wilson said. "Nice work. That's the three."

Macomber felt a drunken elation.

"How many times did you shoot?" he asked.

"Just three," Wilson said. "You killed the first bull. The biggest one. I helped you finish the other two. Afraid they might have got into cover. You had them killed. I was just mopping up a little. You shot damn well."

"Let's go to the car," said Macomber. "I want a drink."

"Got to finish off that buff first," Wilson told him. The buffalo was on his knees and he jerked his head furiously and bellowed in pig-eyed, roaring rage as they came toward him.

"Watch he doesn't get up," Wilson said. Then, "Get a little broadside and take him in the neck just behind the ear."

Macomber aimed carefully at the center of the huge, jerking, rage-driven neck and shot. At the shot the head dropped forward.

"That does it," said Wilson. "Got the spine. They're a hell of a looking thing, aren't they?"

"Let's get the drink," said Macomber. In his life he had never felt so good.

In the car Macomber's wife sat very white faced. "You were marvellous, darling," she said to Macomber. "What a ride."

"Was it rough?" Wilson asked.

"It was frightful. I've never been more frightened in my life."

"Let's all have a drink," Macomber said.

"By all means," said Wilson. "Give it to the Memsahib." She drank the neat whisky from the flask and shuddered a little when she swallowed. She handed the flask to Macomber who handed it to Wilson.

"It was frightfully exciting," she said. "It's given me a dreadful headache. I didn't know you were allowed to shoot them from cars though."

"No one shot from cars," said Wilson coldly.

"I mean chase them from cars."

"Wouldn't ordinarily," Wilson said. "Seemed sporting enough to me though while we were doing it. Taking more chance driving that way across the plain full of holes and one thing and another than hunting on foot. Buffalo could have charged us each time we shot if he liked. Gave him every chance. Wouldn't mention it to any one though. It's illegal if that's what you mean."

"It seemed very unfair to me," Margot said, "chasing those big helpless things in a motor car."

"Did it?" said Wilson.

"What would happen if they heard about it in Nairobi?"

"I'd lose my license for one thing. Other unpleasantnesses," Wilson said, taking a drink from the flask. "I'd be out of business."

"Really?"

"Yes, really."

"Well," said Macomber, and he smiled for the first time all day. "Now she has something on you."

"You have such a pretty way of putting things, Francis," Margot Macomber said. Wilson looked at them both. If a four-letter man marries a five-letter woman, he was thinking, what number of letters would their children be? What he said was, "We lost a gun-bearer. Did you notice it?"

"My God, no," Macomber said.

"Here he comes," Wilson said. "He's all right. He must have fallen off when we left the first bull."

Approaching them was the middle-aged gun-bearer, limping along in his knitted cap, khaki tunic, shorts and rubber sandals, gloomy-faced and disgusted looking. As he came up he called out to Wilson in Swahili and they all saw the change in the white hunter's face.

"What does he say?" asked Margot.

"He says the first bull got up and went into the bush," Wilson said with no expression in his voice.

"Oh," said Macomber blankly.

"Then it's going to be just like the lion," said Margot, full of anticipation.

"It's not going to be a damned bit like the lion," Wilson told her.

"Did you want another drink, Macomber?"

"Thanks, yes," Macomber said. He expected the feeling he had had about the lion to come back but it did not. For the first time in his life he really felt wholly without fear. Instead of fear he had a feeling of definite elation.

"We'll go and have a look at the second bull," Wilson said. "I'll tell the driver to put the car in the shade."

"What are you going to do?" asked Margaret Macomber.

"Take a look at the buff," Wilson said.

"I'll come."

"Come along."

The three of them walked over to where the second buffalo bulked blackly in the open, head forward on the grass, the massive horns swung wide.

"He's a very good head," Wilson said. "That's close to a fifty-inch spread."

Macomber was looking at him with delight.

"He's hateful looking," said Margot. "Can't we go into the shade?"

"Of course," Wilson said. "Look," he said to Macomber, and pointed. "See that patch of bush?"

"Yes."

"That's where the first bull went in. The gun-bearer said when he fell off the bull was down. He was watching us helling along and the other two buff galloping. When he looked up there was the bull up and looking at him. Gun-bearer ran like hell and the bull went off slowly into that bush."

"Can we go in after him now?" asked Macomber eagerly.

Wilson looked at him appraisingly. Damned if this isn't a strange one, he thought. Yesterday he's scared sick and today he's a ruddy[2] fire eater.

"No, we'll give him a while."

"Let's please go into the shade," Margot said. Her face was white and she looked ill.

They made their way to the car where it stood under a single, wide-spreading tree and all climbed in.

"Chances are he's dead in there," Wilson remarked. "After a little we'll have a look."

Macomber felt a wild unreasonable happiness that he had never known before.

"By God, that was a chase," he said. "I've never felt any such feeling. Wasn't it marvellous, Margot?"

"I hated it."

"Why?"

"I hated it," she said bitterly. "I loathed it."

"You know I don't think I'd ever be afraid of anything again," Macomber said to Wilson. "Something happened in me after we first saw the buff and started after him. Like a dam bursting. It was pure excitement."

"Cleans out your liver," said Wilson. "Damn funny things happen to people."

2. Euphemism for the stronger "bloody."

Macomber's face was shining. "You know something did happen to me," he said. "I feel absolutely different."

His wife said nothing and eyed him strangely. She was sitting far back in the seat and Macomber was sitting forward talking to Wilson who turned sideways talking over the back of the front seat.

"You know, I'd like to try another lion," Macomber said. "I'm really not afraid of them now. After all, what can they do to you?"

"That's it," said Wilson. "Worst one can do is kill you. How does it go? Shakespeare. Damned good. See if I can remember. Oh, damned good. Used to quote it to myself at one time. Let's see. 'By my troth, I care not; a man can die but once; we owe God a death and let it go which way it will he that dies this year is quit for the next.'[3] Damned fine, eh?"

He was very embarrassed, having brought out this thing he had lived by, but he had seen men come of age before and it always moved him. It was not a matter of their twenty-first birthday.

It had taken a strange chance of hunting, a sudden precipitation into action without opportunity for worrying beforehand, to bring this about with Macomber, but regardless of how it had happened it had most certainly happened. Look at the beggar now, Wilson thought. It's that some of them stay little boys so long, Wilson thought. Sometimes all their lives. Their figures stay boyish when they're fifty. The great American boy-men. Damned strange people. But he liked this Macomber now. Damned strange fellow. Probably meant the end of cuckoldry too. Well, that would be a damned good thing. Damned good thing. Beggar had probably been afraid all his life. Don't know what started it. But over now. Hadn't had time to be afraid with the buff. That and being angry too. Motor car too. Motor cars made it familiar. Be a damn fire eater now. He'd seen it in the war work the same way. More of a change than any loss of virginity. Fear gone like an operation. Something else grew in its place. Main thing a man had. Made him into a man. Women knew it too. No bloody fear.

From the far corner of the seat Margaret Macomber looked at the two of them. There was no change in Wilson. She saw Wilson as she had seen him the day before when she had first realized what his great talent was. But she saw the change in Francis Macomber now.

"Do you have that feeling of happiness about what's going to happen?" Macomber asked, still exploring his new wealth.

"You're not supposed to mention it," Wilson said, looking in the other's face. "Much more fashionable to say you're scared. Mind you, you'll be scared too, plenty of times."

"But you *have* a feeling of happiness about action to come?"

"Yes," said Wilson. "There's that. Doesn't do to talk too much about all this. Talk the whole thing away. No pleasure in anything if you mouth it up too much."

"You're both talking rot," said Margot. "Just because you've chased

3. Shakespeare, *Henry IV Part 2*, III, 2, 250–55. There are some differences in punctuation, and after "owe God a death," the following is omitted: "I'll ne'er bear a base mind. An't be my destiny, so; an't be not, so. No man's too good to serve's prince."

some helpless animals in a motor car you talk like heroes."

"Sorry," said Wilson. "I have been gassing too much." She's worried about it already, he thought.

"If you don't know what we're talking about why not keep out of it?" Macomber asked his wife.

"You've gotten awfully brave, awfully suddenly," his wife said contemptuously, but her contempt was not secure. She was very afraid of something.

Macomber laughed, a very natural hearty laugh. "You know I *have,*" he said. "I really have."

"Isn't it sort of late?" Margot said bitterly. Because she had done the best she could for many years back and the way they were together now was no one person's fault.

"Not for me," said Macomber.

Margot said nothing but sat back in the corner of the seat.

"Do you think we've given him time enough?" Macomber asked Wilson cheerfully.

"We might have a look," Wilson said. "Have you any solids left?"

"The gun-bearer has some."

Wilson called in Swahili and the older gun-bearer, who was skinning out one of the heads, straightened up, pulled a box of solids out of his pocket and brought them over to Macomber, who filled his magazine and put the remaining shells in his pocket.

"You might as well shoot the Springfield," Wilson said. "You're used to it. We'll leave the Mannlicher in the car with the Memsahib. Your gun-bearer can carry your heavy gun. I've this damned cannon. Now let me tell you about them." He had saved this until the last because he did not want to worry Macomber. "When a buff comes he comes with his head high and thrust straight out. The boss of the horns covers any sort of a brain shot. The only shot is straight into the nose. The only other shot is into his chest or, if you're to one side, into the neck or the shoulders. After they've been hit once they take a hell of a lot of killing. Don't try anything fancy. Take the easiest shot there is. They've finished skinning out that head now. Should we get started."

He called to the gun-bearers, who came up wiping their hands, and the older one got into the back.

"I'll only take Kongoni," Wilson said. "The other can watch to keep the birds away."

As the car moved slowly across the open space toward the island of brushy trees that ran in a tongue of foliage along a dry water course that cut the open swale, Macomber felt his heart pounding and his mouth was dry again, but it was excitement, not fear.

"Here's where he went in," Wilson said. Then to the gun-bearer in Swahili, "Take the blood spoor."

The car was parallel to the patch of bush. Macomber, Wilson and the gun-bearer got down. Macomber, looking back, saw his wife, with the rifle by her side, looking at him. He waved to her and she did not wave back.

The brush was very thick ahead and the ground was dry. The middle-aged gun-bearer was sweating heavily and Wilson had his hat down over his eyes and his red neck showed just ahead of

Macomber. Suddenly the gun-bearer said something in Swahili to Wilson and ran forward.

"He's dead in there," Wilson said. "Good work," and he turned to grip Macomber's hand and as they shook hands, grinning at each other, the gun-bearer shouted wildly and they saw him coming out of the brush sideways, fast as a crab, and the bull coming, nose out, mouth tight closed, blood dripping, massive head straight out, coming in a charge, his little pig eyes bloodshot as he looked at them. Wilson, who was ahead was kneeling shooting, and Macomber, as he fired, unhearing his shot in the roaring of Wilson's gun, saw fragments like slate burst from the huge boss of the horns, and the head jerked, he shot again at the wide nostrils and saw the horns jolt again and fragments fly, and he did not see Wilson now and, aiming carefully, shot again with the buffalo's huge bulk almost on him and his rifle almost level with the on-coming head, nose out, and he could see the little wicked eyes and the head started to lower and he felt a sudden white-hot, blinding flash explode inside his head and that was all he ever felt.

Wilson had ducked to one side to get in a shoulder shot. Macomber had stood solid and shot for the nose, shooting a touch high each time and hitting the heavy horns, splintering and chipping them like hitting a slate roof, and Mrs. Macomber, in the car, had shot at the buffalo with the 6.5 Mannlicher as it seemed about to gore Macomber and had hit her husband about two inches up and a little to one side of the base of his skull.

Francis Macomber lay now, face down, not two yards from where the buffalo lay on his side and his wife knelt over him with Wilson beside her.

"I wouldn't turn him over," Wilson said.

The woman was crying hysterically.

"I'd get back in the car," Wilson said. "Where's the rifle?"

She shook her head, her face contorted. The gun-bearer picked up the rifle.

"Leave it as it is," said Wilson. Then, "Go get Abdulla so that he may witness the manner of the accident."

He knelt down, took a handkerchief from his pocket, and spread it over Francis Macomber's crew-cropped head where it lay. The blood sank into the dry, loose earth.

Wilson stood up and saw the buffalo on his side, his legs out, his thinly-haired belly crawling with ticks. "Hell of a good bull," his brain registered automatically. "A good fifty inches, or better. Better." He called to the driver and told him to spread a blanket over the body and stay by it. Then he walked over to the motor car where the woman sat crying in the corner.

"That was a pretty thing to do," he said in a toneless voice. "He *would* have left you too."

"Stop it," she said.

"Of course it's an accident," he said. "I know that."

"Stop it," she said.

"Don't worry," he said. "There will be a certain amount of unpleasantness but I will have some photographs taken that will be very useful at the inquest. There's the testimony of the gun-bearers and the driver too. You're perfectly all right."

"Stop it," she said.

"There's a hell of a lot to be done," he said. "And I'll have to send a truck off to the lake to wireless for a plane to take the three of us into Nairobi. Why didn't you poison him? That's what they do in England."

"Stop it. Stop it. Stop it," the woman cried.

Wilson looked at her with his flat blue eyes.

"I'm through now," he said. "I was a little angry. I'd begun to like your husband."

"Oh, please stop it," she said. "Please, please stop it."

"That's better," Wilson said. "Please is much better. Now I'll stop."

p. 1936

2 FOCUS AND VOICE

Who is telling us the story—whose words are we reading? Where does this person stand with relation to what is going on in the story? In narrative someone is always between us and the events—a viewer, a speaker, or both; narrative, unlike drama, is always mediated. The way a story is mediated—the way the distance and angle of perspective and the language mold the subject matter—is a key element in fictional structure.

This mediation, or structuring, is usually called **point of view,** a perfectly satisfactory term for the angle of vision, the point from which the people, events, and other details (the history) are viewed. But there are also the words of the story between us and the history, and the words are not always those of the person who is the viewing point. So we shall distinguish between the two, calling the viewing aspect the **focus** and the verbal aspect the **voice.**

Focus acts much as a movie camera does, choosing what we can look at and the angle at which we can view it, framing, proportioning, emphasizing, even distorting. Plot is a structure that places us in a time relationship to the history; focus places us in a spatial relationship.

There are several things to notice about focus at any given point in a story. Is it fixed or mobile; that is, does it stay at more or less the same angle to, and at the same distance from, the characters and action, or does it move around or in and out? In the first three and a half paragraphs of *An Occurrence at Owl Creek Bridge*, for example, we seem to be seeing through the lens of a camera that can swing left or right, up or down, but stays pretty much at the same angle and distance from the bridge. In *The Lottery* that seems true of the focus for the entire story (unless you feel the camera moves in a little closer toward the end). In *Owl Creek Bridge,* however, by the middle of the fourth paragraph we're inside the mind of the man who's about to be hanged: "The arrangement commended itself to his judgment. . . . He looked a moment. . . . A piece of dancing driftwood caught his attention. . . . How slowly it appeared to move!" From now on we are inside the condemned man's head. The focus is more limited in scope—for almost all of the rest of the story we can see and hear only what he sees and hears. But because the focus is internal as well as limited, we can also know what he thinks. This limited, internal focus, used here as well as in *The Most Dangerous Game,* is usually called the **centered** or **central consciousness.**

The centered consciousness has been a popular, perhaps *the* most popular focus in fiction of the past hundred years—through most of the history of the modern short story, in fact—and its tightly controlled range and concentration on a single individual seem particularly suited for the short form. During much of this period, fiction, both long and short, has been in one sense realistic—that is, treating the everyday and the natural. It has become increasingly clear, however, that to the individual, what is real is what is perceived (**psychological realism**). The centered consciousness, in which things, people, and events are perceived through the filter of the individual character's consciousness, has therefore been ideally appropriate. It is a comfortable focus for readers, too. On the one hand, they can identify with someone whose thoughts and perception they share, even if the character is fallible, like Rainsford in *The Most Dangerous Game* or Young Goodman Brown, or even reprehensible, like the womanizing Gurov at the beginning of Chekhov's *The Lady with the Dog.* On the other hand, readers are distanced enough from the focal character to escape. The third person keeps us "other"—we are outside a bit, even as we identify—and the camera eye can pull back, as it cannot do spatially from the first-person narrator.

First-person stories, like *The Summer My Grandmother Was Supposed to Die,* are always limited too, and almost all the time are internal as well (though Montresor, in *The Cask of Amontillado,* hides his plans from us), and though they cannot retract spatially from the narrator, they not only can be but almost always are withdrawn temporally. That is, the "I" telling the story is older than the "I" experiencing the events of the story. Indeed, it may be this temporal distancing in first-person narration that seems to give the centered-consciousness, third-person narration the edge in excitement and suspense; though both types of stories usually use the past tense, the first-person past seems less a narrative convention and more a real pastness than does the third-person past.

The psychological realism gained by having a limited narrator exacts a price from the reader. If you don't hold the author (or the story) responsible for the absolute truth, validity, accuracy, and opinions of the focal character—if he or she is just telling us what he or she thinks, feels, sees—we must accept the possibility that the character's vision may be unreliable. At a significant point in *Owl Creek Bridge,* for example, you will find that the camera pulls back from Peyton

Farquhar and we are made to recognize to what extent his consciousness is a reliable witness to what has been going on. The history here is only an occurrence; the limited focus structures the mere occurrence into a story.

There is no doubt about reliability at the end of *Owl Creek Bridge,* nor in a story like *The Tree of Knowledge* ("Stories for Further Reading"), but there may be considerable difference of opinion about whether the lawyer-narrator in *Bartleby, the Scrivener* (also in "Stories for Further Reading") is meant to be unreliable. (By the way, **unreliable narrator** is the term most often used to refer to this aspect of fiction, though neither Farquhar nor Peter Brench in *Tree of Knowledge* is in fact the narrator.) One of the great puzzles and glories of the limited focus is the need for readers to be actively engaged in weighing the evidence presented, involving them deeply in the story, even, you might say, in participating in the making of the story out of the history.

When the focus is limited, whether to a first-person narrator or to a centered consciousness, it is tied to that individual. When he or she leaves the room, the camera must go too, and if we are to know what happens in the room when the focal character is gone, some means of bringing the information to that character must be devised, such as a letter or a report by another character. The camera may pull back out of the character's mind or even, as in *Owl Creek Bridge,* above and away from the character, but it does not generally jump around. An **unlimited focus** permits such freedom. In *The Short Happy Life of Francis Macomber* we enter the minds of each of the main characters periodically throughout the story. We get inside Margot Macomber's consciousness on the first page as she looks at Wilson and knows she hasn't seen him before, and on another page Macomber and Robert Wilson "both saw that she was going to cry. Wilson had seen it coming for a long time and he dreaded it. Macomber was past dreading it." Throughout, the story seems free to dip inside one consciousness or another, and can move with any of the characters. This unlimited, internal/external focus is called **omniscient.** Though the camera eye in *The Lottery* seems unlimited in that it can focus on one character or another and to some degree move in or out, we are never allowed to get into any character's mind; the focus is consistently external. It is almost as if we were standing back from the crowd watching and listening, or in an audience watching a play. That's why this focus is sometimes called **dramatic.**

There are no laws governing focus in fiction, but there is a general feeling that once a focus is chosen that ought to be the law for that story. Do you feel manipulated when the focus, which has been on Rainsford for the entire length of *The Most Dangerous Game,* shifts, very near the end, from him to the general, apparently just to heighten our suspense? Do you feel betrayed by the fact that we are not allowed to enter Margot Macomber's mind at one crucial moment, even though the focus has shifted freely at less crucial times?

Focus and voice often coincide. There is no discrepancy that I can see (or hear) between the viewing and the telling in *The Cask of*

Amontillado, for example. But wouldn't that always be true in first-person narration, where the "I" who sees is the same person as the "I" who tells the story? Not necessarily. Look at *The Summer My Grandmother Was Supposed to Die.* The "I" telling the story is older than the "I" experiencing the events of the story. Notice how many phrases there are like "years later I was shown the telegram" and "In those days . . ." So, too, the language of the story is clearly not that of a young boy: "She arrived punctually at noon"; "I've been told that to study Talmud with him had been a rare pleasure"; "lots of slender volumes of sermons, chassidic tales, and rabbinical commentaries." Such expressions may deal with incidents and information within the boy's perception, but the language in which they are expressed is clearly beyond him.

The voice in *Owl Creek Bridge,* like the focus, at the beginning of the story is not centered in Peyton Farquhar, but even when the focus narrows on him the voice telling the story is not his; note, for example, "As these thoughts, *which have here to be set down in words,* were flashed into the doomed man's brain" (emphasis added). The discrepancy may prepare a careful reader for later developments in the story.

At times, too, the voice may help to define the narration more fully and more precisely than can the position of the focus alone. The dispassionate narrator of *The Lottery* seems to know all about the history of the lottery and about most of the townspeople's feelings about it, but only from reports of what they said or from general knowledge. It is as if that narrator is a member of the community, an onlooker or participant somewhere in the crowd, where the focus of narration seems located. But the language of the narration, though simple and direct, is not so provincial and colloquial as the language we hear about us in the dialogue. The voice seems that of an educated outsider, present today in the crowd perhaps, but coolly observing the villagers, almost as if they were specimens.

I have used the common term **narrator** in the usual way—to mean the person who tells the story. You will have noticed that often the narrator really is a person in the story, like Muttel, the narrator in *The Summer My Grandmother Was Supposed to Die.* But how about the narrator in *Owl Creek Bridge* or in *Macomber*? Who is it who sets down Farquhar's words and can say things like this: "Death is a dignitary who when he comes announced is to be received with formal manifestations of respect, even by those most familiar with him. In the code of military etiquette silence and fixity are forms of deference." Where is he or she standing? What kind of person is this narrator? It seems even more difficult to imagine or identify than the voice of *The Lottery.* In such cases we tend to identify the narrator with the author; we call the narrator of this story "Bierce," of *Macomber* "Hemingway." This is not necessarily wrong, but it can be misleading. We can dig up a few facts about the author's life and read them into the story, or, worse, read the character or detail of the story into the author's life. It is more prudent, therefore, especially on the basis of a single story, not to speak of the author but of the author's

persona, the voice or figure of the author who tells and structures the story, who may or may not resemble in nature or values the actual person of the author. Mary Ann Evans wrote novels under the name of George Eliot; the first-person narrator speaks of "himself." That male narrator may be a good example of the persona or representative that most authors construct to "write" their stories.

We say *write* the stories. The narrator of *Owl Creek Bridge* has to "set down in words" what Farquhar is thinking. But, just as poets write of singing their songs (poems), so we often speak of telling a story, and we speak of a narrator, which means a teller (and we say we speak when we are writing). There are stories, usually with first-person narrators, that make much of the convention of oral storytelling: *My Man Bovanne,* for example, or Faulkner's *Spotted Horses.* Often these stories not only have an "oral" taleteller but imply a certain audience. Sometimes, as in Mark Twain's *Celebrated Jumping Frog,* there is a narrator who tells the story within the story to someone else who retells it or writes it down, and the nature and response of this **auditor** can be a significant part of the meaning and effect of the story.

To see how focus and voice structure history into story, you might want to try rewriting *The Lottery* with the same focus but with a different voice (perhaps that of one of the villagers), or *Macomber* with any one character as the focus, or *The Summer My Grandmother Was Supposed to Die* with the focus and perhaps with the voice of Muttel's mother.

AMBROSE BIERCE

An Occurrence at Owl Creek Bridge

I

A man stood upon a railroad bridge in northern Alabama, looking down into the swift water twenty feet below. The man's hands were behind his back, the wrists bound with a cord. A rope closely encircled his neck. It was attached to a stout cross-timber above his head and the slack fell to the level of his knees. Some loose boards laid upon the sleepers[1] supporting the metals of the railway supplied a footing for him and his executioners—two private soldiers of the Federal army, directed by a sergeant who in civil life may have been a deputy sheriff. At a short remove upon the same temporary platform was an officer in the uniform of his rank, armed. He was a captain. A sentinel at each end of the bridge stood with his rifle in the position known as "support," that is to say, vertical in front of the left shoulder, the hammer resting on the forearm thrown straight across the chest—a for-

1. Crossties that support railroad track.

mal and unnatural position, enforcing an erect carriage of the body. It did not appear to be the duty of these two men to know what was occurring at the center of the bridge; they merely blockaded the two ends of the foot planking that traversed it.

Beyond one of the sentinels nobody was in sight; the railroad ran straight away into a forest for a hundred yards, then, curving, was lost to view. Doubtless there was an outpost farther along. The other bank of the stream was open ground—a gentle acclivity topped with a stockade of vertical tree trunks, loopholed for rifles, with a single embrasure through which protruded the muzzle of a brass cannon commanding the bridge. Midway of the slope between bridge and fort were the spectators—a single company of infantry in line, at "parade rest," the butts of the rifles on the ground, the barrels inclining slightly backward against the right shoulder, the hands crossed upon the stock. A lieutenant stood at the right of the line, the point of his sword upon the ground, his left hand resting upon his right. Excepting the group of four at the center of the bridge, not a man moved. The company faced the bridge, staring stonily, motionless. The sentinels, facing the banks of the stream, might have been statues to adorn the bridge. The captain stood with folded arms, silent, observing the work of his subordinates, but making no sign. Death is a dignitary who when he comes announced is to be received with formal manifestations of respect, even by those most familiar with him. In the code of military etiquette silence and fixity are forms of deference.

The man who was engaged in being hanged was apparently about thirty-five years of age. He was a civilian, if one might judge from his habit, which was that of a planter. His features were good—a straight nose, firm mouth, broad forehead, from which his long, dark hair was combed straight back, falling behind his ears to the collar of his well-fitting frock coat. He wore a mustache and pointed beard, but no whiskers; his eyes were large and dark gray, and had a kindly expression which one would hardly have expected in one whose neck was in the hemp. Evidently this was no vulgar assassin. The liberal military code makes provision for hanging many kinds of persons, and gentlemen are not excluded.

The preparations being complete, the two private soldiers stepped aside and each drew away the plank upon which he had been standing. The sergeant turned to the captain, saluted and placed himself immediately behind that officer, who in turn moved apart one pace. These movements left the condemned man and the sergeant standing on the two ends of the same plank, which spanned three of the cross-ties of the bridge. The end upon which the civilian stood almost, but not quite, reached a fourth. This plank had been held in place by the weight of the captain; it was now held by that of the sergeant. At a signal from the former the latter would step aside, the plank would tilt and the condemned man go down between two ties. The arrangement commended itself to his judgment as simple and effective. His face had not been covered nor his eyes bandaged. He looked a moment at his "unsteadfast footing," then let his gaze wander to the swirling water of the stream racing madly beneath his feet. A piece of dancing driftwood caught his attention and his eyes followed it down the current. How slowly it appeared to move! What a sluggish stream!

He closed his eyes in order to fix his last thoughts upon his wife and children. The water, touched to gold by the early sun, the brooding mists under the banks at some distance down the stream, the fort, the soldiers, the piece of drift—all had distracted him. And now he became conscious of a new disturbance. Striking through the thought of his dear ones was a sound which he could neither ignore nor understand, a sharp, distinct, metallic percussion like the stroke of a blacksmith's hammer upon the anvil; it had the same ringing quality. He wondered what it was, and whether immeasurably distant or near by—it seemed both. Its recurrence was regular, but as slow as the tolling of a death knell. He awaited each stroke with impatience and—he knew not why—apprehension. The intervals of silence grew progressively longer; the delays became maddening. With their greater infrequency the sounds increased in strength and sharpness. They hurt his ear like the thrust of a knife; he feared he would shriek. What he heard was the ticking of his watch.

He unclosed his eyes and saw again the water below him. "If I could free my hands," he thought, "I might throw off the noose and spring into the stream. By diving I could evade the bullets and, swimming vigorously, reach the bank, take to the woods and get away home. My home, thank God, is as yet outside their lines; my wife and little ones are still beyond the invader's farthest advance."

As these thoughts, which have here to be set down in words, were flashed into the doomed man's brain rather than evolved from it the captain nodded to the sergeant. The sergeant stepped aside.

II

Peyton Farquhar was a well-to-do planter, of an old and highly respected Alabama family. Being a slave owner and like other slave owners a politician he was naturally an original secessionist and ardently devoted to the Southern cause. Circumstances of an imperious nature, which it is unnecessary to relate here, had prevented him from taking service with the gallant army that had fought the disastrous campaigns ending with the fall of Corinth,[2] and he chafed under the inglorious restraint, longing for the release of his energies, the larger life of the soldier, the opportunity for distinction. That opportunity, he felt, would come, as it comes to all in war time. Meanwhile he did what he could. No service was too humble for him to perform in aid of the South, no adventure too perilous for him to undertake if consistent with the character of a civilian who was at heart a soldier, and who in good faith and without too much qualification assented to at least a part of the frankly villainous dictum that all is fair in love and war.

One evening while Farquhar and his wife were sitting on a rustic bench near the entrance to his grounds, a gray-clad soldier rode up to

2. Corinth, Mississippi, captured by General Grant in April 1862.

the gate and asked for a drink of water. Mrs. Farquhar was only too happy to serve him with her own white hands. While she was fetching the water her husband approached the dusty horseman and inquired eagerly for news from the front.

"The Yanks are repairing the railroads," said the man, "and are getting ready for another advance. They have reached the Owl Creek bridge, put it in order and built a stockade on the north bank. The commandant has issued an order, which is posted everywhere, declaring that any civilian caught interfering with the railroad, its bridges, tunnels or trains will be summarily hanged. I saw the order."

"How far is it to the Owl Creek bridge?" Farquhar asked.

"About thirty miles."

"Is there no force on this side the creek?"

"Only a picket post half a mile out, on the railroad, and a single sentinel at this end of the bridge."

"Suppose a man—a civilian and student of hanging—should elude the picket post and perhaps get the better of the sentinel," said Farquhar, smiling, "what could he accomplish?"

The soldier reflected. "I was there a month ago," he replied. "I observed that the flood of last winter had lodged a great quantity of driftwood against the wooden pier at this end of the bridge. It is now dry and would burn like tow."

The lady had now brought the water, which the soldier drank. He thanked her ceremoniously, bowed to her husband and rode away. An hour later, after nightfall, he repassed the plantation, going northward in the direction from which he had come. He was a Federal scout.

III

As Peyton Farquhar fell straight downward through the bridge he lost consciousness and was as one already dead. From this state he was awakened—ages later, it seemed to him—by the pain of a sharp pressure upon his throat, followed by a sense of suffocation. Keen, poignant agonies seemed to shoot from his neck downward through every fiber of his body and limbs. These pains appeared to flash along well-defined lines of ramification and to beat with an inconceivably rapid periodicity. They seemed like streams of pulsating fire heating him to an intolerable temperature. As to his head, he was conscious of nothing but a feeling of fulness—of congestion. These sensations were unaccompanied by thought. The intellectual part of his nature was already effaced; he had power only to feel, and feeling was torment. He was conscious of motion. Encompassed in a luminous cloud, of which he was now merely the fiery heart, without material substance, he swung through unthinkable arcs of oscillation, like a vast pendulum. Then all at once, with terrible suddenness, the light about him shot upward with the noise of a loud plash; a frightful roaring was in his ears, and all was cold and dark. The power of thought was restored; he knew that the rope had broken and he had fallen into the stream. There was no additional strangulation; the noose about his neck was already suffocating him and kept the water from his lungs.

To die of hanging at the bottom of a river!—the idea seemed to him ludicrous. He opened his eyes in the darkness and saw above him a gleam of light, but how distant, how inaccessible! He was still sinking, for the light became fainter and fainter until it was a mere glimmer. Then it began to grow and brighten, and he knew that he was rising toward the surface—knew it with reluctance, for he was now very comfortable. "To be hanged and drowned," he thought, "that is not so bad; but I do not wish to be shot. No; I will not be shot; that is not fair."

He was not conscious of an effort, but a sharp pain in his wrist apprised him that he was trying to free his hands. He gave the struggle his attention, as an idler might observe the feat of a juggler, without interest in the outcome. What splendid effort!—what magnificent, what superhuman strength! Ah, that was a fine endeavor! Bravo! The cord fell away; his arms parted and floated upward, the hands dimly seen on each side in the growing light. He watched them with a new interest as first one and then the other pounced upon the noose at his neck. They tore it away and thrust it fiercely aside, its undulations resembling those of a water snake. "Put it back, put it back!" He thought he shouted these words to his hands, for the undoing of the noose had been succeeded by the direct pang that he had yet experienced. His neck ached horribly; his brain was on fire; his heart, which had been fluttering faintly, gave a great leap, trying to force itself out at his mouth. His whole body was racked and wrenched with an insupportable anguish! But his disobedient hands gave no heed to the command. They beat the water vigorously with quick, downward strokes, forcing him to the surface. He felt his head emerge; his eyes were blinded by the sunlight; his chest expanded convulsively, and with a supreme and crowning agony his lungs engulfed a great draught of air, which instantly he expelled in a shriek!

He was now in full possession of his physical senses. They were, indeed, preternaturally keen and alert. Something in the awful disturbance of his organic system had so exalted and refined them that they made record of things never before perceived. He felt the ripples upon his face and heard their separate sounds as they struck. He looked at the forest on the bank of the stream, saw the individual trees, the leaves and the veining of each leaf—saw the very insects upon them: the locusts, the brilliant-bodied flies, the gray spiders stretching their webs from twig to twig. He noted the prismatic colors in all the dewdrops upon a million blades of grass. The humming of the gnats that danced above the eddies of the stream, the beating of the dragonflies' wings, the strokes of the waterspiders' legs, like oars which had lifted their boat—all these made audible music. A fish slid along beneath his eyes and he heard the rush of its body parting the water.

He had come to the surface facing down the stream; in a moment the visible world seemed to wheel slowly round, himself the pivotal point, and he saw the bridge, the fort, the soldiers upon the bridge, the captain, the sergeant, the two privates, his executioners. They were in silhouette against the blue sky. They shouted and gesticulated, pointing at him. The captain had drawn his pistol, but did not fire; the others were unarmed. Their movements were grotesque and horrible, their forms gigantic.

Suddenly he heard a sharp report and something struck the water smartly within a few inches of his head, spattering his face with spray. He heard a second report, and saw one of the sentinels with his rifle at his shoulder, a light cloud of blue smoke rising from the muzzle. The man in the water saw the eye of the man on the bridge gazing into his own through the sights of the rifle. He observed that it was a gray eye and remembered having read that gray eyes were keenest, and that all famous marksmen had them. Nevertheless, this one had missed.

A counter-swirl had caught Farquhar and turned him half round; he was again looking into the forest on the bank opposite the fort. The sound of a clear, high voice in a monotonous singsong now rang out behind him and came across the water with a distinctness that pierced and subdued all other sounds, even the beating of the ripples in his ears. Although no soldier, he had frequented camps enough to know the dread significance of that deliberate, drawling, aspirated chant; the lieutenant on shore was taking a part in the morning's work. How coldly and pitilessly—with what an even, calm intonation, presaging, and enforcing tranquility in the men—with what accurately measured intervals fell those cruel words:

"Attention, company! . . . Shoulder arms! . . . Ready! . . . Aim! . . . Fire!"

Farquhar dived—dived as deeply as he could. The water roared in his ears like the voice of Niagara, yet he heard the dulled thunder of the volley and, rising again toward the surface, met shining bits of metal, singularly flattened, oscillating slowly downward. Some of them touched him on the face and hands, then fell away, continuing their descent. One lodged between his collar and neck; it was uncomfortably warm and he snatched it out.

As he rose to the surface, gasping for breath, he saw that he had been a long time under water; he was perceptibly farther downstream —nearer to safety. The soldiers had almost finished reloading; the metal ramrods flashed all at once in the sunshine as they were drawn from the barrels, turned in the air, and thrust into their sockets. The two sentinels fired again, independently and ineffectually.

The hunted man saw all this over his shoulder; he was now swimming vigorously with the current. His brain was as energetic as his arms and legs; he thought with the rapidity of lightning.

"The officer," he reasoned, "will not make that martinet's error a second time. It is as easy to dodge a volley as a single shot. He has probably already given the command to fire at will. God help me, I cannot dodge them all!"

An appalling plash within two yards of him was followed by a loud, rushing sound, diminuendo, which seemed to travel back through the air to the fort and died in an explosion which stirred the very river to its deeps! A rising sheet of water curved over him, fell down upon him, blinded him, strangled him! The cannon had taken a hand in the game. As he shook his head free from the commotion of the smitten water he heard the deflected shot humming through the air ahead, and in an instant it was cracking and smashing the branches in the forest beyond.

"They will not do that again," he thought; "the next time they will use a charge of grape.[3] I must keep my eye upon the gun; the smoke will apprise me—the report arrives too late; it lags behind the missile. That is a good gun."

Suddenly he felt himself whirled round and round—spinning like a top. The water, the banks, the forests, the now distant bridge, fort and men—all were commingled and blurred. Objects were represented by their colors only; circular horizontal streaks of color—that was all he saw. He had been caught in a vortex and was being whirled on with a velocity of advance and gyration that made him giddy and sick. In a few moments he was flung upon the gravel at the foot of the left bank of the stream—the southern bank—and behind a projecting point which concealed him from his enemies. The sudden arrest of his motion, the abrasion of one of his hands on the gravel, restored him, and he wept with delight. He dug his fingers into the sand, threw it over himself in handfuls and audibly blessed it. It looked like diamonds, rubies, emeralds; he could think of nothing beautiful which it did not resemble. The trees upon the bank were giant garden plants; he noted a definite order in their arrangement, inhaled the fragrance of their blooms. A strange, roseate light shone through the spaces among their trunks and the wind made in their branches the music of aeolian harps. He had no wish to perfect his escape—was content to remain in that enchanting spot until retaken.

A whiz and rattle of grapeshot among the branches high above his head roused him from his dream. The baffled cannoneer had fired him a random farewell. He sprang to his feet, rushed up the sloping bank, and plunged into the forest.

All that day he traveled, laying his course by the rounding sun. The forest seemed interminable; nowhere did he discover a break in it, not even a woodman's road. He had not known that he lived in so wild a region. There was something uncanny in the revelation.

By nightfall he was fatigued, footsore, famishing. The thought of his wife and children urged him on. At last he found a road which led him in what he knew to be the right direction. It was as wide and straight as a city street, yet it seemed untraveled. No fields bordered it, no dwelling anywhere. Not so much as the barking of a dog suggested human habitation. The black bodies of the trees formed a straight wall on both sides, terminating on the horizon in a point, like a diagram in a lesson in perspective. Overhead, as he looked up through this rift in the wood, shone great golden stars looking unfamiliar and grouped in strange constellations. He was sure they were arranged in some order which had a secret and malign significance. The wood on either side was full of singular noises, among which—

3. Grapeshot, a cluster of small iron balls that scatter when fired from cannon.

once, twice, and again—he distinctly heard whispers in an unknown tongue.

His neck was in pain and lifting his hand to it he found it horribly swollen. He knew that it had a circle of black where the rope had bruised it. His eyes felt congested; he could no longer close them. His tongue was swollen with thirst; he relieved its fever by thrusting it forward from between his teeth into the cold air. How softly the turf had carpeted the untraveled avenue—he could no longer feel the roadway beneath his feet!

Doubtless, despite his suffering, he had fallen asleep while walking, for now he sees another scene—perhaps he has merely recovered from a delirium. He stands at the gate of his own home. All is as he left it, and all bright and beautiful in the morning sunshine. He must have traveled the entire night. As he pushes upon the gate and passes up the wide white walk, he sees a flutter of female garments; his wife, looking fresh and cool and sweet, steps down from the veranda to meet him. At the bottom of the steps she stands waiting, with a smile of ineffable joy, an attitude of matchless grace and dignity. Ah, how beautiful she is! He springs forward with extended arms. As he is about to clasp her he feels a stunning blow upon the back of the neck; a blinding white light blazes all about him with a sound like the shock of a cannon—then all is darkness and silence!

Peyton Farquhar was dead; his body, with a broken neck, swung gently from side to side beneath the timbers of the Owl Creek bridge.

1891

SHIRLEY JACKSON

The Lottery

The morning of June 27th was clear and sunny, with the fresh warmth of a full-summer day; the flowers were blossoming profusely and the grass was richly green. The people of the village began to gather in the square, between the post office and the bank, around ten o'clock; in some towns there were so many people that the lottery took two days and had to be started on June 26th, but in this village, where there were only about three hundred people, the whole lottery took less than two hours, so it could begin at ten o'clock in the morning and still be through in time to allow the villagers to get home for noon dinner.

The children assembled first, of course. School was recently over for the summer, and the feeling of liberty sat uneasily on most of them; they tended to gather together quietly for a while before they broke into boisterous play, and their talk was still of the classroom and the teacher, of books and reprimands. Bobby Martin had already stuffed his pockets full of stones, and the other boys soon followed his example, selecting the smoothest and roundest stones; Bobby and Harry Jones and Dickie Delacroix—the villagers pronounced this name "Dellacroy" —eventually made a great pile of stones in one corner of the square and guarded it against the raids of the other boys. The girls stood aside, talking among themselves, looking over their shoulders at the boys, and the very small children rolled in the dust or clung to the hands of their older brothers or sisters.

Soon the men began to gather, surveying their own children, speaking of planting and rain, tractors and taxes. They stood together, away from the pile of stones in the corner, and their jokes were quiet and they smiled rather than laughed. The women, wearing faded house dresses and sweaters, came shortly after their menfolk. They greeted one another and exchanged bits of gossip as they went to join their husbands. Soon the women, standing by their husbands, began to call to their children, and the chidren came reluctantly, having to be called four or five times. Bobby Martin ducked under his mother's grasping hand and ran, laughing, back to the pile of stones. His father spoke up sharply, and Bobby came quickly and took his place between his father and his oldest brother.

The lottery was conducted—as were the square dances, the teenage club, the Halloween program—by Mr. Summers, who had time and energy to devote to civic activities. He was a round-faced, jovial man and he ran the coal business, and people were sorry for him, because he had no children and his wife was a scold. When he arrived in the square, carrying the black wooden box, there was a murmur of conversation among the villagers, and he waved and called, "Little late today, folks." The postmaster, Mr. Graves, followed him, carrying a three-legged stool, and the stool was put in the center of the square and Mr. Summers set the black box down on it. The villagers kept their distance, leaving a space between themselves and the stool, and when Mr. Summers said, "Some of you fellows want to give me a hand?" there was a hesitation before two men, Mr. Martin and his oldest son, Baxter, came forward to hold the box steady on the stool while Mr. Summers stirred up the papers inside it.

The original paraphernalia for the lottery had been lost long ago, and the black box now resting on the stool had been put into use even before Old Man Warner, the oldest man in town, was born. Mr. Summers spoke frequently to the villagers about making a new box, but no one liked to upset even as much tradition as was represented by the black box. There was a story that the present box had been made with some pieces of the box that had preceded it, the one that had been constructed when the first people settled down to make a village here. Every year, after the lottery, Mr. Summers began talking again about a new box, but every year the subject was allowed to fade off without anything's being done. The black box grew shabbier each year; by now it was no longer completely black but splintered badly along one side to show the original wood color, and in some places faded or stained.

Mr. Martin and his oldest son, Baxter, held the black box securely on the stool until Mr. Summers had stirred the papers thoroughly with his hand. Because so much of the ritual had been forgotten or discarded, Mr. Summers had been successful in having slips of paper substituted for the chips of wood that had been used for generations. Chips of wood, Mr. Summers had argued, had been all very well when the village was tiny, but now that the population was more than three hundred and likely to keep on growing, it was necessary to use something that would fit more easily into the black box. The night before the lottery, Mr. Summers and Mr. Graves made up the slips of paper and put them in the box, and it was then taken to the safe of Mr. Summers' coal company and locked up until Mr. Summers was ready to take it to the square next morning. The rest of the year, the box was put away, sometimes one place, sometimes another; it had spent one year in Mr. Graves's barn and another year underfoot in the post office, and sometimes it was set on a shelf in the Martin grocery and left there.

There was a great deal of fussing to be done before Mr. Summers declared the lottery open. There were the lists to make up—of heads of families, heads of households in each family, members of each household in each family. There was the proper swearing-in of Mr. Summers by the postmaster, as the official of the lottery; at one time, some people remembered, there had been a recital of some sort, performed by the official of the lottery, a perfunctory, tuneless chant that had been rattled off duly each year; some people believed that the official of the lottery used to stand just so when he said or sang it, others believed that he was supposed to walk among the people, but years and years ago this part of the ritual had been allowed to lapse. There had been, also, a ritual salute, which the official of the lottery had had to use in addressing each person who came up to draw from the box, but this also had changed with time, until now it was felt necessary only for the official to speak to each person approaching. Mr. Summers was very good at all this; in his clean white shirt and blue jeans, with one hand resting carelessly on the black box, he seemed very proper and important as he talked interminably to Mr. Graves and the Martins.

Just as Mr. Summers finally left off talking and turned to the assembled villagers, Mrs. Hutchinson came hurriedly along the path to the square, her sweater thrown over her shoulders, and slid into place in the back of the crowd. "Clean forgot what day it was," she said to Mrs. Delacroix, who stood next to her, and they both laughed softly. "Thought my old man was out back stacking wood," Mrs. Hutchinson went on, "and then I looked out the window and the kids was gone, and then I remembered it was the twenty-seventh and came a-running." She dried her hands on her apron, and Mrs. Delacroix said, "You're in time, though. They're still talking away up there."

Mrs. Hutchinson craned her neck to see through the crowd and found her husband and children standing near the front. She tapped Mrs. Delacroix on the arm as a farewell and began to make her way through the crowd. The people separated good-humoredly to let her through; two or three people said, in voices just loud enough to be heard across the crowd, "Here comes your Missus, Hutchinson," and "Bill, she made it after all." Mrs. Hutchinson reached her husband, and Mr. Summers, who had been waiting, said cheerfully, "Thought we were going to have to get on without you, Tessie." Mrs. Hutchinson said, grinning, "Wouldn't have me leave m'dishes in the sink, now, would you, Joe?," and soft laughter ran through the crowd as the people stirred back into position after Mrs. Hutchinson's arrival.

"Well, now," Mr. Summers said soberly, "guess we better get started, get this over with, so's we can go back to work. Anybody ain't here?"

"Dunbar," several people said. "Dunbar, Dunbar."

Mr. Summers consulted his list. "Clyde Dunbar," he said. "That's right. He's broke his leg, hasn't he? Who's drawing for him?"

"Me, I guess," a woman said, and Mr. Summers turned to look at her. "Wife draws for her husband," Mr. Summers said. "Don't you have a grown boy to do it for you, Janey?" Although Mr. Summers and everyone else in the village knew the answer perfectly well, it was the business of the official of the lottery to ask such questions formally. Mr. Summers waited with an expression of polite interest while Mrs. Dunbar answered.

"Horace's not but sixteen yet," Mrs. Dunbar said regretfully. "Guess I gotta fill in for the old man this year."

"Right," Mr. Summers said. He made a note on the list he was holding. Then he asked, "Watson boy drawing this year?"

A tall boy in the crowd raised his hand. "Here," he said. "I'm drawing for m'mother and me." He blinked his eyes nervously and ducked his head as several voices in the crowd said things like "Good fellow, Jack," and "Glad to see your mother's got a man to do it."

"Well," Mr. Summers said, "guess that's everyone. Old Man Warner make it?"

"Here," a voice said, and Mr. Summers nodded.

A sudden hush fell on the crowd as Mr. Summers cleared his throat and looked at the list. "All ready?" he called. "Now, I'll read the names—heads of families first—and the men come up and take a paper out of the box. Keep the paper folded in your hand without looking at it until everyone has had a turn. Everything clear?"

The people had done it so many times that they only half listened to the directions; most of them were quiet, wetting their lips, not looking around. Then Mr. Summers raised one hand high and said, "Adams." A man disengaged himself from the crowd and came forward. "Hi, Steve," Mr. Summers said, and Mr. Adams said, "Hi, Joe." They grinned at one another humorlessly and nervously. Then Mr. Adams reached into the black box and took out a folded paper. He held it firmly by one corner as he turned and went hastily back to his place in the crowd, where he stood a little apart from his family, not looking down at his hand.

"Allen," Mr. Summers said. "Anderson. . . . Bentham."

"Seems like there's no time at all between lotteries any more," Mrs. Delacroix said to Mrs. Graves in the back row. "Seems like we got through with the last one only last week."

"Time sure goes fast," Mrs. Graves said.

"Clark. . . . Delacroix."

"There goes my old man," Mrs. Delacroix said. She held her breath while her husband went forward.

"Dunbar," Mr. Summers said, and Mrs. Dunbar went steadily to the box while one of the women said, "Go on, Janey," and another said, "There she goes."

"We're next," Mrs. Graves said. She watched while Mr. Graves came around from the side of the box, greeted Mr. Summers gravely, and selected a slip of paper from the box. By now, all through the crowd there were men holding the small folded papers in their large hands, turning them over and over nervously. Mrs. Dunbar and her two sons stood together, Mrs. Dunbar holding the slip of paper.

"Harburt. . . . Hutchinson."

"Get up there, Bill," Mrs. Hutchinson said, and the people near her laughed.

"Jones."

"They do say," Mr. Adams said to Old Man Warner, who stood next to him, "that over in the north village they're talking of giving up the lottery."

Old Man Warner snorted. "Pack of crazy fools," he said. "Listening to the young folks, nothing's good enough for *them*. Next thing you know, they'll be wanting to go back to living in caves, nobody work any more, live *that* way for a while. Used to be a saying about 'Lottery in June, corn be heavy soon.' First thing you know, we'd all be eating stewed chickweed and acorns. There's *always* been a lottery," he added petulantly. "Bad enough to see young Joe Summers up there joking with everybody."

"Some places have already quit lotteries," Mrs. Adams said.

"Nothing but trouble in *that*," Old Man Warner said stoutly. "Pack of young fools."

"Martin." And Bobby Martin watched his father go forward. "Overdyke. . . . Percy."

"I wish they'd hurry," Mrs. Dunbar said to her older son. "I wish they'd hurry."

"They're almost through," her son said.

"You get ready to run tell Dad," Mrs. Dunbar said.

Mr. Summers called his own name and then stepped forward precisely and selected a slip from the box. Then he called, "Warner."

"Seventy-seventh year I been in the lottery," Old Man Warner said as he went through the crowd. "Seventy-seventh time."

"Watson." The tall boy came awkwardly through the crowd. Someone said, "Don't be nervous, Jack," and Mr. Summers said, "Take your time, son."

"Zanini."

After that, there was a long pause, a breathless pause, until Mr. Summers, holding his slip of paper in the air, said, "All right, fellows." For a minute, no one moved, and then all the slips of paper were opened. Suddenly, all the women began to speak at once, saying, "Who is it?," "Who's got it?," "Is it the Dunbars?," "Is it the Watsons?" Then the voices began to say, "It's Hutchinson. It's Bill," "Bill Hutchinson's got it."

"Go tell your father," Mrs. Dunbar said to her older son.

People began to look around to see the Hutchinsons. Bill Hutchinson was standing quiet staring down at the paper in his hand. Suddenly, Tessie Hutchinson shouted to Mr. Summers, "You didn't give him time enough to take any paper he wanted. I saw you. It wasn't fair."

"Be a good sport, Tessie," Mrs. Delacroix called, and Mrs. Graves said, "All of us took the same chance."

"Shut up, Tessie," Bill Hutchinson said.

"Well, everyone," Mr. Summers said, "that was done pretty fast, and now we've got to be hurrying a little more to get done in time." He consulted his next list. "Bill," he said, "you draw for the Hutchinson family. You got any other households in the Hutchinsons?"

"There's Don and Eva," Mrs. Hutchinson yelled. "Make *them* take their chance!"

"Daughters draw with their husbands' families, Tessie," Mr. Summers said gently. "You know that as well as anyone else."

"It wasn't *fair*," Tessie said.

"I guess not, Joe," Bill Hutchinson said regretfully. "My daughter draws with her husband's family, that's only fair. And I've got no other family except the kids."

"Then, as far as drawing for families is concerned, it's you," Mr. Summers said in explanation, "and as far as drawing for households is concerned, that's you, too. Right?"

"Right," Bill Hutchinson said.

"How many kids, Bill?" Mr. Summers asked formally.

"Three," Bill Hutchinson said. "There's Bill, Jr., and Nancy, and little Dave. And Tessie and me."

"All right, then," Mr. Summers said. "Harry, you got their tickets back?"

Mr. Graves nodded and held up the slips of paper. "Put them in the box, then," Mr. Summers directed. "Take Bill's and put it in."

"I think we ought to start over," Mrs. Hutchinson said, as quietly as she could. "I tell you it wasn't *fair*. You didn't give him time enough to choose. *Every*body saw that."

Mr. Graves had selected the five slips and put them in the box, and he dropped all the papers but those onto the ground, where the breeze caught them and lifted them off.

"Listen, everybody," Mrs. Hutchinson was saying to the people around her.

"Ready, Bill?" Mr. Summers asked, and Bill Hutchinson, with one quick glance around at his wife and children, nodded.

"Remember," Mr. Summers said, "take the slips and keep them folded until each person has taken one. Harry, you help little Dave." Mr. Graves took the hand of the little boy, who came willingly with him up to the box. "Take a paper out of the box, Davy," Mr. Summers said. Davy put his hand into the box and laughed. "Take just *one* paper." Mr. Summers said. "Harry, you hold it for him." Mr. Graves took the child's hand and removed the folded paper from the tight fist and held it while little Dave stood next to him and looked up at him wonderingly.

"Nancy next," Mr. Summers said. Nancy was twelve, and her school friends breathed heavily as she went forward, switching her skirt, and took a slip daintily from the box. "Bill, Jr.," Mr. Summers said, and Billy, his face red and his feet over-large, nearly knocked the box over as he got a paper out. "Tessie," Mr. Summers said. She hesitated for a minute, looking around defiantly, and then set her lips and went up to the box. She snatched a paper out and held it behind her.

"Bill," Mr. Summers said, and Bill Hutchinson reached into the box and felt around, bringing his hand out at last with the slip of paper in it.

The crowd was quiet. A girl whispered, "I hope it's not Nancy," and the sound of the whisper reached the edges of the crowd.

"It's not the way it used to be," Old Man Warner said clearly. "People ain't the way they used to be."

"All right," Mr. Summers said. "Open the papers. Harry, you open little Dave's."

Mr. Graves opened the slip of paper and there was a general sigh through the crowd as he held it up and everyone could see that it was blank. Nancy and Bill, Jr., opened theirs at the same time, and both beamed and laughed, turning around to the crowd and holding their slips of paper above their heads.

"Tessie," Mr. Summers said. There was a pause, and then Mr. Summers looked at Bill Hutchinson, and Bill unfolded his paper and showed it. It was blank.

"It's Tessie," Mr. Summers said, and his voice was hushed. "Show us her paper, Bill."

Bill Hutchinson went over to his wife and forced the slip of paper out of her hand. It had a black spot on it, the black spot Mr. Summers had made the night before with the heavy pencil in the coal-company office. Bill Hutchinson held it up, and there was a stir in the crowd.

"All right, folks," Mr. Summers said. "Let's finish quickly."

Although the villagers had forgotten the ritual and lost the original black box, they still remembered to use stones. The pile of stones the boys had made earlier was ready; there were stones on the ground with the blowing scraps of paper that had come out of the box. Mrs. Delacroix selected a stone so large she had to pick it up with both hands and turned to Mrs. Dunbar. "Come on," she said. "Hurry up."

Mrs. Dunbar had small stones in both hands, and she said, gasping for breath, "I can't run at all. You'll have to go ahead and I'll catch up with you."

The children had stones already, and someone gave little Davy Hutchinson a few pebbles.

Tessie Hutchinson was in the center of a cleared space by now, and she held her hands out desperately as the villagers moved in on her. "It isn't fair," she said. A stone hit her on the side of the head.

Old Man Warner was saying, "Come on, come on, everyone." Steve Adams was in the front of the crowd of villagers, with Mrs. Graves beside him.

"It isn't fair, it isn't right," Mrs. Hutchinson screamed, and then they were upon her.

1948

MORDECAI RICHLER

The Summer My Grandmother Was Supposed to Die

Dr. Katzman discovered the gangrene on one of his monthly visits. "She won't last a month," he said.

He repeated that the second month, the third, and the fourth, and now she lay dying in the heat of the back bedroom.

"If only she'd die," my mother said. "Oh, God, why doesn't she die? God in heaven, what's she holding on for?"

The summer my grandmother was supposed to die we did not chip in with the Breenbaums to take a cottage in the Laurentians.[1] It wouldn't have been practical. The old lady couldn't be moved, the nurse came daily and the doctor twice a week, and so it seemed best to stay in the city and wait for her to die or, as my mother said, pass away. It was a hot summer, her bedroom was just behind the kitchen, and when we sat down to eat we could smell her. The dressings on my grandmother's left leg had to be changed several times a day and, according to Dr. Katzman, her condition was hopeless. "It's in the hands of the Almighty," he said.

"It won't be long now," my father said, "and she'll be better off, if you know what I mean."

"Please," my mother said.

A nurse came every day from the Royal Victorian Order.[2] She arrived punctually at noon and at five to twelve I'd join the rest of the boys under the outside staircase to look up her dress as she climbed to our second-story flat. Miss Monohan favored lacy pink panties and that was better than waiting under the stairs for Cousin Bessie, for instance. She wore enormous cotton bloomers, rain or shine.

I was sent out to play as often as possible, because my mother felt it was not good for me to see somebody dying. Usually I'd just roam the scorched streets shooting the breeze. There was Arty, Gas sometimes, Hershey, Stan, and me. We talked about everything from A to Z.

"Why is it," Arty wanted to know, "that Tarzan never shits?"

"Dick Tracy too."

"Or Wonder Woman."

"She's a dame."

"So?"

"Jees, wouldn't it be something if Superman crapped in the sky? He could just be flying over Waverly Street when, whamo, Mr. Rabinovitch catches it right in the kisser."

Mr. Rabinovitch was our Hebrew teacher.

"But there's Tarzan," Arty insisted, "in the jungle, week in and week out, and never once does he need to go to the toilet. It's not real, that's all."

Arty told me, "Before your grandma dies she's going to roll her eyes and gurgle. That's what they call the death-rattle."

"Aw, you know everything. Big shot."

"I *read* it, you jerk," Arty said, whacking me one, "in Perry Mason."

Home again I'd find my mother weeping.

"She's dying by inches," she said to my father one stifling night, "and none of them even come to see her. Oh, such children! They should only rot in hell."

"They're not behaving right. It's certainly not according to Hoyle," my father said.

"When I think of all the money and effort that went into making

1. Mountains in eastern Canada between Hudson Bay and the St. Lawrence River.

2. The Victorian Order of Nurses for Canada.

a rabbi out of Israel—the way Mother doted on him—and for what? Oh, what's the world coming to? God."

"It's not right."

Dr. Kaztman was amazed. "I never believed she'd last this long. Really, it must be will-power alone that keeps her going. And your excellent care."

"I want her to die, Doctor. That's not my mother in the back room. It's an animal. I want her to please please die."

"Hush. You don't mean it. You're tired." And Dr. Katzman gave my father some pills for my mother to take. "A remarkable woman," he said. "A born nurse."

At night in bed my brother Harvey and I used to talk about our grandmother. "After she dies," I said, "her hair will go on growing for another twenty-four hours."

"Sez who?"

"Arty. It's a scientific fact. Do you think Uncle Lou will come from New York for the funeral?"

"Sure."

"Boy, that means another fiver for me. You too."

"You shouldn't say things like that, kiddo, or *her ghost will come back to haunt you.*"

"Well," I said, "I'll be able to go to her funeral, anyway. I'm not too young any more."

I was only six years old when my grandfather died, and I wasn't allowed to go to his funeral.

I have only one memory of my grandfather. Once he called me into his study, set me down on his lap, and made a drawing of a horse for me. On the horse he drew a rider. While I watched and giggled he gave the rider a beard and the round fur-trimmed cap of a rabbi.

My grandfather was a Zaddik,[3] one of the Righteous, and I've been told that to study Talmud with him had been a rare pleasure. I wasn't allowed to go to his funeral, but years after I was shown the telegram of condolence that had come from Eire and Poland and Israel and even Japan. My grandfather had written many books: a translation of the Zohar[4] into modern Hebrew—some twenty years' work—and lots of slender volumes of sermons, chassidic tales, and rabbinical commentaries. His books had been published in Warsaw and later in New York. He had been famous.

"At the funeral," my mother told me, "they had to have six motorcycle policemen to control the crowds. It was such a heat that twelve women fainted—and I'm *not* counting Mrs. Waxman from upstairs. With her, you know, *anything* to fall into a man's arms. Even Pinsky's. And did I tell you that there was even a French-Canadian priest there?"

"No kidding?"

"The priest was a real big *knacker*.[5] A bishop maybe. He used to study with the *zeyda*.[6] The *zeyda* was some personality, you know.

3. "Righteous man" in Hebrew.

4. "The Book of Splendor," the central part of the Kabbalah, the esoteric teachings of Judaism and the source of Jewish mysticism.

5. Big shot.

6. Grandfather.

Spiritual and wordly-wise at the same time. Such personalities they don't make any more. Today, rabbis and peanuts are the same size."

But, according to my father, the *zeyda* (his father-in-law) hadn't been as famous as all that. "There are things I could say," he told me. "There was another side to him."

My grandfather had come from generations and generations of rabbis, his youngest son was a rabbi, but none of his grandchildren would be one. My brother Harvey was going to be a dentist and at the time, 1937, I was interested in flying and my cousin Jerry was already a communist. I once heard Jerry say, "Our grandpappy wasn't all he was cracked up to be." When the men at the kosher bakeries went out on strike he spoke up against them on the streets where they were picketing and in the *shule*.[7] It was of no consequence to him that they were grossly underpaid. His superstitious followers had to have bread. "Grandpappy," Jerry said, "was a prize reactionary."

A week after my grandfather died my grandmother suffered a stroke. Her right side was completely paralyzed. She couldn't speak. At first, it's true, my grandmother could say a few words and move her right hand enough to write her name in Hebrew. Her name was Malka. But her condition soon began to deteriorate.

My grandmother had six children and seven stepchildren, for my grandfather had been married before. His first wife had died in the old country. Two years later he had married my grandmother, the only daughter of the richest man in the village, and their marriage had been a singularly happy one. My grandmother had been a beautiful girl. She had also been a wise, resourceful, and patient wife. Qualities, I fear, indispensable to life with a Zaddik. For the synagogue had paid my grandfather no stipulated salary and much of the money he had picked up here and there he had habitually distributed among rabbinical students, needy immigrants, and widows. A vice, and such it was to his hard-pressed family, which made him as unreliable a provider as a drunkard. And indeed, to carry the analogy further, my grandmother had had to make many hurried trips to the pawnbroker with her jewelry. Not all of it had been redeemed, either. But her children had been looked after. The youngest, her favorite, was a rabbi in Boston, the eldest was the actor-manager of a Yiddish theater in New York, and another was a lawyer. One daughter lived in Toronto, two in Montreal. My mother was the youngest daughter, and when my grandmother had her stroke there was a family meeting and it was decided that my mother would take care of her. This was my father's fault. All the other husbands spoke up—they protested their wives had too much work, they could never manage it—but my father detested quarrels, and he was silent. So my grandmother came to stay with us.

Her bedroom, the back bedroom, had actually been promised to me for my seventh birthday. But all that was forgotten now, and I had to go on sharing a bedroom with my brother Harvey. So naturally I was resentful when each morning before I left for school my mother said, "Go in and kiss the *baba*[8] good-bye."

7. Synagogue.

8. Grandma.

All the same I'd go into the bedroom and kiss my grandmother hastily. She'd say "Bouyo-bouyo," for that was the only sound she could make. And after school it was, "Go in and tell the *baba* you're home."

"I'm home, *baba*."

"Bouyo-bouyo."

During those first hopeful months—"Twenty years ago who would have thought there'd be a cure for diabetes?" my father asked; "where there's life there's hope, you know"—she'd smile at me and try to speak, her eyes charged with effort. And even later there were times when she pressed my head urgently to her bosom with her surprisingly strong left arm. But as her illness dragged on and on and she became a condition in the house, something beyond hope or reproach, like the leaky icebox, there was less recognition and more ritual in those kisses. I came to dread her room. A clutter of sticky medicine bottles and the cracked toilet chair beside the bed; glazed but imploring eyes and a feeble smile, the wet slap of her lips against my cheeks. I flinched from her touch. After two years of it I protested to my mother. "Look, what's the use of telling her I'm going or I'm here. She doesn't even recognize me any more."

"Don't be fresh. She's your grandmother."

My uncle who was in the theater in New York sent money regularly to help support my grandmother and, for the first few months, so did the other children. But once the initial and sustaining excitement had passed and it became likely that my grandmother might linger in her invalid condition for two or maybe even three more years, the checks began to drop off, and the children seldom came to our house any more. Anxious weekly visits—"and how is she today, poor lamb?"—quickly dwindled to a dutiful monthly looking in, then a semi-annual visit, and these always on the way to somewhere.

"The way they act," my father said, "you'd think that if they stayed long enough to take off their coats we'd make them take the *baba* home with them."

When the children did come to visit, my mother made it difficult for them.

"It's killing me," she said. "I have to lift her onto that chair three times a day maybe. Have you any idea how heavy she is? And what makes you think I always catch her in time? Sometimes I have to change her bed twice a day. That's a job I'd like to see your wife do," she said to my uncle, the rabbi.

"We could send her to the Old People's Home," the rabbi said.

"Now there's an idea," my father said.

But my mother began to sob. "Not as long as I'm alive," she said. And she gave my father a stony look. "Say something."

"It wouldn't be according to Hoyle."

"You want to be able to complain to everybody in town about all the other children," the rabbi said. "You've got a martyr complex."

"Everybody has a point of view, you know. You know what I mean?" my father said. "So what's the use of fighting?"

Meanwhile, Dr. Katzman came once a month to examine my grandmother. "It's remarkable, astonishing," he'd say each time. "She's as strong as a horse."

"Some life for a person," my father said. "She can't speak—she doesn't recognize anybody—what is there for her?"

The doctor was a cultivated man; he spoke often for women's clubs, sometimes on Yiddish literature and other times, his rubicund face hot with impatience, the voice taking on a doomsday tone, on the cancer threat.

"Who are we to judge?" he asked.

Every evening, during the first months of my grandmother's illness, my mother read her a story by Sholem Aleichem.[9] "Tonight she smiled," my mother would say. "She understood. I can tell." And my father, my brother, and I would not comment. Once a week my mother used to give the old lady a manicure. Sunny afternoons she'd lift her into a wheelchair and put her out in the sun. Somebody always had to stay in the house in case my grandmother called. Often, during the night, she would begin to wail unaccountably, and my mother would get up and rock the old lady in her arms for hours. But in the fourth year of my grandmother's illness the strain and fatigue began to tell on my mother. Besides looking after my grandmother—"and believe you me," the doctor assured her with a clap on the back, "it would be a full-time job for a professional nurse"—she had to keep house for a husband and two sons. She began to quarrel with my father and she became sharp with Harvey and me. My father started to spend his evenings playing pinochle at Tansky's Cigar & Soda. Weekends he took Harvey and me to visit his brothers and sisters. And everywhere he went people had little bits of advice for him.

"Sam, you might as well be a bachelor. You're just going to have to put your foot down for once."

"Yeah, in your face maybe."

My cousin Libby, who was at McGill,[1] said, "This could have a very damaging effect on the development of your boys. These are their formative years, Uncle Samuel, and the omnipresence of death in the house . . ."

"What you need," my father said, "is a boy friend. *And how.*"

At Tansky's Cigar & Soda it was, "Come clean, Sam. It's no hardship. If I know you, the old lady's got a big insurance policy and when the time comes . . ."

My mother lost lots of weight. After dinner she'd fall asleep in her chair in the middle of Lux Radio Theater.[2] One minute she'd be sewing a patch on my breeches or be making a list of girls to call for a bingo party (proceeds for the Talmud Torah),[3] and the next she'd be snoring. Then, one morning, she just couldn't get out of bed, and Dr. Katzman came round a week before his regular visit. "Well, well, this won't do, will it?" He sat in the kitchen with my father and the two men drank apricot brandy out of small glasses.

"Your wife is a remarkable woman," Dr. Katzman said.

9. "Peace be with you," pen name of Yiddish author and humorist Shalom Rabinovitz (1859–1916).

1. University in Montreal.

2. Radio weekly drama sponsored by Lux soap.

3. Orthodox Jewish school for boys.

"You don't say?"

"She's got a gallstone condition."

My father shrugged. "Have another one for the road," he said.

"Thank you, but I have several more calls to make." Dr. Katzman rose, sighing. "There she lies in that back room, poor old woman," he said, "hanging desperately onto life. There's food for thought there."

My grandmother's children met again, and the five of them sat around my mother's bed embarrassed, irritated, and quick to take insult. All except my uncle who was in the theater. He sucked a cigar and drank whisky. He teased my mother, the rabbi, and my aunts, and if not for him I think they would have been at each other's throats. It was decided, over my mother's protests, to send my grandmother to the Old People's Home on Esplanade Street. An ambulance came to take my grandmother away and Dr. Katzman said, "It's for the best." But my father had been in the back bedroom when the old lady had held on tenaciously to the bedpost, not wanting to be moved by the two men in white—"Easy does it, granny," the younger one had said—and afterwards he could not go in to see my mother. He went out for a walk.

"She looked at me with such a funny expression," he told my brother. "Is it my fault?"

My mother stayed in bed for another two weeks. My father cooked for us and we hired a woman to do the housework. My mother put on weight quickly, her cheeks regained their normal pinkish hue and, for the first time in months, she actually joked with Harvey and me. She became increasingly curious about our schools and whether or not we shined our shoes regularly. She began to cook again, special dishes for my father, and she resumed old friendships with women on the parochial school board. The change reflected on my father. Not only did his temper improve, but he stopped going to Tansky's every other night, and began to come home early from work. Life at home had never been so rich. But my grandmother's name was never mentioned. The back bedroom remained empty and I continued to share a room with Harvey. I couldn't see the point and so one evening I said, "Look, why don't I move into the back bedroom?"

My father glared at me across the table.

"But it's empty like."

My mother left the table. And the next afternoon she put on her best dress and coat and new spring hat.

"Where are you going?" my father asked.

"To see my mother."

"Don't go looking for trouble."

"It's been a month. Maybe they're not treating her right."

"They're experts."

"Did you think I was never going to visit her? I'm not inhuman, you know."

"All right, go," he said.

But after she'd gone my father went to the window and said, "Son-of-a-bitch."

Harvey and I sat outside on the steps watching the cars go by. My father sat on the balcony above, cracking peanuts. It was six o'clock, maybe later, when the ambulance turned the corner, slowed down, and parked right in front of the house.

"Son-of-a-bitch," my father said. "I knew it."

My mother got out first, her eyes red and swollen, and hurried upstairs to make my grandmother's bed.

"I'm sorry, Sam, I had to do it."

"You'll get sick again, that's what."

"You think she doesn't recognize people. From the moment she saw me she cried and cried. Oh, it was terrible."

"They're experts there. They know how to handle her better than you do."

"Experts? Expert murderers you mean. She's got bedsores, Sam. Those dirty little Irish nurses they don't change her linen often enough, they hate her. She must have lost twenty pounds there."

"Another month and you'll be flat on your back again."

"Sam, what could I do? Please Sam."

"She'll outlive all of us. Even Muttel.[4] I'm going out for a walk."

She was back and I was to blame.

My father became a regular at Tansky's Cigar & Soda again and every morning I had to go in and kiss my grandmother. She began to look like a man. Little hairs had sprouted on her chin, she had a spiky gray mustache and, of course, she was practically bald. This near-baldness, I guess, sprang from the fact that she had been shaving her head ever since she had married my grandfather the rabbi.[5] My grandmother had four different wigs, but she had not worn one since the first year of her illness. She wore a little pink cap instead. And so, as before, she said, "bouyo-bouyo," to everything.

Once more uncles and aunts sent five-dollar bills, though erratically, to help pay for my grandmother's support. Elderly people, former followers of my grandfather, came to inquire after the old lady's health. They sat in the back bedroom with her for hours, leaning on their canes, talking to themselves, rocking, always rocking to and fro. "The Holy Shakers," my father called them, and Harvey and I avoided them, because they always wanted to pinch our cheeks, give us a dash of snuff and laugh when we sneezed, or offer us a sticky old candy from a little brown bag with innumerable creases in it. When the visit was done the old people would unfailingly sit in the kitchen with my mother for another hour, watching her make lockshen[6] or bake bread. My mother always served them lemon tea and they would talk about my grandfather, recalling his books, his sayings, and his charitable deeds.

And so another two years passed, with no significant change in my grandmother's condition. But fatigue, bad temper, and even morbidity enveloped my mother again. She fought with her brothers and sisters and once, when I stepped into the living room, I found her sitting with her head in her hands, and she looked up at me with such anguish that I was frightened.

4. The narrator's Yiddish name; could be the equivalent of Mordecai.
5. Married Orthodox Jewish women customarily either shave their heads or cover their hair.
6. Noodles.

"What did I do now?" I asked.

"If, God forbid, I had a stroke, would you send me to the Old People's Home?"

"Don't be a joke. Of course not."

"I hope that never in my life do I have to count on my children for anything."

The summer my grandmother was supposed to die, the seventh year of her illness, my brother took a job as a shipper and he kept me awake at night with stories about the factory. "What we do, see, is clear out the middle of a huge pile of lengths of material. That makes for a kind of secret cave. A hideout. Well, then you coax one of the *shiksas*[7] inside and hi-diddle-diddle."

One night Harvey waited until I had fallen asleep and then he wrapped himself in a white sheet, crept up to my bed, and shouted, "Bouyo-bouyo."

I hit him. He shouted.

"Children. Children, please," my mother called. "I must get some rest."

As my grandmother's condition worsened—from day to day we didn't know when she'd die—I was often sent out to eat at my aunt's or at my other grandmother's house. I was hardly ever at home. On Saturday mornings I'd get together with the other guys and we'd walk all the way past the mountain to Eaton's, which was our favorite department store for riding up and down escalators and stealing.

In those days they let boys into the left-field bleachers free during the week and we spent many an afternoon at the ball park. The Montreal Royals, part of the Dodger farm system, was some ball club too. There was Jackie Robinson and Roy Campanella, Honest John Gabbard, Chuck Connors, and Kermit Kitman was our hero. It used to kill us to see that crafty little hebe[8] running around there with all those tall dumb *goyim*.[9] "Hey, Kitman," we'd yell. "Hey, hey, sho-head,[1] if your father knew you played ball on *shabus*—"[2] Kitman, unfortunately, was all field and no hit. He never made the majors. "There goes Kermit Kitman," we'd yell, after he'd gone down swinging again, "the first Jewish strike-out king of the International League." This we usually followed up by bellowing some choice imprecations in Yiddish.

It was after one of these games, on a Friday afternoon, that I came home to find a small crowd gathered in front of the house.

"That's the grandson."

"Poor kid."

Old people stood silent and expressionless across the street staring at our front door. A taxi pulled up and my aunt hurried out, hiding her face in her hands.

"After so many years," somebody said.

7. Gentile girls.
8. Hebrew, Jew.
9. Gentiles.
1. Possibly *shorn-head* (?), referring to short hair or crew cut of athlete, in contrast to traditional long locks of Orthodox Jews (?).
2. Sabbath.

"And probably next year they'll discover a cure. Isn't that *always* the case?"

I took the stairs two at a time. The flat was full. Uncles and aunts from my father's side of the family, odd old people, Dr. Katzman, Harvey, neighbors, were all standing around and talking in hushed voices in the living room. I found my father in the kitchen, getting out the apricot brandy. "Your grandmother's dead," he said.

"She didn't suffer," somebody said. "She passed away in her sleep."

"A merciful death."

"Where's Maw?"

"In the bedroom with . . . you'd better not go in," my father said.

"I want to see her."

My mother's face was long with grief. She wore a black shawl, and glared down at a knot of handkerchief clutched in a fist that had been cracked by washing soda. "Don't come in here," she said.

Several bearded, round-shouldered men in black shiny coats stood round the bed. I couldn't see my grandmother.

"Your grandmother's dead."

"Daddy told me."

"Go and wash your face and comb your hair. You'll have to get your own supper."

"O.K."

"One minute. The *baba* left some jewelry. The ring is for Harvey's wife and the necklace is for yours."

"Who's getting married?"

"Better go and wash your face. And remember behind the ears, Muttel."

Telegrams were sent, long-distance calls were made, and all through the evening relatives and neighbors came and went like swarms of fish when crumbs have been dropped into the water.

"When my father died," my mother said, "they had to have *six* motorcycle policemen to control the crowds. Twelve people fainted, such a heat . . ."

The man from the funeral parlor came.

"There goes the only Jewish businessman in town," my Uncle Harry said, "who wishes all his customers were Germans."

"This is no time for jokes."

"Listen, life goes on."

My cousin Jerry had begun to use a cigarette holder. "Everyone's going to be sickeningly sentimental," he said. "Soon the religious mumbo-jumbo starts. I can hardly wait."

Tomorrow was the Sabbath and so, according to the law, my grandmother couldn't be buried until Sunday. She would have to lie on the floor all night. Two old grizzly women in white came to move and wash the body and a professional mourner arrived to sit up and pray for her.

"I don't trust his face," my mother said. "He'll fall asleep. You watch him, Sam."

"A fat lot of good prayers will do her now."

"Will you just watch him, please."

"I'll watch him, I'll watch him." My father was livid about my

Uncle Harry. "The way he's gone after that apricot brandy you'd think that guy never saw a bottle in his life before."

Harvey and I were sent to bed, but we couldn't sleep. My aunt was sobbing over the body in the living room—"That dirty hypocrite," my mother said—there was the old man praying, coughing, and spitting into his handkerchief each time he woke; and hushed voices and whimpering from the kitchen, where my father and mother sat. Harvey was in a good mood, he let me have a few puffs of his cigarette.

"Well, kiddo, this is our last night together. Tomorrow you can take over the back bedroom."

"*Are you crazy?*"

"You always wanted it for yourself."

"She died in there, but. You think I'm going to sleep in there?"

"Good night. Happy dreams, kiddo."

"Hey, let's talk some more."

Harvey told me a ghost story. "Did you know that when they hang a man," he said, "the last thing that happens is that he has an orgasm?"

"A what?"

"Forget it. I forgot you were still in kindergarten."

"I know plenty. Don't worry."

"At the funeral they're going to open her coffin to throw dirt in her face. It's supposed to be earth from Eretz.[3] They open it and you're going to have to look." Harvey stood up on his bed, holding his hands over his head like claws. He made a hideous face. "Bouyo-bouyo. Who's that sleeping in my bed? Woo-woo."

My uncle who was in the theater, the rabbi, and my aunt from Toronto, all came to Montreal for the funeral. Dr. Katzman came too.

"As long as she was alive," my mother said, "he couldn't even send five dollars a month. Some son! What a rabbi! I don't want him in my house, Sam. I can't bear the sight of him."

"You don't mean a word of that and you know it," Dr. Katzman said.

"Maybe you'd better give her a sedative," the rabbi said.

"Sam. Sam, will you say something, please."

My father stepped up to the rabbi, his face flushed. "I'll tell you this straight to your face, Israel," he said. "You've gone down in my estimation."

"Really," the rabbi said, smiling a little.

My father's face burned a deeper red. "Year by year," he said, "your stock has gone down with me."

And my mother began to weep bitterly, helplessly, without control. She was led unwillingly to bed. While my father tried his best to comfort her, as he said consoling things, Dr. Katzman plunged a needle into her arm. "There we are," he said.

I went to sit in the sun on the outside stairs with Arty. "I'm going to the funeral," I said.

"I couldn't go anyway."

Arty was descended from the tribe of high priests and so was not

3. Eretz Yisrael, the Land of Israel.

allowed to be in the presence of a dead body. I was descended from the Yisroelis.[4]

"The lowest of the low," Arty said.

"Aw."

My uncle, the rabbi, and Dr. Katzman stepped into the sun to light cigarettes.

"It's remarkable that she held out for so long," Dr. Katzman said.

"Remarkable?" my uncle said. "It's written that if a man has been married twice he will spend as much time with his first wife in heaven as he did on earth. My father, may he rest in peace, was married to his first wife for seven years and my mother, may she rest in peace, has managed to keep alive for seven years. Today in heaven she will be able to join my father, may he rest in peace."

Dr. Katzman shook his head, he pursed his lips. "It's amazing," he said. "The mysteries of the human heart. Astonishing."

My father hurried outside. "Dr. Katzman, please. It's my wife. Maybe the injection wasn't strong enough? She just doesn't stop crying. It's like a tap. Could you come please?"

"Excuse me," Dr. Katzman said to my uncle.

"Of course."

My uncle approached Arty and me.

"Well, boys," he said, "what would you like to be when you grow up?"

1961

3 CHARACTERIZATION

In a good many stories we read we know very little about the narrator, who is a disembodied offstage voice, without an identity or a personal history, without influence on the action, without qualities other than those that a voice and style may suggest. So it is in most of the earlier stories in this volume—*The Most Dangerous Game, Macomber, Owl Creek Bridge,* and especially *The Lottery*. Poe's narrator, however, not only tells us the story but acts out the action; without him we not only would not know the story, there just would not be any. Richler's narrator looks back into his past; he is there in the story, speaking, listening, reacting—so he is, then, a **character.** Hazel, in *My Man Bovanne,* is both character and narrator. In fiction a character is simply someone who acts, appears, or is referred to in a work, so that narrators may or may not be characters.

The whole cast of characters is called the **dramatis personae** (literally, characters or actors of the drama). Most discussions of char-

4. The lowest of the three categories into which the Jewish people are traditionally divided.

acter, however, concentrate on the narrator or on the main characters. The most common term for the character with the leading male role is **hero,** the "good guy" who opposes the **villain,** or "bad guy." The leading female character is the **heroine.** Heroes are usually larger than life, stronger, better than most human beings, almost godlike (and there's even a brand of heroes nowadays so close to being godlike that they are called superheroes). In most modern fiction, however, the leading character is much more ordinary, more like the rest of us, as is the father in Sherwood Anderson's *The Egg* or the grandfather in *The Artificial Nigger,* a story in the next chapter, or almost anyone played by Dustin Hoffman. Such a character is called the **antihero,** not because he opposes the hero but because he is not like a hero in stature or perfection. An older and more neutral term than *hero* for the leading character, a term that does not imply either the presence or absence of outstanding virtue (and with the added advantage of referring equally to male and female), is **protagonist,** whose opponent is not the villain but the **antagonist.** You might get into long and pointless arguments by calling Hazel, Raskolnikov in *Crime and Punishment,* or Bonnie's Clyde or Clyde's Bonnie a hero or heroine, so it can be useful to have the more neutral term 'protagonist.'

Because we see more of the major characters over a longer period of time, we learn more about them, and we think of them as more complex and frequently therefore more "realistic" than the minor characters. They can grow and change, as Macomber does, as the father does in *The Egg,* and as Judith does in Doris Lessing's *Our Friend Judith;* by the end of these stories all these have acted in a way not predictable from what we learned earlier in the story about their character and their past actions. Characters who can thus "surprise convincingly," an influential critic says, are **round characters.** Major or minor characters who have only a single trait (or very few traits), and who remain consistent throughout the story, are called **flat characters.** Perhaps the most famous and beloved flat characters are those of Dickens, but Poe's characters are rather flat, and those in *The Lottery* seem so too.

I mention the characters of Dickens to bring out the point that flat characters, though less complex than round characters, are not necessarily inferior artistically. You may recall admirably presented flat characterizations in other media: Shakespeare's Falstaff, Charlie Chaplin's Little Tramp, Little Orphan Annie, the "Jack Benny" portrayed by Jack Benny, Archie Bunker.

Nor are all notable flat characters comic. Dickens's Fagin (in *Oliver Twist*) and Scrooge (in *A Christmas Carol*) are memorable, flat, and unfunny. Nor are flat characters necessarily uninteresting psychological types. Doesn't Iago (in *Othello*) fit the description of a flat character? How does his characterization differ from that of Montresor? Are both flat? equally flat? well presented? equally well presented?

Descriptive terms like *flat* and *round* have a disconcerting way of magically turning into value judgments, a transformation we must constantly discourage. Such terms also seem magically to turn into pigeonholes, so I said that Poe's characters were only "rather" flat, and said that those in *The Lottery* "seem" to be flat. Like *hero, round* and *flat* are useful but not wholly precise terms: they designate extremes or tendencies, matters of degree. Still, it will surely sharpen our perception and deepen our understanding of stories to try to define just how much we know about someone like Wilson in *Macomber,* or Hazel, the delightful narrator of *Bovanne,* to what degree they can be summed up in a phrase or sentence, to what degree they are flat, round, or lumpy.

Though most of Dickens's flat characters are highly individualized, not to say unique, some, like Fagin, the avaricious Jewish moneylender, are **stereotypes.** Stereotypes are characters based on conscious or unconscious cultural assumptions that sex, age, ethnic or national identification, occupation, marital status, and so on are predictably accompanied by certain character traits, actions, even values.

The stereotype may be very useful in creating a round character, one who can surprise convincingly: Macomber is a spoiled, rich American; Judith, according to a Canadian woman, "one of your typical English spinsters." Both Macomber and Judith, however, act in ways that deny the limitations of the stereotype, which is, after all, only a quick—and somewhat superficial—form of classification, and classification is a common first step in definitions. One of the chief ways we have of describing or defining is by placing the thing to be defined in a category and then distinguishing it from the other members of that category. A good deal of **characterization**—the art, craft, method of presentation or even creation of fictional personages—involves a similar process. Characters are almost inevitably identified by category—by sex, age, nationality, occupation, etc. We soon learn that the father in *The Egg* is a male middle-aged American Midwestern farmer, that the narrator of *My Man Bovanne* is a middle-aged urban black woman, and, as we have seen, that Judith is an English spinster.

Not all generalizations involve cultural stereotypes, of course. Some may involve generalized character traits that the story or narrator defines for us (and that we must accept unless events in the story prove otherwise). The father in *The Egg* is said to have been "intended by nature to be a cheerful, kindly man" with "no notion of trying to rise in the world." Bovanne is said to be "just a nice old gent from the block," the kind of man whose conversation is "Comfy and cheery."

You may have noticed something that may seem odd at first: putting a character in more than one general group makes that character more of an individual. The category *middle-aged* includes the father in *The Egg,* the narrator of *Bovanne,* and Judith. That the first is male separates him from the other two; that Judith is British distinguishes her from the other two; that the narrator of *Bovanne* is black separates her from both the father and Judith, though she is American like the first and a woman like the second. So Hazel is to some degree particularized by being identified as a member of three general categories. Similarly, there are more cheerful men and there are more kindly men than there are men who are both cheerful and kindly, and there are still fewer men who are cheerful, kindly, and without ambition.

Physical characteristics also serve as categories. Bovanne is blind. Before we are introduced to him, we are told that blind people hum, and that a blind man called Shakey Bee hums. Only then are we told that there is a blind man named Bovanne who also has the habit of humming. As physical characteristics are multiplied, as with other categories, the result is more and more particularizing or individualizing. That the father in *The Egg* at forty-five is bald and "a little fat" narrows the category of middle-aged male only slightly, but that Judith is beautiful though a fortyish English spinster considerably narrows that category, and detailed physical description makes it possible to visualize her rather fully, almost to recognize her as an individual:

> Judith is tall, small-breasted, slender. Her light brown hair is parted in the center and cut straight around her neck. A high straight forehead, straight nose, a full grave mouth are setting for her eyes, which are green, large and prominent. Her lids are very white, fringed with gold, and molded close over the eyeball. . . .

There are many other ways in which a character is characterized and individualized besides stereotyping and "de-stereotyping," and besides classifying and particularizing by physical description. In most cases we see what characters do and hear what they say; we sometimes learn what they think, and what other people think or say about them; we often know what kind of clothes they wear, what and how much they own, treasure, or covet; we may be told about their childhood, parents, or some part or parts of their past. We learn a bit about Hazel, the narrator of *Bovanne,* from her age, sex, ethnic identification. We learn a great deal more from the way she talks to her children and they to her, from the fact that men call her "long distance and in the middle of the night for a little Mama comfort," the fact that she carried her baby daughter strapped to her chest until the baby was nearly two years old, and from her short, low-cut dress. We even know what she is thinking. We are not privileged to know what the father in *The Egg* thinks from moment to moment, though we are told his general motives, and we do learn how he acts, what others think of him, and, finally, how he feels. And we know more of his earlier life than we know of Hazel's.

No matter how many methods of characterization are employed, however, at some point the particularization of the individual stops. Few characters are described down to the ridges of their fingerprints. No matter how individualized the character may be, he or she remains a member of a number of groups, and we make certain assumptions about the character based on our fixed or stereotyped notions of the groups. To destroy a stereotype, a story must introduce a stereotype to destroy. And somehow the de-stereotyped character, no matter how particularized, remains to some degree representative. If Judith turns out to be not as prudish and prissy as the stereotype of the English spinster has led us to believe, we may well conclude that the stereotype is false and Judith is more representative of the real English spinster than the stereotype is. Indeed, this tendency to generalize from the particulars of a story extends beyond cultural groups sometimes to human character at large: if Francis Macomber can change his ways after years of habitual conduct, then human character, the story might seem to say, is not permanently fixed at birth, in infancy, childhood, ever. If decent and ordinary people like those in *The Lottery* can cast destructive stones, human beings may not be entirely good by nature.

One of the reasons it is so difficult to discuss characters is precisely because the principles of definition and evaluation of fictional characters (not of their characterization) are the same as those we use for real people, an area of violent controversy and confusion. The very term *character* itself, when it refers not to a fictional personage but to a combination of qualities in a human being, is somewhat ambiguous. It usually has moral overtones, often favorable (a man of character); it is sometimes neutral but evaluative (character reference). Judgment about character (not characterization, remember) usually involves moral terms like *good* and *bad* or *strong* and *weak*. *Personality* usually implies that which distinguishes or individualizes a person, and the judgment called for is not so much moral as social —*pleasing* or *displeasing*. An older term, *nature* (it is his nature to be so or do such), usually implies something inherent or inborn, something fixed and thus predictable. The **existential character** implies the opposite; that is, whatever our past, our conditioning, our pattern of previous behavior, we can, by an act of will, change all that right this minute, as Macomber does.

Fictional characters thus frequently seem to be part of the history that lies behind the story or beyond the story as part of our own world, to exist in a reality that is detachable from the words and events of the story in which they appear. We feel we might recognize Tom Jones, Jane Eyre, or Sherlock Holmes on the street, and we might be able to anticipate what they might say or do in *our* world, outside the story. Fictional characters are neither real nor detachable, of course, and they exist only in the words of the works in which they are presented. We must not forget the distinction between the character and the method by which he or she is presented, the characterization; so we must be careful to distinguish the good character, meaning someone whom, if real, we would consider virtuous, and the good characterization, meaning a fictional person who, no matter what his or her morality or behavior, is well presented.

To recognize that characters are not finally detachable, that they have roles, functions, limitations, and their very existence in the context of other elements in the story, and not to confuse them with real people, character with characterization, is not to say that we may not learn about real people from characters in fiction or learn to understand fictional characters in part from what we know about real people. Indeed, it may be worth paying particular attention to how stories create the images of people and what those images assume about human character precisely because this process and these assumptions are so similar to the way we get to know and understand real people. We may be able to enrich both our reading and our lives.

SHERWOOD ANDERSON

The Egg

My father was, I am sure, intended by nature to be a cheerful, kindly man. Until he was thirty-four years old he worked as a farmhand for a man named Thomas Butterworth whose place lay near the town of Bidwell, Ohio. He had then a horse of his own, and on Saturday evenings drove into town to spend a few hours in social intercourse with other farmhands. In town he drank several glasses of beer and stood about in Ben Head's saloon—crowded on Saturday evenings with visiting farmhands. Songs were sung and glasses thumped on the bar. At ten o'clock father drove home along a lonely country road, made his horse comfortable for the night, and himself went to bed, quite happy in his position in life. He had at that time no notion of trying to rise in the world.

It was in the spring of his thirty-fifth year that father married my mother, then a country schoolteacher, and in the following spring I came wriggling and crying into the world. Something happened to the two people. They became ambitious. The American passion for getting up in the world took possession of them.

It may have been that mother was responsible. Being a schoolteacher she had no doubt read books and magazines. She had, I presume, read of how Garfield,[1] Lincoln, and other Americans rose from poverty to fame and greatness, and as I lay beside her—in the days of her lying-in—she may have dreamed that I would some day rule men and cities. At any rate she induced father to give up his place as a farmhand, sell his horse, and embark on an independent enterprise of his own. She was a tall silent woman with a long nose and troubled gray eyes. For herself she wanted nothing. For father and myself she was incurably ambitious.

The first venture into which the two people went turned out badly. They rented ten acres of poor stony land on Grigg's Road, eight miles from Bidwell, and launched into chicken-raising. I grew into boyhood on the place and got my first impression of life there. From the beginning they were impressions of disaster, and if, in my turn, I am a gloomy man inclined to see the darker side of life, I attribute it to the fact that what should have been for me the happy joyous days of childhood were spent on a chicken farm.

One unversed in such matters can have no notion of the many and tragic things that can happen to a chicken. It is born out of an egg, lives for a few weeks as a tiny fluffy thing such as you will see pictured on Easter cards, then becomes hideously naked, eats quantities of corn and meal bought by the sweat of your father's brow, gets diseases called pip, cholera, and other names, stands looking with stupid eyes at the sun, becomes sick and dies. A few hens and now and then a rooster, intended to serve God's mysterious ends, struggle through to

1. James Abram Garfield (1831–1881), twentieth President of the United States, was born on a frontier farm in Ohio, spent his early years in poverty, worked as farmer, canal boatman, carpenter, sent himself through Williams College, to become teacher, principal, Congressman, President; like Lincoln, he was assassinated.

maturity. The hens lay eggs out of which come other chickens and the dreadful cycle is thus made complete. It is all unbelievably complex. Most philosophers must have been raised on chicken farms. One hopes for so much from a chicken and is so dreadfully disillusioned. Small chickens, just setting out on the journey of life, look so bright and alert and they are in fact so dreadfully stupid. They are so much like people they mix one up in one's judgments of life. If disease does not kill them, they wait until your expectations are thoroughly aroused and then walk under the wheels of a wagon—to go squashed and dead back to their maker. Vermin infest their youth, and fortunes must be spent for curative powders. In later life I have seen how a literature has been built up on the subject of fortunes to be made out of the raising of chickens. It is intended to be read by the gods who have just eaten of the tree of the knowledge of good and evil.[2] It is a hopeful literature and declares that much may be done by simple ambitious people who own a few hens. Do not be led astray by it. It was not written for you. Go hunt for gold on the frozen hills of Alaska, put your faith in the honesty of a politician, believe if you will that the world is daily growing better and that good will triumph over evil, but do not read and believe the literature that is written concerning the hen. It was not written for you.

I, however, digress. My tale does not primarily concern itself with the hen. If correctly told it will center on the egg. For ten years my father and mother struggled to make our chicken farm pay and then they gave up that struggle and began another. They moved into the town of Bidwell, Ohio, and embarked in the restaurant business. After ten years of worry with incubators that did not hatch, and with tiny—and in their own way lovely—balls of fluff that passed on into semi-naked pullethood and from that into dead henhood, we threw all aside and, packing our belongings on a wagon, drove down Grigg's Road toward Bidwell, a tiny caravan of hope looking for a new place from which to start on our upward journey through life.

We must have been a sad-looking lot, not, I fancy, unlike refugees fleeing from a battlefield. Mother and I walked in the road. The wagon that contained our goods had been borrowed for the day from Mr. Albert Griggs, a neighbor. Out of its sides stuck the legs of cheap chairs, and at the back of the pile of beds, tables, and boxes filled with kitchen utensils was a crate of live chickens, and on top of that the baby carriage in which I had been wheeled about in my infancy. Why we stuck to the baby carriage I don't know. It was unlikely other children would be born and the wheels were broken. People who have few possessions cling tightly to those they have. That is one of the facts that make life so discouraging.

Father rode on top of the wagon. He was then a bald-headed man of forty-five, a little fat, and from long association with mother and the chickens he had become habitually silent and discouraged. All during our ten years on the chicken farm he had worked as a laborer on

2. See *Genesis* 2:9 and 3, esp. 3:22–23: "And the Lord God said, Behold, the man is become as one of us, to know good and evil; and now, lest he put forth his hand, and take also of the tree of life, and eat, and live for ever:/ Therefore the Lord God sent him forth from the Garden of Eden, to till the ground from whence he was taken."

neighboring farms and most of the money he had earned had been spent for remedies to cure chicken diseases, on Wilmer's White Wonder Cholera Cure or Professor Bidlow's Egg Producer or some other preparations that mother found advertised in the poultry papers. There were two little patches of hair on father's head just above his ear. I remember that as a child I used to sit looking at him when he had gone to sleep in a chair before the stove on Sunday afternoons in the winter. I had at that time already begun to read books and have notions of my own, and the bald path that led over the top of his head was, I fancied, something like a broad road, such a road as Caesar might have made on which to lead his legions out of Rome and into the wonders of an unknown world. The tufts of hair that grew above father's ears were, I thought, like forests. I fell into a half-sleeping, half-waking state and dreamed I was a tiny thing going along the road into a far beautiful place where there were no chicken farms and where life was a happy eggless affair.

One might write a book concerning our flight from the chicken farm into town. Mother and I walked the entire eight miles—she to be sure that nothing fell from the wagon and I to see the wonders of the world. On the seat of the wagon beside father was his greatest treasure. I will tell you of that.

On a chicken farm, where hundreds and even thousands of chickens come out of eggs, surprising things sometimes happen. Grotesques are born out of eggs as out of people. The accident does not often occur—perhaps once in a thousand births. A chicken is, you see, born that has four legs, two pairs of wings, two heads, or what not. The things do not live. They go quickly back to the hand of their maker that has for a moment trembled. The fact that the poor little things could not live was one of the tragedies of life to father. He had some sort of notion that if he could but bring into henhood or roosterhood a five-legged hen or a two-headed rooster his fortune would be made. He dreamed of taking the wonder about the county fairs and of growing rich by exhibiting it to other farmhands.

At any rate, he saved all the little monstrous things that had been born on our chicken farm. They were preserved in alcohol and put each in its own glass bottle. These he had carefully put into a box, and on our journey into town it was carried on the wagon seat beside him. He drove the horses with one hand and with the other clung to the box. When we got to our destination, the box was taken down at once and the bottles removed. All during our days as keepers of a restaurant in the town of Bidwell, Ohio, the grotesques in their little glass bottles sat on a shelf back of the counter. Mother sometimes protested, but father was a rock on the subject of his treasure. The grotesques were, he declared, valuable. People, he said, liked to look at strange and wonderful things.

Did I say that we embarked in the restaurant business in the town of Bidwell, Ohio? I exaggerated a little. The town itself lay at the foot of a low hill and on the shore of a small river. The railroad did not run through the town and the station was a mile away to the north at a place called Pickleville. There had been a cider mill and pickle factory at the station, but before the time of our coming they had both gone out of business. In the morning and in the evening busses came down to the station along a road called Turner's Pike from the hotel on the main street of Bidwell. Our going to the out-of-the-way place to embark in the restaurant business was mother's idea. She talked of it for a year and then one day went off and rented an empty store building opposite the railroad station. It was her idea that the restaurant would be profitable. Traveling men, she said, would be always waiting around to take trains out of town and town people would come to the station to await incoming trains. They would come to the restaurant to buy pieces of pie and drink coffee. Now that I am older I know that she had another motive in going. She was ambitious for me. She wanted me to rise in the world, to get into a town school and become a man of the towns.

At Pickleville father and mother worked hard, as they always had done. At first there was the necessity of putting our place into shape to be a restaurant. That took a month. Father built a shelf on which he put tins of vegetables. He painted a sign on which he put his name in large red letters. Below his name was the sharp command—"EAT HERE"—that was so seldom obeyed. A showcase was bought and filled with cigars and tobacco. Mother scrubbed the floor and the walls of the room. I went to school in the town and was glad to be away from the farm, from the presence of the discouraged, sad-looking chickens. Still I was not very joyous. In the evening I walked home from school along Turner's Pike and remembered the children I had seen playing in the town schoolyard. A troop of little girls had gone hopping about and singing. I tried that. Down along the frozen road I went hopping solemnly on one leg. "Hippity Hop To The Barber Shop,"[3] I sang shrilly. Then I stopped and looked doubtfully about. I was afraid of being seen in my gay mood. It must have seemed to me that I was doing a thing that should not be done by one who, like myself, had been raised on a chicken farm where death was a daily visitor.

Mother decided that our restaurant should remain open at night. At ten in the evening a passenger train went north past our door followed by a local freight. The freight crew had switching to do in Pickleville, and when the work was done they came to our restaurant for hot coffee and food. Sometimes one of them ordered a fried egg. In the morning at four they returned north-bound and again visited us. A little trade began to grow up. Mother slept at night and during the day tended the restaurant and fed our boarders while father slept. He slept in the same bed mother had occupied during the night and I went off to the town of Bidwell and to school. During the long nights, while mother and I slept, father cooked meats that were to go into sandwiches for the lunch baskets of our boarders. Then an idea in regard to getting up in the world came into his head. The American spirit took hold of him. He also became ambitious.

In the long nights when there was little to do, father had time to think. That was his undoing. He decided that he had in the past been an unsuccessful man because he had not been cheerful enough and that in the future he would adopt a cheerful outlook on life. In the early morning he came upstairs and got into bed with mother. She woke and the two talked. From my bed in the corner I listened.

3. Children's song and dance: "Hippety hop to the barber shop to buy a stick of candy./ One for you, and one for me, and one for Sister Annie."

It was father's idea that both he and mother should try to entertain the people who came to eat at our restaurant. I cannot now remember his words, but he gave the impression of one about to become in some obscure way a kind of public entertainer. When people, particularly young people from the town of Bidwell, came into our place, as on very rare occasions they did, bright entertaining conversation was to be made. From father's words I gathered that something of the jolly innkeeper effect was to be sought. Mother must have been doubtful from the first, but she said nothing discouraging. It was father's notion that a passion for the company of himself and mother would spring up in the breasts of the younger people of the town of Bidwell. In the evening bright happy groups would come singing down Turner's Pike. They would troop shouting with joy and laughter into our place. There would be song and festivity. I do not mean to give the impression that father spoke so elaborately of the matter. He was, as I have said, an uncommunicative man. "They want some place to go. I tell you they want some place to go," he said over and over. That was as far as he got. My own imagination has filled in the blanks.

For two or three weeks this notion of father's invaded our house. We did not talk much, but in our daily lives tried earnestly to make smiles take the place of glum looks. Mother smiled at the boarders and I, catching the infection, smiled at our cat. Father became a little feverish in his anxiety to please. There was, no doubt, lurking somewhere in him, a touch of the spirit of the showman. He did not waste much of his ammunition on the railroad men he served at night, but seemed to be waiting for a young man or woman from Bidwell to come in to show what he could do. On the counter in the restaurant there was a wire basket kept always filled with eggs, and it must have been before his eyes when the idea of being entertaining was born in his brain. There was something pre-natal about the way eggs kept themselves connected with the development of his idea. At any rate, an egg ruined his new impulse in life. Late one night I was awakened by a roar of anger coming from father's throat. Both mother and I sat upright in our beds. With trembling hands she lighted a lamp that stood on a table by her head. Downstairs the front door of our restaurant went shut with a bang and in a few minutes father tramped up the stairs. He held an egg in his hand and his hand trembled as though he were having a chill. There was a half-insane light in his eyes. As he stood glaring at us I was sure he intended throwing the egg at either mother or me. Then he laid it gently on the table beside the lamp and dropped on his knees beside mother's bed. He began to cry like a boy, and I, carried away by his grief, cried with him. The two of us filled the little upstairs room with our wailing voices. It is ridiculous, but of the picture we made I can remember only the fact that mother's hand continually stroked the bald path that ran across the top of his head. I have forgotten what mother said to him and how she induced him to tell her of what had happened downstairs. His explanation also has gone out of my mind. I remember only my own grief and fright and the shiny path over father's head glowing in the lamplight as he knelt by the bed.

As to what happened downstairs. For some unexplainable reason I know the story as well as though I had been a witness to my father's discomfiture. One in time gets to know many unexplainable things. On that evening young Joe Kane, son of a merchant of Bidwell, came to Pickleville to meet his father, who was expected on the ten-o-clock evening train from the South. The train was three hours late and Joe came into our place to loaf about and to wait for its arrival. The local freight train came in and the freight crew were fed. Joe was left alone in the restaurant with father.

From the moment he came into our place the Bidwell young man must have been puzzled by my father's actions. It was his notion that father was angry at him for hanging around. He noticed that the restaurant-keeper was apparently disturbed by his presence and he thought of going out. However, it began to rain and he did not fancy the long walk to town and back. He bought a five-cent cigar and ordered a cup of coffee. He had a newspaper in his pocket and took it out and began to read. "I'm waiting for the evening train. It's late," he said apologetically.

For a long time father, whom Joe Kane had never seen before, remained silently gazing at his visitor. He was no doubt suffering from at attack of stage fright. As so often happens in life he had thought so much and so often of the situation that now confronted him that he was somewhat nervous in its presence.

For one thing, he did not know what to do with his hands. He thrust one of them nervously over the counter and shook hands with Joe Kane. "How-de-do," he said. Joe Kane put his newspaper down and stared at him. Father's eyes lighted on the basket of eggs that sat on the counter and he began to talk. "Well," he began hesitatingly, "well, you have heard of Christopher Columbus, eh?" He seemed to be angry. "That Christopher Columbus was a cheat," he declared emphatically. "He talked of making an egg stand on its end. He talked, he did, and then he went and broke the end of the egg."[4]

My father seemed to his visitor to be beside himself at the duplicity of Christopher Columbus. He muttered and swore. He declared it was wrong to teach children that Christopher Columbus was a great man when, after all, he cheated at the critical moment. He had declared he would make an egg stand on end and then, when his bluff had been called, he had done a trick. Still grumbling at Columbus, father took an egg from the basket on the counter and began to walk up and down. He rolled the egg between the palms of his hands. He smiled genially. He began to mumble words regarding the effect to be produced on an egg by the electricity that comes out of the human body. He declared that, without breaking its shell and by virtue of rolling it back and forth in his hands, he could stand the egg on its end. He explained that the warmth of his hands and the gentle rolling move-

4. Washington Irving, attributing it to the 16th-century Italian historian Benzoni, recounts, in *The Life and Voyages of Christopher Columbus,*

> the well-known anecdote of the egg. A shallow courtier . . . impatient of the honors paid to Columbus . . . abruptly asked him whether he thought that, in case he had not discovered the Indies, there were not other men in Spain who would have been capable of the enterprise? To this Columbus made no immediate reply, but, taking an egg, invited the company to make it stand on one end. Everyone attempted it, but in vain; whereupon he struck it upon the table so as to break the end, and left it standing on the broken part: illustrating in this simple manner that when he had once shown the way to the New World nothing was easier than to follow it.

ment he gave the egg created a new center of gravity, and Joe Kane was mildly interested. "I have handled thousands of eggs," father said. "No one knows more about eggs than I do."

He stood the egg on the counter and it fell on its side. He tried the trick again and again, each time rolling the egg between the palms of his hands and saying the words regarding the wonders of electricity and the laws of gravity. When after a half-hour's effort he did succeed in making the egg stand for a moment, he looked up to find that his visitor was no longer watching. By the time he had succeeded in calling Joe Kane's attention to the success of his effort, the egg had rolled over and lay on its side.

Afire with the showman's passion and at the same time a good deal disconcerted by the failure of his first effort, father now took the bottles containing the poultry monstrosities down from their place on the shelf and began to show them to his visitor. "How would you like to have seven legs and two heads like this fellow?" he asked, exhibiting the most remarkable of his treasures. A cheerful smile played over his face. He reached over the counter and tried to slap Joe Kane on the shoulder as he had seen men do in Ben Head's saloon when he was a young farmhand and drove to town on Saturday evenings. His visitor was made a little ill by the sight of the body of the terribly deformed bird floating in the alcohol in the bottle and got up to go. Coming from behind the counter, father took hold of the young man's arm and led him back to his seat. He grew a little angry and for a moment had to turn his face away and force himself to smile. Then he put the bottles back on the shelf. In an outburst of generosity he fairly compelled Joe Kane to have a fresh cup of coffee and another cigar at his expense. Then he took a pan and filling it with vinegar, taken from a jug that sat beneath the counter, he declared himself about to do a new trick. "I will heat this egg in this pan of vinegar," he said. "Then I will put it through the neck of a bottle without breaking the shell. When the egg is inside the bottle it will resume its normal shape and the shell will become hard again. Then I will give the bottle with the egg in it to you. You can take it about with you wherever you go. People will want to know how you got the egg in the bottle. Don't tell them. Keep them guessing. That is the way to have fun with this trick."

Father grinned and winked at his visitor. Joe Kane decided that the man who confronted him was mildly insane but harmless. He drank the cup of coffee that had been given him and began to read his paper again. When the egg had been heated in vinegar, father carried it on a spoon to the counter and going into a back room got an empty bottle. He was angry because his visitor did not watch him as he began to do his trick, but nevertheless went cheerfully to work. For a long time he struggled, trying to get the egg to go through the neck of the bottle. He put the pan of vinegar back on the stove, intending to reheat the egg, then picked it up and burned his fingers. After a second bath in the hot vinegar, the shell of the egg had been softened a little, but not enough for his purpose. He worked and worked and a spirit of desperate determination took possession of him. When he thought that at last the trick was about to be consummated, the delayed train came in at the station and Joe Kane started to go nonchalantly out at the door. Father made a last desperate effort to conquer the egg and make it do the thing that would establish his reputation as one who knew how to entertain guests who came into his restaurant. He worried the egg. He attempted to be somewhat rough with it. He swore and the sweat stood out on his forehead. The egg broke under his hand. When the contents spurted over his clothes, Joe Kane, who had stopped at the door, turned and laughed.

A roar of anger rose from my father's throat. He danced and shouted a string of inarticulate words. Grabbing another egg from the basket on the counter, he threw it, just missing the head of the young man as he dodged through the door and escaped.

Father came upstairs to mother and me with an egg in his hand. I do not know what he intended to do. I imagine he had some idea of destroying it, of destroying all eggs, and that he intended to let mother and me see him begin. When, however, he got into the presence of mother, something happened to him. He laid the egg gently on the table and dropped on his knees by the bed as I have already explained. He later decided to close the restaurant for the night and to come upstairs and get into bed. When he did so, he blew out the light and after much muttered conversation both he and mother went to sleep. I suppose I went to sleep also, but my sleep was troubled. I awoke at dawn and for a long time looked at the egg that lay on the table. I wondered why eggs had to be and why from the egg came the hen who again laid the egg. The question got into my blood. It has stayed there, I imagine, because I am the son of my father. At any rate, the problem remains unsolved in my mind. And that, I conclude, is but another evidence of the complete and final triumph of the egg—at least as far as my family is concerned.

1920

TONI CADE BAMBARA

My Man Bovanne

Blind people got a hummin jones[1] if you notice. Which is understandable completely once you been around one and notice what no eyes will force you into to see people, and you get past the first time, which seems to come out of nowhere, and it's like you in church again with fat-chest ladies and old gents gruntin a hum low in the throat to whatever the preacher be saying. Shakey Bee bottom lip all swole up with Sweet Peach[2] and me explainin how come the sweet-potato bread was a dollar-quarter this time stead of dollar regular and he say uh hunh he understand, then he break into this *thizzin* kind of hum which is quiet, but fiercesome just the same, if

1. A compelling need.

2. A brand of dipping snuff.

you ain't ready for it. Which I wasn't. But I got used to it and the onliest time I had to say somethin bout it was when he was playin checkers on the stoop one time and he commenst to hummin quite churchy seem to me. So I says, "Look here Shakey Bee, I can't beat you and Jesus too." He stop.

So that's how come I asked My Man Bovanne to dance. He ain't my man mind you, just a nice ole gent from the block that we all know cause he fixes things and the kids like him. Or used to fore Black Power got hold their minds and mess em around till they can't be civil to ole folks. So we at this benefit for my niece's cousin who's runnin for somethin with this Black party somethin or other behind her. And I press up close to dance with Bovanne who blind and I'm hummin and he hummin, chest to chest like talkin. Not jammin my breasts into the man. Wasn't bout tits. Was bout vibrations. And he dug it and asked me what color dress I had on and how my hair was fixed and how I was doin without a man, not nosy but nice-like, and who was at this affair and was the canapés dainty-stingy or healthy enough to get hold of proper. Comfy and cheery is what I'm tryin to get across. Touch talkin like the heel of the hand on the tambourine or on a drum.

But right away Joe Lee come up on us and frown for dancin so close to the man. My own son who knows what kind of warm I am about; and don't grown men all call me long distance and in the middle of the night for a little Mama comfort? But he frown. Which ain't right since Bovanne can't see and defend himself. Just a nice old man who fixes toasters and busted irons and bicycles and things and changes the lock on my door when my men friends get messy. Nice man. Which is not why they invited him. Grass roots you see. Me and Sister Taylor and the woman who does heads at Mamies and the man from the barber shop, we all there on account of we grass roots. And I ain't never been souther than Brooklyn Battery and no more country than the window box on my fire escape. And just yesterday my kids tellin me to take them countrified rags off my head and be cool. And now can't get Black enough to suit em. So everybody passin sayin My Man Bovanne. Big deal, keep steppin and don't even stop a minute to get the man a drink or one of them cute sandwiches or tell him what's goin on. And him standin there with a smile ready case someone do speak he want to be ready. So that's how come I pull him on the dance floor and we dance squeezin past the tables and chairs and all them coats and people standin round up in each other face talkin bout this and that but got no use for this blind man who mostly fixed skates and skooters for all these folks when they was just kids. So I'm pressed up close and we touch talkin with the hum. And here come my daughter cuttin her eye[3] at me like she do when she tell me about my "apolitical" self like I got hoof and mouf disease and there ain't no hope at all. And I don't pay her no mind and just look up in Bovanne shadow face and tell him his stomach like a drum and he laugh. Laugh real loud. And here come my youngest, Task, with a tap on my elbow like he the third grade

3. Giving a sharp look.

monitor and I'm cuttin up on the line to assembly.

"I was just talkin on the drums," I explained when they hauled me into the kitchen. I figured drums was my best defense. They can get ready for drums what with all this heritage business. And Bovanne stomach just like that drum Task give me when he come back from Africa. You just touch it and it hum thizzm, thizzm. So I stuck to the drum story. "Just drummin that's all."

"Mama, what are you talkin about?"

"She had too much to drink," say Elo to Task cause she don't hardly say nuthin to me direct no more since that ugly argument about my wigs.

"Look here Mama," say Task, the gentle one. "We just tryin to pull your coat. You were makin a spectacle of yourself out there dancing like that."

"Dancin like what?"

Task run a hand over his left ear like his father for the world and his father before that.

"Like a bitch in heat," say Elo.

"Well uhh, I was goin to say like one of them sex-starved ladies gettin on in years and not too discriminating. Know what I mean?"

I don't answer cause I'll cry. Terrible thing when your own children talk to you like that. Pullin me out the party and hustlin me into some stranger's kitchen in the back of a bar just like the damn police. And ain't like I'm old old. I can still wear me some sleeveless dresses without the meat hangin off my arm. And I keep up with some thangs through my kids. Who ain't kids no more. To hear them tell it. So I don't say nuthin.

"Dancin with that tom," say Elo to Joe Lee, who leanin on the folks' freezer. "His feet can smell a cracker a mile away and go into their shuffle number post haste. And them eyes. He could be a little considerate and put on some shades. Who wants to look into them blown-out fuses that–"

"Is this what they call the generation gap?" I say.

"Generation gap," spits Elo, like I suggested castor oil and fricassee possum in the milk-shakes or somethin. "That's a white concept for a white phenomenon. There's no generation gap among Black people. We are a col–"

"Yeh, well never mind," says Joe Lee. "The point is Mama . . . well, it's pride. You embarrass yourself and us too dancin like that."

"I wasn't shame." Then nobody say nuthin. Them standin there in they pretty clothes with drinks in they hands and gangin up on me, and me in the third-degree chair and nary a olive to my name. Felt just like the police got hold to me.

"First of all," Task say, holdin up his hand and tickin off the offenses, "the dress. Now that dress is too short, Mama, and too low-cut for a woman your age. And Tamu's going to make a speech tonight to kick off the campaign and will be introducin you and expecting you to organize the council of elders–"

"Me? Didn nobody ask me nuthin. You mean Nisi? She change her name?"

"Well, Norton was supposed to tell you about it. Nisi wants to introduce you and then encourage the older folks to form a Council of the Elders to act as an advisory—"

"And you going to be standing there with your boobs out and that wig on your head and that hem up to your ass. And people'll say, 'Ain't that the horny bitch that was grindin with the blind dude?' "

"Elo, be cool a minute," say Task, gettin to the next finger. "And then there's the drinkin. Mama, you know you can't drink cause next thing you know you be laughin loud and carryin on," and he grab another finger for the loudness. "And then there's the dancin. You been tattooed on the man for four records straight and slow draggin even on the fast numbers. How you think that look for a woman your age?"

"What's my age?"

"What?"

"I'm axin you all a simple question. You keep talkin bout what's proper for a woman my age. How old am I anyhow?" And Joe Lee slams his eyes shut and squinches up his face to figure. And Task run a hand over his ear and stare into his glass like the ice cubes goin calculate for him. And Elo just starin at the top of my head like she goin rip the wig off any minute now.

"Is your hair braided up under that thing? If so, why don't you take it off? You always did do a neat cornroll."[4]

"Uh huh," cause I'm thinkin how she couldn't undo her hair fast enough talking bout cornroll so countrified. None of which was the subject. "How old, I say?"

"Sixtee-one or—"

"You a damn lie Joe Lee Peoples."

"And that's another thing," say Task on the fingers.

"You know what you all can kiss," I say, gettin up and brushin the wrinkles out my lap.

"Oh, Mama," Elo say, puttin a hand on my shoulder like she hasn't done since she left home and the hand landin light and not sure it supposed to be there. Which hurt me to my heart. Cause this was the child in our happiness fore Mr. Peoples die. And I carried that child strapped to my chest till she was nearly two. We was close is what I'm tryin to tell you. Cause it was more me in the child than the others. And even after Task it was the girlchild I covered in the night and wept over for no reason at all less it was she was a chub-chub like me and not very pretty, but a warm child. And how did things get to this, that she can't put a sure hand on me and say Mama we love you and care about you and you entitled to enjoy yourself cause you a good woman?

"And then there's Reverend Trent," say Task, glancin from left to right like they hatchin a plot and just now lettin me in on it. "You were suppose to be talking with him tonight, Mama, about giving us his basement for campaign headquarters and—"

"Didn nobody tell me nuthin. If grass roots mean you kept in the dark I can't use it. I really can't. And Reven Trent a fool anyway the

4. Cornrow, a hairstyle in which all the hair is interwoven from the scalp into small braids.

way he tore into the widow man up there on Edgecomb cause he wouldn't take in three of them foster children and the woman not even comfy in the ground yet and the man's mind messed up and—"

"Look here," say Task. "What we need is a family conference so we can get all this stuff cleared up and laid out on the table. In the meantime I think we better get back into the other room and tend to business. And in the meantime, Mama, see if you can't get to Reverend Trent and—"

"You want me to belly rub with the Reven, that it?"

"Oh damn," Elo say and go through the swingin door.

"We'll talk about all this at dinner. How's tomorrow night, Joe Lee?" While Joe Lee being self-important I'm wonderin who's doin the cookin and how come no body ax me if I'm free and do I get a corsage and things like that. Then Joe nod that it's O.K. and he go through the swingin door and just a little hubbub come through from the other room. Then Task smile his smile, lookin just like his daddy, and he leave. And it just me in this stranger's kitchen, which was a mess I wouldn't never let my kitchen look like. Poison you just to look at the pots. Then the door swing the other way and it's My Man Bovanne standin there sayin Miss Hazel but lookin at the deep fry and then at the steam table, and most surprised when I come up on him from the other direction and take him on out of there. Pass the folks pushin up towards the stage where Nisi and some other people settin and ready to talk, and folks gettin to the last of the sandwiches and the booze fore they settle down in one spot and listen serious. And I'm thinkin bout tellin Bovanne what a lovely long dress Nisi got on and the earrings and her hair piled up in a cone and the people bout to hear how we all gettin screwed and gotta form our own party and everybody there listenin and lookin. But instead I just haul the man on out of there, and Joe Lee and his wife look at me like I'm terrible, but they ain't said boo to the man yet. Cause he blind and old and don't nobody there need him since they grown up and don't need they skates fixed no more.

"Where we goin, Miss Hazel?" Him knowin all the time.

"First we gonna buy you some dark sunglasses. Then you comin with me to the supermarket so I can pick up tomorrow's dinner, which is goin to be a grand thing proper and you invited. Then we goin to my house."

"That be fine. I surely would like to rest my feet." Bein cute, but you got to let men play out they little show, blind or not. So he chat on bout how tired he is and how he appreciate me takin him in hand this way. And I'm thinkin I'll have him change the lock on my door first thing. Then I'll give the man a nice warm bath with jasmine leaves in the water and a little Epsom salt on the sponge to do his back. And then a good rubdown with rose water and olive oil. Then a cup of lemon tea with a taste in it. And a little talcum, some of that fancy stuff Nisi mother sent over last Christmas. And then a massage, a good face massage round the forehead which is the worryin part. Cause you gots to take care of the older folks. And let them know they still needed to run the mimeo machine and keep the spark plugs clean and fix the mailboxes for folks who might help us get the breakfast program goin, and the school for the little kids and the campaign and all. Cause old folks in the nation. That what Nisi was sayin and I mean to do my part.

"I imagine you are a very pretty woman, Miss Hazel."

"I surely am," I say just like the hussy my daughter always say I was.

1972

DORIS LESSING

Our Friend Judith

I stopped inviting Judith to meet people when a Canadian woman remarked, with the satisfied fervor of one who has at last pinned a label on a rare specimen: "She is, of course, one of your typical English spinsters."

This was a few weeks after an American sociologist, having elicited from Judith the facts that she was fortyish, unmarried, and living alone, had inquired of me: "I suppose she has given up?" "Given up what?" I asked; and the subsequent discussion was unrewarding.

Judith did not easily come to parties. She would come after pressure, not so much—one felt—to do one a favor, but in order to correct what she believed to be a defect in her character. "I really ought to enjoy meeting new people more than I do," she said once. We reverted to an earlier pattern of our friendship: odd evenings together, an occasional visit to the cinema, or she would telephone to say: "I'm on my way past you to the British Museum. Would you care for a cup of coffee with me? I have twenty minutes to spare."

It is characteristic of Judith that the word "spinster," used of her, provoked fascinated speculation about other people. There are my aunts, for instance: aged seventy-odd, both unmarried, one an ex-missionary from China, one a retired matron of a famous London hospital. These two old ladies live together under the shadow of the cathedral in a country town. They devote much time to the Church, to good causes, to letter writing with friends all over the world, to the grandchildren and the great-grandchildren of relatives. It would be a mistake, however, on entering a house in which nothing has been moved for fifty years, to diagnose a condition of fossilized late-Victorian integrity. They read every book reviewed in the *Observer* or the *Times*,[1] so that I recently got a letter from Aunt Rose inquiring whether I did not think that the author of *On the Road*[2] was not—perhaps?—exaggerating his difficulties. They know a good deal about music, and write letters of encouragement to young composers they

1. Prestigious London newspapers representing roughly the younger more liberal establishment and the Establishment proper.
2. Jack Kerouac (1922–69), leader of the beatniks, 1950s forerunners of the hippies. Kerouac heroes felt themselves completely cut off from and victimized by American society.

feel are being neglected—"You must understand that anything new and original takes time to be understood." Well-informed and critical Tories, they are as likely to dispatch telegrams of protest to the Home Secretary[3] as letters of support. These ladies, my aunts Emily and Rose, are surely what is meant by the phrase "English spinster." And yet, once the connection has been pointed out, there is no doubt that Judith and they are spiritual cousins, if not sisters. Therefore it follows that one's pitying admiration for women who have supported manless and uncomforted lives needs a certain modification?

One will, of course, never know; and I feel now that it is entirely my fault that I shall never know. I had been Judith's friend for upwards of five years before the incident occurred which I involuntarily thought of—stupidly enough—as the first time Judith's mask slipped.

A mutual friend, Betty, had been given a cast-off Dior[4] dress. She was too short for it. Also she said: "It's not a dress for a married woman with three children and a talent for cooking. I don't know why not, but it isn't." Judith was the right build. Therefore one evening the three of us met by appointment in Judith's bedroom, with the dress. Neither Betty nor I was surprised at the renewed discovery that Judith was beautiful. We had both often caught each other, and ourseslves, in moments of envy when Judith's calm and severe face, her undemonstratively perfect body, succeeded in making everyone else in a room or a street look cheap.

Judith is tall, small-breasted, slender. Her light brown hair is parted in the center and cut straight around her neck. A high straight forehead, straight nose, a full grave mouth are setting for her eyes, which are green, large and prominent. Her lids are very white, fringed with gold, and molded close over the eyeball, so that in profile she has the look of a staring gilded mask. The dress was of dark green glistening stuff, cut straight, with a sort of loose tunic. It opened simply at the throat. In it Judith could of course evoke nothing but classical images. Diana, perhaps, back from the hunt, in a relaxed moment? A rather intellectual wood nymph who had opted for an afternoon in the British Museum Reading Room? Something like that. Neither Betty nor I said a word, since Judith was examining herself in a long mirror, and must know she looked magnificent.

Slowly she drew off the dress and laid it aside. Slowly she put on the old cord skirt and woolen blouse she had taken off. She must have surprised a resigned glance between us, for she then remarked, with the smallest of mocking smiles: "One surely ought to stay in character, wouldn't you say?" She added, reading the words out of some invisible book, written not by her, since it was a very vulgar book, but perhaps by one of us: "It does everything *for* me, I must admit."

"After seeing you in it," Betty cried out, defying her, "I can't bear for anyone else to have it. I shall simply put it away." Judith shrugged, rather irritated. In the shapeless skirt and blouse, and with-

3. Head of the British government department responsible for domestic matters.

4. Famous French designer of high fashions.

out makeup, she stood smiling at us, a woman at whom forty-nine out of fifty people would not look twice.

A second revelatory incident occurred soon after. Betty telephoned me to say that Judith had a kitten. Did I know that Judith adored cats? "No, but of course she would," I said.

Betty lived in the same street as Judith and saw more of her than I did. I was kept posted about the growth and habits of the cat and its effect on Judith's life. She remarked for instance that she felt it was good for her to have a tie and some responsibility. But no sooner was the cat out of kittenhood than all the neighbors complained. It was a tomcat, ungelded, and making every night hideous. Finally the landlord said that either the cat or Judith must go, unless she was prepared to have the cat "fixed."[5] Judith wore herself out trying to find some person, anywhere in Britain, who would be prepared to take the cat. This person would, however, have to sign a written statement not to have the cat "fixed." When Judith took the cat to the vet to be killed, Betty told me she cried for twenty-four hours.

"She didn't think of compromising? After all, perhaps the cat might have preferred to live, if given the choice?"

"Is it likely I'd have the nerve to say anything so sloppy to Judith? It's the nature of a male cat to rampage lustfully about, and therefore it would be morally wrong for Judith to have the cat fixed, simply to suit her own convenience."

"She said that?"

"She wouldn't have to *say* it, surely?"

A third incident was when she allowed a visiting young American, living in Paris, the friend of a friend and scarcely known to her, to use her flat while she visited her parents over Christmas. The young man and his friends lived it up for ten days of alcohol and sex and marijuana, and when Judith came back it took a week to get the place clean again and the furniture mended. She telephoned twice to Paris, the first time to say that he was a disgusting young thug and if he knew what was good for him he would keep out of her way in the future; the second time to apologize for losing her temper. "I had a choice either to let someone use my flat, or to leave it empty. But having chosen that you should have it, it was clearly an unwarrantable infringement of your liberty to make any conditions at all. I do most sincerely ask your pardon." The moral aspects of the matter having been made clear, she was irritated rather than not to receive letters of apology from him—fulsome, embarrassed, but above all, baffled.

It was the note of curiosity in the letters—he even suggested coming over to get to know her better—that irritated her most. "What do you suppose he means?" she said to me. "He lived in my flat for ten days. One would have thought that should be enough, wouldn't you?"

The facts about Judith, then, are all in the open, unconcealed, and plain to anyone who cares to study them; or, as it became plain she feels, to anyone with the intelligence to interpret them.

5. Gelded, castrated.

She has lived for the last twenty years in a small two-room flat high over a busy West London street. The flat is shabby and badly heated. The furniture is old, was never anything but ugly, is now frankly rickety and fraying. She has an income of two hundred pounds[6] a year from a dead uncle. She lives on this and what she earns from her poetry, and from lecturing on poetry to night classes and extramural university classes.

She does not smoke or drink, and eats very little, from preference, not self-discipline.

She studied poetry and biology at Oxford, with distinction.

She is a Castlewell. That is, she is a member of one of the academic upper-middle-class families, which have been producing for centuries a steady supply of brilliant but sound men and women who are the backbone of the arts and sciences in Britain. She is on cool good terms with her family, who respect her and leave her alone.

She goes on long walking tours, by herself, in such places as Exmoor[7] or West Scotland.

Every three or four years she publishes a volume of poems.

The walls of her flat are completely lined with books. They are scientific, classical and historical; there is a great deal of poetry and some drama. There is not one novel. When Judith says: "Of course I don't read novels," this does not mean that novels have no place, or a small place, in literature; or that people should not read novels; but that it must be obvious she can't be expected to read novels.

I had been visiting her flat for years before I noticed two long shelves of books, under a window, each shelf filled with the works of a single writer. The two writers are not, to put it at the mildest, the kind one would associate with Judith. They are mild, reminiscent, vague and whimsical. Typical English *belles-lettres,* in fact, and by definition abhorrent to her. Not one of the books in the two shelves has been read; some of the pages are still uncut. Yet each book is inscribed or dedicated to her: gratefully, admiringly, sentimentally and, more than once, amorously. In short, it is open to anyone who cares to examine these two shelves, and to work out dates, to conclude that Judith from the age of fifteen to twenty-five had been the beloved young companion of one elderly literary gentleman, and from twenty-five to thirty-five the inspiration of another.

During all that time she had produced her own poetry, and the sort of poetry, it is quite safe to deduce, not at all likely to be admired by her two admirers. Her poems are always cool and intellectual; that is their form, which is contradicted or supported by a gravely sensuous texture. They are poems to read often; one has to, to understand them.

I did not ask Judith a direct question about these two eminent but rather fusty lovers. Not because she would not have answered, or because she would have found the question impertinent, but because such questions are clearly unnecessary. Having those two shelves of books where they are, and books she could not conceivably care for,

6. About $500–$550 at the time of the story, but probably close to one-third or even one-half of a subsistence income.

7. Swampy or heathery wastelands in western Britain, from southwestern coast to north of England.

for their own sake, is publicly giving credit where credit is due. I can imagine her thinking the thing over, and deciding it was only fair, or perhaps honest, to place the books there; and this despite the fact that she would not care at all for the same attention to be paid to her. There is something almost contemptuous in it. For she certainly despises people who feel they need attention.

For instance, more than once a new emerging wave of "modern" young poets have discovered her as the only "modern" poet among their despised and well-credited elders. This is because, since she began writing at fifteen, her poems have been full of scientific, mechanical and chemical imagery. This is how she thinks, or feels.

More than once has a young poet hastened to her flat, to claim her as an ally, only to find her totally and by instinct unmoved by words like "modern," "new," "contemporary." He has been outraged and wounded by her principle, so deeply rooted as to be unconscious, and to need no expression but a contemptuous shrug of the shoulders, that publicly seeking or to want critical attention is despicable. It goes without saying that there is perhaps one critic in the world she has any time for. He has sulked off, leaving her on her shelf, which she takes it for granted is her proper place, to be read by an appreciative minority.

Meanwhile she gives her lectures, walks alone through London, writes her poems, and is seen sometimes at a concert or a play with a middle-aged professor of Greek, who has a wife and two children.

Betty and I had speculated about this professor, with such remarks as: Surely she must sometimes be lonely? Hasn't she ever wanted to marry? What about that awful moment when one comes in from somewhere at night to an empty flat?

It happened recently that Betty's husband was on a business trip, her children visiting, and she was unable to stand the empty house. She asked Judith for a refuge until her own home filled again.

Afterwards Betty rang me up to report: "Four of the five nights Professor Adams came in about ten or so."

"Was Judith embarrassed?"

"Would you expect her to be?"

"Well, if not embarrassed, at least conscious there was a situation?"

"No, not at all. But I must say I don't think he's good enough for her. He can't possibly understand her. He calls her Judy."

"Good God."

"Yes. But I was wondering. Suppose the other two called her Judy '—little Judy'—imagine it! Isn't it awful? But it does rather throw a light on Judith?"

"It's rather touching."

"I suppose it's touching. But *I* was embarrassed—oh, not because of the situation. Because of how she was, with him. 'Judy, is there another cup of tea in that pot?' And she, rather daughterly and demure, pouring him one."

"Three of the nights he went to her bedroom with her—very casual about it, because she was being. But he was not there in the mornings. So I asked her. You know how it is when you ask her a question. As if you've been having long conversations on that very subject for years and years, and she is merely continuing where you left off last. So when she says something surprising, one feels such a fool to be surprised?"

"Yes. And then?"

"I asked her if she was sorry not to have children. She said yes, but one couldn't have everything."

"One can't have everything, she said?"

"Quite clearly feeling she *has* nearly everything. She said she thought it was a pity, because she would have brought up children very well."

"When you come to think of it, she would, too."

"I asked about marriage, but she said on the whole the role of a mistress suited her better."

"She used the word 'mistress'?"

"You must admit it's the accurate word."

"I suppose so."

"And then she said that while she liked intimacy and sex and everything, she enjoyed waking up in the morning alone and *her own person*."

"Yes, *of course*."

"Of course. abut now she's bothered because the professor would like to marry her. Or he feels he ought. At least, he's getting all guilty and obsessive about it. She says she doesn't see the point of divorce, and anyway, surely it would be very hard on his poor old wife after all these years, particularly after bringing up two children so satisfactorily. She talks about his wife as if she's a kind of nice old charwoman, and it wouldn't be *fair* to sack her, you know. Anyway. What with one thing and another. Judith's going off to Italy soon in order *to collect herself*."

"But how's she going to pay for it?"

"Luckily the Third Program's[8] commissioning her to do some arty programs. They offered her a choice of The Cid—El Thid,[9] you know —and the Borgias. Well, the Borghese, then. And Judith settled for the Borgias."

"The Borgias," I said, "*Judith?*"

"Yes, quite. I said that too, in that tone of voice. She saw my point. She says the epic is right up her street, whereas the Renaissance has never been on her wave length. Obviously it couldn't be, all the magnificence and cruelty and *dirt*. But of course chivalry and a high moral code and all those idiotically noble goings-on are right on her wave length."

"Is the money the same?"

"Yes. But is it likely Judith would let money decide? No, she said that one should always choose something new, that isn't up one's street. Well, because it's better for her character, and so on, to get herself unsettled by the Renaissance. She didn't say *that*, of course."

"Of course not."

8. British Broadcasting Corporation public radio service (and now also television channel) specializing in classical music, literature and plays, lectures, etc.

9. Castilian, standard Spanish, pronunciation of El Cid, the title of an eleventh-century soldier-hero and hero of many works of literature.

Judith went to Florence; and for some months postcards informed us tersely of her doings. Then Betty decided she must go by herself for a holiday. She had been appalled by the discovery that if her husband was away for a night she couldn't sleep; and when he went to Australia for three weeks, she stopped living until he came back. She had discussed this with him, and he had agreed that if she really felt the situation to be serious, he would dispatch her by air, to Italy, in order to recover her self-respect. As she put it.

I got this letter from her: "It's no use, I'm coming home. I might have known. Better face it, once you're really married you're not fit for man nor beast. And if you remember what I used to be like! *Well!* I moped around Milan. I sunbathed in Venice, then I thought my tan was surely worth something, so I was on the point of starting an affair with another lonely soul, but I lost heart, and went to Florence to see Judith. She wasn't there. She'd gone to the Italian Riviera. I had nothing better to do, so I followed her. When I saw the place I wanted to laugh, it's so much not Judith, you know, all those palms and umbrellas and gaiety at all costs and ever such an ornamental blue sea. Judith is in an enormous stone room up on the hillside above the sea, with grape vines all over the place. You should see her, she's got beautiful. It seems for the last fifteen years she's been going to Soho[1] every Saturday morning to buy food at an Italian shop. I must have looked surprised, because she explained she liked Soho. I suppose because all that dreary vice and nudes and prostitutes and everything prove how right she is to be as she is? She told the people in the shop she was going to Italy, and the *signora*[2] said, what a coincidence, she was going back to Italy too, and she did hope an old friend like Miss Castlewell would visit her there. Judith said to me: 'I felt lacking, when she used the word friend. Our relations have always been formal. Can you understand it?' she said to me. 'For fifteen years,' I said to her. She said: 'I think I must feel it's a kind of imposition, don't you know, expecting people to feel friendship for one.' *Well.* I said: 'You ought to understand it, because you're like that yourself.' 'Am I?' she said. 'Well, think about it,' I said. But I could see she didn't want to think about it. Anyway, she's here, and I've spent a week with her. The widow Maria Rineiri inherited her mother's house, so she came home, from Soho. On the ground floor is a tatty little *rosticceria*[3] patronized by the neighbors. They are all working people. This isn't tourist country, up on the hill. The widow lives above the shop with her little boy, a nasty little brat of about ten. Say what you like, the English are the only people who know how to bring up children, I don't care if that's insular. Judith's room is at the back, with a balcony. Underneath her room is the barber's shop, and the barber is Luigi Rineiri, the widow's younger brother. Yes, I was keeping him until the last. He is about forty, tall dark handsome, a great *bull*, but rather a sweet fatherly bull. He has cut Judith's hair and made it lighter. Now it looks like a sort of gold helmet.

1. A section of London roughly equivalent to Greenwich Village in New York—foreign restaurants and groceries, haunt of writers, painters, etc.—but in recent years increasingly known for prostitutes and pornography.
2. Proprietress.
3. Grill.

Judith is all brown. The widow Rineiri has made her a white dress and a green dress. They fit, for a change. When Judith walks down the street to the lower town, all the Italian males take one look at the golden girl and melt in their own oil like ice cream. Judith takes all this in her stride. She sort of acknowledges the homage. Then she strolls into the sea and vanishes into the foam. She swims five miles every day. *Naturally.* I haven't asked Judith whether she has collected herself, because you can see she hasn't. The widow Rineiri is matchmaking. When I noticed this I wanted to laugh, but luckily I didn't because Judith asked me, really wanting to know: 'Can you see me married to an Italian barber?' (Not being snobbish, but stating the position, so to speak.) 'Well yes,' I said, 'you're the only woman I know who I can see married to an Italian barber.' Because it wouldn't matter who she married, she'd always be her *own person*. 'At any rate, for a time,' I said. At which she said, asperously:[4] 'You can use phrases like for a time in England but not in Italy.' Did you ever see England, at least London, as the home of license, liberty and free love? No, neither did I, but of course she's right. Married to Luigi it would be the family, the neighbors, the church and the *bambini*.[5] All the same she's thinking about it, believe it or not. Here she's quite different, all relaxed and free. She's melting in the attention she gets. The widow mothers her and makes her coffee all the time, and listens to a lot of good advice about how to bring up that nasty brat of hers. Unluckily she doesn't take it. Luigi is crazy for her. At mealtimes she goes to the *trattoria*[6] in the upper square and all the workmen treat her like a goddess. Well, a film star then. I said to her, you're mad to come home. For one thing her rent is ten bob[7] a week, and you eat *pasta* and drink red wine till you bust for about one and sixpence. No, she said, it would be nothing but self-indulgence to stay. Why? I said. She said, she's got nothing to stay for. (Ho ho.) And besides, she's done her research on the Borghese, though so far she can't see her way to an honest presentation of the facts. What made these people tick? she wants to know. And so she's only staying because of the cat. I forgot to mention the cat. This is a town of cats. The Italians here love their cats. I wanted to feed a stray cat at the table, but the waiter said no; and after lunch, all the waiters came with trays crammed with leftover food and stray cats came from everywhere to eat. And at dark when the tourists go in to feed and the beach is empty—you know how empty and forlorn a beach is at dusk?—well cats appear from everywhere. The beach seems to move, then you see it's cats. They go stalking along the thin inch of gray water at the edge of the sea, shaking their paws crossly at each step, snatching at the dead little fish, and throwing them with their mouths up onto the dry sand. Then they scamper after them. You've never seen such a snarling and fighting. At dawn when the fishing boats come in to the empty beach, the cats are there in dozens. The fishermen throw them bits of fish. The cats snarl and fight over it. Judith gets up early and

4. Sharply, harshly.
5. Children.
6. Restaurant.
7. Shillings. There are twenty shillings to the pound; *one and sixpence* below is one and a half shillings. Living in Italy at the time was very inexpensive by British standards.

goes down to watch. Sometimes Luigi goes too, being tolerant. Because what he really likes is to join the evening promenade with Judith on his arm around and around the square of the upper town. Showing her off. Can you *see* Judith? But she does it. Being tolerant. But she smiles and enjoys the attention she gets, there's no doubt of it.

"She has a cat in her room. It's a kitten really, but it's pregnant. Judith says she can't leave until the kittens are born. The cat is too young to have kittens. Imagine Judith. She sits on her bed in that great stone room, with her bare feet on the stone floor, and watches the cat, and tries to work out why a healthy uninhibited Italian cat always fed on the best from the *rosticceria* should be neurotic. Because it is. When it sees Judith watching it gets nervous and starts licking at the roots of its tail. But Judith goes on watching, and says about Italy that the reason why the English love the Italians is because the Italians make the English feel superior. They have no discipline. And that's a despicable reason for one nation to love another. Then she talks about Luigi and says he has no sense of guilt, but a sense of sin; whereas she has no sense of sin but she has guilt. I haven't asked her if this has been an insuperable barrier, because judging from how she looks, it hasn't. She says she would rather have a sense of sin, because sin can be attoned for, and if she understood sin, perhaps she would be more at home with the Renaissance. Luigi is very healthy, she says, and not neurotic. He is a Catholic of course. He doesn't mind that she's an atheist. His mother has explained to him that the English are all pagans, but good people at heart. I suppose he thinks a few smart sessions with the local priest would set Judith on the right path for good and all. Meanwhile the cat walks nervously around the room, stopping to lick, and when it can't stand Judith watching it another second, it rolls over on the floor, with its paws tucked up, and rolls up its eyes, and Judith scratches its lumpy pregnant stomach and tells it to relax. It makes *me* nervous to see her, it's not like her. I don't know why. Then Luigi shouts up from the barber's shop, then he comes up and stands at the door laughing, and Judith laughs, and the widow says: Children, enjoy yourselves. And off they go, walking down to the town eating ice cream. The cat follows them. It won't let Judith out of its sight, like a dog. When she swims miles out to sea, the cat hides under a beach hut until she comes back. Then she carries it back up the hill, because that nasty little boy chases it. *Well.* I'm coming home tomorrow thank God, to my dear old Billy, I was mad ever to leave him. There is something about Judith and Italy that has upset me, I don't know what. The point is, what on earth can Judith and Luigi *talk* about? Nothing. How can they? And of course it doesn't matter. So I turn out to be a prude as well. See you next week."

It was my turn for a dose of the sun, so I didn't see Betty. On my way back from Rome I stopped off in Judith's resort and walked up through narrow streets to the upper town, where, in the square with the vine-covered *trattoria* at the corner, was a house with ROSTICCERIA written in black paint on a cracked wooden board over a low door. There was a door curtain of red beads, and flies settled on the beads. I opened the beads with my hands and looked into a small dark room with a stone counter. Loops of salami hung from metal hooks. A glass bell covered some plates of cooked meats. There were flies on the salami and on the glass bell. A few tins on the wooden shelves, a couple of pale loaves, some wine casks and an open case of sticky pale green grapes covered with fruit flies seemed to be the only stock. A single wooden table with two chairs stood in a corner, and two workmen sat there, eating lumps of sausage and bread. Through another bead curtain at the back came a short, smoothly fat, slender-limbed woman with graying hair. I asked for Miss Castlewell, and her face changed. She said in an offended, offhand way: "Miss Castlewell left last week." She took a white cloth from under the counter, and flicked at the flies on the glass bell. "I'm a friend of hers," I said, and she said: "*Si,*"[8] and put her hands palm down on the counter and looked at me, expressionless. The workmen got up, gulped down the last of their wine, nodded and went. She *ciao'*d[9] them; and looked back at me. Then, since I didn't go, she called: "Luigi!" A shout came from the back room, there was a rattle of beads, and in came first a wiry sharp-faced boy, and then Luigi. He was tall, heavy-shouldered, and his black rough hair was like a cap, pulled low over his brows. He looked good-natured, but at the moment uneasy. His sister said something, and he stood beside her, an ally, and confirmed: "Miss Castlewell went away." I was on the point of giving up, when through the bead curtain that screened off a dazzling light eased a thin tabby cat. It was ugly and it walked uncomfortably, with its back quarters bunched up. The child suddenly let out a "Ssssss" through his teeth, and the cat froze. Luigi said something sharp to the child, and something encouraging to the cat, which sat down, looked straight in front of it, then began frantically licking at its flanks. "Miss Castlewell was offended with us," said Mrs. Rineiri suddenly, and with dignity. "She left early one morning. We did not expect her to go." I said: "Perhaps she had to go home and finish some work."

Mrs. Rineiri shrugged, then sighed. Then she exchanged a hard look with her brother. Clearly the subject had been discussed, and closed forever.

"I've known Judith a long time," I said, trying to find the right note. "She's a remarkable woman. She's a poet." But there was no response to this at all. Meanwhile the child, with a fixed bared-teeth grin, was staring at the cat, narrowing his eyes. Suddenly he let out another "Sssssss" and added a short high yelp. The cat shot backwards, hit the wall, tried desperately to claw its way up the wall, came to its senses and again sat down and began its urgent, undirected licking at its fur. This time Luigi cuffed the child, who yelped in earnest, and then ran out into the street past the cat. Now that the way was clear the cat shot across the floor, up onto the counter, and bounded past Luigi's shoulder and straight through the bead curtain into the barber's shop, where it landed with a thud.

"Judith was sorry when she left us," said Mrs. Rineiri uncertainly. "She was crying."

8. "Yes."

9. Said good-bye to.

"I'm sure she was."

"And so," said Mrs. Rineiri, with finality, laying her hands down again, and looking past me at the bead curtain. That was the end. Luigi nodded brusquely at me, and went into the back. I said goodbye to Mrs. Rineiri and walked back to the lower town. In the square I saw the child, sitting on the running board of a lorry[1] parked outside the *trattoria*, drawing in the dust with his bare toes, and directing in front of him a blank, unhappy stare.

I had to go through Florence, so I went to the address Judith had been at. No, Miss Castlewell had not been back. Her papers and books were still here. Would I take them back with me to England? I made a great parcel and brought them back to England.

I telephoned Judith and she said she had already written for the papers to be sent, but it was kind of me to bring them. There had seemed to be no point, she said, in returning to Florence.

"Shall I bring them over?"

"I would be very grateful, of course."

Judith's flat was chilly, and she wore a bunchy sage-green woolen dress. Her hair was still a soft gold helmet, but she looked pale and rather pinched. She stood with her back to a single bar of electric fire—lit because I demanded it—with her legs apart and her arms folded. She contemplated me.

"I went to the Rineiris' house."

"Oh. Did you?"

"They seemed to miss you."

She said nothing.

"I saw the cat too."

"Oh. Oh, I suppose you and Betty discussed it?" This was with a small unfriendly smile.

"Well, Judith, you must see we were likely to?"

She gave this her consideration and said: "I don't understand why people discuss other people. Oh—I'm not criticizing you. But I don't see why you are so interested. I don't understand human behavior and I'm not particularly interested."

"I think you should write to the Rineiris."

"I wrote and thanked them, of course."

"I don't mean that."

"You and Betty have worked it out?"

"Yes, we talked about it. We thought we should talk to you, so you should write to the Rineiris."

"Why?"

"For one thing, they are both very fond of you."

"Fond," she said smiling.

"Judith, I've never in my life felt such an atmosphere of being let down."

Judith considered this. "When something happens that shows one there is really a complete gulf in understanding, what is there to say?"

"It could scarcely have been a complete gulf in understanding. I suppose you are going to say we are being interfering?"

1. Truck.

Judith showed distaste. "That is a very stupid word. And it's a stupid idea. No one can interfere with me if I don't let them. No, it's that I don't understand people. I don't understand why you or Betty should care. Or why the Rineiris should, for that matter," she added with the small tight smile.

"Judith!"

"If you've behaved stupidly, there's no point in going on. You put an end to it."

"What happened? Was it the cat?"

"Yes, I suppose so. But it's not important." She looked at me, saw my ironical face, and said: "The cat was too young to have kittens. That is all there was to it."

"Have it your way. But that is obviously not all there is to it."

"What upsets me is that I don't understand at all why I was so upset then."

"What happened? Or don't you want to talk about it?"

"I don't give a damn whether I talk about it or not. You really do say the most extraordinary things, you and Betty. If you want to know, I'll tell you. What does it matter?"

"I would like to know, of course."

"*Of course!*" she said. "In your place I wouldn't care. Well, I think the essence of the thing was that I must have had the wrong attitude to that cat. Cats are supposed to be independent. They are supposed to go off by themselves to have their kittens. This one didn't. It was climbing up on to my bed all one night and crying for attention. I don't like cats on my bed. In the morning I saw she was in pain. I stayed with her all that day. Then Luigi—he's the brother, you know."

"Yes."

"Did Betty mention him? Luigi came up to say it was time I went for a swim. He said the cat should look after itself. I blame myself very much. That's what happens when you submerge yourself in somebody else."

Her look at me was now defiant; and her body showed both defensiveness and aggression. "Yes. It's true. I've always been afraid of it. And in the last few weeks I've behaved badly. It's because I let it happen."

"Well, go on."

"I left the cat and swam. It was late, so it was only for a few minutes. When I came out of the sea the cat had followed me and had had a kitten on the beach. That little beast Michele—the son, you know?—well, he always teased the poor thing, and now he had frightened her off the kitten. It was dead, though. He held it up by the tail and waved it at me as I came out of the sea. I told him to bury it. He scooped two inches of sand away and pushed the kitten in—on the beach, where people are all day. So I buried it properly. He had run off. He was chasing the poor cat. She was terrified and running up the town. I ran too. I caught Michele and I was so angry I hit him. I don't believe in hitting children. I've been feeling beastly about it ever since."

"You were angry."

"It's no excuse. I would never have believed myself capable of hitting a child. I hit him very hard. He went off, crying. The poor cat had got under a big lorry parked in the square. Then she screamed. And then a most remarkable thing happened. She screamed just once, and all at once cats just materialized. One minute there was just one cat, lying under a lorry, and the next, dozens of cats. They sat in a big circle around the lorry, all quite still, and watched my poor cat."

"Rather moving," I said.

"Why?"

"There is no evidence one way or the other," I said in inverted commas, "that the cats were there out of concern for a friend in trouble."

"No," she said energetically. "There isn't. It might have been curiosity. Or anything. How do we know? However, I crawled under the lorry. There were two paws sticking out of the cat's back end. The kitten was the wrong way round. It was stuck. I held the cat down with one hand and I pulled the kitten out with the other." She held out her long white hands. They were still covered with fading scars and scratches. "She bit and yelled, but the kitten was alive. She left the kitten and crawled across the square into the house. Then all the cats got up and walked away. It was the most extraordinary thing I've ever seen. They vanished again. One minute they were all there, and then they had vanished. I went after the cat, with the kitten. Poor little thing, it was covered with dust—being wet, don't you know. The cat was on my bed. There was another kitten coming, but it got stuck too. So when she screamed and screamed I just pulled it out. The kittens began to suck. One kitten was very big. It was a nice fat black kitten. It must have hurt her. But she suddenly bit out—snapped, don't you know, like a reflex action, at the back of the kitten's head. It died, just like that. Extraordinary, isn't it?" she said, blinking hard, her lips quivering. "She was its mother, but she killed it. Then she ran off the bed and went downstairs into the shop under the counter. I called to Luigi. You know, he's Mrs. Rineiri's brother."

"Yes, I know."

"He said she was too young, and she was badly frightened and very hurt. He took the alive kitten to her but she got up and walked away. She didn't want it. Then Luigi told me not to look. But I followed him. He held the kitten by the tail and he banged it against the wall twice. Then he dropped it into the rubbish heap. He moved aside some rubbish with his toe, and put the kitten there and pushed rubbish over it. Then Luigi said the cat should be destroyed. He said she was badly hurt and it would always hurt her to have kittens."

"He hasn't destroyed her. She's still alive. But it looks to me as if he were right."

"Yes, I expect he was."

"What upset you—that he killed the kitten?"

"Oh no, I expect the cat would if he hadn't. But that isn't the point, is it?"

"What is the point?"

"I don't think I really know." She had been speaking breathlessly, and fast. Now she said slowly: "It's not a question of right or wrong, is it? Why should it be? It's a question of what one is. That night Luigi wanted to go promenading with me. For him, that was *that.* Something had to be done, and he'd done it. But I felt ill. He was very nice to me. He's a very good person," she said, defiantly.

"Yes, he looks it."

"That night I couldn't sleep. I was blaming myself. I should never have left the cat to go swimming. Well, and then I decided to leave the next day. And I did. And that's all. The whole thing was a mistake from start to finish."

"Going to Italy at all?"

"Oh, to go for a holiday would have been all right."

"You've done all that work for nothing? You mean you aren't going to make use of all that research?"

"No. It was a mistake."

"Why don't you leave it a few weeks and see how things are then?"

"Why?"

"You might feel differently about it."

"What an extraordinary thing to say. Why should I? Oh, you mean, time passing, healing wounds—that sort of thing? What an extraordinary idea. It's always seemed to me an extraordinary idea. No, right from the beginning I've felt ill at ease with the whole business, not myself at all."

"Rather irrationally, I should have said."

Judith considered this, very seriously. She frowned while she thought it over. Then she said: "But if one cannot rely on what one feels, what can one rely on?"

"On what one thinks, I should have expected you to say."

"Should you? Why? Really, you people are all very strange. I don't understand you." She turned off the electric fire, and her face closed up. She smiled, friendly and distant, and said: "I don't really see any point at all in discussing it."

1963

4 SYMBOLS

One of the chief devices for bridging the gap between the writer's and the reader's vision is the **symbol.** A symbol is commonly defined as something that stands for something else, but that may need some qualification. Though a member of a class may stand for or represent the class, it is not really a symbol. Symbols are generally **figurative**; that is, they explicitly or implicitly compare or merge two *unlike* things. A senator may represent a state, but he is not a symbol of that state, for the state is a governmental unit and the senator, as a member of the government, *literally* represents the state. A flower, on the other hand, though it may be a native of the state, may very well be a symbol of the state; it has little to do with governing the state, and so represents it only figuratively. When a figure is expressed as an explicit comparison, often signaled by *like* or *as*, it is called a **simile**: "eyes as blue as the sky"; "the baby brother I'd never known looked out from the depths of his private life, like an animal waiting to be coaxed into the light" (*Sonny's Blues*). An implicit comparison or identification of one thing with another unlike itself, without a verbal signal but just seeming to say "A *is* B," is called a **metaphor**: "The sea was a sheet of glass"; "the grass was a green carpet"; "there was a boiling wave of dogs about them" (*The Old People*). Sometimes all figures are loosely referred to as metaphors.

An **allegory** is like a metaphor in that one thing (usually nonrational, abstract, religious) is implicitly spoken of in terms of something that is concrete and usually sensuous (perceptible by the senses), but the comparison in allegory is extended to include a whole work or a large portion of a work. It is therefore usually part of a whole system of equivalencies. *The Pilgrim's Progress* is probably the most famous prose allegory in English: its central character is named Christian; he was born in the City of Destruction and sets out for the Celestial City, passes through the Slough of Despond and Vanity Fair, meets men named Pliable and Obstinate, and so on.

A symbol can be as brief and local as a metaphor or as extended as an allegory, and like an allegory usually speaks in concrete terms of the non- or super-rational, the abstract, that which is not immediately perceived by the senses. Though some allegories can be complex, with many layers or levels of equivalency, and some symbols can be very simple, with paraphrasable equivalencies, allegory usually refers to a one-to-one relationship (as the names from *The Pilgrim's Progress* imply), and literary symbols usually have highly complex or even inexpressible equivalencies. *The Lottery* may be considered a symbolic story, but precisely what it "stands for" is extremely difficult to express briefly and satisfactorily—New England Puritanism? man's cruelty to man? original sin? the dulling of human sensibility by ritualistic actions?

When an entire story, like *The Lottery*, is symbolic, it is sometimes called a **myth** or **mythic.** *Myth* originally meant a story of communal origin that provided an explanation or religious interpretation of man, nature, the universe, and the relation between them; from the vantage point of another culture or set of beliefs, the word usually implied that the story was false. We speak of classical myths, but Christians do not speak of Christian myth. We also apply the term *myth* now to stories by individuals, sophisticated authors, but often there is still the implication that the mythic story relates to a communal or group experience whereas a symbolic story may be more personal or private. It is hard to draw the line firmly: *The Lottery* and *The Old People* seem to have clearly national, American implications, while *The Rocking-Horse Winner* may be a private Lawrencian symbol or a myth of modern bourgeois society. A plot or character element that recurs in cultural or cross-cultural myths, such as episodes involving descent into the underworld (as in the sewer incident in *The Artificial*

Nigger?) or images of the devil (as in *Young Goodman Brown*), is now widely called an **archetype.**

There is another figure of speech, which seems to border on the one hand on representation and on the other on symbol—the **synecdoche,** a figure in which the part stands for the whole ("Jaws"). At the other boundary line of the symbol, totally nonrepresentational but not quite a symbol, is the **sign,** an arbitrary mark that is assigned a meaning (#, $, %, &, =, to use examples that are handy on the typewriter).

Is there no nonarbitrary reason why snakes are commonly symbolic of evil? Sure, some snakes are poisonous, but for some people so are bees, and a lot of snakes are not only harmless but actually helpful ecologically. (In Kipling's *The Jungle Book* the python Ka is frightening but on the side of Law and Order.) Through repeated use over the centuries, the snake has become a traditional symbol of Evil —not just danger, sneakiness, repulsiveness, but theological, absolute Evil. Had Macomber been startled by a snake during the lion hunt, we would not necessarily have said, "Aha—snake, symbol of Evil," though that potential meaning would have hovered around the incident, perhaps, and sent us looking backward and forward in the story for supporting evidence that this snake was indeed being used symbolically. (I can recall none.) However, when we discover that the stranger in *Young Goodman Brown* has a walking stick upon which is carved the image of a snake, we are much more likely to find it such a symbol because of other, related potential symbols or meanings in the context. The term *Goodman* in the title of the story sets up the distinct possibility that Brown (how common a name) stands for more than a "mere" individual young man. (That this expectation is aroused in part because most of us are ignorant of the fact that in colonial New England *Goodman* was used to mean husband does not cancel the fact that it does—and no doubt did—suggest more than the title.) Brown's bride is named Faith—a common name among the early Puritans, but, together with Goodman, suggesting symbolic possibilities. Then, just before the stranger with the walking stick appears, Brown says, "What if the devil himself should be at my very elbow!"

A single item, even something as traditionally fraught with meaning as a snake or a rose, becomes a symbol only when its potentially symbolic meaning is confirmed by something else in the story, just as a point needs a second point to define a line. Multiple symbols or potential symbols, or these plus other kinds of direct and indirect hints, such as Brown's mention of the devil, are among the ways in which details may be identified as symbols (for interpreting symbols is relatively easy once you know what is and what is probably not a symbol).

One form of what may be called an indirect hint is repetition. That an "old maid" like Judith should have a cat seems so ordinary it borders on the trite. When she chooses to have her male cat put to death rather than neutered, it makes us sit up and take notice, doesn't it? This choice may suggest something about the unconventional in her character, but we probably don't think of the cat in itself representing anything. What happens, though, when there appears another cat, a female this time, whose sex life calls forth strange behavior on Judith's part? And when the killing of a kitten interrupts Judith's affair with Luigi? It is difficult to say when or if the literal cats shade off into symbols, they remain so solidly cats, things, in the story. All we can say for sure is that cats become more important in reading and understanding this story than, say, the cask of Amontillado does in the Poe story. The cask remains a thing pure and simple. Repetition, then, calls attention to details and may alert us to potential symbolic overtones, but it does not necessarily turn a thing into a symbol; nor is it important, so long as we get the suggestions of significance, whether we agree entirely on what—or when—is a symbol.

Direct hints may take the form of explicit statements. (Authors are not so anxious to hide their meanings as some readers are prone to believe.) Sherwood Anderson calls his story *The Egg,* and chickens and eggs figure in most of the incidents. To make sure you know he's writing about more than chickens and eggs, he says things like: "A few hens and now and then a rooster, intended to serve God's mysterious ends, struggle through to maturity. . . . Most philosophers must have been raised on chicken farms." And in case that slips by you: "One hopes for so much from a chicken and is so dreadfully disillusioned. Small chickens, just setting out on the journey of life, look so bright and alert and they are *in* fact so dreadfully stupid. They are so much like people they mix one up in one's judgments of life."

We also may be alerted to the fact that something is standing for something else when the something does not seem to make literal sense in itself. It does not take us long to realize that *Young Goodman Brown* is not entirely as realistic a story as *Bovanne* or *Macomber*. When things do not seem explicable in terms of everyday reality, we often look beyond them for some meaning, as we do in *The Lottery*.

We must remember, however, that symbols do not exist solely for the transmission of a meaning we can paraphrase; they do not disappear from the story, our memory, or our response once their "meaning" has been sucked out of them, any more than Francis Macomber ceases to exist as an individual after we recognize his representative or universal nature. Faith's pink ribbons, eggs, Judith's cats are all objects in their stories, whatever meanings or suggestions of meanings they have given rise to.

As I've often implied and occasionally said, few symbols can be exhausted, translated into an abstract phrase or equivalent: the "something else" that the "something" stands for is ultimately allusive. When you get to the scene in *The Artificial Nigger* in which Nelson and his grandfather are brought back together by their puzzlement over the function of the statue of a little black jockey, a once-common and now unlamentably rare suburban lawn decoration, try to paraphrase exactly what the "artificial nigger" stands for. Or explain with certainty what Faith's pink ribbon symbolizes. It is not that the statue and the ribbon mean nothing but that they mean so many things that no one equivalence will do; even an abstract statement seems to reduce rather than fully explain the significance for the reader. Yes, the "artificial nigger" is a mystery that unites the boy and his grandfather in their ignorance, but is that the whole meaning of the story's description of the statue as "some monument to another's victory that brought them together in their common defeat"? Do any other incidents involving blacks in the story—on the train, on the city streets—relate to the statue? How does "artificial" fit in? And how about the tone? The phrase is offensive, isn't it, and suggests prejudice and ignorance. But the incident and their ignorance are a little funny, too, and pathetic. Are this incident and this symbol representative of or disruptive of the tone of the story as a whole? It seems to me the statue appropriately encapsulates the unsettling, frightening, and revealing experiences of grandfather and grandson in the city, but I'm not sure I could say everything I thought the "artificial nigger" means or all the feelings it generates. So, too, reading *Young Goodman Brown,* you might want to think about how many things Faith's pink ribbon suggests.

The unparaphrasable nature of these images is not vagueness but richness, not disorder but complexity.

NATHANIEL HAWTHORNE

Young Goodman Brown

Young Goodman Brown came forth, at sunset, into the street of Salem village,[1] but put his head back, after crossing the threshold, to exchange a parting kiss with his young wife. And Faith, as the wife was aptly named, thrust her own pretty head into the street, letting the wind play with the pink ribbons of her cap, while she called to Goodman Brown.

"Dearest heart," whispered she, softly and rather sadly, when her lips were close to his ear, "pr'y thee, put off your journey until sunrise, and sleep in your own bed tonight. A lone woman is troubled with such dreams and such thoughts, that she's afeard of herself, sometimes. Pray, tarry with me this night, dear husband, of all nights in the year!"

"My love and my Faith," replied young Goodman Brown, "of all nights in the year, this one night must I tarry away from thee. My journey, as thou callest it, forth and back again, must needs be done 'twixt now and sunrise. What, my sweet, pretty wife, dost thou doubt me already, and we but three months married!"

"Then, God bless you!" said Faith, with the pink ribbons, "and may you find all well, when you come back."

"Amen!" cried Goodman Brown. "Say thy prayers, dear Faith, and go to bed at dusk, and no harm will come to thee."

1. Salem, Massachusetts, Hawthorne's birthplace (1804) was the scene of the famous witch trials of 1692; *Goodman:* husband, master of household.

So they parted; and the young man pursued his way, until, being about to turn the corner by the meeting-house, he looked back, and saw the head of Faith still peeping after him, with a melancholy air, in spite of her pink ribbons.

"Poor little Faith!" thought he, for his heart smote him. "What a wretch am I, to leave her on such an errand! She talks of dreams, too. Methought, as she spoke, there was trouble in her face, as if a dream had warned her what work is to be done tonight. But, no, no! 'twould kill her to think it. Well; she's a blessed angel on earth; and after this one night, I'll cling to her skirts and follow her to Heaven."

With this excellent resolve for the future, Goodman Brown felt himself justfiied in making more haste on his present evil purpose. He had taken a dreary road, darkened by all the gloomiest trees of the forest, which barely stood aside to let the narrow path creep through, and closed immediately behind. It was all as lonely as could be; and there is this peculiarity in such a solitude, that the traveler knows not who may be concealed by the innumerable trunks and the thick boughs overhead; so that, with lonely footsteps, he may yet be passing through an unseen multitude.

"There may be a devilish Indian behind every tree," said Goodman Brown, to himself; and he glanced fearfully behind him, as he added, "What if the devil himself should be at my very elbow!"

His head being turned back, he passed a crook of the road, and looking forward again, beheld the figure of a man, in grave and decent attire, seated at the foot of an old tree. He arose, at Goodman Brown's approach, and walked onward, side by side with him.

"You are late, Goodman Brown," said he. "The clock of the Old South[2] was striking as I came through Boston; and that is full fifteen minutes agone."

"Faith kept me back awhile," replied the young man, with a tremor in his voice, caused by the sudden appearance of his companion, though not wholly unexpected.

It was now deep dusk in the forest, and deepest in that part of it where these two were journeying. As nearly as could be discerned, the second traveler was about fifty years old, apparently in the same rank of life as Goodman Brown, and bearing a considerable resemblance to him, though perhaps more in expression than features. Still, they might have been taken for father and son. And yet, though the elder person was as simply clad as the younger, and as simple in manner too, he had an indescribable air of one who knew the world, and would not have felt abashed at the governor's dinner table, or in King William's [3] court, were it possible that his affairs should call him thither. But the only thing about him, that could be fixed upon as remarkable, was his staff, which bore the likeness of a great black snake, so curiously wrought, that it might almost be seen to twist and wriggle itself, like a living serpent. This, of course, must have been an ocular deception, assisted by the uncertain light.

2. The Third Church of Boston, established in 1669 in opposition to the requirement of church membership for political rights and thus a landmark of religious freedom.

3. William III—William of Orange—1650-1702, ruled England from 1689 to 1702, until 1694 jointly with his wife, Mary II.

"Come, Goodman Brown!" cried his fellow-traveler, "this is a dull pace for the beginning of a journey. Take my staff, if you are so soon weary."

"Friend," said the other, exchanging his slow pace for a full stop, "having kept covenant by meeting thee here, it is my purpose now to return whence I came. I have scruples, touching the matter thou wot'st of."

"Sayest thou so?" replied he of the serpent, smiling apart. "Let us walk on, nevertheless, reasoning as we go, and if I convince thee not, thou shalt turn back. We are but a little way in the forest, yet."

"Too far, too far!" exclaimed the goodman, unconsciously resuming his walk. "My father never went into the woods on such an errand, nor his father before him. We have been a race of honest men and good Christians, since the days of the martyrs. And shall I be the first of the name of Brown, that ever took this path, and kept—"

"Such company, thou wouldst say," observed the elder person, interpreting his pause. "Well said, Goodman Brown! I have been as well acquainted with your family as with ever a one among the Puritans; and that's no trifle to say. I helped your grandfather, the constable, when he lashed the Quaker woman so smartly through the streets of Salem. And it was I that brought your father a pitch-pine knot, kindled at my own hearth, to set fire to an Indian village, in King Philip's war.[4] They were my good friends, both; and many a pleasant walk have we had along this path, and returned merrily after midnight. I would fain be friends with you, for their sake."

"If it be as thou sayest," replied Goodman Brown, "I marvel they never spoke of these matters. Or, verily, I marvel not, seeing that the least rumor of the sort would have driven them from New England. We are a people of prayer, and good works, to boot, and abide no such wickedness."

"Wickedness or not," said the traveler with the twisted staff, "I have a very general acquaintance here in New England. The deacons of many a church have drunk the communion wine with me; the selectmen, of divers towns, make me their chairman; and a majority of the Great and General Court are firm supporters of my interest. The governor and I, too—but these are state secrets."

"Can this be so!" cried Goodman Brown, with a stare of amazement at his undisturbed companion. "Howbeit, I have nothing to do with the governor and council; they have their own ways, and are no rule for a simple husbandman, like me. But, were I to go on with thee, how should I meet the eye of that good old man, our minister, at Salem village? Oh, his voice would make me tremble, both Sabbath-day and lecture-day!"[5]

Thus far, the elder traveler had listened with due gravity, but now burst into a fit of irrepressible mirth, shaking himself so violently, that his snake-like staff actually seemed to wriggle in sympathy.

"Ha! ha! ha!" shouted he, again and again; then composing him-

4. Metacom or Metacomet, chief of the Wampanoag Indians, known as King Philip, led a war against the New England colonists in 1675–76 which devastated many frontier communities.

5. The day—in the New England colonies usually a Thursday—appointed for a periodical lecture, the lecture being less formal than a sermon or delivered on a different occasion.

self, "Well, go on, Goodman Brown, go on; but pr'y thee, don't kill me with laughing!"

"Well, then, to end the matter at once," said Goodman Brown, considerably nettled, "there is my wife, Faith. It would break her dear little heart; and I'd rather break my own!"

"Nay, if that be the case," answered the other, "e'en[6] go thy ways, Goodman Brown. I would not, for twenty old women like the one hobbling before us, that Faith should come to any harm."

As he spoke, he pointed his staff at a female figure on the path, in whom Goodman Brown recognized a very pious and exemplary dame, who had taught him his catechism, in youth, and was still his moral and spiritual adviser, jointly with the minister and Deacon Gookin.

"A marvel, truly, that Goody[7] Cloyse should be so far in the wilderness, at nightfall!" said he. "But, with your leave, friend, I shall take a cut through the woods, until we have left this Christian woman behind. Being a stranger to you, she might ask whom I was consorting with, and whither I was going."

"Be it so," said his fellow-traveler. "Betake you to the woods, and let me keep the path."

Accordingly, the young man turned aside, but took care to watch his companion, who advanced softly along the road, until he had come within a staff's length of the old dame. She, meanwhile, was making the best of her way, with singular speed for so aged a woman, and mumbling some indistinct words, a prayer, doubtless, as she went. The traveler put forth his staff, and touched her withered neck with what seemed the serpent's tail.

"The devil!" screamed the pious old lady.

"Then Goody Cloyse knows her old friend?" observed the traveler, confronting her, and leaning on his writhing stick.

"Ah, forsooth, and is it your worship, indeed?" cried the good dame. "Yea, truly is it, and in the very image of my old gossip, Goodman Brown, the grandfather of the silly fellow that now is. But—would your worship believe it?—my broomstick hath strangely disappeared, stolen, as I suspect, by that unhanged witch, Goody Cory, and that, too, when I was all anointed with the juice of smallage and cinque-foil and wolf's-bane—"

"Mingled with fine wheat and the fat of a new-born babe," said the shape of old Goodman Brown.

"Ah, your worship knows the receipt," cried the old lady, cackling aloud. "So, as I was saying, being all ready for the meeting, and no horse to ride on, I made up my mind to foot it; for they tell me, there is a nice young man to be taken into communion tonight. But now your good worship will lend me your arm, and we shall be there in a twinkling."

"That can hardly be," answered her friend. "I may not spare you my arm, Goody Cloyse, but here is my staff, if you will."

So saying, he threw it down at her feet, where, perhaps, it assumed life, being one of the rods which its owner had formerly lent to the

6. Just.

7. Short for "goodwife" or housewife.

Egyptian Magi.[8] Of this fact, however, Goodman Brown could not take cognizance. He had cast up his eyes in astonishment, and looking down again, beheld neither Goody Cloyse nor the serpentine staff, but his fellow-traveler alone, who waited for him as calmly as if nothing had happened.

"That old woman taught me my catechism!" said the young man; and there was a world of meaning in this simple comment.

They continued to walk onward, while the elder traveler exhorted his companion to make good speed and persevere in the path, discoursing so aptly, that his arguments seemed rather to spring up in the bosom of his auditor, than to be suggested by himself. As they went, he plucked a branch of maple, to serve for a walking stick, and began to strip it of the twigs and little boughs, which were wet with evening dew. The moment his fingers touched them, they became strangely withered and dried up, as with a week's sunshine. Thus the pair proceeded, at a good free pace, until suddenly, in a gloomy hollow of the road, Goodman Brown sat himself down on the stump of a tree, and refused to go any farther.

"Friend," said he, stubbornly, "my mind is made up. Not another step will I budge on this errand. What if a wretched old woman do choose to go to the devil, when I thought she was going to Heaven! Is that any reason why I should quit my dear Faith, and go after her?"

"You will think better of this, by-and-by," said his acquaintance, composedly. "Sit here and rest yourself awhile; and when you feel like moving again, there is my staff to help you along."

Without more words, he threw his companion the maple stick, and was as speedily out of sight, as if he had vanished into the deepening gloom. The young man sat a few moments, by the roadside, applauding himself greatly, and thinking with how clear a conscience he should meet the minister, in his morning walk, nor shrink from the eye of good old Deacon Gookin. And what calm sleep would be his, that very night, which was to have been spent so wickedly, but purely and sweetly now, in the arms of Faith! Amidst these pleasant and praiseworthy meditations, Goodman Brown heard the tramp of horses along the road, and deemed it advisable to conceal himself within the verge of the forest, conscious of the guilty purpose that had brought him thither, though now so happily turned from it.

On came the hoof-tramps and the voices of the riders, two grave old voices, conversing soberly as they drew near. These mingled sounds appeared to pass along the road, within a few yards of the young man's hiding-place; but owing, doubtless, to the depth of the gloom, at that particular spot, neither the travelers nor their steeds were visible. Though their figures brushed the small boughs by the wayside, it could not be seen that they intercepted, even for a moment, the faint gleam from the strip of bright sky, athwart which they must have passed. Goodman Brown alternately crouched and stood on tiptoe, pulling aside the branches, and thrusting forth

8. *Exodus* 7:9–12. The Lord instructs Moses to have his prophet Aaron throw down his rod before the Pharaoh, whereupon it will be turned into a serpent, and by which miracle the Pharaoh will be persuaded to let the Jews go into the wilderness to sacrifice to God. The Pharaoh has his magicians (Magi) do likewise, "but Aaron's rod swallowed up their rods."

his head as far as he durst, without discerning so much as a shadow. It vexed him the more, because he could have sworn, were such a thing possible, that he recognized the voices of the minister and Deacon Gookin, jogging along quietly, as they were wont to do, when bound to some ordination or ecclesiastical council. While yet within hearing, one of the riders stopped to pluck a switch.

"Of the two, reverend Sir," said the voice like the deacon's, "I had rather miss an ordination-dinner than tonight's meeting. They tell me that some of our community are to be here from Falmouth[9] and beyond, and others from Connecticut and Rhode Island; besides several of the Indian powows, who, after their fashion, know almost as much deviltry as the best of us. Moreover, there is a goodly young woman to be taken into communion."

"Mighty well, Deacon Gookin!" replied the solemn old tones of the minister. "Spur up, or we shall be late. Nothing can be done, you know, until I get on the ground."

The hoofs clattered again, and the voices, talking so strangely in the empty air, passed on through the forest, where no church had ever been gathered, nor solitary Christian prayed. Whither, then, could these holy men be journeying, so deep into the heathen wilderness? Young Goodman Brown caught hold of a tree, for support, being ready to sink down on the ground, faint and overburdened with the heavy sickness of his heart. He looked up to the sky, doubting whether there really was a Heaven above him. Yet there was the blue arch, and the stars brightening in it.

"With Heaven above, and Faith below, I will yet stand firm against the devil!" cried Goodman Brown.

While he still gazed upward, into the deep arch of the firmament, and had lifted his hands to pray, a cloud, though no wind was stirring, hurried across the zenith, and hid the brightening stars. The blue sky was still visible, except directly overhead, where this black mass of cloud was sweeping swiftly northward. Aloft in the air, as if from the depths of the cloud, came a confused and doubtful sound of voices. Once, the listener fancied that he could distinguish the accents of townspeople of his own, men and women, both pious and ungodly, many of whom he had met at the communion-table, and had seen others rioting at the tavern. The next moment, so indistinct were the sounds, he doubted whether he had heard aught but the murmur of the old forest, whispering without a wind. Then came a stronger swell of those familiar tones, heard daily in the sunshine, at Salem village, but never, until now, from a cloud of night. There was one voice, of a young woman, uttering lamentations, yet with an uncertain sorrow, and entreating for some favor, which, perhaps, it would grieve her to obtain. And all the unseen multitude, both saints and sinners, seemed to encourage her onward.

"Faith!" shouted Goodman Brown, in a voice of agony and desperation; and the echoes of the forest mocked him, crying—"Faith! Faith!" as if bewildered wretches were seeking her, all through the wilderness.

9. A port in extreme southern Massachusetts; Salem is in northern Massachusetts.

The cry of grief, rage, and terror, was yet piercing the night, when the unhappy husband held his breath for a response. There was a scream, drowned immediately in a louder murmur of voices, fading into far-off laughter, as the dark cloud swept away, leaving the clear and silent sky above Goodman Brown. But something fluttered lightly down through the air, and caught on the branch of a tree. The young man seized it, and beheld a pink ribbon.

"My Faith is gone!" cried he, after one stupefied moment. "There is no good on earth; and sin is but a name. Come, devil! for to thee is this world given."

And maddened with despair, so that he laughed loud and long, did Goodman Brown grasp his staff and set forth again, at such a rate, that he seemed to fly along the forest path, rather than to walk or run. The road grew wilder and drearier, and more faintly traced, and vanished at length, leaving him in the heart of the dark wilderness, still rushing onward, with the instinct that guides mortal man to evil. The whole forest was peopled with frightful sounds; the creaking of the trees, the howling of wild beasts, and the yell of Indians; while, sometimes, the wind tolled like a distant church bell, and sometimes gave a broad roar around the traveler, as if all Nature were laughing him to scorn. But he was himself the chief horror of the scene, and shrank not from its other horrors.

"Ha! ha! ha!" roared Goodman Brown, when the wind laughed at him. "Let us hear which will laugh loudest! Think not to frighten me with your deviltry! Come witch, come wizard, come Indian powow, come devil himself! and here comes Goodman Brown. You may as well fear him as he fear you!"

In truth, all through the haunted forest, there could be nothing more frightful than the figure of Goodman Brown. On he flew, among the black pines, brandishing his staff with frenzied gestures, now giving vent to an inspiration of horrid blasphemy, and now shouting forth such laughter, as set all the echoes of the forest laughing like demons around him. The fiend in his own shape is less hideous, than when he rages in the breast of man. Thus sped the demoniac on his course, until, quivering among the trees, he saw a red light before him, as when the felled trunks and branches of a clearing have been set on fire, and throw up their lurid blaze against the sky, at the hour of midnight. He paused, in a lull of the tempest that had driven him onward, and heard the swell of what seemed a hymn, rolling solemnly from a distance, with the weight of many voices. He knew the tune; it was a familiar one in the choir of the village meeting-house. The verse died heavily away, and was lengthened by a chorus, not of human voices, but of all the sounds of the benighted wilderness, pealing in awful harmony together. Goodman Brown cried out; and his cry was lost to his own ear, by its unison with the cry of the desert.

In the interval of silence, he stole forward, until the light glared full upon his eyes. At one extremity of an open space, hemmed in by the dark wall of the forest, arose a rock, bearing some rude, natural resemblance either to an altar or a pulpit, and surrounded by four blazing pines, their tops aflame, their stems untouched, like candles at an evening meeting. The mass of foliage, that had overgrown the summit of the rock, was all on fire, blazing high into the night, and fitfully illuminating the whole field. Each pendent twig and leafy festoon was in a blaze. As the red light arose and fell, a numerous congregation alternately shone forth, then disappeared in shadow, and again grew, as it were, out of the darkness, peopling the heart of the solitary woods at once.

"A grave and dark-clad company!" quoth Goodman Brown.

In truth, they were such. Among them, quivering to-and-fro, between gloom and splendor, appeared faces that would be seen, next day, at the council-board of the province, and others which, Sabbath after Sabbath, looked devoutly heavenward, and benignantly over the crowded pews, from the holiest pulpits in the land. Some affirm, that the lady of the governor was there. At least, there were high dames well known to her, and wives of honored husbands, and widows, a great multitude, and ancient maidens, all of excellent repute, and fair young girls, who trembled, lest their mothers should espy them. Either the sudden gleams of light, flashing over the obscure field, bedazzled Goodman Brown, or he recognized a score of the church-members of Salem village, famous for their especial sanctity. Good old Deacon Gookin had arrived, and waited at the skirts of that venerable saint, his revered pastor. But, irreverently consorting with these grave, reputable, and pious people, these elders of the church, these chaste dames and dewy virgins, there were men of dissolute lives and women of spotted fame, wretches given over to all mean and filthy vice, and suspected even of horrid crimes. It was strange to see, that the good shrank not from the wicked, nor were the sinners abashed by the saints. Scattered, also, among their pale-faced enemies, were the Indian priests, or powows, who had often scared their native forest with more hideous incantations than any known to English witchcraft.

"But, where is Faith?" thought Goodman Brown; and, as hope came into his heart, he trembled.

Another verse of the hymn arose, a slow and mournful strain, such as the pious love, but joined to words which expressed all that our nature can conceive of sin, and darkly hinted at far more. Unfathomable to mere mortals is the lore of fiends. Verse after verse was sung, and still the chorus of the desert swelled between, like the deepest tone of a mighty organ. And, with the final peal of that dreadful anthem, there came a sound, as if the roaring wind, the rushing streams, the howling beasts, and every other voice of the unconverted wilderness, were mingling and according with the voice of guilty man, in homage to the prince of all. The four blazing pines threw up a loftier flame, and obscurely discovered shapes and visages of horror on the smoke-wreaths, above the impious assembly. At the same moment, the fire on the rock shot redly forth, and formed a glowing arch above its base, where now appeared a figure. With reverence be it spoken, the figure bore no slight similitude, both in garb and manner, to some grave divine of the New England churches.

"Bring forth the converts!" cried a voice, that echoed through the field and rolled into the forest.

At the word, Goodman Brown stepped forth from the shadow of the trees, and approached the congregation, with whom he felt a loathful brotherhood, by the sympathy of all that was wicked in his heart. He could have well nigh sworn, that the shape of his own dead father beckoned him to advance, looking downward from a smoke-wreath, while a woman, with dim features of despair, threw out her hand to warn him back. Was it his mother? But he had no power to retreat one step, nor to resist, even in thought, when the minister and good old Deacon Gookin seized his arms, and led him to the blazing rock. Thither came also the slender form of a veiled female, led between Goody Cloyse, that pious teacher of the catechism, and Martha Carrier, who had received the devil's promise to be queen of hell. A rampant hag was she! And there stood the proselytes, beneath the canopy of fire.

"Welcome, my children," said the dark figure, "to the communion of your race! Ye have found, thus young, your nature and your destiny. My children, look behind you!"

They turned; and flashing forth, as it were, in a sheet of flame, the fiend-worshippers were seen; the smile of welcome gleamed darkly on every visage.

"There," resumed the sable form, "are all whom ye have reverenced from youth. Ye deemed them holier than yourselves, and shrank from your own sin, contrasting it with their lives of righteousness, and prayerful aspirations heavenward. Yet, here are they all, in my worshipping assembly! This night it shall be granted you to know their secret deeds; how hoary-bearded elders of the church have whispered wanton words to the young maids of their households; how many a woman, eager for widow's weeds, has given her husband a drink at bedtime, and let him sleep his last sleep in her bosom; how beardless youths have made haste to inherit their fathers' wealth; and how fair damsels—blush not, sweet ones!—have dug little graves in the garden, and bidden me, the sole guest, to an infant's funeral. By the sympathy of your human hearts for sin, ye shall scent out all the places—whether in church, bedchamber, street, field, or forest—where crime has been committed, and shall exult to behold the whole earth one stain of guilt, one mighty bloodspot. Far more than this! It shall be yours to penetrate, in every bosom, the deep mystery of sin, the fountain of all wicked arts, and which inexhaustibly supplies more evil impulses than human power—than my power, at its utmost!—can make manifest in deeds. And now, my children, look upon each other."

They did so; and, by the blaze of the hell-kindled torches, the wretched man beheld his Faith, and the wife her husband, trembling before that unhallowed altar.

"Lo! there ye stand, my children," said the figure, in a deep and solemn tone, almost sad, with its despairing awfulness, as if his once angelic nature could yet mourn for our miserable race. "Depending upon one another's hearts, ye had still hoped, that virtue were not all a dream. Now are ye undeceived! Evil is the nature of mankind. Evil must be your only happiness. Welcome, again, my children, to the communion of your race!"

"Welcome!" repeated the fiend-worshippers, in one cry of despair and triumph.

And there they stood, the only pair, as it seemed, who were yet hesitating on the verge of wickedness, in this dark world. A basin was hollowed, naturally, in the rock. Did it contain water, reddened by the lurid light? or was it blood? or, perchance, a liquid flame? Herein did the Shape of Evil dip his hand, and prepare to lay the mark of baptism upon their foreheads, that they might be partakers of the mystery of sin, more conscious of the secret guilt of others, both in deed and thought, than they could now be of their own. The husband cast one look at his pale wife, and Faith at him. What polluted wretches would the next glance shew them to each other, shuddering alike at what they disclosed and what they saw!

"Faith! Faith!" cried the husband. "Look up to Heaven, and resist the Wicked One!"

Whether Faith obeyed, he knew not. Hardly had he spoken, when he found himself amid calm night and solitude, listening to a roar of the wind, which died heavily away through the forest. He staggered against the rock and felt it chill and damp, while a hanging twig, that had been on fire, besprinkled his cheek with the coldest dew.

The next morning, young Goodman Brown came slowly into the street of Salem village, staring around him like a bewildered man. The good old minister was taking a walk along the graveyard, to get an appetite for breakfast and meditate his sermon, and bestowed a blessing, as he passed, on Goodman Brown. He shrank from the venerable saint, as if to avoid an anathema. Old Deacon Gookin was at domestic worship, and the holy words of his prayer were heard though the open window. "What God doth the wizard pray to?" quoth Goodman Brown. Goody Cloyse, that excellent old Christian, stood in the early sunshine, at her own lattice, catechizing a little girl, who had brought her a pint of morning's milk. Goodman Brown snatched away the child, as from the grasp of the fiend himself. Turning the corner by the meeting-house, he spied the head of Faith, with the pink ribbons, gazing anxiously forth, and bursting into such joy at sight of him, that she skipped along the street, and almost kissed her husband before the whole village. But, Goodman Brown looked sternly and sadly into her face, and passed on without a greeting.

Had Goodman Brown fallen asleep in the forest, and only dreamed a wild dream of a witch-meeting?

Be it so, if you will. But, alas! it was a dream of evil omen for young Goodman Brown. A stern, a sad, a darkly meditative, a distrustful, if not a desperate man, did he become, from the night of that fearful dream. On the Sabbath day, when the congregation were singing a holy psalm, he could not listen, because an anthem of sin rushed loudly upon his ear, and drowned all the blessed strain. When the minister spoke from the pulpit, with power and fervid eloquence, and, with his hand on the open Bible, of the sacred truths of our religion, and of saint-like lives and triumphant deaths, and of future bliss or misery unutterable, then did Goodman Brown turn pale, dreading, lest the roof should thunder down upon the gray blasphemer and his hearers. Often, awakening suddenly at midnight, he shrank from the bosom of Faith, and at morning or eventide, when the family knelt down at prayer, he scowled, and muttered to himself, and gazed sternly at his wife, and turned away. And when he had lived long, and was borne to his grave, a hoary corpse, followed by Faith, an aged woman, and children and grandchildren, a goodly procession, besides neighbors, not a few, they carved no hopeful verse upon his tombstone; for his dying hour was gloom.

1846

FLANNERY O'CONNOR

The Artificial Nigger

Mr. Head awakened to discover that the room was full of moonlight. He sat up and stared at the floor boards—the color of silver—and then at the ticking on his pillow, which might have been brocade, and after a second, he saw half of the moon five feet away in his shaving mirror, paused as if it were waiting for his permission to enter. It rolled forward and cast a dignifying light on everything. The straight chair against the wall looked stiff and attentive as if it were awaiting an order and Mr. Head's trousers, hanging to the back of it, had an almost noble air, like the garment some great man had just flung to his servant; but the face on the moon was a grave one. It gazed across the room and out the window where it floated over the horse stall and appeared to contemplate itself with the look of a young man who sees his old age before him.

Mr. Head could have said to it that age was a choice blessing and that only with years does a man enter into that calm understanding of life that makes him a suitable guide for the young. This, at least, had been his own experience.

He sat up and grasped the iron posts at the foot of his bed and raised himself until he could see the face on the alarm clock which sat on an overturned bucket beside the chair. The hour was two in the morning. The alarm on the clock did not work but he was not dependent on any mechanical means to awaken him. Sixty years had not dulled his responses; his physical reactions, like his moral ones, were guided by his will and strong character, and these could be seen plainly in his features. He had a long tube-like face with a long rounded open jaw and a long depressed nose. His eyes were alert but quiet, and in the miraculous moonlight they had a look of composure and of ancient wisdom as if they belonged to one of the great guides of men. He might have been Vergil summoned in the middle of the night to go to Dante, or better, Raphael, awakened by a blast of God's light to fly to the side of Tobias.[1] The only dark spot in the room was Nelson's pallet, underneath the shadow of the window.

1. Vergil, Publius Vergilius Maro (70–19 B.C.), author of the *Aeneid*, in *The Divine Comedy* of Dante Alighieri (1265–1321), is summoned by Beatrice (*Inferno*, II, 49–70) to assist Dante and serves as his guide through Hell and Purgatory; the angel Raphael in the Book of Tobit in the *Apocrypha* serves as Tobias's instructor and companion in the overcoming of the demon Asmodeus.

Nelson was hunched over on his side, his knees under his chin and his heels under his bottom. His new suit and hat were in the boxes that they had been sent in and these were on the floor at the foot of the pallet where he could get his hands on them as soon as he woke up. The slop jar, out of the shadow and made snow-white in the moonlight, appeared to stand guard over him like a small personal angel. Mr. Head lay back down, feeling entirely confident that he could carry out the moral mission of the coming day. He meant to be up before Nelson and to have the breakfast cooking by the time he awakened. The boy was always irked when Mr. Head was the first up. They would have to leave the house at four to get to the railroad junction by five-thirty. The train was to stop for them at five forty-five and they had to be there on time for this train was stopping merely to accommodate them.

This would be the boy's first trip to the city though he claimed it would be his second because he had been born there. Mr. Head had tried to point out to him that when he was born he didn't have the intelligence to determine his whereabouts but this had made no impression on the child at all and he continued to insist that this was to be his second trip. It would be Mr. Head's third trip. Nelson had said, "I will've already been there twict and I ain't but ten."

Mr. Head had contradicted him.

"If you ain't been there in fifteen years, how you know you'll be able to find your way about?" Nelson had asked. "How you know it hasn't changed some?"

"Have you ever," Mr. Head had asked, "seen me lost?"

Nelson certainly had not but he was a child who was never satisfied until he had given an impudent answer and he replied, "It's nowhere around here to get lost at."

"The day is going to come," Mr. Head prophesied, "when you'll find you ain't as smart as you think you are." He had been thinking about this trip for several months but it was for the most part in moral terms that he conceived it. It was to be a lesson that the boy would never forget. He was to find out from it that he had no cause for pride merely because he had been born in a city. He was to find out that the city is not a great place. Mr. Head meant him to see everything there is to see in a city so that he would be content to stay at home for the rest of his life. He fell asleep thinking how the boy would at last find out that he was not as smart as he thought he was.

He was awakened at three-thirty by the smell of fatback frying and he leaped off his cot. The pallet was empty and the clothes boxes had been thrown open. He put on his trousers and ran into the other room. The boy had a corn pone on cooking and had fried the meat. He was sitting in the half-dark at the table, drinking cold coffee out of a can. He had on his new suit and his new gray hat pulled low over his eyes. It was too big for him but they had ordered it a size large because they expected his head to grow. He didn't say anything but his entire figure suggested satisfaction at having arisen before Mr. Head.

Mr. Head went to the stove and brought the meat to the table in the skillet. "It's no hurry," he said. "You'll get there soon enough and it's no guarantee you'll like it when you do neither," and he sat down across from the boy whose hat teetered back slowly to reveal a fiercely expressionless face, very much the same shape as the old man's. They were grandfather and grandson but they looked enough alike to be brothers and brothers not too far apart in age, for Mr. Head had a youthful expression by daylight, while the boy's look was ancient, as if he knew everything already and would be pleased to forget it.

Mr. Head had once had a wife and daughter and when the wife died, the daughter ran away and returned after an interval with Nelson. Then one morning, without getting out of bed, she died and left Mr. Head with sole care of the year-old child. He had made the mistake of telling Nelson that he had been born in Atlanta. If he hadn't told him that, Nelson couldn't have insisted that this was going to be his second trip.

"You may not like it a bit," Mr. Head continued. "It'll be full of niggers."

The boy made a face as if he could handle a nigger.

"All right," Mr. Head said. "You ain't ever seen a nigger."

"You wasn't up very early," Nelson said.

"You ain't ever seen a nigger," Mr. Head repeated. "There hasn't been a nigger in this county since we run that one out twelve years ago and that was before you were born." He looked at the boy as if he were daring him to say he had ever seen a Negro.

"How you know I never saw a nigger when I lived there before?" Nelson asked. "I probably saw a lot of niggers."

"If you seen one you didn't know what he was," Mr. Head said, completely exasperated. "A six-month-old child don't know a nigger from anybody else."

"I reckon I'll know a nigger if I see one," the boy said and got up and straightened his slick sharply creased gray hat and went outside to the privy.

They reached the junction some time before the train was due to arrive and stood about two feet from the first set of tracks. Mr. Head carried a paper sack with some biscuits and a can of sardines in it for their lunch. A coarse-looking orange-colored sun coming up behind the east range of mountains was making the sky a dull red behind them, but in front of them it was still gray and they faced a gray transparent moon, hardly stronger than a thumbprint and completely without light. A small tin switch box and a black fuel tank were all there was to mark the place as a junction; the tracks were double and did not converge again until they were hidden behind the bends at either end of the clearing. Trains passing appeared to emerge from a tunnel of trees and, hit for a second by the cold sky, vanish terrified into the woods again. Mr. Head had had to make special arrangements with the ticket agent to have this train stop and he was secretly afraid it would not, in which case, he knew Nelson would say, "I never thought no train was going to stop for you." Under the useless morning moon the tracks looked white and fragile. Both the old man and the child stared ahead as if they were awaiting an apparition.

Then suddenly, before Mr. Head could make up his mind to turn back, there was a deep warning bleat and the train appeared, gliding very slowly, almost silently around the bend of trees about two hundred yards down the track, with one yellow front light shining. Mr. Head was still not certain it would stop and he felt it would make an even bigger idiot of him if it went by slowly. But he and Nelson, however, were prepared to ignore the train if it passed them.

The engine charged by, filling their noses with the smell of hot metal and then the second coach came to a stop exactly where they were standing. A conductor with the face of an ancient bloated bulldog was on the step as if he expected them, though he did not look as if it mattered one way or the other to him if they got on or not. "To the right," he said.

Their entry took only a fraction of a second and the train was already speeding on as they entered the quiet car. Most of the travelers were still sleeping, some with their heads hanging off the chair arms, some stretched across two seats, and some sprawled out with their feet in the aisle. Mr. Head saw two unoccupied seats and pushed Nelson toward them. "Get in there by the winder," he said in his normal voice which was very loud at this hour of the morning. "Nobody cares if you set there because it's nobody in it. Sit right there."

"I heard you," the boy muttered. "It's no use in you yelling," and he sat down and turned his head to the glass. There he saw a pale ghost-like face scowling at him beneath the brim of a pale ghost-like hat. His grandfather, looking quickly too, saw a different ghost, pale but grinning, under a black hat.

Mr. Head sat down and settled himself and took out his ticket and started reading aloud everything that was printed on it. People began to stir. Several woke up and stared at him. "Take off your hat," he said to Nelson and took off his own and put it on his knee. He had a small amount of white hair that had turned tobacco-colored over the years and this lay flat across the back of his head. The front of his head was bald and creased. Nelson took off his hat and put it on his knee and they waited for the conductor to come ask for their tickets.

The man across the aisle from them was spread out over two seats, his feet propped on the window and his head jutting into the aisle. He had on a light blue suit and a yellow shirt unbuttoned at the neck. His eyes had just opened and Mr. Head was ready to introduce himself when the conductor came up from behind and growled, "Tickets."

When the conductor had gone, Mr. Head gave Nelson the return half of his ticket and said, "Now put that in your pocket and don't lose it or you'll have to stay in the city."

"Maybe I will," Nelson said as if this were a reasonable suggestion.

Mr. Head ignored him. "First time this boy has ever been on a train," he explained to the man across the aisle, who was sitting up now on the edge of his seat with both feet on the floor.

Nelson jerked his hat on again and turned angrily to the window.

"He's never seen anything before," Mr. Head continued. "Ignorant as the day he was born, but I mean for him to get his fill once and for all."

The boy leaned forward, across his grandfather and toward the stranger. "I was born in the city," he said. "I was born there. This is my second trip." He said it in a high positive voice but the man across the aisle didn't look as if he understood. There were heavy purple circles under his eyes.

Mr. Head reached across the aisle and tapped him on the arm. "The thing to do with a boy," he said sagely, "is to show him all it is to show. Don't hold nothing back."

"Yeah," the man said. He gazed down at his swollen feet and lifted the left one about ten inches from the floor. After a minute he put it down and lifted the other. All through the car people began to get up and move about and yawn and stretch. Separate voices could be heard here and there and then a general hum. Suddenly Mr. Head's serene expression changed. His mouth almost closed and a light, fierce and cautious both, came into his eyes. He was looking down the length of the car. Without turning, he caught Nelson by the arm and pulled him forward. "Look," he said.

A huge coffee-colored man was coming slowly forward. He had on a light suit and a yellow satin tie with a ruby pin in it. One of his hands rested on his stomach which rode majestically under his buttoned coat, and in the other he held the head of a black walking stick that he picked up and set down with a deliberate outward motion each time he took a step. He was proceeding very slowly, his large brown eyes gazing over the heads of the passengers. He had a small white mustache and white crinkly hair. Behind him there were two young women, both coffee-colored, one in a yellow dress and one in a green. Their progress was kept at the rate of his and they chatted in low throaty voices as they followed him.

Mr. Head's grip was tightening insistently on Nelson's arm. As the procession passed them, the light from a sapphire ring on the brown hand that picked up the cane reflected in Mr. Head's eye, but he did not look up nor did the tremendous man look at him. The group proceeded up the rest of the aisle and out of the car. Mr. Head's grip on Nelson's arm loosened. "What was that?" he asked.

"A man," the boy said and gave him an indignant look as if he were tired of having his intelligence insulted.

"What kind of a man?" Mr. Head persisted, his voice expressionless.

"A fat man," Nelson said. He was beginning to feel that he had better be cautious.

"You don't know what kind?" Mr. Head said in a final tone.

"An old man," the boy said and had a sudden foreboding that he was not going to enjoy the day.

"That was a nigger," Mr. Head said and sat back.

Nelson jumped up on the seat and stood looking backward to the end of the car but the Negro had gone.

"I'd of thought you'd know a nigger since you seen so many when you was in the city on your first visit," Mr. Head continued. "That's his first nigger," he said to the man across the aisle.

The boy slid down into the seat. "You said they were black," he said in an angry voice. "You never said they were tan. How do you expect me to know anything when you don't tell me right?"

"You're just ignorant is all," Mr. Head said and he got up and moved over in the vacant seat by the man across the aisle.

Nelson turned backward again and looked where the Negro had disappeared. He felt that the Negro had deliberately walked down the aisle in order to make a fool of him and he hated him with a fierce raw fresh hate; and also, he understood now why his grandfather disliked them. He looked toward the window and the face there seemed to suggest that he might be inadequate to the day's exactions. He wondered if he would even recognize the city when they came to it.

After he had told several stories, Mr. Head realized that the man he was talking to was asleep and he got up and suggested to Nelson that they walk over the train and see the parts of it. He particularly wanted the boy to see the toilet so they went first to the men's room and examined the plumbing. Mr. Head demonstrated the ice-water cooler as if he had invented it and showed Nelson the bowl with the single spigot where the travelers brushed their teeth. They went through several cars and came to the diner.

This was the most elegant car in the train. It was painted a rich egg-yellow and had a wine-colored carpet on the floor. There were wide windows over the tables and great spaces of the rolling view were caught in miniature in the sides of the coffee pots and in the glasses. Three very black Negroes in white suits and aprons were running up and down the aisle, swinging trays and bowing and bending over the travelers eating breakfast. One of them rushed up to Mr. Head and Nelson and said, holding up two fingers, "Space for two!" but Head replied in a loud voice, "We eaten before we left!"

The waiter wore large brown spectacles that increased the size of his eye whites. "Stan' aside then please," he said with an airy wave of the arm as if he were brushing aside flies.

Neither Nelson nor Mr. Head moved a fraction of an inch. "Look," Mr. Head said.

The near corner of the diner, containing two tables, was set off from the rest by a saffron-colored curtain. One table was set but empty but at the other, facing them, his back to the drape, sat the tremendous Negro. He was speaking in a soft voice to the two women while he buttered a muffin. He had a heavy sad face and his neck bulged over his white collar on either side. "They rope them off," Mr. Head explained. Then he said, "Let's go see the kitchen," and they walked the length of the diner but the black waiter was coming fast behind them.

"Passengers are not allowed in the kitchen!" he said in a haughty voice. "Passengers are NOT allowed in the kitchen!"

Mr. Head stopped where he was and turned. "And there's good reason for that," he shouted into the Negro's chest, "because the cockroaches would run the passengers out!"

All the travelers laughed and Mr. Head and Nelson walked out, grinning. Mr. Head was known at home for his quick wit and Nelson felt a sudden keen pride in him. He realized the old man would be his only support in the strange place they were approaching. He would be entirely alone in the world if he were ever lost from his grandfather. A terrible excitement shook him and he wanted to take hold of Mr. Head's coat and hold on like a child.

As they went back to their seats they could see through the passing windows that the countryside was becoming speckled with small houses and shacks and that a highway ran alongside the train. Cars sped by on it, very small and fast. Nelson felt that there was less breath in the air than there had been thirty minutes ago. The man across the aisle had left and there was no one near for Mr. Head to hold a conversation with so he looked out the window, through his own reflection, and read aloud the names of the buildings they were passing. "The Dixie Chemical Corp!" he announced. "Southern Maid Flour! Dixie Doors! Southern Belle Cotton Products! Patty's Peanut Butter! Southern Mammy Cane Syrup!"

"Hush up!" Nelson hissed.

All over the car people were beginning to get up and take their luggage off the overhead racks. Women were putting on their coats and hats. The conductor stuck his head in the car and snarled, "Firstopppppmry,"[2] and Nelson lunged out of his sitting position, trembling. Mr. Head pushed him down by the shoulder.

"Keep your seat," he said in dignified tones. "The first stop is on the edge of town. The second stop is at the main railroad station." He had come by this knowledge on his first trip when he had got off at the first stop and had had to pay a man fifteen cents to take him into the heart of town. Nelson sat back down, very pale. For the first time in his life, he understood that his grandfather was indispensable to him.

The train stopped and let off a few passengers and glided on as if it had never ceased moving. Outside, behind rows of brown rickety houses, a line of blue buildings stood up, and beyond them a pale rose-gray sky faded away to nothing. The train moved into the railroad yard. Looking down, Nelson saw lines and lines of silver tracks multiplying and criss-crossing. Then before he could start counting them, the face in the window stared out at him, gray but distinct, and he looked the other way. The train was in the station. Both he and Mr. Head jumped up and ran to the door. Neither noticed that they had left the paper sack with the lunch in it on the seat.

They walked stiffly through the small station and came out of a heavy door into the squall of traffic. Crowds were hurrying to work. Nelson didn't know where to look. Mr. Head leaned against the side of the building and glared in front of him.

Finally Nelson said, "Well, how do you see what all it is to see?"

Mr. Head didn't answer. Then as if the sight of people passing had given him the clue, he said, "You walk," and started off down the street. Nelson followed, steadying his hat. So many sights and sounds were flooding in on him that for the first block he hardly knew what he was seeing. At the second corner, Mr. Head turned and looked behind him at the station they had left, a putty-colored terminal with a concrete dome on top. He thought that if he could keep the dome always in sight, he would be able to get back in the afternoon to catch the train again.

As they walked along, Nelson began to distinguish details and take note of the store windows, jammed with every kind of equipment—hardware, drygoods, chicken feed, liquor. They passed one that Mr. Head called his particular attention to where you walked in and sat on a chair with your feet upon two rests and let a Negro polish your shoes. They walked slowly and stopped and stood at the entrances so he could see what went on in each place but they did not go into any of them. Mr. Head was determined not to go into any city store because

2. "First stop, Emory," station in suburban Atlanta.

on his first trip here, he had got lost in a large one and had found his way out only after many people had insulted him.

They came in the middle of the next block to a store that had a weighing machine in front of it and they both in turn stepped up on it and put in a penny and received a ticket. Mr. Head's ticket said, "You weigh 120 pounds. You are upright and brave and all your friends admire you." He put the ticket in his pocket, surprised that the machine should have got his character correct but his weight wrong, for he had weighed on a grain scale not long before and knew he weighed 110. Nelson's ticket said, "You weigh 98 pounds. You have a great destiny ahead of you but beware of dark women." Nelson did not know any women and he weighed only 68 pounds but Mr. Head pointed out that the machine had probably printed the number upsidedown, meaning the 9 for a 6.

They walked on and at the end of five blocks the dome of the terminal sank out of sight and Mr. Head turned to the left. Nelson could have stood in front of every store window for an hour if there had not been another more interesting one next to it. Suddenly he said, "I was born here!" Mr. Head turned and looked at him with horror. There was a sweaty brightness about his face. "This is where I come from!" he said.

Mr. Head was appalled. He saw the moment had come for drastic action. "Lemme show you one thing you ain't seen yet," he said and took him to the corner where there was a sewer entrance. "Squat down," he said, "and stick you head in there," and he held the back of the boy's coat while he got down and put his head in the sewer. He drew it back quickly, hearing a gurgling in the depths under the sidewalk. Then Mr. Head explained the sewer system, how the entire city was underlined with it, how it contained all the drainage and was full of rats and how a man could slide into it and be sucked along down endless pitchblack tunnels. At any minute any man in the city might be sucked into the sewer and never heard from again. He described it so well that Nelson was for some seconds shaken. He connected the sewer passages with the entrance to hell and understood for the first time how the world was put together in its lower parts. He drew away from the curb.

Then he said, "Yes, but you can stay away from the holes," and his face took on that stubborn look that was so exasperating to his grandfather. "This is where I come from!" he said.

Mr. Head was dismayed but he only muttered, "You'll get your fill," and they walked on. At the end of two more blocks he turned to the left, feeling that he was circling the dome; and he was correct for in a half-hour they passed in front of the railroad station again. At first Nelson did not notice that he was seeing the same stores twice but when they passed the one where you put your feet on the rests while the Negro polished your shoes, he perceived that they were walking in a circle.

"We done been here!" he shouted. "I don't believe you know where you're at!"

"The direction just slipped my mind for a minute," Mr. Head said and they turned down a different street. He still did not intend to let the dome get too far away and after two blocks in their new direction, he turned to the left. This street contained two- and three-story wooden dwellings. Anyone passing on the sidewalk could see into the rooms and Mr. Head, glancing through one window, saw a woman lying on an iron bed, looking out, with a sheet pulled over her. Her knowing expression shook him. A fierce-looking boy on a bicycle came driving down out of nowhere and he had to jump to the side to keep from being hit. "It's nothing to them if they knock you down," he said. "You better keep closer to me."

They walked on for some time on streets like this before he remembered to turn again. The houses they were passing now were all unpainted and the wood in them looked rotten; the street between was narrower. Nelson saw a colored man. Then another. Then another. "Niggers live in these houses," he observed.

"Well come on and we'll go somewhere else," Mr. Head said. "We didn't come to look at niggers," and they turned down another street but they continued to see Negroes everywhere. Nelson's skin began to prickle and they stepped along at a faster pace in order to leave the neighborhood as soon as possible. There were colored men in their undershirts standing in the doors and colored women rocking on the sagging porches. Colored children played in the gutters and stopped what they were doing to look at them. Before long they began to pass rows of stores with colored customers in them but they didn't pause at the entrances of these. Black eyes in black faces were watching them from every direction. "Yes," Mr. Head said, "this is where you were born—right here with all these niggers."

Nelson scowled. "I think you done got us lost," he said.

Mr. Head swung around sharply and looked for the dome. It was nowhere in sight. "I ain't got us lost either," he said. "You're just tired of walking."

"I ain't tired, I'm hungry," Nelson said. "Give me a biscuit."

They discovered then that they had lost the lunch.

"You were the one holding the sack," Nelson said. "I would have kepaholt of it."

"If you want to direct this trip, I'll go on by myself and leave you right here," Mr. Head said and was pleased to see the boy turn white. However, he realized they were lost and drifting farther every minute from the station. He was hungry himself and beginning to be thirsty and since they had been in the colored neighborhood, they had both begun to sweat. Nelson had on his shoes and he was unaccustomed to them. The concrete sidewalks were very hard. They both wanted to find a place to sit down but this was impossible and they kept on walking, the boy muttering under his breath, "First you lost the sack and then you lost the way," and Mr. Head growling from time to time, "Anybody wants to be from this nigger heaven can be from it!"

By now the sun was well forward in the sky. The odor of dinners cooking drifted out to them. The Negroes were all at their doors to see them pass. "Whyn't you ast one of these niggers the way?" Nelson said. "You got us lost."

"This is where you were born," Mr. Head said. "You can ast one yourself if you want to."

Nelson was afraid of the colored men and he didn't want to be laughed at by the colored children. Up ahead he saw a large colored woman leaning in a doorway that opened onto the sidewalk. Her hair stood straight out from her head for about four inches all around and she was resting on bare brown feet that turned pink at the sides. She had on a pink dress that showed her exact shape. As they came abreast of her, she lazily lifted one hand to her head and her fingers disappeared into her hair.

Nelson stopped. He felt his breath drawn up by the woman's dark eyes. "How do you get back to town?" he said in a voice that did not sound like his own.

After a minute she said, "You in town now," in a rich low tone that made Nelson feel as if a cool spray had been turned on him.

"How do you get back to the train?" he said in the same reed-like voice.

"You can catch you a car," she said.

He understood she was making fun of him but he was too paralyzed even to scowl. He stood drinking in every detail of her. His eyes traveled up from her great knees to her forehead and then made a triangular path from the glistening sweat on her neck down and across her tremendous bosom and over her bare arm back to where her fingers lay hidden in her hair. He suddenly wanted her to reach down and pick him up and draw him against her and then he wanted to feel her breath on his face. He wanted to look down and down into her eyes while she held him tighter and tighter. He had never had such a feeling before. He felt as if he were reeling down through a pitchblack tunnel.

"You can go a block down yonder and catch you a car take you to the railroad station, Sugarpie," she said.

Nelson would have collapsed at her feet if Mr. Head had not pulled him roughly away. "You act like you don't have any sense!" the old man growled.

They hurried down the street and Nelson did not look back at the woman. He pushed his hat sharply forward over his face which was already burning with shame. The sneering ghost he had seen in the train window and all the foreboding feelings he had on the way returned to him and he remembered that his ticket from the scale had said to beware of dark women and that his grandfather's had said he was upright and brave. He took hold of the old man's hand, a sign of dependence that he seldom showed.

They headed down the street toward the car tracks where a long yellow rattling trolley was coming. Mr. Head had never boarded a streetcar and he let that one pass. Nelson was silent. From time to time his mouth trembled slightly but his grandfather, occupied with his own problems, paid him no attention. They stood on the corner and neither looked at the Negroes who were passing, going about their business just as if they had been white, except that most of them stopped and eyed Mr. Head and Nelson. It occurred to Mr. Head that since the streetcar ran on tracks, they could simply follow the tracks. He gave Nelson a slight push and explained that they would follow the tracks on into the railroad station, walking, and they set off.

Presently to their great relief they began to see white people again and Nelson sat down on the sidewalk against the wall of a building. "I got to rest myself some," he said. "You lost the sack and the direction. You can just wait on me to rest myself."

"There's the tracks in front of us," Mr. Head said. "All we got to do is keep them in sight and you could have remembered the sack as good as me. This is where you were born. This is your old home town. This is your second trip. You ought to know how to do," and he squatted down and continued in this vein but the boy, easing his burning feet out of his shoes, did not answer.

"And standing there grinning like a chim-pan-zee while a nigger woman gives you directions. Great Gawd!" Mr. Head said.

"I never said I was nothing but born here," the boy said in a shaky voice. "I never said I would or wouldn't like it. I never said I wanted to come. I only said I was born here and I never had nothing to do with that. I want to go home. I never wanted to come in the first place. It was all your big idea. How you know you ain't following the tracks in the wrong direction?"

This last had occurred to Mr. Head too. "All these people are white," he said.

"We ain't passed here before," Nelson said. This was a neighborhood of brick buildings that might have been lived in or might not. A few empty automobiles were parked along the curb and there was an occasional passer-by. The heat of the pavement came up through Nelson's thin suit. His eyelids began to droop, and after a few minutes his head tilted forward. His shoulders twitched once or twice and then he fell over on his side and lay sprawled in an exhausted fit of sleep.

Mr. Head watched him silently. He was very tired himself but they could not both sleep at the same time and he could not have slept anyway because he did not know where he was. In a few minutes Nelson would wake up, refreshed by his sleep and very cocky, and would begin complaining that he had lost the sack and the way. You'd have a mighty sorry time if I wasn't here, Mr. Head thought; and then another idea occurred to him. He looked at the sprawled figure for several minutes; presently he stood up. He justified what he was going to do on the grounds that it is sometimes necessary to teach a child a lesson he won't forget, particularly when the child is always reasserting his position with some new impudence. He walked without a sound to the corner about twenty feet away and sat down on a covered garbage can in the alley where he could look out and watch Nelson wake up alone.

The boy was dozing fitfully, half conscious of vague noises and black forms moving up from some dark part of him into the light. His face worked in his sleep and he had pulled his knees up under his chin. The sun shed a dull dry light on the narrow street; everything looked like exactly what it was. After a while Mr. Head, hunched like an old monkey on the garbage can lid, decided that if Nelson didn't wake up soon, he would make a loud noise by bamming his foot against the can. He looked at his watch and discovered that it was two o'clock. Their train left at six and the possibility of missing it was too awful for him to think of. He kicked his foot backwards on the can and a hollow boom reverberated in the alley.

Nelson shot up onto his feet with a shout. He looked where his grandfather should have been and stared. He seemed to whirl several times and then, picking up his feet and throwing his head back, he dashed down the street like a wild maddened pony. Mr. Head jumped off the can and galloped after but the child was almost out of sight. He saw a streak of gray disappearing diagonally a block ahead. He ran as fast as he could, looking both ways down every intersection, but without sight of him again. Then as he passed the third intersection completely winded, he saw about half a block down the street a scene that stopped him altogether. He crouched behind a trash box to watch and get his bearings.

Nelson was sitting with both legs spread out and by his side lay an elderly woman, screaming. Groceries were scattered about the sidewalk. A crowd of women had already gathered to see justice done and Mr. Head distinctly heard the old woman on the pavement shout, "You've broken my ankle and your daddy'll pay for it! Every nickel! Police! Police!" Several of the women were plucking at Nelson's shoulder but the boy seemed too dazed to get up.

Something forced Mr. Head from behind the trash box and forward, but only at a creeping pace. He had never in his life been accosted by a policeman. The women were milling around Nelson as if they might suddenly all dive on him at once and tear him to pieces, and the old woman continued to scream that her ankle was broken and to call for an officer. Mr. Head came on so slowly that he could have been taking a backward step after each forward one, but when he was about ten feet away, Nelson saw him and sprang. The child caught him around the hips and clung panting against him.

The women all turned on Mr. Head. The injured one sat up and shouted, "You sir! You'll pay every penny of my doctor's bill that your boy has caused. He's a juve-nile delinquent! Where is an officer? Somebody take this man's name and address!"

Mr. Head was trying to detach Nelson's fingers from the flesh in the back of his legs. The old man's head had lowered itself into his collar like a turtle; his eyes were glazed with fear and caution.

"Your boy has broken my ankle!" the old woman shouted. "Police!"

Mr. Head sensed the approach of the policeman from behind. He stared straight ahead at the women who were massed in their fury like a solid wall to block his escape. "This is not my boy," he said. "I never seen him before."

He felt Nelson's fingers fall out of his flesh.

The women dropped back, staring at him with horror, as if they were so repulsed by a man who could deny his own image and likeness that they could not bear to lay hands on him. Mr. Head walked on, through a space they silently cleared, and left Nelson behind. Ahead of him he saw nothing but a hollow tunnel that had once been the street.

The boy remained standing where he was, his neck craned forward and his hands hanging by his sides. His hat was jammed on his head so that there were no longer any creases in it. The injured woman got up and shook her fist at him and the others gave him pitying looks, but he didn't notice any of them. There was no policeman in sight.

In a minute he began to move mechanically, making no effort to catch up with his grandfather but merely following at about twenty paces. They walked on for five blocks in this way. Mr. Head's shoulders were sagging and his neck hung forward at such an angle that it was not visible from behind. He was afraid to turn his head. Finally he cut a short hopeful glance over his shoulder. Twenty feet behind him, he saw two small eyes piercing into his back like pitchfork prongs.

The boy was not of a forgiving nature but this was the first time he had ever had anything to forgive. Mr. Head had never disgraced himself before. After two more blocks, he turned and called over his shoulder in a high desperately gay voice, "Let's us go get a Co' Cola somewheres!"

Nelson, with a dignity he had never shown before, turned and stood with his back to his grandfather.

Mr. Head began to feel the depth of his denial. His face as they walked on became all hollows and bare ridges. He saw nothing they were passing but he perceived that they had lost the car tracks. There was no dome to be seen anywhere and the afternoon was advancing. He knew that if dark overtook them in the city, they would be beaten and robbed. The speed of God's justice was only what he expected for himself, but he could not stand to think that his sins would be visited upon Nelson and that even now, he was leading the boy to his doom.

They continued to walk on block after block through an endless section of small brick houses until Mr. Head almost fell over a water spigot sticking up about six inches off the edge of a grass plot. He had not had a drink of water since early morning but he felt he did not deserve it now. Then he thought that Nelson would be thirsty and they would both drink and be brought together. He squatted down and put his mouth to the nozzle and turned a cold stream of water into his throat. Then he called out in the high desperate voice, "Come on and getcher some water!"

This time the child stared through him for nearly sixty seconds. Mr. Head got up and walked on as if he had drunk poison. Nelson, though he had not had water since some he had drunk out of a paper cup on the train, passed by the spigot, disdaining to drink where his grandfather had. When Mr. Head realized this, he lost all hope. His face in the waning afternoon light looked ravaged and abandoned. He could feel the boy's steady hate, traveling at an even pace behind him and he knew that (if by some miracle they escaped being murdered in the city) it would continue just that way for the rest of his life. He knew that now he was wandering into a black strange place where nothing was like it had even been before, a long old age without respect and an end that would be welcome because it would be the end.

As for Nelson, his mind had frozen around his grandfather's treachery as if he were trying to preserve it intact to present at the final judgment. He walked without looking to one side or the other, but every now and then his mouth would twitch and this was when he felt, from some remote place inside himself, a black mysterious form reach up as if it would melt his frozen vision in one hot grasp.

The sun dropped down behind a row of houses and hardly noticing, they passed into an elegant suburban section where mansions were set back from the road by lawns with birdbaths on them. Here everything was entirely deserted. For blocks they didn't pass even a dog. The big white houses were like partially submerged icebergs in the distance. There were no sidewalks, only drives and these wound around and around in endless ridiculous circles. Nelson made no move to come nearer to Mr. Head. The old man felt that if he saw a sewer entrance he would drop down into it and let himself be carried away; and he could imagine the boy standing by, watching with only a slight interest, while he disappeared.

A loud bark jarred him to attention and he looked up to see a fat man approaching with two bulldogs. He waved both arms like someone shipwrecked on a desert island. "I'm lost!" he called. "I'm lost and can't find my way and me and this boy have got to catch this train and I can't find the station. Oh Gawd I'm lost! Oh hep me Gawd I'm lost!"

The man, who was bald-headed and had on golf knickers, asked him what train he was trying to catch and Mr. Head began to get out his tickets, trembling so violently he could hardly hold them. Nelson had come up to within fifteen feet and stood watching.

"Well," the fat man said, giving him back the tickets, "you won't have time to get back to town to make this but you can catch it at the suburb stop. That's three blocks from here," and he began explaining how to get there.

Mr. Head stared as if he were slowly returning from the dead and when the man had finished and gone off with the dogs jumping at his heels, he turned to Nelson and said breathlessly, "We're going to get home!"

The child was standing about ten feet away, his face bloodless under the gray hat. His eyes were triumphantly cold. There was no light in them, no feeling, no interest. He was merely there, a small figure, waiting. Home was nothing to him.

Mr. Head turned slowly. He felt he knew now what time would be like without seasons and what heat would be like without light and what man would be like without salvation. He didn't care if he never made the train and if it had not been for what suddenly caught his attention, like a cry out of the gathering dusk, he might have forgotten there was a station to go to.

He had not walked five hundred yards down the road when he saw, within reach of him, the plaster figure of a Negro sitting bent over on a low yellow brick fence that curved around a wide lawn. The Negro was about Nelson's size and he was pitched forward at an unsteady angle because the putty that held him to the wall had cracked. One of his eyes was entirely white and he held a piece of brown watermelon.

Mr. Head stood looking at him silently until Nelson stopped at a little distance. Then as the two of them stood there, Mr. Head breathed, "An artificial nigger!"

It was not possible to tell if the artificial Negro were meant to be young or old; he looked too miserable to be either. He was meant to look happy because his mouth was stretched up at the corners but the chipped eye and the angle he was cocked at gave him a wild look of misery instead.

"An artificial nigger!" Nelson repeated in Mr. Head's exact tone.

The two of them stood there with their necks forward at almost the same angle and their shoulders curved in almost exactly the same way and their hands trembling identically in their pockets. Mr. Head looked like an ancient child and Nelson like a miniature old man. They stood gazing at the artificial Negro as if they were faced with some great mystery, some monument to another's victory that brought them together in their common defeat. They could both feel it dissolving their differences like an action of mercy. Mr. Head had never known before what mercy felt like because he had been too good to deserve any, but he felt he knew now. He looked at Nelson and understood that he must say something to the child to show that he was still wise and in the look the boy returned he saw a hungry need for that assurance. Nelson's eyes seemed to implore him to explain once and for all the mystery of existence.

Mr. Head opened his lips to make a lofty statement and heard himself say, "They ain't got enough real ones here. They got to have an artificial one."

After a second, the boy nodded with a strange shivering about his mouth, and said, "Let's go home before we get ourselves lost again."

Their train glided into the suburb stop just as they reached the station and they boarded it together, and ten minutes before it was due to arrive at the junction, they went to the door and stood ready to jump off if it did not stop; but it did, just as the moon, restored to its full splendor, sprang from a cloud and flooded the clearing with light. As they stepped off, the sage grass was shivering gently in shades of silver and the clinkers under their feet glittered with a fresh black light. The treetops, fencing the junction like the protecting walls of a garden, were darker than the sky which was hung with gigantic white clouds illuminated like lanterns.

Mr. Head stood very still and felt the action of mercy touch him again but this time he knew that there were no words in the world that could name it. He understood that it grew out of agony, which is not denied to any man and which is given in strange ways to children. He understood it was all a man could carry into death to give his Maker and he suddenly burned with shame that he had so little of it to take with him. He stood appalled, judging himself with the thoroughness of God, while the action of mercy covered his pride like a flame and consumed it. He had never thought himself a great sinner before but he saw now that his true depravity had been hidden from him lest it cause him despair. He realized that he was forgiven for sins from the beginning of time, when he had conceived in his own heart the sin of Adam, until the present, when he had denied poor Nelson. He saw that no sin was too monstrous for him to claim as his own, and since God loved in proportion as He forgave, he felt ready at that instant to enter Paradise.

Nelson, composing his expression under the shadow of his hat brim, watched him with a mixture of fatigue and suspicion, but as the train glided past them and disappeared like a frightened serpent into the woods, even his face lightened and he muttered, "I'm glad I've went once, but I'll never go back again!"

1955

5 THEME

If you ask what a story is "about," an author is likely to answer by telling you the **subject.** Indeed, many authors tell you the subject in their titles: *An Occurrence at Owl Creek Bridge, The Lottery, Our Friend Judith, Her First Ball.* Though a subject is always concrete, it may be stated at somewhat greater length than the few words of a title: "a man's thoughts as he faces execution for spying during the Civil War" (*Owl Creek Bridge*); "a young girl's excitement at her first grown-up dance and an incident that temporarily depresses her" (*Her First Ball*).

A friend might be more likely to tell you what a story is about by giving you a summary of the action: "This guy shoots a lion but is too chicken to go in and put it out of its misery, so his wife . . ." (We sometimes call this a **plot summary,** but you will notice that this summary is of the history—that's the way people usually tell us about a story—while the plot is an arrangement or structuring of that history; in *Macomber,* remember, the lion incident is not told to us first, though it did happen first.)

Your teacher may well tell you what a story is about by summarizing its **theme.** Some refer to the central idea, the thesis, or even the message of a story, and that is roughly what we mean by theme: a generalization or abstraction from the story.

The subject of *Young Goodman Brown* may be said to be a coven (witches' meeting), or, more fully, "a young colonial New England husband is driven mad by finding everyone he thought good and pure attending a witches' meeting." The theme may be "everyone partakes of evil," or, more succinctly, "the Fall." The theme of *The Artificial Nigger* similarly may be said to be redemption. There are, as you can see, degrees of generalization and abstraction; subject (a young man finds that everyone is evil) shades off into theme, which itself can be more or less general and abstract.

Discussions of literature in or out of class sometimes seem to suggest that stories exist for their themes, that we read only to get the "point" or message. But most themes, you must admit, are somewhat less than earth-shattering. That all men (and women) are evil may be debatable, but it certainly isn't news. That living beings, human and otherwise, should not be divided into exploiters (hunters) and exploited (hunted)—the apparent theme of *The Most Dangerous Game*—is, if acceptable, pretty obvious, something we don't need to read fifteen pages of fiction to find out. No wonder, then, that some of our more skeptical friends contend that stories are only elaborate ways of "saying something simple"; that literature is a game in which authors hide their meanings under shells of words.

Of course, reading fifteen pages of a story like *The Most Dangerous Game* can be fun. Could it be that we really read fiction for the fun, and all our talk about themes is just hiding from our puritan natures the fact that we are goofing off, pretending there's some high moral purpose in it all ("football builds character")?

I don't believe that articulating the theme of a story is either the purpose of, or the excuse for, reading fiction, or that authors hide their meanings like Easter eggs. In order to relate his or her unique vision of reality to an absent and unknown reader, a writer must find a way of communicating, some common ground on which he or she can meet the various unique individuals who will read the story. Common experiences, common assumptions, common language, and commonplaces offer such ground. Readers reach out from their own subjective worlds toward that new and different vision of the author with the help of the common elements (the general), and especially through the commonplaces of theme, bringing back the particulars and generalizations of the story to their own reading and living experience. The reader sees a spoiled Easterner on safari in Africa overcome his cowardice in an attempt to put a dangerous animal out of its misery. Generalizing, the reader may conclude that what the story says (its theme) is that life (or happy life) is more than survival, that honor is more important than existence, and that when one's values change one's behavior can be changed. Not planning to go on safari in the very near future, the reader may test out the experience of the story by translating it through its theme to his or her own experience: does this mean that I can change long-standing patterns of behavior that I know are wrong? Do I have any ideals I believe greater than life itself?

We should not confuse these questions with the story, but the significance of any story is modified to some extent by the reader's experience of books and life. (If this suggests that only a reader who had read and experienced everything and understood it all perfectly could read a story perfectly, it is not unintentional.) This does not imply that you are to reduce every story to the dimensions of what you already know and feel, but rather that you reach out to the story and bring it back to your own experience as an addition and modification. If you're going to make a story yours, and if you are going to make it more than a yarn about a guy who drinks a lot, has an unfaithful wife, and hunts lions and water buffalos, you will translate it somehow into terms that, while not necessarily psychological or moral precepts, alter or broaden to some degree your own vision of yourself, others, life in general.

When I discussed symbols, I said that even while a symbol suggests a meaning beyond the particulars of the fiction, it remains a detail in the fictional world—the snakelike staff of the stranger in *Young Goodman Brown* remains a staff, the "artificial nigger" remains a statue. Some critics would say that this is true also of theme and that theme is related to the history as integrally as symbolic meaning is to detail; that is, rather than *Young Goodman Brown* telling us something we did not know before, or making hard truths palatable, its theme and its history modify each other. The theme as I've stated it relates to spiritual evil, the kind of evil suggested by the snake and Satan figures. There are other things in the story that seem to suggest the theme has to do with moral evil (specifically, sexuality) in addition to or as part of spiritual evil: the fact that Brown is a newlywed, that Faith wears pink (coquettish?) ribbons, and that she, whom Brown thought so pure and innocent, shows up at the meeting of witches and sinners. So any paraphrase of the theme needs to take both kinds of evil into account, and perhaps even to indicate what the story implies about the relationship between sex and virtue. A statement that can do justice to all the complexity and all the particulars of the story is not likely to take the simple form of a message. Indeed, it is the complex particularity of literature, its ultimate irreducibility, that makes critics and teachers reject *message* (which suggests a simple packaged statement) as a suitable term even for the paraphrasable thematic content of a story.

Young Goodman Brown is an allegorical story whose details do function as symbols with paraphrasable meanings, yet even its theme refuses to be reduced to a simple statement. How much more resistant, then, are more realistic stories that are not allegorical and whose details do not function as allegorical symbols. *Her First Ball* is a short, rather simple story that seems to have a simple theme overtly enunciated by one of the characters: Leila's elderly partner suggests that her first ball is "only the beginning of her last ball." That youth and life itself are fleeting (scarcely a new truth, but one that we must be reminded of from time to time, no doubt) would seem to be the simple theme of this story. But the scene with the elderly partner is not the end of the story. Leila goes on to dance with a young partner, doesn't recognize her former partner, has fun, and seems to have completely forgotten the man's "message." What is the story "saying"? Is her forgetting "bad" or "sad," or "good"? Does the theme suggest the thoughtlessness of youth, the incommunicability of experience, trapping us in inescapable patterns, dooming us to repeat the experiences of our predecessors? Or is it better for Leila to live while she's young, to make the most of life, rather than dwelling on life's brevity? The specifics of the story modify and enrich all the generalizations we can abstract from it, while these themes and questions, if we recognize them, modify and enrich our reading, our experience of the story.

I realize I have been talking as if a theme or themes spring out at the reader, while to some of you my inference of themes may seem more like pulling rabbits out of hats. But if you have been watching carefully you will have caught my left hand prestidigitating. You will have noticed, for example, that I derived the theme of theological evil in *Young Goodman Brown* from the symbols (the snake-staff, Satan figure, names) and that physical details like pink ribbons and the narrative situation (the three-month marriage) which had sexual implications were tested against the theme to see if I would have to modify my paraphrase. In *Her First Ball* a character raises a general issue that is tested by subsequent events in the story and modified by them. In *The Most Dangerous Game* the opening conversation raises thematic issues (the morality of hunting) that are dramatically reinforced by the subsequent action of the story (Rainsford now the hunted rather than hunter). In *The Lady with the Dog* you will see Gurov conjecturing or generalizing to himself—once by the sea, for example, when the sea's indifference to life and death seems, paradoxically, to suggest that life or the life force goes on in a "never-ceasing movement toward perfection," and later when he concludes that everyone's life, like his own, really goes on in secret and "revolves around mystery." We must try somehow to bring these two overt generalizations into some kind of accord, some vision that includes them both. We must decide whether the events in the story confirm Gurov's view, whether we can trust him, or whether, like Leila's partner, he speaks seeming truth that needs serious modification.

There are, of course, other means by which details suggest generalizations or meaning or by which meaning may be abstracted from detail. You no doubt noticed in the first footnote to *The Artificial Nigger* there are two **allusions**, references outside the story (in this case to literature and the Bible, but allusions can encompass history or other areas common to the culture). They have to do with someone guiding someone else through a realm of spirits or the underworld. In the story, the grandfather sets out to guide Nelson through Atlanta, and at one point he has Nelson stick his head into a sewer, telling him that at any time "a man could slide into it and be sucked along down endless pitchblack tunnels." Nelson quite naturally "connected the sewer passages with the entrance to hell." The descent to hell is a common narrative pattern, a common element in cross-cultural myths: an **archetype.** So allusion and archetype as well as symbols and plot, narrative voice, and character are elements that contribute to and must be accounted for in paraphrasing a theme. That is why theme is important, and why it comes last in a discussion of the elements of fiction.

But remember, the theme is an inadequate abstraction from the story; the story and its details do not disappear or lose significance once distilled into theme, nor could you reconstruct a story merely from its paraphrased theme. Indeed, theme and story, history and structure, do not so much interact, are not so much interrelated, as they are fused, inseparable.

How would you paraphrase the theme of *Lady with the Dog*? On the one hand, your definition of the theme will depend on what you think of Gurov and Anna: are they having a rather commonplace affair out of boredom and desperation and deceiving themselves into believing it's some sort of grand passion and ideal love, or is their vision of their relationship, no matter how difficult that relationship is, the true one? On the other hand, your view of their relationship depends on your apprehension and acceptance of the theme; your guess about their future and your evaluation of their love may well depend on whether you believe there is a benign force or current underneath the surface of life that moves irresistibly toward something we can call "the good." The story defines and evaluates the theme, the theme interprets the details and evaluates them. That's what I meant when I said that history and structure, story and theme interact.

A story is a compound of elements, not a mixture. In a sense, though they are useful, may be necessary, and seem reasonable or even obvious, the elements of fiction—plot, focus and voice, character, symbol, and theme, as well as others we have not talked about—do not really exist. They are convenient ways for us to extricate inextricable threads from the fabric of fiction. As the Old Master, Henry James, himself said a hundred years ago:

> A novel is a living thing, all one and continuous, like any other organism, and in proportion as it lives will it be found . . . that in each of its parts there is something of each of the other parts. The critic who over the close texture of a finished work shall pretend to trace a geography of items will mark some frontiers as artificial, I fear, as any that have been known to history. . . . What is character but the determination of incident? What is incident but the illustration of character?

KATHERINE MANSFIELD

Her First Ball

Exactly when the ball began Leila would have found it hard to say. Perhaps her first real partner was the cab. It did not matter that she shared the cab with the Sheridan girls and their brother. She sat back in her own little corner of it, and the bolster on which her hand rested felt like the sleeve of an unknown young man's dress suit; and away they bowled, past waltzing lampposts and houses and fences and trees.

"Have you really never been to a ball before, Leila? But, my child, how too weird—" cried the Sheridan girls.

"Our nearest neighbor was fifteen miles," said Leila softly, gently opening and shutting her fan.

Oh, dear, how hard it was to be indifferent like the others! She tried not to smile too much; she tried not to care. But every single thing was so new and exciting . . . Meg's tuberoses, Jose's long loop of amber, Laura's little dark head, pushing above her white fur like a flower through snow. She would remember for ever. It even gave her a pang to see her cousin Laurie throw away the wisps of tissue paper he pulled from the fastenings of his new gloves. She would like to have kept those wisps as a keepsake, as a remembrance. Laurie leaned forward and put his hand on Laura's knee.

"Look here, darling," he said. "The third and the ninth as usual. Twig?"

Oh, how marvellous to have a brother! In her excitement Leila felt that if there had been time, if it hadn't been impossible, she couldn't have helped crying because she was an only child, and no brother had ever said "Twig?" to her; no sister would ever say, as Meg said to Jose that moment, "I've never known your hair go up more successfully than it has tonight!"

But, of course, there was no time. They were at the drill hall already; there were cabs in front of them and cabs behind. The road was bright on either side with moving fan-like lights, and on the pavement gay couples seemed to float through the air; little satin shoes chased each other like birds.

"Hold on to me, Leila; you'll get lost," said Laura.

"Come on, girls, let's make a dash for it," said Laurie.

Leila put two fingers on Laura's pink velvet cloak, and they were somehow lifted past the big golden lantern, carried along the passage, and pushed into the little room marked "Ladies." Here the crowd was so great there was hardly space to take off their things; the noise was deafening. Two benches on either side were stacked high with wraps. Two old women in white aprons ran up and down tossing fresh armfuls. And everybody was pressing forward trying to get at the little dressing table and mirror at the far end.

A great quivering jet of gas lighted the ladies' room. It couldn't wait; it was dancing already. When the door opened again and there came a burst of tuning from the drill hall, it leaped almost to the ceiling.

Dark girls, fair girls were patting their hair, tying ribbons again, tucking handkerchiefs down the fronts of their bodices, smoothing marble-white gloves. And because they were all laughing it seemed to Leila that they were all lovely.

"Aren't there any invisible hairpins?" cried a voice. "How most extraordinary! I can't see a single invisible hairpin."

"Powder my back, there's a darling," cried some one else.

"But I must have a needle and cotton. I've torn simply miles and miles of the frill," wailed a third.

Then, "Pass them along, pass them along!" The straw basket of programs was tossed from arm to arm. Darling little pink-and-silver programs, with pink pencils and fluffy tassels. Leila's fingers shook as she took one out of the basket. She wanted to ask someone, "Am I meant to have one too?" but she had just time to read: "Waltz 3. *Two, Two in a Canoe.* Polka 4. *Making the Feathers Fly,*" when Meg cried, "Ready, Leila?" and they pressed their way through the crush in the passage towards the big double doors of the drill hall.

Dancing had not begun yet, but the band had stopped tuning, and the noise was so great it seemed that when it did begin to play it would never be heard. Leila, pressing close to Meg, looking over Meg's shoulder, felt that even the little quivering colored flags strung across the ceiling were talking. She quite forgot to be shy; she forgot how in the middle of dressing she had sat down on the bed with one shoe off and one shoe on and begged her mother to ring up her cousins and say she couldn't go after all. And the rush of longing she had had to be sitting on the veranda of their forsaken upcountry home, listening to the baby owls crying "More pork" in the moonlight, was changed to a rush of joy so sweet that it was hard to bear alone. She clutched her fan, and, gazing at the gleaming, golden floor, the azaleas, the lanterns, the stage at one end with its red carpet and gilt chairs and the band in a corner, she thought breathlessly, "How heavenly; how simply heavenly!"

All the girls stood grouped together at one side of the doors, the men at the other, and the chaperones in dark dresses, smiling rather foolishly, walked with little careful steps over the polished floor towards the stage.

"This is my little country cousin Leila. Be nice to her. Find her partners; she's under my wing," said Meg, going up to one girl after another.

Strange faces smiled at Leila—sweetly, vaguely. Strange voices answered, "Of course, my dear." But Leila felt the girls didn't really see her. They were looking towards the men. Why didn't the men begin? What were they waiting for? There they stood, smoothing their gloves, patting their glossy hair and smiling among themselves. Then, quite suddenly, as if they had only just made up their minds that that was what they had to do, the men came gliding over the parquet. There was a joyful flutter among the girls. A tall, fair man flew up to Meg, seized her program, scribbled something; Meg passed him on to Leila. "May I have the pleasure?" He ducked and smiled. There came a dark man wearing an eyeglass, then cousin Laurie with a friend, and Laura with a little freckled fellow whose tie was crooked. Then quite an old man—fat, with a big bald patch on his head—took her program and murmured, "Let me see, let me see!" And he was a long time comparing his program, which looked black with names, with hers. It seemed to give him so much trouble that Leila was ashamed. "Oh, please don't bother," she said eagerly. But instead of replying the fat man wrote something, glanced at her again. "Do I remember this bright little face?" he said softly. "Is it known to me of yore?" At that moment the band began playing; the fat man disappeared. He was tossed away on a great wave of music that came flying over the gleaming floor, breaking the groups up into couples, scattering them, sending them spinning. . . .

Leila had learned to dance at boarding school. Every Saturday afternoon the boarders were hurried off to a little corrugated iron mission hall where Miss Eccles (of London) held her "select" classes. But the difference between that dusty-smelling hall—with calico texts on the walls, the poor terrified little woman in a brown velvet toque with rabbit's ears thumping the cold piano, Miss Eccles poking the girls' feet with her long white wand—and this was so tremendous that Leila was sure if her partner didn't come and she had to listen to that marvelous music and to watch the others sliding, gliding over the golden floor, she would die at least, or faint, or lift her arms and fly out of one of those dark windows that showed the stars.

"Ours, I think—" Some one bowed, smiled, and offered her his arm; she hadn't to die after all. Some one's hand pressed her waist, and she floated away like a flower that is tossed into a pool.

"Quite a good floor, isn't it?" drawled a faint voice close to her ear.

"I think it's most beautifully slippery," said Leila.

"Pardon!" The faint voice sounded surprised. Leila said it again. And there was a tiny pause before the voice echoed, "Oh, quite!" and she was swung round again.

He steered so beautifully. That was the great difference between dancing with girls and men, Leila decided. Girls banged into each other, and stamped on each other's feet; the girl who was gentleman always clutched you so.

The azaleas were separate flowers no longer; they were pink and white flags streaming by.

"Were you at the Bells' last week." the voice came again. It sounded tired. Leila wondered whether she ought to ask him if he would like to stop.

"No, this is my first dance," said she.

Her partner gave a little gasping laugh. "Oh, I say," he protested.

"Yes, it is really the first dance I've ever been to." Leila was most fervent. It was such a relief to be able to tell somebody. "You see, I've lived in the country all my life up until now. . . ."

At that moment the music stopped, and they went to sit on two chairs against the wall. Leila tucked her pink satin feet under and fanned herself, while she blissfully watched the other couples passing and disappearing through the swing doors.

"Enjoying yourself, Leila?" asked Jose, nodding her golden head.

Laura passed and gave her the faintest little wink; it made Leila wonder for a moment whether she was quite grown up after all. Certainly her partner did not say very much. He coughed, tucked his handkerchief away, pulled down his waistcoat, took a minute thread off his sleeve. But it didn't matter. Almost immediately the band started, and her second partner seemed to spring from the ceiling.

"Floor's not bad," said the new voice. Did one always begin with the floor? And then, "Were you at the Neaves' on Tuesday?" And again Leila explained. Perhaps it was a little strange that her partners were not more interested. For it was thrilling. Her first ball! She was only at the beginning of everything. It seemed to her that she had never known what the night was like before. Up till now it had been dark, silent, beautiful very often—oh, yes—but mournful somehow. Solemn. And now it would never be like that again—it had opened dazzling bright.

"Care for an ice?" said her partner. And they went through the swing doors, down the passage, to the supper room. Her cheeks burned, she was fearfully thirsty. How sweet the ices looked on little glass plates, and how cold the frosted spoon was, iced too! And when they came back to the hall there was the fat man waiting for her by the door. It gave her quite a shock again to see how old he was; he ought to have been on the stage with the fathers and mothers. And when Leila compared him with her other partners he looked shabby. His waistcoat was creased, there was a button off his glove, his coat looked as if it was dusty with French chalk.

'Come along, little lady," said the fat man. He scarcely troubled to clasp her, and they moved away so gently, it was more like walking than dancing. But he said not a word about the floor. "Your first dance, isn't it?" he murmured.

"How *did* you know?"

"Ah," said the fat man, "that's what it is to be old!" He wheezed faintly as he steered her past an awkward couple. "You see, I've been doing this kind of thing for the last thirty years."

"Thirty years?" cried Leila. Twelve years before she was born!

"It hardly bears thinking about, does it?" said the fat man gloomily.

Leila looked at his bald head, and she felt quite sorry for him.

"I think it's marvelous to be still going on," she said kindly.

"Kind little lady," said the fat man, and he pressed her a little closer, and hummed a bar of the waltz. "Of course," he said, "you can't hope to last anything like as long as that. No-o," said the fat man, "long before that you'll be sitting up there on the stage, looking on, in your nice black velvet. And these pretty arms will have turned into little short fat ones, and you'll beat time with such a different kind of fan—a black bony one." The fat man seemed to shudder. "And you'll smile away like the poor old dears up there, and point to your daughter, and tell the elderly lady next to you how some dreadful man tried to kiss her at the club ball. And your heart will ache, ache"—the fat man squeezed her closer still, as if he really was sorry for that poor heart—"because no one wants to kiss you now. And you'll say how unpleasant these polished floors are to walk on, how dangerous they are. Eh, Mademoiselle Twinkletoes?" said the fat man softly.

Leila gave a light little laugh, but she did not feel like laughing. Was it—could it all be true? It sounded terribly true. Was this first ball only the beginning of her last ball after all? At that the music seemed to change; it sounded sad, sad it rose upon a great sigh. Oh, how quickly things changed! Why didn't happiness last for ever? For ever wasn't a bit too long.

"I want to stop," she said in a breathless voice. The fat man led her to the door.

"No," she said, "I won't go outside. I won't sit down. I'll just stand here, thank you." She leaned against the wall, tapping with her foot, pulling up her gloves and trying to smile. But deep inside her a little girl threw her pinafore over her head and sobbed. Why had he spoiled it all?

"I say, you know," said the fat man, "you mustn't take me seriously, little lady."

"As if I should!" said Leila, tossing her small dark head and sucking her underlip. . . .

Again the couples paraded. The swing doors opened and shut. Now new music was given out by the bandmaster. But Leila didn't want to dance any more. She wanted to be home, or sitting on the veranda listening to those baby owls. When she looked through the dark windows at the stars, they had long beams like wings. . . .

But presently a soft, melting, ravishing tune began, and a young man with curly hair bowed before her. She would have to dance, out of politeness, until she could find Meg. Very stiffly she walked into the middle; very haughtily she put her hand on his sleeve. But in one minute, in one turn, her feet glided, glided. The lights, the azaleas, the dresses, the pink faces, the velvet chairs, all became one beautiful flying wheel. And when her next partner bumped her into the fat man and he said, "Par*don*," she smiled at him more radiantly than ever. She didn't even recognize him again.

1922

ANTON CHEKHOV

The Lady with the Dog

1

People were telling one another that a newcomer had been seen on the promenade—a lady with a dog. Dmitri Dmitrich Gurov had been a fortnight in Yalta, and was accustomed to its ways, and he, too, had begun to take an interest in fresh arrivals. From his seat in Vernet's outdoor café, he caught sight of a young woman in a toque, passing along the promenade; she was fair and not very tall; after her trotted a white pomeranian.

Later he encountered her in the municipal park, and in the square, several times a day. She was always alone, wearing the same toque, and the pomeranian always trotted at her side. Nobody knew who she was, and people referred to her simply as "the lady with the dog."

"If she's here without her husband, and without any friends," thought Gurov, "it wouldn't be a bad idea to make her acquaintance."

He was not yet forty, but had a twelve-year-old daughter and two schoolboy sons. He had been talked into marrying in his second year at college, and his wife now looked nearly twice as old as he was. She was a tall, black-browed woman, erect, dignified, imposing, and, as she said of herself, a "thinker." She was a great reader, omitted the "hard sign"[1] at the end of words in her letters, and called her husband "Dimitri" instead of Dmitri; and though he secretly considered her shallow, narrow-minded, and dowdy, he stood in awe of her, and disliked being at home. It was long since he had first begun deceiving her and he was now constantly unfaithful to her, and this was no doubt why he spoke slightingly of women, to whom he referred as *the lower race*.

He considered that the ample lessons he had received from bitter experience entitled him to call them whatever he liked, but without this "lower race" he could not have existed a single day. He was bored and ill-at-ease in the company of men, with whom he was always cold and reserved, but felt quite at home among women, and knew exactly what to say to them, and how to behave; he could even be silent in their company without feeling the slightest awkwardness. There was an elusive charm in his appearance and disposition which attracted women and caught their sympathies. He knew this and was himself attracted to them by some invisible force.

Repeated and bitter experience had taught him that every fresh intimacy, while at first introducing such pleasant variety into everyday life, and offering itself as a charming, light adventure, inevitably developed, among decent people (especially in Moscow, where they are so irresolute and slow to move), into a problem of excessive complication leading to an intolerably irksome situation. But every time he encountered an attractive woman he forgot all about this experience, the

1. Conventional sign that was used following consonants; to omit it was then "progressive," and it has in fact been eliminated in the reformed alphabet adopted by the Soviet government.

desire for life surged up in him, and everything suddenly seemed simple and amusing.

One evening, then, while he was dining at the restaurant in the park, the lady in the toque came strolling up and took a seat at a neighboring table. Her expression, gait, dress, coiffure, all told him that she was from the upper classes, that she was married, that she was in Yalta for the first time, alone and bored. . . . The accounts of the laxity of morals among visitors to Yalta are greatly exaggerated, and he paid no heed to them, knowing that for the most part they were invented by people who would gladly have transgressed themselves, had they known how to set about it. But when the lady sat down at a neighboring table a few yards away from him, the stories of easy conquests, of excursions to the mountains, came back to him, and the seductive idea of a brisk transitory liaison, an affair with a woman whose very name he did not know, suddenly took possession of his mind.

He snapped his fingers at the pomeranian, and when it trotted up to him, shook his forefinger at it. The pomeranian growled. Gurov shook his finger again.

The lady glanced at him and instantly lowered her eyes.

"He doesn't bite," she said, and blushed.

"May I give him a bone?" he asked, and on her nod of consent added in friendly tones: "Have you been in Yalta long?"

"About five days."

"And I am dragging out my second week here."

Neither spoke for a few minutes.

"The days pass quickly, and yet one is so bored here," she said, not looking at him.

"It's the thing to say it's boring here. People never complain of boredom in God-forsaken holes like Belyev or Zhizdra, but when they get here it's: 'Oh, the dullness! Oh, the dust!' You'd think they'd come from Granada,[2] to say the least."

She laughed. Then they both went on eating in silence, like complete strangers. But after dinner they left the restaurant together, and embarked upon the light, jesting talk of people free and contented, for whom it is all the same where they go, or what they talk about. They strolled along, remarking on the strange light over the sea. The water was a warm, tender purple, the moonlight lay on its surface in a golden strip. They said how close it was, after the hot day. Gurov told her he was from Moscow, that he was really a philologist,[3] but worked in a bank; that he had at one time trained himself to sing in a private opera company, but had given up the idea; that he owned two houses in Moscow. . . . And from her he learned that she had grown up in Petersburg, but had got married in the town of S., where she had been living two years, that she would stay another month in Yalta, and that perhaps her husband, who also needed a rest, would join her. She was quite unable to explain whether her husband was a member of the gubernia[4] council, or on the board of the Zemstvo,[5] and was greatly

2. City in southern Spain, site of the Alhambra and once capital of the Moorish kingdom.
3. In the older sense, classical scholar.
4. Czarist province.
5. In Czarist Russia an elective provincial council responsible for local government.

amused at herself for this. Further, Gurov learned that her name was Anna Sergeyevna.

Back in his own room he thought about her, and felt sure he would meet her the next day. It was inevitable. As he went to bed he reminded himself that only a very short time ago she had been a schoolgirl, like his own daughter, learning her lessons; he remembered how much there was of shyness and constraint in her laughter, in her way of conversing with a stranger—it was probably the first time in her life that she found herself alone, and in a situation in which men could follow her and watch her, and speak to her, all the time with a secret aim she could not fail to divine. He recalled her slender, delicate neck, her fine gray eyes.

"And yet there's something pathetic about her," he thought to himself as he fell asleep.

2

A week had passed since the beginning of their acquaintance. It was a holiday. Indoors it was stuffy, but the dust rose in clouds out of doors, and people's hats blew off. It was a thirsty day and Gurov kept going to the outdoor café for fruit-drinks and ices to offer Anna Sergeyevna. The heat was overpowering.

In the evening, when the wind had dropped, they walked to the pier to see the steamer come in. There were a great many people strolling about the landing-place; some, bunches of flowers in their hands, were meeting friends. Two peculiarities of the smart Yalta crowd stood out distinctly—the elderly ladies all tried to dress very young, and there seemed to be an inordinate number of generals about.

Owing to the roughness of the sea the steamer arrived late, after the sun had gone down, and it had to maneuver for some time before it could get alongside the pier. Anna Sergeyevna scanned the steamer and passengers through her lorgnette, as if looking for someone she knew, and when she turned to Gurov her eyes were glistening. She talked a great deal, firing off abrupt questions and forgetting immediately what it was she had wanted to know. Then she lost her lorgnette in the crush.

The smart crowd began dispersing, features could no longer be made out, the wind had quite dropped, and Gurov and Anna Sergeyevna stood there as if waiting for someone else to come off the steamer. Anna Sergeyevna had fallen silent, every now and then smelling her flowers, but not looking at Gurov.

"It's turned out a fine evening," he said. "What shall we do? We might go for a drive."

She made no reply.

He looked steadily at her and suddenly took her in his arms and kissed her lips, and the fragrance and dampness of the flowers closed round him, but the next moment he looked behind him in alarm—had anyone seen them?

"Let's go to your room," he murmured.

And they walked off together, very quickly.

Her room was stuffy and smelled of some scent she had bought in the Japanese shop. Gurov looked at her, thinking to himself: "How full of strange encounters life is!" He could remember carefree, good-natured women who were exhilarated by love-making and grateful to him for the happiness he gave them, however short-lived; and there had been others—his wife among them—whose caresses were insincere, affected, hysterical, mixed up with a great deal of quite unnecessary talk, and whose expression seemed to say that all this was not just love-making or passion, but something much more significant; then there had been two or three beautiful, cold women, over whose features flitted a predatory expression, betraying a determination to wring from life more than it could give, women no longer in their first youth, capricious, irrational, despotic, brainless, and when Gurov had cooled to these, their beauty aroused in him nothing but repulsion, and the lace trimming on their underclothes reminded him of fish-scales.

But here the timidity and awkwardness of youth and inexperience were still apparent; and there was a feeling of embarrassment in the atmosphere, as if someone had just knocked at the door. Anna Sergeyevna, "the lady with the dog," seemed to regard the affair as something very special, very serious, as if she had become a fallen woman, an attitude he found odd and disconcerting. Her features lengthened and drooped, and her long hair hung mournfully on either side of her face. She assumed a pose of dismal meditation, like a repentant sinner in some classical painting.

"It isn't right," she said. "You will never respect me anymore."

On the table was a watermelon. Gurov cut himself a slice from it and began slowly eating it. At least half an hour passed in silence.

Anna Sergeyevna was very touching, revealing the purity of a decent, naïve woman who had seen very little of life. The solitary candle burning on the table scarcely lit up her face, but it was obvious that her heart was heavy.

"Why should I stop respecting you?" asked Gurov. "You don't know what you're saying."

"May God forgive me!" she exclaimed, and her eyes filled with tears. "It's terrible."

"No need to seek to justify yourself."

"How can I justify myself? I'm a wicked, fallen woman, I despise myself and have not the least thought of self-justification. It isn't my husband I have deceived, it's myself. And not only now, I have been deceiving myself for ever so long. My husband is no doubt an honest, worthy man, but he's a flunkey. I don't know what it is he does at his office, but I know he's a flunkey. I was only twenty when I married him, and I was devoured by curiosity, I wanted something higher. I told myself that there must be a different kind of life. I wanted to live, to live. . . . I was burning with curiosity . . . you'll never understand that, but I swear to God I could no longer control myself, nothing could hold me back, I told my husband I was ill, and I came here. . . . And I started going about like one possessed, like a madwoman . . . and now I have become an ordinary, worthless woman, and everyone has the right to despise me."

Gurov listened to her, bored to death. The naïve accents, the remorse, all was so unexpected, so out of place. But for the tears in her eyes, she might have been jesting or play-acting.

"I don't understand," he said gently. "What is it you want?"

She hid her face against his breast and pressed closer to him.

"Do believe me, I implore you to believe me," she said. "I love all that is honest and pure in life, vice is revolting to me, I don't know what I'm doing. The common people say they are snared by the devil. And now I can say that I have been snared by the devil, too."

"Come, come," he murmured.

He gazed into her fixed, terrified eyes, kissed her, and soothed her with gentle affectionate words, and gradually she calmed down and regained her cheerfulness. Soon they were laughing together again.

When, a little later, they went out, there was not a soul on the promenade, the town and its cypresses looked dead, but the sea was still roaring as it dashed against the beach. A solitary fishing-boat tossed on the waves, its lamp blinking sleepily.

They found a droshky[6] and drove to Oreanda.

"I discovered your name in the hall, just now," said Gurov, "written up on the board. Von Diederitz. Is your husband a German?"

"No. His grandfather was, I think, but he belongs to the Orthodox church himself."

When they got out of the droshky at Oreanda they sat down on a bench not far from the church, and looked down at the sea, without talking. Yalta could be dimly discerned through the morning mist, and white clouds rested motionless on the summits of the mountains. Not a leaf stirred, the grasshoppers chirruped, and the monotonous hollow roar of the sea came up to them, speaking of peace, of the eternal sleep lying in wait for us all. The sea had roared like this long before there was any Yalta or Oreanda, it was roaring now, and it would go on roaring, just as indifferently and hollowly, when we have passed away. And it may be that in this continuity, this utter indifference to life and death, lies the secret of our ultimate salvation, of the stream of life on our planet, and of its never-ceasing movement toward perfection.

Side by side with a young woman, who looked so exquisite in the early light, soothed and enchanted by the sight of all this magical beauty—sea, mountains, clouds and the vast expanse of the sky—Gurov told himself that, when you came to think of it, everything in the world is beautiful really, everything but our own thoughts and actions, when we lose sight of the higher aims of life, and of our dignity as human beings.

Someone approached them—a watchman, probably—looked at them and went away. And there was something mysterious and beautiful even in this. The steamer from Feodosia could be seen coming toward the pier, lit up by the dawn, its lamps out.

"There's dew on the grass," said Anna Sergeyevna, breaking the silence.

"Yes. Time to go home."

They went back to the town.

After this they met every day at noon on the promenade, lunching and dining together, going for walks, and admiring the sea. She complained of sleeplessness, of palpitations, asked the same questions over and over again, alternately surrendering to jealousy and the fear that he did not really respect her. And often, when there was nobody in sight in the square or the park, he would draw her to him and kiss her

6. Horse-drawn, four-wheeled open carriage.

passionately. The utter idleness, these kisses in broad daylight, accompanied by furtive glances and the fear of discovery, the heat, the smell of the sea, and the idle, smart, well-fed people continually crossing their field of vision, seemed to have given him a new lease on life. He told Anna Sergeyevna she was beautiful and seductive, made love to her with impetuous passion, and never left her side, while she was always pensive, always trying to force from him the admission that he did not respect her, that he did not love her a bit, and considered her just an ordinary woman. Almost every night they drove out of town, to Oreanda, the waterfall, or some other beauty spot. And these excursions were invariably a success, each contributing fresh impressions of majestic beauty.

All this time they kept expecting her husband to arrive. But a letter came in which he told his wife that he was having trouble with his eyes, and implored her to come home as soon as possible. Anna Sergeyevna made hasty preparations for leaving.

"It's a good thing I'm going," she said to Gurov. "It's the intervention of fate."

She left Yalta in a carriage, and he went with her as far as the railway station. The drive took nearly a whole day. When she got into the express train, after the second bell had been rung, she said:

"Let me have one more look at you. . . . One last look. That's right."

She did not weep, but was mournful, and seemed ill, the muscles of her cheeks twitching.

"I shall think of you . . . I shall think of you all the time," she said. "God bless you! Think kindly of me. We are parting for ever, it must be so, because we ought never to have met. Good-bye—God bless you."

The train steamed rapidly out of the station, its lights soon disappearing, and a minute later even the sound it made was silenced, as if everything were conspiring to bring this sweet oblivion, this madness, to an end as quickly as possible. And Gurov, standing alone on the platform and gazing into the dark distance, listened to the shrilling of the grasshoppers and the humming of the telegraph wires, with a feeling that he had only just waked up. And he told himself that this had been just one more of the many adventures in his life, and that it, too, was over, leaving nothing but a memory. . . . He was moved and sad, and felt a slight remorse. After all, this young woman whom he would never again see had not been really happy with him. He had been friendly and affectionate with her, but in his whole behavior, in the tones of his voice, in his very caresses, there had been a shade of irony, the insulting indulgence of the fortunate male, who was, moreover, almost twice her age. She had insisted in calling him good, remarkable, high-minded. Evidently he had appeared to her different from his real self, in a word he had involuntarily deceived her. . . .

There was an autumnal feeling in the air, and the evening was chilly.

"It's time for me to be going north, too," thought Gurov, as he walked away from the platform. "High time!"

3

When he got back to Moscow it was beginning to look like winter, the stoves were heated every day, and it was still dark when the children got up to go to school and drank their tea, so that the nurse had to light the lamp for a short time. Frost had set in. When the first snow falls, and one goes for one's first sleigh-ride, it is pleasant to see the white ground, the white roofs; one breathes freely and lightly, and remembers the days of one's youth. The ancient lime-trees and birches, white with rime, have a good-natured look, they are closer to the heart than cypresses and palms, and beneath their branches one is no longer haunted by the memory of mountains and the sea.

Gurov had always lived in Moscow, and he returned to Moscow on a fine frosty day, and when he put on his fur-lined overcoat and thick gloves, and sauntered down Petrovka Street, and when, on Saturday evening, he heard the church bells ringing, his recent journey and the places he had visited lost their charm for him. He became gradually immersed in Moscow life, reading with avidity three newspapers a day, while declaring he never read Moscow newspapers on principle. Once more he was caught up in a whirl of restaurants, clubs, banquets, and celebrations, once more glowed with the flattering consciousness that well-known lawyers and actors came to his house, that he played cards in the Medical Club opposite a professor.

He had believed that in a month's time Anna Sergeyevna would be nothing but a vague memory, and that hereafter, with her wistful smile, she would only occasionally appear to him in dreams, like others before her. But the month was now well over and winter was in full swing, and all was as clear in his memory as if he had only parted with Anna Sergeyevna the day before. And his recollections grew ever more insistent. When the voices of his children at their lessons reached him in his study through the evening stillness, when he heard a song, or the sounds of a musical-box in a restaurant, when the wind howled in the chimney, it all came back to him: early morning on the pier, the misty mountains, the steamer from Feodosia, the kisses. He would pace up and down his room for a long time, smiling at his memories, and then memory turned into dreaming, and what had happened mingled in his imagination with what was going to happen. Anna Sergeyevna did not come to him in his dreams, she accompanied him everywhere, like his shadow, following him everywhere he went. When he closed his eyes, she seemed to stand before him in the flesh, still lovelier, younger, tenderer than she had really been, and looking back, he saw himself, too, as better than he had been in Yalta. In the evenings she looked out at him from the bookshelves, the fireplace, the corner; he could hear her breathing, the sweet rustle of her skirts. In the streets he followed women with his eyes, to see if there were any like her. . . .

He began to feel an overwhelming desire to share his memories with someone. But he could not speak of his love at home, and outside his home who was there for him to confide in? Not the tenants living in his house, and certainly not his colleagues at the bank. And what was there to tell? Was it love that he had felt? Had there been anything exquisite, poetic, anything instructive or even amusing about his relations with Anna Sergeyevna? He had to content himself with uttering vague generalizations about love and women, and nobody guessed what he meant, though his wife's dark eyebrows twitched as she said:

"The role of a coxcomb doesn't suit you a bit, Dimitri."

One evening, leaving the Medical Club with one of his card-partners, a government official, he could not refrain from remarking:

"If you only knew what a charming woman I met in Yalta!"

The official got into his sleigh, and just before driving off turned and called out:

"Dmítri Dmitrich!"

"Yes?"

"You were quite right, you know—the sturgeon was just a *leetle* off."

These words, in themselves so commonplace, for some reason infuriated Gurov, seemed to him humiliating, gross. What savage manners, what people! What wasted evenings, what tedious, empty days! Frantic card-playing, gluttony, drunkenness, perpetual talk always about the same thing. The greater part of one's time and energy went on business that was no use to anyone, and on discussing the same thing over and over again, and there was nothing to show for it all but a stunted, earth-bound existence and a round of trivialities, and there was nowhere to escape to, you might as well be in a madhouse or a convict settlement.

Gurov lay awake all night, raging, and went about the whole of the next day with a headache. He slept badly on the succeeding nights, too, sitting up in bed, thinking, or pacing the floor of his room. He was sick of his children, sick of the bank, felt not the slightest desire to go anywhere or talk about anything.

When the Christmas holidays came, he packed his things, telling his wife he had to go to Petersburg in the interests of a certain young man, and set off for the town of S. To what end? He hardly knew himself. He only knew that he must see Anna Sergeyevna, must speak to her, arrange a meeting, if possible.

He arrived at S. in the morning and engaged the best room in the hotel, which had a carpet of gray military frieze, and a dusty ink-pot on the table, surmounted by a headless rider, holding his hat in his raised hand. The hall porter told him what he wanted to know: von Diederitz had a house of his own in Staro-Goncharnaya Street. It wasn't far from the hotel, he lived on a grand scale, luxuriously, kept carriage-horses, the whole town knew him. The hall porter pronounced the name "Drideritz."

Gurov strolled over to Staro-Goncharnaya Street and discovered the house. In front of it was a long gray fence with inverted nails hammered into the tops of the palings.

"A fence like that is enough to make anyone want to run away," thought Gurov, looking at the windows of the house and the fence.

He reasoned that since it was a holiday, her husband would probably be at home. In any case it would be tactless to embarrass her by calling at the house. And a note might fall into the hands of the husband, and bring about catastrophe. The best thing would be to wait about on the chance of seeing her. And he walked up and down the street, hovering in the vicinity of the fence, watching for his chance. A beggar entered the gate, only to be attacked by dogs; then, an hour later, the faint, vague sounds of a piano reached his ears. That would be Anna Sergeyevna playing. Suddenly the front door opened and an old woman came out, followed by a familiar white pomeranian. Gurov tried to call to it, but his heart beat violently, and in his agitation he could not remember its name.

He walked on, hating the gray fence more and more, and now ready to tell himself irately that Anna Sergeyevna had forgotten him, had already, perhaps, found distraction in another—what could be more natural in a young woman who had to look at this accursed fence from morning to night? He went back to his hotel and sat on the sofa in his room for some time, not knowing what to do, then he ordered dinner, and after dinner, had a long sleep.

"What a foolish, restless business," he thought, waking up and looking toward the dark windowpanes. It was evening by now. "Well, I've had my sleep out. And what am I to do in the night?"

He sat up in bed, covered by the cheap gray quilt, which reminded him of a hospital blanket, and in his vexation he fell to taunting himself.

"You and your lady with a dog . . . there's adventure for you! See what you get for your pains."

On his arrival at the station that morning he had noticed a poster announcing in enormous letters the first performance at the local theater of *The Geisha.*[7] Remembering this, he got up and made for the theater.

"It's highly probable that she goes to first-nights," he told himself.

The theater was full. It was a typical provincial theater, with a mist collecting over the chandeliers, and the crowd in the gallery fidgeting noisily. In the first row of the stalls[8] the local dandies stood waiting for the curtain to go up, their hands clasped behind them. There, in the front seat of the Governor's box, sat the Governor's daughter, wearing a boa, the Governor himself hiding modestly behind the drapes, so that only his hands were visible. The curtain stirred, the orchestra took a long time tuning up their instruments. Gurov's eyes roamed eagerly over the audience as they filed in and occupied their seats.

Anna Sergeyevna came in, too. She seated herself in the third row of the stalls and when Gurov's glance fell on her, his heart seemed to stop, and he knew in a flash that the whole world contained no one nearer or dearer to him, no one more important to his happiness. This little woman, lost in the provincial crowd, in no way remarkable, holding a silly lorgnette in her hand, now filled his whole life, was his grief, his joy, all that he desired. Lulled by the sounds coming from the wretched orchestra, with its feeble, amateurish violinists, he thought how beautiful she was . . . thought and dreamed. . . .

Anna Sergeyevna was accompanied by a tall, round-shouldered young man with small whiskers, who nodded at every step before taking the seat beside her and seemed to be continually bowing to someone. This must be her husband, whom, in a fit of bitterness, at Yalta, she had called a "flunkey." And there really was something of the lackey's servility in his lanky figure, his side-whiskers, and the little bald spot on the top of his head. And he smiled sweetly, and the badge of some scientific society gleaming in his buttonhole was like the number on a footman's livery.

The husband went out to smoke in the first interval, and she was

7. Operetta by Sidney Jones (1861–1946) which toured Eastern Europe in 1898–99.

8. Seats at the front of a theater, near the stage and separated from nearby seats by a railing.

left alone in her seat. Gurov, who had taken a seat in the stalls, went up to her and said in a trembling voice, with a forced smile: "How d'you do?"

She glanced up at him and turned pale, then looked at him again in alarm, unable to believe her eyes, squeezing her fan and lorgnette in one hand, evidently struggling to overcome a feeling of faintness. Neither of them said a word. She sat there, and he stood beside her, disconcerted by her embarrassment, and not daring to sit down. The violins and flutes sang out as they were tuned, and there was a tense sensation in the atmosphere, as if they were being watched from all the boxes. At last she got up and moved rapidly toward one of the exits. He followed her and they wandered aimlessly along corridors, up and down stairs; figures flashed by in the uniforms of legal officials, high-school teachers, and civil servants, all wearing badges; ladies' coats hanging on pegs, flashed by; there was a sharp draft, bringing with it an odor of cigarette stubs. And Gurov, whose heart was beating violently, thought:

"What on earth are all these people, this orchestra for? . . ."

The next minute he suddenly remembered how, after seeing Anna Sergeyevna off that evening at the station, he had told himself that all was over, and they would never meet again. And how far away the end seemed to be now!

She stopped on a dark narrow staircase over which was a notice bearing the inscription "To the upper circle."

"How you frightened me!" she said, breathing heavily, still pale and half-stunned. "Oh, how you frightened me! I'm almost dead! Why did you come? Oh, why?"

"But, Anna," he said, in low, hasty tones. "But, Anna. . . . Try to understand . . . do try. . . ."

She cast him a glance of fear, entreaty, love, and then gazed at him steadily, as if to fix his features firmly in her memory.

"I've been so unhappy," she continued, taking no notice of his words. "I could think of nothing but you the whole time, I lived on the thoughts of you. I tried to forget—why, oh, why did you come?"

On the landing above them were two schoolboys, smoking and looking down, but Gurov did not care, and, drawing Anna Sergeyevna toward him, began kissing her face, her lips, her hands.

"What are you doing, oh, what are you doing?" she said in horror, drawing back. "We have both gone mad. Go away this very night, this moment. . . . By all that is sacred, I implore you. . . . Somebody is coming."

Someone was ascending the stairs.

"You must go away," went on Anna Sergeyevna in a whisper. "D'you hear me, Dmitri Dmitrich? I'll come to you in Moscow. I have never been happy, I am unhappy now, and I shall never be happy—never! Do not make me suffer still more! I will come to you in Moscow, I swear it! And now we must part! My dear one, my kind one, my darling, we must part."

She pressed his hand and hurried down the stairs, looking back at him continually, and her eyes showed that she was in truth unhappy. Gurov stood where he was for a short time, listening, and when all was quiet went to look for his coat, and left the theater.

4

And Anna Sergeyevna began going to Moscow to see him. Every two or three months she left the town of S., telling her husband that she was going to consult a specialist on female diseases, and her husband believed her and did not believe her. In Moscow she always stayed at the "Slavyanski Bazaar," sending a man in a red cap to Gurov the moment she arrived. Gurov went to her, and no one in Moscow knew anything about it.

One winter morning he went to see her as usual (the messenger had been to him the evening before, but had not found him at home). His daughter was with him for her school was on the way, and he thought he might as well see her to it.

"It is three degrees above zero,"[9] said Gurov to his daughter, "and yet it is snowing. You see it is only above zero close to the ground, the temperature in the upper layers of the atmosphere is quite different."

"Why doesn't it ever thunder in winter, Papa?"

He explained this, too. As he was speaking, he kept reminding himself that he was going to a rendezvous and that not a living soul knew about it, or, probably, ever would. He led a double life—one in public, in the sight of all whom it concerned, full of conventional truth and conventional deception, exactly like the lives of his friends and acquaintances, and another which flowed in secret. And, owing to some strange, possibly quite accidental chain of circumstances, everything that was important, interesting, essential, everything about which he was sincere and never deceived himself, everything that composed the kernel of his life, went on in secret, while everything that was false in him, everything that composed the husk in which he hid himself and the truth which was in him—his work at the bank, discussions at the club, his "lower race," his attendance at anniversary celebrations with his wife—was on the surface. He began to judge others by himself, no longer believing what he saw, and always assuming that the real, the only interesting life of every individual goes on as under cover of night, secretly. Every individual existence revolves around mystery, and perhaps that is the chief reason that all cultivated individuals insisted so strongly on the respect due to personal secrets.

After leaving his daughter at the door of her school Gurov set off for the "Slavyanski Bazaar." Taking off his overcoat in the lobby, he went upstairs and knocked softly on the door. Anna Sergeyevna, wearing the gray dress he liked most, exhausted by her journey and by suspense, had been expecting him since the evening before. She was pale and looked at him without smiling, but was in his arms almost before he was fairly in the room. Their kiss was lingering, prolonged, as if they had not met for years.

"Well, how are you?" he asked. "Anything new?"

"Wait. I'll tell you in a minute. . . . I can't. . . ."

She could not speak, because she was crying. Turning away, she held her handkerchief to her eyes.

"I'll wait till she's had her cry out," he thought, and sank into a chair.

9. Probably Réaumur thermometer; about 39 degrees Fahrenheit.

He rang for tea, and a little later, while he was drinking it, she was still standing there, her face to the window. She wept from emotion, from her bitter consciousness of the sadness of their life; they could only see one another in secret, hiding from people, as if they were thieves. Was not their life a broken one?

"Don't cry," he said.

It was quite obvious to him that this love of theirs would not soon come to an end, and that no one could say when this end would be. Anna Sergeyevna loved him ever more fondly, worshipped him, and there would have been no point in telling her that one day it must end. Indeed, she would not have believed him.

He moved over and took her by the shoulders, intending to fondle her with light words, but suddenly he caught sight of himself in the looking-glass.

His hair was already beginning to turn gray. It struck him as strange that he should have aged so much in the last few years. The shoulders on which his hands lay were warm and quivering. He felt a pity for this life, still so warm and exquisite, but probably soon to fade and droop like his own. Why did she love him so? Women had always believed him different from what he really was, had loved in him not himself but the man their imagination pictured him, a man they had sought for eagerly all their lives. And afterwards when they discovered their mistake, they went on loving him just the same. And not one of them had ever been happy with him. Time had passed, he had met one woman after another, become intimate with each, parted with each, but had never loved. There had been all sorts of things between them, but never love.

And only now, when he was gray-haired, had he fallen in love properly, thoroughly, for the first time in his life.

He and Anna Sergeyevna loved one another as people who are very close and intimate, as husband and wife, as dear friends love one another. It seemed to them that fate had intended them for one another, and they could not understand why she should have a husband, and he a wife. They were like two migrating birds, the male and the female, who had been caught and put into separate cages. They forgave one another all that they were ashamed of in the past, in their present, and felt that this love of theirs had changed them both.

Formerly, in moments of melancholy, he had consoled himself by the first argument that came into his head, but now arguments were nothing to him, he felt profound pity, desired to be sincere, tender.

"Stop crying, my dearest," he said. "You've had your cry, now stop. . . . Now let us have a talk, let us try and think what we are to do."

Then they discussed their situation for a long time, trying to think how they could get rid of the necessity for hiding, deception, living in different towns, being so long without meeting. How were they to shake off these intolerable fetters?

"How? How?" he repeated, clutching his head. "How?"

And it seemed to them that they were within an inch of arriving at a decision, and that then a new, beautiful life would begin. And they both realized that the end was still far, far away, and that the hardest, the most complicated part was only just beginning.

1899

Kinds and Modes

6 A KIND: INITIATION

Themes are useful for grouping stories together for comparison, both to highlight similarities and to reveal differences in history and structure and so to discover the uniqueness of the work. Types of character—stereotypes—are useful for the same purpose: to show both the common qualities and the unique combination of qualities in a particular character in a story. Though all grouping or classification, used poorly, can blur distinctions and make all members of a group seem the same, when used well it does not blur but brings into focus the individuality of the individual thing or being.

Literary criticism lacks the specific and agreed-on system of classification of biology, so that its terms are not so fixed as *phylum, genus, species,* even in the editors' own usage. In general, we use the term **genre** for the largest commonly agreed-on categories: fiction, poetry, drama. When I'm trying to be consistent, I use the term **subgenre** for the divisions of fiction—novel, novella, short story, etc. A **kind** is a species or subcategory within a subgenre.

There is one kind of short story that is so common that there are those who maintain it is not a kind but is equivalent to the subgenre short story itself. That pervasive kind is the **initiation** story, in which a character—often but not always a child or young person—first learns a significant, even life-determining truth about the universe, about reality, about society, about people or a person, or about himself or herself. Such a subject tends to dictate the main outlines of the action of the story: it begins with the protagonist in a state of innocence or mistaken belief (exposition); it leads up to the moment of illumination or the discovery of the truth (rising action to climax or turning point), and ends usually with some indication of the result of that discovery (falling action to conclusion). This kind is particularly suitable to a short story because it lends itself to brief treatment: the illumination is more or less sudden—there is no need for lengthy development, for multiple scenes or settings, for much time to pass, for too many complications of action or a large cast of characters—yet it can encapsulate a whole life or important segment of a life and wide-ranging, significant themes.

If you've been reading this anthology from the beginning, you have already run into a number of initiation stories, and you may have some idea of what kinds of truths their protagonists discover. Young Goodman Brown discovered the universality of evil in human beings. Nelson Head (*The Artificial Nigger*) discovered the ubiquity of evil in the world outside his Edenic rural home, while his grandfather—not a young person, but described as having a youthful expression and looking more like Nelson's brother than his grandfather—learns of his own capacity for evil. Leila (*Her First Ball*) comes across the truth that youth is fleeting (you cannot say she really learns it, since by the end of that very short story she has forgotten it). We have also seen that one may retreat from the truth physically or psychologically, as do Brown and Nelson, or remain unchanged or revert to one's former state, as Leila does.

Since to the young all things seem possible—one can be a doctor, novelist, tennis star, saint, and swinger, serially or simultaneously—many of the truths learned in initiation stories have to do with limitation. The girl in *Boys and Girls* learns that she is "only a girl." Fortunately, growing up is not just loss, and there are positive or "happy" initiation stories. The boy in *The Old People* is initiated first into "manhood," and takes his place among "the hunters," and then into a more exclusive, privileged fraternity, that of the owners or, as Faulkner would no doubt prefer it, "custodians" of the land.

Sometimes the initiation takes place as an unscheduled event. At other times there is a scheduled event, a ritual or **rite of passage,** such as a formal entry into society (*Her First Ball*) or a baptism (*O Yes*), which is the occasion for the initiation into adulthood or into the group. What do we usually think of as the purpose of a debut? How does the society intend to induct its new member? As you read *Her First Ball,* think about these questions and watch how Leila's debut fulfills its ritual role, how it differs from it, and how it may induct Leila into society more truly than intended. So, too, in *O Yes* (originally called *The Baptism*), Parialee is intentionally and ritualistically inducted into her cultural role and is led by the larger (white) society into a predetermined role without ritual. And isn't Carol, who is only a spectator at the first baptism, baptized too in this second predetermined but unritualistic way? The ritual in *The Old People* is formal, communal, and ceremonial. The formalities of the rite in this story may bring to the surface elements in the pattern that lie beneath the surface in other stories.

By the time you finish this chapter you should have some idea of the variations possible within the initiation story, and as you go on to read such stories as *The Horse Dealer's Daughter, The Secret Sharer,* and *Tanhum* and think back over *The Egg* and *Macomber,* you should have a still better idea of the range of stories in this kind. Adults may be initiated as well as children and adolescents; the truths may be bitter or pleasing, cosmic, social, psychological; the initiates may change forever, retreat, shrug off what they have learned. By seeing all these stories as part of the large group of initiation stories you may the more readily notice the differences in the protagonists, in the learning experience, in the results of the initiation on the protagonists and whether they are permanent or temporary, life-denying or life-enhancing. You may, in other words, have gone a long way toward defining the unique vision of the story, its precise and individual illumination of reality. And that's the function of classification in the first place.

JAMES JOYCE

Araby

North Richmond Street, being blind,[1] was a quiet street except at the hour when the Christian Brothers'[2] School set the boys free. An uninhabited house of two stories stood at the blind end, detached from its neighbors in a square ground. The other houses of the street, conscious of decent lives within them, gazed at one another with brown imperturbable faces.

The former tenant of our house, a priest, had died in the back drawing room. Air, musty from having been long enclosed, hung in all the rooms, and the waste room behind the kitchen was littered with old useless papers. Among these I found a few paper-covered books, the pages of which were curled and damp: *The Abbot,* by Walter Scott, *The Devout Communicant* and *The Memoirs of Vidocq.*[3] I liked the last best because its leaves were yellow. The wild garden behind the house contained a central apple tree and a few straggling bushes under one of which I found the late tenant's rusty bicycle pump. He had been a very charitable priest; in his will he had left all his money to institutions and the furniture of his house to his sister.

When the short days of winter came dusk fell before we had well eaten our dinners. When we met in the street the houses had grown somber. The space of sky above us was the color of ever-changing violet and towards it the lamps of the street lifted their feeble lanterns. The cold air stung us and we played till our bodies glowed. Our shouts echoed in the silent street. The career of our play brought us through the dark muddy lanes behind the houses where we ran the gantlet of the rough tribes from the cottages, to the back doors of the dark dripping gardens where odors arose from the ashpits,[4] to the dark odorous stables where a coachman smoothed and combed the horse or shook music from the buckled harness. When we returned to the street light from the kitchen windows had filled the areas. If my uncle was seen turning the corner we hid in the shadow until we had seen him safely housed. Or if Mangan's sister came out on the doorstep to call her brother in to his tea we watched her from our shadow peer up and down the street. We waited to see whether she would remain or go in and, if she remained, we left our shadow and walked up to Mangan's steps resignedly. She was waiting for us, her figure defined by the light from the half-opened door. Her brother always teased her before he obeyed and I stood by the railings looking at her. Her dress swung as she moved her body and the soft rope of her hair tossed from side to side.

1. Dead-end street. The story takes place in Dublin.
2. Conservative Irish lay order.
3. The 1820 novel by Sir Walter Scott (1771–1834) is a romance about the Catholic Mary Queen of Scots (1542–87), who was beheaded; a Catholic religious tract: *The Devout Communicant: or Pious Meditations and Aspirations for the Three Days Before and Three Days After Receiving the Holy Eucharist* (1813); François Vidocq (1775–1857), a French criminal who became chief of detectives, who died poor and disgraced for his part in a crime that he solved, and who probably did not write the book called his memoirs.
4. Where fireplace ashes were dumped.

Every morning I lay on the floor in the front parlor watching her door. The blind was pulled down to within an inch of the sash so that I could not be seen. When she came out on the doorstep my heart leaped. I ran to the hall, seized my books and followed her. I kept her brown figure always in my eye and, when we came near the point at which our ways diverged, I quickened my pace and passed her. This happened morning after morning. I had never spoken to her, except for a few casual words, and yet her name was like a summons to all my foolish blood.

Her image accompanied me even in places the most hostile to romance. On Saturday evenings when my aunt went marketing I had to go to carry some of the parcels. We walked through the flaring streets, jostled by drunken men and bargaining women, amid the curses of laborers, the shrill litanies of shop-boys who stood on guard by the barrels of pigs' cheeks, the nasal chanting of street-singers, who sang a *come-all-you* about O'Donovan Rossa,[5] or a ballad about the troubles in our native land. These noises converged in a single sensation of life for me: I imagined that I bore my chalice safely through a throng of foes. Her name sprang to my lips at moments in strange prayers and praises which I myself did not understand. My eyes were often full of tears (I could not tell why) and at times a flood from my heart seemed to pour itself out into my bosom. I thought little of the future. I did not know whether I would ever speak to her or not or, if I spoke to her, how I could tell her of my confused adoration. But my body was like a harp and her words and gestures were like fingers running upon the wires.

One evening I went into the back drawing room in which the priest had died. It was a dark rainy evening and there was no sound in the house. Through one of the broken panes I heard the rain impinge upon the earth, the fine incessant needles of water playing in the sodden beds. Some distant lamp or lighted window gleamed below me. I was thankful that I could see so little. All my senses seemed to desire to veil themselves and, feeling that I was about to slip from them, I pressed the palms of my hands together until they trembled, murmuring: *O love! O love!* many times.

At last she spoke to me. When she addressed the first words to me I was so confused that I did not know what to answer. She asked me was I going to *Araby*.[6] I forget whether I answered yes or no. It would be a splendid bazaar, she said; she would love to go.

—And why can't you? I asked.

While she spoke she turned a silver bracelet round and round her wrist. She could not go, she said, because there would be a retreat that week in her convent. Her brother and two other boys were fighting for their caps and I was alone at the railings. She held one of the spikes, bowing her head towards me. The light from the lamp opposite our door caught the white curve of her neck, lit up her hair that rested there and, falling, lit up the hand upon the railing.

5. A song, of which there were many, which began "Come, all you Irishmen." Jeremiah ("Dynamite Rossa") O'Donovan (1831–1915) was a militant Irish nationalist who fought on despite terms in prison and banishment.

6. A bazaar billed as a "Grand Oriental Fête," Dublin, May 1894.

It fell over one side of her dress and caught the white border of a petticoat, just visible as she stood at ease.

—It's well for you, she said.

—If I go, I said, I will bring you something.

What innumerable follies laid waste my waking and sleeping thoughts after that evening! I wished to annihilate the tedious intervening days. I chafed against the work of school. At night in my bedroom and by day in the classroom her image came between me and the page I strove to read. The syllables of the word *Araby* were called to me through the silence in which my soul luxuriated and cast an Eastern enchantment over me. I asked for leave to go to the bazaar on Saturday night. My aunt was surprised and hoped it was not some Freemason[7] affair. I answered few questions in class. I watched my master's face pass from amiability to sternness; he hoped I was not beginning to idle. I could not call my wandering thoughts together. I had hardly any patience with the serious work of life which, now that it stood between me and my desire, seemed to me child's play, ugly monotonous child's play.

On Saturday morning I reminded my uncle that I wished to go to the bazaar in the evening. He was fussing at the hallstand, looking for the hat brush, and answered me curtly:

—Yes, boy, I know.

As he was in the hall I could not go into the front parlor and lie at the window. I left the house in bad humor and walked slowly towards the school. The air was pitilessly raw and already my heart misgave me.

When I came home to dinner my uncle had not yet been home. Still it was early. I sat staring at the clock for some time and, when its ticking began to irritate me, I left the room. I mounted the staircase and gained the upper part of the house. The high cold empty gloomy rooms liberated me and I went from room to room singing. From the front window I saw my companions playing below in the street. Their cries reached me weakened and indistinct and, leaning my forehead against the cool glass, I looked over at the dark house where she lived. I may have stood there for an hour, seeing nothing but the brown-clad figure cast by my imagination, touched discreetly by the lamplight at the curved neck, at the hand upon the railings and at the border below the dress.

When I came downstairs again I found Mrs. Mercer sitting at the fire. She was an old garrulous woman, a pawnbroker's widow, who collected used stamps for some pious purpose. I had to endure the gossip of the tea-table. The meal was prolonged beyond an hour and still my uncle did not come. Mrs. Mercer stood up to go: she was sorry she couldn't wait any longer, but it was after eight o'clock and she did not like to be out late, as the night air was bad for her. When she had gone I began to walk up and down the room, clenching my fists. My aunt said:

—I'm afraid you may put off your bazaar for this night of Our Lord.

7. The Masons, or Freemasons, were considered enemies of the Catholics.

At nine o'clock I heard my uncle's latchkey in the hall door. I heard him talking to himself and heard the hall stand rocking when it had received the weight of his overcoat. I could interpret these signs. When he was midway through his dinner I asked him to give me the money to go to the bazaar. He had forgotten.

—The people are in bed and after their first sleep now, he said.

I did not smile. My aunt said to him energetically:

—Can't you give him the money and let him go? You've kept him late enough as it is.

My uncle said he was very sorry he had forgotten. He said he believed in the old saying: *All work and no play makes Jack a dull boy.* He asked me where I was going and, when I had told him a second time he asked me did I know *The Arab's Farewell to His Steed.*[8] When I left the kitchen he was about to recite the opening lines of the piece to my aunt.

I held a florin[9] tightly in my hand as I strode down Buckingham Street towards the station. The sight of the streets thronged with buyers and glaring with gas recalled to me the purpose of my journey. I took my seat in a third-class carriage of a deserted train. After an intolerable delay the train moved out of the station slowly. It crept onward among ruinous houses and over the twinkling river. At Westland Row Station a crowd of people pressed to the carriage doors; but the porters moved them back, saying that it was a special train for the bazaar. I remained alone in the bare carriage. In a few minutes the train drew up beside an improvised wooden platform. I passed out on to the road and saw by the lighted dial of a clock that it was ten minutes to ten. In front of me was a large building which displayed the magical name.

I could not find any sixpenny entrance and, fearing that the bazaar would be closed, I passed in quickly through a turnstile, handing a shilling to a weary-looking man. I found myself in a big hall girdled at half its height by a gallery. Nearly all the stalls were closed and the greater part of the hall was in darkness. I recognized a silence like that which pervades a church after a service. I walked into the center of the bazaar timidly. A few people were gathered about the stalls which were still open. Before a curtain, over which the words *Café Chantant*[1] were written in colored lamps, two men were counting money on a salver. I listened to the fall of the coins.

Remembering with difficulty why I had come, I went over to one of the stalls and examined porcelain vases and flowered tea-sets. At the door of the stall a young lady was talking and laughing with two young gentlemen. I remarked their English accents[2] and listened vaguely to their conversation.

—O, I never said such a thing!

—O, but you did!

—O, but I didn't!

—Didn't she say that?

8. Or *The Arab's Farewell to His Horse,* sentimental nineteenth-century poem by Caroline Norton. The speaker has sold the horse.

9. Two-shilling piece; thus four times the "sixpenny entrance" fee.

1. Café with music.

2. Remember, the story is set in Ireland.

—Yes. I heard her.

—O, there's a . . . fib!

Observing me the young lady came over and asked me did I wish to buy anything. The tone of her voice was not encouraging; she seemed to have spoken to me out of a sense of duty. I looked humbly at the great jars that stood like eastern guards at either side of the dark entrance to the stall and murmured:

—No, thank you.

The young lady changed the position of one of the vases and went back to the two young men. They began to talk of the same subject. Once or twice the young lady glanced at me over her shoulder.

I lingered before her stall, though I knew my stay was useless, to make my interest in her wares seem the more real. Then I turned away slowly and walked down the middle of the bazaar. I allowed the two pennies to fall against the sixpence in my pocket. I heard a voice call from one end of the gallery that the light was out. The upper part of the hall was now completely dark.

Gazing up into the darkness I saw myself as a creature driven and derided by vanity; and my eyes burned with anguish and anger.

1914

ALICE MUNRO

Boys and Girls

My father was a fox farmer. That is, he raised silver foxes, in pens; and in the fall and early winter, when their fur was prime, he killed them and skinned them and sold their pelts to the Hudson's Bay Company or the Montreal Fur Traders. These companies supplied us with heroic calendars to hang, one on each side of the kitchen door. Against a background of cold blue sky and black pine forests and treacherous northern rivers, plumed adventurers planted the flags of England or of France; magnificent savages bent their backs to the portage.

For several weeks before Christmas, my father worked after supper in the cellar of our house. The cellar was whitewashed, and lit by a hundred-watt bulb over the worktable. My brother Laird and I sat on the top step and watched. My father removed the pelt inside-out from the body of the fox, which looked surprisingly small, mean and rat-like, deprived of its arrogant weight of fur. The naked, slippery bodies were collected in a sack and buried at the dump. One time the hired man, Henry Bailey, had taken a swipe at me with this sack, saying, "Christmas present!" My mother thought that was not funny. In fact she disliked the whole pelting operation—that was what the killing, skinning, and preparation of the furs was called—and wished it did not have to take place in the house. There was the smell. After the pelt had been stretched inside-out on a long board my father scraped away delicately, removing the little clotted webs of blood vessels, the bubbles of fat; the smell of blood and animal fat, with the strong primitive odor of the fox itself, penetrated all parts of the house. I found it reassuringly seasonal, like the smell of oranges and pine needles.

Henry Bailey suffered from bronchial troubles. He would cough and cough until his narrow face turned scarlet, and his light blue, derisive eyes filled up with tears; then he took the lid off the stove, and, standing well back, shot out a great clot of phlegm—hsss—straight into the heart of the flames. We admired him for this performance and for his ability to make his stomach growl at will, and for his laughter, which was full of high whistlings and gurglings and involved the whole faulty machinery of his chest. It was sometimes hard to tell what he was laughing at, and always possible that it might be us.

After we had been sent to bed we could still smell fox and still hear Henry's laugh, but these things, reminders of the warm, safe, brightly lit downstairs world, seemed lost and diminished, floating on the stale cold air upstairs. We were afraid at night in the winter. We were not afraid of *outside* though this was the time of year when snowdrifts curled around our house like sleeping whales and the wind harassed us all night, coming up from the buried fields, the frozen swamp, with its old bugbear chorus of threats and misery. We were afraid of *inside*, the room where we slept. At this time the upstairs of our house was not finished. A brick chimney went up one wall. In the middle of the floor was a square hole, with a wooden railing around it; that was where the stairs came up. On the other side of the stairwell were the things that nobody had any use for any more—a soldiery roll of linoleum, standing on end, a wicker baby carriage, a fern basket, china jugs and basins with cracks in them, a picture of the Battle of Balaclava,[1] very sad to look at. I had told Laird, as soon as he was old enough to understand such things, that bats and skeletons lived over there; whenever a man escaped from the county jail, twenty miles away, I imagined that he had somehow let himself in the window and was hiding behind the linoleum. But we had rules to keep us safe. When the light was on, we were safe as long as we did not step off the square of worn carpet which defined our bedroom-space; when the light was off no place was safe but the beds themselves. I had to turn out the light kneeling on the end of my bed, and stretching as far as I could to reach the cord.

In the dark we lay on our beds, our narrow life rafts, and fixed our eyes on the faint light coming up the stairwell, and sang songs. Laird sang "Jingle Bells," which he would sing any time, whether it was Christmas or not, and I sang "Danny Boy." I loved the sound of my own voice, frail and supplicating, rising in the dark. We could make out the tall frosted shapes of the windows now, gloomy and white. When I came to the part, *When I am dead, as dead I well may be*—a fit of shivering caused not by the cold sheets but by pleasurable emotion almost silenced me. *You'll kneel and say, an Ave there above me*—What was an Ave? Every day I forgot to find out.

1. An indecisive Crimean War battle fought on October 25, 1854.

Laird went straight from singing to sleep. I could hear his long, satisfied, bubbly breaths. Now for the time that remained to me, the most perfectly private and perhaps the best time of the whole day, I arranged myself tightly under the covers and went on with one of the stories I was telling myself from night to night. These stories were about myself, when I had grown a little older; they took place in a world that was recognizably mine, yet one that presented opportunities for courage, boldness and self-sacrifice, as mine never did. I rescued people from a bombed building (it discouraged me that the real war had gone on so far away from Jubilee). I shot two rabid wolves who were menacing the schoolyard (the teachers cowered terrified at my back). I rode a fine horse spiritedly down the main street of Jubilee, acknowledging the townspeople's gratitude for some yet-to-be-worked-out piece of heroism (nobody ever rode a horse there, except King Billy in the Orangemen's Day[2] parade). There was always riding and shooting in these stories, though I had only been on a horse twice—bareback because we did not own a saddle—and the second time I had slid right around and dropped under the horse's feet; it had stepped placidly over me. I really was learning to shoot, but I could not hit anything yet, not even tin cans on fence posts.

Alive, the foxes inhabited a world my father made for them. It was surrounded by a high guard fence, like a medieval town, with a gate that was padlocked at night. Along the streets of this town were ranged large, sturdy pens. Each of them had a real door that a man could go through, a wooden ramp along the wire, for the foxes to run up and down on, and a kennel—something like a clothes chest with airholes—where they slept and stayed in winter and had their young. There were feeding and watering dishes attached to the wire in such a way that they could be emptied and cleaned from the outside. The dishes were made of old tin cans, and the ramps and kennels of odds and ends of old lumber. Everything was tidy and ingenious; my father was tirelessly inventive and his favorite book in the world was Robinson Crusoe.[3] He had fitted a tin drum on a wheelbarrow, for bringing water down to the pens. This was my job in summer, when the foxes had to have water twice a day. Between nine and ten o'clock in the morning, and again after supper, I filled the drum at the pump and trundled it down through the barnyard to the pens, where I parked it, and filled my watering can and went along the streets. Laird came too, with his little cream and green gardening can, filled too full and knocking against his legs and slopping water on his canvas shoes. I had the real watering can, my father's, though I could only carry it three-quarters full.

The foxes all had names, which were printed on a tin plate and hung beside their doors. They were not named when they were born,

2. The Orange Society is an Irish Protestant group named after William of Orange, who, as King William III of England, defeated the Catholic James II. The Society sponsors an annual procession on July 12 to commemorate the victory of William III at the Battle of the Boyne.

3. Novel (1719) by Daniel Defoe that is about a man shipwrecked on a desert island and that goes into great detail about his ingenious contraptions.

but when they survived the first year's pelting and were added to the breeding stock. Those my father had named were called names like Prince, Bob, Wally and Betty. Those I had named were called Star or Turk, or Maureen or Diana. Laird named one Maud after a hired girl we had when he was little, one Harold after a boy at school, and one Mexico, he did not say why.

Naming them did not make pets out of them, or anything like it. Nobody but my father ever went into the pens, and he had twice had blood-poisoning from bites. When I was bringing them their water they prowled up and down on the paths they had made inside their pens, barking seldom—they saved that for nighttime, when they might get up a chorus of community frenzy—but always watching me, their eyes burning, clear gold, in their pointed, malevolent faces. They were beautiful for their delicate legs and heavy, aristocratic tails and the bright fur sprinkled on dark down their backs—which gave them their name—but especially for their faces, drawn exquisitely sharp in pure hostility, and their golden eyes.

Besides carrying water I helped my father when he cut the long grass, and the lamb's quarter and flowering money-musk, that grew between the pens. He cut with the scythe and I raked into piles. Then he took a pitchfork and threw fresh-cut grass all over the top of the pens, to keep the foxes cooler and shade their coats, which were browned by two much sun. My father did not talk to me unless it was about the job we were doing. In this he was quite different from my mother, who, if she was feeling cheerful, would tell me all sorts of things—the name of a dog she had had when she was a little girl, the names of boys she had gone out with later on when she was grown up, and what certain dresses of hers had looked like—she could not imagine now what had become of them. Whatever thoughts and stories my father had were private, and I was shy of him and would never ask him questions. Nevertheless I worked willingly under his eyes, and with a feeling of pride. One time a feed salesman came down into the pens to talk to him and my father said, "Like to have you meet my new hired man." I turned away and raked furiously, red in the face with pleasure.

"Could of fooled me," said the salesman. "I thought it was only a girl."

After the grass was cut, it seemed suddenly much later in the year. I walked on stubble in the earlier evening, aware of the reddening skies, the entering silences, of fall. When I wheeled the tank out of the gate and put the padlock on, it was almost dark. One night at this time I saw my mother and father standing talking on the little rise of ground we called the gangway, in front of the barn. My father had just come from the meathouse; he had his stiff bloody apron on, and a pail of cut-up meat in his hand.

It was an odd thing to see my mother down at the barn. She did not often come out of the house unless it was to do something—hang out the wash or dig potatoes in the garden. She looked out of place, with her bare lumpy legs, not touched by the sun, her apron still on and damp across the stomach from the supper dishes. Her hair was tied up in a kerchief, wisps of it falling out. She would tie her hair up like this in the morning, saying she did not have time to do it properly, and it would stay tied up all day. It was true, too; she really did not have time. These days our back porch was piled with baskets of peaches and grapes and pears, bought in town, and onions and tomatoes and cucumbers grown at home, all waiting to be made into jelly and jam and preserves, pickles and chili sauce. In the kitchen there was a fire in the stove all day, jars clinked in boiling water, sometimes a cheesecloth bag was strung on a pole between two chairs straining blue-black grape pulp for jelly. I was given jobs to do and I would sit at the table peeling peaches that had been soaked in the hot water, or cutting up onions, my eyes smarting and streaming. As soon as I was done I ran out of the house, trying to get out of earshot before my mother thought of what she wanted me to do next. I hated the hot dark kitchen in summer, the green blinds and the flypapers, the same old oilcloth table and wavy mirror and bumpy linoleum. My mother was too tired and preoccupied to talk to me, she had no heart to tell about the Normal School Graduation Dance; sweat trickled over her face and she was always counting under her breath, pointing at jars, dumping cups of sugar. It seemed to me that work in the house was endless, dreary and peculiarly depressing; work done out of doors, and in my father's service, was ritualistically important.

I wheeled the tank up to the barn, where it was kept, and I heard my mother saying, "Wait till Laird gets a little bigger, then you'll have a real help."

What my father said I did not hear. I was pleased by the way he stood listening, politely as he would to a salesman or a stranger, but with an air of wanting to get on with his real work. I felt my mother had no business down here and I wanted him to feel the same way. What did she mean about Laird? He was no help to anybody. Where was he now? Swinging himself sick on the swing, going around in circles, or trying to catch caterpillars. He never once stayed with me till I was finished.

"And then I can use her more in the house," I heard my mother say. She had a dead-quiet, regretful way of talking about me that always made me uneasy. "I just get my back turned and she runs off. It's not like I had a girl in the family at all."

I went and sat on a feed bag in the corner of the barn, not wanting to appear when this conversation was going on. My mother, I felt, was not to be trusted. She was kinder than my father and more easily fooled, but you could not depend on her, and the real reasons for the things she said and did were not to be known. She loved me, and she sat up late at night making a dress of the difficult style I wanted, for me to wear when school started, but she was also my enemy. She was always plotting. She was plotting now to get me to stay in the house more, although she knew I hated it (*because* she knew I hated it) and keep me from working for my father. It seemed to me she would do this simply out of perversity, and to try her power. It did not occur to me that she could be lonely, or jealous. No grown-up could be; they were too fortunate. I sat and kicked my heels monotonously against a feed bag, raising dust, and did not come out till she was gone.

At any rate, I did not expect my father to pay any attention to what she said. Who could imagine Laird doing my work—Laird remembering the padlock and cleaning out the watering dishes with a leaf on the end of a stick, or even wheeling the tank without it tumbling over? It showed how little my mother knew about the way things really were.

I have forgotten to say what the foxes were fed. My father's bloody apron reminded me. They were fed horsemeat. At this time most farmers still kept horses, and when a horse got too old to work, or broke a leg or got down and would not get up, as they sometimes did, the owner would call my father, and he and Henry went out to the farm in the truck. Usually they shot and butchered the horse there, paying the farmer from five to twelve dollars. If they had already too much meat on hand, they would bring the horse back alive, and keep it for a few days or weeks in our stable, until the meat was needed. After the war the farmers were buying tractors and gradually getting rid of horses altogether, so it sometimes happened that we got a good healthy horse, that there was just no use for any more. If this happened in the winter we might keep the horse in our stable till spring, for we had plenty of hay and if there was a lot of snow—and the plow did not always get our road cleared—it was convenient to be able to go to town with a horse and cutter.[4]

The winter I was eleven years old we had two horses in the stable. We did not know what names they had had before, so we called them Mack and Flora. Mack was an old black workhorse, sooty and indifferent. Flora was a sorrel mare, a driver. We took them both out in the cutter. Mack was slow and easy to handle. Flora was given to fits of violent alarm, veering at cars and even at other horses, but we loved her speed and high-stepping, her general air of gallantry and abandon. On Saturdays we went down to the stable and as soon as we opened the door on its cosy, animal-smelling darkness Flora threw up her head, rolled her eyes, whinnied despairingly and pulled herself through a crisis of nerves on the spot. It was not safe to go into her stall; she would kick.

This winter also I began to hear a great deal more on the theme my mother had sounded when she had been talking in front of the barn. I no longer felt safe. It seemed that in the minds of the people around me there was a steady undercurrent of thought, not to be deflected, on this one subject. The word *girl* had formerly seemed to me innocent and unburdened, like the word *child*; now it appeared that it was no such thing. A girl was not, as I had supposed, simply what I was; it was what I had to become. It was a definition, always touched with emphasis, with reproach and disappointment. Also it was a joke on me. Once Laird and I were fighting, and for the first time ever I had to use all my strength against him; even so, he caught and pinned my arm for a moment, really hurting me. Henry saw this, and laughed, saying, "Oh, that there Laird's gonna show you, one

4. A small, light, one-horse sleigh.

of these days!" Laird was getting a lot bigger. But I was getting bigger too.

My grandmother came to stay with us for a few weeks and I heard other things. "Girls don't slam doors like that." "Girls keep their knees together when they sit down." And worse still, when I asked some questions, "That's none of girls' business." I continued to slam the doors and sit as awkwardly as possible, thinking that by such measures I kept myself free.

When spring came, the horses were let out in the barnyard. Mack stood against the barn wall trying to scratch his neck and haunches, but Flora trotted up and down and reared at the fences, clattering her hooves against the rails. Snow drifts dwindled quickly, revealing the hard gray and brown earth, the familiar rise and fall of the ground, plain and bare after the fantastic landscape of winter. There was a great feeling of opening-out, of release. We just wore rubbers now, over our shoes; our feet felt ridiculously light. One Saturday we went out to the stable and found all the doors open, letting in the unaccustomed sunlight and fresh air. Henry was there, just idling around looking at his collection of calendars which were tacked up behind the stalls in a part of the stable my mother had probably never seen.

"Come to say goodbye to your old friend Mack?" Henry said. "Here, you give him a taste of oats." He poured some oats into Laird's cupped hands and Laird went to feed Mack. Mack's teeth were in bad shape. He ate very slowly, patiently shifting the oats around in his mouth, trying to find a stump of a molar to grind it on. "Poor old Mack," said Henry mournfully. "When a horse's teeth's gone, he's gone. That's about the way."

"Are you going to shoot him today?" I said. Mack and Flora had been in the stable so long I had almost forgotten they were going to be shot.

Henry didn't answer me. Instead he started to sing in a high, trembly, mocking-sorrowful voice, *Oh, there's no more work, for poor Uncle Ned, he's gone where the good darkies go.*[5] Mack's thick, blackish tongue worked diligently at Laird's hand. I went out before the song was ended and sat down on the gangway.

I had never seen them shoot a horse, but I knew where it was done. Last summer Laird and I had come upon a horse's entrails before they were buried. We had thought it was a big black snake, coiled up in the sun. That was around in the field that ran up beside the barn. I thought that if we went inside the barn, and found a wide crack or a knothole to look through, we would be able to see them do it. It was not something I wanted to see; just the same, if a thing really happened, it was better to see it, and know.

My father came down from the house, carrying the gun.

"What are you doing here?" he said.

"Nothing."

"Go on up and play around the house."

5. Lines from the Stephen Foster song "Old Uncle Ned."

He sent Laird out of the stable. I said to Laird, "Do you want to see them shoot Mack?" and without waiting for an answer led him around to the front door of the barn, opened it carefully, and went in. "Be quiet or they'll hear us," I said. We could hear Henry and my father talking in the stable, then the heavy, shuffling steps of Mack being backed out of his stall.

In the loft it was cold and dark. Thin, crisscrossed beams of sunlight fell through the cracks. The hay was low. It was a rolling country, hills and hollows, slipping under our feet. About four feet up was a beam going around the walls. We piled hay up in one corner and I boosted Laird up and hoisted myself. The beam was not very wide; we crept along it with our hands flat on the barn walls. There were plenty of knotholes, and I found one that gave me the view I wanted—a corner of the barnyard, the gate, part of the field. Laird did not have a knothole and began to complain.

I showed him a widened crack between two boards. "Be quiet and wait. If they hear you you'll get us in trouble."

My father came in sight carrying the gun. Henry was leading Mack by the halter. He dropped it and took out his cigarette papers and tobacco; he rolled cigarettes for my father and himself. While this was going on Mack nosed around in the old, dead grass along the fence. Then my father opened the gate and they took Mack through. Henry led Mack way from the path to a patch of ground and they talked together, not loud enough for us to hear. Mack again began searching for a mouthful of fresh grass, which was not to be found. My father walked away in a straight line, and stopped short at a distance which seemed to suit him. Henry was walking away from Mack too, but sideways, still negligently holding on to the halter. My father raised the gun and Mack looked up as if he had noticed something and my father shot him.

Mack did not collapse at once but swayed, lurched sideways and fell, first on his side; then he rolled over on his back and, amazingly, kicked his legs for a few seconds in the air. At this Henry laughed, as if Mack had done a trick for him. Laird, who had drawn a long, groaning breath of surprise when the shot was fired, said out loud, "He's not dead." And it seemed to me it might be true. But his legs stopped, he rolled on his side again, his muscles quivered and sank. The two men walked over and looked at him in a business-like way; they bent down and examined his forehead where the bullet had gone in, and now I saw his blood on the brown grass.

"Now they just skin him and cut him up," I said. "Let's go." My legs were a little shaky and I jumped gratefully down into the hay. "Now you've seen how they shoot a horse," I said in a congratulatory way, as if I had seen it many times before. "Let's see if any barn cat's had kittens in the hay." Laird jumped. He seemed young and obedient again. Suddenly I remembered how, when he was little, I had brought him into the barn and told him to climb the ladder to the top beam. That was in the spring, too, when the hay was low. I had done it out of a need for excitement, a desire for something to happen so that I could tell about it. He was wearing a little bulky brown and white checked coat, made down from one of mine. He went all the way up just as I told him, and sat down on the top beam with the hay far below him on one side, and the barn floor and some old machinery on the other. Then I ran screaming to my father, "Laird's up on the top beam!" My father came, my mother came, my father went up the ladder talking very quietly and brought Laird down under his arm, at which my mother leaned against the ladder and began to cry. They said to me, "Why weren't you watching him?" but nobody ever knew the truth. Laird did not know enough to tell. But whenever I saw the brown and white checked coat hanging in the closet, or at the bottom of the rag bag, which was where it ended up, I felt a weight in my stomach, the sadness of unexorcised guilt.

I looked at Laird, who did not even remember this, and I did not like the look on this thin, winter-pale face. His expression was not frightened or upset, but remote, concentrating. "Listen," I said, in an unusually bright and friendly voice, "you aren't going to tell, are you?"

"No," he said absently.

"Promise."

"Promise," he said. I grabbed the hand behind his back to make sure he was not crossing his fingers. Even so, he might have a nightmare; it might come out that way. I decided I had better work hard to get all thoughts of what he had seen out of his mind—which, it seemed to me, could not hold very many things at a time. I got some money I had saved and that afternoon we went into Jubilee and saw a show, with Judy Canova,[6] at which we both laughed a great deal. After that I thought it would be all right.

Two weeks later I knew they were going to shoot Flora. I knew from the night before, when I heard my mother ask if the hay was holding out all right, and my father said, "Well, after tomorrow there'll just be the cow, and we should be able to put her out to grass in another week." So I knew it was Flora's turn in the morning.

This time I didn't think of watching it. That was something to see just one time. I had not thought about it very often since, but sometimes when I was busy, working at school, or standing in front of the mirror combing my hair and wondering if I would be pretty when I grew up, the whole scene would flash into my mind: I would see the easy, practiced way my father raised the gun, and hear Henry laughing when Mack kicked his legs in the air. I did not have any great feeling of horror and opposition, such as a city child might have had; I was too used to seeing the death of animals as a necessity by which we lived. Yet I felt a little ashamed, and there was a new wariness, a sense of holding-off, in my attitude to my father and his work.

It was a fine day, and we were going around the yard picking up tree branches that had been torn off in winter storms. This was something we had been told to do, and also we wanted to use them to make a teepee. We heard Flora whinny, and then my father's voice and Henry's shouting, and we ran down to the barnyard to see what was going on.

6. American comedian best known for her yodeling in hillbilly movies of the 1940s.

The stable door was open. Henry had just brought Flora out, and she had broken away from him. She was running free in the barnyard, from one end to the other. We climbed up on the fence. It was exciting to see her running, whinnying, going up on her hind legs, prancing and threatening like a horse in a Western movie, an unbroken ranch horse, though she was just an old driver, an old sorrel mare. My father and Henry ran after her and tried to grab the dangling halter. They tried to work her into a corner, and they had almost succeeded when she made a run between them, wild-eyed, and disappeared around the corner of the barn. We heard the rails clatter down as she got over the fence, and Henry yelled, "She's into the field now!"

That meant she was in the long L-shaped field that ran up by the house. If she got around the center, heading towards the lane, the gate was open; the truck had been driven into the field this morning. My father shouted to me, because I was on the other side of the fence, nearest the lane, "Go shut the gate!"

I could run very fast. I ran across the garden, past the tree where our swing was hung, and jumped across a ditch into the lane. There was the open gate. She had not got out, I could not see her up on the road; she must have run to the other end of the field. The gate was heavy. I lifted it out of the gravel and carried it across the roadway. I had it halfway across when she came in sight, galloping straight towards me. There was just time to get the chain on. Laird came scrambling through the ditch to help me.

Instead of shutting the gate, I opened it as wide as I could. I did not make any decision to do this, it was just what I did. Flora never slowed down; she galloped straight past me, and Laird jumped up and down, yelling, "Shut it, shut it!" even after it was too late. My father and Henry appeared in the field a moment too late to see what I had done. They only saw Flora heading for the township road. They would think I had not got there in time.

They did not waste any time asking about it. They went back to the barn and got the gun and the knives they used, and put these in the truck; then they turned the truck around and came bouncing up the field toward us. Laird called to them, "Let me go too, let me go too!" and Henry stopped the truck and they took him in. I shut the gate after they were all gone.

I supposed Laird would tell. I wondered what would happen to me. I had never disobeyed my father before, and I could not understand why I had done it. Flora would not really get away. They would catch up with her in the truck. Or if they did not catch her this morning somebody would see her and telephone us this afternoon or tomorrow. There was no wild country here for her to run to, only farms. What was more, my father had paid for her, we needed the meat to feed the foxes, we needed the foxes to make our living. All I had done was make more work for my father who worked hard enough already. And when my father found out about it he was not going to trust me any more; he would know that I was not entirely on his side. I was on Flora's side, and that made me no use to anybody, not even to her. Just the same, I did not regret it; when she came running at me and I held the gate open, that was the only thing I could do.

I went back to the house, and my mother said, "What's all the commotion?" I told her that Flora had kicked down the fence and got away. "Your poor father," she said, "now he'll have to go chasing over the countryside. Well, there isn't any use planning dinner before one." She put up the ironing board. I wanted to tell her, but thought better of it and went upstairs and sat on my bed.

Lately I had been trying to make my part of the room fancy, spreading the bed with old lace curtains, and fixing myself a dressing table with some leftovers of cretonne for a skirt. I planned to put up some kind of barricade between my bed and Laird's, to keep my section separate from his. In the sunlight, the lace curtains were just dusty rags. We did not sing at night any more. One night when I was singing Laird said, "You sound silly," and I went right on but the next night I did not start. There was not so much need to anyway, we were no longer afraid. We knew it was just old furniture over there, old jumble and confusion. We did not keep to the rules. I still stayed awake after Laird was asleep and told myself stories, but even in these stories something different was happening, mysterious alterations took place. A story might start off in the old way, with a spectacular danger, a fire or wild animals, and for a while I might rescue people; then things would change around, and instead, somebody would be rescuing me. It might be a boy from our class at school, or even Mr. Campbell, our teacher, who tickled girls under the arms. And at this point the story concerned itself at great length with what I looked like—how long my hair was, and what kind of dress I had on; by the time I had these details worked out the real excitement of the story was lost.

It was later than one o'clock when the truck came back. The tarpaulin was over the back, which meant there was meat in it. My mother had to heat dinner up all over again. Henry and my father had changed from their bloody overalls into ordinary working overalls in the barn, and they washed their arms and necks and faces at the sink, and splashed water on their hair and combed it. Laird lifted his arm to show off a streak of blood. "We shot old Flora," he said, "and cut her up in fifty pieces."

"Well I don't want to hear about it," my mother said. "And don't come to my table like that."

My father made him go and wash the blood off.

We sat down and my father said grace and Henry pasted his chewing gum on the end of his fork, the way he always did; when he took it off he would have us admire the pattern. We began to pass the bowls of steaming, overcooked vegetables. Laird looked across the table at me and said proudly, distinctly, "Anyway it was her fault Flora got away."

"What?" my father said.

"She could of shut the gate and she didn't. She just open' it up and Flora run out."

"Is that right?" my father said.

Everybody at the table was looking at me. I nodded, swallowing food with great difficulty. To my shame, tears flooded my eyes.

My father made a curt sound of disgust. "What did you do that for?"

I did not answer. I put down my fork and waited to be sent from the table, still not looking up.

But this did not happen. For some time nobody said anything, then Laird said matter-of-factly, "She's crying."

"Never mind," my father said. He spoke with resignation, even good humor, the words which absolved and dismissed me for good. "She's only a girl," he said.

I didn't protest that, even in my heart. Maybe it was true.

1968

TILLIE OLSEN

O Yes

For Margaret Heaton, who always taught.

1

They are the only white people there, sitting in the dimness of the Negro church that had once been a corner store, and all through the bubbling, swelling, seething of before the services, twelve-year-old Carol clenches tight her mother's hand, the other resting lightly on her friend, Parialee Phillips, for whose baptism she has come.

The white-gloved ushers hurry up and down the aisle, beckoning people to their seats. A jostle of people. To the chairs angled to the left for the youth choir, to the chairs angled to the right for the ladies' choir, even up to the platform, where behind the place for the dignitaries and the mixed choir, the new baptismal tank gleams—and as if pouring into it from the ceiling, the blue-painted River of Jordan, God standing in the waters, embracing a brown man in a leopard skin and pointing to the letters of gold:

REJOICE

GOD IS LOVE

I AM THE WAY THE TRUTH THE LIFE

At the clear window, the crucified Christ embroidered on the starched white curtain leaps in the wind of the sudden singing. And the choirs march in. Robes of wine, of blue, of red.

"We stands and sings too," says Parialee's mother, Alva, to Helen; though already Parialee has pulled Carol up. Singing, little Lucinda Phillips fluffs out her many petticoats; singing, little Bubbie bounces up and down on his heels.

Any day now I'll reach that land of freedom,
Yes, o yes
Any day now, know that promised land

The youth choir claps and taps to accent the swing of it. Beginning to tap, Carol stiffens. "Parry, look. Somebody from school."

"Once more once," says Parialee, in the new way she likes to talk now.

"Eddie Garlin's up there. He's in my math."

"Couple cats from Franklin Jr. chirps in the choir. No harm or alarm."

Anxiously Carol scans the faces to see who else she might know, who else might know her, but looks quickly down to Lucinda's wide skirts, for it seems Eddie looks back at her, sullen or troubled, though it is hard to tell, faced as she is into the window of curtained sunblaze.

I know my robe will fit me well
I tried it on at the gates of hell

If it were a record she would play it over and over, Carol thought, to untwine the intertwined voices, to search how the many rhythms rock apart and yet are one glad rhythm.

When I get to heaven gonna sing and shout
Nobody be able to turn me out

"That's Mr. Chairback Evans going to invocate," Lucinda leans across Parry to explain. "He don't invoke good like Momma."

"Shhhh."

"Momma's the only lady in the church that invocates. She made the prayer last week. (Last month, Lucy.) I made the children's 'nouncement last time. (That was way back Thanksgiving.) And Bubbie's 'nounced too. Lots of times."

"Lucy-inda. SIT!"

Bible study announcements and mixed-choir practice announcements and Teen Age Hearts meeting announcements.

If Eddie said something to her about being there, worried Carol, if he talked to her right in front of somebody at school.

Messengers of Faith announcements and Mamboettes announcement and Committee for the Musical Tea.

Parry's arm so warm. Not realizing, starting up the old game from grade school, drumming a rhythm on the other's arm to see if the song could be guessed. "Parry, guess."

But Parry is pondering the platform.

The baptismal tank? "Parry, are you scared . . . the baptizing?"

"This cat? No." Shaking her head so slow and scornful, the barrette in her hair, sun fired, strikes a long rail of light. And still ponders the platform.

New Strangers Baptist Church invites you and Canaan Fair Singers announcements and Battle of Song and Cosmopolites meet. "O Lord, I couldn't find no ease," a solo. The ladies' choir:

O what you say seekers, o what you say seekers,
Will you never turn back no more?

The mixed choir sings:

Ezekiel saw that wheel of time
Every spoke was of humankind . . .

And the slim worn man in the pin-stripe suit starts his sermon On the Nature of God. How God is long-suffering. Oh, how long he has suffered. Calling the roll of the mighty nations, that rose and fell and now are dust for grinding the face of man.

O voice of drowsiness and dream to which Carol does not need to listen. As long ago. Parry warm beside her too, as it used to be, there in the classroom at Mann Elementary, and the feel of drenched in sun and dimness and dream. Smell and sound of the chalk wearing itself away to nothing, rustle of books, drumming tattoo of fingers on her arm: *Guess.*

And as the preacher's voice spins happy and free, it is the used-to-be play-yard. Tag. Thump of the volley ball. Ecstasy of the jump rope. Parry, do pepper. Carol, do pepper. Parry's bettern Carol, Carol's bettern Parry. . . .

Did someone scream?

It seemed someone screamed—but all were sitting as before, though the sun no longer blared through the windows. She tried to see up where Eddie was, but the ushers were standing at the head of the aisle now, the ladies in white dresses like nurses or waitresses wear, the men holding their white-gloved hands up so one could see their palms.

"And God is Powerful," the preacher was chanting. "Nothing for him to scoop out the oceans and pat up the mountains. Nothing for him to scoop up the miry clay and create man. Man, I said, create Man."

The lady in front of her moaned *"O yes"* and others were moaning *"O yes."*

"And when the earth mourned the Lord said, Weep not, for all will be returned to you, every dust, every atom. And the tired dust settles back, goes back. Until that Judgment Day. That great day."

"O yes."

The ushers were giving out fans. Carol reached for one and Parry said: "What *you* need one for?" but she took it anyway.

"You think Satchmo can blow; you think Muggsy can blow; you think Dizzy can blow?"[1] He was straining to an imaginary trumpet now, his head far back and his voice coming out like a trumpet.

"Oh Parry, he's so good."

"Well. Jelly jelly."

"Nothing to Gabriel on that great getting-up morning. And the horn wakes up Adam, and Adam runs to wake up Eve, and Eve moans; Just one more minute, let me sleep, and Adam yells, Great Day, woman, don't you know it's the Great Day?"

"Great Day, Great Day," the mixed choir behind the preacher rejoices:

When our cares are past
when we're home at last . . .

"And Eve runs to wake up Cain." Running round the platform, stooping and shaking imaginary sleepers, "and Cain runs to wake up Abel." Looping, scalloping his voice—"Grea-aaa-aat Daaaay." All the choirs thundering:

1. Louis Armstrong (1900–1971); Francis ("Muggsy") Spanier (1906–1967); John ("Dizzy") Gillespie (b. 1917), all famous black jazz trumpeters.

Great Day
When the battle's fought
And the victory's won

Exultant spirals of sound. And Carol caught into it (Eddie forgotten, the game forgotten) chanting with Lucy and Bubbie: "*Great Day.*"

"Ohhhhhhhhhh," his voice like a trumpet again, "the re-unioning. Ohhhhhhhhh, the rejoicing. After the ages immemorial of longing."

Someone *was* screaming. And an awful thrumming sound with it, like feet and hands thrashing around, like a giant jumping of a rope.

"*Great Day.*" And no one stirred or stared as the ushers brought a little woman out into the aisle, screaming and shaking, just a little shrunk-up woman, not much taller than Carol, the biggest thing about her her swollen hands and the cascades of tears wearing her face.

The shaking inside Carol too. Turning and trembling to ask: "What? . . . that lady?" But Parry still ponders the platform; little Lucy loops the chain of her bracelet round and round; and Bubbie sits placidly, dreamily. Alva Phillips is up fanning a lady in front of her; two lady ushers are fanning other people Carol cannot see. And her mother, her mother looks in a sleep.

Yes. He raised up the dead from the grave. He made old death behave.

O Yes

Yes. Yes. From all over, hushed.

He was your mother's rock. Your father's mighty tower. And he gave us a little baby. A little baby to love.

I am so glad

Yes, your friend, when you're friendless. Your father when you're fatherless. Way maker. Door opener.

Yes

When it seems you can't go on any longer, he's there. You can, he says, you can.

Yes

And that burden you been carrying—ohhhhh that burden—not for always will it be. No, not for always.

Stay with me, Lord

I will put my Word in you and it is power. I will put my Truth in you and it is power.

O Yes

Out of your suffering I will make you to stand as a stone. A tried stone. Hewn out of the mountains of ages eternal.

Yes

Ohhhhhhhhhhh. Out of the mire I will lift your feet. Your tired feet from so much wandering. From so much work and wear and hard times.

Yes

From so much journeying—and never the promised land. And I'll wash them in the well your tears made. And I'll shod them in the gospel of peace, and of feeling good. Ohhhhhhhhh.

O Yes.

Behind Carol, a trembling wavering scream. Then the thrashing. Up above, the singing:

They taken my blessed Jesus and flogged him to the woods

And they made him hew out his cross and they dragged him to
Calvary
Shout brother, Shout shout shout. He never cried a word.

Powerful throbbing voices. Calling and answering to each other.

They taken my blessed Jesus and whipped him up the hill
With a knotty whip and a raggedy thorn he never cried a word
Shout, sister. Shout shout shout. He never cried a word.

Go tell the people the Saviour has risen
Has risen from the dead and will live forevermore
And won't have to die no more.
Halleloo.
Shout, brother, shout
We won't have to die no more!

A single exultant lunge of shriek. Then the thrashing. All around a clapping. Shouts with it. The piano whipping, whipping air to a froth. Singing now.

I once was lost who now am found
Was blind who now can see

On Carol's fan, a little Jesus walked on wondrously blue waters to where bearded disciples spread nets out of a fishing boat. If she studied the fan—became it—it might make a wall around her. If she could make what was happening (*what* was happening?) into a record small and round to listen to far and far as if into a seashell—the stamp and rills and spirals all tiny (but never any screaming).

wade wade in the water

Jordan's water is chilly and wild
I've got to get home to the other side
God's going to trouble the waters

Ladders of screamings. The music leaps and prowls. Drumming feet of ushers running. And still little Lucy fluffs her skirts, loops the chain on her bracelet; still Bubbie sits and rocks dreamily; and only eyes turn for an instant to the aisle—as if nothing were happening. "Mother, let's go home," Carol begs, but her mother holds her so tight. Alva Phillips, strong Alva, rocking too and chanting, *O Yes*. No, do not look.

Wade,
Sea of trouble all mingled with fire
Come on my brethren it's time to go higher
Wade wade

The voices in great humming waves, slow, slow (when did it become the humming?), everyone swaying with it too, moving like in slow waves and singing, and up where Eddie is, a new cry, wild and open, "O help me, Jesus," and when Carol opens her eyes she closes them again, quick, but still can see the new known face from school (not Eddie), the thrashing, writhing body, struggling against the ushers with the look of grave and loving support on their faces, and hear the torn, tearing cry: "Don't take me away, life everlasting, don't take me away."

And now the rhinestones in Parry's hair glitter wicked, the white hands of the ushers, fanning, foam in the air; the blue-painted waters of Jordan swell and thunder; Christ spirals on his cross in the window, and she is drowned under the sluice of the slow singing and the sway.

So high up and forgotten the waves and the world, so stirless the deep cool green and the wrecks of what had been. Here now Hostess Foods, where Alva Phillips works her nights—but different from that time Alva had taken them through before work, for it is all sunken under water, the creaking loading platform where they had left the night behind; the closet room where Alva's swaddles of sweaters, boots, and cap hung, the long hall lined with pickle barrels, the sharp freezer door swinging open.

Bubbles of breath that swell. A gulp of numbing air. She swims into the chill room where the huge wheels of cheese stand, and Alva swims too, deftly oiling each machine: slicers and wedgers and the convey, that at her touch start to roll and grind. The light of day blazes up and Alva is holding a cup, saying: Drink this, baby.

"DRINK IT." Her mother's voice and the numbing air demanding her to pay attention. Up through the waters and into the car.

"That's right, lambie, now lie back." Her mother's lap.

"Mother."

"Shhhhh. You almost fainted, lambie."

Alva's voice. "You gonna be all right, Carol . . . Lucy, I'm telling you for the last time, you and Buford get back into that church. Carol is *fine*."

"Lucyinda, if I had all your petticoats I could float." Crying. "Why didn't you let me wear my full skirt with the petticoats, Mother."

"Shhhhh, lamb." Smoothing her cheek. "Just breathe, take long deep breaths."

". . . How you doing now, you little ol' consolation prize?" It is Parry, but she does not come in the car or reach to Carol through the open window: "No need to cuss and fuss. You going to be sharp as a tack, Jack."

Answering automatically: "And cool as a fool."

Quick, they look at each other.

"Parry, we have to go home now, don't we, Mother? I almost fainted, didn't I, Mother? . . . Parry, I'm sorry I got sick and have to miss your baptism."

"Don't feel sorry. I'll feel better you not there to watch. It was our mommas wanted you to be there, not me."

"Parry!" Three voices.

"Maybe I'll come over to play kickball after. If you feeling better. Maybe. Or bring the pogo." Old shared joys in her voice: "Or any little thing."

In just a whisper: "Or any little thing. Parry. Good-bye, Parry."

And why does Alva have to talk now?

"You all right? You breathin' deep like your momma said? Was it too close 'n hot in there? Did something scare you, Carrie?"

Shaking her head to lie, "No."

"I blame myself for not paying attention. You not used to people letting go that way. Lucy and Bubbie, Parialee, they used to it. They been coming since they lap babies."

"Alva, that's all right. Alva, Mrs. Phillips."

"You *was* scared. Carol, it's something to study about. You'll feel better if you understand."

Trying not to listen.

"You not used to hearing what people keeps inside, Carol. You know how music can make you feel things? Glad or sad or like you can't sit still? That was religion music, Carol."

"I have to breathe deep, Mother said."

"Not everybody feels religion the same way. Some it's in their mouth, but some it's like a hope in their blood, their bones. And they singing songs every word that's real to them, Carol, every word out of they own life. And the preaching finding lodgment in their hearts."

The screaming was tuning up in her ears again, high above Alva's patient voice and the waves lapping and fretting.

"Maybe somebody's had a hard week, Carol, and they locked up with it. Maybe a lot of hard weeks bearing down."

"Mother, my head hurts."

"And they're home, Carol, church is home. Maybe the only place they can feel how they feel and maybe let it come out. So they can go on. And it's all right."

"Please, Alva. Mother, tell Alva my head hurts."

"Get Happy, we call it, and most it's good feeling, Carol, when you got all that locked up inside you."

"Tell her we have to go home. It's all right, Alva. Please, Mother. Say good-bye. Good-bye."

When I was carrying Parry and her father left me, and I fifteen years old, one thousand miles away from home, sin-sick and never really believing, as still I don't believe all, scorning, for what have it done to help, waiting there in the clinic and maybe sleeping, a voice called: Alva, Alva. So mournful and so sweet: Alva. Fear not, I have loved you from the foundation of the universe. And a little small child tugged on my dress. He was carrying a parade stick, on the end of it a star that outshined the sun. Follow me, he said. And the real sun went down and he hidden his stick. How dark it was, how dark. I could feel the darkness with my hands. And when I could see, I screamed. Dump trucks run, dumping bodies in hell, and a convey line run, never ceasing with souls, weary ones having to stamp and shove them along, and the air like fire. Oh I never want to hear such screaming. Then the little child jumped on a motorbike making a path no bigger than my little finger. But first he greased my feet with the hands of my momma when I was a knee baby. They shined like the sun was on them. Eyes he placed all around my head, and as I journeyed upward after him, it seemed I heard a mourning: "Mama Mama you must help carry the world." The rise and fall of nations I saw. And the voice called again Alva Alva, and I flew into a world of light, multitudes singing, Free, free, I am so glad.

2

Helen began to cry, telling her husband about it.

"You and Alva ought to have your heads examined, taking her there cold like that," Len said. "All right, wreck my best handkerchief. Anyway, now that she's had a bath, her Sunday dinner. . . ."

"And been fussed over," seventeen-year-old Jeannie put in.

"She seems good as new. Now *you* forget it, Helen."

"I can't. Something . . . deep happened. If only I or Alva had told her what it would be like. . . . But I didn't realize."

You don't realize a lot of things, Mother, Jeannie said, but not aloud.

"So Alva talked about it after instead of before. Maybe it meant more that way."

"Oh Len, she didn't listen."

"You don't know if she did or not. Or what there was in the experience for her. . . ."

Enough to pull that kid apart two ways even more, Jeannie said, but still not aloud.

"I was so glad she and Parry were going someplace together again. Now that'll be between them too. Len, they really need, miss each other. What happened in a few months? When I think of how close they were, the hours of makebelieve and dressup and playing ball and collecting. . . ."

"Grow up, Mother." Jeannie's voice was harsh. "Parialee's collecting something else now. Like her own crowd. Like jivetalk and rhythmandblues. Like teachers who treat her like a dummy and white kids who treat her like dirt; boys who think she's really something and chicks who. . . ."

"Jeannie, I know. It hurts."

"Well, maybe it hurts Parry too. Maybe. At least she's got a crowd. Just don't let it hurt Carol though, 'cause there's nothing she can do about it. That's all through, her and Parialee Phillips, put away with their paper dolls."

"No, Jeannie, no."

"It's like Ginger and me. Remember Ginger, my best friend in Horace Mann. But you hardly noticed when it happened to us, did you . . . because she was white? Yes, Ginger, who's got two kids now, who quit school year before last. Parry's never going to finish either. What's she got to do with Carrie any more? They're going different places. Different places, different crowds. And they're sorting. . . ."

"Now wait, Jeannie. Parry's just as bright, just as capable."

"They're in junior high, Mother. Don't you know about junior high? How they sort? And it's all where you're going. Yes and Parry's colored and Carrie's white. And you have to watch everything, what you wear and how you wear it and who you eat lunch with and how much homework you do and how you act to the teacher and what you laugh at. . . . And run with your crowd."

"It's that final?" asked Len. "Don't you think kids like Carol and Parry can show it doesn't *have* to be that way."

"They can't. They can't. They don't let you."

"No need to shout," he said mildly. "And who do you mean by 'they' and what do you mean by 'sorting'?"

How they sort. A foreboding of comprehension whirled within Helen. What was it Carol had told her of the Welcome Assembly the first day in junior high? The models showing How to Dress and How Not to Dress and half the girls in their loved new clothes watching their counterparts up on the stage—*their* straight skirt, their sweater, their earrings, lipstick, hairdo—"How Not to Dress," "a bad reputation for your school." It was nowhere in Carol's description, yet picturing it now, it seemed to Helen that a mute cry of violated dignity hung in the air. Later there had been a story of going to another Low 7 homeroom on an errand and seeing a teacher trying to wipe the forbidden lipstick off a girl who was fighting back and cursing. Helen could hear Carol's frightened, self-righteous tones: ". . . and I hope they expel her; she's the kind that gives Franklin Jr. a bad rep; she doesn't care about anything and always gets into fights." Yet there was nothing in these incidents to touch the heavy comprehension that waited. . . . Homework, the wonderings those times Jeannie and Carol needed help: "What if there's no one at home to give the help, and the teachers with their two hundred and forty kids a day can't or don't or the kids don't ask and they fall hopelessly behind, what then?"—but this too was unrelated. And what had it been that time about Parry? "Mother, Melanie and Sharon won't go if they know Parry's coming." Then of course you'll go with Parry, she's been your friend longer, she had answered, but where was it they were going and what had finally happened? Len, my head hurts, she felt like saying, in Carol's voice in the car, but Len's eyes were grave on Jeannie who was saying passionately:

"If you think it's so goddam important why do we have to live here where it's for real; why don't we move to Ivy like Betsy (yes, I know, money), where it's the deal to be buddies, in school anyway, three colored kids and their father's a doctor or judge or something big wheel and one always gets elected President or head song girl or something to prove oh how we're democratic. . . . What do you want of that poor kid anyway? Make up your mind. Stay friends with Parry—but be one of the kids. Sure. Be a brain—but not a square. Rise on up, college prep, but don't get separated. Yes, stay one of the kids, but. . . ."

"Jeannie. You're not talking about Carol at all, are you, Jeannie? Say it again. I wasn't listening. I was trying to think."

"She will not say it again," Len said firmly, "you look about ready to pull a Carol. One a day's our quota. And you, Jeannie, we'd better cool it. Too much to talk about for one session. . . . Here, come to the window and watch the Carol and Parry you're both so all worked up about."

In the wind and the shimmering sunset light, half the children of the block are playing down the street. Leaping, bouncing, hallooing, tugging the kites of spring. In the old synchronized understanding, Carol and Parry kick, catch, kick, catch. And now Parry jumps on her pogo stick (the last time), Carol shadowing her, and Bubbie, arching his body in a semicircle of joy, bounds after them, high, higher, higher.

And the months go by and supposedly it is forgotten, except for the now and then when, self-important, Carol will say: I really truly did nearly faint, didn't I, Mother, that time I went to church with Parry?

And now seldom Parry and Carol walk the hill together. Melanie's mother drives by to pick up Carol, and the several times Helen has suggested Parry, too, Carol is quick to explain: "She's already left" or "She isn't ready; she'll make us late."

And after school? Carol is off to club or skating or library or someone's house, and Parry can stay for kickball only on the rare afternoons when she does not have to hurry home where Lucy, Bubbie, and the cousins wait to be cared for, now Alva works the four to twelve-thirty shift.

No more the bending together over the homework. All semester the teachers have been different, and rarely Parry brings her books home, for where is there space or time and what is the sense? And the phone never rings with: what you going to wear tomorrow, are you bringing your lunch, or come on over, let's design some clothes for the Katy Keane comic-book contest. And Parry never drops by with Alva for Saturday snack to or from grocery shopping.

And the months go by and the sorting goes on and seemingly it is over until that morning when Helen must stay home from work, so swollen and feverish is Carol with mumps.

> The afternoon before, Parry had come by, skimming up the stairs, spilling books and binders on the bed: Hey frail, lookahere and wail, your momma askin for homework, what she got against YOU? . . . looking quickly once then not looking again and talking fast. . . . Hey, you bloomed. You gonna be your own pumpkin, hallowe'en? Your momma know yet it's mu-umps? And lumps. Momma says: no distress, she'll be by tomorrow morning see do you need anything while your momma's to work. . . . (Singing: *whole lotta shakin goin on.*) All your 'signments is inside; Miss Rockface says the teachers to write 'em cause I mightn't get it right all right.
>
> > *But did not tell:* Does your mother work for Carol's mother? Oh, you're neighbors! Very well, I'll send along a monitor to open Carol's locker but you're only to take these things I'm writing down, nothing else. Now say after me: Miss Campbell is trusting me to be a good responsible girl. And go right to Carol's house. After school. Not stop anywhere on the way. Not lose anything. And only take. What's written on the list.
>
> You really gonna mess with that book stuff? Sign on *mine* says do-not-open-until-eX-mas. . . . That Mrs. Fernandez doll she didn't send nothin, she was the only, says feel better and read a book to report if you feel like and I'm the most for takin care for you; she's my most, wish I could get her but she only teaches 'celerated. . . . Flicking the old read books on the shelf but not opening to mock-declaim as once she used to . . . Vicky, Eddie's g.f.[2] in Rockface office, she's on suspended for sure, yellin to Rockface: you bitchkitty don't you give me no more bad shit. That Vicky she can sure sling-ating-ring it. Staring out the window as if the tree not there in which they had hid out and rocked so often. . . . For sure. (*Keep mo-o-vin.*[3]) Got me a new pink top and lilac skirt. Look sharp with this purple?

2. Girl friend.
3. Words from "Whole Lotta Shakin' Goin' On" mentioned earlier in the passage and continued later; a famous Jerry Lee Lewis record of 1957.

Cinching in the wide belt as if delighted with what newly swelled above and swelled below. Wear it Saturday night to Sweet's, Sounds of Joy, Leroy and Ginny and me goin if Momma'll stay home. IF. (*Shake my baby shake.*) How come old folks still likes to party? Huh? Asking of Rembrandt's weary old face looking from the wall.[4] How come (softly) you long-gone you. Touching her face to his quickly, lightly. NEXT mumps is your buddybud Melanie's turn to tote your stuff. I'm gettin the hoovus groovus. Hey you so unneat, don't care what you bed with. Removing the books and binders, ranging them on the dresser one by one, marking lipstick faces—bemused or mocking or amazed—on each paper jacket. Better. Fluffing out smoothing the quilt with exaggerated energy. Any little thing I can get, cause I gotta blow. Tossing up and catching their year-ago, arm-in-arm graduation picture, replacing it deftly, upside down, into its mirror crevice. Joe. Bring you joy juice or fizz water or kickapoo? Adding a frown line to one bookface. Twanging the paper fishkite, the Japanese windbell overhead, setting the mobile they had once made of painted eggshells and decorated straws to twirling and rocking. And is gone.

She talked to the lipstick faces after, in her fever, tried to stand on her head to match the picture, twirled and twanged with the violent overhead.

Sleeping at last after the disordered night. Having surrounded herself with the furnishings of that world of childhood she no sooner learned to live in comfortably, then had to leave.

The dollhouse stands there to arrange and rearrange; the shell and picture card collections to re-sort and remember; the population of dolls given away to little sister, borrowed back, propped all round to dress and undress and caress.

She has thrown off her nightgown because of the fever, and her just budding breast is exposed where she reaches to hold the floppy plush dog that had been her childhood pillow.

Not for anything would her mother have disturbed her. Except that in the unaccustomedness of a morning at home, in the bruised restlessness after the sleepless night, Helen clicks on the radio—and the storm of singing whirls into the room:

. . . of trouble all mingled with fire
Come on my brethren we've got to go higher
Wade, wade. . . .

And Carol runs down the stairs, shrieking and shrieking. "Turn it off, Mother, turn it off." Hurling herself at the dial and wrenching it so it comes off in her hand.

"Ohhhhh," choked and convulsive, while Helen tries to hold her, to quiet.

"Mother, why did they sing and scream like that?"

"At Parry's church?"

"Yes." Rocking and strangling the cries. "I hear it all the time." Clinging and beseeching. ". . . What was it, Mother? Why?"

4. Rembrandt van Rijn (1600–1669), the great Dutch painter, produced perhaps 100 self-portraits.

Emotion, Helen thought of explaining, *a characteristic of the religion of all oppressed peoples, yes your very own great-grandparents*—thought of saying. And discarded.

Aren't you now, haven't you had feelings in yourself so strong they had to come out some way? ("what howls restrained by decorum")—thought of saying. And discarded.

Repeat Alva: *hope . . . every word out of their own life. A place to let go. And church is home*. And discarded.

The special history of the Negro people—history?—just you try living what must be lived every day—thought of saying. And discarded.

And said nothing.

And said nothing.

And soothed and held.

"Mother, a lot of the teachers and kids don't like Parry when they don't even know what she's like. Just because. . ." Rocking again, convulsive and shamed. "And I'm not really her friend any more."

No news. Betrayal and shame. Who betrayed? Whose shame? Brought herself to say aloud: "But may be friends again. As Alva and I are."

The sobbing a whisper. "That girl Vicky who got that way when I fainted, she's in school. She's the one keeps wearing the lipstick and they wipe it off and she's always in trouble and now maybe she's expelled. Mother."

"Yes, lambie."

"She acts so awful outside but I remember how she was in church and whenever I see her now I have to wonder. And hear . . . like I'm her, Mother, like I'm her." Clinging and trembling. "Oh why do I have to feel it happens to me too?

"Mother, I want to forget about it all, and not care,—like Melanie. Why can't I forget? *Oh why is it like it is and why do I have to care?*"

Caressing, quieting.

Thinking: *caring asks doing. It is a long baptism into the seas of humankind, my daughter. Better immersion than to live untouched. . . . Yet how will you sustain?*

Why is it like it is?

Sheltering her daughter close, mourning the illusion of the embrace.

And why do I have to care?

While in her, her own need leapt and plunged for the place of strength that was not—where one could scream or sorrow while all knew and accepted, and gloved and loving hands waited to support and understand.

1956

WILLIAM FAULKNER

The Old People

At first there was nothing. There was the faint, cold, steady rain, the gray and constant light of the late November dawn, with the voices of the hounds converging somewhere in it and toward them. Then Sam Fathers, standing just behind the boy as he had been standing when the boy shot his first running rabbit with his first gun and almost with the first load it ever carried, touched his shoulder and he began to shake, not with any cold. Then the buck was there. He did not come into sight; he was just there, looking not like a ghost but as if all of light were condensed in him and he were the source of it, not only moving in it but disseminating it, already running, seen first as you always see the deer, in that split second after he has already seen you, already slanting away in that first soaring bound, the antlers even in that dim light looking like a small rocking-chair balanced on his head.

"Now," Sam Fathers said, "shoot quick, and slow."

The boy did not remember that shot at all. He would live to be eighty, as his father and his father's twin brother and their father in his turn had lived to be, but he would never hear that shot nor remember even the shock of the gun-butt. He didn't even remember what he did with the gun afterward. He was running. Then he was standing over the buck where it lay on the wet earth still in the attitude of speed and not looking at all dead, standing over it shaking and jerking, with Sam Fathers beside him again, extending the knife. "Don't walk up to him in front," Sam said. "If he ain't dead, he will cut you all to pieces with his feet. Walk up to him from behind and take him by the horn first, so you can hold his head down until you can jump away. Then slip your other hand down and hook your fingers in his nostrils."

The boy did that—drew the head back and the throat taut and drew Sam Fathers' knife across the throat and Sam stooped and dipped his hands in the hot smoking blood and wiped them back and forth across the boy's face. Then Sam's horn rang in the wet gray woods and again and again; there was a boiling wave of dogs about them, with Tennie's Jim and Boon Hogganbeck whipping them back after each had had a taste of the blood, then the men, the true hunters—Walter Ewell whose rifle never missed, and Major de Spain and old General Compson and the boy's cousin, McCaslin Edmonds, grandson of his father's sister, sixteen years his senior and, since both he and McCaslin were only children and the boy's father had been nearing seventy when he was born, more his brother than his cousin and more his father than either—sitting their horses and looking down at them: at the old man of seventy who had been a Negro for two generations now but whose face and bearings were still those of the Chickasaw chief who had been his father; and the white boy of twelve with the prints of the bloody hands on his face, who had nothing to do now but stand straight and not let the trembling show.

"Did he do all right, Sam?" his cousin McCaslin said.

"He done all right," Sam Fathers said.

They were the white boy, marked forever, and the old dark man sired on both sides by savage kings, who had marked him, whose bloody hands had merely formally consecrated him to that which, under the man's tutelage, he had already accepted, humbly and joyfully, with abnegation and with pride too; the hands, the touch, the first worthy blood which he had been found at last worthy to draw, joining him and the man forever, so that the man would continue to live past the boy's seventy years and then eighty years, long after the man himself had entered the earth as chiefs and kings entered it;—the child, not yet a man, whose grandfather had lived in the same country and in almost the same manner as the boy himself would grow up to live, leaving his descendants in the land in his turn as his grandfather had done, and the old man past seventy whose grandfathers had owned the land long before the white men ever saw it and who had vanished from it now with all their kind, what of blood they left behind them running now in another race and for a while even in bondage and now drawing toward the end of its alien and irrevocable course, barren, since Sam Fathers had no children.

His father was Ikkemotubbe himself, who had named himself Doom. Sam told the boy about that—how Ikkemotubbe, old Issetibbeha's sister's son, had run away to New Orleans in his youth and returned seven years later with a French companion calling himself the Chevalier Soeur-Blonde de Vitry, who must have been the Ikkemotubbe of his family too and who was already addressing Ikkemotubbe as *Du Homme;*[1]—returned, came home again, with his foreign Aramis[2] and the quadroon slave woman who was to be Sam's mother, and a gold-laced hat and coat and a wicker wine-hamper containing a litter of month-old puppies and a gold snuff-box filled with a white powder resembling fine sugar. And how he was met at the River landing by three or four companions of his bachelor youth, and while the light of a smoking torch gleamed on the glittering braid of the hat and coat Doom squatted in the mud of the land and took one of the puppies from the hamper and put a pinch of the white powder on its tongue and the puppy died before the one who was holding it could cast it away. And how they returned to the Plantation where Issetibbeha, dead now, had been succeeded by his son, Doom's fat cousin Moketubbe, and the next day Moketubbe's eight-year-old son died suddenly and that afternoon, in the presence of Moketubbe and most of the others (the People, Sam Fathers called them) Doom produced another puppy from the wine-hamper and put a pinch of the white powder on its tongue and Moketubbe abdicated and Doom became in fact The Man which his French friend already called him. And how on the day after that, during the ceremony of accession, Doom pronounced a marriage between the pregnant quadroon and one of the slave men which he had just inherited (that was how Sam Fathers got his name, which in Chickasaw had been Had-Two-Fathers) and two years later sold the man and woman and the child who was his own son to his white neighbor, Carothers McCaslin.

That was seventy years ago. The Sam Fathers whom the boy knew was already sixty—a man not tall, squat rather, almost sedentary, flabby-looking though he actually was not, with hair like a horse's mane which even at seventy showed no trace of white and a face which

1. Mistaken or provincialized French for "The Man," with overtones of nobility. French nobility usually have, following their title, *de* or *d'* followed by a place name indicating their residence or seat—e.g., Duc d'Orléans. Even if "The Man," *l'homme,* were preceded by *de,* the proper form would be *de l'homme.*

2. One of Alexandre Dumas' three musketeers.

showed no age until he smiled, whose only visible trace of Negro blood was a slight dullness of the hair and the fingernails, and something else which you did notice about the eyes, which you noticed because it was not always there, only in repose and not always then—something not in their shape nor pigment but in their expression, and the boy's cousin McCaslin told him what that was: not the heritage of Ham, not the mark of servitude but of bondage; the knowledge that for a while that part of his blood had been the blood of slaves. "Like an old lion or a bear in a cage," McCaslin said. "He was born in the cage and has been in it all his life; he knows nothing else. Then he smells something. It might be anything, any breeze blowing past anything and then into his nostrils. But there for a second was the hot sand or the cane-brake that he never even saw himself, might not even know if he did see it and probably does know he couldn't hold his own with it if he got back to it. But that's not what he smells then. It was the cage he smelled. He hadn't smelled the cage until that minute. Then the hot sand or the brake blew into his nostrils and blew away, and all he could smell was the cage. That's what makes his eyes look like that."

"Then let him go!" the boy cried. "Let him go!"

His cousin laughed shortly. Then he stopped laughing, making the sound that is. It had never been laughing. "His cage ain't McCaslins," he said. "He was a wild man. When he was born, all his blood on both sides, except the little white part, knew things that had been tamed out of our blood so long ago that we have not only forgotten them, we have to live together in herds to protect ourselves from our own sources. He was the direct son not only of a warrior but of a chief. Then he grew up and began to learn things, and all of a sudden one day he found out that he had been betrayed, the blood of the warriors and chiefs had been betrayed. Not by his father," he added quickly. "He probably never held it against old Doom for selling him and his mother into slavery, because he probably believed the damage was already done before then and it was the same warriors' and chiefs' blood in him and Doom both that was betrayed through the black blood which his mother gave him. Not betrayed by the black blood and not wilfully betrayed by his mother, but betrayed by her all the same, who had bequeathed him not only the blood of slaves but even a little of the very blood which had enslaved it; himself his own battleground, the scene of his own vanquishment and the mausoleum of his defeat. His cage aint us," McCaslin said. "Did you ever know anybody yet, even your father and Uncle Buddy, that ever told him to do or not do anything that he ever paid any attention to?"

That was true. The boy first remembered him as sitting in the door of the plantation blacksmith-shop, where he sharpened plow-points and mended tools and even did rough carpenter-work when he was not in the woods. And sometimes, even when the woods had not drawn him, even with the shop cluttered with work which the farm waited on, Sam would sit there, doing nothing at all for half a day or a whole one, and no man, neither the boy's father and twin uncle in their day nor his cousin McCaslin after he became practical though not yet titular master, ever to say to him, "I want this finished by sundown" or "why wasn't this done yesterday?" And once each year, in the late fall, in

November, the boy would watch the wagon, the hooped canvas top erected now, being loaded—the food, hams and sausage from the smokehouse, coffee and flour and molasses from the commissary, a whole beef killed just last night for the dogs until there would be meat in camp, the crate containing the dogs themselves, then the bedding, the guns, the horns and lanterns and axes, and his cousin McCaslin and Sam Fathers in their hunting clothes would mount to the seat and with Tennie's Jim sitting on the dog-crate they would drive away to Jefferson, to join Major de Spain and General Compson and Boon Hogganbeck and Walter Ewell and go on into the big bottom of the Tallahatchie where the deer and bear were, to be gone two weeks. But before the wagon was even loaded the boy would find that he could watch no longer. He would go away, running almost, to stand behind the corner where he could not see the wagon and nobody could see him, not crying, holding himself rigid except for trembling, whispering to himself: "Soon now. Soon now. Just three more years" (or two more or one more) "and I will be ten. Then Cass said I can go."

White man's work, when Sam did work. Because he did nothing else: farmed no allotted acres of his own, as the other ex-slaves of old Carothers McCaslin did, performed no field-work for daily wages as the younger and newer Negroes did—and the boy never knew just how that had been settled between Sam and old Carothers, or perhaps with old Carothers' twin sons after him. For, although Sam lived among the Negroes, in a cabin among the other cabins in the quarters, and consorted with Negroes (what of consorting with anyone Sam did after the boy got big enough to walk alone from the house to the blacksmith-shop and then to carry a gun) and dressed like them and talked like them and even went with them to the Negro church now and then, he was still the son of that Chickasaw chief and the Negroes knew it. And, it seemed to the boy, not only Negroes. Boon Hogganbeck's grandmother had been a Chickasaw woman too, and although the blood had run white since and Boon was a white man, it was not chief's blood. To the boy at least, the difference was apparent immediately you saw Boon and Sam together, and even Boon seemed to know it was there—even Boon, to whom in his tradition it had never occurred that anyone might be better born than himself. A man might be smarter, he admitted that, or richer (luckier, he called it) but not better born. Boon was a mastiff, absolutely faithful, dividing his fidelity equally between Major de Spain and the boy's cousin McCaslin, absolutely dependent for his very bread and dividing that impartially too between Major de Spain and McCaslin, hardy, generous, courageous enough, a slave to all the appetites and almost unratiocinative. In the boy's eyes at least it was Sam Fathers, the Negro, who bore himself not only toward his cousin McCaslin and Major de Spain but toward all white men, with gravity and dignity and without servility or recourse to that impenetrable wall of ready and easy mirth which Negroes sustain between themselves and white men, bearing himself toward his cousin McCaslin not only as one man to another but as an older man to a younger.

He taught the boy the woods, to hunt, when to shoot and when not to shoot, when to kill and when not to kill, and better, what to do with it afterward. Then he would talk to the boy, the two of them sitting beneath the close fierce stars on a summer hilltop while they waited for the hounds to bring the fox back within hearing, or beside a fire in the November or December woods while the dogs worked out a coon's trail along the creek, or fireless in the pitch dark and heavy dew of April mornings while they squatted beneath a turkey-roost. The boy would never question him; Sam did not react to questions. The boy would just wait and then listen and Sam would begin, talking about the old days and the People whom he had not had time ever to know and so could not remember (he did not remember ever having seen his father's face), and in place of whom the other race into which his blood had run supplied him with no substitute.

And as he talked about those old times and those dead and vanished men of another race from either that the boy knew, gradually to the boy those old times would cease to be old times and would become a part of the boy's present, not only as if they had happened yesterday but as if they were still happening, the men who walked through them actually walking in breath and air and casting an actual shadow on the earth they had not quitted. And more: as if some of them had not happened yet but would occur tomorrow, until at last it would seem to the boy that he himself had not come into existence yet, that none of his race nor the other subject race which his people had brought with them into the land had come here yet; that although it had been his grandfather's and then his father's and uncle's and was now his cousin's and someday would be his own land which he and Sam hunted over, their hold upon it actually was as trivial and without reality as the now faded and archaic script in the chancery book[3] in Jefferson which allocated it to them and that it was he, the boy, who was the guest here and Sam Fathers' voice the mouthpiece of the host.

Until three years ago there had been two of them, the other a full-blood Chickasaw, in a sense even more incredibly lost than Sam Fathers. He called himself Jobaker, as if it were one word. Nobody knew his history at all. He was a hermit, living in a foul little shack at the forks of the creek five miles from the plantation and about that far from any other habitation. He was a market hunter and fisherman and he consorted with nobody, black or white; no Negro would even cross his path and no man dared approach his hut except Sam. And perhaps once a month the boy would find them in Sam's shop—two old men squatting on their heels on the dirt floor, talking in a mixture of Negroid English and flat hill dialect and now and then a phrase of that old tongue which as time went on and the boy squatted there too listening, he began to learn. Then Jobaker died. That is, nobody had seen him in some time. Then one morning Sam was missing, nobody, not even the boy, knew when nor where, until that night when some Negroes hunting in the creek bottom saw the sudden burst of flame and approached. It was Jobaker's hut, but before they got anywhere near it, someone shot at them from the shadows beyond it. It was Sam who fired, but nobody ever found Jobaker's grave.

The next morning, sitting at breakfast with his cousin, the boy saw Sam pass the dining-room window and he remembered then that never in his life before had he seen Sam nearer the house than the blacksmith-

3. Public records or archives.

shop. He stopped eating even; he sat there and he and his cousin both heard the voices from beyond the pantry door, then the door opened and Sam entered, carrying his hat in his hand but without knocking as anyone else on the place except a house servant would have done, entered just far enough for the door to close behind him and stood looking at neither of them—the Indian face above the nigger clothes, looking at something over their heads or at something not even in the room.

"I want to go," he said. "I want to go to the Big Bottom to live."

"To live?" the boy's cousin said.

"At Major de Spain's and your camp, where you go to hunt," Sam said. "I could take care of it for your all while you aint there. I will build me a little house in the woods, if you rather I didn't stay in the big one."

"What about Isaac here?" his cousin said. "How will you get away from him? Are you going to take him with you?" But still Sam looked at neither of them, standing just inside the room with that face which showed nothing, which showed that he was an old man only when it smiled.

"I want to go," he said. "Let me go."

"Yes," the cousin said quietly. "Of course. I'll fix it with Major de Spain. You want to go soon?"

"I'm going now," Sam said. He went out. And that was all. The boy was nine then; it seemed perfectly natural that nobody, not even his cousin McCaslin, should argue with Sam. Also, since he was nine now, he could understand that Sam could leave him and their days and nights in the woods together without any wrench. He believed that he and Sam both knew that this was not only temporary but that the exigencies of his maturing, of that for which Sam had been training him all his life some day to dedicate himself, required it. They had settled that one night last summer while they listened to the hounds bringing a fox back up the creek valley; now the boy discerned in that very talk under the high, fierce August stars a presage, a warning, of this moment today. "I done taught you all there is of this settled country," Sam said. "You can hunt it good as I can now. You are ready for the Big Bottom now, for bear and deer. Hunter's meat," he said. "Next year you will be ten. You will write your age in two numbers and you will be ready to become a man. Your pa" (Sam always referred to the boy's cousin as his father, establishing even before the boy's orphanhood did that relation between them not of the ward to his guardian and kinsman and chief and head of his blood, but of the child to the man who sired his flesh and his thinking too.) "promised you can go with us then." So the boy could understand Sam's going. But he couldn't understand why now, in March, six months before the moon for hunting.

"If Jobaker's dead like they say," he said, "and Sam hasn't got anybody but us at all kin to him, why does he want to go to the Big Bottom now, when it will be six months before we get there?"

"Maybe that's what he wants," McCaslin said. "Maybe he wants to get away from you a little while."

But that was all right. McCaslin and other grown people often said things like that and he paid no attention to them, just as he paid no attention to Sam saying he wanted to go to the Big Bottom to live. After all, he would have to live there for six months, because there would be no use in going at all if he was going to turn right around and come back. And, as Sam himself had told him, he already knew all about hunting in this settled country that Sam or anybody else could teach him. So it would be all right. Summer, then the bright days after the first frost, then the cold and himself on the wagon with McCaslin this time and the moment would come and he would draw the blood, the big blood which would make him a man, a hunter, and Sam would come back home with them and he too would have outgrown the child's pursuit of rabbits and 'possums. Then he too would make one before the winter fire, talking of the old hunts and the hunts to come as hunters talked.

So Sam departed. He owned so little that he could carry it. He walked. He would neither let McCaslin send him in the wagon, nor take a mule to ride. No one saw him go even. He was just gone one morning, the cabin which had never had very much in it, vacant and empty, the shop in which there never had been very much done, standing idle. Then November came at last, and now the boy made one—himself and his cousin McCaslin and Tennie's Jim, and Major de Spain and General Compson and Walter Ewell and Boon and old Uncle Ash to do the cooking, waiting for them in Jefferson with the other wagon, and the surrey in which he and McCaslin and General Compson and Major de Spain would ride.

Sam was waiting at the camp to meet them. If he was glad to see them, he did not show it. And if, when they broke camp two weeks later to return home, he was sorry to see them go, he did not show that either. Because he did not come back with them. It was only the boy who returned, returning solitary and alone to the settled familiar land, to follow for eleven months the childish business of rabbits and such while he waited to go back, having brought with him, even from his brief first sojourn, an unforgettable sense of the big woods—not a quality dangerous or particularly inimical, but profound, sentient, gigantic and brooding, amid which he had been permitted to go to and fro at will, unscathed, why he knew not, but dwarfed and, until he had drawn honorably blood worthy of being drawn, alien.

Then November, and they would come back. Each morning Sam would take the boy out to the stand allotted him. It would be one of the poorer stands of course, since he was only ten and eleven and twelve and he had never even seen a deer running yet. But they would stand there, Sam a little behind him and without a gun himself, as he had been standing when the boy shot the running rabbit when he was eight years old. They would stand there in the November dawns, and after a while they would hear the dogs. Sometimes the chase would sweep up and past quite close, belling and invisible; once they heard the two heavy reports of Boon Hogganbeck's old gun with which he had never killed anything larger than a squirrel and that sitting, and twice they heard the flat unreverberant clap of Walter Ewell's rifle, following which you did not even wait to hear his horn.

"I'll never get a shot," the boy said. "I'll never kill one."

"Yes, you will," Sam said. "You wait. You'll be a hunter. You'll be a man."

But Sam wouldn't come out. They would leave him there. He would come as far as the road where the surrey waited, to take the riding horses back, and that was all. The men would ride the horses and Uncle Ash and Tennie's Jim and the boy would follow in the wagon with Sam, with the camp equipment and the trophies, the meat, the heads, the antlers, the good ones, the wagon winding on among the tremendous gums and cypresses and oaks where no axe save that of the hunter had ever sounded between the impenetrable walls of cane and brier—the two changing yet constant walls just beyond which the wilderness whose mark he had brought away forever on his spirit even from that first two weeks seemed to lean, stooping a little, watching them and listening, not quite inimical because they were too small, even those such as Walter and Major de Spain and old General Compson who had killed many deer and bear, their sojourn too brief and too harmless to excite to that, but just brooding, secret, tremendous, almost inattentive.

Then they would emerge, they would be out of it, the line as sharp as the demarcation of a doored wall. Suddenly skeleton cotton- and corn-fields would flow away on either hand, gaunt and motionless beneath the gray rain; there would be a house, barns, fences, where the hand of man had clawed for an instant, holding, the wall of the wilderness behind them now, tremendous and still and seemingly impenetrable in the gray and fading light, the very tiny orifice through which they had emerged apparently swallowed up. The surrey would be waiting, his cousin McCaslin and Major de Spain and General Compson and Walter and Boon dismounted beside it. Then Sam would get down from the wagon and mount one of the horses and, with the others on a rope behind him, he would turn back. The boy would watch him for a while against that tall and secret wall, growing smaller and smaller against it, never looking back. Then he would enter it, returning to what the boy believed, and thought that his cousin McCaslin believed, was his loneliness and solitude.

2

So the instant came. He pulled trigger and Sam Fathers marked his face with the hot blood which he had spilled and he ceased to be a child and became a hunter and a man. It was the last day. They broke camp that afternoon and went out, his cousin and Major de Spain and General Compson and Boon on the horses. Walter Ewell and the Negroes in the wagon with him and Sam and his hide and antlers. There could have been (and were) other trophies in the wagon. But for him they did not exist, just as for all practical purposes he and Sam Fathers were still alone together as they had been that morning. The wagon wound and jolted between the slow and shifting yet constant walls from beyond and above which the wilderness watched them pass, less than inimical now and never to be inimical again since the buck still and forever leaped, the shaking gun-barrels coming constantly and forever steady at last, crashing, and still out of his instant of immortality the buck sprang, forever immortal;—the wagon jolting and bouncing on, the moment of the buck, the shot, Sam Fathers and himself and the blood with which Sam had marked him forever one with the wilderness which had accepted him since Sam said that he had done all right, when suddenly Sam reined back and stopped the wagon and they all heard the unmistakable and unforgettable sound of a deer breaking cover.

Then Boon shouted from beyond the bend of the trail and while they sat motionless in the halted wagon. Walter and the boy already reaching for their guns, Boon came galloping back, flogging his mule with his hat, his face wild and amazed as he shouted down at them. Then the other riders came around the bend, also spurring.

"Get the dogs!" Boon cried. "Get the dogs! If he had a nub on his head, he had fourteen points! Laying right there by the road in that pawpaw[4] thicket! If I'd a knowed he was there, I could have cut his throat with my pocket knife!"

"Maybe that's why he run," Walter said. "He saw you never had your gun." He was already out of the wagon with his rifle. Then the boy was out too with his gun, and the other riders came up and Boon got off his mule somehow and was scrabbling and clawing among the duffel[5] in the wagon, still shouting, "Get the dogs! Get the dogs!" And it seemed to the boy too that it would take them forever to decide what to do—the old men in whom the blood ran cold and slow, in whom during the intervening years between them and himself the blood had become a different and colder substance from that which ran in him and even in Boon and Walter.

"What about it, Sam?" Major de Spain said. "Could the dogs bring him back?"

"We wont need the dogs," Same said. "If he dont hear the dogs behind him, he will circle back in here about sundown to bed."

"All right," Major de Spain said. "You boys take the horses. We'll go on out to the road in the wagon and wait there." He and General Compson and McCaslin got into the wagon and Boon and Walter and Sam and the boy mounted the horses and turned back and out of the trail. Sam led them for an hour through the gray and unmarked afternoon whose light was little different from what it had been at dawn and which would become darkness without any graduation between. Then Sam stopped them.

"This is far enough," he said. "He'll be coming upwind, and he dont want to smell the mules." They tied the mounts in a thicket. Sam led them on foot now, unpathed through the markless afternoon, the boy pressing close behind him, the two others, or so it seemed to the boy, on his heels. But they were not. Twice Sam turned his head slightly and spoke back to him across his shoulder, still walking: "You got time. We'll get there fore he does."

So he tried to go slower. He tried deliberately to decelerate the dizzy rushing of time in which the buck which he had not even seen was moving, which it seemed to him must be carrying the buck farther and farther and more and more irretrievably away from them even though there were no dogs behind him now to make him run, even though, according to Sam, he must have completed his circle now and was heading back toward them. They went on; it could have been another hour or twice that or less than half, the boy could not have said. Then they were on a ridge. He had never been in here before and he

4. Papaw, tree of custard apple family. 5. Campers' personal gear.

could not see that it was a ridge. He just knew that the earth had risen slightly because the underbrush had thinned a little, the ground sloping invisibly away toward a dense wall of cane. Sam stopped. "This is it," he said. He spoke to Walter and Boon: "Follow this ridge and you will come to two crossings. You will see the tracks. If he crosses, it will be at one of these three."

Walter looked about for a moment. "I know it," he said. "I've even seen your deer. I was in here last Monday. He aint nothing but a yearling."

"A yearling?" Boon said. He was panting from the walking. His face still looked a little wild. "If the one I saw was any yearling, I'm still in kindergarden."

"Then I must have seen a rabbit," Walter said. "I always heard you quit school altogether two years before the first grade."

Boon glared at Walter. "If you dont want to shoot him, get out of the way," he said. "Set down somewhere. By God, I—"

"Aint nobody going to shoot him standing here," Sam said quietly.

"Sam's right," Walter said. He moved, slanting the worn, silver-colored barrel of his rifle downward to walk with it again. "A little more moving and a little more quiet too. Five miles is still Hogganbeck range, even if he wasn't downwind." They went on. The boy could still hear Boon talking, though presently that ceased too. Then once more he and Sam stood motionless together against a tremendous pin oak in a little thicket, and again there was nothing. There was only the soaring and somber solitude in the dim light, there was the thin murmur of the faint cold rain which had not ceased all day. Then, as if it had waited for them to find their positions and become still, the wilderness breathed again. It seemed to lean inward above them, above himself and Sam and Walter and Boon in their separate lurking-places, tremendous, attentive, impartial and omniscient, the buck moving in it somewhere, not running yet since he had not been pursued, not frightened yet and never fearsome but just alert also as they were alert, perhaps already circling back, perhaps quite near, perhaps conscious also of the eye of the ancient immortal Umpire. Because he was just twelve then, and that morning something had happened to him: in less than a second he had ceased forever to be the child he was yesterday. Or perhaps that made no difference, perhaps even a city-bred man, let alone a child, could not have understood it; perhaps only a country-bred one could comprehend loving the life he spills. He began to shake again.

"I'm glad it's started now," he whispered. He did not move to speak; only his lips shaped the expiring words: "Then it will be gone when I raise the gun—"

Nor did Sam. "Hush," he said.

"Is he that near?" the boy whispered. "Do you think—"

"Hush," Sam said. So he hushed. But he could not stop the shaking. He did not try, because he knew it would go away when he needed the steadiness—had not Sam Fathers already consecrated and absolved him from weakness and regret too?—not from love and pity for all which lived and ran and then ceased to live in a second in the very midst of splendor and speed, but from weakness and regret. So they stood motionless, breathing deep and quiet and steady. If there had been any sun, it would be near to setting now; there was a condensing, a densifying, of what he had thought was the gray and unchanging light until he realized suddenly that it was his own breathing, his heart, his blood—something, all things, and that Sam Fathers had marked him indeed, not as a mere hunter, but with something Sam had had in his turn of his vanished and forgotten people. He stopped breathing then; there was only his heart, his blood, and in the following silence the wilderness ceased to breathe also, leaning, stooping overhead with its breath held, tremendous and impartial and waiting. Then the shaking stopped too, as he had known it would, and he drew back the two heavy hammers of the gun.

Then it had passed. It was over. The solitude did not breathe again yet; it had merely stopped watching him and was looking somewhere else, even turning its back on him, looking on away up the ridge at another point, and the boy knew as well as if he had seen him that the buck had come to the edge of the cane and had either seen or scented them and faded back into it. But the solitude did not breathe again. It should have suspired again then but it did not. It was still facing, watching, what it had been watching and it was not here, not where he and Sam stood; rigid, not breathing himself, he thought, cried *No! No!*, knowing already that it was too late, thinking with the old despair of two and three years ago: *I'll never get a shot.* Then he heard it—the flat single clap of Walter Ewell's rifle which never missed. Then the mellow sound of the horn came down the ridge and something went out of him and he knew then he had never expected to get the shot at all.

"I reckon that's it," he said. "Walter got him." He had raised the gun slightly without knowing it. He lowered it again and had lowered one of the hammers and was already moving out of the thicket when Sam spoke.

"Wait."

"Wait?" the boy cried. And he would remember that—how he turned upon Sam in the truculence of a boy's grief over the missed opportunity, the missed luck. "What for? Dont you hear that horn?"

And he would remember how Sam was standing. Sam had not moved. He was not tall, squat rather and broad, and the boy had been growing fast for the past year or so and there was not much difference between them in height, yet Sam was looking over the boy's head and up the ridge toward the sound of the horn and the boy knew that Sam did not even see him; that Sam knew he was still there beside him but he did not see the boy. Then the boy saw the buck. It was coming down the ridge, as if it were walking out of the very sound of the horn which related its death. It was not running, it was walking, tremendous, unhurried, slanting and tilting its head to pass the antlers through the undergrowth, and the boy standing with Sam beside him now instead of behind him as Sam always stood, and the gun still partly aimed and one of the hammers still cocked.

Then it saw them. And still it did not begin to run. It just stopped for an instant, taller than any man, looking at them; then its muscles suppled, gathered. It did not even alter its course, not fleeing, not even running, just moving with that winged and effortless ease with which deer move, passing within twenty feet of them, its head high and the eye not proud and not haughty but just full and wild and unafraid, and Sam standing beside the boy now, his right arm raised at full length, palm-outward, speaking in that tongue which the boy had learned from listening to him and Jobaker in the blacksmith shop, while up the ridge Walter Ewell's horn was still blowing them in to a dead buck.

"Oleh, Chief," Sam said. "Grandfather."

When they reached Walter, he was standing with his back toward them, quite still, bemused almost, looking down at his feet. He didn't look up at all.

"Come here, Sam," he said quietly. When they reached him he still did not look up, standing above a little spike buck which had still been a fawn last spring. "He was so little I pretty near let him go," Walter said. "But just look at the track he was making. It's pretty near big as a cow's. If there were any more tracks here beside the ones he is laying in, I would swear there was another buck here that I never even saw."

3

It was dark when they reached the road where the surrey waited. It was turning cold, the rain had stopped, and the sky was beginning to blow clear. His cousin and Major de Spain and General Compson had a fire going. "Did you get him?" Major de Spain said.

"Got a good-sized swamp-rabbit with spike horns," Walter said. He slid the little buck down from his mule. The boy's cousin McCaslin looked at it.

"Nobody saw the big one?" he said.

"I dont even believe Boon saw it," Walter said. "He probably jumped somebody's stray cow in that thicket." Boon started cursing, swearing at Walter and at Sam for not getting the dogs in the first place and at the buck and all.

"Never mind," Major de Spain said. "He'll be here for us next fall. Let's get started home."

It was after midnight when they let Walter out at his gate two miles from Jefferson and later still when they took General Compson to his house and then returned to Major de Spain's, where he and McCaslin would spend the rest of the night, since it was still seventeen miles home. It was cold, the sky was clear now; there would be a heavy frost by sunup and the ground was already frozen beneath the horses' feet and the wheels and beneath their own feet as they crossed Major de Spain's yard and entered the house, the warm dark house, feeling their way up the dark stairs until Major de Spain found a candle and lit it, and into the strange room and the big deep bed, the still cold sheets until they began to warm to their bodies and at last the shaking stopped and suddenly he was telling McCaslin about it while McCaslin listened, quietly until he had finished. "You dont believe it," the boy said. "I know you dont—"

"Why not?" McCaslin said. "Think of all that has happened here, on this earth. All the blood hot and strong for living, pleasuring, that has soaked back into it. For grieving and suffering too, of course, but still getting something out of it for all that, getting a lot out of it, because after all you dont have to continue to bear what you believe is suffering; you can always choose to stop that, put an end to that. And even suffering and grieving is better than nothing; there is only one thing worse than not being alive, and that's shame. But you cant be alive forever, and you always wear out life long before you have exhausted the possibilities of living. And all that must be somewhere; all that could not have been invented and created just to be thrown away. And the earth is shallow; there is not a great deal of it before you come to the rock. And the earth dont want to just keep things, hoard them; it wants to use them again. Look at the seed, the acorns, at what happens even to carrion when you try to bury it: it refuses too, seethes and struggles too until it reaches light and air again, hunting the sun still. And they—" the boy saw his hand in silhouette for a moment against the window beyond which, accustomed to the darkness now, he could see sky where the scoured and icy stars glittered "—they dont want it, need it. Besides, what would it want, itself, knocking around out there, when it never had enough time about the earth as it was, when there is plenty of room about the earth, plenty of places still unchanged from what they were when the blood used and pleasured in them while it was still blood?"

"But we want them," the boy said. "We want them too. There is plenty of room for us and them too."

"That's right," McCaslin said. "Suppose they dont have substance, cant cast a shadow—"

"But I saw it!" the boy cried. "I saw him!"

"Steady," McCaslin said. For an instant his hand touched the boy's flank beneath the covers. "Steady. I know you did. So did I. Sam took me in there once after I killed my first deer."

1942

7 A MODE: FANTASY

There is a looser and wider-ranging system of literary classification than genres and kinds, one that looks at works (or even parts of works) not as organisms but in terms of **modes,** ways of perceiving or presenting experience. If we call the conventional literary genres poetry, drama, fiction, we call the conventional modes the **poetic** (or **lyric**), the **dramatic,** and the **narrative.** A work that is classified in the subgenre short story, within the genre fiction, may have passages in the poetic mode—passages marked by heightened and highly figurative language, intensification of rhythms and emotions, often focusing on the ideal or spiritual. The final paragraphs of *The Artificial Nigger,* Gurov standing by the sea or contemplating the nails in the gray fence around Anna's home in *Lady with the Dog,* the boy wandering through the Dublin streets full of frustration and shame in *Araby* are examples of poetic passages. Some portion of a story, even a whole story, may be in the dramatic mode, like a play with unmediated or unnarrated dialogue or action. In *The Most Dangerous Game,* General Zaroff and Rainsford's conversation at their first dinner seems like a scene from a play; it could be transferred to the stage almost without change. *The Lottery,* made up of dialogue and seemingly objective descriptions of action, comes about as close as a short story can to being fully dramatic, short of being reduced to pure dialogue.

Befitting the looseness of the term, modes do not descend in an orderly way through subheadings, as do genres through subgenres and kinds. **Fantasy,** for example, a literary mode involving the consciously unreal—places, societies, or beings that never existed, do not exist, or do not yet exist, or with qualities that are beyond or counter to the ordinary or commonsensical—can be found in fiction, poetry, or drama.

Fantastic fiction sometimes signals its fictionality immediately or very soon: "Once upon a time . . ."; "The story begins about a million kilometers sunward of Mars. . . ." At other times, it goes to some lengths to establish its "reality": many eighteenth-century novels about medieval castles and ghosts (Gothic novels) pretend to be editions of some monk's dusty manuscript, for example. Still other stories, such as *Dotson Gerber* and *A Very Old Man with Enormous Wings,* simply treat the incredible—a buried corpse growing, a man with wings—as perfectly natural, if not perfectly common.

Much fantasy has as its aim to stretch or expand our consciousness, our perception and conception of reality, sometimes even questioning our beliefs about the nature of reality. Some stories seek to open us up to possibilities by disorienting us, alternating or mixing the realistic, the fictional, the fantastic in dizzying patterns. *The Garden of Forking Paths* begins realistically, with documentation and an essay-like manner that makes it seem not like a story at all. Then the confession begins, and we recognize that we are in the midst of a common fictional kind, the spy story or thriller. The shift does not bother us too much —it's like the dusty-manuscript device, and the fictional kind we've entered on is so familiar that we're reasonably comfortable. Suddenly the spy story shifts once again, toward fantasy and, just as we're getting used to fantasy, to mysterious Chinese gardens and riddles. The fantasy is used to question whether it is the fantastic that is incredible, or whether our assumption that time is uniform and absolute is merely arbitrary and too restrictive—itself a fantasy. Given eternity, we must admit that everything that might possibly happen *will* happen. So when we make a choice, the choice we did not make but might have made will yet be made; its potential must be realized; it must exist somewhere in the vastness of eternity in a world of events parallel to our own. No wonder, then, when we return to the world of the spy story, which, though fictional, operates within the same notions of uniform, absolute time, it seems credible that the writer of the confession is not concerned with whether he lives or dies, realities that are now "unreal, insignificant."

I don't think what I have told you about *Forking Paths* will destroy your interest in the story—indeed, everyone can probably do with a little help in reading this fascinating story for the first time. Its questioning of our assumptions about reality is not too different from what's going on in modern thought. It is precisely because history, psychology, science, philosophy—almost all the intellectual disciplines—have in recent years most urgently called into question our long-standing assumptions about reality that fantasy seems so congenial a mode for us today.

From the middle of the nineteenth century to the middle of ours, the rise of the novel and the rise of realism were assumed to be the same thing, and we looked back on literary history as progress toward the literal, the factual, the ordinary (just as some art historians saw the Renaissance and what followed as demonstrating progress in man's ability to represent things "as they really are"). Long narratives that dwelled on the extraordinary, unusual, bizarre, or supernatural were called **romances,** as opposed to the more realistic **novel.**

The early modern short story leaned more heavily toward romance. Poe was perhaps our most widely respected writer, and you can see that *The Cask of Amontillado* is not exactly a story of everyday life. Late in the century, with de Maupassant in France and Chekhov in Russia (see *The Lady with the Dog*), the realistic short story seemed to have caught up with the novel.

But already in the nineteenth century "common sense" notions of realism were beginning to give way before the discovery of worlds beyond our unaided senses, observable through microscope and telescope. Darwin, with his notion that species themselves were not fixed but moving and changing in time, made the solid earth under our feet a little less solid. With the rise of psychology, which too was meant to capture more realms for consciousness and science, we became more and more aware that there were realities only dreamed of in our philosophies. When physics, the most advanced and scientific of the sciences, began to tell us that all our knowledge is, if not subjective, at least limited to what the human brain and its instruments can perceive, and is altered by our perception, we were not so sure anymore that reality was what existed "out there" or that we were contained between our hat and boots.

Perhaps the unsettling "retrogression" of science toward subjectivity has spurred on our most recent spate of the unreal or superreal; perhaps it was the nightmare of a human reality that could create a barbaric holocaust at Dachau or a scientific one at Hiroshima that made *rationality* and *science* and *realism* less automatically terms of positive value. Even the positive side of scientific achievement—space travel, walking on the moon, television and laser beams—destroyed our sense of a real and stable world and opened up other possibilities.

A generation or two ago, *Rosemary's Baby* or *The Exorcist* could have had only one ending—a rational explanation for the appearance of the supernatural. Few viewers or readers then would take seriously a work that was not embedded in a world of more or less everyday reality. The supernatural or fantastic in such a world had to be explained away as a dream, hallucination, or other psychological aberration, or as a hoax of some sort, set up to take in the foolish or credulous. Similarly, we would have had to explain away stories like *The Lottery* and García Márquez's *Very Old Man* by treating them as allegories. Now we can accept them as symbolic, as experiences that cannot be explained away or reduced to everyday terms, but exist on their own terms, explaining in fantasy more than we might in our discursive prose, our scientific formulas, graphs, and charts.

Not all fantasies seek to undermine conventional assumptions about reality or even to set up alternative, symbolic ways of comprehending reality. *Dotson Gerber* seems to use a fantastic event as a comic catalyst to clarify certain destructive tendencies in contemporary society, though it may imply that our actuality is itself a kind of fantasy land. The fantasy land of science fiction is usually the future—not so much never-never as never-yet land—which does not necessarily undermine or question conventional reality but projects potential consequences of present knowledge. There are those who maintain that for this very reason it is a mistake to call sci fi fantasy. Fantasy, they say, involves the incredible or impossible. Science fiction, while it may take place in the future or outside earthly reality, is neither incredible nor impossible but wholly logical, often based on real scientific principles. Others say that's exactly why it's fantasy: historical reality is never predictable, and certainly not by that fantasy called logic.

Science-fiction people are passionate, dedicated, and argumentative, so if it's risky to suggest that science fiction is in the mode of fantasy, it's even riskier to try to define science fiction as a kind, even though everyone will grant that generic definitions are at best only loose approximations. Approximately, science fiction is a narrative about events outside the bounds of Earth history in which science or advanced technology is often centrally important. The term *Earth history* allows for both space travel (to imaginary life on real or imaginary planets) in the present and time travel to prehistory. Science and technology in the stories can be important as a means of transhistorical travel, or in the operation of that imaginary world, or simply, as in *Hide and Seek*, in their preponderant role in the working out of the details of the plot. I'm sure this loose baggy monster of a definition leaves something out or includes too much, but at least it separates *Hide and Seek* from the other three fantasy stories here, and from *The Lottery* and *The Rocking-Horse Winner*, and, in "Stories for Further Reading," from *The Kugelmass Episode* and *A Hunger Artist*. (What would you say about *The Ones Who Walk Away from Omelas*?)

ARTHUR C. CLARKE

Hide and Seek

We were walking back through the woods when Kingman saw the gray squirrel. Our bag was a small but varied one—three grouse, four rabbits (one, I am sorry to say, an infant in arms) and a couple of pigeons. And contrary to certain dark forecasts, both the dogs were still alive.

The squirrel saw us at the same moment. It knew that it was marked for immediate execution as a result of the damage it had done to the trees on the estate, and perhaps it had lost close relatives to Kingman's gun. In three leaps it had reached the base of the nearest tree, and vanished behind it in a flicker of gray. We saw its face once more, appearing for a moment round the edge of its shield a dozen feet from the ground; but though we waited, with guns leveled hopefully at various branches, we never saw it again.

Kingman was very thoughtful as we walked back across the lawn to the magnificent old house. He said nothing as we handed our victims to the cook—who received them without much enthusiasm—and only emerged from his reverie when we were sitting in the smoking room and he remembered his duties as a host.

"That tree-rat," he said suddenly (he always called them "tree-rats," on the grounds that people were too sentimental to shoot the dear little squirrels), "it reminded me of a very peculiar experience that happened shortly before I retired. Very shortly indeed, in fact."

"I thought it would," said Carson dryly. I gave him a glare: he'd been in the Navy and had heard Kingman's stories before, but they were still new to me.

"Of course," Kingman remarked, slightly nettled, "if you'd rather I didn't . . ."

"Do go on," I said hastily. "You've made me curious. What connection there can possibly be between a gray squirrel and the Second Jovian War I can't imagine."

Kingman seemed mollified.

"I think I'd better change some names," he said thoughtfully, "but I won't alter the places. The story begins about a million kilometers sunward of Mars. . . ."

K.15 was a military intelligence operative. It gave him considerable pain when unimaginative people called him a spy, but at the moment he had much more substantial grounds for complaint. For some days now a fast enemy cruiser had been coming up astern, and though it was flattering to have the undivided attention of such a fine ship and so many highly trained men, it was an honor that K.15 would willingly have forgone.

What made the situation doubly annoying was the fact that his friends would be meeting him off Mars in about twelve hours, aboard a ship quite capable of dealing with a mere cruiser—from which you will gather that K.15 was a person of some importance. Unfortunately, the most optimistic calculation showed that the pursuers would be within accurate gun range in six hours. In some six hours five minutes, therefore, K.15 was likely to occupy an extensive and still expanding volume of space.

There might just be time for him to land on Mars, but that would be one of the worst things he could do. It would certainly annoy the aggressively neutral Martians, and the political complications would be frightful. Moreover, if his friends *had* to come down to the planet to rescue him, it would cost them more than ten kilometers a second in fuel—most of their operational reserve.

He had only one advantage, and that a very dubious one. The commander of the cruiser might guess that he was heading for a rendezvous, but he would not know how close it was or how large was the ship that was coming to meet him. If he could keep alive for only twelve hours, he would be safe. The "if" was a somewhat considerable one.

K.15 looked moodily at his charts, wondering if it was worthwhile to burn the rest of his fuel in a final dash. But a dash to where? He would be completely helpless then, and the pursuing ship might still have enough in her tanks to catch him as he flashed outward into the empty darkness, beyond all hope of rescue—passing his friends as they came sunward at a relative speed so great that they could do nothing to save him.

With some people, the shorter the expectation of life, the more sluggish are the mental processes. They seem hypnotized by the approach of death, so resigned to their fate that they do nothing to avoid it. K.15, on the other hand, found that his mind worked better in such a desperate emergency. It began to work now as it had seldom done before.

Commander Smith—the name will do as well as any other—of the cruiser *Doradus* was not unduly surprised when K.15 began to decelerate. He had half expected the spy to land on Mars, on the principle that internment was better than annihilation, but when the plotting room brought the news that the little scout ship was heading for Phobos, he felt completely baffled. The inner moon was nothing but a jumble of rock some twenty kilometers across, and not even the economical Martians had ever found any use for it. K.15 must be pretty desperate if he thought it was going to be of any greater value to him.

The tiny scout had almost come to rest when the radar operator lost it against the mass of Phobos. During the braking maneuver, K.15 had squandered most of his lead and the *Doradus* was now only minutes away—though she was now beginning to decelerate lest she overrun him. The cruiser was scarcely three thousand kilometers from Phobos when she came to a complete halt: of K.15's ship, there was still no sign. It should be easily visible in the telescopes, but it was probably on the far side of the little moon.

It reappeared only a few minutes later, traveling under full thrust on a course directly away from the sun. It was accelerating at almost five gravities—and it had broken its radio silence. An automatic recorder was broadcasting over and over again this interesting message:

"I have landed on Phobos and am being attacked by a Z-class cruiser. Think I can hold out until you come, but hurry."

The message wasn't even in code, and it left Commander Smith a sorely puzzled man. The assumption that K.15 was still aboard the ship and that the whole thing was a ruse was just a little too naïve. But it might be a double bluff: the message had obviously been left in plain language so that he would receive it and be duly confused. He could afford neither the time nor the fuel to chase the scout if K.15

really had landed. It was clear that reinforcements were on the way, and the sooner he left the vicinity the better. The phrase "Think I can hold out until you come" might be a piece of sheer impertinence, or it might mean that help was very near indeed.

Then K.15's ship stopped blasting. It had obviously exhausted its fuel, and was doing a little better than six kilometers a second away from the sun. K.15 *must* have landed, for his ship was now speeding helplessly out of the solar system. Commander Smith didn't like the message it was broadcasting, and guessed that it was running into the track of an approaching warship at some indefinite distance, but there was nothing to be done about that. The *Doradus* began to move toward Phobos, anxious to waste no time.

On the face of it, Commander Smith seemed the master of the situation. His ship was armed with a dozen heavy guided missiles and two turrets of electromagnetic guns. Against him was one man in a space suit, trapped on a moon only twenty kilometers across. It was not until Commander Smith had his first good look at Phobos, from a distance of less than a hundred kilometers, that he began to realize that, after all, K.15 might have a few cards up his sleeve.

To say that Phobos has a diameter of twenty kilometers, as the astronomy books invariably do, is highly misleading. The word "diameter" implies a degree of symmetry which Phobos most certainly lacks. Like those other lumps of cosmic slag, the asteroids, it is a shapeless mass of rock floating in space with, of course, no hint of an atmosphere and not much more gravity. It turns on its axis once every seven hours thirty-nine minutes, thus keeping the same face always to Mars—which is so close that appreciably less than half the planet is visible, the poles being below the curve of the horizon. Beyond this, there is very little more to be said about Phobos.

K.15 had no time to enjoy the beauty of the crescent world filling the sky above him. He had thrown all the equipment he could carry out of the air lock, set the controls, and jumped. As the little ship went flaming out toward the stars he watched it go with feelings he did not care to analyze. He had burned his boats with a vengeance, and he could only hope that the oncoming battleship would intercept the radio message as the empty vessel went racing by into nothingness. There was also a faint possibility that the enemy cruiser might go in pursuit, but that was rather too much to hope for.

He turned to examine his new home. The only light was the ocher radiance of Mars, since the sun was below the horizon, but that was quite sufficient for his purpose and he could see very well. He stood in the center of an irregular plain about two kilometers across, surrounded by low hills over which he could leap rather easily if he wished. There was a story he remembered reading long ago about a man who had accidentally jumped off Phobos: that wasn't quite possible—though it was on Deimos—because the escape velocity was still about ten meters a second. But unless he was careful, he might easily find himself at such a height that it would take hours to fall back to the surface—and that would be fatal. For K.15's plan was a simple one: he must remain as close to the surface of Phobos as possible—

and diametrically opposite the cruiser. The *Doradus* could then fire all her armament against the twenty kilometers of rock, and he wouldn't even feel the concussion. There were only two serious dangers, and one of these did not worry him greatly.

To the layman, knowing nothing of the finer details of astronautics, the plan would have seemed quite suicidal. The *Doradus* was armed with the latest in ultrascientific weapons: moreover, the twenty kilometers which separated her from her prey represented less than a second's flight at maximum speed. But Commander Smith knew better, and was already feeling rather unhappy. He realized, only too well, that of all the machines of transport man has ever invented, a cruiser of space is far and away the least maneuverable. It was a simple fact that K.15 could make half a dozen circuits of his little world while her commander was persuading the *Doradus* to make even one.

There is no need to go into technical details, but those who are still unconvinced might like to consider these elementary facts. A rocket-driven spaceship can, obviously, only accelerate along its major axis —that is, "forward." Any deviation from a straight course demands a physical turning of the ship, so that the motors can blast in another direction. Everyone knows that this is done by internal gyros or tangential steering jets, but very few people know just how long this simple maneuver takes. The average cruiser, fully fueled, has a mass of two or three thousand tons, which does not make for rapid footwork. But things are even worse than this, for it isn't the mass, but the moment of inertia that matters here—and since a cruiser is a long, thin object, its moment of inertia is slightly colossal. The sad fact remains (though it is seldom mentioned by astronautical engineers) that it takes a good ten minutes to rotate a spaceship through one hundred and eighty degrees, with gyros of any reasonable size. Control jets aren't much quicker, and in any case their use is restricted because the rotation they produce is permanent and they are liable to leave the ship spinning like a slow-motion pinwheel, to the annoyance of all inside.

In the ordinary way, these disadvantages are not very grave. One has millions of kilometers and hundreds of hours in which to deal with such minor matters as a change in the ship's orientation. It is definitely against the rules to move in ten-kilometer-radius circles, and the commander of the *Doradus* felt distinctly aggrieved. K.15 wasn't playing fair.

At the same moment that resourceful individual was taking stock of the situation, which might very well have been worse. He had reached the hills in three jumps and felt less naked than he had out in the open plain. The food and equipment he had taken from the ship he had hidden where he hoped he could find it again, but since his suit could keep him alive for over a day that was the least of his worries. The small packet that was the cause of all the trouble was still with him, in one of those numerous hiding places a well-designed space suit affords.

There was an exhilarating loneliness about his mountain eyrie, even though he was not quite as lonely as he would have wished. Forever fixed in his sky, Mars was waning almost visibly as Phobos swept above the night side of the planet. He could just make out the lights of some of the Martian cities, gleaming pinpoints marking the junctions of the invisible canals. All else was stars and silence and a line of jagged peaks so close it seemed he could almost touch them. Of the *Doradus* there was still no sign. She was presumably carrying out a careful telescopic examination of the sunlighted side of Phobos.

Mars was a very useful clock: when it was half full the sun would rise and, very probably, so would the *Doradus.* But she might approach from some quite unexpected quarter: she might even—and this was the one real danger—she might even have landed a search party.

This was the first possiblity that had occurred to Commander Smith when he saw just what he was up against. Then he realized that the surface area of Phobos was over a thousand square kilometers and that he could not spare more than ten men from his crew to make a search of that jumbled wilderness. Also, K.15 would certainly be armed.

Considering the weapons which the *Doradus* carried, this last objection might seem singularly pointless. It was very far from being so. In the ordinary course of business, sidearms and other portable weapons are as much use to a space cruiser as are cutlasses and crossbows. The *Doradus* happened, quite by chance—and against regulations at that—to carry one automatic pistol and a hundred rounds of ammunition. Any search party would therefore consist of a group of unarmed men looking for a well-concealed and very desperate individual who could pick them off at his leisure. K.15 was breaking the rules again.

The terminator of Mars was now a perfectly straight line, and at almost the same moment the sun came up, not so much like thunder as like a salvo of atomic bombs. K.15 adjusted the filters of his visor and decided to move. It was safer to stay out of the sunlight, not only because here he was less likely to be detected in the shadow but also because his eyes would be much more sensitive there. He had only a pair of binoculars to help him, whereas the *Doradus* would carry an electronic telescope of twenty-centimeter aperture at least.

It would be best, K.15 decided, to locate the cruiser if he could. It might be a rash thing to do, but he would feel much happier when he knew exactly where she was and could watch her movements. He could then keep just below the horizon, and the glare of the rockets would give him ample warning of any impending move. Cautiously launching himself along an almost horizontal trajectory, he began the circumnavigation of his world.

The narrowing crescent of Mars sank below the horizon until only one vast horn reared itself enigmatically against the stars. K.15 began to feel worried: there was still no sign of the *Doradus*. But this was hardly surprising, for she was painted black as night and might be a good hundred kilometers away in space. He stopped, wondering if he had done the right thing after all. Then he noticed that something quite large was eclipsing the stars almost vertically overhead, and was moving swiftly even as he watched. His heart stopped for a moment: then he was himself again, analyzing the situation and trying to discover how he had made so disastrous a mistake.

It was some time before he realized that the black shadow slipping across the sky was not the cruiser at all, but something almost equally deadly. It was far smaller, and far nearer, than he had at first thought. The *Doradus* had sent her television-homing guided missiles to look for him.

This was the second danger he had feared, and there was nothing he could do about it except to remain as inconspicuous as possible. *Doradus* now had many eyes searching for him, but these auxiliaries had very severe limitations. They had been built to look for sunlit spaceships against a background of stars, not to search for a man hiding in a dark jungle of rock. The definition of their television systems was low, and they could only see in the forward direction.

There were rather more men on the chessboard now, and the game was a little deadlier, but his was still the advantage.

The torpedo vanished into the night sky. As it was traveling on a nearly straight source in this low-gravitational field, it would soon be leaving Phobos behind, and K.15 waited for what he knew must happen. A few minutes later, he saw a brief stabbing of rocket exhausts and guessed that the projectile was swinging slowly back on its course. At almost the same moment he saw another flare far away in the opposite quarter of the sky, and wondered just how many of these infernal machines were in action. From what he knew of Z-class cruisers—which was a good deal more than he should—there were four missile-control channels, and they were probably all in use.

He was suddenly struck by an idea so brilliant that he was quite sure it couldn't possibly work. The radio on his suit was a tunable one, covering an unusually wide band, and somewhere not far away the *Doradus* was pumping out power on everything from a thousand megacycles upward. He switched on the receiver and began to explore.

It came in quickly—the raucous whine of a pulse transmitter not far away. He was probably only picking up a subharmonic, but that was quite good enough. It D/F'ed[1] sharply, and for the first time K.15 allowed himself to make long-range plans about the future. The *Doradus* had betrayed herself: as long as she operated her missiles, he would know exactly where she was.

He moved cautiously forward toward the transmitter. To his surprise the signal faded, then increased sharply again. This puzzled him until he realized that he must be moving through a diffraction zone. Its width might have told him something useful if he had been a good-enough physicist, but he couldn't imagine what.

The *Doradus* was hanging about five kilometers above the surface, in full sunlight. Her "nonreflecting" paint was overdue for renewal, and K.15 could see her clearly. Since he was still in darkness, and the shadow line was moving away from him, he decided that he was as safe here as anywhere. He settled down comfortably so that he could just see the cruiser and waited, feeling fairly certain than none of the guided projectiles would come so near the ship. By now, he calculated, the commander of the *Doradus* must be getting pretty mad. He was perfectly correct.

1. Detected or found the direction (thus D/F, direction finder) of the transmitter.

After an hour, the cruiser began to heave herself round with all the grace of a bogged hippopotamus. K.15 guessed what was happening. Commander Smith was going to have to look at the antipodes, and was preparing for the perilous fifty-kilometer journey. He watched very carefully to see the orientation the ship was adopting, and when she came to rest again was relieved to see that she was almost broadside to him. Then, with a series of jerks that could not have been very enjoyable aboard, the cruiser began to move down to the horizon. K.15 followed her at a comfortable walking pace—if one could use the phrase—reflecting that this was a feat very few people had ever performed. He was particularly careful not to overtake her on one of his kilometer-long glides, and kept a close watch for any missiles that might be coming up astern.

It took the *Doradus* nearly an hour to cover the fifty kilometers. This, as K.15 amused himself by calculating, represented considerably less than a thousandth of her normal speed. Once she found herself going off into space at a tangent, and rather than waste time turning end over end again fired off a salvo of shells to reduce speed. But she made it at last, and K.15 settled down for another vigil, wedged between two rocks where he could just see the cruiser and he was quite sure she couldn't see him. It occurred to him that by this time Commander Smith might have grave doubts as to whether he really was on Phobos at all, and he felt like firing off a signal flare to reassure him. However, he resisted the temptation.

There would be little point in describing the events of the next ten hours, since they differed in no important detail from those that had gone before. The *Doradus* made three other moves, and K.15 stalked her with the care of a big-game hunter following the spoor of some elephantine beast. Once, when she would have led him out into full sunlight, he let her fall below the horizon until he could only just pick up her signals. But most of the time he kept her just visible, usually low down behind some convenient hill.

Once a torpedo exploded some kilometers away, and K.15 guessed that some exasperated operator had seen a shadow he didn't like—or else that a technician had forgotten to switch off a proximity fuse. Otherwise nothing happened to enliven the proceedings: in fact, the whole affair was becoming rather boring. He almost welcomed the sight of an occasional guided missile drifting inquisitively overhead, for he did not believe that they could see him if he remained motionless and in reasonable cover. If he could have stayed on the part of Phobos exactly opposite the cruiser he would have been safe even from these, he realized, since the ship would have no control there in the moon's radio-shadow.[2] But he could think of no reliable way in which he could be sure of staying in the safety zone if the cruiser moved again.

The end came very abruptly. There was a sudden blast of steering jets, and the cruiser's main drive burst forth in all its power and splendor. In seconds the *Doradus* was shrinking sunward, free at last,

2. Since radio waves move in a straight line, so long as K.15 keeps the moon Phobos between himself and the *Doradus*, the ship cannot successfully fire radio-guided missles at him.

thankful to leave, even in defeat, this miserable lump of rock that had so annoyingly balked her of her legitimate prey. K.15 knew what had happened, and a great sense of peace and relaxation swept over him. In the radar room of the cruiser, someone had seen an echo of disconcerting amplitude approaching with altogether excessive speed. K.15 now had only to switch on his suit beacon and to wait. He could even afford the luxury of a cigarette.

"Quite an interesting story," I said, "and I see now how it ties up with that squirrel. But it does raise one or two queries in my mind."

"Indeed?" said Rupert Kingman politely.

I always like to get to the bottom of things, and I knew that my host had played a part in the Jovian War about which he very seldom spoke. I decided to risk a long shot in the dark.

"May I ask how you happen to know so much about this unorthodox military engagement? It isn't possible, is it, that *you* were K.15?"

There was an odd sort of strangling noise from Carson. Then Kingman said, quite calmly: "No, I wasn't."

He got to his feet and went off toward the gun room.

"If you'll excuse me a moment, I'm going to have another shot at that tree-rat. Maybe I'll get him this time." Then he was gone.

Carson looked at me as if to say: "This is another house you'll never be invited to again." When our host was out of earshot he remarked in a coldly cynical voice:

"You've done it. What did you have to say that for?"

"Well, it seemed a safe guess. How else could he have known all that?"

"As a matter of fact, I believe he met K.15 after the War: they must have had an interesting conversation together. But I thought you knew that Rupert was retired from the service with only the rank of lieutenant commander. The Court of Inquiry could never see his point of view. After all, it just wasn't reasonable that the commander of the fastest ship in the Fleet couldn't catch a man in a space suit."

p. 1949

JORGE LUIS BORGES

The Garden of Forking Paths*

On page 22 of Liddell Hart's *History of World War I* you will read that an attack against the Serre-Montauban[1] line by thirteen British

*Translated by Donald A. Yates.

1. Liddell Hart's work is entitled *The Real War, 1914–1918* (1930) and *A History of the World War, 1914–1918* in the enlarged English-language edition (1934). The events of July 1916 do not appear on page 22 in the first and are unlikely to appear so early in any edition. A line between Serre and Montauban forms a defensive position about a hundred miles north-northeast of Paris, north of the Somme River. There is a dizzying mixture of factual references and fiction in this story, the most unlikely often being the factual.

divisions (supported by 1,400 artillery pieces), planned for the 24th of July, 1916, had to be postponed until the morning of the 29th. The torrential rains, Captain Liddell Hart comments, caused this delay, an insignificant one, to be sure.

The following statement, dictated, reread and signed by Dr. Yu Tsun, former professor of English at the *Hochschule* at Tsingtao,[2] throws an unsuspected light over the whole affair. The first two pages of the document are missing.

". . . and I hung up the receiver. Immediately afterwards, I recognized the voice that had answered in German. It was that of Captain Richard Madden. Madden's presence in Viktor Runeberg's apartment meant the end of our anxieties and—but this seemed, *or should have seemed,* very secondary to me—also the end of our lives. It meant that Runeberg had been arrested or murdered.[3] Before the sun set on that day, I would encounter the same fate. Madden was implacable. Or rather, he was obliged to be so. An Irishman at the service of England, a man accused of laxity and perhaps of treason, how could he fail to seize and be thankful for such a miraculous opportunity: the discovery, capture, maybe even the death of two agents of the German Reich? I went up to my room; absurdly I locked the door and threw myself on my back on the narrow iron cot. Through the window I saw the familiar roofs and the cloud-shaded six o'clock sun. It seemed incredible to me that that day without premonitions or symbols should be the one of my inexorable death. In spite of my dead father, in spite of having been a child in a symmetrical garden of Hai Feng,[4] was I—now—going to die? Then I reflected that everything happens to a man precisely, precisely *now.* Centuries of centuries and only in the present do things happen; countless men in the air, on the face of the earth and the sea, and all that really is happening is happening to me . . . The almost intolerable recollection of Madden's horselike face banished these wanderings. In the midst of my hatred and terror (it means nothing to me now to speak of terror, now that I have mocked Richard Madden, now that my throat yearns for the noose) it occurred to me that that tumultuous and doubtless happy warrior did not suspect that I possessed the Secret. The name of the exact location of the new British artillery park on the River Ancre.[5] A bird streaked across the gray sky and blindly I translated it into an airplane and that airplane into many (against the French sky) annihilating the artillery station with vertical bombs. If only my mouth, before a bullet shattered it, could cry out that secret name so it could be heard in Germany . . . My human voice was very weak. How might I make it carry to the ear of the Chief? To the ear of that sick and hateful man who knew nothing of Runeberg and me save that we were in Staffordshire[6] and who was wait-

2. The high school in what was the capital of the German colonial enclave until the First World War.

3. An hypothesis both hateful and odd. The Prussian spy Hans Rabener, alias Viktor Runeberg, attacked with drawn automatic the bearer of the warrant for his arrest, Captain Richard Madden. The latter, in self-defense, inflicted the wound which brought about Runeberg's death. (Borges's note.)

4. Chinese gardens usually aim for the appearance of nature, so a symmetrical garden would be unusual. Hai Feng seems fictional, as many names here are, but Hai-fang is Chinese for the Vietnamese city of Haiphong and is near the Yunnan province mentioned later.

5. River in northeastern France.

6. County in English midlands.

ing in vain for our report in his arid office in Berlin, endlessly examining newspapers . . . I said out loud: *I must flee.* I sat up noiselessly, in a useless perfection of silence, as if Madden were already lying in wait for me. Something—perhaps the mere vain ostentation of proving my resources were nil—made me look through my pockets. I found what I knew I would find. The American watch, the nickel chain and the square coin, the key ring with the incriminating useless keys to Runeberg's apartment, the notebook, a letter which I resolved to destroy immediately (and which I did not destroy), a crown, two shillings and a few pence,[7] the red-and-blue pencil, the handkerchief, the revolver with one bullet. Absurdly, I took it in my hand and weighed it in order to inspire courage within myself. Vaguely I thought that a pistol report can be heard at a great distance. In ten minutes my plan was perfected. The telephone book listed the name of the only person capable of transmitting the message; he lived in a suburb of Fenton, less than a half hour's train ride away.

I am a cowardly man. I say it now, now that I have carried to its end a plan whose perilous nature no one can deny. I know its execution was terrible. I didn't do it for Germany, no. I care nothing for a barbarous country which imposed upon me the abjection of being a spy. Besides, I know of a man from England—a modest man—who for me is no less great than Goethe. I talked with him for scarcely an hour, but during that hour he was Goethe . . . I did it because I sensed that the Chief somehow feared people of my race—for the innumerable ancestors who merge within me. I wanted to prove to him that a yellow man could save his armies. Besides, I had to flee from Captain Madden. His hands and his voice could call at my door at any moment. I dressed silently, bade farewell to myself in the mirror, went downstairs, scrutinized the peaceful street and went out. The station was not far from my home, but I judged it wise to take a cab. I argued that in this way I ran less risk of being recognized; the fact is that in the deserted street I felt myself visible and vulnerable, infinitely so. I remember that I told the cab driver to stop a short distance before the main entrance. I got out with voluntary, almost painful slowness; I was going to the village of Ashgrove but I bought a ticket for a more distant station. The train left within a very few minutes, at eight-fifty. I hurried; the next one would leave at nine-thirty. There was hardly a soul on the platform. I went through the coaches; I remember a few farmers, a woman dressed in mourning, a young boy who was reading with fervor the *Annals* of Tacitus,[8] a wounded and happy soldier. The coaches jerked forward at last. A man whom I recognized ran in vain to the end of the platform. It was Captain Richard Madden. Shattered, trembling, I shrank into the far corner of the seat, away from the dreaded window.

From this broken state I passed into an almost abject felicity. I told myself that the duel had already begun and that I had won the first encounter by frustrating, even if for forty minutes, even if by a

7. Though the two dollars' worth of coins would be worth quite a bit more at present, it still is not much for a middle-class person to be carrying.

8. The Annals of Cornelius Tacitus (55?–117?) treat the history of Rome from the death of Augustus in 14 to the end of Nero's reign in 68, and the military events of the period.

stroke of fate, the attack of my adversary. I argued that this slightest of victories foreshadowed a total victory. I argued (no less fallaciously) that my cowardly felicity proved that I was a man capable of carrying out the adventure successfully. From this weakness I took strength that did not abandon me. I foresee that man will resign himself each day to more atrocious undertakings; soon there will be no one but warriors and brigands; I give them this counsel: *The author of an atrocious undertaking ought to imagine that he has already accomplished it, ought to impose upon himself a future as irrevocable as the past.* Thus I proceeded as my eyes of a man already dead registered the elapsing of that day, which was perhaps the last, and the diffusion of the night. The train ran gently along, amid ash trees. It stopped, almost in the middle of the fields. No one announced the name of the station. "Ashgrove?" I asked a few lads on the platform. "Ashgrove," they replied. I got off.

A lamp enlightened the platform but the faces of the boys were in shadow. One questioned me, "Are you going to Dr. Stephen Albert's house?" Without waiting for my answer, another said, "The house is a long way from here, but you won't get lost if you take this road to the left and at every crossroads turn again to your left." I tossed them a coin (my last), descended a few stone steps and started down the solitary road. It went downhill, slowly. It was of elemental earth; overhead the branches were tangled; the low, full moon seemed to accompany me.

For an instant, I thought that Richard Madden in some way had penetrated my desperate plan. Very quickly, I understood that that was impossible. The instructions to turn always to the left reminded me that such was the common procedure for discovering the central point of certain labyrinths. I have some understanding of labyrinths: not for nothing am I the great grandson of that Ts'ui Pên who was governor of Yunnan[9] and who renounced worldly power in order to write a novel that might be even more populous than the *Hung Lu Meng*[1] and to construct a labyrinth in which all men would become lost. Thirteen years he dedicated to these heterogeneous tasks, but the hand of a stranger murdered him—and his novel was incoherent and no one found the labyrinth. Beneath English trees I meditated on that lost maze: I imagined it inviolate and perfect at the secret crest of a mountain; I imagined it erased by rice fields or beneath the water; I imagined it infinite, no longer composed of octagonal kiosks and returning paths, but of rivers and provinces and kingdoms . . . I thought of a labyrinth of labyrinths, of one sinuous spreading labyrinth that would encompass the past and the future and in some way involve the stars. Absorbed in these illusory images, I forgot my destiny of one pursued. I felt myself to be, for an unknown period of time, an abstract perceiver of the world. The vague, living countryside, the moon, the remains of the day worked on me, as well as the slope of the road, which eliminated any possibility of weariness. The

9. Southwesternmost of China's eighteen traditional provinces; beautiful but sparsely populated, damp and malarial (the name means "Cloudy South"); not an ideal diplomatic assignment.

1. *Dream of the Red Chamber*, long, semiautobiographical novel by Ts'ao Chan (1715–1763) about the decay of a wealthy noble family.

afternoon was intimate, infinite. The road descended and forked among the now confused meadows. A high-pitched, almost syllabic music approached and receded in the shifting of the wind, dimmed by leaves and distance. I thought that a man can be an enemy of other men, of the moments of other men, but not of a country: not of fireflies, words, gardens, streams of water, sunsets. Thus I arrived before a tall, rusty gate. Between the iron bars I made out a poplar grove and a pavilion. I understood suddenly two things, the first trivial, the second almost unbelievable: the music came from the pavilion, and the music was Chinese. For precisely that reason I had openly accepted it without paying it any heed. I do not remember whether there was a bell or whether I knocked with my hand. The sparkling of the music continued.

From the rear of the house within a lantern approached: a lantern that the trees sometimes striped and sometimes eclipsed, a paper lantern that had the form of a drum and the color of the moon. A tall man bore it. I didn't see his face for the light blinded me. He opened the door and said slowly, in my own language: "I see that the pious Hsi P'êng persists in correcting my solitude. You no doubt wish to see the garden?"

I recognized the name of one of our consuls and I replied, disconcerted, "The garden?"

"The garden of forking paths."

Something stirred in my memory and I uttered with incomprehensible certainty, "The garden of my ancestor Ts'ui Pên."

"Your ancestor? Your illustrious ancestor? Come in."

The damp path zigzagged like those of my childhood. We came to a library of Eastern and Western books. I recognized bound in a yellow silk several volumes of the Lost Encyclopedia, edited by the Third Emperor of the Luminous Dynasty[2] but never printed. The record on the phonograph revolved next to a bronze phoenix. I also recall a *famille rose*[3] vase and another, many centuries older, of that shade of blue which our craftsmen copied from the potters of Persia . . .

Stephen Albert observed me with a smile. He was, as I have said, very tall, sharp-featured, with gray eyes and a gray beard. He told me that he had been a missionary in Tientsin "before aspiring to become a Sinologist."

We sat down—I on a long, low divan, he with his back to the window and a tall circular clock. I calculated that my pursuer, Richard Madden, could not arrive for at least an hour. My irrevocable determination could wait.

"An astounding fate, that of Ts'ui Pên," Stephen Albert said. "Governor of his native province, learned in astronomy, in astrology and in the tireless interpretation of the canonical books,[4] chess player, famous poet and calligrapher—he abandoned all this in order to com-

2. The "Luminous" Dynasty is the Ming; its third emperor, Yung-lo, reigned 1402–1424. He commissioned a compilation of all significant work done on Chinese history, government, philosophy, geography, etc., which, though incomplete, ran to over 11,000 of the small Chinese volumes—too long to be printed.

3. "Rose family" Chinese porcelain, characterized by rose glaze over the decoration.

4. The Confucian classics which officials had to know thoroughly and apply to contemporary social and political issues.

pose a book and a maze. He renounced the pleasures of both tyranny and justice, of his populous couch, of his banquets and even of erudition—all to close himself up for thirteen years in the Pavilion of the Limpid Solitude.[5] When he died, his heirs found nothing save chaotic manuscripts. His family, as you may be aware, wished to condemn them to the fire, but his executor—a Taoist or Buddhist monk—insisted on their publication."

"We descendants of Ts'ui Pên," I replied, "continue to curse that monk. Their publication was senseless. The book is an indeterminate heap of contradictory drafts. I examined it once: in the third chapter the hero dies, in the fourth he is alive. As for the other undertaking of Ts'ui Pên, his labyrinth . . ."

"Here is Ts'ui Pên's labyrinth," he said, indicating a tall lacquered desk.

"An ivory labyrinth!" I exclaimed. "A minimum labyrinth."

"A labyrinth of symbols," he corrected. "An invisible labyrinth of time. To me, a barbarous Englishman, has been entrusted the revelation of this diaphanous mystery. After more than a hundred years, the details are irretrievable; but it is not hard to conjecture what happened. Ts'ui Pên must have said once: *I am withdrawing to write a book*. And another time: *I am withdrawing to construct a labyrinth*. Everyone imagined two works; to no one did it occur that the book and the maze were one and the same thing. The Pavilion of the Limpid Solitude stood in the center of a garden that was perhaps intricate; that circumstance could have suggested to the heirs a physical labyrinth. Ts'ui Pên died; no one in the vast territories that were his came upon the labyrinth; the confusion of the novel suggested to me that *it* was the maze. Two circumstances gave me the correct solution of the problem. One: the curious legend that Ts'ui Pên had planned to create a labyrinth which would be strictly infinite. The other: a fragment of a letter I discovered."

Albert rose. He turned his back on me for a moment; he opened a drawer of the black and gold desk. He faced me and in his hands he held a sheet of paper that had once been crimson, but was now pink and tenuous and cross-sectioned. The fame of Ts'ui Pên as a calligrapher had been justly won. I read, uncomprehendingly and with fervor, these words written with a minute brush by a man of my blood: *I leave to the various futures (not to all) my garden of forking paths*. Wordlessly, I returned the sheet. Albert continued:

"Before unearthing this letter, I had questioned myself about the ways in which a book can be infinite. I could think of nothing other than a cyclic volume, a circular one. A book whose last page was identical with the first, a book which had the possibility of continuing indefinitely. I remembered too that night which is at the middle of the Thousand and One Nights when Scheherazade (through a magical oversight of the copyist) begins to relate word for word the story of the Thousand and One Nights, establishing the risk of coming once again to the night when she must repeat it, and thus on to infinity. I imagined as well a Platonic, hereditary work, transmitted

5. The names of both Ts'ui Pên and the Pavilion seem fictitious.

from father to son, in which each new individual adds a chapter or corrects with pious care the pages of his elders. These conjectures diverted me; but none seemed to correspond, not even remotely, to the contradictory chapters of Ts'ui Pên. In the midst of this perplexity, I received from Oxford the manuscript you have examined. I lingered, naturally, on the sentence: *I leave to the various futures (not to all) my garden of forking paths.* Almost instantly, I understood: 'the garden of forking paths' was the chaotic novel; the phrase 'the various futures (not to all)' suggested to me the forking in time, not in space. A broad rereading of the work confirmed the theory. In all fictional works, each time a man is confronted with several alternatives, he chooses one and eliminates the others; in the fiction of Ts'ui Pên, he chooses—simultaneously—all of them. *He creates,* in this way, diverse futures, diverse times which themselves also proliferate and fork. Here, then, is the explanation of the novel's contradictions. Fang, let us say, has a secret; a stranger calls at his door; Fang resolves to kill him. Naturally, there are several possible outcomes: Fang can kill the intruder, the intruder can kill Fang, they both can escape, they both can die, and so forth. In the work of Ts'ui Pên, all possible outcomes occur; each one is the point of departure for other forkings. Sometimes, the paths of this labyrinth converge: for example, you arrive at this house, but in one of the possible pasts you are my enemy, in another, my friend. If you will resign yourself to my incurable pronunciation, we shall read a few pages."

His face, within the vivid circle of the lamplight, was unquestionably that of an old man, but with something unalterable about it, even immortal. He read with slow precision two versions of the same epic chapter. In the first, an army marches to a battle across a lonely mountain; the horror of the rocks and shadows makes the men undervalue their lives and they gain an easy victory. In the second, the same army traverses a palace where a great festival is taking place; the resplendent battle seems to them a continuation of the celebration and they win the victory. I listened with proper veneration to these ancient narratives, perhaps less admirable in themselves than the fact that they had been created by my blood and were being restored to me by a man of a remote empire, in the course of a desperate adventure, on a Western isle. I remember the last words, repeated in each version like a secret commandment: *Thus fought the heroes, tranquil their admirable hearts, violent their swords, resigned to kill and to die.*

From that moment on, I felt about me and within my dark body an invisible, intangible swarming. Not the swarming of the divergent, parallel and finally coalescent armies, but a more inaccessible, more intimate agitation that they in some manner prefigured. Stephen Albert continued:

"I don't believe that your illustrious ancestor played idly with these variations. I don't consider it credible that he would sacrifice thirteen years to the infinite execution of a rhetorical experiment. In your country, the novel is a subsidiary form of literature; in Ts'ui Pên's time it was a despicable form. Ts'ui Pên was a brilliant novelist, but he was also a man of letters who doubtless did not consider himself a mere novelist. The testimony of his contemporaries proclaims—and his life fully confirms—his metaphysical and mystical interests. Philosophic controversy usurps a good part of the novel. I know that of all problems, none disturbed him so greatly nor worked upon him so much as the abysmal problem of time. Now then, the latter is the only problem that does not figure in the pages of the *Garden*. He does not even use the word that signifies *time*. How do you explain this voluntary omission?"

I proposed several solutions—all unsatisfactory. We discussed them. Finally, Stephen Albert said to me:

"In a riddle whose answer is chess, what is the only prohibited word?"

I thought a moment and replied, "The word *chess*."

"Precisely," said Albert. "*The Garden of Forking Paths* is an enormous riddle, or parable, whose theme is time; this recondite cause prohibits its mention. To omit a word always, to resort to inept metaphors and obvious periphrases, is perhaps the most emphatic way of stressing it. That is the tortuous method preferred, in each of the meanderings of his indefatigable novel, by the oblique Ts'ui Pên. I have compared hundreds of manuscripts, I have corrected the errors that the negligence of the copyists has introduced, I have guessed the plan of this chaos, I have re-established—I believe I have re-established—the primordial organization, I have translated the entire work: it is clear to me that not once does he employ the word 'time.' The explanation is obvious: *The Garden of Forking Paths* is an incomplete, but not false, image of the universe as Ts'ui Pên conceived it. In contrast to Newton and Schopenhauer, your ancestor did not believe in a uniform, absolute time. He believed in an infinite series of times, in a growing, dizzying net of divergent, convergent and parallel times. This network of times which approached one another, forked, broke off, or were unaware of one another for centuries, embraces *all* possibilities of time. We do not exist in the majority of these times; in some you exist, and not I; in others I, and not you; in others, both of us. In the present one, which a favorable fate has granted me, you have arrived at my house; in another, while crossing the garden, you found me dead; in still another, I utter these same words, but I am a mistake, a ghost."

"In every one," I pronounced, not without a tremble to my voice, "I am grateful to you and revere you for your re-creation of the garden of Ts'ui Pên."

"Not in all," he murmured with a smile. "Time forks perpetually toward innumerable futures. In one of them I am your enemy."

Once again I felt the swarming sensation of which I have spoken. It seemed to me that the humid garden that surrounded the house was infinitely saturated with invisible persons. Those persons were Albert and I, secret, busy and multiform in other dimensions of time. I raised my eyes and the tenuous nightmare dissolved. In the yellow and black garden there was only one man; but this man was as strong as a statue . . . this man was approaching along the path and he was Captain Richard Madden.

"The future already exists," I replied, "but I am your friend. Could I see the letter again?"

Albert rose. Standing tall, he opened the drawer of the tall desk; for the moment his back was to me. I had readied the revolver. I fired with extreme caution. Albert fell uncomplainingly, immediately. I swear his death was instantaneous—a lightning stroke.

The rest is unreal, insignificant. Madden broke in, arrested me. I have been condemned to the gallows. I have won out abominably; I have communicated to Berlin the secret name of the city they must attack. They bombed it yesterday; I read it in the same papers that offered to England the mystery of the learned Sinologist Stephen Albert, who was murdered by a stranger, one Yu Tsun. The Chief had deciphered this mystery. He knew my problem was to indicate (through the uproar of the war) the city called Albert[6] and that I had found no other means to do so than to kill a man of that name. He does not know (no one can know) my innumerable contrition and weariness.

For Victoria Ocampo p. 1958

HAL BENNETT

Dotson Gerber Resurrected

We saw the head of Mr. Dotson Gerber break ground at approximately nine o'clock on a bright Saturday morning in March out near our collard patch, where Poppa had started to dig a well and then filled it in. Of course, none of us knew then that the shock of red hair and part of a head sprouting from the abandoned well belonged to Mr. Dotson Gerber, who'd been missing from his farm since early last fall. We were black folk, and the fact that a white man like Mr. Dotson Gerber was missing from his home was of small importance to us. Unless that white man suddenly started growing from the ground near our collard patch like Mr. Dotson Gerber was doing now for Momma, my sister Millicent and me. We'd come running because of a commotion the chickens had made, thinking that a lynx or a weasel might have got after them. And found Mr. Dotson Gerber's head instead.

"Good Jesus," Millicent said, "I do think I'm going to faint." Millicent had been prone to fainting ever since she'd seen two black men kissing behind some boxes in the factory where she worked. Now she was getting ready to faint again. But Momma snatched her roughly by the apron.

"Girl, you *always* fainting, you don't hardly give other people a chance." And Momma fainted dead away, which left Millicent conscious for the time being and looking very desperate. But she didn't faint and I was glad of that, because I certainly didn't want to be

6. City on the Paris side (southwest) of the River Ancre.

alone with Mr. Dotson Gerber sprouting from the ground. A dozen or so chickens were still raising a ruckus about the unexpected appearance of a white man's head where they were accustomed to picking for grain. Screeching at the top of her voice, Millicent shooed the chickens away while I tugged Momma into the shade and propped her against the barn. Then we went back to looking at Mr. Dotson Gerber.

I have mentioned the well that Poppa started to dig because it was apparent that Mr. Dotson Gerber had been planted standing up in that hole. Which, of course, explained why his head was growing out first. Although, as I have said, neither Millicent nor I knew then that what we were looking at belonged to Mr. Dotson Gerber. It took Poppa to tell us that.

He came riding on Miss Tricia from the stable, where he'd been saddling her. "Why you children making all that noise out there?" he called from the road. When we didn't answer, he yanked the reins and rode Miss Tricia toward us. "Millicent, was that you I heard hollering? What you all doing out here?" Poppa asked again.

"There's a white man growing from the ground," I said.

Poppa nearly fell off Miss Tricia. "A *what?*"

"A white man. He's growing from that hole where you started to dig the well."

"I *know* I'm going to faint now," Millicent said. And she wrapped her hands around her throat as though to choke herself into unconsciousness. But Poppa and I both ignored her and she was too curious to faint right then. So she stopped choking herself and watched Poppa jump down from Miss Tricia to inspect the head. He walked all around it, poking it from time to time with his shoe.

"That'd be Mr. Dotson Gerber," he finally pronounced.

By this time, Momma had revived and was watching Poppa with the rest of us. "Poppa, how you know that's Mr. Dotson Gerber? Why, he could be any old white man! There's hardly enough of him above ground for anybody to recognize."

"I know it's Mr. Dotson Gerber because I planted him there," Poppa said. He told us how Mr. Gerber had come out to the farm last fall to inspect the well that he was digging, which had been part of Mr. Gerber's job here in Alcanthia County.[1] "He kept calling me Uncle," Poppa said, with some bitterness. "I told him respectfully that my name is Walter Beaufort, or that he could even call me *Mr.* Beaufort, if he'd a mind to. After all, things have changed so much nowadays, I told him I certainly wouldn't think any less of him if he called me Mr. Beaufort. I told him that black people don't appreciate white folks' calling us Uncle any longer. But he just kept on calling me that, so I hit him on the head with my shovel." We all looked at Mr. Dotson Gerber's head; and it was true that there was a wide gash in his skull that could only have been caused by a shovel. "I didn't intend to kill him," Poppa said. "I just wanted to teach him some respect. After all, things *have* changed. But when I found out he was dead, I stood him up in that hole I was digging and covered him up. I never expected to see him growing out of the ground this way."

1. Both this and Burnside mentioned below seem to be fictional; Dillwyn, mentioned later, is a very small town in Buckingham County, Virginia.

"Well, that's not the problem now," Millicent said. "The problem now is, what are we going to do with him?"

Momma moved a step closer to Mr. Gerber and cautiously poked him with her toe. "If it weren't for that red hair," she said, "somebody might mistake him for a cabbage."

"He don't look like no cabbage to me," Millicent said. It was clear that she was annoyed because Momma had fainted before she'd had a chance to.

"I didn't say he looked like a cabbage," Momma said. "I said somebody might mistake him for a cabbage."

"He too red to be a cabbage," Millicent said stubbornly. "Anyway, we still ought to do something about him. It just don't look right, a white man growing like this on a colored person's farm. Suppose some white people see it?"

The 9:10 Greyhound to Richmond went by then. Momma and Poppa shaded their eyes to watch it speed down the far road; but Millicent and I were of today's generation and we hardly looked. Although there had been a time when the passing of the Richmond bus was the most exciting event of everybody's day in Burnside. But the years in between had brought many changes. There was electricity now, and television and telephones. Several factories and supermarkets had opened up on the highway, so that farming became far less profitable than working in the factories and spending weekly wages in the glittering markets, where everything that had formerly come from soil was sold now in tin cans and plastic wrappers. Because nobody in Burnside farmed anymore. Like almost everyone else, Momma and Poppa and Millicent all worked in the factories. And Momma bought at the supermarkets, like everyone else. The land around us, given over to weeds, was overgrown now like a graveyard in those first green days of spring.

Momma and Poppa watched the bus until it disappeared. "That Greyhound, she sure do go," Momma said. "It's Saturday now and I bet she's crowded with nigger men going to Richmond for them white hussies on Clay Street."

Millicent grunted. "Let them help themselves," she said bitterly. "After what I seen, a nigger man don't mean a thing to me no more."

"You're right there, sugar," Momma agreed. "A nigger man, he ain't worth a damn."

Millicent curled her lip and she and Momma looked at Poppa and me as though there were something dirty and pathetic about being a black man. I had seen this expression on their faces before—a wan kind of pity mixed with distaste and the sad realization that being a black man is next to being nothing at all. And the black woman is always telling the black man that with her eyes and lips and hips, telling him by the way she moves beside him on the road and underneath him in the bed. *Nigger, oh, I love you, but I know you ain't never going to be as good as a white man.* That's the way Momma and Millicent looked at Poppa and me while they cut us dead right there on the spot. They almost fell over each other, talking about how low and no-good nigger men are. And they weren't just joking; they really meant it. I saw it in their faces and it hurt me to my heart. I just didn't know what to do. I reached out and caught Poppa's arm, that's how hurt I was. He seemed to understand, because he wrapped his arm around me and I could feel some of his strength draining into me. So Momma and Millicent stood there ridiculing us on one side of Mr. Dotson Gerber's head, and Poppa and I stood there on the other.

Then, when Momma and Millicent were all through with their tirade, Poppa said very quietly, "I'm riding in to Dillwyn now. I'm going to turn myself over to the sheriff for killing Mr. Gerber here."

There was a kind of joy in Poppa's voice that I suppose no black woman can ever understand, and Momma and Millicent looked at Poppa as though he had suddenly lost his mind. But I was sixteen years old, which is old enough to be a man if you're black, and I understood why Poppa was so happy about killing that white man. Until now, he'd always had to bury his rich, black male rage in the far corner of some infertile field, lest it do harm to him and to the rest of us as well. But by telling that he'd killed that white man, he would undo all the indignities he had ever suffered in the name of love.

Now Momma looked afraid. "Turn yourself in to the sheriff? What you talking about, Walter Beaufort? What kind of foolishness you talking?" She tried humor to change Poppa's somber mood, laughing in a big hullabaloo. "I bet you been hitting the plum wine again," she said joyously.

But Poppa shook his head. "You always accuse me of that when you want to make light of what I'm saying. But I haven't been near that plum wine, not today. And what I'm saying is plain enough. I've killed a white man and I want somebody to know it."

"*We* know it," Momma said. "Ain't that good enough?"

"I want them to know it," Poppa said. "I want them to know he's dead and I want them to know why he's dead."

"Because he didn't call you Mister?" Momma said. There wasn't a white man in Alcanthia County who didn't call her Auntie, and she started to rage scornfully at the idea of Poppa's rebelling at being called Uncle. "Now, I could see it if you said you were going to hide out for a while, killing that white man and all that—"

But Poppa stopped her with an angry jerk of his hand. "It's not that way at all, Hattie. I don't aim to hide no more. I been hiding too long already—if you understand what I mean. The time's come for me to stop hiding. I'm going to Dillwyn and tell the sheriff what I've done."

Momma jumped straight up in the air. "Walter Beaufort, you gone *crazy* or something? No, I don't understand what you mean. Why didn't you tell the sheriff last year? Why you got to tell him now? Nobody even knows you killed Mr. Gerber. And to give yourself up now, that don't make no sense at all."

"Some things don't never make no sense," Poppa said. He cocked his eye at me. "You coming with me to the sheriff, boy? Somebody's got to ride Miss Tricia back here to home."

I got up onto Miss Tricia with him and we rode off to find the sheriff.

"I think I'm going to faint," I heard Millicent say behind me. But when I looked around, she was still standing there with her mouth hanging open.

As Poppa and I went up the road, Momma's voice followed us like an angry wind. "You see what I mean about *niggers,* Millicent?" Moaning sadly, half happy and afraid at the same time, a kind of turbulent satisfaction marred her voice as she shrieked at Millicent. "You see what I mean about *niggers,* child?"

"That black bitch," Poppa muttered. I don't know whether he knew I heard him or not. He kicked Miss Tricia viciously in the ribs and the mule leaped into a surprised gallop, heading to Dillwyn for Poppa to give himself up to the sheriff. After the way Momma and Millicent had carried on, I didn't see what else he could do.

Even here in Burnside, we had heard that black is beautiful. But I don't think that many of us believed it, because black is ugly and desperate and degraded wherever the white man is sitting on your neck. Still, Millicent and I had worn Afros for a while to show our black pride; but they were too hard to keep clean here in the country, there is so much dust and dirt blowing about. And our kind of hair picks up everything that goes by. Besides, the white people who owned the factories took Afro hairdos as a sign of militancy and threatened to fire everybody who wore one. So everybody went back to getting their hair cut short or straightening it like before.

I was thinking about that as I rode with Poppa to the sheriff's office. I thought about Millicent, too, and the black men she'd seen kissing in the factory. She never would tell who they were, and sometimes I wondered whether it might not have been just a story that she made up to justify her saying that all black men are sissies. At any rate, she complained quite openly that no black man had made love to her since last Halloween, which was almost five months ago, and this probably explained why she was so jumpy and threatening to faint all the time.

As for me, I thought I knew why no black men were interested in Millicent. For one thing, they could go to Richmond and Charlottesville and get white women, now that they had money to spend on the whores there. Also, the black men I'd talked to told me that they didn't find black women so desirable anymore, the way they were dressing and acting and perfuming themselves like white women on television, now that they had money to do so.

So the black men went to Richmond and paid white women, because their own women were trying to act white. And the black women were turning their backs on their own men, because—if Millicent was any example—they thought that black men were sissies. It was all very confusing.

I was old enough to have had myself a woman or two by then. But I was very hung up on Mrs. Palmer and her five daughters; I hope you know what I mean. There was a time when black people said that doing something like that to yourself would make you crazy. Now they said that it would make you turn white. Which was sufficient reason for some black boys to stop. But not me. I actually did it more. But all that happened was that sometimes I felt dizzy and depressed.

Sometimes I felt weak. But I never did turn white.

Sheriff Dave Young's office was closed when we got to Dillwyn. Some white men sitting around told us that the sheriff was away to a Christian conference. "He's a deacon in the white Baptist church, you know. He'll be away for the rest of the week." There were some hounds lying around, sleeping in the dust, and one or two of them opened a drowsy eye and looked at Poppa and me without curiosity. The white men looked at us as though we were two hounds who had by some miracle managed to get up onto a mule. That's the way white men are in the South. As for Poppa and me, we looked right through those white men, which is really a very good way of rebelling by pretending that you're looking at nothing. There are other sly ways that we Southern black people have of rebelling—like grinning, or licking our tongue out behind the white man's back, spitting in his water when he's not looking, imitating his way of talking—which is why so many Northern black people think that Southern black people are such natural clowns, when what we're really doing is rebelling. Not as dramatic as a Molotov cocktail or a pipe bomb, but it certainly is satisfying, and a whole lot safer, too. Furthermore, it must be said that we do not hate whites here as black people apparently do in the North. Although we nearly always view them with pity and suspicion, for *they* think that we hate them, as they might well do if the tables were reversed.

"Uncle, is there any particular reason why you want to see the sheriff?"

"No, sir, no, sir, none at all," Poppa said. He thanked them the way he was supposed to, grinning a little, and rode away.

"Where we going now, Poppa? Back to home?"

He shook his head. "We going to Mr. Dotson Gerber's house up the street yonder. I expect his wife is home. I expect she'd like to know what happened to her husband."

When we got to Mrs. Dotson Gerber's, there was a decrepit old white lady sitting in a rocking chair on her porch and waving a small Confederate flag over the banister, like a child does at a parade. She was the mother of Mr. Dotson Gerber's wife. And while colored people said quite openly that the old lady was touched in the head, white people claimed that she had arthritis; and they said that she waved the Confederate flag to exercise her arm, as though to conceal from black people the fact that any white had ever lost his mind.

She waved the flag and rocked every once in a while, pushing at the banister with spidery legs that ended in two fluffy slippers that had once been white. Her pale-blue eyes were as sharp as a hawk's behind her wire-rimmed glasses; but it was hard to tell whether she was looking into the past or the future, waving and rocking, smiling from time to time.

Poppa got down from Miss Tricia and walked over to the fence. "Good morning, ma'am," he said respectfully. It was dangerous not to be respectful, just in case the old white woman wasn't crazy and really did have arthritis in her arm. She could raise a ruckus for Poppa's disrespecting her that could cause him to wind up on the end of a rope. "I came to see Mrs. Dotson Gerber, ma'am," Poppa said politely, while the old lady rocked and waved the flag outrageously. She might have been saluting Lee's army marching proudly on its way to Appomattox, which was only a few miles away. Her eyes grew large and happy. But she didn't pay any attention at all to Poppa, even when he asked a second and a third time for Mrs. Dotson Gerber. She had arthritis, all right, that old woman. She had arthritis in the brain, that's where she had it.

Just then, Mrs. Dotson Gerber came to the screen door. Drying her hands on a pink apron, she inspected Poppa for a minute, as though trying to figure out whether he was safe or not. "Is that you, Uncle Walter?" She squinted through the screen. "Did you want to talk to me?"

"Yes, ma'am, Mrs. Gerber. I did come to talk to you. I got something to tell you."

"I certainly don't see why you came to my front door," Mrs. Gerber said peevishly, coming out onto the porch. "I *never* receive colored people at my front door, and I'm sure you know that, Uncle Walter. Besides, it bothers my mother's arthritis, people talking all around her." She inspected the crazy old woman, who was waving the Confederate flag and rocking vigorously.

"Well, ma'am . . . I'm sorry I came to your front door. I certainly do know better than that. But I've come to tell you about your husband."

Mrs. Gerber seemed to stop breathing. "My husband?" She dashed from the porch and stood at the fence near Poppa. "You know where my husband is?"

"Yes, ma'am. He's out in my collard patch—where my collard patch used to be."

"What's he doing out there?"

Poppa looked embarrassed. "He came to inspect the well I was digging. We got in an argument and I hit him with my shovel."

Mrs. Gerber turned very white, indeed. "You killed him?"

"I'm afraid so, ma'am. I buried him there in the well."

Mrs. Gerber tapped her bottom teeth with her forefinger. She was a sort of pretty white woman and certainly a lot younger than Mr. Dotson Gerber had been. Behind her on the porch, the crazy old woman rocked on, waving the flag at Southern armies that only she could see. "Momma's arthritis isn't too good today," Mrs. Gerber said absently, patting her hair. After a while, she said, "So Dotson is dead. All of us wondered what happened when he didn't come home last year. Knowing him, I was almost certain that he'd gone and got himself killed." But she didn't seem too upset. "Actually, Uncle Walter, you've done me a big favor. Dotson used to treat my poor mother something terrible, laughing at her arthritis all the time." She patted her hair again, although every strand seemed to be perfectly in place. "I suppose you know that I'm to get married again this summer to a very respectable man here in Alcanthia?"

"No, ma'am, I didn't know that."

"Well, I'm surprised," Mrs. Gerber said. "I thought that colored people knew everything. Anyway, he's a very respectable man. Very decent and very intelligent, too, I need not say. We both figured that Dotson was dead after all these months. That's why we decided to get married." She looked at Poppa almost gently. "But I never supposed you'd be the one to kill him, Uncle Walter. Why, you've even been here and done a little work for Dotson and me around the house."

"Yes, ma'am."

"He really must've provoked you, Uncle Walter. What did he do?"

"He kept calling me Uncle. I asked him not to, but he kept on."

"Yes, that sounds like Dotson. He could be mean that way. I suppose you want me to stop calling you Uncle, too?"

"I'd appreciate it if you would, ma'am. I mean, it's an actual fact that I'm not your uncle, so I'd appreciate your not calling me that."

Now Mrs. Gerber nibbled on her thumb. Her mother rocked on and on, waving the flag. "All right, I'll stop calling you Uncle," Mrs. Gerber said, "if you promise not to tell anybody about my husband being buried out there in your collard patch. After all, I'm planning on being married to a very decent man. It would be a big embarrassment to me—and to him, too—if anybody found out about Dotson being buried in a collard patch. As much as he hates collard greens." It was clear from the tone of her voice that the disgrace lay not in Mr. Dotson Gerber's being dead but in his being buried in our collard patch.

"There ain't no collards there now," Poppa said, trying to placate Mrs. Gerber some. "Why, we haven't done any farming for years."

"But collards *were* there," Mrs. Gerber said, almost stomping her foot. "And Dotson couldn't stand collards. I just hope you won't tell anybody else about this, Uncle Walter. I don't know what my fiancé would say if he knew about this. Considering that he's willing to marry me and to put up with Momma's arthritis in the bargain, I certainly wouldn't want him to know about Dotson. Why, I don't know what he'd do if he ever found out about Dotson. You haven't told anybody else, have you?"

"I went to tell the sheriff, but he's out of town until next week."

"You went to tell the sheriff?" She seemed absolutely horrified. "Mr. Beaufort, I know I have no right asking you to think about me and my feelings in all this. But you ought to at least think about your own family. You know what they'll do to you if they find out about this?"

"I know," Poppa said.

"And you don't care?"

"I certainly do care. I don't want to die. I want to live. But I've killed me a white man. That's not something that somebody like me does every day. I think I want folks to know about it."

"But why now?" she cried. "Why didn't you say something before? Before I went out and got myself engaged?"

"It didn't seem important before. Besides, Mr. Gerber was still in the ground then. He ain't in the ground anymore, not exactly."

From time to time, white people had gone past and looked at Poppa and Mrs. Gerber as they talked. "I think you all ought to go around to the back door," Mrs. Gerber said. "My husband-to-be certainly wouldn't like it known that I stood on my own front porch and carried on a conversation with colored people . . ." She turned very red then and took a step or two away, as though she was afraid that Poppa might hit her with a shovel. But Poppa started laughing very gently, the way a man does when he weighs the value of things and finds out that what is important to other people seems absurd to him. And he looked at Mrs. Gerber with a kind of amused pity darkening his eyes, as though he realized now that no white person could ever understand why he wanted him to know about Mr. Dotson Gerber.

"We're going on home," Poppa said. "And don't you worry none about Mr. Gerber, ma'am. We'll take care of him. Your husband-to-be won't ever find out."

"What do you intend to do?" Mrs. Gerber wanted to know.

Poppa's face lit up with a great big grin. Not the kind of tame, painful grin that a black man puts on when he's rebelling. But a large, beautiful grin that showed all of his teeth and gums. "I'm going to plant collard greens around him," Poppa said.

Mrs. Gerber wrinkled her nose in distaste. "Dotson certainly wouldn't like that, if he knew. And you mean *over* him, don't you?"

Now Poppa and I both laughed. We hadn't told her that Mr. Gerber was growing straight up from the ground. And she wouldn't have believed us if we had told her. That's how white people are. "Good-bye, ma'am," Poppa said to Mrs. Gerber. She nodded and went into her house. On the porch, her mother waved the Confederate flag triumphantly. The rocker squeaked like the tread of strident ghosts. We climbed up onto Miss Tricia and rode home.

And we were nearly halfway there before I finally figured out why that old crazy white woman was on Mrs. Gerber's porch. They kept her there instead of buying a doorbell and using electricity. That way, when people talked to her, Mrs. Gerber heard them and came outside to see who it was. Smart. Sometimes I had to give it to white people. They were very smart indeed.

Momma and Millicent were waiting for us when we got home. "Did you tell the sheriff?" Momma said. She looked haggard and very unhappy.

"The sheriff wasn't there," Poppa said. "He won't be home until next week." With Momma and Millicent following us, he rode Miss Tricia out to the collard patch and gave me the reins. "Take her to the stable, boy." But I watched while he knelt and worked the dirt into a mound around Mr. Gerber's head. "There, that ought to do it," Poppa said. "Tomorrow, I'm going to plant me some collard greens here." He stood up happily and wiped his hands on the seat of his overalls.

Momma's mouth dropped open. She ran to Mr. Dotson Gerber's head and tried to stomp it back into the ground. But Poppa stopped her firmly. "You've gone stark crazy!" Momma cried.

Poppa slapped her right in the mouth. She spun around like a top. He slapped her again and sent her spinning the other way. "I don't want no more trouble out of you," Poppa said.

Momma melted against him like warm cheese. "All right, sugar. You won't have no more trouble out of me, sugar."

I rode Miss Tricia down to the stable. Millicent had enough sense to keep her mouth shut for a change, and Momma and Poppa went on up to the house with their arms wrapped around each other. I hadn't seen them together like that for years.

And that is how Poppa started farming again. Helped on by sun and spring rain, Mr. Dotson Gerber and the collards grew rapidly together. It would not be an exaggeration to say that Mr. Gerber's body growing there seemed to fertilize the whole field. Although in no time at all, he was taller than the collards and still growing. Most of his chest and arms was out of the ground by the end of March. And by the middle of April, he had cleared the ground down to his ankles. With his tattered clothes and wild red hair, his large blue eyes wide and staring, he seemed more some kind of monster than a resurrected man. The sun and wind had burned his skin nearly as black as ours. And while there was small chance of anybody seeing him—people in Burnside didn't visit anymore, now that most of them worked in the factories—Poppa still thought it might be a good idea to cover Mr. Gerber up. "You'd better put a sack over his head and some gloves on his hands," he said. Later on, Poppa put a coat and some sunglasses on Mr. Gerber, along with an old straw hat. He propped a stick behind Mr. Gerber and passed another one through the sleeves of Mr. Gerber's coat for him to rest his arms on. He really looked like a scarecrow then, and we stopped worrying about people finding out about him. In truth, however, it must be said that Mr. Gerber made a very poor scarecrow, indeed, because the birds hardly paid any attention to him. It was fortunate for us that birds don't especially like collard greens.

Poppa worked a few hours in the collard patch every night after he came home from the factory. Momma helped him sometimes. Sometimes Millicent and I helped him, too. Then one day, Poppa quit his job at the factory and hitched Miss Tricia to the plow. "You farming again?" Momma asked him. She had been very tame with Poppa since he'd slapped her.

"I'm farming again," Poppa said.

Momma just nodded. "That's very nice, sugar. That's really very nice."

In no time at all, Poppa had planted all the old crops that used to grow on our farm—all kinds of vegetables, wheat, corn. He went to Dillwyn and bought a couple of pigs and a cow. All the neighbors knew what he was doing. But they kept on working at the factories and spending their money at the supermarkets. Until one day, a neighbor woman showed up to buy some collard greens. Poppa sold her a large basketful for a dollar. "I'm just sick to death of store-bought food," she said.

"I know what you mean," Poppa said. "You come back, you hear?" In a little while, other people came to buy tomatoes, string beans, white potatoes, golden corn from the tall green stalks.

Summer droned on. Poppa worked his crops. Word reached us

that Mrs. Dotson Gerber had married her decent white man. After school had let out, I had begun to help Poppa full time. Momma finally quit her job at the factory and helped, too. But mostly, she took care of selling and managing the money that we were making. As for Millicent, I spied her one day making love down in the pea patch. And that black man she was with, he certainly was no sissy. That was all Millicent needed and all a black man needed, too—someplace green and growing to make love in. I never heard Millicent talk about fainting after that, although she did talk about getting married.

Around the end of summer, Sheriff Dave Young came to our farm. "Some of the fellows said you were looking for me," he told Poppa. "But I figured it wasn't really too important, since you never came back."

"It wasn't important, Sheriff."

He bought a watermelon that Poppa let him have very cheap. "You got a good business going here," Sheriff Young said. "Some of the white farmers been talking about doing the same thing."

"It'd be good if they did," Poppa said. The sheriff put his watermelon into his car and drove away.

When fall came and the leaves turned red and gold and brown, Mr. Dotson Gerber turned like all the other growing things and shriveled away to nothing. Poppa seemed very satisfied then, looking over his fields. And I knew how he must have felt, standing there looking at Mr. Dotson Gerber and all the other dead things that would live again next spring.

The Greyhound to Richmond went by and Poppa shielded his eyes to watch. I think that I understood everything about him then and it hurt me so much that I deliberately turned my back. The lesson of that summer seemed a particularly bitter one, because we had done everything and we had done nothing. Mr. Doston Gerber would certainly be growing in my father's fields every spring forever. And my father, my poor father would always watch and admire the Greyhound to Richmond. The same way that in the deepest and sincerest and blackest part of himself he would always hate himself and believe that God is the greatest white man of all.

"That Greyhound, she sure do run," Poppa said. He sounded very satisfied, indeed. God knew he'd killed a white man. With God knowing, that was knowledge enough. But I was thinking about how it feels to be black and forever afraid. And about the white man, god*damn* him, how he causes everything. Even when He is God. Even when he is dead.

p. 1970

GABRIEL GARCÍA MÁRQUEZ

A Very Old Man with Enormous Wings*

A TALE FOR CHILDREN

On the third day of rain they had killed so many crabs inside the house that Pelayo had to cross his drenched courtyard and throw them into the sea, because the newborn child had a temperature all night and they thought it was due to the stench. The world had been sad since Tuesday. Sea and sky were a single ash-gray thing and the sands of the beach, which on March nights glimmered like powdered light, had become a stew of mud and rotten shellfish. The light was so weak at noon that when Pelayo was coming back to the house after throwing away the crabs, it was hard for him to see what it was that was moving and groaning in the rear of the courtyard. He had to go very close to see that it was an old man, a very old man, lying face down in the mud, who, in spite of his tremendous efforts, couldn't get up, impeded by his enormous wings.

Frightened by that nightmare, Pelayo ran to get Elisenda, his wife, who was putting compresses on the sick child, and he took her to the rear of the courtyard. They both looked at the fallen body with mute stupor. He was dressed like a ragpicker. There were only a few faded hairs left on his bald skull and very few teeth in his mouth, and his pitiful condition of a drenched great-grandfather had taken away any sense of grandeur he might have had. His huge buzzard wings, dirty and half-plucked, were forever entangled in the mud. They looked at him so long and so closely that Pelayo and Elisenda very soon overcame their surprise and in the end found him familiar. Then they dared speak to him, and he answered in an incomprehensible dialect with a strong sailor's voice. That was how they skipped over the inconvenience of the wings and quite intelligently concluded that he was a lonely castaway from some foreign ship wrecked by the storm. And yet, they called in a neighbor woman who knew everything about life and death to see him, and all she needed was one look to show them their mistake.

"He's an angel," she told them. "He must have been coming for the child, but the poor fellow is so old that the rain knocked him down."

On the following day everyone knew that a flesh-and-blood angel was held captive in Pelayo's house. Against the judgment of the wise neighbor woman, for whom angels in those times were the fugitive survivors of a celestial conspiracy, they did not have the heart to club him to death. Pelayo watched over him all afternoon from the kitchen, armed with his bailiff's club, and before going to bed he dragged him out of the mud and locked him up with the hens in the wire chicken coop. In the middle of the night, when the rain stopped, Pelayo and Elisenda were still killing crabs. A short time afterward the child woke up without a fever and with a desire to eat. Then they

* Translated by Gregory Rabassa.

felt magnanimous and decided to put the angel on a raft with fresh water and provisions for three days and leave him to his fate on the high seas. But when they went out into the courtyard with the first light of dawn, they found the whole neighborhood in front of the chicken coop having fun with the angel, without the slightest reverence, tossing him things to eat through the openings in the wire as if he weren't a supernatural creature but a circus animal.

Father Gonzaga arrived before seven o'clock, alarmed at the strange news. By that time onlookers less frivolous than those at dawn had already arrived and they were making all kinds of conjectures concerning the captive's future. The simplest among them thought that he should be named mayor of the world. Others of sterner mind felt that he should be promoted to the rank of five-star general in order to win all wars. Some visionaries hoped that he could be put to stud in order to implant on earth a race of winged wise men who could take charge of the universe. But Father Gonzaga, before becoming a priest, had been a robust woodcutter. Standing by the wire, he reviewed his catechism in an instant and asked them to open the door so that he could take a close look at that pitiful man who looked more like a huge decrepit hen among the fascinated chickens. He was lying in a corner drying his open wings in the sunlight among the fruit peels and breakfast leftovers that the early risers had thrown him. Alien to the impertinences of the world, he only lifted his antiquarian eyes and murmured something in his dialect when Father Gonzaga went into the chicken coop and said good morning to him in Latin. The parish priest had his first suspicion of an imposter when he saw that he did not understand the language of God or know how to greet His ministers. Then he noticed that seen close up he was much too human: he had an unbearable smell of the outdoors, the back side of his wings was strewn with parasites and his main feathers had been mistreated by terrestrial winds, and nothing about him measured up to the proud dignity of angels. Then he came out of the chicken coop and in a brief sermon warned the curious against the risks of being ingenuous. He reminded them that the devil had the bad habit of making use of carnival tricks in order to confuse the unwary. He argued that if wings were not the essential element in determining the difference between a hawk and an airplane, they were even less so in the recognition of angels. Nevertheless, he promised to write a letter to his bishop so that the latter would write to his primate so that the latter would write to the Supreme Pontiff in order to get the final verdict from the highest courts.

His prudence fell on sterile hearts. The news of the captive angel spread with such rapidity that after a few hours the courtyard had the bustle of a marketplace and they had to call in troops with fixed bayonets to disperse the mob that was about to knock the house down. Elisenda, her spine all twisted from sweeping up so much marketplace trash, then got the idea of fencing in the yard and charging five cents admission to see the angel.

The curious came from far away. A traveling carnival arrived with a flying acrobat who buzzed over the crowd several times, but no one paid any attention to him because his wings were not those of an angel but, rather, those of a sidereal bat. The most unfortunate invalids on earth came in search of health: a poor woman who since childhood had been counting her heartbeats and had run out of numbers; a Portuguese man who couldn't sleep because the noise of the stars disturbed him; a sleepwalker who got up at night to undo the things he had done while awake; and many others with less serious ailments. In the midst of that shipwreck disorder that made the earth tremble, Pelayo and Elisenda were happy with fatigue, for in less than a week they had crammed their rooms with money and the line of pilgrims waiting their turn to enter still reached beyond the horizon.

The angel was the only one who took no part in his own act. He spent his time trying to get comfortable in his borrowed nest, befuddled by the hellish heat of the oil lamps and sacramental candles that had been placed along the wire. At first they tried to make him eat some mothballs, which, according to the wisdom of the wise neighbor woman, were the food prescribed for angels. But he turned them down, just as he turned down the papal lunches[1] that the penitents brought him, and they never found out whether it was because he was an angel or because he was an old man that in the end he ate nothing but eggplant mush. His only supernatural virtue seemed to be patience. Especially during the first days, when the hens pecked at him, searching for the stellar parasites that proliferated in his wings, and the cripples pulled out feathers to touch their defective parts with, and even the most merciful threw stones at him, trying to get him to rise so they could see him standing. The only time they succeeded in arousing him was when they burned his side with an iron for branding steers, for he had been motionless for so many hours that they thought he was dead. He awoke with a start, ranting in his hermetic language and with tears in his eyes, and he flapped his wings a couple of times, which brought on a whirlwind of chicken dung and lunar dust and a gale of panic that did not seem to be of this world. Although many thought that his reaction had been one not of rage but of pain, from then on they were careful not to annoy him, because the majority understood that his passivity was not that of a hero taking his ease but that of a cataclysm in repose.

Father Gonzaga held back the crowd's frivolity with formulas of maidservant inspiration while awaiting the arrival of a final judgment on the nature of the captive. But the mail from Rome showed no sense of urgency. They spent their time finding out if the prisoner had a navel, if his dialect had any connection with Aramaic, how many times he could fit on the head of a pin, or whether he wasn't just a Norwegian with wings. Those meager letters might have come and gone until the end of time if a providential event had not put an end to the priest's tribulations.

It so happened that during those days, among so many other carnival attractions, there arrived in town the traveling show of the woman who had been changed into a spider for having disobeyed her parents. The admission to see her was not only less than the ad-

1. Choice, extremely expensive meals.

mission to see the angel, but people were permitted to ask her all manner of questions about her absurd state and to examine her up and down so that no one would ever doubt the truth of her horror. She was a frightful tarantula the size of a ram and with the head of a sad maiden. What was most heart-rending, however, was not her outlandish shape but the sincere affliction with which she recounted the details of her misfortune. While still practically a child she had sneaked out of her parents' house to go to a dance, and while she was coming back through the woods after having danced all night without permission, a fearful thunderclap rent the sky in two and through the crack came the lightning bolt of brimstone that changed her into a spider. Her only nourishment came from the meatballs that charitable souls chose to toss into her mouth. A spectacle like that, full of so much human truth and with such a fearful lesson, was bound to defeat without even trying that of a haughty angel who scarcely deigned to look at mortals. Besides, the few miracles attributed to the angel showed a certain mental disorder, like the blind man who didn't recover his sight but grew three new teeth, or the paralytic who didn't get to walk but almost won the lottery, and the leper whose sores sprouted sunflowers. Those consolation miracles, which were more like mocking fun, had already ruined the angel's reputation when the woman who had been changed into a spider finally crushed him completely. That was how Father Gonzaga was cured forever of his insomnia and Pelayo's courtyard went back to being as empty as during the time it had rained for three days and crabs walked through the bedrooms.

The owners of the house had no reason to lament. With the money they saved they built a two-story mansion with balconies and gardens and high netting so that crabs wouldn't get in during the winter, and with iron bars on the windows so that angels wouldn't get in. Pelayo also set up a rabbit warren close to town and gave up his job as bailiff for good, and Elisenda bought some satin pumps with high heels and many dresses of iridescent silk, the kind worn on Sunday by the most desirable women in those times. The chicken coop was the only thing that didn't receive any attention. If they washed it down with creolin[2] and burned tears of myrrh inside it every so often, it was not in homage to the angel but to drive away the dungheap stench that still hung everywhere like a ghost and was turning the new house into an old one. At first, when the child learned to walk, they were careful that he not get too close to the chicken coop. But then they began to lose their fears and got used to the smell, and before the child got his second teeth he'd gone inside the chicken coop to play, where the wires were falling apart. The angel was no less standoffish with him than with other mortals, but he tolerated the most ingenious infamies with the patience of a dog who had no illusions. They both came down with chicken pox at the same time. The doctor who took care of the child couldn't resist the temptation to listen to the angel's heart, and he found so much whistling in the heart and so many sounds in his kidneys that it seemed impossible for him to be alive.

2. A disinfectant.

What surprised him most, however, was the logic of his wings. They seemed so natural on that completely human organism that he couldn't understand why other men didn't have them too.

When the child began school it had been some time since the sun and rain had caused the collapse of the chicken coop. The angel went dragging himself about here and there like a stray dying man. They would drive him out of the bedroom with a broom and a moment later find him in the kitchen. He seemed to be in so many places at the same time that they grew to think that he'd been duplicated, that he was reproducing himself all through the house, and the exasperated and unhinged Elisenda shouted that it was awful living in that hell full of angels. He could scarcely eat and his antiquarian eyes had also become so foggy that he went about bumping into posts. All he had left were the bare cannulae of his last feathers. Pelayo threw a blanket over him and extended him the charity of letting him sleep in the shed, and only then did they notice that he had a temperature at night, and was delirious with the tongue twisters of an old Norwegian. That was one of the few times they became alarmed, for they thought he was going to die and not even the wise neighbor woman had been able to tell them what to do with dead angels.

And yet he not only survived his worst winter, but seemed improved with the first sunny days. He remained motionless for several days in the farthest corner of the courtyard, where no one would see him, and at the beginning of December some large, stiff feathers began to grow on his wings, the feathers of a scarecrow, which looked more like another misfortune of decrepitude. But he must have known the reason for those changes, for he was quite careful that no one should notice them, that no one should hear the sea chanteys that he sometimes sang under the stars. One morning Elisenda was cutting some bunches of onions for lunch when a wind that seemed to come from the high seas blew into the kitchen. Then she went to the window and caught the angel in his first attempts at flight. They were so clumsy that his fingernails opened a furrow in the vegetable patch and he was on the point of knocking the shed down with the ungainly flapping that slipped on the light and couldn't get a grip on the air. But he did manage to gain altitude. Elisenda let out a sigh of relief, for herself and for him, when she saw him pass over the last houses, holding himself up in some way with the risky flapping of a senile vulture. She kept watching him even when she was through cutting the onions and she kept on watching until it was no longer possible for her to see him, because then he was no longer an annoyance in her life but an imaginary dot on the horizon of the sea.

1972

8 THE SHORT STORY AND OTHER NARRATIVES

Elsewhere in this book I have talked about short stories without ever defining the term, assuming that the selections were short stories (and so far they have been), and that they could be discussed as such.

This chapter, however, includes seven brief narratives that are short and that tell stories, but that are not really *short stories.* The distinction between the narratives in this chapter and the short stories in the other chapters should lead us toward a definition of the short story as a fictional genre.

Short stories are short. Short stories can be very short indeed, perhaps no longer than a few words, though the median length is about 8,000 words (a dozen or so pages in this book). The longer short stories get, the more they become something else (see "A Preface to the Novel," p. 529).

Short stories are written down (the root of the word *literature* means *letter*). **Narrative,** a mode that includes stories and accounts, real or fictional, usually connecting a series of events, derives from a root word meaning *to tell,* and began indeed as an oral form, long before there were alphabets or writing, no doubt—stories told around a campfire (if there were campfires). Narrative is still an essentially oral form in many cultures and exists as an oral form in all—in our culture as jokes, anecdotes, tall tales, and so forth. All of the stories in this volume are written down—or printed, rather—but most in this chapter were first "told," and were probably passed down by word of mouth from generation to generation. These tales are not necessarily "primitive" in the sense of artless or unsophisticated, for oral narrative has its own qualities and requires its own skills in construction, but they do not as a rule follow the same structural patterns of rising and falling action or of causal, logical connection or articulation that we customarily find in short stories.

Short stories are original. An Eskimo, Lamba, or Kiowa narrative is presented as a story that belongs not to the teller but to the culture as a whole; a tale that has existed in one form or another over a long time, perhaps from the dawn of the culture itself. Though some short stories may use traditional patterns—the journey in *The Artificial Nigger,* the scapegoat in *The Lottery* or *The Ones Who Walk Away from Omelas*—or traditional material—like the ritual initiation in *The Old People* or the trickster in *Jumping Frog*—the story itself, in its details and in most of its elements, is new or original. Originality implies and sometimes emphasizes the author or creator of the story. The Eskimo, Lamba, or Kiowa narrator is usually effaced, and if he has any identity it is usually either that of an elder whose memory goes back to historical events or to tales he heard as a child or youth from his elders, or that of the performer, newly presenting old tales. Even short stories such as *My Man Bovanne* and *Spotted Horses,* which sound like oral narratives written down, deal with unique, new, or original events and characters, and are "told" by narrators who participate in or observe the "actual" story.

One universal kind of communal oral narrative whose origins lie in the shadowy past is the **myth,** a tale that has to do with matters beyond human memory or knowledge: the gods, the origins of the world, of man, of the tribe, or of various animals and plants. Another common kind is the **legend,** the tale of a human hero, often with divine qualities, and his exploits, often with divine assistance. **Fables** —narratives in prose or verse that point a moral and often use animals as characters—were originally an oral form. They proved so popular that not only were many written down, but more were invented, and the fable has become a literary genre, as we can see in *The Zebra Storyteller.* **Parables** are short narratives that make or illustrate a moral point; they are sometimes short allegories in which each of the details contributes to that moral meaning. They often begin as oral narratives and are later written down as the sayings of great teachers. *The Brigand and the Sage* is such a parable. Most of us are familiar with the parables in the New Testament, such as that of the talents (Matthew 25: 14–30) or of the Good Samaritan (Luke 10: 30–37).

Short stories are fictional. Though the short story as we are defining it is a subgenre of the genre fiction, even the assertion that a short story is fictional needs qualification. I read the autobiographical portions of N. Scott Momaday's *The Way to Rainy Mountain* as nonfiction. I think Momaday wants me to believe that what he says about himself and his experiences is true and that he believes it to be true. It is not necessary that it *be* true: memory inevitably distorts somewhat, and some details he "remembers," he may have dreamed or heard from older friends or relatives so often that he only thinks he remembers them. On the other hand, I read Mordecai Richler's *The Day My Grandmother Was Supposed to Die* as fiction, as a short story. While it is conceivable that every word of the story is true, that Richler may be reporting an episode from his childhood (the narrator's Yiddish name Muttel can be translated Mordecai), Richler has structured the piece like a short story—with beginning, middle, and end, for example—and we can read it as a story without concern for its actuality. This appearance of arrangement and structuring, of being made, of being *artificial,* in its best sense, is sometimes as important as the relation of a story to actuality in defining its fictionality. (Both *artificial* and *fiction* come from root words having to do with *making* or *molding.*)

Short stories are narratives. This, surely, would seem to need no qualification. The middle sections of the Momaday selections, however—especially the passages from the work of an anthropologist—we recognize not as narrative but as *exposition,* a subgenre of nonfictional prose that serves to explain, or as a mixture of exposition and description. But all narratives are "impure," having passages of description and exposition in them. What we mean when we say a short story is a narrative is not that every word, sentence, or passage is in some special narrative language that could be identified as such outside the context of the story, but only that the piece as a whole tells a story and that the non-narrative elements contribute to that story.

The short story, then, may be defined as a brief, written, original, fictional narrative in prose.

This chapter makes no attempt to represent all the various kinds of narratives other than the short story, nor does it sample representative narratives that preceded the short story in Western culture. To some extent it represents prose narratives that are most "other": primarily oral narratives; non-Western narratives from American Indian, Eskimo, African, Middle Eastern, and Oriental cultures; and even a bit of nonfictional narrative. It seeks to push toward the outer limits of narrative, to the most strange and different.

The purpose is not only to make us less provincial in thinking about brief narratives, but to open us up to what in fact has been happening in the short story of our own time. A tendency toward the realistic or everyday was long thought to be one of the defining qualities of the modern short story—and a few years ago I might easily have added *realistic* to the list of adjectives in my generic definition. As suggested in the previous chapter, "Fantasy," the line from Poe through Maupassant to Chekhov and Joyce was long considered the history of artistic progress—not just in the quality of the individual authors named, which may be valid enough, but in writers' mastery of the art of representing reality. Just as the camera jolted painters in the last hundred years or so to open their eyes to alternative ways of looking at reality and lead them to non-Western traditions of representation as one means of broadening human vision, so the writer of narrative, such as Spencer Holst or Gabriel García Márquez, seems to have turned to older oral or other modes. One way of reading *The Way to Rainy Mountain* is to use the nonfiction narrative sections to understand the "reality" behind the Kiowa myths and legends and oral history; another, however, is to recognize that Momaday and the anthropologist he quotes in exposition and autobiography are also only giving fallible human versions of reality, not necessarily more valid (though more acceptable because more familiar) than the Kiowa. Many recent stories, such as Grace Paley's *A Conversation with My Father,* acknowledge within the narrative the artificiality or arbitrariness of narrative itself, the inevitable subjective distortion of reality by an author, the imposition of art upon the actual.

A Note on Dates

Oral narrative is, by its very nature, difficult if not impossible to date accurately. Some of the Kiowa legends that N. Scott Momaday reports in the 1960s probably go back two or three centuries, but they have been passed on to him by his elders. So, too, the Iroquois, Lamba, and Eskimo stories are both old and new. Chuang Tzu lived about the fourth century B.C. but some of the stories and sayings attributed to him have no doubt been added and most have been changed. Sir Richard Burton's translation of *The Thousand Nights and a Night* was published between 1885 and 1888; Western translations date to the early eighteenth century. The actual origin of the tales is obscure, though Harun-al-Rashid, the Persian caliph in the tales, reigned from A.D. 786 to 809. Some of the tales may well have earlier Indian origins.

CORNPLANTER

The Great Mosquito*

An immense bird preyed upon the red men in all parts of the country. Their homes were at no time safe from its ravages. Often it would carry away children playing beside the wigwams, or, like a bolt of lightning, dart from the sky and strike a woman or man bleeding and dying to the earth. Whole fields of corn had been destroyed in a single night by its ravages, and its coming was so swift and terrible that the Indians hardly dared stir from the shelter of their houses. A strong party of Cayugas and Onondagas[1] finally determined upon its death, no matter at what cost to themselves. A young warrior offered himself for the sacrifice. He was provided with a quantity of rawhide thongs, and repaired to one of the open spaces, where it was believed the dreaded monster would discover and descend upon him. The young brave was to bind one of the thongs upon the bird's feet or upon some portion of its body, if possible, before he killed him, and then his companions, rushing from their place of concealment, would try to slay the enemy that had been snared with such difficulty. The preparations were elaborately made, and the young brave went forth on his dangerous mission.

Three days he sat, chanting his death-song and awaiting the coming of his terrible fate. On the morning of the fourth day the sky was suddenly darkened and the watchers saw that the great bird was slowly circling above the heroic young Cayuga. He ceased his chanting, and, standing upright, shouted defiance to the almost certain death that awaited him.

With a scream that turned the hearts of the waiting Indians cold with terror, the bird dropped upon its victim like a panther on his prey. A short and terrible struggle took place and then the concealed warriors rushed forth to finish the work of their brave young companion, who had succeeded in throwing one of the thongs over the great mosquito's neck. They brought willing and ready hands to the battle, and the arrows poured upon the struggling mass like a storm of hail. After a long encounter the bird was killed, and the young Cayuga smiled in triumph as his last glance rested upon the dead body of the monster.

Runners were at once dispatched to the villages to inform the Indians of the victory, and soon vast numbers of them came to look upon their long-dreaded enemy that had been slain at such cost. Its body was larger than that of the largest bear they had ever seen, and the breadth of its outstretched wings was as great as the height of three men. Its talons were as long as arrows, and its monstrous beak was lined with sharp teeth. There was much rejoicing over the great mosquito's death, and for several days feasting and dancing were held in honor of the bravery of those who had rid the country

* Translated by William Canfield.

1. Two American Indian nations within the Iroquois Confederacy, which was founded about 1570 in New York state.

of such a terrible scourge. Soon, however, swarms of the poisonous little flies that have been the pests of all nations since that time, infested the woods, and the Indians discovered that they came from the body of the dead bird. Too late they realized that the body of the great mosquito should have been burned when it was first slain, for fire is ever the destroyer of evil spirits.

OHAYOHOK

A Human Kayak*

This is the story of two brothers who lived in the south part of the village of Keengegan. They had just passed the tests that would permit them to be considered among the regular hunters of the village. After each had brought home a seal and delivered it to the old chief, who would cut it up and pass the meat around to all the homes, they became producers instead of dependents. It was in the spring of the year. The warm south winds had broken up the great ice fields and had brought with them a great abundance of seal to become the prey of *Innuit*[1] hunters. On this particular day the two brothers agreed to go out to the edge of the shore ice and hunt seal. How proud their old father, the Chief, would be to see his two sons dragging their first seal over the ice to the village. Thereafter, they would be considered full-fledged hunters and would take their place with the other hunters.

Taking their bows, arrows, spears, *pooksaks*,[2] and other necessary hunting equipment, they traveled almost half of the day before they came to the edge of the shore ice. Around the open patches of water, they hunted until darkness began to overtake them. This brought them to the realization that they had better return to the village regardless of the fact that they had failed to kill a single seal and would be the subjects of many chiding remarks and laughter when they reached the village empty-handed. When they came to a point about halfway on their homeward journey, they discovered that they were on a very large pan of ice which had broken away from the shore and had already left a wide stretch of water between them and the village. The wind and current carried them farther and farther away on their enormous raft of ice. As darkness fell, they could see the land gradually disappearing from sight.

Their plight offered no serious difficulties to the problem of procuring food. They could always rely on their bows and arrows and spears to provide the food they would need. But they realized that unless their ice raft brought them again to land they would finally find themselves in the land of Peeleeuktuk, the land of missing men,

* Translated by Clark M. Garber.
1. "People," i.e., Eskimo people.
2. Hunter's bag, usually sealskin.

from which no man ever returned. Then their relatives and friends would hear of them no more. In their feather parkas and fur pants and *mukluks*[3] they could not freeze, or even suffer from the cold. As long as they could kill seal or other game, they were in no danger of starving.

The boys could hardly wait for daylight to come the next morning so they could set to work building a shelter of snow and ice blocks. In this kind of a shelter, even though it were small, they would be safe from the blizzards which so often raged across the ocean ice. In their little snow hut they lived for many days while their big raft of ice carried them farther and farther from home. Apparently the spirits of the sea were unfavorable to them because they had been so careless as to get caught on the drifting ice. Therefore the seal and other game animals failed to come near them. It was not long until they became very hungry. One day, when the older boy returned from a hunt for food he found his brother had fallen sick in their snow hut. Thereupon a great fear began to creep into their hearts. A longing to return to their father's *innie*[4] possessed them and made them very sad.

On the following day, the younger brother said, "One has conversed with the spirits during the night. They have said that one's body will turn cold in death before two more suns pass."

On the second day thereafter, the younger brother went to their customary lookout on top of a large ice ridge to search with his keen eyes the endless expanse of ice for some sign of land. Toward midday, he sighted a low dark streak of land. Waiting long enough to be sure that they were approaching the shore, he rushed back to the snow hut thinking that such glad tidings would bring rapid recovery to his brother. When he entered the hut, he found his brother dead. Thus his brother's body had turned cold in death just as he had said it would. What could he do now? Land was in sight and the big ice raft on which he was drifting would soon touch the shore. He could not leave his brother's body on the drifting ice. That would offend the spirits of the sea animals beyond repair and would bring famine upon all his people.

There was only one thing to do. Dragging his brother's body by the parka hood, he came as quickly as possible to the edge of the ice nearest to the land. But here he was again thwarted in his purpose. The large ice floe had already touched the shore and was again drifting away from the land. How to get to land across the rapidly widening open water, and at the same time take his brother's body ashore, gave him a problem almost beyond his ability to solve. At length, after many trials and failures, he struck upon the plan of using his brother's body as a means to reach the shore. With his hunting knife he quickly opened the body of his brother and removed the viscera. Then he lashed the shaft of his harpoon to the back of the corpse in order to hold it rigid. He then placed the corpse in the water with the face turned up, and carefully assumed a position within the body cavity, as he would sit in his kayak. In this manner he had converted

3. Fur or leather boots.

4. Underground house.

the body of his brother into a human kayak. After much hard paddling with his bare hands and very slow progress, he finally reached the shore ice safely.

By this time he was becoming very weak from hunger. However, he managed, by great will power and effort, to drag his brother's body to the mountain side and bury it among the rocks. Then he began journeying along the beach in the direction of his home. Day after day he walked alowly along the rock-strewn shore and sandy beach. After many days of slow and difficult traveling with nothing to eat but bits of decaying matter which he picked up along the beach, he came upon a village. When he first caught sight of the village, his strength suddenly left him and he fell prone upon the ground. By sheer will power he forced himself to crawl along on his hands and knees. In this manner he came to the first *innie* of the village. Darkness had fallen, so there were no people about to witness his slow and laborious approach. When he crawled into the entrance of the *innie,* he came upon a mother dog with a litter of pups. There his progress was halted with great commotion.

The *innie* door opened and out through the tunnellike entrance came a beautiful girl to discover the cause of such an unusual disturbance. No sooner did she discover the young man in his weak and starving condition than she sounded an alarm and summoned help from within. Her father came to help her, and soon the young man was lying upon a soft bed of skins noisily devouring a large dish of *okpone,* blood stew. Under the kind treatment of these good people and the excellent food, which the very nice girl prepared for him, his strength soon returned. In a few days, he was ready to add his hunting skill to the problem of keeping food supplied for the family. It was not long until he had become the best hunter in the village. Thereupon he married the lovely girl who had saved him and had nursed him back to health. Thereafter, for a long time, he lived with his wife's people and became the main support of her family.

Until many moons later, life ran along smoothly for the young hunter and his wife. One day his wife came to him and said with much concern, "One's man is a very good hunter. Every time he goes hunting he returns after a short time with a very fine catch. How does one do it?"

"Someday one will tell his woman all about it," replied the young husband.

When another moon had passed, his wife again asked him about his wonderful skill as a hunter. To her query he replied, "First you must get your man some water from the ocean." With her small pail, she hastened to the beach and dipped it full of salty brine. Returning quickly to the *innie,* she placed the pail of water on the floor before her husband. From his parka sleeve her husband drew the skin of a bird. He wet the bird skin in his mouth and then stretched it over his body, thereby transforming himself into a bird. Then he began to fly about inside of the *innie*. After flying about the *innie* for a while, he suddenly dived into the pail of water and came out with a small fish in his beak. Flying as high as possible in the *innie,* he dropped the little fish onto the floor. To the great amazement of his wife, the little fish suddenly turned into a seal. Again the bird man dived into the pail of water and this time brought up a larger fish. This one turned into an *oogrook*[5] when dropped upon the floor. Suddenly the bird man flew through the window of the *innie*. His wife called to him, "Come back my husband. Come back my man. Do not leave your woman in this way."

"This is why one did not wish to tell his lovely wife about his hunting skill. Now one must leave his woman and never return," replied the young birdlike husband, as he flew over the *innie* endeavoring to find his bearings.

In his bird plumage, the young hunter began the journey to his own home. When he arrived in the village of his own people after many days of flying along the coast, his people did not know him from the other birds which flew about the village. Many times, he slept near his mother's *innie* but she did not know that this little bird was one of her long-lost sons. All the time, the little bird stayed near the window of his mother's *eeah*, kitchen, where the smoke from the seal oil lamps and stoves came out. At length the smoke and soot had turned his plumage black so that he looked like a raven.

One day, he fell asleep while perched on the edge of the *eeah* window, and fell into the kitchen. His mother struck him with a wooden spoon with which she was stirring the *okpone*, blood stew. The blow bursted the bird plumage open and out stepped her son. His mother's feelings at finding her long-lost son so unexpectedly brought tears of joy which were mingled with sobs of sorrow when she learned about the death of her other son.

Thereafter, the young man used the bird skin when hunting food for his own people. It brought him great success, and soon he was a very rich man. At length he found himself a wife among his own people. Unfortunately she gave him nothing but girl babies but she was a very devoted wife and kept his *innie* in good order. As his fortune increased his desire for sons became greater. He must have sons to carry on his skill and position among the people. Eventually, he took a second wife who was especially skilled at sewing, tanning and making fur garments. His second wife gave him four sons who, like their father, grew to be famous hunters.

AFRICAN FOLK TALE

What a Little Thing Did*

And one daughter and a son were born. And a man, her cousin, married the girl; and on the morrow he went hunting. His first father-in-law died, and his mother-in-law remained. One day a certain man

5. Large bearded seal.

* As told by Clement M. Doke in *Lamba Folk-Lore* (1927). The Awalamba live in what is now Zambia and Zaire in central Africa.

came and said, "I want to marry your mother-in-law, my son-in-law." And that son-in-law of his said, "Marry, am I to deny my mother-in-law?" And sure enough he came and married his mother-in-law.

One day he said to his son-in-law, "Come, son-in-law, let us go into the bush,[1] that we may eat some honey." Ah, and the son-in-law went with him into the bush. Then as they went along, the father-in-law said, "Son-in-law, here are the bees!" When the son-in-law had gone, he found the bees in a grass-stalk,[2] and the son-in-law thought, "What sort of a father-in-law is this, who calls me to bees in a grass-stalk?" And he cut out the honey from the grass-stalk there. Then his father-in-law said, "Eat the honey that you have cut out." The son-in-law refused, saying, "I have not yet eaten honey from a grass-stalk." And his father-in-law ate alone.

And again they went on. Again he located bees in a tremendously high Wanga[3] tree. Again he called his son-in-law; and when the son-in-law came he said, "Here are bees in the Wanga tree." And he replied, "Am I to climb right high up there?" And his father-in-law said, "Go!" And the son-in-law climbed up above, and the son-in-law cut out the bees, and called saying, "Father-in-law, now I have cut out the honey; give me some bark rope that I may tie up the bark dish." And his father-in-law stripped a bundle of bark rope, and his father-in-law hoisted it up above, and he tied the bark plate. Then he said, "Now father-in-law, take the honey that I have tied." And his father-in-law took the honey, and put it down, and the son-in-law came down from above. And he ordered his son-in-law saying. "Eat up the honey, son-in-law!" And the son-in-law refused even as he had done at the first over the honey from the grass-stalk. Then he carried the honey. And off they went to the village, and slept.

Again when morning dawned, he went early to his son-in-law. And he said, "Son-in-law, let us go today also, and let us cut out some honey." And the son-in-law came out, and off they both went, he and his father-in-law. Again his father-in-law did the same as he had priorly done, and again located it in a grass-stalk; and he called saying, "Father,[4] cut out these bees here." And the son-in-law came, and found them just in the grass-stalk. The son-in-law just stared, saying, "My father-in-law is a worry to me; he is always locating bees in a grass-stalk; he is acting as though he has tricks." Then he said, "Son-in-law, cut out the bees!" Then the son-in-law began to cut them out from the grass-stalk, and took out a barkplate. Then his father-in-law said, "Father, let us eat the honey." And the son-in-law refused, saying, "I don't eat honey from a grass-stalk." Then his father-in-law said, "Carry it, and let us go on walking"; and they departed, and off they went, son-in-law as well. Then as they passed along, he said, "There are some more bees here!" And when the son-in-law went, he found them even in a Wanga tree. And he said, "Climb up, son-in-law!" And the other said, "My father-in-law compels me, he wants his son-in-law to die." And the son-in-law climbed up above to a great

1. Uncleared scrubland.
2. An impossible place in which to find a nest of bees. (Doke's note)
3. A tree of such hard wood that natives seldom attempt to cut out a nest of bees located in it. (Doke's note)
4. Form of address.

height in the Wanga tree; and the son-in-law cut out the honey up there. Then he said, "Now I have cut out the honey, bring the bark rope!" And his father-in-law, who remained below stripped off the bark rope. And he who was above tied up the honey. And he said, "Now take the honey that I have tied up." And then his father-in-law went to the foot of the tree, and held out his hands, that the plate might come into his hands; and the father-in-law received the honey; and placed it on the ground. And the son-in-law descended from above where he was. Then his father-in-law said, "Son-in-law, let us eat the honey." And the son-in-law said, "No, I shall not eat it!" and he refused. Then the other said, "Carry the honey then, and let us go to the village." And they reached the village, and slept.

When it was morning, the father-in-law said, "Come, son-in-law, today also into the bush, and let us cut out some honey." Again he located bees, saying, "Son-in-law, here are some bees in a grass-stalk." The son-in-law came and found the bees even in the grass-stalk, even as he had done before. And the son-in-law said, "Every day you are locating bees right in a grass-stalk, father-in-law; why do you do this?" But his father-in-law said, "Cut out the bees, son-in-law!" And so the son-in-law began to cut out the bees from the grass-stalk, and removed a bark plate, and took the honey. Then his father-in-law said, "Son-in-law, let us eat the honey." His son-in-law refused. Then he said, "Take the honey, and let us go walking on." And the son-in-law took the plate of honey, and carried it. Then off he went with his father-in-law. And then where his father-in-law passed, he located them on the top of a Wanga tree; and then he called his son-in-law saying, "Cut out these bees here." And his son-in-law came; and he stared at them in the Wanga tree, saying, "To what a height my father-in-law sends me to cut out bees!" And the son-in-law climbed up, and cut out the honey.

And he said (to himself), "Today I won't call for a bark plate from below, I will remove a plate from the side of my leg." And he removed a plate from the side of his leg, and it was just there on his leg that he stripped off the string; and he tied the plate with the string that he stripped off from his very leg. Then his father-in-law said, "Lower the honey, son-in-law." And he said, "Hold out your hands, and take the honey." And his father-in-law received the honey. Then his father-in-law said, "What about this string, son-in-law, where did you strip it off?" Then his father-in-law went to the village, saying in his heart, "This son-in-law of mine is a man of tricks." And he reached the village and slept.

When morning came, he went early to his son-in-law. He said, "Today also let us go out walking." Where they went his father-in-law came upon a herd of buffalo. And the son-in-law said, "Wait, father-in-law, let me stalk them." And his father-in-law refused saying, "Stop, let me go, and let me kill them." And he took one arrow, and set it in the bow-string, and shot the arrow, and it went into an animal, and went through this one, and went through that one and it died, and it went through that one and it died, and it went through that one and it died; and the last one also it entered, and he who shot the arrow also entered the animals. Then the son-in-law said, "My father-in-law who killed these animals, where has he gone?" And he went to the first animal, and said, "Father-in-law come out!" He did not come out. And he reached another, and said, "Father-in-law come out!" But his father-in-law did not come out. And to another, but he did not come out. Then it was that he reached the last, and said, "Father-in-law come out, let us go to the village!" Then it was that his father-in-law came out with his bow in his hand. And off they went to the village; and the son-in-law was thinking all the while of his father-in-law's tricks. And the people came to fetch that meat to take it to the village.

Again another day the son-in-law and his father-in-law went into the bush to kill animals. Where they went they came upon many eland. And the father-in-law said, "I am going, let me kill them!" But the son-in-law said, "Let me go today, I know how to kill animals." And the son-in-law took one arrow, and shot it into the herd of eland. It went through this one, and it died; and it went through this one, and it died; and it went through this one, and it died; and when it came to the last one, the arrow went right through, and entered a wild orange. The wild orange fell into the water, and a crocodile swallowed the orange. And in its turn a hippopotamus swallowed the crocodile. The father-in-law went to the animals, and said, "Son-in-law come out!" He did not come out. And he reached another, and said, "Son-in-law come out!" He did not come out. And yet another, but he did not come out. And the last one, but he did not come out. Then he said, "But where has my son-in-law gone? I have finished asking all the animals!" And the father-in-law went off along to the village.

When it was morning, he said, "Where am I to find my son-in-law? Today I am going to dig a pitfall at the side of the river." And he dug the pitfall, and left it covered over, and went away. In the morning when he went early, he found that a hippopotamus had died in it. And he went to the village and said, "Come, mates, let us cut up a hippo, it has died in the pitfall."

And they pierced that hippopotamus, and took out a crocodile from the stomach of the hippopotamus. Then he said, "But where is my son-in-law?" He said, "Now men, pierce this crocodile." And they pierced the crocodile, and took out a wild orange. Then he said, "My son-in-law, come out!" Then it was that he came out of the wild orange with his bow in his hand. His father-in-law sat and marveled, saying, "Son-in-law of mine, why do you do these wonderful things to me, because you have worried me, and have entered many animals?" And he went to the village with his father-in-law, and the people carried that meat.

And he went out early with his son-in-law to cut out honey; and again located bees in a very tall Wanga tree. And he said, "Son-in-law cut out these bees in the Wanga tree." And the son-in-law came, and climbed that Wanga tree, and the son-in-law cut out the honey. And he said, "Father-in-law, take this honey that I have cut out!" Ah, and he received the honey; and then the son-in-law fell hurtling down, and broke and smashed to pieces, and not even a little bit of him was seen; and he entirely crumbled up, and turned into dust. His father-in-law became afraid, and said, "Today my son-in-law is dead, he has broken to pieces." And off he went to the village, and reached the village and said, "My son-in-law is dead, I don't see him."

There where he remained, he revived, and joined himself together piece by piece, and changed into a woman. In the morning his father-in-law came saying, "Just let me go to where my son-in-law died." When he had gone some distance, he met that woman. He said, "Woman, where have you come from?" She said, "I have come from here in this country." Then he said, "I am going to divorce my old wife, and I shall marry this beautiful one that I have seen." All the time it was his son-in-law who had turned into a woman. And she said, "Marry me then." There and then he built a zareba. And night fell. And he lay with that woman. When it was morning, he wanted to return to the village, to fetch something to smoke; and off he went to the village. Where the woman remained, she turned back into the man that she was before. On the father-in-law's return, to his surprise he found the dwelling empty, she had gone out. Then he began calling out, "O my wife, where have you gone?" And she didn't reply; how could she when she had already gone to the village. Then where she went, she turned back into the very son-in-law; and then it was that his father-in-law said, "My son-in-law has bothered me, now I am going to gather all the people together, that I may tell them how sons-in-law behave." Then it was that he gathered together all his companions. And he said, "Friends do you associate with a son-in-law who is always performing wonderful miracles?" And his companions asked, "What has he done?" He said, "I saw some honey in a Wanga tree; my son-in-law went to cut it out, and he peeled off a bark plate from the side of his leg!" Then all the people said, "Is that what your son-in-law does?" He said, "Yes!" Then all his companions said, "You son-in-law of his, explain what your father-in-law has said." And he said, "It was my father-in-law who began by locating bees in a grass-stalk. Again another day he located bees in a Wanga tree; and I went up above to cut them out. And that was why I started, for why should my father-in-law start his cunning? And so I too one day revealed my cunning, that of peeling a bark plate off my leg." And he added, "And my falling from a tall tree also was in order that my father-in-law might today be met by a devil!"

Then everybody said, "It was you, father-in-law, who began it!" Then the son-in-law said, "That was why I changed into a woman; and you did not know me, you thought I was a woman, and all the time I was your son-in-law." That was how they settled the case.

CHUANG TZU

The Brigand and the Sage*

Confucius was on friendly terms with the sage Liu-hsia Hui. Liu-hsia Hui had a younger brother who was known as the Brigand Chih.

* Translated by Arthur Waley.

This brigand and the nine thousand followers who formed his band swept through the country, pillaging and despoiling every kingdom under Heaven, burrowing their way into houses, wrenching doors, driving off men's cattle and horses, seizing their wives and daughters. In his greed for gain the brigand forgot all ties of kinship, paid no heed to father, mother, or brothers young and old, and made no offerings to his ancestors. Whenever he approached a town, if it was a big place the people manned the city-walls and if it was a small place they ensconced themselves behind their barrows. The whole countryside groaned under the affliction.

Confucius said to Liu-hsia Hui, "A father who is worthy of the name ought to be able to correct his son; an elder brother who is worthy of the name ought to be capable of instructing his younger brother. If it is not the duty of fathers to call their sons to order and of elder brothers to instruct their younger brothers, the whole importance that we attach to those relationships at once disappears. But here are you, admittedly one of the most gifted men of your generation; yet your younger brother is known as 'the Brigand Chih,' has become a curse to the whole land, and you have failed to teach him better ways. Forgive me for saying so, but I blush on your behalf. I hope you will not take it amiss if I go in your stead and have a talk with him." "You say," replied Liu-hsia Hui, "that a father ought to be able to correct his son, that an elder brother ought to be capable of instructing his younger brother. But suppose the son does not listen to his father, suppose the younger brother does not accept the elder brother's advice? In the present case even such eloquence as yours cannot possibly have the slightest effect. My brother Chih is a remarkable man. His passions, once aroused, leap like a fountain; his calculations are swift as a whirlwind. Not only is he strong enough to defy every foe; he is also clever enough to justify every crime. Humor him, and he is friendly; thwart him and he flies into a rage. On such occasions the language he uses is far from flattering; I certainly advise you not to go near him."

Confucius did not listen to this warning, but taking his disciple Yen Hui to drive the carriage and putting Tzu-kung on his right, he set off to visit the Brigand Chih. The brigand and his men happened at the time to be resting on the southern slopes of the T'ai-shan, and were enjoying a supper of minced human liver. Confucius got down from his carriage and went toward the camp. Being confronted by a sentinel he said to him: "Pray inform the General that K'ung Ch'iu[1] of the land of Lu, having heard of his Excellency as a champion of morality, has come to pay his respects." And so saying he prostrated himself twice before the sentinel with solemnity. When the message was brought, the Brigand Chih fell into a mighty rage. His eyes blazed like fiery comets, his hair stood on end so that his hat was lifted off his head. "Why this is that crafty fraud from Lu, K'ung Ch'iu, isn't it? Tell him from me that it is mere talk for the sake of talking—all this random chatter about his heroes king Wên and king Wu. Dresses up in a forked hat that looks as though a tree had taken root on his head, puts the whole flank of a dead ox round his belly and then chatters

1. I.e., Confucius. (Waley's note)

unceasingly, heaping nonsense upon nonsense; eats what others have grown, wears what others have woven, wags his lips and drums his tongue, deluding all the rulers under heaven with his own private notions of right and wrong and preventing the scholars who come to him from every corner of the land from using the powers that are in them! Pretends to be interested only in filial piety and brotherly obedience, but spends his time currying favor with landed lords, with the rich and great! Tell the fellow that he is a scoundrel for whom no punishment would be too great, and that if he does not clear out of here at once, we shall add his liver to our morning stew."

The message was delivered; but Confucius again asked for an interview. "Being fortunate enough to know your brother Liu-hsia Hui," he said, "I desire to look at your feet beneath the curtain."[2]

The sentinel brought in the message, and this time the brigand Chih said, "Bring him in!" Confucius advanced at a brisk trot,[3] carefully avoided treading upon the brigand's mat, ran backwards a few steps, and prostrated himself twice.

The brigand was evidently in a great rage. His feet were planted wide apart, he was fingering the blade of his sword, his eyes glared, and finally with a voice like that of a suckling tigress he roared out, "Come here, Ch'iu! And remember, if what you say is acceptable to me, you live; if it is not acceptable, you die!"

"I have heard," said Confucius, "that there are among the men of the world three kinds of personal power (*tê*). To grow to a stature so commanding, to possess beauty and grace so incomparable as to delight the eyes of all men, high or humble, young or old—this is the highest sort of power. To have a knowledge that embraces heaven above and earth below, to have abilities that can cope with every possible situation—this is the second and lower sort of power. To be bold, ruthless, undeterred by any hazard, a gatherer of multitudes and a causer of wars—this is the third and lowest kind of personal power. To possess any one of these three is sufficient to set a man with his face turned to the south and to give him the title of Lonely One.[4] You, my General, possess all three. Your stature is 8 feet 2 inches,[5] your countenance is dazzling, your lips are as though smeared with cinnabar, your teeth are like a row of shells; your voice booms like the tone-note of the scale. And yet for all this, men call you the Brigand Chih! I confess I am ashamed on your behalf and cannot reconcile myself to this. But if you will listen to me, I will go as your ambassador to the courts of Wu and Yüeh in the south, of Ch'i and Lu in the north, of Sung and Wei in the east, of Chin and Ch'u in the west,[6] and arrange that a great walled city shall be built for you, several hundred leagues in circumference, with quarters for many hundred thousand inhabitants. You shall be raised to the dignity of a feudal prince, and under your sway the whole world shall begin anew. You will lay down your arms, disband your followers, gather

2. I.e., to be allowed even the most cursory contact with you. (Waley's note)

3. A sign of respect. (Waley's note)

4. When the ruler faces his subjects, he alone faces to the south; his subjects face north. He is the Lonely One (Orphan) because his position is unique and perhaps also because the father whom he has succeeded is necessarily dead. (Waley's note)

5. About 5 feet 8 inches in our measurement. (Waley's note)

6. The geography of this promise is somewhat confused. (Waley's note)

about you brothers old and young, and see to it that they lack nothing; and make due offering to your ancestors. You will thus be behaving like a Sage and Hero and at the same time giving to the world that for which it ardently longs."

"Listen here," cried the Brigand Chih, in a great rage. "It is only the ignorant low rabble who allow themselves to be beguiled by promises of gain or scolded into altering their ways. My tall stature and my good looks which delight the eyes of all who see me—these are advantages that I inherited from my parents. I am the person most likely to be aware of them and stand in no need of your approbation. Moreover, it is commonly said that those who are prone to praise men to their faces, are quick to speak ill of them behind their backs.

"And now as to your talk of a great city and a multitude of inhabitants—this is merely an attempt to dazzle me by promises of gain, and is treating me as though I were a common, witless peasant. And even if such success were attainable, how long would it be secured? The biggest city cannot be larger than the world. The Emperors Yao and Shun[7] possessed the whole world, yet their sons and grandsons had not so much as a pin-point of land. T'ang of the Yin dynasty, Wu of the Chou dynasty rose to be Sons of Heaven; but their posterity is extinct. Was not this just because what they sought and won was far too large a prize? . . . Neither Yao nor Shun could set a son upon the throne; both made way for subjects. T'ang of Yin banished his sovereign; King Wu of Chou slew Chieh[8] of Yin. And from that day onward the strong have crushed the weak, the many have maltreated the few; nor since the time of T'ang and Wu has there been a single ruler who was not as great a ruffian as they. Yet here come you, earnestly applying yourself to the Way of king Wên and king Wu and using every sophistry under heaven in order to inculcate it upon generations to come. You dress up in a wide cloak and belt of clipped bull's hide, and by your cant and humbug delude the princes of the world into giving you the wealth and honors that are your only real ambition. There can be no greater brigand than you, and instead of talking so much about the Brigand Chih, I wonder people do not call you the Brigand Confucius! . . .

"There is no need for you to say a word more. If you could tell me about the affairs of ghosts or hobgoblins, it would be another matter. About them I admit I know nothing at all. But concerning human affairs nothing you say can possibly carry me any further. I shall have heard it all before. I, on the other hand, intend to tell you something about man and his natural desires. He has an eye that longs for beauty, an ear that longs for music, a mouth that longs for sweet flavors, ambitions and energies that crave fulfillment. Some few may live to eighty years, some fewer to a hundred; but one who lives till sixty has still not died young. And during these sixty years, if we take away the time that is spent in sickness, mourning and trouble, in all this time there will not be more than four or five days in each month when his lips are opened and laughter comes.

"Heaven and earth are illimitable; to man a term is set. Furnished

7. Legendary "good kings." (Waley's note)

8. Semi-legendary tyrant. (Waley's note)

only with the scrap of time that is his span, he is committed to a place amid the illimitables. A flash, and all is over, like a racehorse seen through a crack. He who by the enjoyment of his senses can use this brief moment to the full alone can claim to have found the Way. All that you acclaim, I utterly discard. Be off with you as fast as you can, and never dare prate to me again! This Way of yours is nothing but noise and babble, humbug and empty fraud, such as could never help any man to perfect the unalloyed that is within him; is in fact not worth a moment's discussion."

Confucius prostrated himself twice, and retired at full speed. When he had reached the gate of the camp and regained his carriage, his hands were trembling to such an extent that three times the reins fell out of them, there was a cloud before his eyes and his face was ashen gray. He leant over the fore-rail with sunken head, gasping for breath. At last he reached Lu, and outside the eastern gate happened to meet Liu-hsia Hui. "What has become of you lately?" asked Liu-hsia Hui. "I have not seen you for several days. Judging by the appearance of your horses and carriage, I should think you have been on a journey. Is it possible that, despite my warning, you have been to see my brother Chih?" Confucius gazed upwards at the sky and sighed. "I have indeed," he said. "And Chih," said Liu-hsia Hui, "did not take to your ideas any more kindly than I predicted?" "That is true," said Confucius. "I must confess that, as the saying goes, I poulticed myself with moxa[9] when there was nothing wrong with me. I rushed off to dress a tiger's head and plait its beard. Small wonder if I nearly landed in the tiger's maw!"

CHUANG TZU

King Mu and the Wizard*

In the time of king Mu of Chou there came from a land in the far west a wizard who could go into water and fire, pierce metals and stone, turn mountains upside down, make rivers flow backwards, move fortifications and towns, ride on the air without falling, collide with solids without injury. There was indeed no limit to the miracles that he could perform. And not only could he change the outward shape of material things; he could also transform the thoughts of men. King Mu reverenced him like a god, served him like a master, put his own state chambers at the wizard's disposal, gave him for sustenance the animals reared for imperial sacrifice, and for his entertainment chose girls skilled in music and dancing.

But the wizard found the king's palace too cramped and sordid to live in; the choicest delicacies from the king's kitchen he pronounced to

9. An ointment burned on the skin.

* Translated by Arthur Waley.

be coarse and rancid, and he would not eat them. The ladies from the king's harem he would not look at, so foul and hideous did he find them.

The king accordingly set about building a completely new palace, employing all the most skillful workers in clay and wood, the most accomplished decorators in whitewash and ochre; expending indeed so much upon the work that by the time it was complete all his treasuries were empty. The towers were six thousand feet high, and from them one looked down upon the top of the Chung-nan hills. It was named The Tower that hits Heaven. The king chose, from among the virgins of Chêng and Wei, girls of the most transcendent beauty and charm, anointed them with fragrant oils, straightened the curve of their eyebrows, decked them with combs and earrings, clothed them in jackets of the softest gauze, skirts of the thinnest floss, beautified them with white powder and with black, set jade rings at their girdles, strewed the floors with scented herbs, and brought these ladies to the palace till it was full. For the wizard's pleasure continual music was played, Receiving the Clouds, The Six Gems, The Nine Songs of Succession, The Morning Dew; every month he received a supply of costly garments, and every morning he was provided with costly food. But he was still far from content and could only with the greatest difficulty be persuaded to approach this new abode. After some time had passed, during which the magician frequently absented himself, he one day invited the king to accompany him upon a journey. Whereupon the magician began to rise from the ground and the king, clutching at his sleeve, was carried up and up, till they reached the sky. Here they halted, just in front of the magician's house, which was moated with dust of silver and gold and looped with festoons of jade and pearl. It stood out far above the rain and clouds. What it rested upon was hard to say, but it seemed to be supported by a coil of cloud. In this house nothing that his ears and eyes heard or saw, nothing that his nose and mouth smelt or tasted was in the least like what the king was accustomed to in the world of men. This, he thought, must surely be Stainless City, Purple Mystery, Level Sky, Wide Joy—one of the palaces of God. Looking down at the world below he saw what seemed like a hummock in the ground, with some piles of brushwood lying around it, and suddenly realized that this was his own palace with its arbors. Here as it seemed to him he lived for twenty or thirty years without a thought for his kingdom. At last the wizard again invited him to make a journey, and once more they traveled, till they had reached a place where looking up one could not see the sun or moon, looking down one saw neither river nor lake. So fierce a light blazed and flashed that the king's eyes were dazzled and he could not look; so loud a noise jangled and echoed that his ears were deafened and he could not listen. His limbs loosened, his entrails were as though dissolved within him, his thoughts were confused, his energy extinct. "Let us go back," he cried to the wizard, who gave him a push and soon they were falling through space.

The next thing that he knew was that he was sitting just where he had sat when the magician summoned him; the same attendants were still at his side, the wine that they had just served to him was still warm, the food still moist. "Where have I been?" he asked. "Your Majesty," one of his servants answered, "has been sitting there in silence."

It was three days before the king was completely himself again. On his recovery he sent for the wizard and asked him to explain what had happened. "I took you," the wizard replied, "upon a journey of the soul. Your body never moved. The place where you have been living was none other than your own palace; the grounds in which you strolled were in fact your own park.

"Your Majesty, between himself and the understanding of such things, interposes habitual doubts. Could you for a moment divest yourself of them, there is no miracle of mine, no trick with time, that you could not imitate."

The king was very pleased, paid no further heed to affairs of state, amused himself no more with ministers or concubines, but devoted himself henceforth to distant journeys of the soul.

N. SCOTT MOMADAY

from The Way to Rainy Mountain

IV

They lived at first in the mountains. They did not yet know of Tai-me,[1] but this is what they knew: There was a man and his wife. They had a beautiful child, a little girl whom they would not allow to go out of their sight. But one day a friend of the family came and asked if she might take the child outside to play. The mother guessed that would be all right, but she told the friend to leave the child in its cradle and to place the cradle in a tree. While the child was in the tree, a redbird came among the branches. It was not like any bird that you have seen; it was very beautiful, and it did not fly away. It kept still upon a limb, close to the child. After a while the child got out of its cradle and began to climb after the redbird. And at the same time the tree began to grow taller, and the child was borne up into the sky. She was then a woman, and she found herself in a strange place. Instead of a redbird, there was a young man standing before her. The man spoke to her and said: "I have been watching you for a long time, and I knew that I would find a way to bring you here. I have brought you here to be my wife." The woman looked all around; she saw that he was the only living man there. She saw that he was the sun.

1. Legendary creature with feet of deer and body covered with feathers, protector of the Kiowa Indians. Represented by a two-foot green stone doll shaped like a human with robe of white feathers, feather and ermine-skin headdress, blue beads, and painted with symbols of sun and moon; the effigy is kept hidden except during Sun Dance ceremony.

There the land itself ascends into the sky. These mountains lie at the top of the continent, and they cast a long rain shadow on the sea of grasses to the east. They arise out of the last North American wilderness, and they have wilderness names: Wasatch, Bitterroot, Bighorn, Wind River.[2]

I have walked in a mountain meadow bright with Indian paintbrush, lupine, and wild buckwheat, and I have seen high in the branches of a lodgepole pine the male pine grosbeak, round and rose-colored, its dark, striped wings nearly invisible in the soft, mottled light. And the uppermost branches of the tree seemed very slowly to ride across the blue sky.

V

After that the woman grew lonely. She thought about her people, and she wondered how they were getting on. One day she had a quarrel with the sun, and the sun went away. In her anger she dug up the root of a bush which the sun had warned her never to go near. A piece of earth fell from the root, and she could see her people far below. By that time she had given birth; she had a child—a boy by the sun. She made a rope out of sinew and took her child upon her back; she climbed down upon the rope, but when she came to the end, her people were still a long way off, and there she waited with her child on her back. It was evening; the sun came home and found his woman gone. At once he thought of the bush and went to the place where it had grown. There he saw the woman and the child, hanging by the rope halfway down to the earth. He was very angry, and he took up a ring, a gaming wheel, in his hand. He told the ring to follow the rope and strike the woman dead. Then he threw the ring and it did what he told it to do; it struck the woman and killed her, and then the sun's child was all alone.

The plant is said to have been the pomme blanche, *or* pomme de prairie, *of the voyageurs, whose chronicles refer time and again to its use by the Indians. It grows on the high plains and has a farinaceous root that is turniplike in taste and in shape. This root is a healthful food, and attempts have been made to cultivate the plant as a substitute for the potato.*

The anthropologist Mooney wrote in 1896: "Unlike the neighboring Cheyenne and Arapaho, who yet remember that they once lived east of the Missouri and cultivated corn, the Kiowa have no tradition of ever having been an agricultural people or anything but a tribe of hunters."

Even now they are meateaters; I think it is not in them to be farmers. My grandfather, Mammedaty, worked hard to make wheat and cotton

2. Mountains in Utah, Idaho and Montana, and Wyoming. The Kiowa were mountain people from the district around Yellowstone who moved east and south to a knoll on the Oklahoma plain northwest of the Wichita Range.

grow on his land, but it came to very little in the end. Once when I was a small boy I went across the creek to the house where the old woman Keahdinekeah lived. Some men and boys came in from the pasture, where a calf had just been killed and butchered. One of the boys held the calf's liver—still warm and wet with life—in his hand, eating of it with great relish. I have heard that the old hunters of the Plains prized the raw liver and tongue of the buffalo above all other delicacies.

VI

The sun's child was big enough to walk around on the earth, and he saw a camp nearby. He made his way to it and saw that a great spider—that which is called a grandmother—lived there. The spider spoke to the sun's child, and the child was afraid. The grandmother was full of resentment; she was jealous, you see, for the child had not yet been weaned from its mother's breasts. She wondered whether the child were a boy or a girl, and therefore she made two things, a pretty ball and a bow and arrows. These things she left alone with the child all the next day. When she returned, she saw that the ball was full of arrows, and she knew then that the child was a boy and that he would be hard to raise. Time and again the grandmother tried to capture the boy, but he always ran away. Then one day she made a snare out of rope. The boy was caught up in the snare, and he cried and cried, but the grandmother sang to him and at last he fell asleep.

Go to sleep and do not cry.
Your mother is dead, and still you feed
   upon her breasts.
Oo-oo-la-la-la-la, oo-oo.

In the autumn of 1874, the Kiowas were driven southward towards the Staked Plains. Columns of troops were converging upon them from all sides, and they were bone-weary and afraid. They camped on Elk Creek, and the next day it began to rain. It rained hard all that day, and the Kiowas waited on horseback for the weather to clear. Then, as evening came on, the earth was suddenly crawling with spiders, great black tarantulas, swarming on the flood.

I know of spiders. There are dirt roads in the Plains. You see them, and you wonder where and how far they go. They seem very old and untraveled, as if they all led away to deserted houses. But creatures cross these roads: dung beetles and grasshoppers, sidewinders and tortoises. Now and then there comes a tarantula, at evening, always larger than you imagine, dull and dark brown, covered with long, dusty hairs. There is something crochety about them; they stop and go and angle away.

VII

The years went by, and the boy still had the ring which killed his mother. The grandmother spider told him never to throw the ring into the sky, but one day he threw it up, and it fell squarely on top of his head and cut him in two. He looked around, and there was another boy, just like himself, his twin. The two of them laughed and laughed, and then they went to the grandmother spider. She nearly cried aloud when she saw them, for it had been hard enough to raise the one. Even so, she cared for them well and made them fine clothes to wear.

Mammedaty owned horses. And he could remember that it was essentially good to own horses, that it was hard to be without horses. There was a day: Mammedaty got down from a horse for the last time. Of all the tribes of the Plains, the Kiowas owned the greatest number of horses per person.

On summer afternoons I went swimming in the Washita River.[3] *The current was slow, and the warm, brown water seemed to be standing still. It was a secret place. There in the deep shade, inclosed in the dense, overhanging growth of the banks, my mind fixed on the wings of a dragonfly or the flitting motion of a water strider, the great open land beyond was all but impossible to imagine. But it was there, a stone's throw away. Once, from the limb of a tree, I saw myself in the brown water; then a frog leaped from the bank, breaking the image apart.*

XVII

Bad women are thrown away. Once there was a handsome young man. He was wild and reckless, and the chief talked to the wind about him. After that, the man went hunting. A great whirlwind passed by, and he was blind. The Kiowas have no need of a blind man; they left him alone with his wife and child. The winter was coming on and food was scarce. In four days the man's wife grew tired of caring for him. A herd of buffalo came near, and the man knew the sound. He asked his wife to hand him a bow and an arrow. "You must tell me," he said, "when the buffalo are directly in front of me." And in that way he killed a bull, but his wife said that he had missed. He asked for another arrow and killed another bull, but again his wife said that he had missed. Now the man was a hunter, and he knew the sound an arrow makes when it strikes home, but he said nothing. Then his wife helped herself to the meat and ran away with her child. The man was blind; he ate grass and kept himself alive. In seven days a band of Kiowas found him and took him to their camp. There in the firelight a woman was telling a story. She told of how her husband had been killed by enemy warriors. The blind man listened, and he knew her voice. That was a bad woman. At sunrise they threw her away.

In the Kiowa calendars there is graphic proof that the lives of women were hard, whether they were "bad women" or not. Only the captives, who were slaves, held lower status. During the Sun Dance of 1843, a man stabbed his wife in the breast because she accepted Chief Dohasan's invitation to ride with him in the ceremonial procession. And

3. In Oklahoma.

in the winter of 1851–52, Big Bow stole the wife of a man who was away on a raiding expedition. He brought her to his father's camp and made her wait outside in the bitter cold while he went in to collect his things. But his father knew what was going on, and he held Big Bow and would not let him go. The woman was made to wait in the snow until her feet were frozen.

Mammedaty's grandmother, Kau-au-ointy, was a Mexican captive, taken from her homeland when she was a child of eight or ten years. I never knew her, but I have been to her grave at Rainy Mountain.

KAU-AU-OINTY
BORN 1834
DIED 1929
AT REST

She raised a lot of eyebrows, they say, for she would not play the part of a Kiowa woman. From slavery she rose up to become a figure in the tribe. She owned a great herd of cattle, and she could ride as well as any man. She had blue eyes.

1969

from The Thousand Nights and a Night*

. . . but sleep gave no sign of visiting the Caliph that night and he lay awake pondering the mishaps of the three Kalandar[1]-princes and impatient to know the history of the ladies and the two black bitches. No sooner had morning dawned than he went forth and sat upon the throne of his sovereignty; and, turning to Ja'afar,[2] after all his Grandees and Officers of state were gathered together, he said, "Bring me the three ladies and the two bitches and the three Kalandars." So Ja'afar fared forth and brought them all before him (and the ladies were veiled); then the Minister turned to them and said in the Caliph's name, "We pardon you your maltreatment of us and your want of courtesy, in consideration of the kindness which forewent it, and because you knew us not: now however I would have you to know that you stand in presence of the fifth of the sons of Abbas, Harun al-Rashid, brother of Caliph Músá al-Hádi, son of Al-Mansúr; son of Mohammed the brother of Al-Saffáh bin Mohammed who was first of the royal house. Speak therefore before him the truth and the whole truth!" When the ladies heard Ja'afar's words touching the Commander of the Faithful, the eldest came forward and said, "O Prince of True Believers, my story is one which, were it graven with needlegravers upon the eye-corners were a warning for whoso

* Translated by Sir Richard Burton.
1. Beggar monks.
2. The Wazir, or chief counselor of Harun al-Rashid the Caliph. Both are historical personages.

would be warned[3] and an example for whoso can take profit from example."—And Shahrazad perceived the dawn of day and ceased to say her permitted say.

Now when it was the Seventeenth Night,

She said, It has reached me, O auspicious King, that she stood forth before the Commander of the Faithful and began to tell

The Eldest Lady's Tale

Verily a strange tale is mine and it is this:—Those two black bitches are my eldest sisters by one mother and father; and these two others, she who bears upon her the signs of stripes and the third our procuratrix are my sisters by another mother. When my father died, each took her share of the heritage and, after a while my mother also deceased, leaving me and my sisters three thousand dinars; so each daughter received her portion of a thousand dinars and I the same, though the youngest. In due course of time my sisters married with the usual festivities and lived with their husbands, who bought merchandise with their wives' money and set out on their travels together. Thus they threw me off. My brothers-in-law were absent with their wives five years, during which period they spent all the money they had and, becoming bankrupt, deserted my sisters in foreign parts amid stranger folk. After five years my eldest sister returned to me in beggar's gear with her clothes in rags and tatters and a dirty old mantilla;[4] and truly she was in the foulest and sorriest plight. At first sight I did not know my own sister; but presently I recognized her and said, "What state is this?" "O our sister," she replied, "Words cannot undo the done; and the reed of Destiny has run through what Allah decreed." Then I sent her to the bath and dressed her in a suit of my own, and boiled for her a bouillon and brought her some good wine and said to her, "O my sister, you are the eldest, who still stand to us in the place of father and mother; and, as for the inheritance which came to me as to you two, Allah has blessed it and prospered it to me with increase; and my circumstances are easy, for I have made much money by spinning and cleaning silk; and I and you will share my wealth alike." I entreated her with all kindliness and she abode with me a whole year, during which our thoughts and fancies were always full of our other sister. Shortly after she too came home in yet fouler and sorrier plight than that of my eldest sister; and I dealt by her still more honorably than I had done by the first, and each of them had a share of my substance. After a time they said to me, "O our sister, we desire to marry again, for indeed we have not patience to drag on our days without husbands and to lead the lives of widows bewitched"; and I replied, "O eyes of me![5] you have hitherto seen scanty weal in wedlock, for nowadays good men and

3. A common play on the Arabic word *ibrat*, which means both engraving needle and warning or example.

4. Sheet of white calico covering head or hands, worn by poor Egyptian women out of doors.

5. I.e., "My dears." (Burton's note)

true are become rareties and curiosities; nor do I deem your projects advisable, as you have already made trial of matrimony and have failed." But they would not accept my advice and married without my consent: nevertheless I gave them outfit and dowries out of my money; and they fared forth with their mates. In a mighty little time their husbands played them false and, taking whatever they could lay hands upon, ran off and left them in the lurch. Thereupon they came to me ashamed and in abject case and made their excuses to me, saying, "Pardon our fault and do not be angry with us; for although you are younger in years yet are you older in wit; henceforth we will never make mention of marriage; so take us back as your hand-maidens that we may eat our mouthful." I said, "Welcome to you, O my sisters, there is nothing dearer to me than you." And I took them in and redoubled my kindness to them. We ceased not to live after this loving fashion for a full year, when I resolved to sell my wares abroad and first to fit me a conveyance for Bassorah; so I equipped a large ship, and loaded her with merchandise and valuable goods for traffic, and with provisions and all needful for a voyage, and said to my sisters, "Will you stay at home while I travel, or would you prefer to accompany me on the voyage?" "We will travel with you," they answered, "for we cannot bear to be parted from you." So I divided my money into two parts, one to accompany me and the other to be left in charge of a trusty person, for, as I said to myself, "Perhaps some accident may happen to the ship and yet we remain alive; in which case we shall find on our return what may stand us in good stead. I took my two sisters and we went a-voyaging some days and nights; but the master was careless enough to miss his course, and the ship went astray with us and entered a sea other than the sea we sought. For a time we knew naught of this; and the wind blew fair for us ten days, after which the look-out man went aloft to see about him and cried, "Good news!" Then he came down rejoicing and said, "I have seen what seems to be a city as 'twere a pigeon." We rejoiced and, before an hour of the day had passed, the buildings showed plain in the offing and we asked the Captain, "What is the name of yonder city?" and he answered, "By Allah I know not, for I never saw it before and never sailed these seas in my life: but, since our troubles have ended in safety, it remains for you only to land there with your merchandise and, if you find selling profitable, sell and make your market of what is there; and if not, we will rest here two days and provision ourselves and fare away. So we entered the port and the Captain went up town and was absent awhile, after which he returned to us and said, "Arise; go up into the city and marvel at the works of Allah with His creatures and pray to be preserved from His righteous wrath!" So we landed and going up into the city, saw at the gate men holding staves, but when we drew near them, behold, they had been transformed by the anger of Allah and had become stones. Then we entered the city and found all who lived there turned into black stones: not an inhabited house appeared to the espier, nor was there a blower of fire. We were awe-struck at the sight and threaded the market streets where we found the goods and gold and silver left lying in their places; and we were glad and said, "Doubtless there is some mystery in all this." Then we dispersed about the thoroughfares and each busied himself with collecting the wealth and money and rich stuffs, taking scanty heed of friend or comrade. As for myself I went up to the castle which was strongly fortified; and, entering the King's palace by its gate of red gold, found all the vessel of gold and silver, and the King himself seated in the midst of his Chamberlains and Nabobs and Emirs and Wazirs; all clad in raiment which confounded man's art. I drew nearer and saw him sitting on a throne incrusted and inlaid with pearls and gems; and his robes were of gold-cloth adorned with jewels of every kind, each one flashing like a star. Around him stood fifty Mamelukes, white slaves, clothed in silks of diverse sorts holding their drawn swords in their hands; but when I drew near to them lo! all were black stones. My understanding was confounded at the sight, but I walked on and entered the great hall of the harem, whose walls I found hung with tapestries of gold-striped silk and spread with silken carpets embroidered with golden flowers. Here I saw the Queen lying at full length arrayed in robes purfled with fresh young[6] pearls; on her head was a diadem set with many sorts of gems each fit for a ring and around her neck hung collars and necklaces. All her raiment and her ornaments were in natural state but she had been turned into a black stone by Allah's wrath. Presently I espied an open door for which I made straight and found leading to it a flight of seven steps. So I walked up and came upon a place pargeted with marble and spread and hung with gold-worked carpets and tapestry, in the middle of which stood a throne of juniper-wood inlaid with pearls and precious stones and set with bosses of emeralds. In the further wall was an alcove whose curtains, bestrung with pearls, were let down and I saw a light issuing therefrom; so I drew near and perceived that the light came from a precious stone as big as an ostrich egg, set at the upper end of the alcove upon a little chryselephantine couch of ivory and gold; and this jewel, blazing like the sun, cast its rays wide and side. The couch also was spread with all manner of silken stuffs amazing the gazer with their richness and beauty. I marveled much at all this, especially when seeing in that place candles ready lighted; and I said in my mind, "Some one must have lighted these candles." Then I went forth and came to the kitchen and thence to the buttery and the King's treasure-chambers; and continued to explore the palace and to pace from place to place; I forgot myself in my awe and marvel at these matters and I was drowned in thought till the night came on. Then I would have gone forth, but not knowing the gate I lost my way, so I returned to the alcove whither the lighted candles directed me and sat down upon the couch; and wrapping myself in a coverlet, after I had repeated somewhat from the Koran, I would have slept but could not, for restlessness possessed me. When night was at its noon I heard a voice chanting the Koran in sweetest accents; but the tone was weak; so I rose, glad to hear the silence broken, and followed the sound until I reached a closet

6. The pearl is supposed in the East to lose 1 percent per ann. of its splendor and value. (Burton's note)

whose door stood ajar. Then, peeping through a chink, I considered the place and lo! it was an oratory wherein was a prayer-niche[7] with two wax candles burning and lamps hanging from the ceiling. In it too was spread a prayer-carpet whereupon sat a youth fair to see; and before him on its stand[8] was a copy of the Koran, from which he was reading. I marveled to see him alone alive amongst the people of the city and entering saluted him; whereupon he raised his eyes and returned my salam. I said, "Now by the Truth of what you read in Allah's Holy Book, I conjure you to answer my question." He looked at me with a smile and said, "O handmaid of Allah, first tell me the cause of your coming here, and I in turn will tell what has befallen both me and the people of this city, and what was the reason of my escaping their doom." So I told him my story whereat he wondered; and I questioned him of the people of the city, when he replied, "Have patience with me for awhile, O my sister!" and, reverently closing the Holy Book, he laid it up in a satin bag. Then he seated me by his side; and I looked at him and behold, he was as the moon at its full, fair of face and rare of form, soft-sided and slight, of well-proportioned height, and cheek smoothly bright and diffusing light; in brief a sweet, a sugar-stick, even as the poet says of the like of him in these couplets:—

That night th' astrologer a scheme of planets drew, / And lo! a graceful shape of youth appeared in view:
Saturn had stained his locks with Saturninest jet, / And spots of nut-brown musk on rosey side-face blew:[9]
Mars tinctured either cheek with tinct of martial red; / Sagittal shots from eyelids Sagittarius threw:
Dowered him Mercury with bright mercurial wit; / Bore off the Bear[1] what all man's evil glances grew:
Amazed stood Astrophil[2] to sight the marvel-birth / When louted low the Moon at full to buss the Earth.

And of a truth Allah the Most High had robed him in the raiment of perfect grace and had purfled and fringed it with a cheek all beauty and loveliness, even as the poet says of such a one:—

By his eyelids shedding perfume and his fine slim waist I swear, / By the shooting of his shafts barbed with sorcery passing rare;
By the softness of his sides, and glances' lingering light; / And brow of dazzling day-tide ray and night within his hair;
By his eyebrows which deny to who look upon them rest, / Now bidding now forbidding, ever dealing joy and care;
By the rose that decks his cheek, and the myrtle of its moss[3]; / By jacinths bedded in his lips and pearl his smile lays bare;
By his graceful bending neck and the curving of his breast; / Whose polished surface beareth those granados,[4] lovely pair;

7. The arch-headed niche in the mosque wall facing Mecca.
8. A stool of palm-fronds, etc., X-shaped.
9. The Persian poets have a thousand conceits in praise of the "mole." (Burton's note)
1. That is, a bright star in the constellation called The Great Bear drew off the "evil eye" of those who might have envied him his beauty and virtues.
2. The name of the astrologer, from the Greek words for *star* and *lover of knowledge*.
3. Young face hair.
4. Pomegranates (?).

By his heavy hips that quiver as he passeth in his pride; / Or he resteth with that waist which is slim beyond compare;
By the satin of his skin, by that fine unsullied sprite; / By the beauty that containeth all things bright and debonair;
By that ever-open hand; by the candor of his tongue; / By noble blood and high degree whereof he's hope and heir;
Musk from him borrows muskiness she loveth to exhale / And all the airs of ambergris through him perfume the air;
The sun, methinks, the broad bright sun, before my love would pale/ And sans his splendor would appear a paring of his nail.

I glanced at him with one glance of eyes which caused me a thousand sighs; and my heart was at once taken captive; so I asked him, "O my lord and my love, tell me what I questioned you about"; and he answered, "Hearing is obeying! Know, O handmaid of Allah, that this city was the capital of my father who is the King you saw on the throne transfigured by Allah's wrath to a black stone, and the Queen you found in the alcove is my mother. They and all the people of the city were Magians who adored fire instead of the Omnipotent Lord and swore by flame and heat and shade and light, and the spheres revolving day and night. My father never had a son till he was blessed with me near the last of his days; and he reared me till I grew up and prosperity anticipated me in all things. Now it so happened there was with us an old woman well stricken in years, a Moslem who, inwardly believing in Allah and His Apostle, conformed outwardly with the religion of my people; and my father placed thorough confidence in her for he knew her to be trustworthy and virtuous; and he treated her with ever-increasing kindness, believing her to be of his own belief. So when I was well-nigh grown up my father committed me to her charge saying:—Take him and educate him and teach him the rules of our faith; let him have the best instructions and do not cease your fostering care of him. So she took me and taught me the tenets of Al-Islam with the divine orders given in the Koran and the five daily prayers and she made me learn the Koran by rote, often repeating:—Serve none save Allah Almighty! When I had mastered this much of knowledge she said to me:—O my son, keep this matter concealed from your sire and reveal nothing to him lest he slay you. So I hid it from him and I lived like this for a term of days when the old woman died, and the people of the city redoubled in their impiety and arrogance and the error of their ways. One day, while they were as usual, behold, they heard a loud and terrible sound and a crier crying out with a voice like roaring thunder so every ear could hear, far and near:—O folk of this city leave your fire-worshipping and adore Allah the All-compassionate King! At this, fear and terror fell upon the citizens and they crowded to my father (he being King of the city) and asked him:—What is the awesome voice we have heard, for it has confounded us with the excess of its terror?; and he answered:—Let not a voice fright you nor shake your steadfast spirit nor turn you back from the faith which is right. Their hearts inclined to his words and they continued to worship the fire and they persisted in rebellion for a full year from the time they heard the first voice; and on the anniversary came a second cry and a third at the head of the third year, each year once. Still they persisted in their malpractices till one day at break of dawn, judgment and the wrath of Heaven descended upon them with all suddenness, and by the visitation of Allah all were metamorphosed into black stones, they and their beasts and their cattle; and none was saved save myself who at the time was engaged in my devotions. From that day to this I am as you see me, constant in prayer and fasting and reading and reciting the Koran; but I am indeed grown weary by reason of my loneliness, having none to bear me company." Then I said to him (for in very sooth he had won my heart and was the lord of my life and soul), "O youth, will you fare with me to Baghdad city and visit the Olema, men learned in the law and doctors of divinity, and increase your wisdom and understanding and theology? And know that she who stands in your presence will be your handmaid, though she is head of her family and mistress over men and eunuchs and servants and slaves. Indeed my life was no life before it fell in with your youth. I have here a ship laden with merchandise; and in very truth Destiny drove me to this city that I might come to the knowledge of these matters, for it was fated that we should meet." And I continued to persuade him and speak him fair and use every art till he consented."——And Shahrazad perceived the dawn of day and ceased to say her permitted say.

Now when it was the Eighteenth Night,

She continued, It hath reached me, O auspicious King, that the lady ceased not persuading with soft speech the youth to depart with her till he consented and said "Yes." She slept that night lying at his feet and hardly knowing where she was for excess of joy. As soon as the next morning dawned (she pursued, addressing the Caliph), I arose and we entered the treasuries and took whatever was light in weight and great in worth; then we went down side by side from the castle to the city, where we were met by the Captain and my sisters and slaves who had been seeking for me. When they saw me they rejoiced and asked what had kept me, and I told them all I had seen and related to them the story of the young Prince and the transformation with which the citizens had been justly visited. All marveled, but when my two sisters (these two bitches, O Commander of the Faithful!) saw me by the side of my young lover they were jealous of me on his account and were angry and plotted mischief against me. We awaited a fair wind and went on board rejoicing and ready to fly for joy by reason of the goods we had gotten, but my own greatest joyance was in the youth; and we waited awhile till the wind blew fair for us and then we set sail and fared forth. Now as we sat talking, my sisters asked me, "And what will you do with this handsome young man?"; and I answered, "I purpose to make him my husband!" Then I turned to him and said, "O my lord, I have something to propose to you in which you must not cross me; and it is that, when we reach Baghdad, my native city, I offer you my life as your handmaiden in holy matrimony, and you shall be to me baron and I will be femme to thee." He answered, "I hear and

I obey!; you are my lady and my mistress and whatso you do I will not gainsay." Then I turned to my sisters and said, "This is my gain; I content me with this youth and those who have gotten any of my property let them keep it as their gain with my good will." "You say and do well," answered the two, but they imagined mischief against me. We ceased not spooning before a fair wind till we had exchanged the sea of peril for the seas of safety and, in a few days, we made Bassorah-city, whose buildings loomed clear before us as evening fell. But after we had retired to rest and were sound asleep, my two sisters arose and took me up, bed and all, and threw me into the sea: they did the same with the young Prince who, as he could not swim, sank and was drowned and Allah enrolled him in the noble army of Martyrs.[5] As for me would Heaven I had been drowned with him, but Allah deemed that I should be of the saved; so when I awoke and found myself in the sea and saw the ship making off like a flash of lightning, He threw in my way a piece of timber which I bestrided, and the waves tossed me to and fro till they cast me upon an island coast, a high land and an uninhabited one. I landed and walked about the island the rest of the night and, when morning dawned, I saw a rough track barely fit for child of Adam to tread, leading to what proved a shallow ford connecting island and mainland. As soon as the sun had risen I spread my garments to dry in its rays; and ate of the fruits of the island and drank of its waters; then I set out along the foot-track and walked till I reached the mainland. Now when there remained between me and the city but a two hours' journey, behold, a great serpent, the bigness of a date-palm, came fleeing towards me in all haste, gliding along now to the right then to the left till she was close upon me, while her tongue lolled groundwards a span long and swept the dust as she went. She was pursued by a Dragon who was not longer than two lances, and of slender build about the bulk of a spear and, although her terror lent her speed, and she kept wriggling from side to side, he overtook her and seized her by the tail, whereat her tears streamed down and her tongue was thrust out in her agony. I took pity on her and, picking up a stone and calling upon Allah for aid, threw it at the Dragon's head with such force that he died then and there; and the serpent opening a pair of wings flew into the air and disappeared from before my eyes. I sat down marveling over that adventure, but I was weary and, drowsiness overcoming me, I slept where I was for a while. When I awoke I found a jet-black damsel sitting at my feet shampooing them; and by her side stood two black bitches (my sisters, O Commander of the Faithful!). I was ashamed before her[6] and, sitting up, asked her, "O my sister, who and what?"; and she answered, "How soon you have forgotten me! I

5. The Martyrs-category is extensive, including those killed by falling walls; victims of the plague, pleurisy and pregnancy; travelers drowned or otherwise lost when journeying honestly, and chaste lovers who die of "broken hearts," i.e., impaired digestion. Their souls are at once stowed away in the crops of green birds where they remain till Resurrection Day, "eating of the fruits and drinking of the streams of Paradise," a place however, whose topography is wholly uncertain. Thus the young Prince was rewarded with a manner of anti-Purgatory, a preparatory heaven. (Burton's note)

6. She was ashamed to see the lady doing servile duty by rubbing her feet. (Burton's note)

am she for whom you did a good deed and sowed the seed of gratitude and slew her foe; for I am the serpent whom by Allah's aid you did just now deliver from the Dragon. I am a Jinniyah and he was a Jinn who hated me, and none saved my life from him but you. As soon as you freed me from him I flew on the wind to the ship whence your sisters threw you, and removed all that was there to your house. Then I ordered my attendant Marids[7] to sink the ship and I transformed your two sisters into these black bitches; for I know all that has passed between them and you; but as for the youth, of a truth he is drowned." So saying she flew up with me and the bitches, and presently set us down on the terrace-roof of my house, where I found already stored the whole of what property was in my ship, nor was any of it missing. "Now (continued the serpent that was), I swear by all engraven on the seal-ring of Solomon[8] (with whom be peace!) unless you deal to each of these bitches three hundred stripes every day I will come and imprison you forever under the earth." I answered, "Hearkening and obedience!"; and away she flew. But before going she again charged me saying, "I again swear by Him who made the two seas[9] flow (and this be my second oath) if you contradict me I will come and transform you like your sisters." Since then I have never failed, O Commander of the Faithful, to beat them with that number of blows till their blood flows with my tears, I pitying them the while, and well they know that their being scourged is no fault of mine and they accept my excuses. And this is my tale and my history! The Caliph marveled at her adventures and then signed to Ja'afar who said to the second lady, the Portress, "And you, how did you come by the welts and wheals upon your body?" So she began the

Tale of the Portress. . . .

7. One of the tribes of the Jinn, generally but not always hostile to man. (Burton's note)

8. Alluding to the Most High Name, the hundredth name of God. (Burton's note)

9. I.e., the Mediterranean and the Indian Ocean. (Burton's note)

Contexts

9 THE AUTHOR'S WORK

Stories do not exist by themselves. Each is, first of all, part of the author's entire body of work—the **canon**—which, taken together, forms something like a huge single entity, a "superwork."

Even if it were desirable to read a story as a thing in itself, separate from everything else we had ever read or seen and from everything else the author had written, it is in practice impossible. We can *first* look into Chapman's Homer or Faulkner's fiction only once. After we read a second and then a third story by an author, we recognize the voice and have a sense of familiarity, as we would with a growing acquaintance. The author's voice and vision soon create in us certain expectations—of action, structure, characterization, world view, language. We come to expect short sentences from Hemingway, long ones from Faulkner, a certain amount of violence from both; we are not surprised if a Hemingway story is set in Michigan or Montmartre or on Mount Kilimanjaro, but we are surprised if a Faulkner story takes place outside Mississippi (his portion of which, we soon learn, Faulkner calls Yoknapatawpha). We inevitably bring to our interpretations of Mrs. Macomber's actions what we have learned about Hemingway's view of women from his other writings.

When we find an author's vision attractive or challenging, we naturally want to find out more about it, reading not only the literary works in the canon but the author's nonfictional prose—essays, letters, anything we can find that promises a fuller or clearer view of that unique way of looking at the world. Such knowledge is helpful—within limits. It was D. H. Lawrence, whose stories and statements we are about to read, who warned us to trust the tale and not the teller. A statement of beliefs or of intentions is not necessarily the same as what a given work may show or achieve—otherwise we'd all be saints and masters. It works the other way, too: often writers embody in their art what they cannot articulate, what indeed may not be expressible, in discursive prose.

The three short stories and brief selections from Lawrence's letters and criticism in this chapter are meant to make you feel more at home (and interested) in Lawrence's world and to raise questions about the relationship of the individual work to an author's work as a whole. Of course, short stories and a few pages of nonfiction alone cannot adequately represent the career of a writer who was a novelist, poet, critic, and essayist as well as short story writer, nor can three stories represent the richness and variety of the fifty or more that he published. However, as each story comes from a different decade, they do represent somewhat the continuities and changes within the three decades of his career. Two of the stories, *Odour of Chrysanthemums* and *The Horse Dealer's Daughter,* are characteristically set in the coal-mining region of his native English Midlands, the scene of many of his novels, including three of the most famous, which also span his career—*Sons and Lovers* (1913), *The Rainbow* (1915), and *Lady Chatterley's Lover* (1928). The emphasis on the Midlands setting may be justified in terms of the canon, but can be misleading; there is no way in so few selections to represent both the emphasis on the Midlands and the scope of Lawrence's settings—his stories take place all over Western Europe, in the Americas, and in Australia. The London setting of *The Rocking-Horse Winner* only faintly indicates Lawrence's growing cosmopolitanism socially as well as geographically. It also suggests, though superficially, his developing interest in the superreal and the mythic, concerns most fully developed in *The Plumed Serpent* (1926) and *The Man Who Died* (1929), and his movement in content and style away from nineteenth-century notions of realism.

It may be useful to see the first story here (one of Lawrence's very first stories) through the eyes of its first "professional" reader as he remembers the experience. Not long before World War I, a young woman sent to Ford Madox Ford, then editor of *The English Review,* three poems and a short story written by a schoolmaster friend of hers, the then unknown D. H. Lawrence. Ford read the story first and, he recalls, knew immediately that he had a genius on his hands, "a big one." The very title, *Odour of Chrysanthemums,* Ford noted, "makes an impact on the mind," indicates that the writer is observant (not many people realize that chrysanthemums have an odor), and sets the dark autumnal tone of the story. From the very first sentence, Ford goes on to say,

> . . . you know that this fellow with the power of observation is going to write whatever he writes about from the inside. The "Number 4" shows that. He will be the sort of fellow who knows that for the sort of people who work about engines, engines have a sort of individuality. He had to give the engine the personality of a number. . . . "With seven full wagons". . . . The "seven" is good. The ordinary careless writer would say "some small wagons." This man knows what he wants. He sees the scene of his story exactly. He has an authoritative mind.
>
> "It appeared round the corner with loud threats of speed." . . . Good writing; slightly, but not *too* arresting. . . . "But the colt that it startled from among the gorse . . . out-distanced it at a canter." Good again. This fellow does not "state." He doesn't say: "It was coming slowly," or—what would have been a little better—"at seven miles an hour." Because even "seven miles an hour" means nothing definite for the untrained mind. It might mean something for a trainer or pedestrian racers. The imaginative writer writes for all humanity; he does not limit his desired readers to specialists. . . . But anyone knows that an engine that makes a great deal of noise and yet cannot overtake a colt at a canter must be a ludicrously ineffective machine. We know then that this fellow knows his job.

"The gorse still flickered indistinctly in the raw afternoon. . . ." Good too, distinctly good. This is the just-sufficient observation of Nature that gives you, in a single phrase, landscape, time of day, weather, season. It is a raw afternoon in autumn in a rather accented countryside. The engine would not come round a bend if there were not some obstacle to a straight course—a watercourse, a chain of hills. Hills, probably, because gorse grows on dry, broken-up waste country. They won't also be mountains or anything spectacular or the writer would have mentioned them. It is, then, just "country."

Your mind does all this for you without any ratiocination on your part. You are not, I mean, purposedly sleuthing. The engine and the trucks are there, with the white smoke blowing away over hummocks of gorse. Yet there has been practically none of the tiresome thing called descriptive nature, of which the English writer is as a rule so lugubriously lavish. . . . And then the woman comes in, carrying her basket. That indicates her status in life. She does not belong to the comfortable classes. Nor, since the engine is small, with trucks on a dud line, will the story be one of the Kipling-engineering type, with gleaming rails and gadgets, and the smell of oil warmed by the bearings and all the other tiresomenesses.

You are, then, for as long as the story lasts, to be in one of those untidy, unfinished landscapes where locomotives wander innocuously amongst women with baskets. That is to say, you are going to learn how what we used to call "the other half"—though we might as well have said other ninety-nine hundredths—lives. And if you are an editor and that is what you are after, you know that you have got what you want and you can pitch the story straight away into your wicker basket with the few accepted manuscripts and go onto some other occupation. . . . Because this man knows. He knows how to open a story with a sentence of the right cadence for holding the attention. He knows how to construct a paragraph. He knows the life he is writing about in a landscape just sufficiently constructed with a casual word here and there. You can trust him for the rest. . . .

—from "Before the Wars," *Selected Memories, The Bodley Head Ford Madox Ford* (London, 1962), I, 322–323

You will find the same precision of detail, suggesting the author's "inside view," his mastery of his material, in *The Horse Dealer's Daughter*—in paragraph six, for example, or the later description of the cemetery and the pond. You will find it even in that strange and strangely different story *The Rocking-Horse Winner*, in the first description of Paul's riding the horse, for example; in the description of the horse's "lowered face" ("Its red mouth was slightly open, its big eye was wide and glassy-bright") and in the precise accounting of the races, the odds, the money.

Ford read *Odour of Chrysanthemums* outside the context available to us. He did not know anything of the author and had read nothing else by him. Ford was an excellent editor (as well as writer) and to his credit spotted Lawrence's genius, a genius quite different from his own. Lawrence's mastery of detail made Ford trust him, but what he trusted him for seems to have been knowledge of the "other ninety-nine hundredths" of the population, the working class. An English writer of genius with knowledge of the working class was no doubt rare and notable in those pre-war days, and Lawrence's early works are full of details of the lives of miners and their families. But Lawrence, we now know, considered not class but the man–woman relationship the "great relationship of humanity," all others being subsidiary. Because we know that, know of Lawrence's notoriety for describing sexual relations, know his later works in which sexual relations are the major or basic concern—and perhaps because of the emphasis on sex in our own time—in reading *Odour of Chrysanthemums* we focus our attention not on the working-class mores but on the strange relationship between the Bateses. We ponder over Elizabeth's recognition that she not only had never really known her husband as himself despite their marital intimacy, but that by thinking of him only as her husband she had denied his individual selfhood and his otherness. The class element is still in the story, but the context of Lawrence's other works and utterances highlights this other human relationship.

What is implied about "real" or "true" love in the criticism of Elizabeth Bates's possessive love? There is nothing in that story that would specifically suggest the terrible risk of loving or the inexplicable descent of love on the soul beyond all reason and intent, or love as transfiguration and new birth, the kind of love we see in *The Horse Dealer's Daughter*. We cannot legitimately go back and put that kind of love in the earlier story, and yet, knowing Lawrence's later work, we can see its potential definition lying there, can see in what Elizabeth Bates's love was not the shadowy suggestion of what love must be. At least love as defined in *The Horse Dealer's Daughter* is not inconsistent with what real love might be in *Chrysanthemums*. Similarly, the notion of an emotional knowledge deeper than reason, language, and appearance that we see in Fergusson's loving Mabel, the horse dealer's daughter—

> With an inward groan he gave way, and let his heart yield towards her. A sudden gentle smile came on his face. And her eyes, which never left his face, slowly, slowly filled with tears. He watched the strange water rise in her eyes, like some slow fountain coming up. And his heart seemed to burn and melt away in his breast.

—prepares us for the same kind of deep emotional knowledge in the mother of Paul, the rocking-horse rider—

> . . . when her children were present, she always felt the center of her heart go hard. This troubled her, and in her manner she was all the more gentle and anxious for her children, as if she loved them very much. Only she herself knew that at the center of her heart was a hard little place that could not feel love, no, not for anybody. Everybody else said of her: "She is such a good mother. She adores her children." Only she herself, and her children themselves, knew it was not so.

—only in her case the knowledge is of lack of love.

The central, sometimes obsessive concerns and assumptions that permeate an author's work not only relate the individual stories to each other, mutually illuminating and enriching them, but they also serve as the author's trademark. It is not difficult to recognize or even parody a story by Lawrence.

Embodying these larger concerns and underlying such larger structures as plot, focus, and voice are the basic characteristics of the author's language, such as **diction** (choice of words and their use), sentence structure, **rhetorical tropes** (figures of thought and speech), **imagery** and **rhythm**—in other words, the author's style.

Perhaps because of the uniqueness of style, the vocabulary for discussing stylistic elements is not very precise or accessible. We can broadly characterize diction as **formal** (*The Cask of Amontillado*) or **informal** (most of the stories in this collection), and within the broad term *informal* identify a level of language that approximates the speech of ordinary people and call it colloquial (*My Man Bovanne*). But to characterize precisely an author's diction so that it adequately describes his or her work and marks it off from the works of contemporaries is a very difficult task indeed. We can note Hemingway's short sentences and Faulkner's long sentences, but it is hard to get much definition in the stylistic fingerprint of an author merely by measuring the lengths of sentences or tabulating connectives (though these qualities no doubt do subliminally contribute to the effect of the works on readers and do help them identify an author's work).

Diction and sentence structure contribute to the tone of a work, or the implied attitude or stance of the author toward the characters and events, an aspect somewhat analogous to tone of voice. When what is being said and the tone are consistent, it is difficult to separate one from the other; when there seems to be a discrepancy, we have some words that are useful to describe the difference. If the language seems exaggerated, we call it **overstatement.** The narrator of *Spotted Horses* is very fond of overstatement: "Flem Snopes had filled that whole country full of spotted horses," he says, and one "flew right over my team, big as a billboard and flying through the air like a hawk." When Wilson, in *Macomber,* admits that if the authorities discovered they had hunted from cars he would lose his license and there might be "Other unpleasantnesses," he is indulging in a bit of obvious **understatement.** When a word or expression says virtually the opposite of its literal meaning, we have an example of **verbal irony.** Yellow Blossom, in *The Horse-Swap,* has been bragging that he is "a *leetle* of the best man at a horse-swap" that anyone has seen, but when his own words are thrown back at him mockingly later, their meaning is so different that the difference is painful to him. There are also nonverbal forms of irony, the most common of which is **dramatic irony,** in which a character holds a position or has an expectation that is reversed or fulfilled in an unexpected way. Knowing her husband's habit of drinking himself into unconsciousness, Elizabeth Bates expects him to be brought home like a log. How is her expectation fulfilled? She had also said bitterly, "But he needn't come rolling in here in his pit-dirt, for *I* won't wash him," and yet she does. Why is her determination altered? As you read through, or look back over this story, watch for other reversed or unexpectedly fulfilled expectations.

Another and highly emphasized element of style is **imagery.** In its broadest sense imagery includes any sensory detail or evocation in a work. Note how much more imagery in that sense we find in *The Old People* than in, say, *The Lottery.* Imagery in this broad sense, however, is so prevalent in literature that it would take exhaustive statistics to differentiate styles by counting the number of sensory elements per hundred or thousand words, categorizing the images as primarily visual, tactile, etc. In a more restricted sense imagery refers to figurative language (see Chapter 4 on symbols), particularly that which defines an abstraction or any emotional or psychological state with a sensory comparison. The opening paragraph of *Odour of Chrysanthemums* illustrates the broader definition of imagery, and this passage from later in the same story may represent the figurative sense: "Life with its smoky burning gone from him, had left him apart. . . . In her womb was ice of fear. . . ."

We might say that if an author's vision gives us his or her profile, the style gives us a fingerprint—though the fingerprint is unique and definitive, it is also harder to come by than a glimpse of a profile. Ultimately, however, vision and style are less distinguishable from each other than the profile-fingerprint image suggests. For vision and style, just like history and structure, do more than interact: they are inextricably fused or compounded. Let us look back at the Ford passage. He says this of "the gorse, which still flickered indistinctly in the raw afternoon" (though he misquotes it slightly and rather loosely calls it a phrase):

> . . . Good too, distinctly good. This is the just-sufficient observation of Nature that gives you, in a single phrase, landscape, time of day, weather, season.

Is this vision or style? The observation of Nature is clearly vision, but expressing that vision economically, tautly, is style. The two merge.

Whatever else this passage is, it is vintage, typical Lawrence. Perhaps it would take more than just these ten words, but surely in a paragraph or two we know we're in the fictional world that he perceived and that he embodied in his stories, novels, poems in a language of his own created out of that language we share.

D. H. LAWRENCE

Odour of Chrysanthemums

1

The small locomotive engine, Number 4, came clanking, stumbling down from Selston with seven full wagons. It appeared round the corner with loud threats of speed, but the colt that it startled from among the gorse, which still flickered indistinctly in the raw afternoon, out-distanced it at a canter. A woman, walking up the railway line to Underwood, drew back into the hedge, held her basket aside, and watched the footplate of the engine advancing. The trucks thumped heavily past, one by one, with slow inevitable movement, as she stood insignificantly trapped between the jolting black wagons and the hedge; then they curved away towards the coppice where the withered oak leaves dropped noiselessly, while the birds, pulling at the scarlet hips beside the track, made off into the dusk that had already crept into the spinney. In the open, the smoke from the engine sank and cleaved to the rough grass. The fields were dreary and forsaken, and in the marshy strip that led to the whimsey, a reedy pit-pond, the fowls had already abandoned their run among the alders, to roost in the tarred fowl-house. The pit-bank loomed up beyond the pond, flames like red sores licking its ashy sides, in the afternoon's stagnant light. Just beyond rose the tapering chimneys and the clumsy black headstocks of Brinsley Colliery. The two wheels were spinning fast up against the sky, and the winding engine rapped out its little spasms. The miners were being turned up.

The engine whistled as it came into the wide bay of railway lines[1] beside the colliery, where rows of trucks stood in harbor.

Miners, single, trailing and in groups, passed like shadows diverging home. At the edge of the ribbed level of sidings squat a low cottage, three steps down from the cinder track. A large bony vine clutched at the house, as if to claw down the tiled roof. Round the bricked yard grew a few wintry primroses. Beyond, the long garden sloped down to a bush-covered brook course. There were some twiggy apple trees, winter-crack trees, and ragged cabbages. Beside the path hung dishevelled pink chrysanthemums, like pink cloths hung on bushes. A woman came stooping out of the felt-covered fowl-house, half-way down the garden. She closed and padlocked the door, then drew herself erect, having brushed some bits from her white apron.

She was a tall woman of imperious mien, handsome, with definite black eyebrows. Her smooth black hair was parted exactly. For a few moments she stood steadily watching the miners as they passed along the railway: then she turned towards the brook course. Her face was calm and set, her mouth was closed with disillusionment. After a moment she called:

"John!" There was no answer. She waited, and then said distinctly: "Where are you?"

"Here!" replied a child's sulky voice from among the bushes. The woman looked piercingly through the dusk.

"Are you at that brook?" she asked sternly.

For answer the child showed himself before the raspberry-canes that rose like whips. He was a small, sturdy boy of five. He stood quite still, defiantly.

"Oh!" said the mother, conciliated. "I thought you were down at that wet brook—and you remember what I told you——"

The boy did not move or answer.

"Come, come on in," she said more gently, "it's getting dark. There's your grandfather's engine coming down the line!"

1. Flat, level area of railroad tracks, probably bending away.

The lad advanced slowly, with resentful, taciturn movement. He was dressed in trousers and waistcoat of cloth that was too thick and hard for the size of the garments. They were evidently cut down from a man's clothes.

As they went slowly towards the house he tore at the ragged wisps of chrysanthemums and dropped the petals in handfuls along the path.

"Don't do that—it does look nasty," said his mother. He refrained, and she, suddenly pitiful, broke off a twig with three or four wan flowers and held them against her face. When mother and son reached the yard her hand hesitated, and instead of laying the flower aside, she pushed it in her apron-band. The mother and son stood at the foot of the three steps looking across the bay of lines at the passing home of the miners. The trundle of the small train was imminent. Suddenly the engine loomed past the house and came to a stop opposite the gate.

The engine-driver, a short man with round gray beard, leaned out of the cab high above the woman.

"Have you got a cup of tea?" he said in a cheery, hearty fashion.

It was her father. She went in, saying she would mash.[2] Directly, she returned.

"I didn't come to see you on Sunday," began the little gray-bearded man.

"I didn't expect you," said his daughter.

The engine-driver winced; then, reassuming his cheery, airy manner, he said:

"Oh, have you heard then? Well, and what do you think——?"

"I think it is soon enough," she replied.

At her brief censure the little man made an impatient gesture, and said coaxingly, yet with dangerous coldness:

"Well, what's a man to do? It's no sort of life for a man of my years, to sit at my own hearth like a stranger. And if I'm going to marry again it may as well be soon as late—what does it matter to anybody?"

The woman did not reply, but turned and went into the house. The man in the engine-cab stood assertive, till she returned with a cup of tea and a piece of bread and butter on a plate. She went up the steps and stood near the footplace of the hissing engine.

"You needn't 'a' brought me bread an' butter," said her father. "But a cup of tea"—he sipped appreciatively—"it's very nice." He sipped for a moment or two, then: "I hear as Walter's got another bout on," he said.

"When hasn't he?" said the woman bitterly.

"I heerd tell of him in the 'Lord Nelson'[3] braggin' as he was going to spend that b—— afore he went: half a sovereign[4] that was."

"When?" asked the woman.

"A' Sat'day night—I know that's true."

"Very likely," she laughed bitterly. "He gives me twenty-three shillings."

"Aye, it's a nice thing, when a man can do nothing with his money but make a beast of himself!" said the gray-whiskered man. The woman

2. Prepare (tea).
3. A public house, pub.
4. A sovereign is an English pound, then worth $4.86+; there are 20 shillings (see below) to the pound.

turned her head away. Her father swallowed the last of his tea and handed her the cup.

"Aye," he sighed, wiping his mouth. "It's a settler, it is——"

He put his hand on the lever. The little engine strained and groaned, and the train rumbled towards the crossing. The woman again looked across the metals. Darkness was settling over the spaces of the railway and trucks; the miners, in gray somber group, were still passing home. The winding engine pulsed hurriedly, with brief pauses. Elizabeth Bates looked at the dreary flow of men, then she went indoors. Her husband did not come.

The kitchen was small and full of firelight; red coals piled glowing up the chimney mouth. All the life of the room seemed in the white, warm hearth and the steel fender reflecting the red fire. The cloth was laid for tea; cups glinted in the shadows. At the back, where the lowest stairs protruded into the room, the boy sat struggling with a knife and a piece of white wood. He was almost hidden in the shadow. It was half-past four. They had but to await the father's coming to begin tea. As the mother watched her son's sullen little struggle with the wood, she saw herself in his silence and pertinacity; she saw the father in her child's indifference to all but himself. She seemed to be occupied by her husband. He had probably gone past his home, slunk past his own door, to drink before he came in, while his dinner spoiled and wasted in waiting. She glanced at the clock, then took the potatoes to strain them in the yard. The garden and fields beyond the brook were closed in uncertain darkness. When she rose with the saucepan, leaving the drain steaming into the night behind her, she saw the yellow lamps were lit along the high road that went up the hill away beyond the space of the railway lines and the field.

Then again she watched the men trooping home, fewer now and fewer.

Indoors the fire was sinking and the room was dark red. The woman put her saucepan on the hob, and set a batter-pudding near the mouth of the oven. Then she stood unmoving. Directly, gratefully, came quick young steps to the door. Someone hung on the latch a moment, then a little girl entered and began pulling off her outdoor things, dragging a mass of curls, just ripening from gold to brown, over her eyes with her hat.

Her mother chid her for coming late from school, and said she would have to keep her at home the dark winter days.

"Why, mother, it's hardly a bit dark yet. The lamp's not lighted, and my father's not home."

"No, he isn't. But it's a quarter to five! Did you see anything of him?"

The child became serious. She looked at her mother with large wistful blue eyes.

"No, mother, I've never seen him. Why? Has he come up an' gone past, to Old Brinsley? He hasn't, mother, 'cos I never saw him."

"He'd watch that," said the mother bitterly, "he'd take care as you didn't see him. But you may depend upon it, he's seated in the 'Prince o' Wales.' He wouldn't be this late."

The girl looked at her mother piteously.

"Let's have our teas, mother, should we?" said she.

The mother called John to table. She opened the door once more and looked out across the darkness of the lines. All was deserted: she could not hear the winding engines.

"Perhaps," she said to herself, "he's stopped to get some ripping[5] done."

They sat down to tea. John, at the end of the table near the door, was almost lost in the darkness. Their faces were hidden from each other. The girl crouched against the fender slowly moving a thick piece of bread before the fire. The lad, his face a dusky mark on the shadow, sat watching her who was transfigured in the red glow.

"I do think it's beautiful to look in the fire," said the child.

"Do you?" said her mother. "Why?"

"It's so red, and full of little caves—and it feels so nice, and you can fair smell it."

"It'll want mending directly," replied her mother, "and then if your father comes he'll carry on and say there never is a fire when a man comes home sweating from the pit. A public house is always warm enough."

There was silence till the boy said complainingly: "Make haste, our Annie."

"Well, I am doing! I can't make the fire do it no faster, can I?"

"She keeps wafflin'[6] it about so's to make 'er slow," grumbled the boy.

"Don't have such an evil imagination, child," replied the mother.

Soon the room was busy in the darkness with the crisp sound of crunching. The mother ate very little. She drank her tea determinedly, and sat thinking. When she rose her anger was evident in the stern unbending of her head. She looked at the pudding in the fender, and broke out:

"It is a scandalous thing as a man can't even come home to his dinner! If it's crozzled[7] up to a cinder I don't see why I should care. Past his very door he goes to get to a public house, and here I sit with his dinner waiting for him——"

She went out. As she dropped piece after piece of coal on the red fire, the shadows fell on the walls, till the room was almost in total darkness.

"I canna see," grumbled the invisible John. In spite of herself, the mother laughed.

"You know the way to your mouth," she said. She set the dustpan outside the door. When she came again like a shadow on the hearth, the lad repeated, complaining sulkily:

"I canna see."

"Good gracious!" cried the mother irritably, "you're as bad as your father if it's a bit dusk!"

Nevertheless, she took a paper spill from a sheaf on the mantelpiece and proceeded to light the lamp that hung from the ceiling in the middle of the room. As she reached up, her figure displayed itself just rounding with maternity.

"Oh, mother——!" exclaimed the girl.

"What?" said the woman, suspended in the act of putting the lamp-

5. Coal-mining term for taking down the roof of an underground road in order to make it higher.

6. Waving.

7. Shriveled.

glass over the flame. The copper reflector shone handsomely on her, as she stood with uplifted arm, turning to face her daughter.

"You've got a flower in your apron!" said the child, in a little rapture at this unusual event.

"Goodness me!" exclaimed the woman, relieved. "One would think the house was afire." She replaced the glass and waited a moment before turning up the wick. A pale shadow was seen floating vaguely on the floor.

"Let me smell!" said the child, still rapturously, coming forward and putting her face to her mother's waist.

"Go along, silly!" said the mother, turning up the lamp. The light revealed their suspense so that the woman felt it almost unbearable. Annie was still bending at her waist. Irritably, the mother took the flowers out from her apron-band.

"Oh, mother—don't take them out!" Annie cried, catching her hand and trying to replace the sprig.

"Such nonsense!" said the mother, turning away. The child put the pale chrysanthemums to her lips, murmuring:

"Don't they smell beautiful!"

Her mother gave a short laugh.

"No," she said, "not to me. It was chrysanthemums when I married him, and chrysanthemums when you were born, and the first time they ever brought him home drunk, he'd got brown chrysanthemums in his buttonhole."

She looked at the children. Their eyes and their parted lips were wondering. The mother sat rocking in silence for some time. Then she looked at the clock.

"Twenty minutes to six!" In a tone of fine bitter carelessness she continued: "Eh, he'll not come now till they bring him. There he'll stick! But he needn't come rolling in here in his pit-dirt, for *I* won't wash him. He can lie on the floor—Eh, what a fool I've been, what a fool! And this is what I came here for, to this dirty hole, rats and all, for him to slink past his very door. Twice last week—he's begun now——"

She silenced herself, and rose to clear the table.

While for an hour or more the children played, subduedly intent, fertile of imagination, united in fear of the mother's wrath, and in dread of their father's homecoming, Mrs. Bates sat in her rocking-chair making a "singlet" of thick cream-colored flannel, which gave a dull wounded sound as she tore off the gray edge. She worked at her sewing with energy, listening to the children, and her anger wearied itself, lay down to rest, opening its eyes from time to time and steadily watching, its ears raised to listen. Sometimes even her anger quailed and shrank, and the mother suspended her sewing, tracing the footsteps that thudded along the sleepers outside; she would lift her head sharply to bid the children "hush," but she recovered herself in time, and the footsteps went past the gate, and the children were not flung out of their play-world.

But at last Annie sighed, and gave in. She glanced at her wagon of slippers, and loathed the game. She turned plaintively to her mother.

"Mother!"—but she was inarticulate.

John crept out like a frog from under the sofa. His mother glanced up.

"Yes," she said, "just look at those shirtsleeves!"

The boy held them out to survey them, saying nothing. Then somebody called in a hoarse voice away down the line, and suspense bristled in the room, till two people had gone by outside, talking.

"It is time for bed," said the mother.

"My father hasn't come," wailed Annie plaintively. But her mother was primed with courage.

"Never mind. They'll bring him when he does come—like a log." She meant there would be no scene. "And he may sleep on the floor till he wakes himself. I know he'll not go to work tomorrow after this!"

The children had their hands and faces wiped with a flannel.[8] They were very quiet. When they had put on their nightdresses, they said their prayers, the boy mumbling. The mother looked down at them, at the brown silken bush of intertwining curls in the nape of the girl's neck, at the little black head of the lad, and her heart burst with anger at their father, who caused all three such distress. The children hid their faces in her skirts for comfort.

When Mrs. Bates came down, the room was strangely empty, with a tension of expectancy. She took up her sewing and stitched for some time without raising her head. Meantime her anger was tinged with fear.

2

The clock struck eight and she rose suddenly, dropping her sewing on her chair. She went to the stair-foot door, opened it, listening. Then she went out, locking the door behind her.

Something scuffled in the yard, and she started, though she knew it was only the rats with which the place was overrun. The night was very dark. In the great bay of railway lines, bulked with trucks, there was no trace of light, only away back she could see a few yellow lamps at the pit-top, and the red smear of the burning pit-bank on the night. She hurried along the edge of the track, then, crossing the converging lines, came to the stile by the white gates, whence she emerged on the road. Then the fear which had led her shrank. People were walking up to New Brinsley; she saw the lights in the houses; twenty yards farther on were the broad windows of the 'Prince of Wales,' very warm and bright, and the loud voices of men could be heard distinctly. What a fool she had been to imagine that anything had happened to him! He was merely drinking over there at the 'Prince of Wales.' She faltered. She had never yet been to fetch him, and she never would go. So she continued her walk toward the long straggling line of houses, standing back on the highway. She entered a passage between the dwellings.

"Mr. Rigley?—Yes! Did you want him? No, he's not in at this minute."

The raw-boned woman leaned forward from her dark scullery and peered at the other, upon whom fell a dim light through the blind of the kitchen window.

"Is it Mrs. Bates?" she asked in a tone tinged with respect.

"Yes. I wondered if your Master was at home. Mine hasn't come yet."

" 'Asn't 'e! Oh, Jack's been 'ome an' 'ad 'is dinner an' gone out. 'E's just gone for 'alf an hour afore bed-time. Did you call at the 'Prince of Wales'?"

8. Washrag.

"No——"

"No, you didn't like——! It's not very nice." The other woman was indulgent. There was an awkward pause. "Jack never said nothink about—about your Master," she said.

"No!—I expect he's stuck in there!"

Elizabeth Bates said this bitterly, and with recklessness. She knew that the woman across the yard was standing at her door listening, but she did not care. As she turned:

"Stop a minute! I'll just go an' ask Jack if 'e knows anythink," said Mrs. Rigley.

"Oh no—I wouldn't like to put——!"

"Yes, I will, if you'll just step inside an' see as th' childer doesn't come downstairs and set theirselves afire."

Elizabeth Bates, murmuring a remonstrance, stepped inside. The other woman apologized for the state of the room.

The kitchen needed apology. There were little frocks and trousers and childish undergarments on the squab[9] and on the floor, and a litter of playthings everywhere. On the black American cloth[1] of the table were pieces of bread and cake, crusts, slops, and a teapot with cold tea.

"Eh, ours is just as bad," said Elizabeth Bates, looking at the woman, not at the house. Mrs. Rigley put a shawl over her head and hurried out, saying:

"I shanna be a minute."

The other sat, noting with faint disapproval the general untidiness of the room. Then she fell to counting the shoes of various sizes scattered over the floor. There were twelve. She sighed and said to herself: "No wonder!"—glancing at the litter. There came the scratching of two pairs of feet on the yard, and the Rigleys entered. Elizabeth Bates rose. Rigley was a big man, with very large bones. His head looked particularly bony. Across his temple was a blue scar, caused by a wound got in the pit, a wound in which the coal-dust remained blue like tattooing.

" 'Asna 'e come whoam yit?" asked the man, without any form of greeting, but with deference and sympathy. "I couldna say wheer he is—'e's non ower theer!"—he jerked his head to signify the 'Prince of Wales.'

" 'E's 'appen[2] gone up to th' 'Yew,' " said Mrs. Rigley.

There was another pause. Rigley had evidently something to get off his mind:

"Ah left 'im finishin' a stint," he began. "Loose-all[3] 'ad bin gone about ten minutes when we com'n away, an' I shouted: 'Are ter comin', Walt?' an' 'e said: 'Go on, Ah shanna be but a'ef a minnit,' so we com'n ter th' bottom, me an' Bowers, thinkin' as 'e wor just behint, an' 'ud come up i' th' next bantle[4]——"

He stood perplexed, as if answering a charge of deserting his mate. Elizabeth Bates, now again certain of disaster, hastened to reassure him:

"I expect 'e's gone up to th' 'Yew Tree,' as you say. It's not the first time. I've fretted myself into a fever before now. He'll come home when they carry him."

9. Sofa.
1. Enameled oilcloth.
2. Perhaps.
3. Signal to quit work and come to the surface.
4. An open seat or car of the lift or elevator that takes the miners to the surface.

"Ay, isn't it too bad!" deplored the other woman.

"I'll just step up to Dick's an' see if 'e *is* theer," offered the man, afraid of appearing alarmed, afraid of taking liberties.

"Oh, I wouldn't think of bothering you that far," said Elizabeth Bates, with emphasis, but he knew she was glad of his offer.

As they stumbled up the entry, Elizabeth Bates heard Rigley's wife run across the yard and open her neighbor's door. At this, suddenly all the blood in her body seemed to switch away from her heart.

"Mind!"[5] warned Rigley. "Ah've said many a time as Ah'd fill up them ruts in this entry, sumb'dy 'll be breakin' their legs yit."

She recovered herself and walked quickly along with the miner.

"I don't like leaving the children in bed, and nobody in the house," she said.

"No, you dunna!" he replied courteously. They were soon at the gate of the cottage.

"Well, I shanna be many minnits. Dunna you be frettin' now, 'e'll be all right," said the butty.[6]

"Thank you very much, Mr. Rigley," she replied.

"You're welcome!" he stammered, moving away. "I shanna be many minnits."

The house was quiet. Elizabeth Bates took off her hat and shawl, and rolled back the rug. When she had finished, she sat down. It was a few minutes past nine. She was startled by the rapid chuff of the winding engine at the pit, and the sharp whirr of the brakes on the rope as it descended. Again she felt the painful sweep of her blood, and she put her hand to her side, saying aloud: "Good gracious!—it's only the nine o'clock deputy going down," rebuking herself.

She sat still, listening. Half an hour of this, and she was wearied out.

"What am I working myself up like this for?" she said pitiably to herself, "I s'll only be doing myself some damage."

She took out her sewing again.

At a quarter to ten there were footsteps. One person! She watched for the door to open. It was an elderly woman, in a black bonnet and a black woollen shawl—his mother. She was about sixty years old, pale, with blue eyes, and her face all wrinkled and lamentable. She shut the door and turned to her daughter-in-law peevishly.

"Eh, Lizzie, whatever shall we do, whatever shall we do!" she cried.

Elizabeth drew back a little, sharply.

"What is it, mother?" she said.

The elder woman seated herself on the sofa.

"I don't know, child, I can't tell you!"—she shook her head slowly. Elizabeth sat watching her, anxious and vexed.

"I don't know," replied the grandmother, sighing very deeply. "There's no end to my troubles, there isn't. The things I've gone through, I'm sure it's enough——!" She wept without wiping her eyes, the tears running.

"But, mother," interrupted Elizabeth, "what do you mean? What is it?"

The grandmother slowly wiped her eyes. The fountains of her tears

5. Watch out.

6. Buddy, fellow worker.

were stopped by Elizabeth's directness. She wiped her eyes slowly.

"Poor child! Eh, you poor thing!" she moaned. "I don't know what we're going to do, I don't—and you as you are—it's a thing, it is indeed!"

Elizabeth waited.

"Is he dead?" she asked, and at the words her heart swung violently, though she felt a slight flush of shame at the ultimate extravagance of the question. Her words sufficiently frightened the old lady, almost brought her to herself.

"Don't say so, Elizabeth! We'll hope it's not as bad as that; no, may the Lord spare us that, Elizabeth. Jack Rigley came just as I was sittin' down to a glass afore going to bed, an' 'e said: "Appen you'll go down th' line, Mrs. Bates. Walt's had an accident. 'Appen you'll go an' sit wi' 'er till we can get him home.' I hadn't time to ask him a word afore he was gone. An' I put my bonnet on an' come straight down, Lizzie. I thought to myself: 'Eh, that poor blessed child, if anybody should come an' tell her of a sudden, there's no knowin' what'll 'appen to 'er.' You mustn't let it upset you, Lizzie—or you know what to expect. How long is it, six months—or is it five, Lizzie? Ay!"—the old woman shook her head—"time slips on, it slips on! Ay!"

Elizabeth's thoughts were busy elsewhere. If he was killed—would she be able to manage on the little pension and what she could earn? —she counted up rapidly. If he was hurt—they wouldn't take him to the hospital—how tiresome he would be to nurse!—but perhaps she'd be able to get him away from the drink and his hateful ways. She would—while he was ill. The tears offered to come to her eyes at the picture. But what sentimental luxury was this she was beginning? She turned to consider the children. At any rate she was absolutely necessary for them. They were her business.

"Ay!" repeated the old woman, "it seems but a week or two since he brought me his first wages. Ay—he was a good lad, Elizabeth, he was, in his way. I don't know why he got to be such a trouble, I don't. He was a happy lad at home, only full of spirits. But there's no mistake he's been a handful of trouble, he has! I hope the Lord'll spare him to mend his ways. I hope so, I hope so. You've had a sight o' trouble with him, Elizabeth, you have indeed. But he was a jolly enough lad wi' me, he was, I can assure you. I don't know how it is. . . ."

The old woman continued to muse aloud, a monotonous irritating sound, while Elizabeth thought concentratedly, startled once, when she heard the winding-engine chuff quickly, and the brakes skirr with a shriek. Then she heard the engine more slowly, and the brakes made no sound. The old woman did not notice. Elizabeth waited in suspense. The mother-in-law talked, with lapses into silence.

"But he wasn't your son, Lizzie, an' it makes a difference. Whatever he was, I remember him when he was little, an' I learned to understand him and to make allowances. You've got to make allowances for them——"

It was half-past ten, and the old woman was saying: "But it's trouble from beginning to end; you're never too old for trouble, never too old for that——" when the gate banged back, and there were heavy feet on the steps.

"I'll go, Lizzie, let me go," cried the old woman, rising. But Elizabeth was at the door. It was a man in pit-clothes.

"They're bringin' 'im, Missis," he said. Elizabeth's heart halted a moment. Then it surged on again, almost suffocating her.

"Is he—is it bad?" she asked.

The man turned away, looking at the darkness:

"The doctor says 'e'd been dead hours. 'E saw 'im i' th' lamp-cabin."

The old woman, who stood just behind Elizabeth, dropped into a chair, and folded her hands, crying: "Oh, my boy, my boy!"

"Hush!" said Elizabeth, with a sharp twitch of a frown. "Be still, mother, don't waken th' children: I wouldn't have them down for anything!"

The old woman moaned softly, rocking herself. The man was drawing away. Elizabeth took a step forward.

"How was it?" she asked.

"Well, I couldn't say for sure," the man replied, very ill at ease. " 'E wor finishin' a stint an' th' butties 'ad gone, an' a lot o' stuff come down atop 'n 'im.'

"And crushed him?" cried the widow, with a shudder.

"No," said the man, "it fell at th' back of 'im. 'E wor under th' face, an' it niver touched 'im. It shut 'im in. It seems 'e wor smothered."

Elizabeth shrank back. She heard the old woman behind her cry:

"What?—what did 'e say it was?"

The man replied, more loudly: " 'E wor smothered!"

Then the old woman wailed aloud, and this relieved Elizabeth.

"Oh, mother," she said, putting her hand on the old woman, "don't waken th' children, don't waken th' children."

She wept a little, unknowing, while the old mother rocked herself and moaned. Elizabeth remembered that they were bringing him home, and she must be ready. "They'll lay him in the parlor," she said to herself, standing a moment pale and perplexed.

Then she lighted a candle and went into the tiny room. The air was cold and damp, but she could not make a fire, there was no fireplace. She set down the candle and looked round. The candlelight glittered on the luster-glasses[7] on the two vases that held some of the pink chrysanthemums, and on the dark mahogany. There was a cold, deathly smell of chrysanthemums in the room. Elizabeth stood looking at the flowers. She turned away, and calculated whether there would be room to lay him on the floor, between the couch and the chiffonier. She pushed the chairs aside. There would be room to lay him down and to step round him. Then she fetched the old red tablecloth, and another old cloth, spreading them down to save her bit of carpet. She shivered on leaving the parlor; so, from the dresser drawer she took a clean shirt and put it at the fire to air. All the time her mother-in-law was rocking herself in the chair and moaning.

"You'll have to move from there, mother," said Elizabeth. "They'll be bringing him in. Come in the rocker."

The old mother rose mechanically, and seated herself by the fire, continuing to lament. Elizabeth went into the pantry for another

7. Glass pendants around the edge of an ornamental vase.

candle, and there, in the little pent-house[8] under the naked tiles, she heard them coming. She stood still in the pantry doorway, listening. She heard them pass the end of the house, and come awkwardly down the three steps, a jumble of shuffling footsteps and muttering voices. The old woman was silent. The men were in the yard.

Then Elizabeth heard Matthews, the manager of the pit, say: "You go in first, Jim. Mind!"

The door came open, and the two women saw a collier backing into the room, holding one end of a stretcher, on which they could see the nailed pit-boots of the dead man. The two carriers halted, the man at the head stooping to the lintel of the door.

"Wheer will you have him?" asked the manager, a short, white-bearded man.

Elizabeth roused herself and came from the pantry carrying the unlighted candle.

"In the parlor," she said.

"In there, Jim!" pointed the manager, and the carriers backed round into the tiny room. The coat with which they had covered the body fell off as they awkwardly turned through the two doorways, and the women saw their man, naked to the waist, lying stripped for work. The old woman began to moan in a low voice of horror.

"Lay th' stretcher at th' side," snapped the manager, "an' put 'im on th' cloths. Mind now, mind! Look you now——!"

One of the men had knocked off a vase of chrysanthemums. He stared awkwardly, then they set down the stretcher. Elizabeth did not look at her husband. As soon as she could get in the room, she went and picked up the broken vase and the flowers.

"Wait a minute!" she said.

The three men waited in silence while she mopped up the water with a duster.

"Eh, what a job, what a job, to be sure!" the manager was saying, rubbing his brow with trouble and perplexity. "Never knew such a thing in my life, never! He'd no business to ha' been left. I never knew such a thing in my life! Fell over him clean as a whistle, an' shut him in. Not four foot of space, there wasn't—yet it scarce bruised him."

He looked down at the dead man, lying prone, half naked, all grimed with cold-dust.

"'Sphyxiated,' the doctor said. It *is* the most terrible job I've ever known. Seems as if it was done o' purpose. Clean over him, an' shut 'im in, like a mouse-trap"—he made a sharp, descending gesture with his hand.

The colliers standing by jerked aside their heads in hopeless comment.

The horror of the thing bristled upon them all.

Then they heard the girl's voice upstairs calling shrilly: "Mother, mother—who is it? Mother, who is it?"

Elizabeth hurried to the foot of the stairs and opened the door:

"Go to sleep!" she commanded sharply. "What are you shouting about? Go to sleep at once—there's nothing——"

8. Structure, usually with a sloping roof, attached to house.

Then she began to mount the stairs. They could hear her on the boards, and on the plaster floor of the little bedroom. They could hear her distinctly:

"What's the mater now?—what's the matter with you, silly thing?"—her voice was much agitated, with an unreal gentleness.

"I thought it was some men come," said the plaintive voice of the child. "Has he come?"

"Yes, they've brought him. There's nothing to make a fuss about. Go to sleep now, like a good child."

They could hear her voice in the bedroom, they waited whilst she covered the children under the bedclothes.

"Is he drunk?" asked the girl, timidly, faintly.

"No! No—he's not! He—he's asleep."

"Is he asleep downstairs?"

"Yes—and don't make a noise."

There was silence for a moment, then the men heard the frightened child again:

"What's that noise?"

"It's nothing, I tell you, what are you bothering for?"

The noise was the grandmother moaning. She was oblivious of everything, sitting on her chair rocking and moaning. The manager put his hand on her arm and bade her "Sh—sh!!"

The old woman opened her eyes and looked at him. She was shocked by this interruption, and seemed to wonder.

"What time is it?" the plaintive thin voice of the child, sinking back unhappily into sleep, asked this last question.

"Ten o'clock," answered the mother more softly. Then she must have bent down and kissed the children.

Matthews beckoned to the men to come away. They put on their caps and took up the stretcher. Stepping over the body, they tiptoed out of the house. None of them spoke till they were far from the wakeful children.

When Elizabeth came down she found her mother alone on the parlor floor, leaning over the dead man, the tears dropping on him.

"We must lay him out," the wife said. She put on the kettle, then returning knelt at the feet, and began to unfasten the knotted leather laces. The room was clammy and dim with only one candle, so that she had to bend her face almost to the floor. At last she got off the heavy boots and put them away.

"You must help me now," she whispered to the old woman. Together they stripped the man.

When they arose, saw him lying in the naïve dignity of death, the women stood arrested in fear and respect. For a few moments they remained still, looking down, the old mother whimpering. Elizabeth felt countermanded. She saw him, how utterly inviolable he lay in himself. She had nothing to do with him. She could not accept it. Stooping, she laid her hand on him, in claim. He was still warm, for the mine was hot where he had died. His mother had his face between her hands, and was murmuring incoherently. The old tears fell in succession as drops from wet leaves; the mother was not weeping, merely her tears flowed. Elizabeth embraced the body of her husband, with cheek and lips. She seemed to be listening, inquiring, trying to get some connection. But she could not. She was driven away. He was impregnable.

She rose, went into the kitchen, where she poured warm water into a bowl, brought soap and flannel and a soft towel.

"I must wash him," she said.

Then the old mother rose stiffly, and watched Elizabeth as she carefully washed his face, carefully brushing the big blond moustache from his mouth with the flannel. She was afraid with a bottomless fear, so she ministered to him. The old woman, jealous, said:

"Let me wipe him!"—and she kneeled on the other side drying slowly as Elizabeth washed, her big black bonnet sometimes brushing the dark head of her daughter-in-law. They worked thus in silence for a long time. They never forgot it was death, and the touch of the man's dead body gave them strange emotions, different in each of the women; a great dread possessed them both, the mother felt the lie was given to her womb, she was denied; the wife felt the utter isolation of the human soul, the child within her was a weight apart from her.

At last it was finished. He was a man of handsome body, and his face showed no traces of drink. He was blond, full-fleshed, with fine limbs. But he was dead.

"Bless him," whispered his mother, looking always at his face, and speaking out of sheer terror. "Dear lad—bless him!" She spoke in a faint, sibilant ecstasy of fear and mother love.

Elizabeth sank down again to the floor, and put her face against his neck, and trembled and shuddered. But she had to draw away again. He was dead, and her living flesh had no place against his. A great dread and weariness held her: she was so unavailing. Her life was gone like this.

"White as milk he is, clear as a twelve-month baby, bless him, the darling!" the old mother murmured to herself. "Not a mark on him, clear and clean and white, beautiful as ever a child was made," she murmured with pride. Elizabeth kept her face hidden.

"He went peaceful, Lizzie—peaceful as sleep. Isn't he beautiful, the lamb? Ay—he must ha' made his peace, Lizzie. 'Appen he made it all right, Lizzie, shut in there. He'd have time. He wouldn't look like this if he hadn't made his peace. The lamb, the dear lamb. Eh, but he had a hearty laugh. I loved to hear it. He had the heartiest laugh, Lizzie, as a lad——"

Elizabeth looked up. The man's mouth was fallen back, slightly open under the cover of the moustache. The eyes, half shut, did not show glazed in the obscurity. Life with its smoky burning gone from him, had left him apart and utterly alien to her. And she knew what a stranger he was to her. In her womb was ice of fear, because of this separate stranger with whom she had been living as one flesh. Was this what it all meant—utter, intact separateness, obscured by heat of living? In dread she turned her face away. The fact was too deadly. There had been nothing between them, and yet they had come together, exchanging their nakedness repeatedly. Each time he had taken her, they had been two isolated beings, far apart as now. He was no more responsible than she. The child was like ice in her womb. For as she looked at the dead man, her mind, cold and detached, said clearly: "Who am I? What have I been doing? I have been fighting a husband who did not exist. *He* existed all the time. What wrong have I done? What was that I have been living with? There lies the reality, this man." And her soul died in her for fear: she knew she had never seen him, he had never seen her, they had met in the dark and had fought in the dark, not knowing whom they met nor whom they fought. And now she saw, and turned silent in seeing. For she had been wrong. She had said he was something he was not; she had felt familiar with him. Whereas he was apart all the while, living as she never lived, feeling as she never felt.

In fear and shame she looked at his naked body, that she had known falsely. And he was the father of her children. Her soul was torn from her body and stood apart. She looked at his naked body and was ashamed, as if she had denied it. After all, it was itself. It seemed awful to her. She looked at his face, and she turned her own face to the wall. For his look was other than hers, his way was not her way. She had denied him what he was—she saw it now. She had refused him as himself. And this had been her life, and his life. She was grateful to death, which restored the truth. And she knew she was not dead.

And all the while her heart was bursting with grief and pity for him. What had he suffered? What stretch of horror for this helpless man! She was rigid with agony. She had not been able to help him. He had been cruelly injured, this naked man, this other being, and she could make no reparation. There were the children—but the children belonged to life. This dead man had nothing to do with them. He and she were only channels through which life had flowed to issue in the children. She was a mother—but how awful she knew it now to have been a wife. And he, dead now, how awful he must have felt it to be a husband. She felt that in the next world he would be a stranger to her. If they met there, in the beyond, they would only be ashamed of what had been before. The children had come, for some mysterious reason, out of both of them. But the children did not unite them. Now he was dead, she knew how eternally he was apart from her, how eternally he had nothing more to do with her. She saw this episode of her life closed. They had denied each other in life. Now he had withdrawn. An anguish came over her. It was finished then: it had become hopeless between them long before he died. Yet he had been her husband. But how little!

"Have you got his shirt, 'Lizabeth?"

Elizabeth turned without answering, though she strove to weep and behave as her mother-in-law expected. But she could not, she was silenced. She went into the kitchen and returned with the garment.

"It is aired," she said, grasping the cotton shirt here and there to try. She was almost ashamed to handle him; what right had she or anyone to lay hands on him; but her touch was humble on his body. It was hard work to clothe him. He was so heavy and inert. A terrible dread gripped her all the while: that he could be so heavy and utterly inert, unresponsive, apart. The horror of the distance between them was almost too much for her—it was so infinite a gap she must look across.

At last it was finished. They covered him with a sheet and left him lying, with his face bound. And she fastened the door of the little parlor, lest the children should see what was lying there. Then, with peace sunk heavy on her heart, she went about making tidy the kitchen. She knew she submitted to life, which was her immediate master. But from death, her ultimate master, she winced with fear and shame.

1914

D. H. LAWRENCE

The Horse Dealer's Daughter

"Well, Mabel, and what are you going to do with yourself?" asked Joe, with foolish flippancy. He felt quite safe himself. Without listening for an answer, he turned aside, worked a grain of tobacco to the tip of his tongue, and spat it out. He did not care about anything, since he felt safe himself.

The three brothers and the sister sat round the desolate breakfast table, attempting some sort of desultory consultation. The morning's post had given the final tap to the family fortunes, and all was over. The dreary dining room itself, with its heavy mahogany furniture, looked as if it were waiting to be done away with.

But the consultation amounted to nothing. There was a strange air of ineffectuality about the three men, as they sprawled at table, smoking and reflecting vaguely on their own condition. The girl was alone, a rather short, sullen-looking young woman of twenty-seven. She did not share the same life as her brothers. She would have been good-looking, save for the impassive fixity of her face, "bull dog," as her brothers called it.

There was a confused tramping of horses' feet outside. The three men all sprawled round in their chairs to watch. Beyond the dark holly bushes that separated the strip of lawn from the highroad, they could see a cavalcade of shire horses swinging out of their own yard, being taken for exercise. This was the last time. These were the last horses that would go through their hands. The young men watched with critical, callous look. They were all frightened at the collapse of their lives, and the sense of disaster in which they were involved left them no inner freedom.

Yet they were three fine, well-set fellows enough. Joe, the eldest, was a man of thirty-three, broad and handsome in a hot, flushed way. His face was red, he twisted his black mustache over a thick finger, his eyes were shallow and restless. He had a sensual way of uncovering his teeth when he laughed, and his bearing was stupid. Now he watched the horses with a glazed look of helplessness in his eyes, a certain stupor of downfall.

The great draft-horses swung past. They were tied head to tail, four of them, and they heaved along to where a lane branched off from the highroad, planting their great hoofs floutingly in the fine black mud, swinging their great rounded haunches sumptuously, and trotting a few sudden steps as they were led into the lane, round the corner. Every movement showed a massive, slumbrous strength, and a stupidity which held them in subjection. The groom at the head looked back, jerking the leading rope. And the cavalcade moved out of sight up the lane, the tail of the last horse, bobbed up tight and stiff, held out taut from the swinging great haunches as they rocked behind the hedges in a motion-like sleep.

Joe watched with glazed hopeless eyes. The horses were almost like his own body to him. He felt he was done for now. Luckily he was engaged to a woman as old as himself, and therefore her father, who was steward of a neighboring estate, would provide him with a job. He would marry and go into harness. His life was over, he would be a subject animal now.

He turned uneasily aside, the retreating steps of the horses echoing in his ears. Then, with foolish restlessness, he reached for the scraps of bacon-rind from the plates, and making a faint whistling sound, flung them to the terrier that lay against the fender.[1] He watched the dog swallow them, and waited till the creature looked into his eyes. Then a faint grin came on his face, and in a high, foolish voice he said:

"You won't get much more bacon, shall you, you little b——?"

The dog faintly and dismally wagged its tail, then lowered its haunches, circled round, and lay down again.

There was another helpless silence at the table. Joe sprawled uneasily in his seat, not willing to go till the family conclave was dissolved. Fred Henry, the second brother, was erect, clean-limbed, alert. He had watched the passing of the horses with more sang-froid. If he was an animal, like Joe, he was an animal which controls, not one which is controlled. He was master of any horse, and he carried himself with a well-tempered air of mastery. But he was not master of the situations of life. He pushed his coarse brown mustache upwards, off his lip, and glanced irritably at his sister, who sat impassive and inscrutable.

"You'll go and stop with Lucy for a bit, shan't you?" he asked. The girl did not answer.

"I don't see what else you can do," persisted Fred Henry.

"Go as a skivvy,"[2] Joe interpolated laconically.

The girl did not move a muscle.

"If I was her, I should go in for training for a nurse," said Malcolm, the youngest of them all. He was the baby of the family, a young man of twenty-two, with a fresh, jaunty *museau*.[3]

But Mabel did not take any notice of him. They had talked at her and round her for so many years, that she hardly heard them at all.

The marble clock on the mantelpiece softly chimed the half-hour, the dog rose uneasily from the hearthrug and looked at the party

1. Fire-screen or guard.
2. Servant.
3. Face, "mug" (slightly derogatory).

at the breakfast table. But still they sat on in ineffectual conclave.

"Oh, all right," said Joe suddenly, apropos of nothing. "I'll get a move on."

He pushed back his chair, straddled his knees with a downward jerk, to get them free, in horsey fashion, and went to the fire. Still he did not go out of the room; he was curious to know what the others would do or say. He began to charge his pipe, looking down at the dog and saying, in a high, affected voice:

"Going wi' me? Going wi' me are ter? Tha'rt goin' further than tha counts on just now, dost hear?"

The dog faintly wagged its tail, the man stuck out his jaw and covered his pipe with his hands, and puffed intently, losing himself in the tobacco, looking down all the while at the dog with an absent brown eye. The dog looked up at him in mournful distrust. Joe stood with his knees stuck out, in real horsey fashion.

"Have you had a letter from Lucy?" Fred Henry asked of his sister.

"Last week," came the neutral reply.

"And what does she say?"

There was no answer.

"Does she *ask* you to go and stop there?" persisted Fred Henry.

"She says I can if I like."

"Well, then, you'd better. Tell her you'll come on Monday."

This was received in silence.

"That's what you'll do then, is it?" said Fred Henry, in some exasperation.

But she made no answer. There was a silence of futility and irritation in the room. Malcolm grinned fatuously.

"You'll have to make up your mind between now and next Wednesday," said Joe loudly, "or else find yourself lodgings on the curbstone."

The face of the young woman darkened, but she sat on immutable.

"Here's Jack Fergusson!" exclaimed Malcolm, who was looking aimlessly out of the window.

"Where?" exclaimed Joe, loudly.

"Just gone past."

"Coming in?"

Malcolm craned his neck to see the gate.

"Yes," he said.

There was a silence. Mabel sat on like one condemned, at the head of the table. Then a whistle was heard from the kitchen. The dog got up and barked sharply. Joe opened the door and shouted: "Come on."

After a moment a young man entered. He was muffled up in overcoat and a purple woolen scarf, and his tweed cap, which he did not remove, was pulled down on his head. He was of medium height, his face was rather long and pale, his eyes looked tired.

"Hello, Jack! Well, Jack!" exclaimed Malcolm and Joe. Fred Henry merely said, "Jack."

"What's doing?" asked the newcomer, evidently addressing Fred Henry.

"Same. We've got to be out by Wednesday. Got a cold?"

"I have—got it bad, too."

"Why don't you stop in?"[4]

"*Me* stop in? When I can't stand on my legs, perhaps I shall have a chance." The young man spoke huskily. He had a slight Scotch accent.

"It's a knockout, isn't it," said Joe, boisterously, "if a doctor goes round croaking with a cold. Looks bad for the patients, doesn't it?"

The young doctor looked at him slowly.

"Anything the matter with *you*, then?" he asked sarcastically.

"Not as I know of. Damn your eyes, I hope not. Why?"

"I thought you were very concerned about the patients, wondered if you might be one yourself."

"Damn it, no, I've never been patient to no flaming[5] doctor, and hope I never shall be," returned Joe.

At this point Mabel rose from the table, and they all seemed to become aware of her existence. She began putting the dishes together. The young doctor looked at her, but did not address her. He had not greeted her. She went out of the room with the tray, her face impassive and unchanged.

"When are you off then, all of you?" asked the doctor.

"I'm catching the eleven-forty," replied Malcolm. "Are you goin' down wi' th' trap, Joe?"

"Yes, I've told you I'm going down wi' th' trap, haven't I?"

"We'd better be getting her in then. So long, Jack, if I don't see you before I go," said Malcolm, shaking hands.

He went out, followed by Joe, who seemed to have his tail between his legs.

"Well, this is the devil's own," exclaimed the doctor, when he was left alone with Fred Henry. "Going before Wednesday, are you?"

"That's the orders," replied the other.

"Where, to Northampton?"[6]

"That's it."

"The devil!" exclaimed Fergusson, with quiet chagrin.

And there was silence between the two.

"All settled up, are you?" asked Fergusson.

"About."

There was another pause.

"Well, I shall miss yer, Freddy, boy," said the young doctor.

"And I shall miss thee, Jack," returned the other.

"Miss you like hell," mused the doctor.

Fred Henry turned aside. There was nothing to say. Mabel came in again, to finish clearing the table.

"What are *you* going to do, then, Miss Pervin?" asked Fergusson. "Going to your sister's, are you?"

Mabel looked at him with her steady, dangerous eyes, that always made him uncomfortable, unsettling his superficial ease.

"No," she said.

"Well, what in the name of fortune *are* you going to do? Say

4. Stay home.
5. Euphemism for "bloody," roughly equivalent to "darned."
6. Town about 65 miles north and slightly west of London.

what you mean to do," cried Fred Henry, with futile intensity.

But she only averted her head, and continued her work. She folded the white tablecloth, and put on the chenille cloth.

"The sulkiest bitch that ever trod!" muttered her brother.

But she finished her task with perfectly impassive face, the young doctor watching her interestedly all the while. Then she went out.

Fred Henry stared after her, clenching his lips, his blue eyes fixing in sharp antagonism, as he made a grimace of sour exasperation.

"You could bray[7] her into bits, and that's all you'd get out of her," he said, in a small, narrowed tone.

The doctor smiled faintly.

"What's she *going* to do, then?" he asked.

"Strike me if *I* know!" returned the other.

There was a pause. Then the doctor stirred.

"I'll be seeing you tonight, shall I?" he said to his friend.

"Ay—where's it to be? Are we going over to Jessdale?"[8]

"I don't know. I've got such a cold on me. I'll come round to the Moon and Stars, anyway."

"Let Lizzie and May miss their night for once, eh?"

"That's it—if I feel as I do now."

"All's one——"

The two young men went through the passage and down to the back door together. The house was large, but it was servantless now, and desolate. At the back was a small bricked house-yard, and beyond that a big square, graveled fine and red, and having stables on two sides. Sloping, dank, winter-dark fields stretched away on the open sides.

But the stables were empty. Joseph Pervin, the father of the family, had been a man of no education, who had become a fairly large horse dealer. The stables had been full of horses, there was a great turmoil and come-and-go of horses and of dealers and grooms. Then the kitchen was full of servants. But of late things had declined. The old man had married a second time, to retrieve his fortunes. Now he was dead and everything was gone to the dogs, there was nothing but debt and threatening.

For months, Mabel had been servantless in the big house, keeping the home together in penury for her ineffectual brothers. She had kept house for ten years. But previously it was with unstinted means. Then, however brutal and coarse everything was, the sense of money had kept her proud, confident. The men might be foul-mouthed, the women in the kitchen might have bad reputations, her brothers might have illegitimate children. But so long as there was money, the girl felt herself established, and brutally proud, reserved.

No company came to the house, save dealers and coarse men. Mabel had no associates of her own sex, after her sister went away. But she did not mind. She went regularly to church, she attended to her father. And she lived in the memory of her mother, who had died when she was fourteen, and whom she had loved. She had

7. Crush.

8. Apparently a fictional name.

loved her father, too, in a different way, depending upon him, and feeling secure in him, until at the age of fifty-four he married again. And then she had set hard against him. Now he had died and left them all hopelessly in debt.

She had suffered badly during the period of poverty. Nothing, however, could shake the curious sullen, animal pride that dominated each member of the family. Now, for Mabel, the end had come. Still she would not cast about her. She would follow her own way just the same. She would always hold the keys of her own situation. Mindless and persistent, she endured from day to day. Why should she think? Why should she answer anybody? It was enough that this was the end, and there was no way out. She need not pass any more darkly along the main street of the small town, avoiding every eye. She need not demean herself any more, going into the shops and buying the cheapest food. This was at an end. She thought of nobody, not even of herself. Mindless and persistent, she seemed in a sort of ecstasy to be coming nearer to her fulfilment, her own glorification, approaching her dead mother, who was glorified.

In the afternoon she took a little bag, with shears and sponge and a small scrubbing brush, and went out. It was a gray, wintry day, with saddened, dark green fields and an atmosphere blackened by the smoke of foundries not far off. She went quickly, darkly along the causeway, heeding nobody, through the town to the churchyard.

There she always felt secure, as if no one could see her, although as a matter of fact she was exposed to the stare of every one who passed along under the churchyard wall. Nevertheless, once under the shadow of the great looming church, among the graves, she felt immune from the world, reserved within the thick churchyard wall as in another country.

Carefully she clipped the grass from the grave, and arranged the pinky white, small chrysanthemums in the tin cross. When this was done, she took an empty jar from a neighboring grave, brought water, and carefully, most scrupulously sponged the marble headstone and the coping-stone.[9]

It gave her sincere satisfaction to do this. She felt in immediate contact with the world of her mother. She took minute pains, went through the park in a state bordering on pure happiness, as if in performing this task she came into a subtle, intimate connection with her mother. For the life she followed here in the world was far less real than the world of death she inherited from her mother.

The doctor's house was just by the church. Fergusson, being a mere hired assistant, was slave to the countryside. As he hurried now to attend to the outpatients in the surgery, glancing across the graveyard with his quick eye, he saw the girl at her task at the grave. She seemed so intent and remote, it was like looking into another world. Some mystical element was touched in him. He slowed down as he walked, watching her as if spellbound.

She lifted her eyes, feeling him looking. Their eyes met. And each looked again at once, each feeling, in some way, found out by

9. Copestone, stone on top layer.

the other. He lifted his cap and passed on down the road. There remained distinct in his consciousness, like a vision, the memory of her face, lifted from the tombstone in the churchyard, and looking at him with slow, large, portentous eyes. It *was* portentous, her face. It seemed to mesmerize him. There was a heavy power in her eyes which laid hold of his whole being, as if he had drunk some powerful drug. He had been feeling weak and done before. Now the life came back into him, he felt delivered from his own fretted, daily self.

He finished his duties at the surgery as quickly as might be, hastily filling up the bottles of the waiting people with cheap drugs. Then, in perpetual haste, he set off again to visit several cases in another part of his round, before teatime. At all times he preferred to walk if he could, but particularly when he was not well. He fancied the motion restored him.

The afternoon was falling. It was gray, deadened, and wintry, with a slow, moist, heavy coldness sinking in and deadening all the faculties. But why should he think or notice? He hastily climbed the hill and turned across the dark green fields, following the black cinder-track. In the distance, across a shallow dip in the country, the small town was clustered like smouldering ash, a tower, a spire, a heap of low, raw, extinct houses. And on the nearest fringe of the town, sloping into the dip, was Oldmeadow, the Pervins' house. He could see the stables and the outbuildings distinctly, as they lay towards him on the slope. Well, he would not go there many more times! Another resource would be lost to him, another place gone: the only company he cared for in the alien, ugly little town he was losing. Nothing but work, drudgery, constant hastening from dwelling to dwelling among the colliers and the ironworkers. It wore him out, but at the same time he had a craving for it. It was a stimulant to him to be in the homes of the working people, moving as it were through the innermost body of their life. His nerves were excited and gratified. He could come so near, into the very lives of the rough, inarticulate, powerfully emotional men and women. He grumbled, he said he hated the hellish hole. But as a matter of fact it excited him, the contact with the rough, strongly-feeling people was a stimulant applied direct to his nerves.

Below Oldmeadow, in the green, shallow, soddened hollow of fields, lay a square, deep pond. Roving across the landscape, the doctor's quick eye detected a figure in black passing through the gate of the field, down towards the pond. He looked again. It would be Mabel Pervin. His mind suddenly became alive and attentive.

Why was she going down there? He pulled up on the path on the slope above, and stood staring. He could just make sure of the small black figure moving in the hollow of the failing day. He seemed to see her in the midst of such obscurity, that he was like a clairvoyant, seeing rather with the mind's eye than with ordinary sight. Yet he could see her positively enough, whilst he kept his eye attentive. He felt, if he looked away from her, in the thick, ugly, falling dusk, he would lose her altogether.

He followed her minutely as she moved, direct and intent, like something transmitted rather than stirring in voluntary activity, straight down the field towards the pond. There she stood on the bank for a moment. She never raised her head. Then she waded slowly into the water.

He stood motionless as the small black figure walked slowly and deliberately towards the center of the pond, very slowly, gradually moving deeper into the motionless water, and still moving forward as the water got up to her breast. Then he could see her no more in the dusk of the dead afternoon.

"There!" he exclaimed. "Would you believe it?"

And he hastened straight down, running over the wet, soddened fields, pushing through the hedges, down into the depression of callous wintry obscurity. It took him several minutes to come to the pond. He stood on the bank, breathing heavily. He could see nothing. His eyes seemed to penetrate the dead water. Yes, perhaps that was the dark shadow of her black clothing beneath the surface of the water.

He slowly ventured into the pond. The bottom was deep, soft clay, he sank in, and the water clasped dead cold round his legs. As he stirred he could smell the cold, rotten clay that fouled up into the water. It was objectionable in his lungs. Still, repelled and yet not heeding, he moved deeper into the pond. The cold water rose over his thighs, over his loins, upon his abdomen. The lower part of his body was all sunk in the hideous cold element. And the bottom was so deeply soft and uncertain, he was afraid of pitching with his mouth underneath. He could not swim, and was afraid.

He couched a little, spreading his hands under the water and moving them round, trying to feel for her. The dead cold pond swayed upon his chest. He moved again, a little deeper, and again, with his hands underneath, he felt all around under the water. And he touched her clothing. But it evaded his fingers. He made a desperate effort to grasp it.

And so doing he lost his balance and went under, horribly, suffocating in the foul earthy water, struggling madly for a few moments. At last, after what seemed an eternity, he got his footing, rose again into the air and looked around. He gasped, and knew he was in the world. Then he looked at the water. She had risen near him. He grasped her clothing, and drawing her nearer, turned to take his way to land again.

He went very slowly, carefully, absorbed in the slow progress. He rose higher, climbing out of the pond. The water was now only about his legs; he was thankful, full of relief to be out of the clutches of the pond. He lifted her and staggered on to the bank, out of the horror of wet, gray clay.

He laid her down on the bank. She was quite unconscious and running with water. He made the water come from her mouth, he worked to restore her. He did not have to work very long before he could feel the breathing begin again in her; she was breathing naturally. He worked a little longer. He could feel her live beneath his hands; she was coming back. He wiped her face, wrapped her in his overcoat, looked round into the dim, dark gray world, then lifted her and staggered down the bank and across the fields.

It seemed an unthinkably long way, and his burden so heavy he felt he would never get to the house. But at last he was in the stable-yard, and then in the house-yard. He opened the door and went into the house. In the kitchen he laid her down on the hearthrug, and called. The house was empty. But the fire was burning in the grate.

Then again he kneeled to attend to her. She was breathing regularly, her eyes were wide open and as if conscious, but there seemed something missing in her look. She was conscious in herself, but unconscious of her surroundings.

He ran upstairs, took blankets from a bed, and put them before the fire to warm. Then he removed her saturated, earthy-smelling clothing, rubbed her dry with a towel, and wrapped her naked in the blankets. Then he went into the diningroom, to look for spirits. There was a little whisky. He drank a gulp himself, and put some into her mouth.

The effect was instantaneous. She looked full into his face, as if she had been seeing him for some time, and yet had only just become conscious of him.

"Dr. Fergusson?" she said.

"What?" he answered.

He was divesting himself of his coat, intending to find some dry clothing upstairs. He could not bear the smell of the dead, clayey water, and he was mortally afraid for his own health.

"What did I do?" she asked.

"Walked into the pond," he replied. He had begun to shudder like one sick, and could hardly attend to her. Her eyes remained full on him, he seemed to be going dark in his mind, looking back at her helplessly. The shuddering became quieter in him, his life came back in him, dark and unknowing, but strong again.

"Was I out of my mind?" she asked, while her eyes were fixed on him all the time.

"Maybe, for the moment," he replied. He felt quiet, because his strength had come back. The strange fretful strain had left him.

"Am I out of my mind now?" she asked.

"Are you?" he reflected a moment. "No," he answered truthfully, "I don't see that you are." He turned his face aside. He was afraid now, because he felt dazed, and felt dimly that her power was stronger than his, in this issue. And she continued to look at him fixedly all the time. "Can you tell me where I shall find some dry things to put on?" he asked.

"Did you dive into the pond for me?" she asked.

"No," he answered. "I walked in. But I went in overhead as well."

There was silence for a moment. He hesitated. He very much wanted to go upstairs to get into dry clothing. But there was another desire in him. And she seemed to hold him. His will seemed to have gone to sleep, and left him, standing there slack before her. But he felt warm inside himself. He did not shudder at all, though his clothes were sodden on him.

"Why did you?" she asked.

"Because I didn't want you to do such a foolish thing," he said.

"It wasn't foolish," she said, still gazing at him as she lay on the floor, with a sofa cushion under her head. "It was the right thing to do. *I* knew best, then."

"I'll go and shift[1] these wet things," he said. But still he had not the power to move out of her presence, until she sent him. It was as if she had the life of his body in her hands, and he could not extricate himself. Or perhaps he did not want to.

Suddenly she sat up. Then she became aware of her own immediate condition. She felt the blankets about her, she knew her own limbs. For a moment it seemed as if her reason were going. She looked round, with wild eye, as if seeking something. He stood still with fear. She saw her clothing lying scattered.

"Who undressed me?" she asked, her eyes resting full and inevitable on his face.

"I did," he replied, "to bring you round."

For some moments she sat and gazed at him awfully, her lips parted.

"Do you love me, then?" she asked.

He only stood and stared at her, fascinated. His soul seemed to melt.

She shuffled forward on her knees, and put her arms round him, round his legs, as he stood there, pressing her breasts against his knees and thighs, clutching him with strange, convulsive certainty, pressing his thighs against her, drawing him to her face, her throat, as she looked up at him with flaring, humble eyes of transfiguration, triumphant in first possession.

"You love me," she murmured, in strange transport, yearning and triumphant and confident. "You love me. I know you love me, I know."

And she was passionately kissing his knees, through the wet clothing, passionately and indiscriminately kissing his knees, his legs, as if unaware of everything.

He looked down at the tangled wet hair, the wild, bare, animal shoulders. He was amazed, bewildered, and afraid. He had never thought of loving her. He had never wanted to love her. When he rescued her and restored her, he was a doctor, and she was a patient. He had had no single personal thought of her. Nay, this introduction of the personal element was very distasteful to him, a violation of his professional honor. It was horrible to have her there embracing his knees. It was horrible. He revolted from it, violently. And yet—and yet—he had not the power to break away.

She looked at him again, with the same supplication of powerful love, and that same transcendent, frightening light of triumph. In view of the delicate flame which seemed to come from her face like a light, he was powerless. And yet he had never intended to love her. He had never intended. And something stubborn in him could not give way.

"You love me," she repeated, in a murmur of deep, rhapsodic assurance. "You love me."

Her hands were drawing him, drawing him down to her. He was

1. Change.

afraid, even a little horrified. For he had, really, no intention of loving her. Yet her hands were drawing him towards her. He put out his hand quickly to steady himself, and grasped her bare shoulder. A flame seemed to burn the hand that grasped her soft shoulder. He had no intention of loving her: his whole will was against his yielding. It was horrible. And yet wonderful was the touch of her shoulders, beautiful the shining of her face. Was she perhaps mad? He had a horror of yielding to her. Yet something in him ached also.

He had been staring away at the door, away from her. But his hand remained on her shoulder. She had gone suddenly very still. He looked down at her. Her eyes were now wide with fear, with doubt, the light was dying from her face, a shadow of terrible grayness was returning. He could not bear the touch of her eyes' question upon him, and the look of death behind the question.

With an inward groan he gave way, and let his heart yield towards her. A sudden gentle smile came on his face. And her eyes, which never left his face, slowly, slowly filled with tears. He watched the strange water rise in her eyes, like some slow fountain coming up. And his heart seemed to burn and melt away in his breast.

He could not bear to look at her any more. He dropped on his knees and caught her head with his arms and pressed her face against his throat. She was very still. His heart, which seemed to have broken, was burning with a kind of agony in his breast. And he felt her slow, hot tears wetting his throat. But he could not move.

He felt the hot tears wet his neck and the hollows of his neck, and he remained motionless, suspended through one of man's eternities. Only now it had become indispensable to him to have her face pressed close to him; he could never let her go again. He could never let her head go away from the close clutch of his arm. He wanted to remain like that for ever, with his heart hurting him in a pain that was also life to him. Without knowing, he was looking down on her damp, soft brown hair.

Then, as it were suddenly, he smelt the horrid stagnant smell of that water. And at the same moment she drew away from him and looked at him. Her eyes were wistful and unfathomable. He was afraid of them, and he fell to kissing her, not knowing what he was doing. He wanted her eyes not to have that terrible, wistful, unfathomable look.

When she turned her face to him again, a faint delicate flush was glowing, and there was again dawning that terrible shining of joy in her eyes, which really terrified him, and yet which he now wanted to see, because he feared the look of doubt still more.

"You love me?" she said, rather faltering.

"Yes." The word cost him a painful effort. Not because it wasn't true. But because it was too newly true, the *saying* seemed to tear open again his newly-torn heart. And he hardly wanted it to be true, even now.

She lifted her face to him, and he bent forward and kissed her on the mouth, gently, with the one kiss that is an eternal pledge. And as he kissed her his heart strained again in his breast. He never intended to love her. But now it was over. He had crossed over the gulf to her, and all that he had left behind had shriveled and become void.

After the kiss, her eyes again slowly filled with tears. She sat still, away from him, with her face drooped aside, and her hands folded in her lap. The tears fell very slowly. There was complete silence. He too sat there motionless and silent on the hearthrug. The strange pain of his heart that was broken seemed to consume him. That he should love her? That this was love! That he should be ripped open in this way! Him, a doctor! How they would all jeer if they knew! It was agony to him to think they might know.

In the curious naked pain of the thought he looked again to her. She was sitting there drooped into a muse. He saw a tear fall, and his heart flared hot. He saw for the first time that one of her shoulders was quite uncovered, one arm bare, he could see one of her small breasts; dimly, because it had become almost dark in the room.

"Why are you crying?" he asked, in an altered voice.

She looked up at him, and behind her tears the consciousness of her situation for the first time brought a dark look of shame to her eyes.

"I'm not crying, really," she said, watching him half frightened.

He reached his hand, and softly closed it on her bare arm.

"I love you! I love you!" he said in a soft, low vibrating voice, unlike himself.

She shrank, and dropped her head. The soft, penetrating grip of his hand on her arm distressed her. She looked up at him.

"I want to go," she said. "I want to go and get you some dry things."

"Why?" he said. "I'm all right."

"But I want to go," she said. "And I want you to change your things."

He released her arm, and she wrapped herself in the blanket, looking at him rather frightened. And still she did not rise.

"Kiss me," she said wistfully.

He kissed her, but briefly, half in anger.

Then, after a second, she rose nervously, all mixed up in the blanket. He watched her in her confusion, as she tried to extricate herself and wrap herself up so that she could walk. He watched her relentlessly, as she knew. And as she went, the blanket trailing, and as he saw a glimpse of her feet and her white leg, he tried to remember her as she was when he had wrapped her in the blanket. But then he didn't want to remember, because she had been nothing to him then, and his nature revolted from remembering her as she was when she was nothing to him.

A tumbling, muffled noise from within the dark house startled him. Then he heard her voice—"There are clothes." He rose and went to the foot of the stairs, and gathered up the garments she had thrown down. Then he came back to the fire, to rub himself down and dress. He grinned at his own appearance when he had finished.

The fire was sinking, so he put on coal. The house was now quite dark, save for the light of a street-lamp that shone in faintly from beyond the holly trees. He lit the gas with matches he found on the mantelpiece. Then he emptied the pockets of his own clothes, and threw all his wet things in a heap into the scullery. After which he gathered up her sodden clothes, gently, and put them in a separate heap on the copper-top[2] in the scullery.

It was six o'clock on the clock. His own watch had stopped. He ought to go back to the surgery. He waited, and still she did not come down. So he went to the foot of the stairs and called:

"I shall have to go."

Almost immediately he heard her coming down. She had on her best dress of black voile, and her hair was tidy, but still damp. She looked at him—and in spite of herself, smiled.

"I don't like you in those clothes," she said.

"Do I look a sight?" he answered.

They were shy of one another.

"I'll make you some tea," she said.

"No, I must go."

"Must you?" And she looked at him again with the wide, strained, doubtful eyes. And again, from the pain of his breast, he knew how he loved her. He went and bent to kiss her, gently, passionately, with his heart's painful kiss.

"And my hair smells so horrible," she murmured in distraction. "And I'm so awful, I'm so awful! Oh, no, I'm too awful." And she broke into bitter, heartbroken sobbing. "You can't want to love me, I'm horrible."

"Don't be silly, don't be silly," he said, trying to comfort her, kissing her, holding her in his arms. "I want you, I want to marry you, we're going to be married, quickly, quickly—tomorrow if I can."

But she only sobbed terribly, and cried:

"I feel awful. I feel awful. I feel I'm horrible to you."

"No, I want you, I want you," was all he answered, blindly, with that terrible intonation which frightened her almost more than her horror lest he should *not* want her.

1922

D. H. LAWRENCE

The Rocking-Horse Winner

There was a woman who was beautiful, who started with all the advantages, yet she had no luck. She married for love, and the love turned to dust. She had bonny children, yet she felt they had been thrust upon her, and she could not love them. They looked at her coldly, as if they were finding fault with her. And hurriedly she felt she must cover up some fault in herself. Yet what it was that she must cover up she never knew. Nevertheless, when her children were present, she always felt the center of her heart go hard. This troubled her, and in her manner she was all the more gentle and anxious for her

2. Top of a washtub or cooking vessel, now usually made of iron.

children, as if she loved them very much. Only she herself knew that at the center of her heart was a hard little place that could not feel love, no, not for anybody. Everybody else said of her: "She is such a good mother. She adores her children." Only she herself, and her children themselves, knew it was not so. They read it in each other's eyes.

There were a boy and two little girls. They lived in a pleasant house, with a garden, and they had discreet servants, and felt themselves superior to anyone in the neighborhood.

Although they lived in style, they felt always an anxiety in the house. There was never enough money. The mother had a small income, and the father had a small income, but not nearly enough for the social position which they had to keep up. The father went into town to some office. But though he had good prospects, these prospects never materialized. There was always the grinding sense of the shortage of money, though the style was always kept up.

At last the mother said: "I will see if *I* can't make something." But she did not know where to begin. She racked her brains, and tried this thing and the other, but could not find anything successful. The failure made deep lines come into her face. Her children were growing up, they would have to go to school. There must be more money, there must be more money. The father, who was always very handsome and expensive in his tastes, seemed as if he never *would* be able to do anything worth doing. And the mother, who had a great belief in herself, did not succeed any better, and her tastes were just as expensive.

And so the house came to be haunted by the unspoken phrase: *There must be more money! There must be more money!* The children could hear it all the time, though nobody said it aloud. They heard it at Christmas, when the expensive and splendid toys filled the nursery. Behind the shining modern rocking-horse, behind the smart doll's house, a voice would start whispering: "There *must* be more money! There *must* be more money!" And the children would stop playing, to listen for a moment. They would look into each other's eyes, to see if they had all heard. And each one saw in the eyes of the other two that they too had heard. "There *must* be more money! There *must* be more money!"

It came whispering from the springs of the still-swaying rocking-horse, and even the horse, bending his wooden, champing head, heard it. The big doll, sitting so pink and smirking in her new pram,[1] could hear it quite plainly, and seemed to be smirking all the more self-consciously because of it. The foolish puppy, too, that took the place of the teddy bear, he was looking so extraordinarily foolish for no other reason but that he heard the secret whisper all over the house: "There *must* be more money!"

Yet nobody ever said it aloud. The whisper was everywhere, and therefore no one spoke it. Just as no one ever says: "We are breathing!" in spite of the fact that breath is coming and going all the time.

"Mother," said the boy Paul one day, "why don't we keep a car of our own? Why do we always use uncle's, or else a taxi?"

"Because we're the poor members of the family," said the mother.

1. Baby carriage.

"But why *are* we, mother?"

"Well—I suppose," she said slowly and bitterly, "it's because your father has no luck."

The boy was silent for some time.

"Is luck money, mother?" he asked, rather timidly.

"No, Paul. Not quite. It's what causes you to have money."

"Oh!" said Paul vaguely. "I thought when Uncle Oscar said *filthy lucker*, it meant money."

"*Filthy lucre* does mean money," said the mother. "But it's lucre, not luck."

"Oh!" said the boy. "Then what *is* luck, mother?"

"It's what causes you to have money. If you're lucky you have money. That's why it's better to be born lucky than rich. If you're rich, you may lose your money. But if you're lucky, you will always get more money."

"Oh! Will you? And is father not lucky?"

"Very unlucky, I should say," she said bitterly.

The boy watched her with unsure eyes.

"Why?" he asked.

"I don't know. Nobody ever knows why one person is lucky and another unlucky."

"Don't they? Nobody at all? Does *nobody* know?"

"Perhaps God. But He never tells."

"He ought to, then. And aren't you lucky either, mother?"

"I can't be, if I married an unlucky husband."

"But by yourself, aren't you?"

"I used to think I was, before I married. Now I think I am very unlucky indeed."

"Why?"

"Well—never mind! Perhaps I'm not really," she said.

The child looked at her to see if she meant it. But he saw, by the lines of her mouth, that she was only trying to hide something from him.

"Well, anyhow," he said stoutly, "I'm a lucky person."

"Why?" said his mother, with a sudden laugh.

He stared at her. He didn't even know why he had said it.

"God told me," he asserted, brazening it out.

"I hope He did, dear!" she said, again with a laugh, but rather bitter.

"He did, mother!"

"Excellent!" said the mother, using one of her husband's exclamations.

The boy saw she did not believe him; or rather, that she paid no attention to his assertion. This angered him somewhat, and made him want to compel her attention.

He went off by himself, vaguely, in a childish way, seeking for the clue to "luck." Absorbed, taking no heed of other people, he went about with a sort of stealth, seeking inwardly for luck. He wanted luck, he wanted it, he wanted it. When the two girls were playing dolls in the nursery, he would sit on his big rocking-horse, charging madly into space, with a frenzy that made the little girls peer at him uneasily.

Wildly the horse careered, the waving dark hair of the boy tossed, his eyes had a strange glare in them. The little girls dared not speak to him.

When he had ridden to the end of his mad little journey, he climbed down and stood in front of his rocking-horse, staring fixedly into its lowered face. Its red mouth was slightly open, its big eye was wide and glassy-bright.

"Now!" he would silently command the snorting steed. "Now, take me to where there is luck! Now take me!"

And he would slash the horse on the neck with the little whip he had asked Uncle Oscar for. He *knew* the horse could take him to where there was luck, if only he forced it. So he would mount again and start on his furious ride, hoping at last to get there. He knew he could get there.

"You'll break your horse, Paul!" said the nurse.

"He's always riding like that! I wish he'd leave off!" said his elder sister Joan.

But he only glared down on them in silence. Nurse gave him up. She could make nothing of him. Anyhow, he was growing beyond her.

One day his mother and his Uncle Oscar came in when he was on one of his furious rides. He did not speak to them.

"Hallo, you young jockey! Riding a winner?" said his uncle.

"Aren't you growing too big for a rocking-horse? You're not a very little boy any longer, you know," said his mother.

But Paul only gave a blue glare from his big, rather close-set eyes. He would speak to nobody when he was in full tilt. His mother watched him with an anxious expression on her face.

At last he suddenly stopped forcing his horse into the mechanical gallop and slid down.

"Well, I got there!" he announced fiercely, his blue eyes still flaring, and his sturdy long legs straddling apart.

"Where did you get to?" asked his mother.

"Where I wanted to go," he flared back at her.

"That's right, son!" said Uncle Oscar. "Don't you stop till you get there. What's the horse's name?"

"He doesn't have a name," said the boy.

"Gets on without all right?" asked the uncle.

"Well, he has different names. He was called Sansovino last week."

"Sansovino, eh? Won the Ascot. How did you know this name?"

"He always talks about horse-races with Bassett," said Joan.

The uncle was delighted to find that his small nephew was posted with all the racing news. Bassett, the young gardener, who had been wounded in the left foot in the war[2] and had got his present job through Oscar Cresswell, whose batman he had been, was a perfect blade[3] of the "turf." He lived in the racing events, and the small boy lived with him.

Oscar Cresswell got it all from Bassett.

"Master Paul comes and asks me, so I can't do more than tell him, sir," said Bassett, his face terribly serious, as if he were speaking of religious matters.

2. World War I, 1914–1918.

3. Dashing young man.

"And does he ever put anything on a horse he fancies?"

"Well—I don't want to give him away—he's a young sport, a fine sport, sir. Would you mind asking him himself? He sort of takes a pleasure in it, and perhaps he'd feel I was giving him away, sir, if you don't mind."

Bassett was serious as a church.

The uncle went back to his nephew and took him off for a ride in the car.

"Say, Paul, old man, do you ever put anything on a horse?" the uncle asked.

The boy watched the handsome man closely.

"Why, do you think I oughtn't to?" he parried.

"Not a bit of it! I thought perhaps you might give me a tip for the Lincoln."[4]

The car sped on into the country, going down to Uncle Oscar's place in Hampshire.

"Honor bright?" said the nephew.

"Honor bright, son!" said the uncle.

"Well, then, Daffodil."

"Daffodil! I doubt it, sonny. What about Mirza?"

"I only know the winner," said the boy. "That's Daffodil."

"Daffodil, eh?"

There was a pause. Daffodil was an obscure horse comparatively.

"Uncle!"

"Yes, son?"

"You won't let it go any further, will you? I promised Bassett."

"Bassett be damned, old man! What's he got to do with it?"

"We're partners. We've been partners from the first. Uncle, he lent me my first five shillings,[5] which I lost. I promised him, honor bright, it was only between me and him; only you gave me that ten-shilling note I started winning with, so I thought you were lucky. You won't let it go any further, will you?"

The boy gazed at his uncle from those big, hot, blue eyes, set rather close together. The uncle stirred and laughed uneasily.

"Right you are, son! I'll keep your tip private. Daffodil, eh? How much are you putting on him?"

"All except twenty pounds," said the boy. "I keep that in reserve."

The uncle thought it a good joke.

"You keep twenty pounds in reserve, do you, you young romancer? What are you betting, then?"

"I'm betting three hundred," said the boy gravely. "But it's between you and me, Uncle Oscar! Honor bright?"

The uncle burst into a roar of laughter.

"It's between you and me all right, you young Nat Gould,"[6] he said, laughing. "But where's your three hundred?"

4. Lincolnshire Handicap race then run at Lincoln Downs. Other races mentioned in the story include the St. Leger Stakes (the Leger) run at Doncaster; the Grand National Steeplechase run at Aintree, the most famous steeplechase in the world; the famous Derby, a mile-and-a-half race for three-year-olds run at Epsom Downs, and the Ascot (above) run at the course of that name in Berkshire.

5. Then just over a dollar. The English pound after World War I fluctuated considerably but was generally less than the $4.86 of the pre-War period and more than $4. There are 20 shillings to the pound.

6. Nathaniel Gould (1857–1919) novelist and journalist whose writings in both genres concerned horse-racing.

"Bassett keeps it for me. We're partners."

"You are, are you! And what is Bassett putting on Daffodil?"

"He won't go quite as high as I do, I expect. Perhaps he'll go a hundred and fifty."

"What, pennies?" laughed the uncle.

"Pounds," said the child, with a surprised look at his uncle. "Bassett keeps a bigger reserve than I do."

Between wonder and amusement Uncle Oscar was silent. He pursued the matter no further, but he determined to take his nephew with him to the Lincoln races.

"Now, son," he said, "I'm putting twenty on Mirza, and I'll put five on for you on any horse you fancy. What's your pick?"

"Daffodil, uncle."

"No, not the fiver on Daffodil!"

"I should if it was my own fiver," said the child.

"Good! Good! Right you are! A fiver for me and a fiver for you on Daffodil."

The child had never been to a race-meeting before, and his eyes were blue fire. He pursed his mouth tight and watched. A Frenchman just in front had put his money on Lancelot. Wild with excitement, he flayed his arms up and down, yelling *"Lancelot! Lancelot!"* in his French accent.

Daffodil came in first, Lancelot second, Mirza third. The child, flushed and with eyes blazing, was curiously serene. His uncle brought him four five-pound notes, four to one.

"What am I to do with these?" he cried, waving them before the boy's eyes.

"I suppose we'll talk to Bassett," said the boy. "I expect I have fifteen hundred now; and twenty in reserve; and this twenty."

His uncle studied him for some moments.

"Look here, son!" he said. "You're not serious about Bassett and that fifteen hundred, are you?"

"Yes, I am. But it's between you and me, uncle. Honor bright?"

"Honor bright all right, son! But I must talk to Bassett."

"If you'd like to be a partner, uncle, with Bassett and me, we could all be partners. Only, you'd have to promise, honor bright, uncle, not to let it go beyond us three. Bassett and I are lucky, and you must be lucky, because it was your ten shillings I started winning with. . . ."

Uncle Oscar took both Bassett and Paul into Richmond Park for an afternoon, and there they talked.

"It's like this, you see, sir," Bassett said. "Master Paul would get me talking about racing events, spinning yarns, you know, sir. And he was always keen on knowing if I'd made or if I'd lost. It's about a year since, now, that I put five shillings on Blush of Dawn for him: and we lost. Then the luck turned, with that ten shillings, he had from you: that we put on Singhalese. And since that time, it's been pretty steady, all things considering. What do you say, Master Paul?"

"We're all right when we're sure," said Paul. "It's when we're not quite sure that we go down."

"Oh, but we're careful then," said Bassett.

"But when are you *sure*?" smiled Uncle Oscar.

"It's Master Paul, sir," said Bassett in a secret, religious voice. "It's as if he had it from heaven. Like Daffodil, now, for the Lincoln. That was as sure as eggs."

"Did you put anything on Daffodil?" asked Oscar Cresswell.

"Yes, sir. I made my bit."

"And my nephew?"

Bassett was obstinately silent, looking at Paul.

"I made twelve hundred, didn't I, Bassett? I told uncle I was putting three hundred on Daffodil."

"That's right," said Bassett, nodding.

"But where's the money?" asked the uncle.

"I keep it safe locked up, sir. Master Paul he can have it any minute he likes to ask for it."

"What, fifteen hundred pounds?"

"And twenty! And *forty*, that is, with the twenty he made on the course."

"It's amazing!" said the uncle.

"If Master Paul offers you to be partners, sir, I would, if I were you: if you'll excuse me," said Bassett.

Oscar Cresswell thought about it.

"I'll see the money," he said.

They drove home again, and, sure enough, Bassett came round to the garden-house with fifteen hundred pounds in notes. The twenty pounds reserve was left with Joe Glee, in the Turf Commission deposit.

"You see, it's all right, uncle, when I'm *sure*! Then we go strong, for all we're worth. Don't we, Bassett?"

"We do that, Master Paul."

"And when are you sure?" said the uncle, laughing.

"Oh, well, sometimes I'm *absolutely* sure, like about Daffodil," said the boy; "and sometimes I have an idea; and sometimes I haven't even an idea, have I, Bassett? Then we're careful, because we mostly go down."

"You do, do you! And when you're sure, like about Daffodil, what makes you sure, sonny?"

"Oh, well, I don't know," said the boy uneasily. "I'm sure, you know, uncle; that's all."

"It's as if he had it from heaven, sir," Bassett reiterated.

"I should say so!" said the uncle.

But he became a partner. And when the Leger was coming on, Paul was "sure" about Lively Spark, which was a quite inconsiderable horse. The boy insisted on putting a thousand on the horse, Bassett went for five hundred, and Oscar Cresswell two hundred. Lively Spark came in first, and the betting had been ten to one against him. Paul had made ten thousand.

"You see," he said, "I was absolutely sure of him."

Even Oscar Cresswell had cleared two thousand.

"Look here, son," he said, "this sort of thing makes me nervous."

"It needn't, uncle! Perhaps I shan't be sure again for a long time."

"But what are you going to do with your money?" asked the uncle.

"Of course," said the boy, "I started it for mother. She said she had no luck, because father is unlucky, so I thought if *I* was lucky, it might stop whispering."

"What might stop whispering?"

"Our house. I *hate* our house for whispering."

"What does it whisper?"

"Why—why"—the boy fidgeted—"why, I don't know. But it's always short of money, you know, uncle."

"I know it, son, I know it."

"You know people send mother writs, don't you, uncle?"

"I'm afraid I do," said the uncle.

"And then the house whispers, like people laughing at you behind your back.. It's awful, that is! I thought if I was lucky—"

"You might stop it," added the uncle.

The boy watched him with big blue eyes, that had an uncanny cold fire in them, and he said never a word.

"Well, then!" said the uncle. "What are we doing?"

"I shouldn't like mother to know I was lucky," said the boy.

"Why not, son?"

"She'd stop me."

"I don't think she would."

"Oh!"—and the boy writhed in an odd way—"I *don't* want her to know, uncle."

"All right, son! We'll manage it without her knowing."

They managed it very easily. Paul, at the other's suggestion, handed over five thousand pounds to his uncle, who deposited it with the family lawyer, who was then to inform Paul's mother that a relative had put five thousand pounds into his hands, which sum was to be paid out a thousand pounds at a time, on the mother's birthday, for the next five years.

"So she'll have a birthday present of a thousand pounds for five successive years," said Uncle Oscar. "I hope it won't make it all the harder for her later."

Paul's mother had her birthday in November. The house had been "whispering" worse than ever lately, and, even in spite of his luck, Paul could not bear up against it. He was very anxious to see the effect of the birthday letter, telling his mother about the thousand pounds.

When there were no visitors, Paul now took his meals with his parents, as he was beyond the nursery control. His mother went into town nearly every day. She had discovered that she had an odd knack of sketching furs and dress materials, so she worked secretly in the studio of a friend who was the chief "artist" for the leading drapers. She drew the figures of ladies in furs and ladies in silk and sequins for the newspaper advertisements. This young woman artist earned several thousand pounds a year, but Paul's mother only made several hundreds, and she was again dissatisfied. She so wanted to be first in something, and she did not succeed, even in making sketches for drapery advertisements.

She was down to breakfast on the morning of her birthday. Paul watched her face as she read her letters. He knew the lawyer's letter. As his mother read it, her face hardened and became more expressionless. Then a cold, determined look came on her mouth. She hid the letter under the pile of others, and said not a word about it.

"Didn't you have anything nice in the post for your birthday, mother?" said Paul.

"Quite moderately nice," she said, her voice cold and absent.

She went away to town without saying more.

But in the afternoon Uncle Oscar appeared. He said Paul's mother had had a long interview with the lawyer, asking if the whole five thousand could not be advanced at once, as she was in debt.

"What do you think, uncle?" said the boy.

"I leave it to you, son."

"Oh, let her have it, then! We can get some more with the other," said the boy.

"A bird in the hand is worth two in the bush, laddie!" said Uncle Oscar.

"But I'm sure to *know* for the Grand National; or the Lincolnshire; or else the Derby. I'm sure to know for one of them," said Paul.

So Uncle Oscar signed the agreement, and Paul's mother touched the whole five thousand. Then something very curious happened. The voices in the house suddenly went mad, like a chorus of frogs on a spring evening. There were certain new furnishings, and Paul had a tutor. He was *really* going to Eton, his father's school, in the following autumn. There were flowers in the winter, and a blossoming of the luxury Paul's mother had been used to. And yet the voices in the house, behind the sprays of mimosa and almond-blossom, and from under the piles of iridescent cushions, simply trilled and screamed in a sort of ecstasy: "There *must* be more money! Oh-h-h; there *must* be more money. Oh, now, now-w! Now-w-w—there *must* be more money! —more than ever! More than ever!"

It frightened Paul terribly. He studied away at his Latin and Greek with his tutor. But his intense hours were spent with Bassett. The Grand National had gone by: he had not "known," and had lost a hundred pounds. Summer was at hand. He was in agony for the Lincoln. But even for the Lincoln he didn't "know," and he lost fifty pounds. He became wild-eyed and strange, as if something were going to explode in him.

"Let it alone, son! Don't you bother about it!" urged Uncle Oscar. But it was as if the boy couldn't really hear what his uncle was saying.

"I've got to know for the Derby! I've got to know for the Derby!" the child reiterated, his big blue eyes blazing with a sort of madness.

His mother noticed how overwrought he was.

"You'd better go to the seaside. Wouldn't you like to go now to the seaside, instead of waiting? I think you'd better," she said, looking down at him anxiously, her heart curiously heavy because of him.

But the child lifted his uncanny blue eyes.

"I couldn't possibly go before the Derby, mother!" he said. "I couldn't possibly!"

"Why not?" she said, her voice becoming heavy when she was opposed. "Why not? You can still go from the seaside to see the Derby with your Uncle Oscar, if that's what you wish. No need for you to wait here. Besides, I think you care too much about these races. It's a bad sign. My family has been a gambling family, and you won't know till you grow up how much damage it has done. But it has done damage. I shall have to send Bassett away, and ask Uncle Oscar not to talk racing to you, unless you promise to be reasonable about it: go away to the seaside and forget it. You're all nerves!"

"I'll do what you like, mother, so long as you don't send me away till after the Derby," the boy said.

"Send you away from where? Just from this house?"

"Yes," he said, gazing at her.

"Why, you curious child, what makes you care about this house so much, suddenly? I never knew you loved it."

He gazed at her without speaking. He had a secret within a secret, something he had not divulged, even to Bassett or to his Uncle Oscar.

But his mother, after standing undecided and a little bit sullen for some moments, said:

"Very well, then! Don't go to the seaside till after the Derby, if you don't wish it. But promise me you won't let your nerves go to pieces. Promise you won't think so much about horse-racing and *events,* as you call them!"

"Oh, no," said the boy casually. "I won't think much about them, mother. You needn't worry. I wouldn't worry, mother, if I were you."

"If you were me and I were you," said his mother, "I wonder what we *should* do!"

"But you know you needn't worry, mother, don't you?" the boy repeated.

"I should be awfully glad to know it," she said wearily.

"Oh, well, you *can,* you know. I mean, you *ought* to know you needn't worry," he insisted.

"Ought I? Then I'll see about it," she said.

Paul's secret of secrets was his wooden horse, that which had no name. Since he was emancipated from a nurse and a nursery-governess, he had had his rocking-horse removed to his own bedroom at the top of the house.

"Surely you're too big for a rocking-horse!" his mother had remonstrated.

"Well, you see, mother, till I can have a *real* horse, I like to have *some* sort of animal about," had been his quaint answer.

"Do you feel he keeps you company?" she laughed.

"Oh, yes! He's very good, he always keeps me company, when I'm there," said Paul.

So the horse, rather shabby, stood in an arrested prance in the boy's bedroom.

The Derby was drawing near, and the boy grew more and more tense. He hardly heard what was spoken to him, he was very frail, and his eyes were really uncanny. His mother had sudden strange seizures of uneasiness about him. Sometimes, for half an hour, she would feel a sudden anxiety about him that was almost anguish. She wanted to rush to him at once, and know he was safe.

Two nights before the Derby, she was at a big party in town, when one of her rushes of anxiety about her boy, her first-born, gripped her heart till she could hardly speak. She fought with the feeling, might and main, for she believed in common sense. But it was too strong. She had to leave the dance and go downstairs to telephone to the country. The children's nursery-governess was terribly surprised and startled at being rung up in the night.

"Are the children all right, Miss Wilmot?"

"Oh, yes, they are quite all right."

"Master Paul? Is he all right?"

"He went to bed as right as a trivet. Shall I run up and look at him?"

"No," said Paul's mother reluctantly. "No! Don't trouble. It's all right. Don't sit up. We shall be home fairly soon." She did not want her son's privacy intruded upon.

"Very good," said the governess.

It was about one o'clock when Paul's mother and father drove up to their house. All was still. Paul's mother went to her room and slipped off her white fur cloak. She had told her maid not to wait up for her. She heard her husband downstairs, mixing a whisky and soda.

And then, because of the strange anxiety at her heart, she stole upstairs to her son's room. Noiselessly she went along the upper corridor. Was there a faint noise? What was it?

She stood, with arrested muscles, outside his door, listening. There was a strange, heavy, and yet not loud noise. Her heart stood still. It was a soundless noise, yet rushing and powerful. Something huge, in violent, hushed motion. What was it? What in God's name was it? She ought to know. She felt that she knew the noise. She knew what it was.

Yet she could not place it. She couldn't say what it was. And on and on it went, like a madness.

Softly, frozen with anxiety and fear, she turned the door-handle.

The room was dark. Yet in the space near the window, she heard and saw something plunging to and fro. She gazed in fear and amazement.

Then suddenly she switched on the light, and saw her son, in his green pajamas, madly surging on the rocking-horse. The blaze of light suddenly lit him up, as he urged the wooden horse, and lit her up, as she stood, blonde, in her dress of pale green and crystal, in the doorway.

"Paul!" she cried. "Whatever are you doing?"

"It's Malabar!" he screamed, in a powerful, strange voice. "It's Malabar!"

His eyes blazed at her for one strange and senseless second, as he ceased urging his wooden horse. Then he fell with a crash to the ground, and she, all her tormented motherhood flooding upon her, rushed to gather him up.

But he was unconscious, and unconscious he remained, with some brain-fever. He talked and tossed, and his mother sat stonily by his side.

"Malabar! It's Malabar! Bassett, Bassett, I *know*! It's Malabar!"

So the child cried, trying to get up and urge the rocking-horse that gave him his inspiration.

"What does he mean by Malabar?" asked the heart-frozen mother.

"I don't know," said the father stonily.

"What does he mean by Malabar?" she asked her brother Oscar.

"It's one of the horses running for the Derby," was the answer.

And, in spite of himself, Oscar Cresswell spoke to Bassett, and himself put a thousand on Malabar: at fourteen to one.

The third day of the illness was critical: they were waiting for a change. The boy, with his rather long, curly hair, was tossing ceaselessly on the pillow. He neither slept nor regained consciousness, and his eyes were like blue stones. His mother sat, feeling her heart had gone, turned actually into a stone.

In the evening, Oscar Cresswell did not come, but Bassett sent a message, saying could he come up for one moment, just one moment? Paul's mother was very angry at the intrusion, but on second thought she agreed. The boy was the same. Perhaps Bassett might bring him to consciousness.

The gardener, a shortish fellow with a little brown moustache and sharp little brown eyes, tiptoed into the room, touched his imaginary cap to Paul's mother, and stole to the bedside, staring with glittering, smallish eyes, at the tossing, dying child.

"Master Paul!" he whispered. "Master Paul! Malabar came in first all right, a clean win. I did as you told me. You've made over seventy thousand pounds, you have; you've got over eighty thousand. Malabar came in all right, Master Paul."

"Malabar! Malabar! Did I say Malabar, mother? Did I say Malabar? Do you think I'm lucky, mother? I knew Malabar, didn't I? Over eighty thousand pounds! I call that lucky, don't you, mother? Over eighty thousand pounds! I knew, didn't I know I knew? Malabar came in all right. If I ride my horse till I'm sure, then I tell you, Bassett, you can go as high as you like. Did you go for all you were worth, Bassett?"

"I went a thousand on it, Master Paul."

"I never told you, mother, that if I can ride my horse, and *get there*, then I'm absolutely sure—oh, absolutely! Mother, did I ever tell you? I *am* lucky!"

"No, you never did," said the mother.

But the boy died in the night.

And even as he lay dead, his mother heard her brother's voice saying to her: "My God, Hester, you're eighty-odd thousand to the good, and a poor devil of a son to the bad. But, poor devil, poor devil, he's best gone out of a life where he rides his rocking-horse to find a winner."

1932

D. H. LAWRENCE

Passages from Essays and Letters

from "Nottingham and the Mining Countryside"

I was born . . . in Eastwood, a mining village of some three thousand souls, about eight miles from Nottingham. . . . It is hilly country. . . . To me it seemed, and still seems, an extremely beautiful countryside, just between the red sandstone and the oak-trees of Nottingham, and the cold limestone, the ash-trees, the stone fences of Derbyshire. To me, as a child and a young man, it was still the old England of the forest and agricultural past; there were no motor-cars, the mines were, in a sense, an accident in the landscape, and Robin Hood and his merry men were not very far away.

. . . The people lived almost entirely by instinct, men of my father's age could not really read. And the pit did not mechanize men. . . . My father loved the pit. He was hurt badly, more than once, but he would never stay away. He loved the contact, the intimacy, as men in the war loved the intense male comradeship of the dark days.

Now the colliers had also an instinct for beauty. The colliers' wives had not. The colliers were deeply alive, instinctively. But they had no daytime ambition, and no daytime intellect. They avoided, really, the rational aspect of life. . . . They didn't even care very profoundly about wages. It was the women, naturally, who nagged on this score. . . . The collier went to the pub and drank in order to continue the intimacy with his mates.

. . . Life for him did not consist of facts, but in a flow. Very often he loved his garden. And very often he had a genuine love of the beauty of flowers. . . .

. . . Most women love flowers as possessions, and as trimmings. They can't look at a flower, and wonder a moment, and pass on. If they see a flower that arrests their attention, they must at once pick it, pluck it. Possession! A possession! Something added on to *me!*

from "Love"

. . . the love between a man and a woman . . . is dual. It is the melting into pure communion, and it is the friction of sheer sensuality, both. In pure communion I become whole in love. And in pure, fierce passion of sensuality, I am burned into essentiality. I am driven from the matrix unto sheer separate distinction. I become my single self, inviolable and unique, as the gems were perhaps once driven into themselves out of the confusion of earths. . . .

from "Women Are So Cocksure"

. . . [My mother] was convinced . . . that a man ought not to drink beer. This conviction developed from the fact, naturally, that my father drank beer. He sometimes drank too much. He sometimes boozed away the money necessary for the young family. When my father came in tipsy, she saw scarlet.

from "Art and Morality"

Apples are always apples! says Vox Populi, Vox Dei.[1]

Sometimes they're sin, sometimes they're a knock on the head, sometimes they're a bellyache, sometimes they're part of a pie, sometimes they're sauce for a goose.

1. The voice of the people [is] the voice of God.

What art has got to do, and will go on doing, is to reveal things in their different relationships. That is to say, you've got to see in the apples the bellyache, Sir Isaac's knock on the cranium, the vast, moist wall through which the insect bores to lay her eggs in the middle, and the untasted, unknown quality which Eve saw hanging on a tree.

from "Morality and the Novel"

The business of art is to reveal the relation between man and his circumambient universe, at the living moment. As mankind is always struggling in the toils of old relationships, art is always ahead of the "times," which themselves are always far in the rear of the living moment.

When Van Gogh paints sunflowers, he reveals, or achieves, the vivid relation between himself, as man, and the sunflowers, as sunflower, at that quick moment of time. His painting does not represent the sunflower itself. We shall never know what the sunflower itself is. And the camera will *visualize* the sunflower far more perfectly than van Gogh can.

The vision on the canvas is a third thing, utterly intangible and inexplicable, the offspring of the sunflower itself and van Gogh himself. . . .

. . . The novel is the highest example of subtle interrelatedness that man has discovered. Everything is true in its own time, place, and circumstance, and untrue outside of its own place, time, circumstance. If you try to nail anything down, in the novel, either it kills the novel, or the novel gets up and walks away with the nail.

. . . Love is a great emotion. But if you set out to write a novel, and you yourself are in the throes of the great predilection for love, love as the supreme, the only emotion worth living for, then you will write an immoral novel.

Because *no* emotion is supreme, or exclusively worth living for. *All* emotions go to the achieving of a living relationship between a human being and the other human being or creature or thing he becomes purely related to. All emotions, including love and hate, and rage and tenderness, go to the adjusting of the oscillating, unestablished balance between two people who amount to anything.

A new relation, a new relatedness hurts somewhat in the attaining; and will always hurt. So life will always hurt. . . .

Each time we strive to a new relation, with anyone or anything, it is bound to hurt somewhat. Because it means the struggle with and the displacing of old connections, and this is never pleasant. And, moreover, between living things at least, an adjustment means also a fight, for each party, inevitably, must "seek its own" in the other, and be denied. When, in the two parties, each of them seeks his own, her own, absolutely, then it is a fight to the death. And this is true of the thing called "passion."

The great relationship for humanity will always be the relation between man and woman. The relation between man and man, woman and woman, parent and child, will always be subsidiary.

And the relation between man and woman will change forever, and will forever be the new central clue to human life. It is the *relation itself* which is the quick and the central clue to life, not the man, nor the woman, nor the children that result from the relationship, as a contingency.

from "Why the Novel Matters"

We have curious ideas of ourselves. We think of ourselves as a body with a spirit in it, or a body with a soul in it, or a body with a mind in it. . . .

It is a funny sort of superstition. Why should I look at my hand, as it so cleverly writes these words, and decide that it is a mere nothing compared to the mind that directs it? Why should I imagine that there is a *me* which is more *me* than my hand is? Since my hand is absolutely alive, me alive.

And that's what you learn, when you're a novelist. And that's what you are liable *not* to know, if you're a parson, or a philosopher, or a scientist, or a stupid person.

Now I absolutely flatly deny that I am a soul, or a body, or a mind, or an intelligence, or a brain, or a nervous system, or a bunch of glands, or any of the rest of these bits of me. The whole is greater than the part. And therefore, I, who am man alive, am greater than my soul, or spirit, or body, or mind, or consciousness, or anything else that is merely a part of me. I am man a man, and alive. I am man alive, and as long as I can, I intend to go on being man alive.

For this reason I am a novelist. And being a novelist, I consider myself superior to the saint, the scientist, the philosopher, and the poet, who are all great masters of different bits of man alive, but never get the whole thing.

We should ask for no absolutes, or absolute. . . . There is no absolute good, there is nothing absolutely right. All things flow and change, and even change is not absolute. . . .

. . . If the one I love remains unchanged and unchanging, I shall cease to love her. It is only because she changes and startles me into change and defies my inertia, and is herself staggered in her inertia by my changing, that I can continue to love her. If she stayed put, I might as well love the pepper-pot.

In life, there is right and wrong, good and bad, all the time. But what is right in one case is wrong in another. And in the novel you see one man becoming a corpse, because of his so-called goodness, another going dead because of his so-called wickedness. Right and wrong is an instinct: but an instinct of the whole consciousness in a man, bodily, mental, spiritual at once. And only in the novel are *all* things given full play, or at least, they may be given full play, when we realize that life itself, and not inert safety, is the reason for living. For out of the full play of all things emerges the only thing that is anything, the wholeness of a man, the wholeness of a woman, man alive, and live woman.

from Autobiographical Sketch

They ask me; "Did you find it very hard to get on and to become a success?" And I have to admit that if I can be said to have got on, and if I can be called a success, then I *did not* find it hard.

I never starved in a garret, nor waited in anguish for the post to bring me an answer from editor or publisher, nor did I struggle in sweat and blood to bring forth mighty works, nor did I ever wake up and find myself famous.

. . . My father was a collier, and only a collier, nothing praiseworthy about him. He wasn't even respectable, in so far as he got drunk rather frequently, never went near a chapel, and was usually rather rude to his little immediate bosses at the pit.

My mother was, I suppose, superior. She came from town, and belonged really to the lower bourgeoisie. She spoke King's English, without an accent, and never in her life could even imitate a sentence of the dialect which my father spoke, and which we children spoke out of doors.

I have *wanted* to feel truly friendly with some, at least of my fellow-men. Yet I have never quite succeeded. Whether I got on *in* the world is a question; but I certainly don't get on very well *with* the world. And whether I am a worldly success or not I really don't know. But I feel, somehow, not much of a human success.

By which I mean that I don't feel there is any very cordial of fundamental contact between me and society, or me and other people. There is a breach. And my contact is with something that is nonhuman, nonvocal.

[Why?] The answer, as far as I can see, has something to do with class. Class makes a gulf, across which all the best human flow is lost. It is not exactly the triumph of the middle classes that has made the deadness, but the triumph of the middle-class *thing*.

As a man from the working class, I feel that the middle class cut off some of my vital vibration when I am with them. I admit them charming and educated and good people often enough. *But they just stop some part of me from working. . . .*

Then why don't I live with my working people? Because their vibration is limited in another direction. They are narrow, but still fairly deep and passionate, whereas the middle class is broad and shallow and passionless.

I cannot make the transfer from my own class into the middle class. I cannot, not for anything in the world, forfeit my passional consciousness and my old blood-affinity with my fellow-men and the animals and the land, for that other thin, spurious mental conceit which is all that is left of the mental consciousness once it has made itself exclusive.

from the Letters

TO A. W. MCLEOD, 26 APRIL 1913

I am so sure that only through a readjustment between men and women, and a making free and healthy of this sex, will she [England] get out of her present atrophy. Oh, Lord, and if I don't "subdue my art to a metaphysic," as somebody very beautifully said of Hardy, I do write because I want folk—English folk—to alter, and have more sense.

TO A. W. MCLEOD, 2 JUNE 1914

I think the only re-sourcing of art, revivifying it, is to make it more the joint work of man and woman. I think *the* one thing to do, is for men to have courage to draw nearer to women, expose themselves to them, and be altered by them; and for women to accept and admit men. That is the start—by bringing themselves together, men and women—revealing themselves to each other, gaining great blind knowledge and suffering and joy, which it will take a big further lapse of civilization to exploit and work out. Because the source of all life and knowledge is in man and woman, and the source of all living is in the interchange and the meeting and mingling of these two: man-life and woman-life, man-knowledge and woman-knowledge, man-being and woman-being.

TO J. B. PINKER, 16 DECEMBER 1915

. . . Tell Arnold Bennett [2] that all rules of construction hold good only for novels which are copies of other novels. A book which is not a copy of other books has its own construction and what he calls faults, he being an old imitator, I call characteristics.

TO ROLF GARDINER, 9 AUGUST 1924

What we need is to smash a few big holes in European suburbanity, let in a little real fresh air.

TO LADY OTTOLINE MORRELL, 5 FEBRUARY 1929

. . . Don't you think it's nonsense when Murry says that my world is not the ordinary man's world and that I am a sort of animal with a sixth sense. Seems to me more likely he's a sort of animal with only four senses—the real sense of touch missing. They all seem determined to make a freak of me—to save their own short-failings, and make them "normal."

2. An early twentieth-century novelist (1867–1931) whose major works—*The Old Wives' Tale* (1908) and *The Clayhanger Trilogy* (1910–15)—treat the middle classes in the pottery country of the English Midlands in a naturalistic manner (usually criticizing the money-grubbing, social-climbing selfishness of the society). In his later years he more or less turned into a hack, though a clever one, and it is to Bennett as a very popular, successful hack that Lawrence is referring.

10 TRADITION

What is a short story? a novel? When we sit down to read a short story, what do we expect? Our expectations, our very notion of what a short story or novel is, have been formed by other short stories and novels we have read or heard about. This body of work—all the stories, novels, even poems and plays—that the author and informed reader are in general familiar with is the literary tradition. Within the literary tradition are less all-inclusive traditions: there is the Western literary tradition, and the tradition of American literature, and the Puritan tradition, and so on. Within a **literary tradition** certain signals or **conventions** are developed with which readers become familiar, and which tell them, for example, whether to expect high adventure or everyday events, even whether there is likely to be a happy ending, an unhappy one, or not much of an ending at all.

Conventions are something like a second layer of language, an aid and structure for communicating meaning. We know from the conventions of punctuation—arbitrary signs such as ?, !, . —how to read certain sentences. We know from the conventions of English word order who did what to whom in the sentence "The girl hit the boy." We know that when type is set in blocks we are reading prose; when it is set in uneven lines beginning with capital letters, we are reading poetry. So we know what kind of story to expect when it begins, "Once upon a time . . ."

Of course, writers don't know exactly who *you* are. They must make certain assumptions and by some of their signals and devices try to make you the kind of reader they want. Sometimes, especially in the case of foreign or older literature, we are not the reader the author had in mind at all, and it is thus up to us either to resign ourselves to missing a good deal of what's going on, or to try to learn enough to become at least a reasonably informed reader.

The writer, then, expects the reader to share a common literary tradition in a general way, to understand most of the signals that further relate the individual work to a body of works, and thus to raise expectations that he can either fulfill or transform. We all know that if a television show is a series, both the young cop and his older partner will more than likely survive (and catch the bad guys), but if it's not a series and the older cop is near retirement, a widower living alone, and very kindly but a little lost, we fully expect him to fall heroically before the final commercial. Sometimes a writer will expect you to know a specific work and keep it in mind while you are reading the new work. A **parody,** or an imitation that makes fun of another work, like *Samurai Night Fever* or Fielding's *Shamela,* which parodies Richardson's *Pamela,* clearly assumes you remember the work being parodied.

As readers, the literary tradition is important to us primarily so that we can get the full enjoyment, the full experience, from reading the work. We want to be familiar with the Gothic tradition—with castles and ghosts—and its science-fiction aspect—the mad scientist, weird experiments—so that when, in *The Most Dangerous Game,* Rainsford comes upon the château in the middle of the jungle and Ivan answers the door, we can have the thrill of expectation—even though it's a false expectation, for it's not being right but being aware that's the important thing. If we know the tradition of the serial ordeal, in which the hero must accomplish three tasks or solve three problems, Rainsford's tricks of survival may build our expectations more intensely.

For writers the tradition is a necessary tool in defining their fictional world, both for themselves and for readers. Most want to write because there is some truth, some vision of reality they want to present that no one has quite got right. They want to tell it like it is, but in order to do so they have to work on what you already know. So they use the most appropriate portion of the tradition to "place" their work or frame it, and then they play off the tradition, or work against it, or define their world and its operations in terms of it, so that you can see the difference and significance more immediately and clearly. The narrator of *Catcher in the Rye,* for example, wants to deny the influence of his home and early years on his current "mad" behavior, so he says he will not tell *his* story the way Dickens told David Copperfield's: "If you really want to hear about it, the first thing you'll probably want to know is where I was born, and what my lousy childhood was like, and how my parents were occupied and all before they had me, and all that David Copperfield kind of crap, but I don't feel like going into it, if you want to know the truth. . . ."

The three stories in this chapter are in the tradition of what has been called "Southwest humor" (*Southwest* meaning the southern frontier wherever it happened to be; in Longstreet's day, then, no farther west than Georgia).

All these stories involve the trickster. The trickster—practical joker, shady trader, underhanded opponent; sometimes heroic, sometimes a rogue, at times a villain, respected or contemptible—appears in European, African, and other folk literature as well as in the American. In the American, as in other traditions, the trickster may be a braggart, like Yellow Blossom in the Longstreet story (and like Odysseus); sometimes more sly, like Longstreet's old man or Faulkner's Flem Snopes; sometimes downright sneaky, like the stranger in Samuel Clemens's story. Very often in the American tradition, as perhaps one might expect, the trick involves trading, as in Longstreet and Faulkner, or other forms of gain such as betting, as in Clemens.

The trickster is usually a local and his victim usually an outsider or stranger, often one who is himself trying to trick and who thus deserves to be bested. Often the stories are anti-urban or anti-intellectual, with the "folk" getting the better of his more sophisticated rival. For some reason, in the American stories within this tradition there is almost always a narrator between us and the trickster. Perhaps it is to insulate us morally from the trickster: the narrator, like the reader, is removed from the action and uninvolved, neither profiting nor losing by the tricks, and so disclaiming responsibility, as it were, for the morality of the action. Perhaps it is to make the tale, often a rather outlandish one, more credible: the narrator, someone like us, is merely reporting what he heard or testifying to the veracity of the story, no matter how strange it seems. Perhaps it is to make the story respectable or comprehensible, for the folk characters speak local dialect and the narrator usually speaks standard American.

Though the humor in these stories is based on verbal exaggeration (**hyperbole** or overstatement) and on physical, knockabout, pratfall, vaudeville-type comic action (**slapstick**), the folk characters, folk humor, dialect, and regional description and mores (**local color**) connect this tradition with the movement toward increased realism in nineteenth-century fiction. Historically the tradition is centered in the generation immediately preceding the Civil War, when American literature was first separating itself from its English predecessors and seeking local roots. (See Hennig Cohen and William B. Dillingham's Introduction to *Humor of the Old Southwest.*) It must have struck a taproot, for after the Civil War we find Clemens and a number of his contemporaries, and in our own century William Faulkner as well as many others (*Dotson Gerber* has many elements of the tradition), writing stories recognizably related to these.

It is more than likely that the later writers had read Longstreet; Faulkner had certainly read Longstreet and Clemens. However, we are not here primarily concerned with **influence**—the direct effect of one writer on another—or with **allusion**—reference within a work to another specific work, such as the early reference to Dante's epic in *The Artificial Nigger,* or Woody Allen's hilarious use of *Madame Bovary* in *The Kugelmass Episode.* What we are focusing on here is the later authors' reliance on reader familiarity not with any specific work but with a sufficient number of stories within the tradition to arouse certain expectations of plot and character, and in some cases voice, language, even setting.

The author can thus assume that the tradition itself, rather than any specific work or works within the tradition, is common knowledge. Clemens can write a story within the tradition that is at the same time a spoof of the tradition. The jumping frog contest is more ridiculous than a horse race or swap, and the trick is a rather blatant and flimsy one. You might think this is just Clemens writing a poor or strained example of the trickster-tricked story, but notice that Simon Wheeler tells story after story about Jim Smiley, and the narrator himself, a stand-in for the reader, recognizes the triteness of the trickster device and flees rather than listen to another such story, about "a yaller one-eyed cow that didn't have no tail." Faulkner shows how a master can revive and transform the tradition. *Spotted Horses* retains the trickster and the trick, the broad verbal humor and the slapstick, but he reveals within the jokes the trickster's essential cruelty and exploitation, and without sentimentality he creates out of comedy almost unbearable pathos.

AUGUSTUS BALDWIN LONGSTREET

The Horse-Swap

During the session of the Supreme Court, in the village of —— about three weeks ago, when a number of people were collected in the principal street of the village, I observed a young man riding up and down the street, as I supposed, in a violent passion. He galloped this way, then that, and then the other; spurred his horse to one group of citizens, then to another, then dashed off at half speed, as if fleeing from danger; and, suddenly checking his horse, returned first in a pace, then in a trot, and then in a canter. While he was performing these various evolutions, he cursed, swore, whooped, screamed, and tossed himself in every attitude which man could assume on horseback. In short, he *cavorted* most magnanimously (a term which, in our tongue, expresses all that I have described, and a little more), and seemed to be setting all creation at defiance. As I like to see all that is passing, I determined to take a position a little nearer to him, and to ascertain, if possible, what it was that affected him so sensibly. Accordingly, I approached a crowd before which he had stopped for a moment, and examined it with the strictest scrutiny. But I could see nothing in it that seemed to have anything to do with the cavorter. Every man appeared to be in good humor, and all minding their own business. Not one so much as noticed the principal figure. Still he went on. After a semicolon pause, which my appearance seemed to produce (for he eyed me closely as I approached), he fetched a whoop, and swore that "he could out-swap any live man, woman, or child that ever walked these hills, or that ever straddled horseflesh since the days of old daddy Adam. Stranger," said he to me, "did you ever see the *Yallow* Blossom from Jasper?"

"No," said I, "but I have often heard of him."

"I'm the boy," continued he; "perhaps a *leetle,* jist a *leetle,* of the best man at a horse-swap that ever trod shoe-leather."

I began to feel my situation a little awkward, when I was relieved by a man somewhat advanced in years, who stepped up and began to survey the "*Yallow Blossom*'s" horse with much apparent interest. This drew the rider's attention, and he turned the conversation from me to the stranger.

"Well, my old coon," said he, "do you want to swap *hosses?*"

"Why, I don't know," replied the stranger; "I believe I've got a beast I'd trade with you for that one, if you like him."

"Well, fetch up your nag, my old cock; you're jist the lark[1] I wanted to get hold of. I am perhaps a *leetle,* jist a *leetle,* of the best man at a horse-swap that ever stole *cracklins* out of his mammy's fat gourd. Where's your *hoss?*"

"I'll bring him presently; but I want to examine your horse a little."

"Oh! look at him," said the Blossom, alighting and hitting him a cut; "look at him. He's the best piece of *hoss*flesh in the thirteen united univarsal worlds. There's no sort o' mistake in little Bullet. He can pick up miles on his feet, and fling 'em behind him as fast as the next man's *hoss,* I don't care where he comes from. And he can keep at it as long as the sun can shine without resting."

During this harangue, little Bullet looked as if he understood it all, believed it, and was ready at any moment to verify it. He was a horse of goodly countenance, rather expressive of vigilance than fire; though

1. Game or trick.

an unnatural appearance of fierceness was thrown into it by the loss of his ears, which had been cropped pretty close to his head. Nature had done but little for Bullet's head and neck; but he managed, in a great measure, to hide their defects by bowing perpetually. He had obviously suffered severely for corn; but if his ribs and hip bones had not disclosed the fact, *he* never would have done it; for he was in all respects as cheerful and happy as if he commanded all the corn-cribs and fodder-stacks in Georgia. His height was about twelve hands; but as his shape partook somewhat of that of the giraffe, his haunches stood much lower. They were short, strait, peaked, and concave. Bullet's tail, however, made amends for all his defects. All that the artist could do to beautify it had been done; and all that horse could do to compliment the artist, Bullet did. His tail was nicked in superior style, and exhibited the line of beauty in so many directions, that it could not fail to hit the most fastidious taste in some of them. From the root it dropped into a graceful festoon; then rose in a handsome curve; then resumed its first direction; and then mounted suddenly upward like a cypress knee to a perpendicular of about two and a half inches. The whole had a careless and bewitching inclination to the right. Bullet obviously knew where his beauty lay, and took all occasions to display it to the best advantage. If a stick cracked, or if anyone moved suddenly about him, or coughed, or hawked, or spoke a little louder than common, up went Bullet's tail like lightning; and if the *going up* did not please, the *coming down* must of necessity, for it was as different from the other movement as was its direction. The first was a bold and rapid flight upward, usually to an angle of forty-five degrees. In this position he kept his interesting appendage until he satisfied himself that nothing in particular was to be done; when he commenced dropping it by half inches, in second beats, then in triple time, then faster and shorter, and faster and shorter still, until it finally died away imperceptibly into its natural position. If I might compare sights to sounds, I should say its *settling* was more like the note of a locust than anything else in nature.

Either from native sprightliness of disposition, from uncontrollable activity, or from an unconquerable habit of removing flies by the stamping of the feet, Bullet never stood still; but always kept up a gentle fly-scaring movement of his limbs, which was peculiarly interesting.

"I tell you, man," proceeded the Yellow Blossom, "he's the best live hoss that ever trod the grit of Georgia. Bob Smart knows the hoss. Come here, Bob, and mount this hoss, and show Bullet's motions." Here Bullet bristled up, and looked as if he had been hunting for Bob all day long, and had just found him. Bob sprang on his back "Boo-oo-oo!" said Bob, with a fluttering noise of the lips; and away went Bullet, as if in a quarter race,[2] with all his beauties spread in handsome style.

"Now fetch him back," said Blossom. Bullet turned and came in pretty much as he went out.

"Now trot him by." Bullet reduced his tail to "*customary*"; sidled to

2. Quarter-mile race.

the right and left airily, and exhibited at least three varieties of trot in the short space of fifty yards.

"Make him pace!"[3] Bob commenced twitching the bridle and kicking at the same time. These inconsistent movements obviously (and most naturally) disconcerted Bullet; for it was impossible for him to learn, from them, whether he was to proceed or stand still. He started to trot, and was told that wouldn't do. He attempted a canter, and was checked again. He stopped, and was urged to go on. Bullet now rushed into the wide field of experiment, and struck out a gait of his own, that completely turned the tables upon his rider, and certainly deserved a patent. It seemed to have derived its elements from the jig, the minuet, and the cotillion. If it was not a pace, it certainly had *pace* in it, and no man would venture to call it anything else; so it passed off to the satisfaction of the owner.

"Walk him!" Bullet was now at home again; and he walked as if money was staked on him.

The stranger, whose name, I afterward learned, was Peter Ketch, having examined Bullet to his heart's content, ordered his son Neddy to go and bring up Kit. Neddy soon appeared upon Kit; a well-formed sorrel of the middle size, and in good order. His *tout ensemble*[4] threw Bullet entirely in the shade, though a glance was sufficient to satisfy anyone that Bullet had the decided advantage of him in point of intellect.

"Why, man," said Blossom, "do you bring such a hoss as that to trade for Bullet? Oh, I see you're no notion of trading."

"Ride him off, Neddy!" said Peter. Kit put off at a handsome lope.

"Trot him back!" Kit came in at a long, sweeping trot, and stopped suddenly at the crowd.

"Well," said Blossom, "let me look at him; maybe he'll do to plow."

"Examine him!" said Peter, taking hold of the bridle close to the mouth; "he's nothing but a tacky. He an't as *pretty* a horse as Bullet, I know; but he'll do. Start 'em together for a hundred and fifty *mile*; and if Kit an't twenty mile ahead of him at the coming out, any man may take Kit for nothing. But he's a monstrous mean horse, gentlemen; any man may see that. He's the scariest horse, too, you ever saw. He won't do to hunt on, no how. Stranger, will you let Neddy have your rifle to shoot off him? Lay the rifle between his ears, Neddy, and shoot at the blaze in that stump. Tell me when his head is high enough."

Ned fired, and hit the blaze; and Kit did not move a hair's breadth.

"Neddy, take a couple of sticks, and beat on that hogshead at Kit's tail."

Ned made a tremendous rattling, at which Bullet took fright, broke his bridle, and dashed off in grand style; and would have stopped all farther negotiations by going home in disgust, had not a traveler arrested him and brought him back; but Kit did not move.

"I tell you, gentlemen," continued Peter, "he's the scariest horse you ever saw. He ain't as gentle as Bullet, but he won't do any harm if you watch him. Shall I put him in a cart, gig, or wagon for you,

3. Display his abilities; a pace is a fast gait.

4. All-together.

stranger? He'll cut the same capers there he does here. He's a monstrous mean horse."

During all this time Blossom was examining him with the nicest scrutiny. Having examined his frame and limbs, he now looked at his eyes.

"He's got a curious look out of his eyes," said Blossom.

"Oh yes, sir," said Peter, "just as blind as a bat. Blind horses always have clear eyes. Make a motion at his eyes, if you please, sir."

Blossom did so, and Kit threw up his head rather as if something pricked him under the chin than as if fearing a blow. Blossom repeated the experiment, and Kit jerked back in considerable astonishment.

"Stone blind, you see, gentlemen," proceeded Peter; "but he's just as good to travel of a dark night as if he had eyes."

"Blame my buttons," said Blossom, "if I like them eyes."

"No," said Peter, "nor I neither. I'd rather have 'em made of diamonds; but they'll do, if they don't show as much white as Bullet's."

"Well," said Blossom, "make a pass at me."[5]

"No," said Peter; "you made the banter,[6] now make your pass."

"Well, I'm never afraid to price my hosses. You must give me twenty-five dollars boot."[7]

"Oh, certainly; say fifty, and my saddle and bridle in. Here, Neddy, my son, take away daddy's horse."

"Well," said Blossom, "I've made my pass, now you make yours."

"I'm for short talk in a horse-swap, and therefore always tell a gentleman at once what I mean to do. You must give me ten dollars."

Blossom swore absolutely, roundly, and profanely, that he never would give boot.

"Well," said Peter, "I didn't care about trading; but you cut such high shines[8] that I thought I'd like to back you out, and I've done it. Gentlemen, you see I've brought him to a hack."[9]

"Come, old man," said Blossom, "I've been joking with you. I begin to think you do want to trade; therefore, give me five dollars and take Bullet. I'd rather lose ten dollars any time than not make a trade, though I hate to fling away a good hoss."

"Well," said Peter, "I'll be as clever as you are. Just put the five dollars on Bullet's back, and hand him over; it's a trade."

Blossom swore again, as roundly as before, that he would not give boot; and, said he, "Bullet wouldn't hold five dollars on his back, no how. But as, I bantered you, if you say an even swap, here's at you."

"I told you," said Peter, "I'd be as clever as you; therefore, here goes two dollars more, just for trade sake. Give me three dollars, and it's a bargain."

Blossom repeated his former assertion; and here the parties stood for a long time, and the bystanders (for many were now collected) began to taunt both parties. After some time, however, it was pretty unanimously decided that the old man had backed Blossom out.

At length Blossom swore he "never would be backed out for three

5. Make me an offer.
6. Challenge.
7. To boot (in addition).
8. Such a big show.
9. Horse in bad physical condition.

dollars after bantering a man"; and, accordingly, they closed the trade.

"Now," said Blossom, as he handed Peter the three dollars, "I'm a man that, when he makes a bad trade, makes the most of it until he can make a better. I'm for no rues and after-claps."[1]

"That's just my way," said Peter; "I never goes to law to mend my bargains."

"Ah, you're the kind of boy I love to trade with. Here's your hoss, old man. Take the saddle and bridle off him, and I'll strip yours; but lift up the blanket easy from Bullet's back, for he's a mighty tender-backed hoss."

The old man removed the saddle, but the blanket stuck fast. He attempted to raise it, and Bullet bowed himself, switched his tail, danced a little, and gave signs of biting.

"Don't hurt him, old man," said Blossom, archly; "take it off easy. I am, perhaps, a leetle of the best man at a horse-swap that ever catched a coon."

Peter continued to pull at the blanket more and more roughly, and Bullet became more and more *cavortish*; insomuch that, when the blanket came off, he had reached the *kicking* point in good earnest.

The removal of the blanket disclosed a sore on Bullet's backbone that seemed to have defied all medical skill. It measured six full inches in length and four in breadth, and had as many features as Bullet had motions. My heart sickened at the sight; and I felt that the brute who had been riding him in that situation deserved the halter.

The prevailing feeling, however, was that of mirth. The laugh became loud and general at the old man's expense, and rustic witticisms were liberally bestowed upon him and his late purchase. These Blossom continued to provoke by various remarks. He asked the old man "if he thought Bullet would let five dollars lie on his back." He declared most seriously that he had owned that horse three months, and had never discovered before that he had a sore back, "or he never should have thought of trading him," etc., etc.

The old man bore it all with the most philosophic composure. He evinced no astonishment at his late discovery, and made no replies. But his son Neddy had not disciplined his feelings quite so well. His eyes opened wider and wider from the first to the last pull of the blanket; and, when the whole sore burst upon his view, astonishment and fright seemed to contend for the mastery of his countenance. As the blanket disappeared, he stuck his hands in his breeches pockets, heaved a deep sigh, and lapsed into a profound reverie, from which he was only roused by the cuts at his father. He bore them as long as he could; and, when he could contain himself no longer, he began, with a certain wildness of expression which gave a peculiar interest to what he uttered: "His back's mighty bad off; but dod drot[2] my soul if he's put it to daddy as bad as he thinks he has, for old Kit's both blind and *deef*, I'll be dod drot if he eint."

"The devil he is," said Blossom.

"Yes, dod drot my soul if he *eint*. You walk him, and see if he *eint*. His eyes don't look like it; but he'd *jist as leve go agin* the house with

1. Regrets or unexpected consequences. 2. God rot, an expletive.

you, or in a ditch, as any how. Now you go try him." The laugh was now turned on Blossom; and many rushed to test the fidelity of the little boy's report. A few experiments established its truth beyond controversy.

"Neddy," said the old man, "you oughtn't to try and make people discontented with their things. Stranger, don't mind what the little boy says. If you can only get Kit rid of them little failings, you'll find him all sorts of a horse. You are a *leetle* the best man at a horse-swap that ever I got hold of; but don't fool away Kit. Come, Neddy, my son, let's be moving; the stranger seems to be getting snappish."

1835

SAMUEL CLEMENS (MARK TWAIN)

The Celebrated Jumping Frog of Calaveras County

In compliance with the request of a friend of mine, who wrote me from the East, I called on good-natured, garrulous old Simon Wheeler, and inquired about my friend's friend, Leonidas W. Smiley, as requested to do, and I hereunto append the result. I have a lurking suspicion that *Leonidas* W. Smiley is a myth; that my friend never knew such a personage; and that he only conjectured that if I asked old Wheeler about him, it would remind him of his infamous *Jim* Smiley, and he would go to work and bore me to death with some exasperating reminiscence of him as long and as tedious as it should be useless to me. If that was the design, it succeeded.

I found Simon Wheeler dozing comfortably by the barroom stove of the dilapidated tavern in the decayed mining camp of Angel's, and I noticed that he was fat and bald-headed, and had an expression of winning gentleness and simplicity upon his tranquil countenance. He roused up, and gave me good day. I told him that a friend of mine had commissioned me to make some inquiries about a cherished companion of his boyhood named *Leonidas* W. Smiley—*Rev. Leonidas* W. Smiley, a young minister of the Gospel, who he had heard was at one time a resident of Angel's Camp. I added that if Mr. Wheeler could tell me anything about this Rev. Leonidas W. Smiley, I would feel under many obligations to him.

Simon Wheeler backed me into a corner and blockaded me there with his chair, and then sat down and reeled off the monotonous narrative which follows this paragraph. He never smiled, he never frowned, he never changed his voice from the gentle-flowing key to which he tuned his initial sentence, he never betrayed the slightest suspicion of enthusiasm; but all through the interminable narrative there ran a vein of impressive earnestness and sincerity, which showed me plainly that, so far from his imagining that there was anything ridiculous or funny about his story, he regarded it as a really important matter, and admired its two heroes as men of transcendent genius in *finesse*. I let him go on in his own way, and never interrupted him once.

"Rev. Leonidas W. H'm, Reverend Le—well, there was a feller here once by the name of *Jim* Smiley, in the winter of '49—or maybe it was the spring of '50—I don't recollect exactly, somehow, though what makes me think it was one or the other is because I remember the big flume[1] warn't finished when he first came to the camp; but anyway, he was the curiousest man about always betting on anything that turned up you ever see, if he could get anybody to bet on the other side; and if he couldn't he'd change sides. Any way that suited the other man would suit *him*—any way just so's he got a bet, *he* was satisfied. But still he was lucky, uncommon lucky; he most always come out winner. He was always ready and laying for a chance; there couldn't be no solit'ry thing mentioned but that feller'd offer to bet on it, and take ary side you please, as I was just telling you. If there was a horse-race, you'd find him flush or you'd find him busted at the end of it; if there was a dog-fight, he'd bet on it; if there was a cat-fight, he'd bet on it; if there was a chicken-fight, he'd bet on it; why, if there was two birds setting on a fence, he would bet you which one would fly first; or if there was a camp-meeting, he would be there reg'lar to bet on Parson Walker, which he judged to be the best exhorter about here, and so he was too, and a good man. If he even see a straddle-bug[2] start to go anywheres, he would bet you how long it would take him to get to—to wherever he was going to, and if you took him up, he would foller that straddle-bug to Mexico but what he would find out where he was bound for and how long he was on the road. Lots of the boys here has seen that Smiley, and can tell you about him. Why, it never made no difference to *him* —he'd bet on *any* thing—the dangdest feller. Parson Walker's wife laid very sick once, for a good while, and it seemed as if they warn't going to save her; but one morning he come in, and Smiley up and asked him how she was, and he said she was considerable better—thank the Lord for his inf'nite mercy—and coming on so smart that with the blessing of Prov'dence she'd get well yet; and Smiley, before he thought, says, 'Well, I'll resk two-and-a-half she don't anyway.'

"Thish-yer Smiley had a mare—the boys called her the fifteen-minute nag, but that was only in fun, you know, because of course she was faster than that—and he used to win money on that horse, for all she was so slow and always had the asthma, or the distemper, or the consumption, or something of that kind. They used to give her two or three hundred yards' start, and then pass her under way; but always at the fag end of the race she'd get excited and desperate like, and come cavoting and straddling up, and scattering her legs around limber, sometimes in the air, and sometimes out to one side among the fences, and kicking up m-o-r-e dust and raising m-o-r-e racket with her coughing and sneezing and blowing her nose—and *always* fetch up at the stand just about a neck ahead, as near as you could cipher it down.

1. Artificial chute or trough for carrying water to gold diggings.

2. Long-legged beetle.

"And he had a little small bull-pup, that to look at him you'd think he warn't worth a cent but to set around and look ornery and lay for a chance to steal something. But as soon as money was up on him he was a different dog; his under-jaw'd begin to stick out like the fo'castle of a steamboat, and his teeth would uncover and shine like the furnaces. And a dog might tackle him and bully-rag him, and bite him, and throw him over his shoulder two or three times, and Andrew Jackson[3]—which was the name of the pup—Andrew Jackson would never let on but what *he* was satisfied, and hadn't expected nothing else—and the bets being doubled and doubled on the other side all the time, till the money was all up; and then all of a sudden he would grab that other dog jest by the j'int of his hind leg and freeze to it—not chaw, you understand, but only just grip and hang on till they throwed up the sponge, if it was a year. Smiley always come out winner on that pup, till he harnessed a dog once that didn't have no hind legs, because they'd been sawed off in a circular saw, and when the thing had gone along far enough, and the money was all up, and he come to make a snatch for his pet holt, he see in a minute how he'd been imposed on, and how the other dog had him in the door, so to speak, and he 'peared surprised, and then he looked sorter discouraged-like, and didn't try no more to win the fight, and so he got shucked out bad. He give Smiley a look, as much as to say his heart was broke, and it was *his* fault, for putting up a dog that hadn't no hind legs for him to take holt of, which was his main dependence in a fight, and then he limped off a piece and laid down and died. It was a good pup, was that Andrew Jackson, and would have made a name for hisself if he'd lived, for the stuff was in him and he had genius—I know it, because he hadn't no opportunities to speak of, and it don't stand to reason that a dog could make such a fight as he could under them circumstances if he hadn't no talent. It always makes me feel sorry when I think of that last fight of his'n, and the way it turned out.

"Well, thish-yer Smiley had rat-tarriers, and chicken cocks, and tom-cats and all them kind of things, till you couldn't rest, and you couldn't fetch nothing for him to bet on but he'd match you. He ketched a frog one day, and took him home, and said he cal'lated to educate him; and so he never done nothing for three months but set in his back yard and learn that frog to jump. And you bet you he *did* learn him, too. He'd give him a little punch behind, and the next minute you'd see that frog whirling in the air like a doughnut—see him turn one summerset, or maybe a couple, if he got a good start, and come down flat-footed and all right, like a cat. He got him up so in the matter of ketching flies, and kep' him in practice so constant, that he'd nail a fly every time as fur as he could see him. Smiley said all a frog wanted was education, and he could do 'most anything—and I believe him. Why, I've seen him set Dan'l Webster[4] down here

3. President of the United States, 1829–1837; called Old Hickory because he was so tough and determined.

4. Famous congressman, senator, orator (1782–1852) whose independence—supporting Jackson on Union, running against him as a Whig, not resigning from Tyler's cabinet when other Whigs did—made him seem to some a great "jumper."

on this floor—Dan'l Webster was the name of the frog—and sing out, 'Flies, Dan'l, flies!' and quicker'n you could wink he'd spring straight up and snake a fly off'n the counter there, and flop down on the floor ag'in as solid as a gob of mud, and fall to scratching the side of his head with his hind foot as indifferent as if he hadn't no idea he'd been doin' any more'n any frog might do. You never see a frog so modest and straightfor'ard as he was, for all he was so gifted. And when it come to fair and square jumping on a dead level, he could get over more ground at one straddle than any animal of his breed you ever see. Jumping on a dead level was his strong suit, you understand; and when it come to that, Smiley would ante up money on him as long as he had a red.[5] Smiley was monstrous proud of his frog, and well he might be, for fellers that had traveled and been everywheres, all said he laid over any frog that ever *they* see.

"Well, Smiley kep' the beast in a little lattice box, and he used to fetch him downtown sometimes and lay for a bet. One day a feller—a stranger in the camp, he was—come acrost him with his box, and says:

" 'What might it be that you've got in the box?'

"And Smiley says, sorter indifferent-like, 'It might be a parrot, or it might be a canary, maybe, but it ain't—it's only just a frog.'

"And the feller took it, and looked at it careful, and turned it round this way and that, and says, 'H'm—so 'tis. Well, what's *he* good for?'

" 'Well,' Smiley says, easy and careless, 'he's good enough for *one* thing, I should judge—he can outjump any frog in Calaveras County.'

"The feller took the box again, and took another long, particular look, and give it back to Smiley, and says, very deliberate, 'Well,' he says, 'I don't see no p'ints about that frog that's any better'n any other frog.'

" 'Maybe you don't,' Smiley says. 'Maybe you understand frogs and maybe you don't understand 'em; maybe you've had experience, and maybe you ain't only a amature, as it were. Anyways, I've got *my* opinion, and I'll resk forty dollars that he can outjump any frog in Calaveras County.'

"And the feller studied a minute, and then says, kinder sadlike, 'Well, I'm only a stranger here, and I ain't got no frog; but if I had a frog, I'd bet you.'

"And then Smiley says, 'That's all right—that's all right—if you'll hold my box a minute, I'll go and get you a frog.' And so the feller took the box, and put up his forty dollars along with Smiley's, and set down to wait.

"So he set there a good while thinking and thinking to himself, and then he got the frog out and prized his mouth open and took a teaspoon and filled him full of quail-shot—filled him pretty near up to his chin—and set him on the floor. Smiley he went to the swamp and slopped around in the mud for a long time, and finally he ketched a frog, and fetched him in, and give him to this feller, and says:

" 'Now, if you're ready, set him alongside of Dan'l, with his fore paws just even with Dan'l's, and I'll give the word.' Then he says,

5. A single (red) penny.

'One—two—three—*git!*' and him and the feller touched up the frogs from behind, and the new frog hopped off lively, but Dan'l give a heave, and hysted up his shoulders—so—like a Frenchman, but it warn't no use—he couldn't budge; he was planted as solid as a church, and he couldn't no more stir than if he was anchored out. Smiley was a good deal surprised, and he was disgusted too, but he didn't have no idea what the matter was, of course.

"The feller took the money and started away; and when he was going out at the door, he sorter jerked his thumb over his shoulder —so—at Dan'l, and says again, very deliberate, 'Well,' he says, 'I don't see no p'ints about that frog that's any better'n any other frog.'

"Smiley he stood scratching his head and looking down at Dan'l a long time, and at last he says, 'I do wonder what in the nation that frog throw'd off for—I wonder if there ain't something the matter with him—he 'pears to look mighty baggy, somehow.' And he ketched Dan'l by the nape of the neck, and hefted him, and says, 'Why blame my cats if he don't weigh five pound!'" and turned him upside down and he belched out a double handful of shot. And then he see how it was, and he was the maddest man—he set the frog down and took out after that feller, but he never ketched him. And—"

[Here Simon Wheeler heard his name called from the front yard, and got up to see what was wanted.] And turning to me as he moved away, he said: "Just set where you are, stranger, and rest easy—I ain't going to be gone a second."

But, by your leave, I did not think that a continuation of the history of the enterprising vagabond *Jim* Smiley would be likely to afford me much information concerning the Rev. *Leonidas* W. Smiley, and so I started away.

At the door I met the sociable Wheeler returning, and he button-holed me and recommended:

"Well, thish-yer Smiley had a yaller one-eyed cow that didn't have no tail, only just a short stump like a bannanner, and—"

However, lacking both time and inclination, I did not wait to hear about the afflicted cow, but took my leave.

1867

WILLIAM FAULKNER

Spotted Horses

Yes, sir. Flem Snopes has filled that whole country full of spotted horses. You can hear folks running them all day and all night, whooping and hollering, and the horses running back and forth across them little wooden bridges ever now and then kind of like thunder. Here I was this morning pretty near halfway to town, with the team ambling along and me setting in the buckboard about half asleep, when all of a sudden something come swurging[1] up outen the bushes and jumped the road clean, without touching hoof to it. It flew right over my team, big as a billboard and flying through the air like a hawk. It taken me thirty minutes to stop my team and untangle the harness and the buckboard and hitch them up again.

That Flem Snopes. I be dog if he ain't a case, now. One morning about ten years ago, the boys was just getting settled down on Varner's porch for a little talk and tobacco, when here come Flem out from behind the counter, with his coat off and his hair all parted like he might have been clerking for Varner for ten years already. Folks all knowed him; it was a big family of them about five miles down the bottom. That year, at least. Share-cropping. They never stayed on any place over a year. Then they would move on to another place, with the chap or maybe the twins of that year's litter. It was a regular nest of them. But Flem. The rest of them stayed tenant farmers, moving ever year, but here come Flem one day, walking out from behind Jody Varner's counter like he owned it. And he wasn't there but a year or two before folks knowed that, if him and Jody was both still in that store in ten years more, it would be Jody clerking for Flem Snopes. Why, that fellow could make a nickel where it wasn't but four cents to begin with. He skun[2] me in two trades, myself, and the fellow that can do that, I just hope he'll get rich before I do; that's all.

All right. So here Flem was, clerking at Varner's, making a nickel here and there and not telling nobody about it. No, sir. Folks never knowed when Flem got the better of somebody lessen the fellow he beat told it. He'd just set there in the store-chair, chewing his tobacco and keeping his own business to hisself, until about a week later we'd find out it was somebody else's business he was keeping to hisself—provided the fellow he trimmed was mad enough to tell it. That's Flem.

We give him ten years to own everthing Jody Varner had. But he never waited no ten years. I reckon you-all know that gal of Uncle Billy Varner's, the youngest one; Eula. Jody's sister. Ever Sunday ever yellow-wheeled buggy and curried riding horse in that country would be hitched to Bill Varner's fence, and the young bucks setting on the porch, swarming around Eula like bees around a honey pot. One of these here kind of big, soft-looking gals that could giggle richer than plowed newground. Wouldn't none of them leave before the others, and so they would set there on the porch until time to go home, with some of them with nine and ten miles to ride and then get up tomorrow and go back to the field. So they would all leave together and they would ride in a clump down to the creek ford and hitch them curried horses and yellow-wheeled buggies and get out and fight one another. Then they would get in the buggies again and go on home.

Well, one day about a year ago, one of them yellow-wheeled buggies and one of them curried saddle-horses quit this country. We heard they was heading for Texas. The next day Uncle Billy and

1. Surging.

2. Skinned, cheated.

Eula and Flem come in to town in Uncle Bill's surrey, and when they come back, Flem and Eula was married. And on the next day we heard that two more of them yellow-wheeled buggies had left the country. They mought have gone to Texas, too. It's a big place.

Anyway, about a month after the wedding, Flem and Eula went to Texas, too. They was gone pretty near a year. Then one day last month, Eula come back, with a baby. We figgered up, and we decided that it was as well-growed a three-months-old baby as we ever see. It can already pull up on a chair. I reckon Texas makes big men quick, being a big place. Anyway, if it keeps on like it started, it'll be chewing tobacco and voting time it's eight years old.

And so last Friday here come Flem himself. He was on a wagon with another fellow. The other fellow had one of these two-gallon hats and a ivory-handled pistol and a box of gingersnaps sticking out of his hind pocket, and tied to the tailgate of the wagon was about two dozen of them Texas ponies, hitched to one another with barbed wire. They was colored like parrots and they was quiet as doves, and ere a one of them would kill you quick as a rattlesnake. Nere a one of them had two eyes the same color, and nere a one of them had ever see a bridle, I reckon; and when that Texas man got down offen the wagon and walked up to them to show how gentle they was, one of them cut his vest clean offen him, same as with a razor.

Flem had done already disappeared; he had went on to see his wife, I reckon, and to see if that ere baby had done gone on to the field to help Uncle Billy plow, maybe. It was the Texas man that taken the horses on to Mrs. Littlejohn's lot. He had a litttle trouble at first, when they come to the gate, because they hadn't never see a fence before, and when he finally got them in and taken a pair of wire cutters and unhitched them and got them into the barn and poured some shell corn into the trough, they durn nigh tore down the barn. I reckon they thought that shell corn was bugs, maybe. So he left them in the lot and he announced that the auction would begin at sunup tomorrow.

That night we was setting on Mrs. Littlejohn's porch. You-all mind the moon was nigh full that night, and we could watch them spotted varmints swirling along the fence and back and forth across the lot same as minnows in a pond. And then now and then they would all kind of huddle up against the barn and rest themselves by biting and kicking one another. We would hear a squeal, and then a set of hoofs would go Bam! against the barn, like a pistol. It sounded just like a fellow with a pistol, in a nest of cattymounts,[3] taking his time.

II

It wasn't ere[4] a man knowed yet if Flem owned them things or not. They just knowed one thing: that they wasn't never going to know for sho if Flem did or not, or if maybe he didn't just get on that wagon at the edge of town, for the ride or not. Even Eck Snopes didn't know, Flem's own cousin. But wasn't nobody surprised at that. We knowed that Flem would skin Eck quick as he would ere a one of us.

3. Panthers.

4. There was not one.

They was there by sunup next morning, some of them come twelve and sixteen miles, with seed-money tied up in tobacco sacks in their overalls, standing along the fence, when the Texas man come out of Mrs. Littlejohn's after breakfast and clumb onto the gate post with that ere white pistol butt sticking outen his hind pocket. He taken a new box of gingersnaps outen his pocket and bit the end offen it like a cigar and spit out the paper, and said the auction was open. And still they was coming up in wagons and a horse-and-mule-back and hitching the teams across the road and coming to the fence. Flem wasn't nowhere in sight.

But he couldn't get them started. He begun to work on Eck, because Eck holp him last night to get them into the barn and feed them that shell corn. Eck got out jist in time. He come outen that barn like a chip of the crest of a busted dam of water, and clumb into the wagon just in time.

He was working on Eck when Henry Armstid come up in his wagon. Eck was saying he was skeered to bid on one of them, because he might get it, and the Texas man says, "Them ponies? Them little horses?" He clumb down offen the gate post and went toward the horses. They broke and run, and him following them, kind of chirping to them, with his hand out like he was fixing to catch a fly, until he got three or four of them cornered. Then he jumped into them, and then we couldn't see nothing for a while because of the dust. It was a big cloud of it, and them blare-eyed, spotted things swoaring outen it twenty foot to a jump, in forty directions without counting up. Then the dust settled and there they was, that Texas man and the horse. He had its head twisted clean around like a owl's head. Its legs was braced and it was trembling like a new bride and groaning like a saw mill, and him holding its head wrung clean around on its neck so it was snuffing sky. "Look it over," he says, with his heels dug too and that white pistol sticking outen his pocket and his neck swole up like a spreading adder's until you could just tell what he was saying, cussing the horse and talking to us all at once: "Look him over, the fiddle-headed son of fourteen fathers. Try him, buy him; you will get the best—" Then it was all dust again, and we couldn't see nothing but spotted hide and mane, and that ere Texas man's boot-heels like a couple of walnuts on two strings, and after a while that two-gallon hat come sailing out like a fat old hen crossing a fence.

When the dust settled again, he was just getting outen the far fence corner, brushing himself off. He come and got his hat and brushed it off and come and clumb onto the gate post again. He was breathing hard. He taken the gingersnap box outen his pocket and et one, breathing hard. The hammer-head horse was still running round and round the lot like a merry-go-round at a fair. That was when Henry Armstid come shoving up to the gate in them patched overalls and one of them dangle-armed shirts of hisn. Hadn't nobody noticed him until then. We was all watching the Texas man and the horses. Even Mrs. Littlejohn; she had done come out and built a fire under the washpot in her back yard, and she would stand at the fence a while and then go back into the house and come out again with a armful of wash and stand at the fence again. Well, here come Henry shoving up, and then we see Mrs. Armstid right behind him, in that ere faded wrapper and sunbonnet and them tennis shoes. "Git on back to that wagon," Henry says.

"Henry," she says.

"Here, boys," the Texas man says; "make room for missus to git up and see. Come on, Henry," he says; "here's your chance to buy that saddle-horse missus has been wanting. What about ten dollars, Henry?"

"Henry," Mrs. Armstid says. She put her hand on Henry's arm. Henry knocked her hand down.

"Git on back to that wagon, like I told you," he says.

Mrs. Armstid never moved. She stood behind Henry, with her hands rolled into her dress, not looking at nothing. "He hain't no more despair[5] than to buy one of them things," she says. "And us not five dollars ahead of the porehouse, he hain't no more despair." It was the truth, too. They ain't never made more than a bare living offen that place of theirs, and them with four chaps and the very clothes they wears she earns by weaving by the firelight at night while Henry's asleep.

"Shut your mouth and git on back to that wagon," Henry says. "Do you want I taken a wagon stake to you here in the big road?"

Well, that Texas man taken one look at her. Then he begun on Eck again, like Henry wasn't even there. But Eck was skeered. "I can git me a snapping turtle or a water moccasin for nothing. I ain't going to buy none."

So the Texas man said he would give Eck a horse. "To start the auction, and because you holp me last night. If you'll start the bidding on the next horse," he says, "I'll give you that fiddle-head horse."

I wish you could have seen them, standing there with their seed-money in their pockets, watching that Texas man give Eck Snopes a live horse, all fixed to call him a fool if he taken it or not. Finally Eck says he'll take it. "Only I just starts the bidding," he says. "I don't have to buy the next one lessen I ain't overtopped." The Texas man said all right, and Eck bid a dollar on the next one, with Henry Armstid standing there with his mouth already open, watching Eck and the Texas man like a mad dog or something. "A dollar," Eck says.

The Texas man looked at Eck. His mouth was already open too, like he had started to say something and what he was going to say had up and died on him. "A dollar?" he says. "One dollar? You mean, *one* dollar, Eck?"

"Durn it," Eck says; "two dollars, then."

Well, sir, I wish you could a seen that Texas man. He taken out that gingersnap box and held it up and looked into it, careful, like it might have been a diamond ring in it, or a spider. Then he throwed it away and wiped his face with a bandanna. "Well," he says. "Well. Two dollars. Two dollars. Is your pulse all right, Eck?" he says. "Do you have ager-sweats[6] at night, maybe?" he says. "Well," he says, "I got to take it. But are you boys going to stand there and see Eck

5. To spare.

6. Cold sweats, as in malaria.

get two horses at a dollar a head?"

That done it. I be dog if he wasn't nigh as smart as Flem Snopes. He hadn't no more than got the words outen his mouth before here was Henry Armstid, waving his hand. "Three dollars," Henry says. Mrs. Armstid tried to hold him again. He knocked her hand off, shoving up to the gate post.

"Mister," Mrs. Armstid says, "we got chaps in the house and not corn to feed the stock. We got five dollars I earned my chaps a-weaving after dark, and him snoring in the bed. And he hain't no more despair."

"Henry bids three dollars," the Texas man says. "Raise him a dollar, Eck, and the horse is yours."

"Henry," Mrs. Armstid says.

"Raise him, Eck," the Texas man says.

"Four dollars," Eck says.

"Five dollars," Henry says, shaking his fist. He shoved up right under the gate post. Mrs. Armstid was looking at the Texas man too.

"Mister," she says, "if you take that five dollars I earned my chaps a-weaving for one of them things, it'll be a curse onto you and yourn during all the time of man."

But it wasn't no stopping Henry. He had shoved up, waving his fist at the Texas man. He opened it; the money was in nickels and quarters, and one dollar bill that looked like a cow's cud. "Five dollars," he says. "And the man that raises it'll have to beat my head off, or I'll beat hisn."

"All right," the Texas man says. "Five dollars is bid. But don't you shake your hand at me."

III

It taken till nigh sundown before the last one was sold. He got them hotted up once and the bidding got up to seven dollars and a quarter, but most of them went around three or four dollars, him setting on the gate post and picking the horses out one at a time by mouth-word, and Mrs. Littlejohn pumping up and down at the tub and stopping and coming to the fence for a while and going back to the tub again. She had done got done too, and the wash was hung on the line in the back yard, and we could smell supper cooking. Finally they was all sold; he swapped the last two and the wagon for a buckboard.

We was all kind of tired, but Henry Armstid looked more like a mad dog than ever. When he bought, Mrs. Armstid had went back to the wagon, setting in it behind them two rabbit-sized, bone-pore mules, and the wagon itself looking like it would fall all to pieces soon as the mules moved. Henry hadn't even waited to pull it outen the road; it was still in the middle of the road and her setting in it, not looking at nothing, ever since this morning.

Henry was right up against the gate. He went up to the Texas man. "I bought a horse and I paid cash," Henry says. "And yet you expect me to stand around here until they are all sold before I can get my horse. I'm going to take my horse outen that lot."

The Texas man looked at Henry. He talked like he might have

been asking for a cup of coffee at the table. "Take your horse," he says.

Then Henry quit looking at the Texas man. He begun to swallow, holding onto the gate. "Ain't you going to help me?" he says.

"It ain't my horse," the Texas man says.

Henry never looked at the Texas man again, he never looked at nobody. "Who'll help me catch my horse?" he says. Never nobody said nothing. "Bring the plowline," Henry says. Mrs. Armstid got outen the wagon and brought the plowline. The Texas man got down offen the post. The woman made to pass him, carrying the rope.

"Don't you go in there, missus," the Texas man says.

Henry opened the gate. He didn't look back. "Come on here," he says.

"Don't you go in there, missus," the Texas man says.

Mrs. Armstid wasn't looking at nobody, neither, with her hands across her middle, holding the rope. "I reckon I better," she says. Her and Henry went into the lot. The horses broke and run. Henry and Mrs. Armstid followed.

"Get him into the corner," Henry says. They got Henry's horse cornered finally, and Henry taken the rope, but Mrs. Armstid let the horse get out. They hemmed it up again, but Mrs. Armstid let it get out again, and Henry turned and hit her with the rope. "Why didn't you head him back?" Henry says. He hit her again. "Why didn't you?" It was about that time I looked around and see Flem Snopes standing there.

It was the Texas man that done something. He moved fast for a big man. He caught the rope before Henry could hit the third time, and Henry whirled and made like he would jump at the Texas man. But he never jumped. The Texas man went and taken Henry's arm and led him outen the lot. Mrs. Armstid come behind them and the Texas man taken some money outen his pocket and he give it into Mrs. Armstid's hand. "Get him into the wagon and take him on home," the Texas man says, like he might have been telling them he enjoyed his supper.

Then here come Flem. "What's that for, Buck?" Flem says.

"Thinks he bought one of them ponies," the Texas man says. "Get him on away, missus."

But Henry wouldn't go. "Give him back that money," he says. "I bought that horse and I aim to have him if I have to shoot him."

And there was Flem, standing there with his hands in his pockets, chewing, like he had just happened to be passing.

"You take your money and I take my horse," Henry says. "Give it back to him," he says to Mrs. Armstid.

"You don't own no horse of mine," the Texas man says. "Get him on home, missus."

Then Henry seen Flem. "You got something to do with these horses," he says. "I bought one. Here's the money for it." He taken the bill outen Mrs. Armstid's hand. He offered it to Flem. "I bought one. Ask him. Here. Here's the money," he says, giving the bill to Flem.

When Flem taken the money, the Texas man dropped the rope he had snatched outen Henry's hand. He had done sent Eck Snopes's boy up to the store for another box of gingersnaps, and he taken the box of gingersnaps, and he taken the box outen his pocket and looked into it. It was empty and he dropped it on the ground. "Mr. Snopes will have your money for you tomorrow," he says to Mrs. Armstid. "You can get it from him tomorrow. He don't own no horse. You get him into the wagon and get him on home." Mrs. Armstid went back to the wagon and got in. "Where's that ere buckboard I bought?" the Texas man says. It was after sundown then. And then Mrs. Littlejohn come out on the porch and rung the supper bell.

IV

I come on in and et supper. Mrs. Littlejohn would bring in a pan of bread or something, then she would go out to the porch a minute and come back and tell us. The Texas man had hitched his team to the buckboard he had swapped them last two horses for, and him and Flem had gone, and then she told that the rest of them that never had ropes had went back to the store with I. O. Snopes to get some ropes, and wasn't nobody at the gate but Henry Armstid, and Mrs. Armstid setting in the wagon in the road, and Eck Snopes and that boy of hisn. "I don't care how many of them fool men gets killed by them things," Mrs. Littlejohn says, "but I ain't going to let Eck Snopes take that boy into that lot again." So she went down to the gate, but she come back without the boy or Eck neither.

"It ain't no need to worry about that boy," I says. "He's charmed." He was right behind Eck last night when Eck went to help feed them. The whole drove of them jumped clean over that boy's head and never touched him. It was Eck that touched him. Eck snatched him into the wagon and taken a rope and frailed the tar outen him.

So I had done et and went to my room and was undressing, long as I had a long trip to make next day; I was trying to sell a machine to Mrs. Bundren up past Whiteleaf; when Henry Armstid opened that gate and went in by hisself. They couldn't make him wait for the balance of them to get back with their ropes. Eck Snopes said he tried to make Henry wait, but Henry wouldn't do it. Eck said Henry walked right up to them and that when they broke, they run clean over Henry like a hay-mow breaking down. Eck said he snatched that boy of hisn out of the way just in time and that them things went through that gate like a creek flood and into the wagons and teams hitched side the road, busting wagon tongues and snapping harness like it was fishing line, with Mrs. Armstid still setting in their wagon in the middle of it like something carved outen wood. Then they scattered, wild horses and tame mules with pieces of harness and single trees dangling offen them, both ways up and down the road.

"There goes ourn, paw!" Eck says his boy said. "There it goes, into Mrs. Littlejohn's house." Eck says it run right up the steps and into the house like a boarder late for supper. I reckon so. Anyway, I was in my room, in my underclothes, with one sock on and one sock in my hand, leaning out the window when the commotion busted out, when I heard something run into the melodeon in the hall; it sounded like a railroad engine. Then the door to my room come sailing in like when you throw a tin bucket top into the wind and I looked over my shoulder and see something that looked like a fourteen-foot pinwheel a-blaring its eyes at me. It had to blare them fast, because I was already done jumped out the window.

I reckon it was anxious, too. I reckon it hadn't never seen barbed wire or shell corn before, but I know it hadn't never seen underclothes before, or maybe it was a sewing-machine agent it hadn't never seen. Anyway, it swirled and turned to run back up the hall and outen the house, when it met Eck Snopes and that boy just coming in, carrying a rope. It swirled again and run down the hall and out the back door just in time to meet Mrs. Littlejohn. She had just gathered up the clothes she had washed, and she was coming onto the back porch with a armful of washing in one hand and a scrubbing board in the other, when the horse skidded up to her, trying to stop and swirl again. It never taken Mrs. Littlejohn no time a-tall.

"Git outen here, you son," she says. She hit it across the face with the scrubbing board; that ere scrubbing board split as neat as ere a axe could have done it, and when the horse swirled to run back up the hall, she hit it again with what was left of the scrubbing board, not on the head this time. "And stay out," she says.

Eck and that boy was halfway down the hall by this time. I reckon that horse looked like a pinwheel to Eck too. "Git to hell outen here, Ad!" Eck says. Only there wasn't time. Eck dropped flat on his face, but the boy never moved. The boy was about a yard tall maybe, in overhalls just like Eck's; that horse swoared over his head without touching a hair. I saw that, because I was just coming back up the front steps, still carrying that ere sock and still in my underclothes, when the horse come onto the porch again. It taken one look at me and swirled again and run to the end of the porch and jumped the banisters and the lot fence like a hen-hawk and lit in the lot running and went out the gate again and jumped eight or ten upside-down wagons and went on down the road. It was a full moon then. Mrs. Armstid was still setting in the wagon like she had done been carved outen wood and left there and forgot.

That horse. It ain't never missed a lick. It was going about forty miles a hour when it come to the bridge over the creek. It would have had a clear road, but it so happened that Vernon Tull was already using the bridge when it got there. He was coming back from town; he hadn't heard about the auction; him and his wife and three daughters and Mrs. Tull's aunt, all setting in chairs in the wagon bed, and all asleep, including the mules. They waked up when the horse hit the bridge one time, but Tull said the first he knew was when the mules tried to turn the wagon around in the middle of the bridge and he seen that spotted varmint run right twixt the mules and run up the wagon tongue like a squirrel. He said he just had time to hit it across the face with his whip-stock, because about that time the mules turned the wagon around on that ere one-way bridge and that horse clumb across one of the mules and jumped down onto the bridge again and went on, with Vernon standing up in the wagon and kicking at it.

Tull said the mules turned in the harness and clumb back into the wagon too, with Tull trying to beat them out again, with the reins wrapped around his wrist. After that he says all he seen was overturned chairs and womenfolks' legs and white drawers shining in the moonlight, and his mules and that spotted horse going on up the road like a ghost.

The mules jerked Tull outen the wagon and drug him a spell on the bridge before the reins broke. They thought at first that he was dead, and while they was kneeling around him, picking the bridge splinters outen him, here come Eck and that boy, still carrying the rope. They was running and breathing a little hard. "Where'd he go?" Eck says.

V

I went back and got my pants and shirt and shoes on just in time to go and help get Henry Armstid outen the trash in the lot. I be dog[7] if he didn't look like he was dead, with his head hanging back and his teeth showing in the moonlight, and a little rim of white under his eyelids. We could still hear them horses, here and there; hadn't none of them got more than four–five miles away yet, not knowing the country, I reckon. So we could hear them and folks yelling now and then: "Whooey. Head him!"

We toted Henry into Mrs. Littlejohn's. She was in the hall; she hadn't put down the armful of clothes. She taken one look at us, and she laid down the busted scrubbing board and taken up the lamp and opened a empty door. "Bring him in here," she says.

We toted him in and laid him on the bed. Mrs. Littlejohn set the lamp on the dresser, still carrying the clothes. "I'll declare, you men," she says. Our shadows was way up the wall, tiptoeing too; we could hear ourselves breathing. "Better get his wife," Mrs. Littlejohn says. She went out, carrying the clothes.

"I reckon we had," Quick says. "Go get her, somebody."

"Whyn't you go?" Winterbottom says.

"Let Ernest git her," Durley says. "He lives neighbors with them."

Ernest went to fetch her. I be dog if Henry didn't look like he was dead. Mrs. Littlejohn come back, with a kettle and some towels. She went to work on Henry, and then Mrs. Armstid and Ernest come in. Mrs. Armstid come to the foot of the bed and stood there, with her hands rolled into her apron, watching what Mrs. Littlejohn was doing, I reckon.

"You men get outen the way," Mrs. Littlejohn says. "Git outside," she says. "See if you can't find something else to play with that will kill some more of you."

"Is he dead?" Winterbottom says.

"It ain't your fault if he ain't," Mrs. Littlejohn says. "Go tell Will Varner to come up here. I reckon a man ain't so different from a mule, come long come short. Except maybe a mule's got more sense."

We went to get Uncle Billy. It was a full moon. We could hear them, now and then, four mile away: "Whooey. Head him." The country was full of them, one on ever wooden bridge in the land, running across it like thunder: "Whooey. There he goes. Head him."

7. Darned.

We hadn't got far before Henry begun to scream. I reckon Mrs. Littlejohn's water had brung him to; anyway, he wasn't dead. We went on to Uncle Billy's. The house was dark. We called to him, and after a while the window opened and Uncle Billy put his head out, peart as a peckerwood,[8] listening. "Are they still trying to catch them durn rabbits?" he says.

He come down, with his britches on over his nightshirt and his suspenders dangling, carrying his horse-doctoring grip. "Yes, sir," he says, cocking his head like a woodpecker; "they're still a-trying."

We could hear Henry before we reached Mrs. Littlejohn's. He was going Ah-Ah-Ah. We stopped in the yard. Uncle Billy went on in. We could hear Henry. We stood in the yard, hearing them on the bridges, this-a-way and that: "Whooey. Whooey."

"Eck Snopes ought to caught hisn," Ernest says.

"Looks like he ought," Winterbottom said.

Henry was going Ah-Ah-Ah steady in the house; then he begun to scream. "Uncle Billy's started," Quick says. We looked into the hall. We could see the light where the door was. Then Mrs. Littlejohn come out.

"Will needs some help," she says. "You, Ernest. You'll do." Ernest went into the house.

"Hear them?" Quick said. "That one was on Four Mile bridge." We could hear them; it sounded like thunder a long way off; it didn't last long:

"Whooey."

We could hear Henry: "Ah-Ah-Ah-Ah-Ah."

"They are both started now," Winterbottom says. "Ernest too."

That was early in the night. Which was a good thing, because it taken a long night for folks to chase them things right and for Henry to lay there and holler, being as Uncle Billy never had none of this here chloryfoam to set Henry's leg with. So it was considerate in Flem to get them started early. And what do you reckon Flem's com-ment was?

That's right. Nothing. Because he wasn't there. Hadn't nobody see him since that Texas man left.

VI

That was Saturday night. I reckon Mrs. Armstid got home about daylight, to see about the chaps. I don't know where they thought her and Henry was. But lucky the oldest one was a gal, about twelve, big enough to take care of the little ones. Which she did for the next two days. Mrs. Armstid would nurse Henry all night and work in the kitchen for hern and Henry's keep, and in the afternoon she would drive home (it was about four miles) to see to the chaps. She would cook up a pot of victuals and leave it on the stove, and the gal would bar the house and keep the little ones quiet. I would hear Mrs. Littlejohn and Mrs. Armstid talking in the kitchen. "How are the chaps making out?" Mrs. Littlejohn says.

"All right," Mrs. Armstid says.

8. Woodpecker.

"Don't they git skeered at night?" Mrs. Littlejohn says.

"Ina May bars the door when I leave," Mrs. Armstid says. "She's got the axe in bed with her. I reckon she can make out."

I reckon they did. And I reckon Mrs. Armstid was waiting for Flem to come back to town; hadn't nobody seen him until this morning; to get her money the Texas man said Flem was keeping for her. Sho. I reckon she was.

Anyway, I heard Mrs. Armstid and Mrs. Littlejohn talking in the kitchen this morning while I was eating breakfast. Mrs. Littlejohn had just told Mrs. Armstid that Flem was in town. "You can ask him for that five dollars," Mrs. Littlejohn says.

"You reckon he'll give it to me?" Mrs. Armstid says.

Mrs. Littlejohn was washing dishes, washing them like a man, like they was made out of iron. "No," she says. "But asking him won't do no hurt. It might shame him. I don't reckon it will, but it might."

"If he wouldn't give it back, it ain't no use to ask," Mrs. Armstid says.

"Suit yourself," Mrs. Littlejohn says. "It's your money."

I could hear the dishes.

"Do you reckon he might give it back to me?" Mrs. Armstid says. "That Texas man said he would. He said I could get it from Mr. Snopes later."

"Then go and ask him for it," Mrs. Littlejohn says.

I could hear the dishes.

"He won't give it back to me," Mrs. Armstid says.

"All right," Mrs. Littlejohn says. "Don't ask him for it, then."

I could hear the dishes; Mrs. Armstid was helping. "You don't reckon he would, do you?" she says. Mrs. Littlejohn never said nothing. It sounded like she was throwing the dishes at one another. "Maybe I better go and talk to Henry about it," Mrs. Armstid says.

"I would," Mrs. Littlejohn says. I be dog if it didn't sound like she had two plates in her hands, beating them together. "Then Henry can buy another five-dollar horse with it. Maybe he'll buy one next time that will out and out kill him. If I thought that, I'd give you back the money, myself."

"I reckon I better talk to him first," Mrs. Armstid said. Then it sounded like Mrs. Littlejohn taken up all the dishes and throwed them at the cookstove, and I come away.

That was this morning. I had been up to Bundren's and back, and I thought that things would have kind of settled down. So after breakfast, I went up to the store. And there was Flem, setting in the store chair and whittling, like he might not have ever moved since he come to clerk for Jody Varner. I. O. was leaning in the door, in his shirt sleeves and with his hair parted too, same as Flem was before he turned the clerking job over to I. O. It's a funny thing about them Snopes: they all looks alike, yet there ain't ere a two of them that claims brothers. They're always just cousins, like Flem and Eck and Flem and I. O. Eck was there too, squatting against the wall, him and that boy, eating cheese and crackers outen a sack; they told me that Eck hadn't been home a-tall. And that Lon Quick hadn't got back to town, even. He followed his horse clean down to Samson's

Bridge, with a wagon and a camp outfit. Eck finally caught one of hisn. It run into a blind lane at Freeman's and Eck and the boy taken and tied their rope across the end of the lane, about three foot high. The horse come to the end of the lane and whirled and run back without ever stopping. Eck says it never seen the rope a-tall. He says it looked just like one of these here Christmas pinwheels. "Didn't it try to run again?" I says.

"No," Eck says, eating a bit of cheese offen his knife blade. "Just kicked some."

"Kicked some?" I says.

"It broke its neck," Eck says.

Well, they was squatting there, about six of them, talking, talking at Flem; never nobody knowed yet if Flem had ere a interest in them horses or not. So finally I come right out and asked him. "Flem's done skun all of us so much," I says, "that we're proud of him. Come on, Flem," I says, "how much did you and that Texas man make offen them horses? You can tell us. Ain't nobody here but Eck that bought one of them; the others ain't got back to town yet, and Eck's your own cousin; he'll be proud to hear, too. How much did you-all make?"

They was all whittling, not looking at Flem, making like they was studying. But you could a heard a pin drop. And I. O. He had been rubbing his back up and down on the door, but he stopped now, watching Flem like a pointing dog. Flem finished cutting the sliver offen his stick. He spit across the porch, into the road. " 'Twarn't none of my horses," he says.

I. O. cackled, like a hen, slapping his legs with both hands. "You boys might just as well quit trying to get ahead of Flem," he said.

Well, about that time I see Mrs. Armstid come outen Mrs. Littlejohn's gate, coming up the road. I never said nothing. I says, "Well, if a man can't take care of himself in a trade, he can't blame the man that trims him."

Flem never said nothing, trimming at the stick. He hadn't seen Mrs. Armstid. "Yes, sir," I says. "A fellow like Henry Armstid ain't got nobody but hisself to blame."

"Course he ain't," I. O. says. He ain't seen her, neither. "Henry Armstid's a born fool. Always is been. If Flem hadn't a got his money, somebody else would."

We looked at Flem. He never moved. Mrs. Armstid come on up the road.

"That's right," I says. "But, come to think of it, Henry never bought no horse." We looked at Flem; you could a heard a match drop. "That Texas man told her to get that five dollars back from Flem next day. I reckon Flem's done already taken that money to Mrs. Littlejohn's and give it to Mrs. Armstid."

We watched Flem. I. O. quit rubbing his back against the door again. After a while Flem raised his head and spit across the porch, into the dust. I. O. cackled, just like a hen. "Ain't he a beating fellow, now?" I. O. says.

Mrs. Armstid was getting closer, so I kept on talking, watching to see if Flem would look up and see her. But he never looked up. I went on talking about Tull, about how he was going to sue Flem, and Flem setting there, whittling his stick, not saying nothing else after he said they wasn't none of his horses.

Then I. O. happened to look around. He seen Mrs. Armstid. "Psssst!" he says. Flem looked up. "Here she comes!" I. O. says. "Go out the back. I'll tell her you done went in to town today."

But Flem never moved. He just set there, whittling, and we watched Mrs. Armstid come up onto the porch, in that ere faded sunbonnet and wrapper and them tennis shoes that made a kind of hissing noise on the porch. She come onto the porch and stopped, her hands rolled into her dress in front, not looking at nothing.

"He said Saturday," she says, "that he wouldn't sell Henry no horse. He said I could get the money from you."

Flem looked up. The knife never stopped. It went on trimming off a sliver same as if he was watching it. "He taken that money off with him when he left," Flem says.

Mrs. Armstid never looked at nothing. We never looked at her, neither, except the boy of Eck's. He had a half-et cracker in his hand, watching her, chewing.

"He said Henry hadn't bought no horse," Mrs. Armstid says. "He said for me to get the money from you today."

"I reckon he forgot about it," Flem said. "He taken that money off with him Saturday." He whittled again. I. O. kept on rubbing his back, slow. He licked his lips. After a while the woman looked up the road, where it went on up the hill, toward the graveyard. She looked up that way for a while, with that boy of Eck's watching her and I. O. rubbing his back slow against the door. Then she turned back toward the steps.

"I reckon it's time to get dinner started," she says.

"How's Henry this morning, Mrs. Armstid?" Winterbottom says.

She looked at Winterbottom; she almost stopped. "He's resting, I thank you kindly," she says.

Flem got up, outen the chair, putting his knife away. He spit across the porch. "Wait a minute, Mrs. Armstid," he says. She stopped again. She didn't look at him. Flem went on into the store, with I. O. done quit rubbing his back now, with his head craned after Flem, and Mrs. Armstid standing there with her hands rolled into her dress, not looking at nothing. A wagon come up the road and passes; it was Freeman, on the way to town. Then Flem come out again, with I. O. still watching him. Flem had one of these little striped sacks of Jody Varner's candy; I bet he still owes Jody that nickel, too. He put the sack into Mrs. Armstid's hand, like he would have put it into a hollow stump. He spit again across the porch. "A little sweetening for the chaps," he says.

"You're right kind," Mrs. Armstid says. She held the sack of candy in her hand, not looking at nothing. Eck's boy was watching the sack, the half-et cracker in his hand; he wasn't chewing now. He watched Mrs. Armstid roll the sack into her apron. "I reckon I better get on back and help with dinner," she says. She turned and went back across the porch. Flem set down in the chair again and opened his knife. He spit across the porch again, past Mrs. Armstid where she hadn't went down the steps yet. Then she went on, in that ere sunbonnet and wrapper all the same color, back down the road toward Mrs. Littlejohn's. You couldn't see her dress move, like a natural woman walking. She looked like a old snag still standing up and moving along on a high water. We watched her turn in at Mrs. Littlejohn's and go outen sight. Flem was whittling. I. O. begun to rub his back on the door. Then he begun to cackle, just like a durn hen.

"You boys might just as well quit trying," I. O. says. "You can't git ahead of Flem. You can't touch him. Ain't he a sight, now?"

I be dog if he ain't. If I had brung a herd of wild cattymounts into town and sold them to my neighbors and kinfolks, they would have lynched me. Yes, sir.

p. 1931

11 SETTING

All stories, like all individuals, are obviously part of their time, place, and culture, and are conditioned by them. The more we understand of the historical and cultural context, the more we may come to understand about a story (or about a person). The close relationship between historical, geographical, and cultural context—or **setting**—on the one hand, and people and events on the other, offers the author a means of reinforcing and communicating his or her vision and the reader therefore a means of understanding more fully the details of the story.

Setting is an important aspect even of the very first story in this collection. Montresor's character and plot can be called Machiavellian (characterized by subtle or unscrupulous cunning; after the Italian Renaissance politician and writer Niccolò Machiavelli, 1469–1527); no wonder Poe's story is set in Renaissance Italy. The Puritan Goodman Brown lives in the reign of King William (1689–1702) in Salem, Massachusetts, where in 1692 the famous witch trials were held—what better place for a story whose subject is a witches' meeting and whose theme is man's natural depravity? Not all of us who live in Atlanta will admit that it is a fit place for a fictional journey through Hell (as in *The Artificial Nigger*), or that rural Georgia (the scene of the novel *Deliverance*) is a fit image for the Garden of Eden, but the traditional image of rural innocence and virtue and urban sinfulness is long established and widely known in our culture, and even those of us who do not accept its validity understand its import. An *English* spinster seems (or seemed) much more prudish and virginal than just any old spinster, Italian lovers seem more sensual than Anglo-Saxon ones, and *Our Friend Judith* takes advantage of that cultural convention. Though few of us know Yalta, Chekhov has little trouble making us understand the contrast of that semitropical resort on the sea, whose very fruit, the melon, is sensuous, and the frozen world of Moscow, of everyday routine and emotions, of fish that's not quite fresh. And in Conrad's *Heart of Darkness* (see below, "Preface to the Novel") the journey to the interior of the Dark Continent and the journey into the dark interior recesses of the human heart are parallel.

I've mentioned a number of other stories here toward the end of our discussions to emphasize what I hope you long ago understood: almost any story can be put in almost any chapter in this book; almost every aspect of fiction can be seen in almost any story. The stories here illustrate how geographical, historical, and cultural contexts may inform a work, but they are not exclusively local-color, historical, or sociological stories.

Beyond the Bayou, like *Heart of Darkness*, makes parallel or analogous psychic areas and geographical ones. La Folle, frightened "out of her senses" during the Civil War, deadens large areas of her emotional life and restricts herself to a narrow corner of her small world. Another trauma opens her to life, and she crosses into the territory "beyond the bayou." Besides this central analogy, the cultural context—the complex racial mix of Louisiana, which made race relations even in the time of slavery and Reconstruction unique, and even the physical nature of the bayou country—subtly modifies and defines the characters and their actions. While we can learn a good deal about that context from the story, we can also learn a good deal about the story from increased awareness of and knowledge of the context.

Charlie, in *Babylon Revisited*, so reflects his historical and cultural context that it is difficult to say whether he is a symbol or a product of his time and nation and social set; is he merely representative, or does the story imply that one's life is virtually determined by and therefore a reflection of its context? During the prosperous, dissolute Roaring Twenties, Charlie was prosperous and dissolute; an American in Paris, he roared with the loudest. Now, in the depressed thirties, he, like the times, has sobered up. Many of the geographical and historical details in these two stories need footnotes in order for us more fully to understand the relation between the individuals and their background and even the authors and their assumptions (since the first story was written nearly a hundred years ago and the second almost fifty). Now, however, even white readers may understand more of what it means to be a black living in Harlem in the mid-twentieth century than such readers would have a hundred years ago or will a hundred years from now. There is some question whether a white reader ever can understand a story like *Sonny's Blues* as well as a black reader can, whether it is ever possible to make the imaginative leap across ethnic, cultural, or historical dividing lines with complete success. Surely detailed knowledge and a sympathetic imagination sensitized by literature may at least help us approach such understanding, and understanding other subjective visions of the world is, after all, what literature is all about.

KATE CHOPIN

Beyond the Bayou

The bayou curved like a crescent around the point of land on which La Folle's cabin stood. Between the stream and the hut lay a big abandoned field, where cattle were pastured when the bayou supplied them with water enough. Through the woods that spread back into unknown regions the woman had drawn an imaginary line, and past this circle she never stepped. This was the form of her only mania.

She was now a large, gaunt black woman, past thirty-five. Her real name was Jacqueline, but everyone on the plantation called her La Folle,[1] because in childhood she had been frightened literally "out of her senses," and had never wholly regained them.

It was when there had been skirmishing and sharpshooting all day in the woods. Evening was near when P'tit Maître,[2] black with powder and crimson with blood, had staggered into the cabin of Jacqueline's mother, his pursuers close at his heels. The sight had stunned her childish reason.

She dwelt alone in her solitary cabin, for the rest of the quarters had long since been removed beyond her sight and knowledge. She had more physical strength than most men, and made her patch of cotton and corn and tobacco like the best of them. But of the world beyond the bayou she had long known nothing, save what her morbid fancy conceived.

People at Bellissime had grown used to her and her way, and they thought nothing of it. Even when "Old Mis' " died, they did not wonder that La Folle had not crossed the bayou, but had stood upon her side of it, wailing and lamenting.

P'tit Maître was now the owner of Bellissime. He was a middle-aged man, with a family of beautiful daughters about him, and a little son whom La Folle loved as if he had been her own. She called him Chéri,[3] and so did every one else because she did.

None of the girls had ever been to her what Chéri was. They had each and all loved to be with her, and to listen to her wondrous stories of things that always happened "yonda, beyon' de bayou."

But none of them had stroked her black hand quite as Chéri did, nor rested their heads against her knee so confidingly, nor fallen asleep in her arms as he used to do. For Chéri hardly did such things

1. The crazy woman.
2. Little Master.
3. Darling.

now, since he had become the proud possessor of a gun, and had had his black curls cut off.

That summer—the summer Chéri gave La Folle two black curls tied with a knot of red ribbon—the water ran so low in the bayou that even the little children at Bellissime were able to cross it on foot, and the cattle were sent to pasture down by the river. La Folle was sorry whan they were gone, for she loved these dumb companions well, and liked to feel that they were there, and to hear them browsing by night up to her own enclosure.

It was Saturday afternoon, when the fields were deserted. The men had flocked to a neighboring village to do their week's trading, and the women were occupied with household affairs—La Folle as well as the others. It was then she mended and washed her handful of clothes, scoured her house, and did her baking.

In this last employment she never forgot Chéri. Today she had fashioned croquignoles[4] of the most fantastic and alluring shapes for him. So when she saw the boy come trudging across the old field with his gleaming little new rifle on his shoulder, she called out gaily to him, "Chéri! Chéri!"

But Chéri did not need the summons, for he was coming straight to her. His pockets all bulged out with almonds and raisins and an orange that he had secured for her from the very fine dinner which had been given that day up at his father's house.

He was a sunny-faced youngster of ten. When he had emptied his pockets, La Folle patted his round red cheek, wiped his soiled hands on her apron, and smoothed his hair. Then she watched him as, with his cakes in his hand, he crossed her strip of cotton back of the cabin, and disappeared into the wood.

He had boasted of the things he was going to do with his gun out there.

"You think they got plenty deer in the wood, La Folle?" he had inquired, with the calculating air of an experienced hunter.

"*Non, non!*" the woman laughed. "Don't you look fo' no deer, Chéri. Dat 's too big. But you bring La Folle one good fat squirrel fo' her dinner to-morrow, an' she goin' be satisfi'."

"One squirrel ain't a bit. I'll bring you mo' 'an one, La Folle," he had boasted pompously as he went away.

When the woman, an hour later, heard the report of the boy's rifle close to the wood's edge, she would have thought nothing of it if a sharp cry of distress had not followed the sound.

She withdrew her arms from the tub of suds in which they had been plunged, dried them upon her apron, and as quickly as her trembling limbs would bear her, hurried to the spot whence the ominous report had come.

It was as she feared. There she found Chéri stretched upon the ground, with his rifle beside him. He moaned piteously:

"I'm dead, La Folle! I'm dead! I'm gone!"

"*Non, non!*" she exclaimed resolutely, as she knelt beside him. "Put you' arm 'roun' La Folle's nake, Chéri. Dat's nuttin'; dat goin' be

4. Biscuits.

nuttin'." She lifted him in her powerful arms.

Chéri had carried his gun muzzle-downward. He had stumbled, he did not know how. He only knew that he had a ball lodged somewhere in his leg, and he thought that his end was at hand. Now, with his head upon the woman's shoulder, he moaned and wept with pain and fright.

"Oh, La Folle! La Folle! it hurt so bad! I can' stan' it, La Folle!"

"Don't cry, *mon bébé,*[5] *mon bébé, mon Chéri!*" the woman spoke soothingly as she covered the ground with long strides. "La Folle goin' mine you; Doctor Bonfils goin' come make *mon Chéri* well agin."

She had reached the abandoned field. As she crossed it with her precious burden, she looked constantly and restlessly from side to side. A terrible fear was upon her—the fear of the world beyond the bayou, the morbid and insane dread she had been under since childhood.

When she was at the bayou's edge she stood there, and shouted for help as if a life depended upon it:

"Oh, P'tit Maître! P'tit Maître! *Venez donc! Au secours! Au secours!*"[6]

No voice responded. Chéri's hot tears were scalding her neck. She called for each and every one upon the place, and still no answer came.

She shouted, she wailed; but whether her voice remained unheard or unheeded, no reply came to her frenzied cries. And all the while Chéri moaned and wept and entreated to be taken home to his mother.

La Folle gave a last despairing look around her. Extreme terror was upon her. She clasped the child close against her breast, where he could feel her heart beat like a muffled hammer. Then shutting her eyes, she ran suddenly down the shallow bank of the bayou, and never stopped till she had climbed the opposite shore.

She stood there quivering an instant as she opened her eyes. Then she plunged into the footpath through the trees.

She spoke no more to Chéri, but muttered constantly, "*Bon Dieu, ayez pitié La Folle! Bon Dieu, ayez pitié moi!*"[7]

Instinct seemed to guide her. When the pathway spread clear and smooth enough before her, she again closed her eyes tightly against the sight of that unknown and terrifying world.

A child, playing in some weeds, caught sight of her as she neared the quarters. The little one uttered a cry of dismay.

"La Folle!" she screamed, in her piercing treble. "La Folle done cross de bayer!"

Quickly the cry passed down the line of cabins.

"Yonda, La Folle done cross de bayou!"

Children, old men, old women, young ones with infants in their arms, flocked to doors and windows to see this awe-inspiring spectacle. Most of them shuddered with superstitious dread of what it might portend. "She totin' Chéri!" some of them shouted.

Some of the more daring gathered about her, and followed at her heels, only to fall back with new terror when she turned her distorted

5. My baby.
6. Come here! Help! Help!
7. Good Lord, have pity on La Folle! Good Lord, have pity on me!

face upon them. Her eyes were bloodshot and the saliva had gathered in a white foam on her black lips.

Some one had run ahead of her to where P'tit Maître sat with his family and guests upon the gallery.

"P'tit Maître! La Folle done cross de bayou! Look her! Look her yonda totin' Chéri!" This startling intimation was the first which they had of the woman's approach.

She was now near at hand. She walked with long strides. Her eyes were fixed desperately before her, and she breathed heavily, as a tired ox.

At the foot of the stairway, which she could not have mounted, she laid the boy in his father's arms. Then the world that had looked red to La Folle suddenly turned black—like that day she had seen powder and blood.

She reeled for an instant. Before a sustaining arm could reach her, she fell heavily to the ground.

When La Folle regained consciousness, she was at home again, in her own cabin and upon her own bed. The moon rays, streaming in through the open door and windows, gave what light was needed to the old black mammy who stood at the table concocting a tisane of fragrant herbs. It was very late.

Others who had come, and found that the stupor clung to her, had gone again. P'tit Maître had been there, and with him Doctor Bonfils, who said that La Folle might die.

But death had passed her by. The voice was very clear and steady with which she spoke to Tante[8] Lizette, brewing her tisane there in a corner.

"Ef you will give me one good drink tisane, Tante Lizette, I b'lieve I'm goin' sleep, me."

And she did sleep; so soundly, so healthfully, that old Lizette without compunction stole softly away to creep back through the moonlit fields to her own cabin in the new quarters.

The first touch of the cool gray morning awoke La Folle. She arose, calmly, as if no tempest had shaken and threatened her existence but yesterday.

She donned her new blue cottonade[9] and white apron, for she remembered that this was Sunday. When she had made for herself a cup of strong black coffee, and drunk it with relish, she quitted the cabin and walked across the old familiar field to the bayou's edge again.

She did not stop there as she had always done before, but crossed with a long, steady stride as if she had done this all her life.

When she had made her way through the brush and scrub cottonwood-trees that lined the opposite bank, she found herself upon the border of a field where the white, bursting cotton, with the dew upon it, gleamed for acres and acres like frosted silver in the early dawn.

La Folle drew a long, deep breath as she gazed across the country. She walked slowly and uncertainly, like one who hardly knows how, looking about her as she went.

8. Aunt.

9. Cotton fabric made to resemble wool.

The cabins, that yesterday had sent a clamor of voices to pursue her, were quiet now. No one was yet astir at Bellissime. Only the birds that darted here and there from hedges were awake, and singing their matins.

When La Folle came to the broad stretch of velvety lawn that surrounded the house, she moved slowly and with delight over the springy turf, that was delicious beneath her tread.

She stopped to find whence came those perfumes that were assailing her senses with memories from a time far gone.

There they were, stealing up to her from the thousand blue violets that peeped out from green, luxuriant beds. There they were, showering down from the big waxen bells of the magnolias far above her head, and from the jessamine clumps around her.

There were roses, too, without number. To right and left palms spread in broad and graceful curves. It all looked like enchantment beneath the sparkling sheen of dew.

When La Folle had slowly and cautiously mounted the many steps that led up to the veranda, she turned to look back at the perilous ascent she had made. Then she caught sight of the river, bending like a silver bow at the foot of Bellissime. Exultation possessed her soul.

La Folle rapped softly upon a door near at hand. Chéri's mother soon cautiously opened it. Quickly and cleverly she dissembled the astonishment she felt at seeing La Folle.

"Ah, La Folle? Is it you, so early?"

"*Oui,*[1] madame. I come ax how my po' li'le Chéri to, 's mo'nin'."

"He is feeling easier, thank you, La Folle. Dr. Bonfils says it will be nothing serious. He's sleeping now. Will you come back when he awakes?"

"*Non,* madame. I'm goin' wait yair tell Chéri wake up." La Folle seated herself upon the topmost step of the veranda.

A look of wonder and deep content crept into her face as she watched for the first time the sun rise upon the new, the beautiful world beyond the bayou.

1894

F. SCOTT FITZGERALD

Babylon Revisited

"And where's Mr. Campbell?" Charlie asked.

"Gone to Switzerland. Mr. Campbell's a pretty sick man, Mr. Wales."

"I'm sorry to hear that. And George Hardt?" Charlie inquired.

"Back in America, gone to work."

"And where is the Snow Bird?"

1. Yes.

"He was in here last week. Anyway, his friend, Mr. Schaeffer, is in Paris."

Two familiar names from the long list of a year and a half ago. Charlie scribbled an address in his notebook and tore out the page.

"If you see Mr. Schaeffer, give him this," he said. "It's my brother-in-law's address. I haven't settled on a hotel yet."

He was not really disappointed to find Paris was so empty. But the stillness in the Ritz bar was strange and portentous. It was not an American bar any more—he felt polite in it, and not as if he owned it. It had gone back into France. He felt the stillness from the moment he got out of the taxi and saw the doorman, usually in a frenzy of activity at this hour, gossiping with a *chasseur*[1] by the servants' entrance.

Passing through the corridor, he heard only a single, bored voice in the once-clamorous women's room. When he turned into the bar he traveled the twenty feet of green carpet with his eyes fixed straight ahead by old habit; and then, with his foot firmly on the rail, he turned and surveyed the room, encountering only a single pair of eyes that fluttered up from a newspaper in the corner. Charlie asked for the head barman, Paul, who in the latter days of the bull market[2] had come to work in his own custom-built car—disembarking, however, with due nicety at the nearest corner. But Paul was at his country house today and Alix giving him information.

"No, no more," Charlie said, "I'm going slow these days."

Alix congratulated him: "You were going pretty strong a couple of years ago."

"I'll stick to it all right," Charlie assured him. "I've stuck to it for over a year and a half now."

"How do you find conditions in America?"

"I haven't been to America for months. I'm in business in Prague, representing a couple of concerns there. They don't know about me down there."

Alix smiled.

"Remember the night of George Hardt's bachelor dinner here?" said Charlie. "By the way, what's become of Claude Fessenden?"

Alix lowered his voice confidentially: "He's in Paris, but he doesn't come here any more. Paul doesn't allow it. He ran up a bill of thirty thousand francs,[3] charging all his drinks and his lunches, and usually his dinner, for more than a year. And when Paul finally told him he had to pay, he gave him a bad check."

Alix shook his head sadly.

"I don't understand it, such a dandy fellow. Now he's all bloated up—" He made a plump apple of his hands.

Charlie watched a group of strident queens installing themselves in a corner.

"Nothing affects them," he thought. "Stocks rise and fall, people loaf or work, but they go on forever." The place oppressed him. He called for the dice and shook with Alix for the drink.

1. Hotel errand boy.
2. Rising stock market. The crash came in October 1929, beginning the Depression.
3. About $7,500. Below, 4 Swiss francs equals 18¢.

"Here for long, Mr. Wales?"

"I'm here for four or five days to see my little girl."

"Oh-h! You have a little girl?"

Outside, the fire-red, gas-blue, ghost-green signs shone smokily through the tranquil rain. It was late afternoon and the streets were in movement; the bistros gleamed. At the corner of the Boulevard des Capucines he took a taxi. The Place de la Concorde moved by in pink majesty; they crossed the logical Seine, and Charlie felt the sudden provincial quality of the Left Bank.[4]

Charlie directed his taxi to the Avenue de l'Opéra, which was out of his way. But he wanted to see the blue hour spread over the magnificent façade, and imagine that the cab horns, playing endlessly the first few bars of *Le Plus que Lent,*[5] were the trumpets of the Second Empire.[6] They were closing the iron grill in front of Brentano's Bookstore, and people were already at dinner behind the trim little bourgeois hedge of Duval's. He had never eaten at a really cheap restaurant in Paris. Five-course dinner, four francs fifty, eighteen cents, wine included. For some odd reason he wished that he had.

As they rolled on to the Left Bank and he felt its sudden provincialism, he thought, "I spoiled this city for myself. I didn't realize it, but the days came along one after another, and then two years were gone, and everything was gone, and I was gone."

He was thirty-five, and good to look at. The Irish mobility of his face was sobered by a deep wrinkle between his eyes. As he rang his brother-in-law's bell in the Rue Palatine, the wrinkle deepened till it pulled down his brows; he felt a cramping sensation in his belly. From behind the maid who opened the door darted a lovely little girl of nine who shrieked "Daddy!" and flew up, struggling like a fish, into his arms. She pulled his head around by one ear and set her cheek against his.

"My old pie," he said.

"Oh, daddy, daddy, daddy, daddy, dads, dads, dads!"

She drew him into the salon, where the family waited, a boy and a girl his daughter's age, his sister-in-law and her husband. He greeted Marion with his voice pitched carefully to avoid either feigned enthusiasm or dislike, but her response was more frankly tepid, though she minimized her expression of unalterable distrust by directing her regard toward his child. The two men clasped hands in a friendly way and Lincoln Peters rested his for a moment on Charlie's shoulder.

The room was warm and comfortably American. The three children moved intimately about, playing through the yellow oblongs that led to other rooms; the cheer of six o'clock spoke in the eager smacks of the fire and the sounds of French activity in the kitchen. But Charlie did not relax; his heart sat up rigidly in his body and he drew confidence from his daughter, who from time to time came close to him, holding in her arms the doll he had brought.

"Really extremely well," he declared in answer to Lincoln's question.

4. South of the Seine River; site of the student quarter and Bohemian section of Paris.

5. "More than Slow," a Debussy piano piece.

6. Reign of Louis Napoleon, 1852–1870; glamorous "good old days."

"There's a lot of business there that isn't moving at all, but we're doing even better than ever. In fact, damn well. I'm bringing my sister over from America next month to keep house for me. My income last year was bigger than it was when I had money. You see, the Czechs——"

His boasting was for a specific purpose; but after a moment, seeing a faint restiveness in Lincoln's eye, he changed the subject:

"Those are fine children of yours, well brought up, good manners."

"We think Honoria's a great little girl too."

Marion Peters came back from the kitchen. She was a tall woman with worried eyes, who had once possessed a fresh American loveliness. Charlie had never been sensitive to it and was always surprised when people spoke of how pretty she had been. From the first there had been an instinctive antipathy between them.

"Well, how do you find Honoria?" she asked.

"Wonderful. I was astonished how much she's grown in ten months. All the children are looking well."

"We haven't had a doctor for a year. How do you like being back in Paris?"

"It seems very funny to see so few Americans around."

"I'm delighted," Marion said vehemently. "Now at least you can go into a store without their assuming you're a millionaire. We've suffered like everybody, but on the whole it's a good deal pleasanter."

"But it was nice while it lasted," Charlie said. "We were a sort of royalty, almost infallible, with a sort of magic around us. In the bar this afternoon"—he stumbled, seeing his mistake—"there wasn't a man I knew."

She looked at him keenly. "I should think you'd have had enough of bars."

"I only stayed a minute. I take one drink every afternoon, and no more."

"Don't you want a cocktail before dinner?" Lincoln asked.

"I take only one drink every afternoon, and I've had that."

"I hope you keep to it," said Marion.

Her dislike was evident in the coldness with which she spoke, but Charlie only smiled; he had larger plans. Her very aggressiveness gave him an advantage, and he knew enough to wait. He wanted them to initiate the discussion of what they knew had brought him to Paris.

At dinner he couldn't decide whether Honoria was most like him or her mother. Fortunate if she didn't combine the traits of both that had brought them to disaster. A great wave of protectiveness went over him. He thought he knew what to do for her. He believed in character; he wanted to jump back a whole generation and trust in character again as the eternally valuable element. Everything else wore out.

He left soon after dinner, but not to go home. He was curious to see Paris by night with clearer and more judicious eyes than those of other days. He bought a *strapontin*[7] for the Casino and watched Josephine Baker go through her chocolate arabesques.

7. Cheap seat in the aisle. Josephine Baker (1906–1975) was a celebrated black singer of the blues in Paris in the 1920s.

After an hour he left and strolled toward Montmartre, up the Rue Pigalle into the Place Blanche. The rain had stopped and there were a few people in evening clothes disembarking from taxis in front of cabarets, and *cocottes*[8] prowling singly or in pairs, and many Negroes. He passed a lighted door from which issued music, and stopped with the sense of familiarity; it was Bricktop's, where he had parted with so many hours and so much money. A few doors farther on he found another ancient rendezvous and incautiously put his head inside. Immediately an eager orchestra burst into sound, a pair of professional dancers leaped to their feet and a maître d'hôtel swooped toward him, crying, "Crowd just arriving, sir!" But he withdrew quickly.

"You have to be damn drunk," he thought.

Zelli's was closed, the bleak and sinister cheap hotels surrounding it were dark; up in the Rue Blanche there was more light and a local, colloquial French crowd. The Poet's Cave had disappeared, but the two great mouths of the Café of Heaven and the Café of Hell still yawned—even devoured, as he watched, the meager contents of a tourist bus—a German, a Japanese, and an American couple who glanced at him with frightened eyes.

So much for the effort and ingenuity of Montmartre. All the catering to vice and waste was on an utterly childish scale, and he suddenly realized the meaning of the word "dissipate"—to dissipate into thin air; to make nothing out of something. In the little hours of the night every move from place to place was an enormous human jump, an increase of paying for the privilege of slower and slower motion.

He remembered thousand-franc notes given to an orchestra for playing a single number, hundred-franc notes tossed to a doorman for calling a cab.

But it hadn't been given for nothing.

It had been given, even the most wildly squandered sum, as an offering to destiny that he might not remember the things most worth remembering, the things that now he would always remember—his child taken from his control, his wife escaped to a grave in Vermont.

In the glare of a *brasserie*[9] a woman spoke to him. He bought her some eggs and coffee, and then, eluding her encouraging stare, gave her a twenty-franc note and took a taxi to his hotel.

II

He woke upon a fine fall day—football weather. The depression of yesterday was gone and he liked the people on the streets. At noon he sat opposite Honoria at Le Grand Vatel, the only restaurant he could think of not reminiscent of champagne dinners and long luncheons that began at two and ended in a blurred and vague twilight.

"Now, how about vegetables? Oughtn't you to have some vegetables?"

"Well, yes."

"Here's *épinards* and *chou-fleur* and carrots and *haricots*."[1]

"I'd like *chou-fleur*."

"Wouldn't you like to have two vegetables?"

8. Prostitutes.
9. Small restaurant and bar.
1. Spinach, cauliflower, and beans.

"I usually only have one at lunch."

The waiter was pretending to be inordinately fond of children. "*Qu'elle est mignonne la petite! Elle parle exactement comme une française.*"[2]

"How about dessert? Shall we wait and see?"

The waiter disappeared. Honoria looked at her father expectantly.

"What are we going to do?"

"First, we're going to that toy store in the Rue Saint-Honoré and buy you anything you like. And then we're going to the vaudeville at the Empire."

She hesitated. "I like it about the vaudeville, but not the toy store."

"Why not?"

"Well, you brought me this doll." She had it with her. "And I've got lots of things. And we're not rich any more, are we?"

"We never were. But today you are to have anything you want."

"All right," she agreed resignedly.

When there had been her mother and a French nurse he had been inclined to be strict; now he extended himself, reached out for a new tolerance; he must be both parents to her and not shut any of her out of communication.

"I want to get to know you," he said gravely. "First let me introduce myself. My name is Charles J. Wales, of Prague."

"Oh, daddy!" her voice cracked with laughter.

"And who are you, please?" he persisted, and she accepted a role immediately: "Honoria Wales, Rue Palatine, Paris."

"Married or single?"

"No, not married. Single."

He indicated the doll. "But I see you have a child, madame."

Unwilling to disinherit it, she took it to her heart and thought quickly: "Yes, I've been married, but I'm not married now. My husband is dead."

He went on quickly, "And the child's name?"

"Simone. That's after my best friend at school."

"I'm very pleased that you're doing so well at school."

"I'm third this month," she boasted. "Elsie"—that was her cousin—"is only about eighteenth, and Richard is about at the bottom."

"You like Richard and Elsie, don't you?"

"Oh, yes. I like Richard quite well and I like her all right."

Cautiously and casually he asked: "And Aunt Marion and Uncle Lincoln—which do you like best?"

"Oh, Uncle Lincoln, I guess."

He was increasingly aware of her presence. As they came in, a murmur of ". . . adorable" followed them, and now the people at the next table bent all their silences upon her, staring as if she were something no more conscious than a flower.

"Why don't I live with you?" she asked suddenly. "Because mamma's dead?"

"You must stay here and learn more French. It would have been hard for daddy to take care of you so well."

2. "What a cute little girl! She talks just like a French girl."

"I don't really need much taking care of any more. I do everything for myself."

Going out of the restaurant, a man and a woman unexpectedly hailed him.

"Well, the old Wales!"

"Hello there, Lorraine. . . . Dunc."

Sudden ghosts out of the past: Duncan Schaeffer, a friend from college. Lorraine Quarrles, a lovely, pale blonde of thirty; one of a crowd who had helped them make months into days in the lavish times of three years ago.

"My husband couldn't come this year," she said, in answer to his question. "We're poor as hell. So he gave me two hundred a month and told me I could do my worst on that. . . . This your little girl?"

"What about coming back and sitting down?" Duncan asked.

"Can't do it." He was glad for an excuse. As always, he felt Lorraine's passionate, provocative attraction, but his own rhythm was different now.

"Well, how about dinner?" she asked.

"I'm not free. Give me your address and let me call you."

"Charlie, I believe you're sober," she said judicially. "I honestly believe he's sober, Dunc. Pinch him and see if he's sober."

Charlie indicated Honoria with his head. They both laughed.

"What's your address?" said Duncan skeptically.

He hesitated, unwilling to give the name of his hotel.

"I'm not settled yet. I'd better call you. We're going to see the vaudeville at the Empire."

"There! That's what I want to do," Lorraine said. "I want to see some clowns and acrobats and jugglers. That's just what we'll do, Dunc."

"We've got to do an errand first," said Charlie. "Perhaps we'll see you there."

"All right, you snob. . . . Good-by, beautiful little girl."

"Good-by."

Honoria bobbed politely.

Somehow, an unwelcome encounter. They liked him because he was functioning, because he was serious; they wanted to see him, because he was stronger than they were now, because they wanted to draw a certain sustenance from his strength.

At the Empire, Honoria proudly refused to sit upon her father's folded coat. She was already an individual with a code of her own, and Charlie was more and more absorbed by the desire of putting a little of himself into her before she crystallized utterly. It was hopeless to try to know her in so short a time.

Between the acts they came upon Duncan and Lorraine in the lobby where the band was playing.

"Have a drink?"

"All right, but not up at the bar. We'll take a table."

"The perfect father."

Listening abstractedly to Lorraine, Charlie watched Honoria's eyes leave their table, and he followed them wistfully about the room, wondering what they saw. He met her glance and she smiled.

"I liked that lemonade," she said.

What had she said? What had he expected? Going home in a taxi afterward, he pulled her over until her head rested against his chest.

"Darling, do you ever think about your mother?"

"Yes, sometimes," she answered vaguely.

"I don't want you to forget her. Have you got a picture of her?"

"Yes, I think so. Anyhow, Aunt Marion has. Why don't you want me to forget her?"

"She loved you very much."

"I loved her too."

They were silent for a moment.

"Daddy, I want to come and live with you," she said suddenly.

His heart leaped; he had wanted it to come like this.

"Aren't you perfectly happy?"

"Yes, but I love you better than anybody. And you love me better than anybody, don't you, now that mummy's dead?"

"Of course I do. But you won't always like me best, honey. You'll grow up and meet somebody your own age and go marry him and forget you ever had a daddy."

"Yes, that's true," she agreed tranquilly.

He didn't go in. He was coming back at nine o'clock and he wanted to keep himself fresh and new for the thing he must say then.

"When you're safe inside, just show yourself in that window."

"All right. Good-by, dads, dads, dads, dads."

He waited in the dark street until she appeared, all warm and glowing, in the window above and kissed her fingers out into the night.

III

They were waiting. Marion sat behind the coffee service in a dignified black dinner dress that just faintly suggested mourning. Lincoln was walking up and down with the animation of one who had already been talking. They were as anxious as he was to get into the question. He opened it almost immediately:

"I suppose you know what I want to see you about—why I really came to Paris."

Marion played with the black stars on her necklace and frowned.

"I'm awfully anxious to have a home," he continued. "And I'm awfully anxious to have Honoria in it. I appreciate your taking in Honoria for her mother's sake, but things have changed now"—he hesitated and then continued more forcibly—"changed radically with me, and I want to ask you to reconsider the matter. It would be silly for me to deny that about three years ago I was acting badly——"

Marion looked up at him with hard eyes.

"—but all that's over. As I told you, I haven't had more than a drink a day for over a year, and I take that drink deliberately, so that the idea of alcohol won't get too big in my imagination. You see the idea?"

"No," said Marion succinctly.

"It's a sort of stunt I set myself. It keeps the matter in proportion."

"I get you," said Lincoln. "You don't want to admit it's got any attraction for you."

"Something like that. Sometimes I forget and don't take it. But I try to take it. Anyhow, I couldn't afford to drink in my position. The people I represent are more than satisfied with what I've done, and I'm bringing my sister over from Burlington to keep house for me, and I want awfully to have Honoria too. You know that even when her mother and I weren't getting along well we never let anything that happened touch Honoria. I know she's fond of me and I know I'm able to take care of her and—well, there you are. How do you feel about it?"

He knew that now he would have to take a beating. It would last an hour or two hours, and it would be difficult, but if he modulated his inevitable resentment to the chastened attitude of the reformed sinner, he might win his point in the end.

Keep your temper, he told himself. You don't want to be justified. You want Honoria.

Lincoln spoke first: "We've been talking it over ever since we got your letter last month. We're happy to have Honoria here. She's a dear little thing, and we're glad to be able to help her, but of course that isn't the question——"

Marion interrupted suddenly. "How long are you going to stay sober, Charlie?" she asked.

"Permanently, I hope."

"How can anybody count on that?"

"You know I never did drink heavily until I gave up business and came over here with nothing to do. Then Helen and I began to run around with——"

"Please leave Helen out of it. I can't bear to hear you talk about her like that."

He stared at her grimly; he had never been certain how fond of each other the sisters were in life.

"My drinking only lasted about a year and a half—from the time we came over until I—collapsed."

"It was time enough."

"It was time enough," he agreed.

"My duty is entirely to Helen," she said. "I try to think what she would have wanted me to do. Frankly, from the night you did that terrible thing you haven't really existed for me. I can't help that. She was my sister."

"Yes."

"When she was dying she asked me to look out for Honoria. If you hadn't been in a sanitarium then, it might have helped matters."

He had no answer.

"I'll never in my life be able to forget the morning when Helen knocked at my door, soaked to the skin and shivering, and said you'd locked her out."

Charlie gripped the sides of the chair. This was more difficult than he expected; he wanted to launch out into a long expostulation and explanation, but he only said: "The night I locked her out—" and she interrupted, "I don't feel up to going over that again."

After a moment's silence Lincoln said: "We're getting off the subject. You want Marion to set aside her legal guardianship and give you Honoria. I think the main point for her is whether she has confidence in you or not."

"I don't blame Marion," Charlie said slowly, "but I think she can have entire confidence in me. I had a good record up to three years ago. Of course, it's within human possibilities I might go wrong any time. But if we wait much longer I'll lose Honoria's childhood and my chance for a home." He shook his head. "I'll simply lose her, don't you see?"

"Yes, I see," said Lincoln.

"Why didn't you think of all this before?" Marion asked.

"I suppose I did, from time to time, but Helen and I were getting along badly. When I consented to the guardianship, I was flat on my back in a sanitarium and the market had cleaned me out. I knew I'd acted badly, and I thought if it would bring any peace to Helen, I'd agree to anything. But now it's different. I'm functioning, I'm behaving damn well, so far as——"

"Please don't swear at me," Marion said.

He looked at her, startled. With each remark the force of her dislike became more and more apparent. She had built up all her fear of life into one wall and faced it toward him. This trivial reproof was possibly the result of some trouble with the cook several hours before. Charlie became increasingly alarmed at leaving Honoria in this atmosphere of hostility against himself; sooner or later it would come out, in a word here, a shake of the head there, and some of that distrust would be irrevocably implanted in Honoria. But he pulled his temper down out of his face and shut it up inside him; he had won a point, for Lincoln realized the absurdity of Marion's remark and asked her lightly since when she had objected to the word "damn."

"Another thing," Charlie said: "I'm able to give her certain advantages now. I'm going to take a French governess to Prague with me. I've got a lease on a new apartment——"

He stopped, realizing that he was blundering. They couldn't be expected to accept with equanimity the fact that his income was again twice as large as their own.

"I suppose you can give her more luxuries than we can," said Marion. "When you were throwing away money we were living along watching every ten francs. . . . I suppose you'll start doing it again."

"Oh, no," he said. "I've learned. I worked hard for ten years, you know—until I got lucky in the market, like so many people. Terribly lucky. It won't happen again."

There was a long silence. All of them felt their nerves straining, and for the first time in a year Charlie wanted a drink. He was sure now that Lincoln Peters wanted him to have his child.

Marion shuddered suddenly; part of her saw that Charlie's feet were planted on the earth now, and her own maternal feeling recognized the naturalness of his desire; but she had lived for a long time with a prejudice—a prejudice founded on a curious disbelief in her sister's happiness, which, in the shock of one terrible night, had turned to hatred for him. It had all happened at a point in her life where the discouragement of ill health and adverse circumstances made it necessary for her to believe in tangible villainy and a tangible villain.

"I can't help what I think!" she cried out suddenly. "How much you were responsible for Helen's death, I don't know. It's something you'll have to square with your own conscience."

An electric current of agony surged through him; for a moment he was almost on his feet, an unuttered sound echoing in his throat. He hung on to himself for a moment, another moment.

"Hold on there," said Lincoln uncomfortably. "I never thought you were responsible for that."

"Helen died of heart trouble," Charlie said dully.

"Yes, heart trouble." Marion spoke as if the phrase had another meaning for her.

Then, in the flatness that followed her outburst, she saw him plainly and she knew he had somehow arrived at control over the situation. Glancing at her husband, she found no help from him, and as abruptly as if it were a matter of no importance, she threw up the sponge.

"Do what you like!" she cried, springing up from her chair. "She's your child. I'm not the person to stand in your way. I think if it were my child I'd rather see her—" She managed to check herself. "You two decide it. I can't stand this. I'm sick. I'm going to bed."

She hurried from the room; after a moment Lincoln said:

"This has been a hard day for her. You know how strongly she feels—" His voice was almost apologetic: "When a woman gets an idea in her head."

"Of course."

"It's going to be all right. I think she sees now that you—can provide for the child, and so we can't very well stand in your way or Honoria's way."

"Thank you, Lincoln."

"I'd better go along and see how she is."

"I'm going."

He was still trembling when he reached the street, but a walk down the Rue Bonaparte to the *quais*[3] set him up, and as he crossed the Seine, fresh and new by the *quai* lamps, he felt exultant. But back in his room he couldn't sleep. The image of Helen haunted him. Helen whom he had loved so until they had senselessly begun to abuse each other's love, tear it into shreds. On that terrible February night that Marion remembered so vividly, a slow quarrel had gone on for hours. There was a scene at the Florida, and then he attempted to take her home, and then she kissed young Webb at a table; after that there was what she had hysterically said. When he arrived home alone he turned the key in the lock in wild anger. How could he know she would arrive an hour later alone, that there would be a snow storm in which she wandered about in slippers, too confused to find a taxi? Then the aftermath, her escaping pneumonia by a miracle, and all the attendant horror. They were "reconciled," but that was the beginning of the end, and Marion, who had seen with her own eyes and who imagined it to be one of many scenes from her sister's martyrdom, never forgot.

Going over it again brought Helen nearer, and in the white, soft

3. Paved walks along the Seine River.

light that steals upon half sleep near morning he found himself talking to her again. She said that he was perfectly right about Honoria and that she wanted Honoria to be with him. She said she was glad he was being good and doing better. She said a lot of other things—very friendly things—but she was in a swing in a white dress, and swinging faster and faster all the time, so that at the end he could not hear clearly all that she said.

IV

He woke up feeling happy. The door of the world was open again. He made plans, vistas, futures for Honoria and himself, but suddenly he grew sad, remembering all the plans he and Helen had made. She had not planned to die. The present was the thing—work to do and someone to love. But not to love too much, for he knew the injury that a father can do to a daughter or a mother to a son by attaching them too closely: afterward, out in the world, the child would seek in the marriage partner the same blind tenderness and, failing probably to find it, turn against love and life.

It was another bright, crisp day. He called Lincoln Peters at the bank where he worked and asked if he could count on taking Honoria when he left for Prague. Lincoln agreed that there was no reason for delay. One thing—the legal guardianship. Marion wanted to retain that a while longer. She was upset by the whole matter, and it would oil things if she felt that the situation was still in her control for another year. Charlie agreed, wanting only the tangible, visible child.

Then the question of a governess. Charles sat in a gloomy agency and talked to a cross Béarnaise and to a buxom Breton peasant,[4] neither of whom he could have endured. There were others whom he would see tomorrow.

He lunched with Lincoln Peters at Griffons, trying to keep down his exultation.

"There's nothing quite like your own child," Lincoln said. "But you understand how Marion feels too."

"She's forgotten how hard I worked for seven years there," Charlie said. "She just remembers one night."

"There's another thing." Lincoln hesitated. "While you and Helen were tearing around Europe throwing money away, we were just getting along. I didn't touch any of the prosperity because I never got ahead enough to carry anything but my insurance. I think Marion felt there was some kind of injustice in it—you not even working toward the end, and getting richer and richer."

"It went just as quick as it came," said Charlie.

"Yes, a lot of it stayed in the hands of *chasseurs* and saxophone players and maitres d'hôtel—well, the big party's over now. I just said that to explain Marion's feeling about those crazy years. If you drop in about six o'clock tonight before Marion's too tired, we'll settle the details on the spot."

Back at his hotel, Charlie found a *pneumatique*[5] that had been re-

4. Woman from Béarn, a region of southwestern France; peasant from Brittany.

5. Express message sent through Paris-wide system of air tubes.

directed from the Ritz bar, where Charlie had left his address for the purpose of finding a certain man.

> Dear Charlie: You were so strange when we saw you the other day that I wondered if I did something to offend you. If so, I'm not conscious of it. In fact, I have thought about you too much for the last year, and it's always been in the back of my mind that I might see you if I came over here. We *did* have such good times that crazy spring, like the night you and I stole the butcher's tricycle, and the time we tried to call on the president and you had the old derby rim and the wire cane. Everybody seems so old lately, but I don't feel old a bit. Couldn't we get together some time today for old time's sake? I've got a vile hangover for the moment, but will be feeling better this afternoon and will look for you about five in the sweatshop at the Ritz.
>
> Always devotedly,
> Lorraine

His first feeling was one of awe that he had actually, in his mature years, stolen a tricycle and pedaled Lorraine all over the Étoile between the small hours and dawn. In retrospect it was a nightmare. Locking out Helen didn't fit in with any other act of his life, but the tricycle incident did—it was one of many. How many weeks or months of dissipation to arrive at that condition of utter irresponsibility?

He tried to picture how Lorraine had appeared to him then—very attractive; Helen was unhappy about it, though she said nothing. Yesterday, in the restaurant, Lorraine had seemed trite, blurred, worn away. He emphatically did not want to see her, and he was glad Alix had not given away his hotel address. It was a relief to think, instead, of Honoria, to think of Sundays spent with her and of saying good morning to her and of knowing she was there in his house at night, drawing her breath in the darkness.

At five he took a taxi and bought presents for all the Peterses—a piquant cloth doll, a box of Roman soldiers, flowers for Marion, big linen handkerchiefs for Lincoln.

He saw, when he arrived in the apartment, that Marion had accepted the inevitable. She greeted him now as though he were a recalcitrant member of the family, rather than a menacing outsider. Honoria had been told she was going; Charlie was glad to see that her tact made her conceal her excessive happiness. Only on his lap did she whisper her delight and the question "When?" before she slipped away with the other children.

He and Marion were alone for a minute in the room, and on an impulse he spoke out boldly:

"Family quarrels are bitter things. They don't go according to any rules. They're not like aches or wounds; they're more like splits in the skin that won't heal because there's not enough material. I wish you and I could be on better terms."

"Some things are hard to forget," she answered. "It's a question of confidence." There was no answer to this and presently she asked, "When do you propose to take her?"

"As soon as I can get a governess. I hoped the day after tomorrow."

"That's impossible. I've got to get her things in shape. Not before Saturday."

He yielded. Coming back into the room, Lincoln offered him a drink.

"I'll take my daily whisky," he said.

It was warm here, it was a home, people together by a fire. The children felt very safe and important; the mother and father were serious, watchful. They had things to do for the children more important than his visit here. A spoonful of medicine was, after all, more important than the strained relations between Marion and himself. They were not dull people, but they were very much in the grip of life and circumstances. He wondered if he couldn't do something to get Lincoln out of his rut at the bank.

A long peal at the doorbell; the *bonne à tout faire*[6] passed through and went down the corridor. The door opened upon another long ring, and then voices, and the three in the salon looked up expectantly; Richard moved to bring the corridor within his range of vision, and Marion rose. Then the maid came back along the corridor, closely followed by the voices, which developed under the light into Duncan Schaeffer and Lorraine Quarrles.

They were gay, they were hilarious, they were roaring with laughter. For a moment Charlie was astounded; unable to understand how they ferreted out the Peterses' address.

"Ah-h-h!" Duncan wagged his finger roguishly at Charlie. "Ah-h-h!"

They both slid down another cascade of laughter. Anxious and at a loss, Charlie shook hands with them quickly and presented them to Lincoln and Marion. Marion nodded, scarcely speaking. She had drawn back a step toward the fire; her little girl stood beside her, and Marion put an arm about her shoulder.

With growing annoyance at the intrusion, Charlie waited for them to explain themselves. After some concentration Duncan said:

"We came to invite you out to dinner. Lorraine and I insist that all this shishi,[7] cagy business 'bout your address got to stop."

Charlie came closer to them, as if to force them backward down the corridor.

"Sorry, but I can't. Tell me where you'll be and I'll phone you in half an hour."

This made no impression. Lorraine sat down suddenly on the side of a chair, and focusing her eyes on Richard, cried, "Oh, what a nice little boy! Come here, little boy." Richard glanced at his mother, but did not move. With a perceptible shrug of her shoulders, Lorraine turned back to Charlie:

"Come and dine. Sure your cousins won' mine. See you so sel'om. Or solemn."

"I can't," said Charlie sharply. "You two have dinner and I'll phone you."

Her voice became suddenly unpleasant. "All right, we'll go. But I remember once when you hammered on my door at four A.M. I was enough of a good sport to give you a drink. Come on, Dunc."

6. Maid of all work.

7. Chichi, showy.

Still in slow motion, with blurred, angry faces, with uncertain feet, they retired along the corridor.

"Good night," Charlie said.

"Good night!" responded Lorraine emphatically.

When he went back into the salon Marion had not moved, only now her son was standing in the circle of her other arm. Lincoln was still swinging Honoria back and forth like a pendulum from side to side.

"What an outrage!" Charlie broke out. "What an absolute outrage!"

Neither of them answered. Charlie dropped into an armchair, picked up his drink, set it down again and said:

"People I haven't seen for two years having the colossal nerve——"

He broke off. Marion had made the sound "Oh!" in one swift, furious breath, turned her body from him with a jerk and left the room.

Lincoln set down Honoria carefully.

"You children go in and start your soup," he said, and when they obeyed, he said to Charlie:

"Marion's not well and she can't stand shocks. That kind of people make her really physically sick."

"I didn't tell them to come here. They wormed your name out of somebody. They deliberately——"

"Well, it's too bad. It doesn't help matters. Excuse me a minute."

Left alone, Charlie sat tense in his chair, In the next room he could hear the children eating, talking in monosyllables, already oblivious to the scene between their elders. He heard a murmur of conversation from a farther room and then the ticking bell of a telephone receiver picked up, and in a panic he moved to the other side of the room and out of earshot.

In a minute Lincoln came back. "Look here, Charlie. I think we'd better call off dinner for tonight. Marion's in bad shape."

"Is she angry with me?"

"Sort of," he said, almost roughly. "She's not strong and——"

"You mean she's changed her mind about Honoria?"

"She's pretty bitter right now. I don't know. You phone me at the bank tomorrow."

"I wish you'd explain to her I never dreamed these people would come here. I'm just as sore as you are."

"I couldn't explain anything to her now."

Charlie got up. He took his coat and hat and started down the corridor. Then he opened the door of the dining room and said in a strange voice, "Good night, children."

Honoria rose and ran around the table to hug him.

"Good night, sweetheart," he said vaguely, and then trying to make his voice more tender, trying to conciliate something, "Good night, dear children."

V

Charlie went directly to the Ritz bar with the furious idea of finding Lorraine and Duncan, but they were not there, and he realized that in any case there was nothing he could do. He had not touched his drink at the Peters, and now he ordered a whisky-and-soda. Paul came over to say hello.

"It's a great change," he said sadly. "We do about half the business we did. So many fellows I hear about back in the States lost everything, maybe not in the first crash, but then in the second. Your friend George Hardt lost every cent, I hear. Are you back in the States?"

"No, I'm in business in Prague."

"I heard that you lost a lot in the crash."

"I did," and he added grimly, "but I lost everything I wanted in the boom."

"Selling short."[8]

"Something like that."

Again the memory of those days swept over him like a nightmare —the people they had met traveling; then people who couldn't add a row of figures or speak a coherent sentence. The little man Helen had consented to dance with at the ship's party, who had insulted her ten feet from the table; the women and girls carried screaming with drink or drugs out of public places——

The men who locked their wives out in the snow, because the snow of twenty-nine wasn't real snow. If you didn't want it to be snow, you just paid some money.

He went to the phone and called the Peterses' apartment; Lincoln answered.

"I called up because this thing is on my mind. Has Marion said anything definite?"

"Marion's sick," Lincoln answered shortly. "I know this thing isn't altogether your fault, but I can't have her go to pieces about it. I'm afraid we'll have to let it slide for six months; I can't take the chance of working her up to this state again."

"I see."

"I'm sorry, Charlie."

He went back to his table. His whisky glass was empty, but he shook his head when Alix looked at it questioningly. There wasn't much he could do now except send Honoria some things; he would send her a lot of things tomorrow. He thought rather angrily that this was just money—he had given so many people money. . . .

"No, no more," he said to another waiter. "What do I owe you?"

He would come back some day; they couldn't make him pay forever. But he wanted his child, and nothing was much good now, beside that fact. He wasn't young any more, with a lot of nice thoughts and dreams to have by himself. He was absolutely sure Helen wouldn't have wanted him to be so alone.

1931

8. Selling at too low a price.

JAMES BALDWIN

Sonny's Blues

I read about it in the paper, in the subway, on my way to work. I read it, and I couldn't believe it, and I read it again. Then perhaps I just stared at it, at the newsprint spelling out his name, spelling out the story. I stared at it in the swinging lights of the subway car, and in the faces and bodies of the people, and in my own face, trapped in the darkness which roared outside.

It was not to be believed and I kept telling myself that, as I walked from the subway station to the high school. And at the same time I couldn't doubt it. I was scared, scared for Sonny. He became real to me again. A great block of ice got settled in my belly and kept melting there slowly all day long, while I taught my classes algebra. It was a special kind of ice. It kept melting, sending trickles of ice water all up and down my veins, but it never got less. Sometimes it hardened and seemed to expand until I felt my guts were going to come spilling out or that I was going to choke or scream. This would always be at a moment when I was remembering some specific thing Sonny had once said or done.

When he was about as old as the boys in my classes his face had been bright and open, there was a lot of copper in it; and he'd had wonderfully direct brown eyes, and great gentleness and privacy. I wondered what he looked like now. He had been picked up, the evening before, in a raid on an apartment downtown, for peddling and using heroin.

I couldn't believe it: but what I mean by that is that I couldn't find any room for it anywhere inside me. I had kept it outside me for a long time. I hadn't wanted to know. I had had suspicions, but I didn't name them, I kept putting them away. I told myself that Sonny was wild, but he wasn't crazy. And he'd always been a good boy, he hadn't ever turned hard or evil or disrespectful, the way kids can, so quick, so quick, especially in Harlem. I didn't want to believe that I'd ever see my brother going down, coming to nothing, all that light in his face gone out, in the condition I'd already seen so many others. Yet it had happened and here I was, talking about algebra to a lot of boys who might, every one of them for all I knew, be popping off needles every time they went to the head.[1] Maybe it did more for them than algebra could.

I was sure that the first time Sonny had ever had horse,[2] he couldn't have been much older than these boys were now. These boys, now, were living as we'd been living then, they were growing up with a rush and their heads bumped abruptly against the low ceiling of their actual possibilities. They were filled with rage. All they really knew were two darknesses, the darkness of their lives, which was now closing in on them, and the darkness of the movies, which had blinded them to that other darkness, and in which they now, vindictively, dreamed, at once more together than they were at any other time, and more alone.

When the last bell rang, the last class ended, I let out my breath. It seemed I'd been holding it for all that time. My clothes were wet—I may have looked as though I'd been sitting in a steam bath, all dressed

1. Lavatory.

2. Heroin.

up, all afternoon. I sat alone in the classroom a long time. I listened to the boys outside, downstairs, shouting and cursing and laughing. Their laughter struck me for perhaps the first time. It was not the joyous laughter which—God knows why—one associates with children. It was mocking and insular, its intent was to denigrate. It was disenchanted, and in this, also, lay the authority of their curses. Perhaps I was listening to them because I was thinking about my brother and in them I heard my brother. And myself.

One boy was whistling a tune, at once very complicated and very simple, it seemed to be pouring out of him as though he were a bird, and it sounded very cool and moving through all that harsh, bright air, only just holding its own through all those other sounds.

I stood up and walked over to the window and looked down into the courtyard. It was the beginning of the spring and the sap was rising in the boys. A teacher passed through them every now and again, quickly, as though he or she couldn't wait to get out of that courtyard, to get those boys out of their sight and off their minds. I started collecting my stuff. I thought I'd better get home and talk to Isabel.

The courtyard was almost deserted by the time I got downstairs. I saw this boy standing in the shadow of a doorway, looking just like Sonny. I almost called his name. Then I saw that it wasn't Sonny, but somebody we used to know, a boy from around our block. He'd been Sonny's friend. He'd never been mine, having been too young for me, and, anyway, I'd never liked him. And now, even though he was a grown-up man, he still hung around that block, still spent hours on the street corners, was always high and raggy. I used to run into him from time to time and he'd often work around to asking me for a quarter or fifty cents. He always had some real good excuse, too, and I always gave it to him, I don't know why.

But now, abruptly, I hated him. I couldn't stand the way he looked at me, partly like a dog, partly like a cunning child. I wanted to ask him what the hell he was doing in the school courtyard.

He sort of shuffled over to me, and he said, "I see you got the papers. So you already know about it."

"You mean about Sonny? Yes, I already know about it. How come they didn't get you?"

He grinned. It made him repulsive and it also brought to mind what he'd looked like as a kid. "I wasn't there. I stay away from them people."

"Good for you." I offered him a cigarette and I watched him through the smoke. "You come all the way down here just to tell me about Sonny?"

"That's right." He was sort of shaking his head and his eyes looked strange, as though they were about to cross. The bright sun deadened his damp dark brown skin and it made his eyes look yellow and showed up the dirt in his kinked hair. He smelled funky.[3] I moved a little away from him and I said, "Well, thanks. But I already know about it and I got to get home."

"I'll walk you a little ways," he said. We started walking. There were a couple of kids still loitering in the courtyard and one of them said goodnight to me and looked strangely at the boy beside me.

3. Obnoxious.

"What're you going to do?" he asked me. "I mean, about Sonny?"

"Look. I haven't seen Sonny for over a year, I'm not sure I'm going to do anything. Anyway, what the hell *can* I do?"

"That's right," he said quickly, "ain't nothing you can do. Can't much help old Sonny no more, I guess."

It was what I was thinking and so it seemed to me he had no right to say it.

"I'm surprised at Sonny, though," he went on—he had a funny way of talking, he looked straight ahead as though he were talking to himself—"I thought Sonny was a smart boy, I thought he was too smart to get hung."

"I guess he thought so too," I said sharply, "and that's how he got hung. And how about you? You're pretty goddamn smart, I bet."

Then he looked directly at me, just for a minute. "I ain't smart," he said. "If I was smart, I'd have reached for a pistol a long time ago."

"Look. Don't tell *me* your sad story, if it was up to me, I'd give you one." Then I felt guilty—guilty, probably, for never having supposed that the poor bastard *had* a story of his own, much less a sad one, and I asked, quickly, "What's going to happen to him now?"

He didn't answer this. He was off by himself some place.

"Funny thing," he said, and from his tone we might have been discussing the quickest way to get to Brooklyn, "when I saw the papers this morning, the first thing I asked myself was if I had anything to do with it. I felt sort of responsible."

I began to listen more carefully. The subway station was on the corner, just before us, and I stopped. He stopped, too. We were in front of a bar and he ducked slightly, peering in, but whoever he was looking for didn't seem to be there. The juke box was blasting away with something black and bouncy and I half watched the barmaid as she danced her way from the juke box to her place behind the bar. And I watched her face as she laughingly responded to something someone said to her, still keeping time to the music. When she smiled one saw the little girl, one sensed the doomed, still-struggling woman beneath the battered face of the semi-whore.

"I never *give* Sonny nothing," the boy said finally, "but a long time ago I come to school high and Sonny asked me how it felt." He paused, I couldn't bear to watch him, I watched the barmaid, and I listened to the music which seemed to be causing the pavement to shake. "I told him it felt great." The music stopped, the barmaid paused and watched the juke box until the music began again. "It did."

All this was carrying me some place I didn't want to go. I certainly didn't want to know how it felt. It filled everything, the people, the houses, the music, the dark, quicksilver barmaid, with menace; and this menace was their reality.

"What's going to happen to him now?" I asked again.

"They'll send him away some place and they'll try to cure him." He shook his head. "Maybe he'll even think he's kicked the habit. Then they'll let him loose"—he gestured, throwing his cigarette into the gutter. "That's all."

"What do you mean, that's *all?*"

But I knew what he meant.

"I *mean,* that's *all.*" He turned his head and looked at me, pulling down the corners of his mouth. "Don't you know what I mean?" he asked, softly.

"How the hell *would* I know what you mean?" I almost whispered it, I don't know why.

"That's right," he said to the air, "how would *he* know what I mean?" He turned toward me again, patient and calm, and yet I somehow felt him shaking, shaking as though he were going to fall apart. I felt that ice in my guts again, the dread I'd felt all afternoon; and again I watched the barmaid, moving about the bar, washing glasses, and singing. "Listen. They'll let him out and then it'll just start all over again. That's what I mean."

"You mean—they'll let him out. And then he'll just start working his way back in again. You mean he'll never kick the habit. Is that what you mean?"

"That's right," he said, cheerfully. "*You* see what I mean."

"Tell me," I said at last, "why does he want to die? He must want to die, he's killing himself, why does he want to die?"

He looked at me in surprise. He licked his lips. "He don't want to die. He wants to live. Don't nobody want to die, ever."

Then I wanted to ask him—too many things. He could not have answered, or if he had, I could not have borne the answers. I started walking. "Well, I guess it's none of my business."

"It's going to be rough on old Sonny," he said. We reached the subway station. "This is your station?" he asked. I nodded. I took one step down. "Damn!" he said, suddenly. I looked up at him. He grinned again. "Damn it if I didn't leave all my money home. You ain't got a dollar on you, have you? Just for a couple of days, is all."

All at once something inside gave and threatened to come pouring out of me. I didn't hate him any more. I felt that in another moment I'd start crying like a child.

"Sure," I said. "Don't sweat." I looked in my wallet and didn't have a dollar, I only had a five. "Here," I said. "That hold you?"

He didn't look at it—he didn't want to look at it. A terrible, closed look came over his face, as though he were keeping the number on the bill a secret from him and me. "Thanks," he said, and now he was dying to see me go. "Don't worry about Sonny. Maybe I'll write him or something."

"Sure," I said. "You do that. So long."

"Be seeing you," he said. I went on down the steps.

And I didn't write Sonny or send him anything for a long time. When I finally did, it was just after my little girl died, he wrote me back a letter which made me feel like a bastard.

Here's what he said:

Dear brother,

You don't know how much I needed to hear from you. I wanted to write you many a time but I dug how much I must have hurt you and so I didn't write. But now I feel like a man who's been trying to climb up out of some deep, real deep and funky hole and just saw the sun up there, outside. I got to get outside.

I can't tell you much about how I got here. I mean I don't know how to tell you. I guess I was afraid of something or I was trying to escape from something and you know I have never been very strong in the head (smile). I'm glad Mama and Daddy are dead and can't see what's happened to their son and I swear if I'd known what I was doing I would never have hurt you so, you and a lot of other fine people who were nice to me and who believed in me.

I don't want you to think it had anything to do with me being a musician. It's more than that. Or maybe less than that. I can't get anything straight in my head down here and I try not to think about what's going to happen to me when I get outside again. Sometime I think I'm going to flip and *never* get outside and sometime I think I'll come straight back. I tell you one thing, though, I'd rather blow my brains out than go through this again. But that's what they all say, so they tell me. If I tell you when I'm coming to New York and if you could meet me, I sure would appreciate it. Give my love to Isabel and the kids and I was sure sorry to hear about little Gracie. I wish I could be like Mama and say the Lord's will be done, but I don't know it seems to me that trouble is the one thing that never does get stopped and I don't know what good it does to blame it on the Lord. But maybe it does some good if you believe it.

Your brother,
Sonny

Then I kept in constant touch with him and I sent him whatever I could and I went to meet him when he came back to New York. When I saw him many things I thought I had forgotten came flooding back to me. This was because I had begun, finally, to wonder about Sonny, about the life that Sonny lived inside. This life, whatever it was, had made him older and thinner and it had deepened the distant stillness in which he had always moved. He looked very unlike my baby brother. Yet, when he smiled, when we shook hands, the baby brother I'd never known looked out from the depths of his private life, like an animal waiting to be coaxed into the light.

"How you been keeping?" he asked me.

"All right. And you?"

"Just fine." He was smiling all over his face. "It's good to see you again."

"It's good to see you."

The seven years' difference in our ages lay between us like a chasm: I wondered if these years would ever operate between us as a bridge. I was remembering, and it made it hard to catch my breath, that I had been there when he was born; and I had heard the first words he had ever spoken. When he started to walk, he walked from our mother straight to me. I caught him just before he fell when he took the first steps he ever took in this world.

"How's Isabel?"

"Just fine. She's dying to see you."

"And the boys?"

"They're fine, too. They're anxious to see their uncle."

"Oh, come on. You know they don't remember me."

"Are you kidding? Of course they remember you."

He grinned again. We got into a taxi. We had a lot to say to each other, far too much to know how to begin.

As the taxi began to move, I asked, "You still want to go to India?"

He laughed. "You still remember that. Hell, no. This place is Indian enough for me."

"It used to belong to them," I said.

And he laughed again. "They damn sure knew what they were doing when they got rid of it."

Years ago, when he was around fourteen, he'd been all hipped on the idea of going to India. He read books about people sitting on rocks, naked, in all kinds of weather, but mostly bad, naturally, and walking barefoot through hot coals and arriving at wisdom. I used to say that it sounded to me as though they were getting away from wisdom as fast as they could. I think he sort of looked down on me for that.

"Do you mind," he asked, "if we have the driver drive alongside the park? On the west side—I haven't seen the city in so long."

"Of course not," I said. I was afraid that I might sound as though I were humoring him, but I hoped he wouldn't take it that way.

So we drove along, between the green of the park and the stony, lifeless elegance of hotels and apartment buildings, toward the vivid, killing streets of our childhood. These streets hadn't changed, though housing projects jutted up out of them now like rocks in the middle of a boiling sea. Most of the houses in which we had grown up had vanished, as had the stores from which we had stolen, the basements in which we had first tried sex, the rooftops from which we had hurled tin cans and bricks. But houses exactly like the houses of our past yet dominated the landscape, boys exactly like the boys we once had been found themselves smothering in these houses, came down into the streets for light and air and found themselves encircled by disaster. Some escaped the trap, most didn't. Those who got out always left something of themselves behind, as some animals amputate a leg and leave it in the trap. It might be said, perhaps, that I had escaped, after all, I was a school teacher; or that Sonny had, he hadn't lived in Harlem for years. Yet, as the cab moved uptown through streets which seemed, with a rush, to darken with dark people, and as I covertly studied Sonny's face, it came to me that what we both were seeking through our separate cab windows was that part of ourselves which had been left behind. It's always at the hour of trouble and confrontation that the missing member aches.

We hit 110th Street and started rolling up Lenox Avenue. And I'd known this avenue all my life, but it seemed to me again, as it had seemed on the day I'd first heard about Sonny's trouble, filled with a hidden menace which was its very breath of life.

"We almost there," said Sonny.

"Almost." We were both too nervous to say anything more.

We live in a housing project. It hasn't been up long. A few days after it was up it seemed uninhabitably new, now, of course, it's already rundown. It looks like a parody of the good, clean, faceless life—God knows the people who live in it do their best to make it a parody. The beat-looking grass lying around isn't enough to make their lives green, the hedges will never hold out the streets, and they know it. The big windows fool no one, they aren't big enough to make space out of no space. They don't bother with the windows, they watch the TV screen instead. The playground is most popular with the children who don't play at jacks, or skip rope, or roller skate, or swing, and they can be found in it after dark. We moved in partly because it's not too far from where I teach, and partly for the kids; but it's really just like the houses in which Sonny and I grew up. The same things happen, they'll have the same things to remember. The moment Sonny and I started into the house I had the feeling that I was simply bringing him back into the danger he had almost died trying to escape.

Sonny has never been talkative. So I don't know why I was sure he'd be dying to talk to me when supper was over the first night. Everything went fine, the oldest boy remembered him, and the youngest boy liked him, and Sonny had remembered to bring something for each of them; and Isabel, who is really much nicer than I am, more open and giving, had gone to a lot of trouble about dinner and was genuinely glad to see him. And she's always been able to tease Sonny in a way that I haven't. It was nice to see her face so vivid again and to hear her laugh and watch her make Sonny laugh. She wasn't, or, anyway, she didn't seem to be, at all uneasy or embarrassed. She chatted as though there were no subject which had to be avoided and she got Sonny past his first, faint stiffness. And thank God she was there, for I was filled with that icy dread again. Everything I did seemed awkward to me, and everything I said sounded freighted with hidden meaning. I was trying to remember everything I'd heard about dope addiction and I couldn't help watching Sonny for signs. I wasn't doing it out of malice. I was trying to find out something about my brother. I was dying to hear him tell me he was safe.

"Safe!" my father grunted, whenever Mama suggested trying to move to a neighborhood which might be safer for children. "Safe, hell! Ain't no place safe for kids, nor nobody."

He always went on like this, but he wasn't, ever, really as bad as he sounded, not even on weekends, when he got drunk. As a matter of fact, he was always on the lookout for "something a little better," but he died before he found it. He died suddenly, during a drunken weekend in the middle of the war, when Sonny was fifteen. He and Sonny hadn't ever got on too well. And this was partly because Sonny was the apple of his father's eye. It was because he loved Sonny so much and was frightened for him, that he was always fighting with him. It doesn't do any good to fight with Sonny. Sonny just moves back, inside himself, where he can't be reached. But the principal reason that they never hit it off is that they were so much alike. Daddy was big and rough and loud-talking, just the opposite of Sonny, but they both had—that same privacy.

Mama tried to tell me something about this, just after Daddy died. I was home on leave from the army.

This was the last time I ever saw my mother alive. Just the same, this picture gets all mixed up in my mind with pictures I had of her when she was younger. The way I always see her is the way she used to be on a Sunday afternoon, say, when the old folks were talking after the big Sunday dinner. I always see her wearing pale blue. She'd be sitting on the sofa. And my father would be sitting in the easy chair, not far from her. And the living room would be full of church folks and relatives. There they sit, in chairs all around the living room, and the night is creeping up outside, but nobody knows it yet. You can see the darkness growing against the windowpanes and you hear the street noises every now and again, or maybe the jangling beat of a tambourine from one of the churches close by, but it's real quiet in the room. For a moment nobody's talking, but every face looks darkening, like the sky outside. And my mother rocks a little from the waist, and my father's eyes are closed. Everyone is looking at something a child can't see. For a minute they've forgotten the children. Maybe a kid is lying on the rug, half asleep. Maybe somebody's got a kid in his lap and is absent-mindedly stroking the kid's head. Maybe there's a kid, quiet and big-eyed, curled up in a big chair in the corner. The silence, the darkness coming, and the darkness in the faces frighten the child obscurely. He hopes that the hand which strokes his forehead will never stop—will never die. He hopes that there will never come a time when the old folks won't be sitting around the living room, talking about where they've come from, and what they've seen, and what's happened to them and their kinfolk.

But something deep and watchful in the child knows that this is bound to end, is already ending. In a moment someone will get up and turn on the light. Then the old folks will remember the children and they won't talk any more that day. And when light fills the room, the child is filled with darkness. He knows that every time this happens he's moved just a little closer to that darkness outside. The darkness outside is what the old folks have been talking about. It's what they've come from. It's what they endure. The child knows that they won't talk any more because if he knows too much about what's happened to *them*, he'll know too much too soon, about what's going to happen to *him*.

The last time I talked to my mother, I remember I was restless. I wanted to get out and see Isabel. We weren't married then and we had a lot to straighten out between us.

There Mama sat, in black, by the window. She was humming an old church song, *Lord, you brought me from a long ways off*. Sonny was out somewhere. Mama kept watching the streets.

"I don't know," she said, "if I'll ever see you again, after you go off from here. But I hope you'll remember the things I tried to teach you."

"Don't talk like that," I said, and smiled. "You'll be here a long time yet."

She smiled, too, but she said nothing. She was quiet for a long time. And I said, "Mama, don't you worry about nothing. I'll be writing all the time, and you be getting the checks. . . ."

"I want to talk to you about your brother," she said, suddenly. "If anything happens to me he ain't going to have nobody to look out for him."

"Mama," I said, "ain't nothing going to happen to you *or* Sonny. Sonny's all right. He's a good boy and he's got good sense."

"It ain't a question of his being a good boy," Mama said, "nor of his having good sense. It ain't only the bad ones, nor yet the dumb ones that gets sucked under." She stopped, looking at me. "Your Daddy once had a brother," she said, and she smiled in a way that made me feel she was in pain. "You didn't never know that, did you?"

"No," I said, "I never knew that," and I watched her face.

"Oh, yes," she said, "your Daddy had a brother." She looked out of the window again. "I know you never saw your Daddy cry. But *I* did—many a time, through all these years."

I asked her, "What happened to his brother? How come nobody's ever talked about him?"

This was the first time I ever saw my mother look old.

"His brother got killed," she said, "when he was just a little younger than you are now. I knew him. He was a fine boy. He was maybe a little full of the devil, but he didn't mean nobody no harm."

Then she stopped and the room was silent, exactly as it had sometimes been on those Sunday afternoons. Mama kept looking out into the streets.

"He used to have a job in the mill," she said, "and, like all young folks, he just liked to perform on Saturday nights. Saturday nights, him and your father would drift around to different place, go to dances and things like that, or just sit around with people they knew, and your father's brother would sing, he had a fine voice, and play along with himself on his guitar. Well, this particular Saturday night, him and your father was coming home from some place, and they were both a little drunk and there was a moon that night, it was bright like day. Your father's brother was feeling kind of good, and he was whistling to himself, and he had his guitar slung over his shoulder. They was coming down a hill and beneath them was a road that turned off from the highway. Well, your father's brother, being always kind of frisky, decided to run down this hill, and he did, with that guitar banging and clanging behind him, and he ran across the road, and he was making water behind a tree. And your father was sort of amused at him and he was still coming down the hill, kind of slow. Then he heard a car motor and that same minute his brother stepped from behind the tree, into the road, in the moonlight. And he started to cross the road. And your father started to run down the hill, he says he don't know why. This car was full of white men. They was all drunk, and when they seen your father's brother they let out a great whoop and holler and they aimed the car straight at him. They was having fun, they just wanted to scare him, the way they do sometimes, you know. But they was drunk. And I guess the boy, being drunk, too, and scared, kind of lost his head. By the time he jumped it was too late. Your father says he heard his brother scream when the car rolled over him, and he heard the wood of that guitar when it give, and he heard them strings go flying, and he heard them white men shouting, and the car kept on a-going and it ain't stopped till this day. And, time your father got down the hill, his brother weren't nothing but blood and pulp."

Tears were gleaming on my mother's face. There wasn't anything I could say.

"He never mentioned it," she said, "because I never let him mention it before you children. Your Daddy was like a crazy man that night and for many a night thereafter. He says he never in his life seen anything as dark as that road after the lights of that car had gone away. Weren't nothing, weren't nobody on that road, just your Daddy and his brother and that busted guitar. Oh, yes. Your Daddy never did really get right again. Till the day he died he weren't sure but that every white man he saw was the man that killed his brother."

She stopped and took out her handkerchief and dried her eyes and looked at me.

"I ain't telling you all this," she said, "to make you scared or bitter or to make you hate nobody. I'm telling you this because you got a brother. And the world ain't changed."

I guess I didn't want to believe this. I guess she saw this in my face. She turned away from me, toward the window again, searching those streets.

"But I praise my Redeemer," she said at last, "that He called your Daddy home before me. I ain't saying it to throw no flowers at myself, but, I declare, it keeps me from feeling too cast down to know I helped your father get safely through this world. Your father always acted like he was the roughest, strongest man on earth. And everybody took him to be like that. But if he hadn't had *me* there—to see his tears!"

She was crying again. Still, I couldn't move. I said, "Lord, Lord, Mama, I didn't know it was like that."

"Oh, honey," she said, "there's a lot that you don't know. But you are going to find out." She stood up from the window and came over to me. "You got to hold on to your brother," she said, "and don't let him fall, no matter what it looks like is happening to him and no matter how evil you gets with him. You going to be evil with him many a time. But don't you forget what I told you, you hear?"

"I won't forget," I said. "Don't you worry, I won't forget. I won't let nothing happen to Sonny."

My mother smiled as though she were amused at something she saw in my face. Then, "You may not be able to stop nothing from happening. But you got to let him know you's *there*."

Two days later I was married, and then I was gone. And I had a lot of things on my mind and I pretty well forgot my promise to Mama until I got shipped home on a special furlough for her funeral.

And, after the funeral, with just Sonny and me alone in the empty kitchen, I tried to find out something about him.

"What do you want to do?" I asked him.

"I'm going to be a musician," he said.

For he had graduated, in the time I had been away, from dancing to the juke box to finding out who was playing what, and what they were doing with it, and he had bought himself a set of drums.

"You mean, you want to be a drummer?" I somehow had the feeling that being a drummer might be all right for other people but not for my brother Sonny.

"I don't think," he said, looking at me very gravely, "that I'll ever be a good drummer. But I think I can play a piano."

I frowned. I'd never played the role of the older brother quite so seriously before, had scarcely ever, in fact, *asked* Sonny a damn thing. I sensed myself in the presence of something I didn't really know how to handle, didn't understand. So I made my frown a little deeper as I asked: "What kind of musician do you want to be?"

He grinned. "How many kinds do you think there are?"

"Be *serious,*" I said.

He laughed, throwing his head back, and then looked at me. "I *am* serious."

"Well, then, for Christ's sake, stop kidding around and answer a serious question. I mean, do you want to be a concert pianist, you want to play classical music and all that, or—or what?" Long before I finished he was laughing again. "For Christ's *sake,* Sonny!"

He sobered, but with difficulty. "I'm sorry. But you sound so—*scared!*" and he was off again.

"Well, you may think it's funny now, baby, but it's not going to be so funny when you have to make your living at it, let me tell you *that.*" I was furious because I knew he was laughing at me and I didn't know why.

"No," he said, very sober now, and afraid, perhaps, that he'd hurt me, "I don't want to be a classical pianist. That isn't what interests me. I mean"—he paused, looking hard at me, as though his eyes would help me to understand, and then gestured helplessly, as though perhaps his hand would help—"I mean, I'll have a lot of studying to do, and I'll have to study *everything,* but, I mean, I want to play *with*—jazz musicians." He stopped. "I want to play jazz," he said.

Well, the word had never before sounded as heavy, as real, as it sounded that afternoon in Sonny's mouth. I just looked at him and I was probably frowning a real frown by this time. I simply couldn't see why on earth he'd want to spend his time hanging around nightclubs, clowning around on bandstands, while people pushed each other around a dance floor. It seemed—beneath him, somehow. I had never thought about it before, had never been forced to, but I suppose I had always put jazz musicians in a class with what Daddy called "good-time people."

"Are you *serious?*"

"Hell, *yes,* I'm serious."

He looked more helpless than ever, and annoyed, and deeply hurt.

I suggested, helpfully: "You mean—like Louis Armstrong?"

His face closed as though I'd struck him. "No. I'm not talking about none of that old-time, down home crap."

"Well, look, Sonny, I'm sorry, don't get mad. I just don't altogether get it, that's all. Name somebody—you know, a jazz musician you admire."

"Bird."

"Who?"

"Bird! Charlie Parker![4] Don't they teach you nothing in the goddamn army?"

I lit a cigarette. I was surprised and then a little amused to discover that I was trembling. "I've been out of touch," I said. "You'll have to be patient with me. Now. Who's this Parker character?"

4. Charlie ("Bird") Parker (1920–1955), for whom Birdland in New York was named, perhaps the greatest saxophonist and innovator of jazz; cofounder, with Dizzy Gillespie, of the new jazz, once called "bebop"; narcotics addict.

"He's just one of the greatest jazz musicians alive," said Sonny, sullenly, his hands in his pockets, his back to me. "Maybe *the* greatest," he added, bitterly, "that's probably why *you* never heard of him."

"All right," I said, "I'm ignorant. I'm sorry. I'll go out and buy all the cat's records right away, all right?"

"It don't," said Sonny, with dignity, "make any difference to me. I don't care what you listen to. Don't do me no favors."

I was beginning to realize that I'd never seen him so upset before. With another part of my mind I was thinking that this would probably turn out to be one of those things kids go through and that I shouldn't make it seem important by pushing it too hard. Still, I didn't think it would do any harm to ask: "Doesn't all this take a lot of time? Can you make a living at it?"

He turned back to me and half leaned, half sat, on the kitchen table. "Everything takes time," he said, "and—well, yes, sure, I can make a living at it. But what I don't seem to be able to make you understand is that it's the only thing I want to do."

"Well, Sonny," I said, gently, "you know people can't always do exactly what they *want* to do—"

"*No*, I don't know that," said Sonny, surprising me. "I think people *ought* to do what they want to do, what else are they alive for?"

"You getting to be a big boy," I said desperately, "it's time you started thinking about your future."

"I'm thinking about my future," said Sonny, grimly. "I think about it all the time."

I gave up. I decided, if he didn't change his mind, that we could always talk about it later. "In the meantime," I said, "you got to finish school." We had already decided that he'd have to move in with Isabel and her folks. I knew this wasn't the ideal arrangement because Isabel's folks are inclined to be dicty[5] and they hadn't especially wanted Isabel to marry me. But I didn't know what else to do. "And we have to get you fixed up at Isabel's."

There was a long silence. He moved from the kitchen table to the window. "That's a terrible idea. You know it yourself."

"Do you have a *better* idea?"

He just walked up and down the kitchen for a minute. He was as tall as I was. He had started to shave. I suddenly had the feeling that I didn't know him at all.

He stopped at the kitchen table and picked up my cigarettes. Looking at me with a kind of mocking, amused defiance, he put one between his lips. "You mind?"

"You smoking already?"

He lit the cigarette and nodded, watching me through the smoke. "I just wanted to see if I'd have the courage to smoke in front of you." He grinned and blew a great cloud of smoke to the ceiling. "It was easy." He looked at my face. "Come on, now. I bet you was smoking at my age, tell the truth."

I didn't say anything but the truth was on my face, and he laughed. But now there was something very strained in his laugh. "Sure. And

5. Snobbish, bossy.

I bet that ain't all you was doing."

He was frightening me a little. "Cut the crap," I said. "We already decided that you was going to go and live at Isabel's. Now what's got into you all of a sudden?"

"*You* decided it," he pointed out. "*I* didn't decide nothing." He stopped in front of me, leaning against the stove, arms loosely folded. "Look, brother. I don't want to stay in Harlem no more, I really don't." He was very earnest. He looked at me, then over toward the kitchen window. There was something in his eyes I'd never seen before, some thoughtfulness, some worry all his own. He rubbed the muscle of one arm. "It's time I was getting out of here."

"Where do you want to *go*, Sonny?"

"I want to join the army. Or the navy, I don't care. If I say I'm old enough, they'll believe me."

Then I got mad. It was because I was so scared. "You must be crazy. You goddamn fool, what the hell do you want to go and join the *army* for?"

"I just told you. To get out of Harlem."

"Sonny, you haven't even finished *school*. And if you really want to be a musician, how do you expect to study if you're in the *army?*"

He looked at me, trapped, and in anguish. "There's ways. I might be able to work out some kind of deal. Anyway, I'll have the G.I. Bill when I come out."

"*If* you come out." We stared at each other. "Sonny, please. Be reasonable. I know the setup is far from perfect. But we got to do the best we can."

"I ain't learning nothing in school," he said. "Even when I go." He turned away from me and opened the window and threw his cigarette out into the narrow alley. I watched his back. "At least, I ain't learning nothing you'd want me to learn." He slammed the window so hard I thought the glass would fly out, and turned back to me. "And I'm sick of the stink of these garbage cans!"

"Sonny," I said, "I know how you feel. But if you don't finish school now, you're going to be sorry later that you didn't." I grabbed him by the shoulders. "And you only got another year. It ain't so bad. And I'll come back and I swear I'll help you do *whatever* you want to do. Just try to put up with it till I come back. Will you please do that? For me?"

He didn't answer and he wouldn't look at me.

"Sonny. You hear me?"

He pulled away. "I hear you. But you never hear anything *I* say."

I didn't know what to say to that. He looked out of the window and then back at me. "OK," he said, and sighed. "I'll try."

Then I said, trying to cheer him up a little, "They got a piano at Isabel's. You can practice on it."

And as a matter of fact, it did cheer him up for a minute. "That's right," he said to himself. "I forgot that." His face relaxed a little. But the worry, the thoughtfulness, played on it still, the way shadows play on a face which is staring into the fire.

But I thought I'd never hear the end of that piano. At first, Isabel would write me, saying how nice it was that Sonny was so serious about his music and how, as soon as he came in from school, or wherever he had been when he was supposed to be at school, he went straight to that piano and stayed there until suppertime. And, after supper, he went back to that piano and stayed there until everybody went to bed. He was at the piano all day Saturday and all day Sunday. Then he bought a record player and started playing records. He'd play one record over and over again, all day long sometimes, and he'd improvise along with it on the piano. Or he'd play one section of the record, one chord, one change, one progression, then he'd do it on the piano. Then back to the record. Then back to the piano.

Well, I really don't know how they stood it. Isabel finally confessed that it wasn't like living with a person at all, it was like living with sound. And the sound didn't make any sense to her, didn't make any sense to any of them—naturally. They began, in a way, to be afflicted by this presence that was living in their home. It was as though Sonny were some sort of god, or monster. He moved in an atmosphere which wasn't like theirs at all. They fed him and he ate, he washed himself, he walked in and out of their door; he certainly wasn't nasty or unpleasant or rude, Sonny isn't any of those things; but it was as though he were all wrapped up in some cloud, some fire, some vision all his own; and there wasn't any way to reach him.

At the same time, he wasn't really a man yet, he was still a child, and they had to watch out for him in all kinds of ways. They certainly couldn't throw him out. Neither did they dare to make a great scene about that piano because even they dimly sensed, as I sensed, from so many thousands of miles away, that Sonny was at that piano playing for his life.

But he hadn't been going to school. One day a letter came from the school board and Isabel's mother got it—there had, apparently, been other letters but Sonny had torn them up. This day, when Sonny came in, Isabel's mother showed him the letter and asked where he'd been spending his time. And she finally got it out of him that he'd been down in Greenwich Village, with musicians and other characters, in a white girl's apartment. And this scared her and she started to scream at him and what came up, once she began—though she denies it to this day—was what sacrifices they were making to give Sonny a decent home and how little he appreciated it.

Sonny didn't play the piano that day. By evening, Isabel's mother had calmed down but then there was the old man to deal with, and Isabel herself. Isabel says she did her best to be calm but she broke down and started crying. She says she just watched Sonny's face. She could tell, by watching him, what was happening with him. And what was happening was that they penetrated his cloud, they had reached him. Even if their fingers had been a thousand times more gentle than human fingers ever are, he could hardly help feeling that they had stripped him naked and were spitting on that nakedness. For he also had to see that his presence, that music, which was life or death to him, had been torture for them and that they had endured it, not at all for his sake, but only for mine. And Sonny couldn't take that. He can take it a little better today than he could then but he's still not very good at it and, frankly, I don't know anybody who is.

The silence of the next few days must have been louder than the sound of all the music ever played since time began. One morning, before she went to work, Isabel was in his room for something and she suddenly realized that all of his records were gone. And she knew for certain that he was gone. And he was. He went as far as the navy would carry him. He finally sent me a postcard from some place in Greece and that was the first I knew that Sonny was still alive. I didn't see him any more until we were both back in New York and the war had long been over.

He was a man by then, of course, but I wasn't willing to see it. He came by the house from time to time, but we fought almost every time we met. I didn't like the way he carried himself, loose and dreamlike all the time, and I didn't like his friends, and his music seemed to be merely an excuse for the life he led. It sounded just that weird and disordered.

Then we had a fight, a pretty awful fight, and I didn't see him for months. By and by I looked him up, where he was living, in a furnished room in the Village, and I tried to make it up. But there were lots of other people in the room and Sonny just lay on his bed, and he wouldn't come downstairs with me, and he treated these other people as though they were his family and I weren't. So I got mad and then he got mad, and then I told him that he might just as well be dead as live the way he was living. Then he stood up and he told me not to worry about him any more in life, that he *was* dead as far as I was concerned. Then he pushed me to the door and the other people looked on as though nothing were happening, and he slammed the door behind me. I stood in the hallway, staring at the door. I heard somebody laugh in the room and then the tears came to my eyes. I started down the steps, whistling to keep from crying, I kept whistling to myself, *You going to need me, baby, one of these cold, rainy days.*

I read about Sonny's trouble in the spring. Little Grace died in the fall. She was a beautiful little girl. But she only lived a little over two years. She died of polio and she suffered. She had a slight fever for a couple of days, but it didn't seem like anything and we just kept her in bed. And we would certainly have called the doctor, but the fever dropped, she seemed to be all right. So we thought it had just been a cold. Then, one day, she was up, playing, Isabel was in the kitchen fixing lunch for the two boys when they'd come in from school, and she heard Grace fall down in the living room. When you have a lot of children you don't always start running when one of them falls, unless they start screaming or something. And, this time, Gracie was quiet. Yet, Isabel says that when she heard that *thump* and then that silence, something happened in her to make her afraid. And she ran to the living room and there was little Grace on the floor, all twisted up, and the reason she hadn't screamed was that she couldn't get her breath. And when she did scream, it was the worst sound, Isabel says, that she'd ever heard in all her life, and she still hears it sometimes in her dreams. Isabel will sometimes wake me up with a low, moaning, strangled sound and I have to be quick to awaken her and hold her to me and where Isabel is weeping against me seems a mortal wound.

I think I may have written Sonny the very day that little Grace was buried. I was sitting in the living room in the dark, by myself, and I suddenly thought of Sonny. My trouble made his real.

One Saturday afternoon, when Sonny had been living with us, or anyway, been in our house, for nearly two weeks, I found myself wandering aimlessly about the living room, drinking from a can of beer, and trying to work up courage to search Sonny's room. He was out, he was usually out whenever I was home, and Isabel had taken the children to see their grandparents. Suddenly I was standing still in front of the living room window, watching Seventh Avenue. The idea of searching Sonny's room made me still. I scarcely dared to admit to myself what I'd be searching for. I didn't know what I'd do if I found it. Or if I didn't.

On the sidewalk across from me, near the entrance to a barbecue joint, some people were holding an old-fashioned revival meeting. The barbecue cook, wearing a dirty white apron, his conked[6] hair reddish and metallic in the pale sun, and a cigarette between his lips, stood in the doorway, watching them. Kids and older people paused in their errands and stood there, along with some older men and a couple of very tough-looking women who watched everything that happened on the avenue, as though they owned it, or were maybe owned by it. Well, they were watching this, too. The revival was being carried on by three sisters in black, and a brother. All they had were their voices and their Bibles and a tambourine. The brother was testifying[7] and while he testified two of the sisters stood together, seeming to say, amen, and the third sister walked around with the tambourine outstretched and a couple of people dropped coins into it. Then the brother's testimony ended and the sister who had been taking up the collection dumped the coins into her palm and transferred them to the pocket of her long black robe. Then she raised both hands, striking the tambourine against the air, and then against one hand, and she started to sing. And the two other sisters and the brother joined in.

It was strange, suddenly, to watch, though I had been seeing these meetings all my life. So, of course, had everybody else down there. Yet, they paused and watched and listened and I stood still at the window. "*'Tis the old ship of Zion,*" they sang, and the sister with the tambourine kept a steady, jangling beat, "*it has rescued many a thousand!*" Not a soul under the sound of their voices was hearing this song for the first time, not one of them had been rescued. Nor had they seen much in the way of rescue work being done around them. Neither did they especially believe in the holiness of the three sisters and the brother, they knew too much about them, knew where they lived, and how. The woman with the tambourine, whose voice dominated the air, whose face was bright with joy, was divided by very little from the woman who stood watching her, a cigarette between her heavy, chapped lips, her hair a cuckoo's nest, her face scarred and swollen from many beatings, and her black eyes glittering like coal. Perhaps they both knew this, which was why, when, as rarely, they addressed each other, they addressed each other as Sister. As the singing filled the air the watching, listening faces underwent a change, the eyes focusing on something within; the music seemed to soothe a poison out of them;

6. Processed: straightened and greased.

7. Publicly professing belief.

and time seemed, nearly, to fall away from the sullen, belligerent, battered faces, as though they were fleeing back to their first condition, while dreaming of their last. The barbecue cook half shook his head and smiled, and dropped his cigarette and disappeared into his joint. A man fumbled in his pockets for change and stood holding it in his hand impatiently, as though he had just remembered a pressing appointment further up the avenue. He looked furious. Then I saw Sonny, standing on the edge of the crowd. He was carrying a wide, flat notebook with a green cover, and it made him look, from where I was standing, almost like a schoolboy. The coppery sun brought out the copper in his skin, he was very faintly smiling, standing very still. Then the singing stopped, the tambourine turned into a collection plate again. The furious man dropped in his coins and vanished, so did a couple of the women, and Sonny dropped some change in the plate, looking directly at the woman with a little smile. He started across the avenue, toward the house. He has a slow, loping walk, something like the way Harlem hipsters walk, only he's imposed on this his own half-beat. I had never really noticed it before.

I stayed at the window, both relieved and apprehensive. As Sonny disappeared from my sight, they began singing again. And they were still singing when his key turned in the lock.

"Hey," he said.

"Hey, yourself. You want some beer?"

"No. Well, maybe." But he came up to the window and stood beside me, looking out. "What a warm voice," he said.

They were singing *If I could only hear my mother pray again!*

"Yes," I said, "and she can sure beat that tambourine."

"But what a terrible song," he said, and laughed. He dropped his notebook on the sofa and disappeared into the kitchen. "Where's Isabel and the kids?"

"I think they went to see their grandparents. You hungry?"

"No." He came back into the living room with his can of beer. "You want to come some place with me tonight?"

I sensed, I don't know how, that I couldn't possibly say no. "Sure. Where?"

He sat down on the sofa and picked up his notebook and started leafing through it. "I'm going to sit in with some fellows in a joint in the Village."

"You mean, you're going to play, tonight?"

"That's right." He took a swallow of his beer and moved back to the window. He gave me a sidelong look. "If you can stand it."

"I'll try," I said.

He smiled to himself and we both watched as the meeting across the way broke up. The three sisters and the brother, heads bowed, were singing *God be with you till we meet again.* The faces around them were very quiet. Then the song ended. The small crowd dispersed. We watched the three women and the lone man walk slowly up the avenue.

"When she was singing before," said Sonny, abruptly, "her voice reminded me for a minute of what heroin feels like sometimes—when it's in your veins. It makes you feel sort of warm and cool at the same time. And distant. And—and sure." He sipped his beer, very deliberately not looking at me. I watched his face. "It makes you feel—in control. Sometimes you've got to have that feeling."

"Do you?" I sat down slowly in the easy chair.

"Sometimes." He went to the sofa and picked up his notebook again. "Some people do."

"In order," I asked, "to play?" And my voice was very ugly, full of contempt and anger.

"Well"—he looked at me with great, troubled eyes, as though, in fact, he hoped his eyes would tell me things he could never otherwise say—"they *think* so. And *if* they think so—!"

"And what do *you* think?" I asked.

He sat on the sofa and put his can of beer on the floor. "I don't know," he said, and I couldn't be sure if he were answering my question or pursuing his thoughts. His face didn't tell me. "It's not so much to *play*. It's to *stand* it, to be able to make it at all. On any level." He frowned and smiled: "In order to keep from shaking to pieces."

"But these friends of yours," I said, "they seem to shake themselves to pieces pretty goddamn fast."

"Maybe." He played with the notebook. And something told me that I should curb my tongue, that Sonny was doing his best to talk, that I should listen. "But of course you only know the ones that've gone to pieces. Some don't—or at least they haven't *yet* and that's just about all *any* of us can say." He paused. "And then there are some who just live, really, in hell, and they know it and they see what's happening and they go right on. I don't know." He sighed, dropped the notebook, folded his arms. "Some guys, you can tell from the way they play, they on something *all* the time. And you can see that, well, it makes something real for them. But of course," he picked up his beer from the floor and sipped it and put the can down again, "they *want* to, too, you've got to see that. Even some of them that say they don't—*some*, not all."

"And what about you?" I asked—I couldn't help it. "What about you? Do *you* want to?"

He stood up and walked to the window and I remained silent for a long time. Then he sighed. "Me," he said. Then: "While I was downstairs before, on my way here, listening to that woman sing, it struck me all of a sudden how much suffering she must have had to go through—to sing like that. It's *repulsive* to think you have to suffer that much."

I said: "But there's no way not to suffer—is there, Sonny?"

"I believe not," he said and smiled, "but that's never stopped anyone from trying." He looked at me. "Has it?" I realized, with this mocking look, that there stood between us, forever, beyond the power of time or forgiveness, the fact that I had held silence—so long!—when he had needed human speech to help him. He turned back to the window. "No, there's no way not to suffer. But you try all kinds of ways to keep from drowning in it, to keep on top of it, and to make it seem—well, like *you*. Like you did something, all right, and now you're suffering for it. You know?" I said nothing. "Well you know," he said, impatiently, "why *do* people suffer? Maybe it's better to do something to give it a reason, *any* reason."

"But we just agreed," I said, "that there's no way not to suffer. Isn't it better, then, just to—take it?"

"But nobody just takes it," Sonny cried, "that's what I'm telling you! *Everybody* tries not to. You're just hung up on the *way* some people try—it's not *your* way!"

The hair on my face began to itch, my face felt wet. "That's not true," I said, "that's not true. I don't give a damn what other people do, I don't even care how they suffer. I just care how *you* suffer." And he looked at me. "Please believe me," I said, "I don't want to see you—die—trying not to suffer."

"I won't," he said flatly, "die trying not to suffer. At least, not any faster than anybody else."

"But there's no need," I said, trying to laugh, "is there? in killing yourself."

I wanted to say more, but I couldn't. I wanted to talk about will power and how life could be—well, beautiful. I wanted to say that it was all within; but was it? or, rather, wasn't that exactly the trouble? And I wanted to promise that I would never fail him again. But it would all have sounded—empty words and lies.

So I made the promise to myself and prayed that I would keep it.

"It's terrible sometimes, inside," he said, "that's what's the trouble. You walk these streets, black and funky and cold, and there's not really a living ass to talk to, and there's nothing shaking, and there's no way of getting it out—that storm inside. You can't talk it and you can't make love with it, and when you finally try to get with it and play it, you realize *nobody's* listening. So *you've* got to listen. You got to find a way to listen."

And then he walked away from the window and sat on the sofa again, as though all the wind had suddenly been knocked out of him. "Sometimes you'll do *anything* to play, even cut your mother's throat." He laughed and looked at me. "Or your brother's." Then he sobered. "Or your own." Then: "Don't worry. I'm all right now and I think I'll *be* all right. But I can't forget—where I've been. I don't mean just the physical place I've been, I mean where I've *been*. And *what* I've been."

"What have you been, Sonny?" I asked.

He smiled—but sat sideways on the sofa, his elbow resting on the back, his fingers playing with his mouth and chin, not looking at me. "I've been something I didn't recognize, didn't know I could be. Didn't know anybody could be." He stopped, looking inward, looking helplessly young, looking old. "I'm not talking about it now because I feel *guilty* or anything like that—maybe it would be better if I did, I don't know. Anyway, I can't really talk about it. Not to you, not to anybody," and now he turned and faced me. "Sometimes, you know, and it was actually when I was most *out* of the world, I felt that I was in it, that I was *with* it, really, and I could play or I didn't really have to *play*, it just came out of me, it was there. And I don't know how I played, thinking about it now, but I know I did awful things, those times, sometimes, to people. Or it wasn't that I *did* anything to them—it was that they weren't real." He picked up the beer can; it was empty; he rolled it between his palms: "And other times—well, I needed a fix, I needed to find a place to lean, I needed to clear a space to *listen*—and I couldn't find it, and I—went crazy, I did terrible things to *me*, I was terrible *for* me." He began pressing the beer can between his hands, I watched the metal begin to give. It glittered, as he played with it like a knife, and I was afraid he would cut himself, but I said nothing. "Oh well. I can never tell you. I was all by myself at the bottom of something, stinking and sweating and crying and shaking, and I smelled it, you know? *my* stink, and I thought I'd die if I couldn't get away from it and yet, all the same, I knew that everything I was doing was just locking me in with it. And I didn't know," he paused, still flattening the beer can, "I didn't know, I still *don't* know, something kept telling me that maybe it was good to smell your own stink, but I didn't think that *that* was what I'd been trying to do—and—who can stand it?" and he abruptly dropped the ruined beer can, looking at me with a small, still smile, and then rose, walking to the window as though it were the lodestone rock. I watched his face, he watched the avenue. "I couldn't tell you when Mama died—but the reason I wanted to leave Harlem so bad was to get away from drugs. And then, when I ran away, that's what I was running from—really. When I came back, nothing had changed, *I* hadn't changed, I was just—older." And he stopped, drumming with his fingers on the windowpane. The sun had vanished, soon darkness would fall. I watched his face. "It can come again," he said, almost as though speaking to himself. Then he turned to me. "It can come again," he repeated. "I just want you to know that."

"All right," I said, at last. "So it can come again. All right."

He smiled, but the smile was sorrowful. "I had to try to tell you," he said.

"Yes," I said. "I understand that."

"You're my brother," he said, looking straight at me, and not smiling at all.

"Yes," I repeated, "yes. I understand that."

He turned back to the window, looking out. "All that hatred down there," he said, "all that hatred and misery and love. It's a wonder it doesn't blow the avenue apart."

We went to the only nightclub on a short, dark street, downtown. We squeezed through the narrow, chattering, jampacked bar to the entrance of the big room, where the bandstand was. And we stood there for a moment, for the lights were very dim in this room and we couldn't see. Then, "Hello, boy," said a voice and an enormous black man, much older than Sonny or myself, erupted out of all that atmospheric lighting and put an arm around Sonny's shoulder. "I been sitting right here," he said, "waiting for you."

He had a big voice, too, and heads in the darkness turned toward us.

Sonny grinned and pulled a little away, and said, "Creole, this is my brother. I told you about him."

Creole shook my hand. "I'm glad to meet you, son," he said, and it was clear that he was glad to meet me *there*, for Sonny's sake. And he smiled, "You got a real musician in *your* family," and he took his arm from Sonny's shoulder and slapped him, lightly, affectionately, with the back of his hand.

"Well. Now I've heard it all," said a voice behind us. This was another musician, and a friend of Sonny's, a coal-black, cheerful-looking man, built close to the ground. He immediately began confiding to me, at the top of his lungs, the most terrible things about Sonny, his teeth gleaming like a lighthouse and his laugh coming up out of him like the beginning of an earthquake. And it turned out that everyone at the bar knew Sonny, or almost everyone; some were musicians, working there, or nearby, or not working, some were simply hangers-on, and some were there to hear Sonny play. I was introduced to all of them and they were all very polite to me. Yet, it was clear that, for them, I was only Sonny's brother. Here, I was in Sonny's world. Or, rather: his kingdom. Here, it was not even a question that his veins bore royal blood.

They were going to play soon and Creole installed me, by myself, at a table in a dark corner. Then I watched them, Creole, and the little black man, and Sonny, and the others, while they horsed around, standing just below the bandstand. The light from the bandstand spilled just a little short of them and, watching them laughing and gesturing and moving about, I had the feeling that they, nevertheless, were being most careful not to step into that circle of light too suddenly: that if they moved into the light too suddenly, without thinking, they would perish in flame. Then, while I watched, one of them, the small black man, moved into the light and crossed the bandstand and started fooling around with his drums. Then—being funny and being, also, extremely ceremonious—Creole took Sonny by the arm and led him to the piano. A woman's voice called Sonny's name and a few hands started clapping. And Sonny, also being funny and being ceremonious, and so touched, I think, that he could have cried, but neither hiding it nor showing it, riding it like a man, grinned, and put both hands to his heart and bowed from the waist.

Creole then went to the bass fiddle and a lean, very bright-skinned brown man jumped up on the bandstand and picked up his horn. So there they were, and the atmosphere on the bandstand and in the room began to change and tighten. Someone stepped up to the microphone and announced them. Then there were all kinds of murmurs. Some people at the bar shushed others. The waitress ran around, frantically getting in the last orders, guys and chicks got closer to each other, and the lights on the bandstand, on the quartet, turned to a kind of indigo. Then they all looked different there. Creole looked about him for the last time, as though he were making certain that all his chickens were in the coop, and then he—jumped and struck the fiddle. And there they were.

All I know about music is that not many people ever really hear it. And even then, on the rare occasions when something opens within, and the music enters, what we mainly hear, or hear corroborated, are personal, private, vanishing evocations. But the man who creates the music is hearing something else, is dealing with the roar rising from the void and imposing order on it as it hits the air. What is evoked in him, then, is of another order, more terrible because it has no words, and triumphant, too, for that same reason. And his triumph, when he triumphs, is ours. I just watched Sonny's face. His face was troubled, he was working hard, but he wasn't with it. And I had the feeling that, in a way, everyone on the bandstand was waiting for him, both waiting for him and pushing him along. But as I began to watch Creole, I realized that it was Creole who held them all back. He had them on a short rein. Up there, keeping the beat with his whole body, wailing on the fiddle, with his eyes half closed, he was listening to everything, but he was listening to Sonny. He was having a dialogue with Sonny. He wanted Sonny to leave the shoreline and strike out for the deep water. He was Sonny's witness that deep water and drowning were not the same thing—he had been there, and he knew. And he wanted Sonny to know. He was waiting for Sonny to do the things on the keys which would let Creole know that Sonny was in the water.

And, while Creole listened, Sonny moved, deep within, exactly like someone in torment. I had never before thought of how awful the relationship must be between the musician and his instrument. He has to fill it, this instrument, with the breath of life, his own. He has to make it do what he wants it to do. And a piano is just a piano. It's made out of so much wood and wires and little hammers and big ones, and ivory. While there's only so much you can do with it, the only way to find this out is to try; to try and make it do everything.

And Sonny hadn't been near a piano for over a year. And he wasn't on much better terms with his life, not the life that stretched before him now. He and the piano stammered, started one way, got scared, stopped; started another way, panicked, marked time, started again; then seemed to have found a direction, panicked again, got stuck. And the face I saw on Sonny I'd never seen before. Everything had been burned out of it, and, at the same time, things usually hidden were being burned in, by the fire and fury of the battle which was occurring in him up there.

Yet, watching Creole's face as they neared the end of the first set, I had the feeling that something had happened, something I hadn't heard. Then they finished, there was scattered applause, and then, without an instant's warning, Creole started into something else, it was almost sardonic, it was *Am I Blue*.[8] And, as though he commanded, Sonny began to play. Something began to happen. And Creole let out the reins. The dry, low, black man said something awful on the drums, Creole answered, and the drums talked back. Then the horn insisted, sweet and high, slightly detached perhaps, and Creole listened, commenting now and then, dry, and driving, beautiful and calm and old. Then they all came together again, and Sonny was part of the family again. I could tell this from his face. He seemed to have found, right there beneath his fingers, a damn brand-new piano. It seemed that he couldn't get over it. Then, for a while, just being happy with Sonny, they seemed to be agreeing with him that brand-new pianos certainly were a gas.

Then Creole stepped forward to remind them that what they were playing was the blues. He hit something in all of them, he hit something in me, myself, and the music tightened and deepened, apprehension began to beat the air. Creole began to tell us what the blues were all about. They were not about anything very new. He and his boys up

8. By Grant Clark and Harry Akst, sung by Ethel Waters in 1929 film, "On with the Show," brilliantly recorded by Billy Holiday, and a favorite blues piece.

there were keeping it new, at the risk of ruin, destruction, madness, and death, in order to find new ways to make us listen. For, while the tale of how we suffer, and how we are delighted, and how we may triumph is never new, it always must be heard. There isn't any other tale to tell, it's the only light we've got in all this darkness.

And this tale, according to that face, that body, those strong hands on those strings, has another aspect in every country, and a new depth in every generation. Listen, Creole seemed to be saying, listen. Now these are Sonny's blues. He made the little black man on the drums know it, and the bright, brown man on the horn. Creole wasn't trying any longer to get Sonny in the water. He was wishing him Godspeed. Then he stepped back, very slowly, filling the air with the immense suggestion that Sonny speak for himself.

Then they all gathered around Sonny and Sonny played. Every now and again one of them seemed to say, amen. Sonny's fingers filled the air with life, his life. But that life contained so many others. And Sonny went all the way back, he really began with the spare, flat statement of the opening phrase of the song. Then he began to make it his. It was very beautiful because it wasn't hurried and it was no longer a lament. I seemed to hear with what burning he had made it his, with what burning we had yet to make it ours, how we could cease lamenting. Freedom lurked around us and I understood, at last, that he could help us to be free if we would listen, that he would never be free until we did. Yet, there was no battle in his face now, I heard what he had gone through, and would continue to go through until he came to rest in earth. He had made it his: that long line, of which we knew only Mama and Daddy. And he was giving it back, as everything must be given back, so that, passing through death, it can live forever. I saw my mother's face again, and felt, for the first time, how the stones of the road she had walked on must have bruised her feet. I saw the moonlit road where my father's brother died. And it brought something else back to me, and carried me past it, I saw my little girl again and felt Isabel's tears again, and I felt my own tears begin to rise. And I was yet aware that this was only a moment, that the world waited outside, as hungry as a tiger, and that trouble stretched above us, longer than the sky.

Then it was over. Creole and Sonny let out their breath, both soaking wet, and grinning. There was a lot of applause and some of it was real. In the dark, the girl came by and I asked her to take drinks to the bandstand. There was a long pause, while they talked up there in the indigo light and after awhile I saw the girl put a Scotch and milk on top of the piano for Sonny. He didn't seem to notice it, but just before they started playing again, he sipped from it and looked toward me, and nodded. Then he put it back on top of the piano. For me, then, as they began to play again, it glowed and shook above my brother's head like the very cup of trembling.[9]

1965

9. See *Isaiah* 51:17, 22–23: "Awake, awake, stand up, O Jerusalem, which hast drunk at the hand of the Lord the cup of his fury; thou hast drunken the dregs of the cup of trembling, and wrung them out. . . . Behold, I have taken out of thine hand the cup of trembling, even the dregs of the cup of my fury; thou shalt no more drink it again: But I will put it into the hands of them that afflict thee; . . . ."

Stories for Further Reading

GEORGE WASHINGTON HARRIS

Mrs. Yardley's Quilting

"Thar's one durn'd nasty muddy job, an' I is jis' glad enuf tu take a ho'n[1] ur two, on the straingth ove hit."

"What have you been doing, Sut?"

"Helpin tu salt ole Missis Yardley down."

"What do you mean by that?"

"Fixin her fur rotten cumfurtably, kiverin her up wif sile, tu keep the buzzards from cheatin the wurms."

"Oh, you have been helping to bury a woman."

"That's hit, by golly! Now why the devil can't I 'splain myself like yu? I ladles out my words at randum, like a calf kickin at yaller-jackids; yu jis' rolls em out tu the pint, like a feller a-layin bricks—every one fits. How is it that bricks fits so clost enyhow? Rocks won't ni du hit."

"Becaze they'se all ove a size," ventured a man with a wen over his eye.

"The devil yu say, hon'ey-head![2] haint reapin-mersheens ove a size? I'd like tu see two ove em fit clost. Yu wait ontil yu sprouts tuther ho'n, afore yu venters tu 'splain mix'd questions. George did yu know ole Missis Yardley?"

"No."

"Well, she wer a curious 'oman in her way, an' she wore shiney specks. Now jis' listen: Whenever yu see a ole 'oman ahine a par ove *shiney* specks, yu keep yer eye skinn'd; they am dang'rus in the extreme. Thar is jis' no knowin' what they ken du. I hed one a-stradil ove me onst, fur kissin her gal. She went fur my har, an' she went fur my skin, ontil I tho't she ment tu kill me, an' wud a-dun hit, ef my hollerin hadent fotch ole Dave Jordan, a *bacheler*, tu my aid. He, like a durn'd fool, cotch her by the laig, an' drug her back'ards ofen me. She jis' kivered him, an' I run, by golly! The nex time I seed him he wer bald headed, an' his face looked like he'd been a-fitin wildcats.

"Ole Missis Yardley wer a great noticer ove littil things, that nobody else ever seed. She'd say right in the middil ove sumbody's serious talk: 'Law sakes! thar goes that yaller slut ove a hen, a-flingin straws over her shoulder; she's arter settin now, an' haint laid but seven aigs. I'll disapint *her*, see ef I don't; I'll put a punkin in her nes', an' a feather in her nose. An' bless my soul! jis' look at that cow wif the wilted ho'n, a-flingin up dirt an' a-smellin the place whar hit cum frum, wif

1. "Horn": a drink.
2. "Horny-head" (because of a wen, or tumor); thus his reference to sporting another horn and becoming wise (like the devil?).

the rale ginuine still-wurim twis'[3] in her tail, too; what upon the face ove the yeath kin she be arter now, the ole fool? watch her, Sally. An' sakes alive jis' look at that ole sow; she's a-gwine in a fas' trot, wif her empty bag a-floppin agin her sides. Thar, she hes stop't, an's a-listenin! massy on us! what a long yearnis grunt she gin; hit cum frum way back ove her kidneys. Thar she goes agin; she's arter no good, sich kerryin on means no good.'

"An' so she wud gabble, no odds who wer a-listenin. She looked like she mout been made at fust 'bout four foot long, an' the common thickness ove wimen when they's at tharsefs,[4] an' then had her har tied tu a stump, a par ove steers hitched to her heels, an' then straiched out a-mos' two foot more—mos' ove the straichin cumin outen her laigs an' naik. Her stockins, a-hangin on the clothesline tu dry, looked like a par ove sabre scabbards, an' her naik looked like a dry beef shank smoked, an' mout been ni ontu es tough. I never felt hit mysef, I didn't, I jis' jedges by looks. Her darter Sal wer bilt at fust 'bout the laingth ove her mam, but wer never straiched eny by a par ove steers an' she wer fat enuf tu kill; she wer taller lyin down than she wer a-standin up. Hit wer her who gin me the 'hump shoulder.' Jis' look at me; haint I'se got a tech ove the dromedary back thar bad? haint I humpy? Well, a-stoopin tu kiss that squatty lard-stan[5] ove a gal is what dun hit tu me. She wer the fairest-lookin gal I ever seed. She allers wore thick woolin stockins 'bout six inches too long fur her laig; they rolled down over her garters, lookin like a par ove life-presarvers up thar. I tell yu she wer a tarin gal enyhow. Luved kissin, wrastlin, an' biled cabbige, an' hated tite clothes, hot weather, an suckit-riders.[6] B'leved strong in married folk's ways, cradles, an' the remishun ove sins, an' didn't b'leve in corsets, fleas, peaners, nur the fashun plates."

"What caused the death of Mrs. Yardley, Sut?"

"Nuffin, only her heart stop't beatin 'bout losin a nine dimunt quilt.[7] True, she got a skeer'd hoss tu run over her, but she'd a-got over that ef a quilt hadn't been mix'd up in the catastrophy. Yu see quilts wer wun ove her speshul gifts; she run strong on the bed-kiver question. Irish chain, star ove Texas, sun-flower, nine-dimunt, saw teeth, checker board, an' shell quilts; blue, an' white, an' yaller an' black coverlids, an' callickercumfurts[8] reigned triumphan' 'bout her hous'. They wer packed in drawers, layin in shelfs full, wer hung four dubbil on lines in the lof, packed in chists, piled on cheers, an' wer everywhar, even ontu the beds, an' wer changed every bed-makin. She told every-body she cud git tu listen tu hit that she ment tu give every durn'd one ove them tu Sal when she got married. Oh, lordy! what es fat a gal es Sal Yardley cud ever du wif half ove em, an' sleepin wif a hus-bun at that, is more nor I ever cud see through. Jis' think ove her onder twenty layer ove quilts in July, an' yu in thar too. Gewhillikins! George, look how I is sweatin' now, an' this is December. I'd 'bout es lief be shet up in a steam biler wif a three-hundred-pound bag ove

3. Still-worm is a spiralling tube in whiskey stills.
4. Full-grown (and not pregnant).
5. Tub or crock of lard.
6. Circuit riders: preachers.
7. Nine-diamond, pattern of quilt; others, like "Irish chain," "star over Texas," are named below.
8. Coverlets (bedspreads) and calico comforters or quilted bedcoverings.

lard, es tu make a bisiness ove sleepin wif that gal—'twould kill a glass-blower.

"Well, tu cum tu the serious part ove this conversashun, that is how the old quilt-mersheen an' coverlid-loom cum tu stop operashuns on this yeath. She hed narrated hit thru the neighborhood that nex Saterday she'd gin a quiltin[9]—three quilts an' one cumfurt tu tie. 'Goblers,[1] fiddils, gals, an' whisky,' wer the words she sent tu the men-folk, an' more tetchin ur wakenin words never drap't ofen an 'oman's tongue. She sed tu the gals, 'Sweet toddy, huggin, dancin, an' huggers in 'bundance.' Them words struck the gals rite in the pit ove the stumick, an' spread a ticklin sensashun bof ways, ontil they scratched thar heads wif one han, an' thar heels wif tuther.

"Everybody, he an' she, what wer baptized b'levers in the righteousnes ove quiltins wer thar, an' hit jis' so happen'd that everybody in them parts, frum fifteen summers tu fifty winters, were unannamus b'levers. Strange, warn't hit? Hit wer the bigges' quiltin ever Missis Yardley hilt, an' she hed hilt hundreds; everybody wer thar, 'scept the constibil an' suckit-rider, two dam easily-spared pussons; the numbers ni ontu even too; jis' a few more boys nur gals; that made hit more exhitin, fur hit gin the gals a chance tu kick an' squeal a littil, wifout runnin eny risk ove not gittin kissed at all, an' hit gin reasonabil grouns fur a few scrimmages amung the he's. Now es kissin an' fitin am the pepper an' salt ove all soshul getherins, so hit were more espishully wif this ove ours. Es I swung my eyes over the crowd, George, I thought quiltins, managed in a morril an' sensibil way, truly am good things—good fur free drinkin, good fur free eatin, good fur free huggin, good fur free dancin, good fur free fitin, an' goodest ove all fur poperlatin a country fas'.

"Thar am a fur-seein wisdum in quiltins, ef they hes proper trimmins: 'vittils, fiddils, an' sperrits in 'bundence.' One holesum quiltin am wuf three old pray'r meetins on the poperlashun pint, purtickerly ef hits hilt in the dark ove the moon, an' runs intu the night a few hours, an' April ur May am the time chosen. The moon don't suit quiltins whar everybody is well acquainted an' already fur along in courtin. She dus help pow'ful tu begin a courtin match onder, but when hit draws ni ontu a head, nobody wants a moon but the ole mammys.

"The mornin cum, still, saft, sunshiney; cocks crowin, hens singin, birds chirpin, tuckeys gobblin—jis' the day tu sun quilts, kick, kiss, squeal, an' make love.

"All the plow-lines an' clotheslines wer straiched tu every post an' tree. Quilts purvailed. Durn my gizzard ef two acres round that ar house warn't jis' one solid quilt, all out a-sunnin, an' tu be seed. They dazzled the eyes, skeered the hosses, gin wimen the heart-burn, an' perdominated.

"To'ards sundown the he's begun tu drap in. Yearnis' needil-drivin cummenced tu lose groun; threads broke ofen, thimbils got los', an' quilts needed anuther roll. Gigglin, winkin, whisperin, smoofin ove har, an' gals a-ticklin one anuther, wer a-gainin every inch ove groun what the needils los'. Did yu ever notis, George, at all soshul getherins,

9. Quilting bee.

1. Turkeys.

when the he's begin tu gather, that the young she's begin tu tickil one anuther an' the ole maids swell thar tails, roach[2] up thar backs, an' sharpen thar nails ontu the bed-posts an' door jams, an' spit an' groan sorter like cats a-courtin? Dus hit mean *rale* rath, ur is hit a dare tu the he's, sorter kivered up wif the outside signs ove danger? I honestly b'leve that the young shes' ticklin means, 'Cum an' take this job ofen our hans.' But that swellin I jis' don't onderstan; dus yu? Hit looks skeery, an' I never tetch one ove em when they am in the swellin way. I may be mistaken'd 'bout the ticklin bisiness too; hit may be dun like a feller chaws poplar bark when he haint got eny terbacker, a-sorter better nur nun make-shif. I dus know one thing tu a certainty: that is, when the he's take hold the ticklin quits, an' ef yu gits one ove the ole maids out tu hersef, then she subsides an' is the smoofes, sleekes, saft thing yu ever seed, an' dam ef yu can't hear her purr, jis' es plain!

"But then, George, gals an' ole maids haint the things tu fool time away on. Hits widders, by golly, what am the rale sensibil, steady-goin, never-skeerin, never-kickin, willin, sperrited, smoof pacers. They cum clost up tu the hoss-block,[3] standin still wif thar purty silky years playin, an' the naik-veins a-throbbin, an' waits fur the word, which ove course yu gives, arter yu finds yer feet well in the stirrup, an' away they moves like a cradil on cushioned rockers, ur a spring buggy runnin in damp san'. A tetch ove the bridil, an' they knows yu want em tu turn, an' they dus hit es willin es ef the idear wer thar own. I be dod rabbited[4] ef a man can't 'propriate happiness by the skinful ef he is in contack wif sumbody's widder, an' is smart. Gin me a willin widder, the yeath over: what they don't know, haint worth larnin. They hes all been tu Jamakey an' larnt how sugar's made, an' knows how tu sweeten wif hit; an' by golly, they is always ready tu use hit. All yu hes tu du is tu find the spoon, an' then drink cumfort till yer blind. Nex tu good sperrits an' my laigs, I likes a twenty-five-year-ole widder, wif roun ankils, an' bright eyes, honestly an' squarly lookin intu yurn, an' sayin es plainly es a partrige sez 'Bob White,' 'Don't be afraid ove me; I hes been thar; yu know hit ef yu hes eny sense, an' thar's no use in eny humbug, old feller—cum ahead!"

"Ef yu onderstans widder nater, they ken save yu a power ove troubil, onsartinty, an' time, an ef you is interprisin yu gits mons'rous well paid fur hit. The very soun ove thar littil shoe-heels speak full trainin, an' hes a knowin click as they tap the floor; an' the rustil ove thar dress sez, 'I dar yu tu ax me.'

"When yu hes made up yer mind tu court one, jis' go at hit like hit wer a job ove rail-maulin. Ware yer workin close, use yer common, every-day moshuns an' words, an' abuv all, fling away yer cinamint ile[5] vial an' burn all yer love songs. No use in tryin tu fool em, fur they sees plum thru yu, a durn'd sight plainer than they dus thru thar veils. No use in a pasted[6] shut; she's been thar. No use in borrowin a cavortin fat hoss; she's been thar. No use in har-dye; she's been thar. No use in cloves, tu kill whisky breff; she's been thar. No

2. Arch.
3. A platform used to mount or dismount a horse or to get into or out of a vehicle.
4. God-confounded.
5. Cinnamon oil perfume.
6. Starched.

use in buyin clost curtains fur yer bed, fur she has been thar. Widders am a speshul means, George, fur ripenin green men, killin off weak ones, an makin 'ternally happy the soun ones.

"Well, es I sed afore, I flew the track an' got ontu the widders. The fellers begun tu ride up an' walk up, sorter slow, like they warn't in a hurry, the durn'd 'saitful[7] raskils, hitchin thar critters tu enything they cud find. One red-comb'd, long-spurr'd, dominecker[8] feller, frum town, in a red an' white grid-iron jackid an' patent leather gaiters,[9] hitched his hoss, a wild, skeery, wall-eyed devil, inside the yard palins, tu a cherry tree lim'. Thinks I, that hoss hes a skeer intu him big enuf tu run intu town, an' perhaps beyant hit, ef I kin only tetch hit off; so I sot intu thinkin.

"One aind ove a long clothesline, wif nine dimunt quilts ontu hit, wer tied tu the same cherry tree that the hoss wer. I tuck my knife and socked hit thru every quilt, 'bout the middil, an' jis' below the rope, an' tied them thar wif bark, so they cudent slip. Then I went tu the back aind, an' ontied hit frum the pos', knottin in a hoe-handil, by the middil, tu keep the quilts frum slippin off ef my bark strings failed, an' laid hit on the groun. Then I went tu the tuther aind: thar wer 'bout ten foot tu spar, a-lyin on the groun arter tyin tu the tree. I tuck hit atwix Wall-eye's hine laigs, an' tied hit fas' tu bof stirrups, an' then cut the cherry tree lim' betwix his bridil an' the tree, almos' off. Now, mine yu thar wer two ur three uther ropes full ove quilts atween me an' the hous', so I wer purty well hid frum thar. I jis' tore off a palin frum the fence, an' tuck hit in bof hans, an' arter raisin hit 'way up yander, I fotch hit down, es hard es I cud, flatsided to'ards the groun, an' hit acksidentally happen'd tu hit Wall-eye, 'bout nine inches ahead ove the root ove his tail. Hit landed so hard that hit made my hans tingle, an' then busted intu splinters. The first thing I did, wer tu feel ove mysef, on the same spot whar hit hed hit the hoss. I cudent help duin hit tu save my life, an' I swar I felt sum ove Wall-eye's sensashun, jis' es plain. The fust thing he did, wer tu tare down the lim' wif a twenty-foot jump, his head to'ards the hous. Thinks I, now yu hev dun hit, yu durn'd wall-eyed fool! tarin down that lim' wer the beginin ove all the troubil, an' the hoss did hit hissef; my conshuns felt clar es a mountin spring, an' I wer in a frame ove mine tu obsarve things es they happen'd, an' they soon begun tu happen purty clost arter one anuther rite then, an' thar, an' tharabouts, clean ontu town, thru hit, an' still wer a-happenin, in the woods beyant thar ni ontu eleven mile frum ole man Yardley's gate, an' four beyant town.

"The fust line ove quilts he tried tu jump, but broke hit down; the nex one he ran onder; the rope cotch ontu the ho'n ove the saddil, broke at bof ainds, an' went along wif the hoss, the cherry tree lim' an' the fust line ove quilts, what I hed proverdensally tied fas' tu the rope. That's what I calls foresight, George. Right furnint[1] the frunt door he cum in contack wif ole Missis Yardley hersef, an' anuther ole 'oman; they wer a-holdin a nine-dimunt quilt spread out,

7. Deceitful.

8. Dominiques: yellow-legged chickens with gray-barred plumage.

9. High-topped shoes.

1. In front of.

a-'zaminin hit an' a-praisin hits perfeckshuns. The durn'd onmanerly, wall-eyed fool run plum over Missis Yardley frum ahine, stompt one hine foot through the quilt takin hit along, a-kickin ontil he made hits corners snap like a whip. The gals screamed, the men hollered wo! an' the ole 'oman wer toted intu the hous' limber es a wet string, an' every word she sed wer, 'Oh, my preshus nine-dimunt quilt!'

"Wall-eye busted thru the palins, an' Dominicker seed 'im, made a mortal rush fur his bitts, wer too late fur them, but in good time fur the strings ove flyin quilts, got tangled amung em, an' the gridiron jackid patren wer los' tu my sight amung star an' Irish chain quilts; he went frum that quiltin at the rate ove thuty miles tu the hour. Nuffin lef on the lot ove the hole consarn, but a nine biler[2] hat, a par ove gloves, an' the jack ove hearts.

"What a onmanerly, suddin way ove leavin places sum folks hev got, enyhow.

"Thinks I, well, that fool hoss, tarin down that cherry tree lim', hes dun sum good, enyhow; hit hes put the ole 'oman outen the way fur the balance ove the quiltin, an' tuck Dominicker outen the way an' outen danger, fur that gridiron jackid wud a-bred a scab on his nose afore midnite; hit wer morrily boun tu du hit.

"Two months arterwards, I tracked the route that hoss tuck in his kalamatus skeer, by quilt rags, tufts ove cotton, bunches ove har, (human an' hoss), an' scraps ove a gridiron jackid stickin ontu the bushes, an' plum at the aind ove hit, whar all signs gin out, I foun a piece ove watch chain an' a hosses head. The places what know'd Dominicker, know'd 'im no more.[3]

"Well, arter they'd tuck the ole 'oman up stairs an' camfired her tu sleep, things begun tu work agin. The widders broke the ice, an' arter a littil gigilin, goblin, an' gabblin, the kissin begun. *Smack!*—'Thar, now,' a widder sed that. *Pop!*—'Oh, don't!' *Pfip!*—'Oh, yu quit!' *Plosh!*—'Go *way* yu awkerd critter, yu kissed me in the eye!' anuther widder sed that. *Bop!*—'Now yu ar satisfied, I recon, big mouf!' *Vip!*—'That haint fair!' *Spat!*—'Oh, lordy! May, cum pull Bill away; he's a-tanglin my har.' *Thut!*—'I jis' d-a-r-e yu tu du that agin!" a widder sed that, too. Hit sounded all 'roun that room like poppin co'n in a hot skillet, an' wer pow'ful sujestif.

"Hit kep on ontil I be durn'd ef *my* bristils didn't begin tu rise, an' sumthin like a cold buckshot wud run down the marrow in my back-bone 'bout every ten secons, an' then run up agin, tolerabil hot. I kep a swallerin wif nuthin tu swaller, an' my face felt swell'd: an' yet I wer fear'd tu make a bulge. Thinks I, I'll ketch one out tu hersef torreckly, an' then I guess we'll rastil. Purty soon Sal Yardley started fur the smoke 'ous, so I jis' gin my head a few short shakes, let down one ove my wings a-trailin, an' sirkiled roun her wif a side twis' in my naik, steppin sidewise, an' a-fetchin up my hinmos' foot wif a sorter jerkin slide at every step. Sez I, 'Too coo-took a-too.' She onderstood hit, an stopt, sorter spreadin her shoulders. An' jis' es I hed pouch'd out my mouf, an' wer a-reachin forrid wif hit, fur the article hitself, sunthin interfared wif me, hit did. George, wer yu ever ontu yer hans

2. Unidentified.
3. Job 7: 9–10 ". . . he that goeth down to the grave shall come up no more. He shall return no more to his house, neither shall his place know him any more."

an' knees, an' let a hell-tarin big, mad ram, wif a ten-yard run, but[4] yu yearnis'ly, jis' onst, right squar ontu the pint ove yer backbone?"

"No, you fool, why do you ask?"

"Kaze I wanted tu know ef yu cud hev a realizin' noshun ove my shock. Hits scarcely worth while tu try tu make yu onderstan the case by words only, onless yu hev been tetched in that way. Gr-eat golly! the fust thing I felt, I tuck hit tu be a back-ackshun yeathquake; an' the fust thing I seed wer my chaw'r terbacker a-flyin' over Sal's head like a skeer'd bat. My mouf wer pouch'd out, ready fur the article hitsef, yu know, an' hit went outen the roun hole like the wad outen a pop-gun—thug! an' the fust thing I know'd, I wer a flyin over Sal's head too, an' a-gainin on the chaw'r terbacker fast. I wer straitened out strait, toes hinemos', middil finger-nails foremos', an' the fust thing I hearn wer, 'Yu dam Shanghi!'[5] Great Jerus-a-lam! I lit ontu my all fours jis' in time tu but the yard gate ofen hits hinges, an' skeer loose sum more hosses—kep on in a four-footed gallop, clean acrost the lane afore I cud straiten up, an' yere I cotch up wif my chaw'r terbacker, stickin flat agin a fence-rail. I hed got so good a start that I thot hit a pity tu spile hit, so I jis' jump'd the fence an' tuck thru the orchurd. I tell yu I dusted these yere close, fur I tho't hit wer arter me.

"Arter runnin a spell, I ventered tu feel roun back thar, fur sum signs ove what hed happened tu me. George, arter two pow'ful hard tugs, I pull'd out the vamp an' sole ove one ove ole man Yardley's big brogans, what he hed los' amung my coattails. Dre'ful! dre'ful! Arter I got hit away frum thar, my flesh went fas' asleep, frum abuv my kidneys tu my knees; about now, fur the fust time, the idear struck me, what hit wer that hed interfar'd wif me, an' los' me the kiss. Hit wer ole Yardley hed kicked me. I walked fur a month like I wer straddlin a thorn hedge. Sich a shock, at sich a time, an' on sich a place—jis' think ove hit! hit am tremenjus, haint hit? The place feels num, right now."

"Well, Sut, how did the quilting come out?"

"How the hell du yu 'speck me tu know? I warn't thar eny more."

1867

HERMAN MELVILLE

Bartleby, the Scrivener

A STORY OF WALL STREET

I am a rather elderly man. The nature of my avocations for the last thirty years has brought me into more than ordinary contact with what would seem an interesting and somewhat singular set of men, of whom as yet nothing that I know of has ever been written:—I mean the law-copyists or scriveners. I have known very many of them, professionally and privately, and if I pleased, could relate divers histories, at which

4. Butt.

5. Chicken with long feathered legs.

good-natured gentlemen might smile, and sentimental souls might weep. But I waive the biographies of all other scriveners for a few passages in the life of Bartleby, who was a scrivener the strangest I ever saw or heard of. While of other law-copyists I might write the complete life, of Bartleby nothing of that sort can be done. I believe that no materials exist for a full and satisfactory biography of this man. It is an irreparable loss to literature. Bartleby was one of those beings of whom nothing is ascertainable, except from the original sources, and in his case those are very small. What my own astonished eyes saw of Bartleby, *that* is all I know of him, except, indeed, one vague report which will appear in the sequel.

Ere introducing the scrivener, as he first appeared to me, it is fit I make some mention of myself, my *employées,* my business, my chambers, and general surroundings; because some such description is indispensable to an adequate understanding of the chief character about to be presented.

Imprimis:[1] I am a man who, from his youth upwards, has been filled with a profound conviction that the easiest way of life is the best. Hence, though I belong to a profession proverbially energetic and nervous, even to turbulence, at times, yet nothing of that sort have I ever suffered to invade my peace. I am one of those unambitious lawyers who never addresses a jury, or in any way draws down public applause; but in the cool tranquillity of a snug retreat, do a snug business among rich men's bonds and mortgages and title-deeds. All who know me, consider me an eminently *safe* man. The late John Jacob Astor,[2] a personage little given to poetic enthusiasm, had no hesitation in pronouncing my first grand point to be prudence; my next, method. I do not speak it in vanity, but simply record the fact, that I was not unemployed in my profession by the late John Jacob Astor; a name which, I admit, I love to repeat, for it hath a rounded and orbicular sound to it, and rings like unto bullion. I will freely add that I was not insensible to the late John Jacob Astor's good opinion.

Some time prior to the period at which this little history begins, my avocations had been largely increased. The good old office, now extinct in the State of New York, of a Master in Chancery,[3] had been conferred upon me. It was not a very arduous office, but very pleasantly remunerative. I seldom lose my temper; much more seldom indulge in dangerous indignation at wrongs and outrages; but I must be permitted to be rash here and declare, that I consider the sudden and violent abrogation of the office of Master in Chancery, by the new Constitution, as a—premature act; inasmuch as I had counted upon a life-lease of the profits, whereas I only received those of a few short years. But this is by the way.

My chambers were up stairs at No. —— Wall Street. At one end they looked upon the white wall of the interior of a spacious skylight shaft, penetrating the building from top to bottom. This view might have been considered rather tame than otherwise, deficient in what landscape painters call "life." But if so, the view from the other end of my chambers offered, at least, a contrast, if nothing more. In that direction

1. In the first place.
2. New York fur merchant and land owner (1763–1848) who died the richest man in the United States.
3. A court of chancery can temper the law, applying "dictates of conscience" or "the principles of natural justice"; the office of Master was abolished in 1847.

my windows commanded an unobstructed view of a lofty brick wall, black by age and everlasting shade; which wall required no spyglass to bring out its lurking beauties, but for the benefit of all near-sighted spectators, was pushed up to within ten feet of my window panes. Owing to the great height of the surrounding buildings, and my chambers being on the second floor, the interval between this wall and mine not a little resembled a huge square cistern.

At the period just preceding the advent of Bartleby, I had two persons as copyists in my employment, and a promising lad as an office-boy. First, Turkey; second, Nippers; third, Ginger Nut. These may seem names the like of which are not usually found in the Directory.[4] In truth they were nicknames, mutually conferred upon each other by my three clerks, and were deemed expressive of their respective persons or characters. Turkey was a short, pursy[5] Englishman of about my own age, that is, somewhere not far from sixty. In the morning, one might say, his face was of a fine florid hue, but after twelve o'clock, meridian —his dinner hour—it blazed like a grate full of Christmas coals; and continued blazing—but, as it were, with a gradual wane—till 6 o'clock, P.M. or thereabouts, after which I saw no more of the proprietor of the face, which gaining its meridian with the sun, seemed to set with it, to rise, culminate, and decline the following day, with the like regularity and undiminished glory. There are many singular coincidences I have known in the course of my life, not the least among which was the fact, that exactly when Turkey displayed his fullest beams from his red and radiant countenance, just then, too, at that critical moment, began the daily period when I considered his business capacities as seriously disturbed for the remainder of the twenty-four hours. Not that he was absolutely idle, or averse to business then; far from it. The difficulty was, he was apt to be altogether too energetic. There was a strange, inflamed, flurried, flighty recklessness of activity about him. He would be incautious in dipping his pen into his inkstand. All his blots upon my documents were dropped there after twelve o'clock, meridian. Indeed, not only would he be reckless and sadly given to making blots in the afternoon, but some days he went further, and was rather noisy. At such times, too, his face flamed with augmented blazonry, as if cannel coal had been heaped on anthracite.[6] He made an unpleasant racket with his chair; spilled his sand-box; in mending his pens, impatiently split them all to pieces, and threw them on the floor in a sudden passion; stood up and leaned over his table, boxing his papers about in a most indecorous manner, very sad to behold in an elderly man like him. Nevertheless, as he was in many ways a most valuable person to me, and all the time before twelve o'clock, meridian, was the quickest, steadiest creature too, accomplishing a great deal of work in a style not easy to be matched—for these reasons, I was willing to overlook his eccentricities, though indeed, occasionally, I remonstrated with him. I did this very gently, however, because, though the civilest, nay, the blandest and most reverential of men in the morning, yet in the afternoon he was disposed, upon provocation, to be slightly rash with his tongue, in fact, insolent. Now, valuing his morning services as I did, and resolved not to lose them; yet, at the same time made un-

4. Post Office Directory.
5. Fat, shortwinded.
6. A fast, bright-burning coal heaped on slow-burning, barely glowing coal.

comfortable by his inflamed ways after twelve o'clock; and being a man of peace, unwilling by my admonitions to call forth unseemly retorts from him; I took upon me, one Saturday noon (he was always worse on Saturdays), to hint to him, very kindly, that perhaps now that he was growing old, it might be well to abridge his labors; in short, he need not come to my chambers after twelve o'clock, but, dinner over, had best go home to his lodgings and rest himself till tea-time. But no; he insisted upon his afternoon devotions. His countenance became intolerably fervid, as he oratorically assured me—gesticulating with a long ruler at the other end of the room—that if his services in the morning were useful, how indispensable, then, in the afternoon?

"With submission, sir," said Turkey on this occasion, "I consider myself your right-hand man. In the morning I but marshal and deploy my columns; but in the afternoon I put myself at their head, and gallantly charge the foe, thus!"—and he made a violent thrust with the ruler.

"But the blots, Turkey," intimated I.

"True,—but, with submission, sir, behold these hairs! I am getting old. Surely, sir, a blot or two of a warm afternoon is not to be severely urged against gray hairs. Old age—even if it blot the page—is honorable. With submission, sir, we *both* are getting old."

This appeal to my fellow-feeling was hardly to be resisted. At all events, I saw that go he would not. So I made up my mind to let him stay, resolving, nevertheless, to see to it, that during the afternoon he had to do with my less important papers.

Nippers, the second on my list, was a whiskered, sallow, and, upon the whole, rather piratical-looking young man of about five and twenty. I always deemed him the victim of two evil powers—ambition and indigestion. The ambition was evinced by a certain impatience of the duties of a mere copyist, an unwarrantable usurpation of strictly professional affairs, such as the original drawing up of legal documents. The indigestion seemed betokened in an occasional nervous testiness and grinning irritability, causing the teeth to audibly grind together over mistakes committed in copying; unnecessary maledictions, hissed, rather than spoken, in the heat of business; and especially by a continual discontent with the height of the table where he worked. Though of a very ingenious mechanical turn. Nippers could never get this table to suit him. He put chips under it, blocks of various sorts, bits of pasteboard, and at last went so far as to attempt an exquisite adjustment by final pieces of folded blotting-paper. But no invention would answer. If, for the sake of easing his back, he brought the table lid at a sharp angle well up towards his chin, and wrote there like a man using the steep roof of a Dutch house for his desk:—then he declared that it stopped the circulation in his arms. If now he lowered the table to his waistbands, and stooped over it in writing, then there was a sore aching in his back. In short, the truth of the matter was, Nippers knew not what he wanted. Or, if he wanted any thing, it was to be rid of a scrivener's table altogether. Among the manifestations of his diseased ambition was a fondness he had for receiving visits from certain ambiguous-looking fellows in seedy coats, whom he called his clients. Indeed I was aware that not only was he, at times, considerable of a ward-politician, but he occasionally did a little business at the

Justices' courts, and was not unknown on the steps of the Tombs.[7] I have good reason to believe, however, that one individual who called upon him at my chambers, and who, with a grand air, he insisted was his client, was no other than a dun,[8] and the alleged title-deed, a bill. But with all his failings, and the annoyances he caused me, Nippers, like his compatriot Turkey, was a very useful man to me; wrote a neat, swift hand; and, when he chose, was not deficient in a gentlemanly sort of deportment. Added to this, he always dressed in a gentlemanly sort of way: and so, incidentally, reflected credit upon my chambers. Whereas with respect to Turkey, I had much ado to keep him from being a reproach to me. His clothes were apt to look oily and smell of eating-houses. He wore his pantaloons very loose and baggy in summer. His coats were execrable; his hat not to be handled. But while the hat was a thing of indifference to me, inasmuch as his natural civility and deference, as a dependent Englishman, always led him to doff it the moment he entered the room, yet his coat was another matter. Concerning his coats, I reasoned with him; but with no effect. The truth was, I suppose, that a man with so small an income, could not afford to sport such a lustrous face and a lustrous coat at one and the same time. As Nippers once observed, Turkey's money went chiefly for red ink. One winter day I presented Turkey with a highly-respectable looking coat of my own, a padded gray coat, of a most comfortable warmth, and which buttoned straight up from the knee to the neck. I thought Turkey would appreciate the favor, and abate his rashness and obstreperousness of afternoons. But no. I verily believe that buttoning himself up in so downy and blanket-like a coat had a pernicious effect upon him; upon the same principle that too much oats are bad for horses. In fact, precisely as a rash, restive horse is said to feel his oats, so Turkey felt his coat. It made him insolent. He was a man whom prosperity harmed.

Though concerning the self-indulgent habits of Turkey I had my own private surmises, yet touching Nippers I was well persuaded that whatever might be his faults in other respects, he was, at least, a temperate young man. But indeed, nature herself seemed to have been his vintner,[9] and at his birth charged him so thoroughly with an irritable, brandy-like disposition, that all subsequent potations were needless. When I consider how, amid the stillness of my chambers, Nippers would sometimes impatiently rise from his seat, and stooping over his table, spread his arms wide apart, seize the whole desk, and move it, and jerk it, with a grim, grinding motion on the floor, as if the table were a perverse voluntary agent, intent on thwarting and vexing him; I plainly perceive that for Nippers, brandy and water were altogether superfluous.

It was fortunate for me that, owing to its peculiar cause—indigestion—the irritability and consequent nervousness of Nippers, were mainly observable in the morning, while in the afternoon he was comparatively mild. So that Turkey's paroxysms only coming on about twelve o'clock, I never had to do with their eccentricities at one time. Their fits relieved each other like guards. When Nippers' was on,

7. Prison in New York City.
8. Bill collector.
9. Wine-seller.

Turkey's was off; and *vice versa.* This was a good natural arrangement under the circumstances.

Ginger Nut, the third on my list, was a lad some twelve years old. His father was a carman,[1] ambitious of seeing his son on the bench instead of a cart, before he died. So he sent him to my office as student at law, errand boy, and cleaner and sweeper, at the rate of one dollar a week. He had a little desk to himself, but he did not use it much. Upon inspection, the drawer exhibited a great array of the shells of various sorts of nuts. Indeed, to this quick-witted youth the whole noble science of the law was contained in a nutshell. Not the least among the employments of Ginger Nut, as well as one which he discharged with the most alacrity, was his duty as cake and apple purveyor for Turkey and Nippers. Copying law papers being proverbially a dry, husky sort of business, my two scriveners were fain to moisten their mouths very often with Spitzenbergs[2] to be had at the numerous stalls nigh the Custom House and Post Office. Also, they sent Ginger Nut very frequently for that peculiar cake—small, flat, round, and very spicy—after which he had been named by them. Of a cold morning when business was but dull, Turkey would gobble up scores of these cakes, as if they were mere wafers—indeed they sell them at the rate of six or eight for a penny—the scrape of his pen blending with the crunching of the crisp particles in his mouth. Of all the fiery afternoon blunders and flurried rashnesses of Turkey, was his once moistening a ginger-cake between his lips, and clapping it on to a mortgage for a seal. I came within an ace of dismissing him then. But he mollified me by making an oriental bow, and saying—"With submission, sir, it was generous of me to find you in[3] stationery on my own account."

Now my original business—that of a conveyancer and title hunter,[4] and drawer-up of recondite documents of all sorts—was considerably increased by receiving the master's office. There was now great work for scriveners. Not only must I push the clerks already with me, but I must have additional help. In answer to my advertisement, a motionless young man one morning stood upon my office threshold, the door being open, for it was summer. I can see that figure now—pallidly neat, pitiably respectable, incurably forlorn! It was Bartleby.

After a few words touching his qualifications, I engaged him, glad to have among my corps of copyists a man of so singularly sedate an aspect, which I thought might operate beneficially upon the flighty temper of Turkey, and the fiery one of Nippers.

I should have stated before that ground glass folding-doors divided my premises into two parts, one of which was occupied by my scriveners, the other by myself. According to my humor I threw open these doors, or closed them. I resolved to assign Bartleby a corner by the folding-doors, but on my side of them, so as to have this quiet man within easy call, in case any trifling thing was to be done. I placed his desk close up to a small side-window in that part of the room, a window which originally had afforded a lateral view of certain grimy backyards and bricks, but which, owing to subsequent erections, commanded at present no view at all, though it gave some light. Within

1. Driver of wagon or cart that hauls goods.
2. Red-and-yellow American apple.
3. Supply you with.
4. Lawyer who draws up deeds for transferring property, and one who searches out legal control of title deeds.

three feet of the panes was a wall, and the light came down from far above, between two lofty buildings, as from a very small opening in a dome. Still further to a satisfactory arrangement, I procured a high green folding screen, which might entirely isolate Bartleby from my sight, though not remove him from my voice. And thus, in a manner, privacy and society were conjoined.

At first Bartleby did an extraordinary quantity of writing. As if long famishing for something to copy, he seemed to gorge himself on my documents. There was no pause for digestion. He ran a day and night line, copying by sunlight and by candlelight. I should have been quite delighted with his application, had he been cheerfully industrious. But he wrote on silently, palely, mechanically.

It is, of course, an indispensable part of a scrivener's business to verify the accuracy of his copy, word by word. Where there are two or more scriveners in an office, they assist each other in this examination, one reading from the copy, the other holding the original. It is a very dull, wearisome, and lethargic affair. I can readily imagine that to some sanguine temperaments it would be altogether intolerable. For example, I cannot credit that the mettlesome poet Byron would have contentedly sat down with Bartleby to examine a law document of, say, five hundred pages, closely written in a crimpy hand.

Now and then, in the haste of business, it had been my habit to assist in comparing some brief document myself, calling Turkey or Nippers for this purpose. One object I had in placing Bartleby so handy to me behind the screen, was to avail myself of his services on such trivial occasions. It was on the third day, I think, of his being with me, and before any necessity had arisen for having his own writing examined, that, being much hurried to complete a small affair I had in hand, I abruptly called to Bartleby. In my haste and natural expectancy of instant compliance, I sat with my head bent over the original on my desk, and my right hand sideways, and somewhat nervously extended with the copy, so that immediately upon emerging from his retreat, Bartleby might snatch it and proceed to business without the least delay.

In this very attitude did I sit when I called to him, rapidly stating what it was I wanted him to do—namely, to examine a small paper with me. Imagine my surprise, nay, my consternation, when without moving from his privacy, Bartleby, in a singularly mild, firm voice, replied, "I would prefer not to."

I sat awhile in perfect silence, rallying my stunned faculties. Immediately it occurred to me that my ears had deceived me, or Bartleby had entirely misunderstood my meaning. I repeated my request in the clearest tone I could assume. But in quite as clear a one came the previous reply, "I would prefer not to."

"Prefer not to," echoed I, rising in high excitement, and crossing the room with a stride. "What do you mean? Are you moon-struck?[5] I want you to help me compare this sheet here—take it," and I thrust it towards him.

"I would prefer not to," said he.

I looked at him steadfastly. His face was leanly composed; his gray

5. Crazy.

eye dimly calm. Not a wrinkle of agitation rippled him. Had there been the least uneasiness, anger, impatience or impertinence in his manner; in other words, had there been anything ordinarily human about him, doubtless I should have violently dismissed him from the premises. But as it was, I should have as soon thought of turning my pale plaster-of-paris bust of Cicero[6] out-of-doors. I stood gazing at him awhile, as he went on with his own writing, and then reseated myself at my desk. This is very strange, thought I. What had one best do? But my business hurried me. I concluded to forget the matter for the present, reserving it for my future leisure. So calling Nippers from the other room, the paper was speedily examined.

A few days after this, Bartleby concluded four lengthy documents, being quadruplicates of a week's testimony taken before me in my High Court of Chancery. It became necessary to examine them. It was an important suit, and great accuracy was imperative. Having all things arranged I called Turkey, Nippers and Ginger Nut from the next room, meaning to place the four copies in the hands of my four clerks, while I should read from the original. Accordingly Turkey, Nippers and Ginger Nut had taken their seats in a row, each with his document in hand, when I called to Bartleby to join this interesting group.

"Bartleby! quick, I am waiting."

I heard a slow scrape of his chair legs on the uncarpeted floor, and soon he appeared standing at the entrance of his hermitage.

"What is wanted?" said he mildly.

"The copies, the copies," said I hurriedly. "We are going to examine them. There"—and I held towards him the fourth quadruplicate.

"I would prefer not to," he said, and gently disappeared behind the screen.

For a few moments I was turned into a pillar of salt,[7] standing at the head of my seated column of clerks. Recovering myself, I advanced towards the screen, and demanded the reason for such extraordinary conduct.

"*Why* do you refuse?"

"I would prefer not to."

With any other man I should have flown outright into a dreadful passion, scorned all further words, and thrust him ignominiously from my presence. But there was something about Bartleby that not only strangely disarmed me, but in a wonderful manner touched and disconcerted me. I began to reason with him.

"These are your own copies we are about to examine. It is labor saving to you, because one examination will answer for your four papers. It is common usage. Every copyist is bound to help examine his copy. Is it not so? Will you not speak? Answer!"

"I prefer not to," he replied in a flute-like tone. It seemed to me that while I had been addressing him, he carefully revolved every statement that I made; fully comprehended the meaning; could not gainsay the irresistible conclusion; but, at the same time, some paramount consideration prevailed with him to reply as he did.

"You are decided, then, not to comply with my request—a request

6. Marcus Tullius Cicero (106–43 B.C.), pro-republican Roman statesman, barrister, writer, who ranks with Demosthenes and Burke as orator.

7. Struck dumb; in *Genesis* 19:26, Lot's wife defies God's command and "looked back from behind him, and she became a pillar of salt."

made according to common usage and common sense?"

He briefly gave me to understand that on that point my judgment was sound. Yes: his decision was irreversible.

It is not seldom the case that when a man is browbeaten in some unprecedented and violently unreasonable way, he begins to stagger in his own plainest faith. He begins, as it were, vaguely to surmise that, wonderful as it may be, all the justice and all the reason is on the other side. Accordingly, if any disinterested persons are present, he turns to them for some reinforcement for his own faltering mind.

"Turkey," said I, "what do you think of this? Am I not right?"

"With submission, sir," said Turkey, with his blandest tone, "I think that you are."

"Nippers," said I, "what do *you* think of it?"

"I think I should kick him out of the office."

(The reader of nice perceptions will here perceive that, it being morning, Turkey's answer is couched in polite and tranquil terms, but Nippers replies in ill-tempered ones. Or, to repeat a previous sentence, Nippers's ugly mood was on duty, and Turkey's off.)

"Ginger Nut," said I, willing to enlist the smallest suffrage[8] in my behalf, "what do *you* think of it?"

"I think, sir, he's a little *luny*," replied Ginger Nut, with a grin.

"You hear what they say," said I, turning towards the screen, "come forth and do your duty."

But he vouchsafed no reply. I pondered a moment in sore perplexity. But once more business hurried me. I determined again to postpone the consideration of this dilemma to my future leisure. With a little trouble we made out to examine the papers without Bartleby, though at every page or two, Turkey deferentially dropped his opinion that this proceeding was quite out of the common; while Nippers, twitching in his chair with a dyspeptic nervousness, ground out between his set teeth occasional hissing maledictions against the stubborn oaf behind the screen. And for his (Nippers's) part, this was the first and the last time he would do another man's business without pay.

Meanwhile Bartleby sat in his hermitage, oblivious to everything but his own peculiar business there.

Some days passed, the scrivener being employed upon another lengthy work. His late remarkable conduct led me to regard his ways narrowly. I observed that he never went to dinner; indeed that he never went anywhere. As yet I had never of my personal knowledge known him to be outside of my office. He was a perpetual sentry in the corner. At about eleven o'clock though, in the morning, I noticed that Ginger Nut would advance toward the opening in Bartleby's screen, as if silently beckoned thither by a gesture invisible to me where I sat. The boy would then leave the office jingling a few pence, and reappear with a handful of ginger-nuts which he delivered in the hermitage, receiving two of the cakes for his trouble.

He lives, then, on ginger-nuts, thought I; never eats a dinner, properly speaking; he must be a vegetarian then; but no; he never eats even vegetables, he eats nothing but ginger-nuts. My mind then ran on in reveries concerning the probable effects upon the human constitution of living entirely on ginger-nuts. Ginger-nuts are so called because they

8. Favorable vote.

contain ginger as one of their peculiar constituents, and the final flavoring one. Now what was ginger? A hot, spicy thing. Was Bartleby hot and spicy? Not at all. Ginger, then, had no effect upon Bartleby. Probably he preferred it should have none.

Nothing so aggravates an earnest person as a passive resistance. If the individual so resisted be of a not inhumane temper, and the resisting one perfectly harmless in his passivity; then, in the better moods of the former, he will endeavor charitably to construe to his imagination what proves impossible to be solved by his judgment. Even so, for the most part, I regarded Bartleby and his ways. Poor fellow! thought I, he means no mischief; it is plain he intends no insolence; his aspect sufficiently evinces that his eccentricities are involuntary. He is useful to me. I can get along with him. If I turn him away, the chances are he will fall in with some less indulgent employer, and then he will be rudely treated, and perhaps driven forth miserably to starve. Yes. Here I can cheaply purchase a delicious self-approval. To befriend Bartleby; to humor him in his strange wilfulness, will cost me little or nothing, while I lay up in my soul what will eventually prove a sweet morsel for my conscience. But this mood was not invariable with me. The passiveness of Bartley sometimes irritated me. I felt strangely goaded on to encounter him in new opposition, to elicit some angry spark from him answerable to my own. But indeed I might as well have essayed to strike fire with my knuckles against a bit of Windsor soap.[9] But one afternoon the evil impulse in me mastered me, and the following little scene ensued:

"Bartleby," said I, "when those papers are all copied, I will compare them with you."

"I would prefer not to."

"How? Surely you do not mean to persist in that mulish vagary?"

No answer.

I threw open the folding-doors near by, and turning upon Turkey and Nippers, exclaimed in an excited manner—

"He says, a second time, he won't examine his papers. What do you think of it, Turkey?"

It was afternoon, be it remembered. Turkey sat glowing like a brass boiler, his bald head steaming, his hands reeling among his blotted papers.

"Think of it?" roared Turkey; "I think I'll just step behind his screen, and black his eyes for him!"

So saying, Turkey rose to his feet and threw his arms into a puglistic position. He was hurrying away to make good his promise, when I detained him, alarmed at the effect of incautiously rousing Turkey's combativeness after dinner.

"Sit down, Turkey," said I, "and hear what Nippers has to say. What do you think of it, Nippers? Would I not be justified in immediately dismissing Bartleby?"

"Excuse me, that is for you to decide, sir. I think his conduct quite unusual, and indeed unjust, as regards Turkey and myself. But it may only be a passing whim."

"Ah," exclaimed I, "you have strangely changed your mind then—you speak very gently of him now."

9. Scented soap, usually brown.

"All beer," cried Turkey; "gentleness is effects of beer—Nippers and I dined together today. You see how gentle *I* am, sir. Shall I go and black his eyes?"

"You refer to Bartleby, I suppose. No, not today, Turkey," I replied; "pray, put up your fists."

I closed the doors, and again advanced towards Bartleby. I felt additional incentives tempting me to my fate. I burned to be rebelled against again. I remembered that Bartleby never left the office.

"Bartleby," said I, "Ginger Nut is away; just step round to the Post Office, won't you? (it was but a three minutes' walk,) and see if there is anything for me."

"I would prefer not to."

"You *will* not?"

"I *prefer* not."

I staggered to my desk, and sat there in a deep study. My blind inveteracy returned. Was there any other thing in which I could procure myself to be ignominiously repulsed by this lean, penniless wight?—my hired clerk? What added thing is there, perfectly reasonable, that he will be sure to refuse to do?

"Bartleby!"

No answer.

"Bartleby," in a louder tone.

No answer.

"Bartleby," I roared.

Like a very ghost, agreeably to the laws of magical invocation, at the third summons, he appeared at the entrance of his hermitage.

"Go to the next room, and tell Nippers to come to me."

"I prefer not to," he respectfully and slowly said, and mildly disappeared.

"Very good, Bartleby," said I, in a quiet sort of serenely severe self-possessed tone, intimating the unalterable purpose of some terrible retribution very close at hand. At the moment I half intended something of the kind. But upon the whole, as it was drawing towards my dinner-hour, I thought it best to put on my hat and walk home for the day, suffering much from perplexity and distress of mind.

Shall I acknowledge it? The conclusion of this whole business was, that it soon became a fixed fact of my chambers, that a pale young scrivener, by the name of Bartleby, had a desk there; that he copied for me at the usual rate of four cents a folio (one hundred words); but he was permanently exempt from examining the work done by him, that duty being transferred to Turkey and Nippers, one of compliment doubtless to their superior acuteness; moreover, said Bartleby was never on any account to be dispatched on the most trivial errand of any sort; and that even if entreated to take upon him such a matter, it was generally understood that he would prefer not to—in other words, that he would refuse point-blank.

As days passed on, I became considerably reconciled to Bartleby. His steadiness, his freedom from all dissipation, his incessant industry (except when he chose to throw himself into a standing revery behind his screen), his great stillness, his unalterableness of demeanor under all circumstances, made him a valuable acquisition. One prime thing was this,—*he was always there;*—first in the morning, continually through the day, and the last at night. I had a singular confidence in his honesty. I felt my most precious papers perfectly safe in his hands. Sometimes to be sure I could not, for the very soul of me, avoid falling into sudden spasmodic passions with him. For it was exceeding difficult to bear in mind all the time those strange peculiarities, privileges, and unheard of exemptions, forming the tacit stipulations on Bartleby's part under which he remained in my office. Now and then, in the eagerness of dispatching pressing business, I would inadvertently summon Bartleby, in a short, rapid tone, to put his finger, say, on the incipient tie of a bit of red tape with which I was about compressing some papers. Of course, from behind the screen the usual answer, "I prefer not to," was sure to come; and then, how could a human creature with the common infirmities of our nature, refrain from bitterly exclaiming upon such perverseness—such unreasonableness? However, every added repulse of this sort which I received only tended to lessen the probability of my repeating the inadvertence.

Here it must be said, that according to the custom of most legal gentlemen occupying chambers in densely-populated law buildings, there were several keys to my door. One was kept by a woman residing in the attic, which person weekly scrubbed and daily swept and dusted my apartments. Another was kept by Turkey for convenience sake. The third I sometimes carried in my own pocket. The fourth I knew not who had.

Now, one Sunday morning I happened to go to Trinity Church, to hear a celebrated preacher, and finding myself rather early on the ground, I thought I would walk round to my chambers for a while. Luckily I had my key with me; but upon applying it to the lock, I found it resisted by something inserted from the inside. Quite surprised, I called out; when to my consternation a key was turned from within; and thrusting his lean visage at me, and holding the door ajar, the apparition of Bartleby appeared, in his shirt sleeves, and otherwise in a strangely tattered dishabille, saying quietly that he was sorry, but he was deeply engaged just then, and—preferred not admitting me at present. In a brief word or two, he moreover added, that perhaps I had better walk round the block two or three times, and by that time he would probably have concluded his affairs.

Now, the utterly unsurmised appearance of Bartleby, tenanting my law-chambers of a Sunday morning, with his cadaverously gentlemanly *nonchalance*, yet withal firm and self-possessed, had such a strange effect upon me, that incontinently I slunk away from my own door, and did as desired. But not without sundry twinges of impotent rebellion against the mild effrontery of this unaccountable scrivener. Indeed, it was his wonderful mildness, chiefly, which not only disarmed me, but unmanned me, as it were. For I consider that one, for the time, is sort of unmanned when he tranquilly permits his hired clerk to dictate to him, and order him away from his own premises. Furthermore, I was full of uneasiness as to what Bartleby could possibly be doing in my office in his shirt sleeves, and in an otherwise dismantled condition of a Sunday morning. Was anything amiss going on? Nay, that was out of the question. It was not to be thought of for a moment that Bartleby was an immoral person. But what could he be doing there?—

copying? Nay again, whatever might be his eccentricities, Bartleby was an eminently decorous person. He would be the last man to sit down to his desk in any state approaching to nudity. Besides, it was Sunday; and there was something about Bartleby that forbade the supposition that he would by any secular occupation violate the proprieties of the day.

Nevertheless, my mind was not pacified; and full of a restless curiosity, at last I returned to the door. Without hindrance I inserted my key, opened it, and entered. Bartleby was not to be seen. I looked round anxiously, peeped behind his screen; but it was very plain that he was gone. Upon more closely examining the place, I surmised that for an indefinite period Bartleby must have ate, dressed, and slept in my office, and that too without plate, mirror, or bed. The cushioned seat of a ricketty old sofa in one corner bore the faint impress of a lean, reclining form. Rolled away under his desk, I found a blanket under the empty grate, a blacking box[1] and brush; on a chair, a tin basin, with soap and a ragged towel; in a newspaper a few crumbs of ginger-nuts and a morsel of cheese. Yes, thought I, it is evident enough that Bartleby has been making his home here, keeping bachelor's hall all by himself. Immediately then the thought came sweeping across me, What miserable friendlessness and loneliness are here revealed! His poverty is great; but his solitude, how horrible! Think of it. Of a Sunday, Wall Street is deserted as Petra;[2] and every night of every day it is an emptiness. This building too, which of weekdays hums with industry and life, at nightfall echoes with sheer vacancy, and all through Sunday is forlorn. And here Bartleby makes his home; sole spectator of a solitude which he has seen all populous—a sort of innocent and transformed Marius brooding among the ruins of Carthage![3]

For the first time in my life a feeling of overpowering stinging melancholy seized me. Before, I had never experienced aught but a not-unpleasing sadness. The bond of a common humanity now drew me irresistibly to gloom. A fraternal melancholy! For both I and Bartleby were sons of Adam. I remembered the bright silks and sparkling faces I had seen that day, in gala trim, swan-like sailing down the Mississippi of Broadway; and I contrasted them with the pallid copyist, and thought to myself, Ah, happiness courts the light, so we deem the world is gay; but misery hides aloof, so we deem that misery there is none. These sad fancyings—chimeras, doubtless, of a sick and silly brain—led on to other and more special thoughts, concerning the eccentricities of Bartleby. Presentiments of strange discoveries hovered round me. The scrivener's pale form appeared to me laid out, among uncaring strangers, in its shivering winding sheet.

Suddenly I was attracted by Bartleby's closed desk, the key in open sight left in the lock.

1. Box of black shoe polish.
2. Once a flourishing Middle Eastern trade center, long in ruins.
3. Gaius (or Caius) Marius (157–86 B.C.), Roman consul and general, expelled from Rome in 88 B.C. by Sulla; when an officer of Sextilius, the governor, forbade him to land in Africa, Marius replied, "Go tell him that you have seen Caius Marius sitting in exile among the ruins of Carthage," applying the example of the fortune of that city to the change of his own condition. The image was so common that a few years after "Bartleby," Dickens apologizes for using it: ". . . like that lumbering Marius among the ruins of Carthage, who has sat heavy on a thousand millions of similes . . ." ("The Calais Night-Mail," in *The Uncommercial Traveller*).

I mean no mischief, seek the gratification of no heartless curiosity, thought I; besides, the desk is mine, and its contents too, so I will make bold to look within. Everything was methodically arranged, the papers smoothly placed. The pigeonholes were deep, and removing the files of documents, I groped into their recesses. Presently I felt something there, and dragged it out. It was an old bandanna handkerchief, heavy and knotted. I opened it, and saw it was a savings' bank.

I now recalled all the quiet mysteries which I had noted in the man. I remembered that he never spoke but to answer; that though at intervals he had considerable time to himself, yet I had never seen him reading—no, not even a newspaper; that for long periods he would stand looking out, at his pale window behind the screen, upon the dead brick wall; I was quite sure he never visited any refectory or eating house; while his pale face clearly indicated that he never drank beer like Turkey, or tea and coffee even, like other men; that he never went anywhere in particular that I could learn; never went out for a walk, unless indeed that was the case at present; that he had declined telling who he was, or whence he came, or whether he had any relatives in the world; that though so thin and pale, he never complained of ill health. And more than all, I remembered a certain unconscious air of pallid—how shall I call it?—of pallid haughtiness, say, or rather an austere reserve about him, which had positively awed me into my tame compliance with his eccentricities, when I had feared to ask him to do the slightest incidental thing for me, even though I might know, from his long-continued motionlessness, that behind his screen he must be standing in one of those dead-wall reveries of his.

Revolving all these things, and coupling them with the recently discovered fact that he made my office his constant abiding place and home, and not forgetful of his morbid moodiness; revolving all these things, a prudential feeling began to steal over me. My first emotions had been those of pure melancholy and sincerest pity; but just in proportion as the forlornness of Bartleby grew and grew to my imagination, did that same melancholy merge into fear, that pity into repulsion. So true it is, and so terrible too, that up to a certain point the thought or sight of misery enlists our best affections; but, in certain special cases, beyond that point it does not. They err who would assert that invariably this is owing to the inherent selfishness of the human heart. It rather proceeds from a certain hopelessness of remedying excessive and organic ill. To a sensitive being, pity is not seldom pain. And when at last it is perceived that such pity cannot lead to effectual succor, common sense bids the soul be rid of it. What I saw that morning persuaded me that the scrivener was the victim of innate and incurable disorder. I might give alms to his body; but his body did not pain him; it was his soul that suffered, and his soul I could not reach.

I did not accomplish the purpose of going to Trinity Church that morning. Somehow, the things I had seen disqualified me for the time from churchgoing. I walked homeward, thinking what I would do with Bartleby. Finally, I resolved upon this;—I would put certain calm questions to him the next morning, touching his history, &c., and if he declined to answer them openly and unreservedly (and I supposed he would prefer not), then to give him a twenty-dollar bill over and above whatever I might owe him, and tell him his services were no longer required; but that if in any other way I could assist him, I would be happy to do so, especially if he desired to return to his native place, wherever that might be, I would willingly help to defray the expenses. Moreover, if, after reaching home, he found himself at any time in want of aid, a letter from him would be sure of a reply.

The next morning came.

"Bartleby," said I, gently calling to him behind his screen.

No reply.

"Bartleby," said I, in a still gentler tone, "come here; I am not going to ask you to do anything you would prefer not to do—I simply wish to speak to you."

Upon this he noiselessly slid into view.

"Will you tell me, Bartleby, where you were born?"

"I would prefer not to."

"Will you tell me *anything* about yourself?"

"I would prefer not to."

"But what reasonable objection can you have to speak to me? I feel friendly towards you."

He did not look at me while I spoke, but kept his glance fixed upon my bust of Cicero, which as I then sat, was directly behind me, some six inches above my head.

"What is your answer, Bartleby?" said I, after waiting a considerable time for a reply, during which his countenance remained immovable, only there was the faintest conceivable tremor of the white attenuated mouth.

"At present I prefer to give no answer," he said, and retired into his hermitage.

It was rather weak in me I confess, but his manner on this occasion nettled me. Not only did there seem to lurk in it a certain calm disdain, but his perverseness seemed ungrateful, considering the undeniable good usage and indulgence he had received from me.

Again I sat ruminating what I should do. Mortified as I was at his behavior, and resolved as I had been to dismiss him when I entered my office, nevertheless I strangely felt something superstitious knocking at my heart, and forbidding me to carry out my purpose, and denouncing me for a villain if I dared to breathe one bitter word against this forlornest of mankind. At last, familiarly drawing my chair behind his screen, I sat down and said: "Bartleby, never mind then about revealing your history; but let me entreat you, as a friend, to comply as far as may be with the usages of this office. Say now you will help to examine papers tomorrow or next day: in short, say now that in a day or two you will begin to be a little reasonable:—say so, Bartleby."

"At present I would prefer not to be a little reasonable," was his mildly cadaverous reply.

Just then the folding-doors opened, and Nippers approached. He seemed suffering from an unusually bad night's rest, induced by severer indigestion than common. He overheard those final words of Bartleby.

"*Prefer not,* eh?" gritted Nippers—"I'd *prefer* him, if I were you, sir," addressing me—"I'd *prefer* him; I'd give him preferences, the stubborn mule! What is it, sir, pray, that he *prefers* not to do now?"

Bartleby moved not a limb.

"Mr. Nippers," said I, "I'd prefer that you would withdraw for the present."

Somehow, of late I had got into the way of involuntarily using this word "prefer" upon all sorts of not exactly suitable occasions. And I trembled to think that my contact with the scrivener had already and seriously affected me in a mental way. And what further and deeper aberration might it not yet produce? This apprehension had not been without efficacy in determining me to summary means.

As Nippers, looking very sour and sulky, was departing, Turkey blandly and deferentially approached.

"With submission, sir," said he, "yesterday I was thinking about Bartleby here, and I think that if he would but prefer to take a quart of good ale every day, it would do much towards mending him and enabling him to assist in examining his papers."

"So you have got the word too," said I, slightly excited.

"With submission, what word, sir?" asked Turkey, respectfully crowding himself into the contracted space behind the screen, and by so doing making me jostle the scrivener. "What word, sir?"

"I would prefer to be left alone here," said Bartleby, as if offended at being mobbed in his privacy.

"*That's* the word, Turkey," said I—"*that's* it."

"Oh, *prefer*? oh yes—queer word. I never use it myself. But, sir, as I was saying, if he would but prefer—"

"Turkey," interrupted I, "you will please withdraw."

"Oh certainly, sir, if you prefer that I should."

As he opened the folding-door to retire, Nippers at his desk caught a glimpse of me, and asked whether I would prefer to have a certain paper copied on blue paper or white. He did not in the least roguishly accent the word *prefer*. It was plain that it involuntarily rolled from his tongue. I thought to myself, surely I must get rid of a demented man, who already has in some degree turned the tongues, if not the heads of myself and clerks. But I thought it prudent not to break the dismission at once.

The next day I noticed that Bartleby did nothing but stand at his window in his dead-wall revery. Upon asking him why he did not write, he said that he had decided upon doing no more writing.

"Why, how now? what next?" exclaimed I, "do no more writing?"

"No more."

"And what is the reason?"

"Do you not see the reason for yourself," he indifferently replied.

I looked steadfastly at him, and perceived that his eyes looked dull and glazed. Instantly it occurred to me, that his unexampled diligence in copying by his dim window for the first few weeks of his stay with me might have temporarily impaired his vision.

I was touched. I said something in condolence with him. I hinted that of course he did wisely in abstaining from writing for a while; and urged him to embrace that opportunity of taking wholesome exercise in the open air. This, however, he did not do. A few days after this, my other clerks being absent, and being in a great hurry to dispatch certain letters by the mail, I thought that, having nothing else earthly to do,

Bartleby would surely be less inflexible than usual, and carry these letters to the post office. But he blankly declined. So, much to my inconvenience, I went myself.

Still added days went by. Whether Bartleby's eyes improved or not, I could not say. To all appearance, I thought they did. But when I asked him if they did, he vouchsafed no answer. At all events, he would do no copying. At last, in reply to my urgings, he informed me that he had permanently given up copying.

"What!" exclaimed I; "suppose your eyes should get entirely well—better than ever before—would you not copy then?"

"I have given up copying," he answered, and slid aside.

He remained, as ever, a fixture in my chamber. Nay—if that were possible—he became still more of a fixture than before. What was to be done? He would do nothing in the office: why should he stay there? In plain fact, he had now become a millstone[4] to me, not only useless as a necklace, but afflictive to bear. Yet I was sorry for him. I speak less than truth when I say that, on his own account, he occasioned me uneasiness. If he would but have named a single relative or friend, I would instantly have written, and urged their taking the poor fellow away to some convenient retreat. But he seemed alone, absolutely alone in the universe. A bit of wreck in the mid-Atlantic. At length, necessities connected with my business tyrannized over all other considerations. Decently as I could, I told Bartleby that in six days' time he must unconditionally leave the office. I warned him to take measures, in the interval, for procuring some other abode. I offered to assist him in this endeavor, if he himself would but take the first step towards a removal. "And when you finally quit me, Bartleby," added I, "I shall see that you go not away entirely unprovided. Six days from this hour, remember."

At the expiration of that period, I peeped behind the screen, and lo! Bartleby was there.

I buttoned up my coat, balanced myself; advanced slowly towards him, touched his shoulder, and said, "The time has come; you must quit this place; I am sorry for you; here is money; but you must go."

"I would prefer not," he replied, with his back still towards me.

"You *must*."

He remained silent.

Now I had an unbounded confidence in this man's common honesty. He had frequently restored to me sixpences and shillings[5] carelessly dropped upon the floor, for I am apt to be very reckless in such shirt-button affairs. The proceeding then which followed will not be deemed extraordinary.

"Bartleby," said I, "I owe you twelve dollars on account; here are thirty-two; the odd twenty are yours.—Will you take it?" and I handed the bills towards him.

But he made no motion.

"I will leave them here then," putting them under a weight on the table. Then taking my hat and cane and going to the door I tranquilly

4. Heavy stone for grinding grain. See *Matthew* 18:6: "But whoso shall offend one of these little ones which believe in me, it were better for him that a millstone were hanged about his neck, and that he were drowned in the depth of the sea."

5. Coins now worth six cents and 12 cents but once worth twice that.

turned and added—"After you have removed your things from these offices, Bartleby, you will of course lock the door—since everyone is now gone for the day but you—and if you please, slip your key underneath the mat, so that I may have it in the morning. I shall not see you again; so good-bye to you. If hereafter in your new place of abode I can be of any service to you, do not fail to advise me by letter. Good-bye, Bartleby, and fare you well."

But he answered not a word; like the last column of some ruined temple, he remained standing mute and solitary in the middle of the otherwise deserted room.

As I walked home in a pensive mood, my vanity got the better of my pity. I could not but highly plume myself on my masterly management in getting rid of Bartleby. Masterly I call it, and such it must appear to any dispassionate thinker. The beauty of my procedure seemed to consist in its perfect quietness. There was no vulgar bullying, no bravado of any sort, no choleric hectoring, and striding to and fro across the apartment, jerking out vehement commands for Bartleby to bundle himself off with his beggarly traps.[6] Nothing of the kind. Without loudly bidding Bartleby depart—as an inferior genius might have done —I *assumed* the ground that depart he must; and upon that assumption built all I had to say. The more I thought over my procedure, the more I was charmed with it. Nevertheless, next morning, upon awakening, I had my doubts,—I had somehow slept off the fumes of vanity. One of the coolest and wisest hours a man has is just after he awakes in the morning. My procedure seemed as sagacious as ever,—but only in theory. How it would prove in practice—there was the rub. It was truly a beautiful thought to have assumed Bartleby's departure; but, after all, that assumption was simply my own, and none of Bartleby's. The great point was, not whether I had assumed that he would quit me, but whether he would prefer so to do. He was more a man of preferences than assumptions.

After breakfast, I walked downtown, arguing the probabilities *pro* and *con*. One moment I thought it would prove a miserable failure, and Bartleby would be found all alive at my office as usual; the next moment it seemed certain that I should see his chair empty. And so I kept veering about. At the corner of Broadway and Canal Street, I saw quite an excited group of people standing in earnest conversation.

"I'll take odds he doesn't," said a voice as I passed.

"Doesn't go?—done!" said I, "put up your money."

I was instinctively putting my hand in my pocket to produce my own, when I remembered that this was an election day. The words I had overheard bore no reference to Bartleby, but to the success or non-success of some candidate for the mayoralty. In my intent frame of mind, I had, as it were, imagined that all Broadway shared in my excitement, and were debating the same question with me. I passed on, very thankful that the uproar of the street screened my momentary absent-mindedness.

As I had intended, I was earlier than usual at my office door. I stood listening for a moment. All was still. He must be gone. I tried the knob. The door was locked. Yes, my procedure had worked to a charm; he

6. Personal belongings, luggage.

indeed must be vanished. Yet a certain melancholy mixed with this: I was almost sorry for my brilliant success. I was fumbling under the door mat for the key, which Bartleby was to have left there for me, when accidentally my knee knocked against a panel, producing a summoning sound, and in response a voice came to me from within—"Not yet; I am occupied."

It was Bartleby.

I was thunderstruck. For an instant I stood like the man who, pipe in mouth, was killed one cloudless afternoon long ago in Virginia, by summer lightning; at his own warm open window he was killed, and remained leaning out there upon the dreamy afternoon, till some one touched him, when he fell.

"Not gone!" I murmured at last. But again obeying that wondrous ascendancy which the inscrutable scrivener had over me, and from which ascendency, for all my chafing, I could not completely escape, I slowly went downstairs and out into the street, and while walking round the block, considered what I should next do in this unheard-of perplexity. Turn the man out by an actual thrusting I could not; to drive him away by calling him hard names would not do; calling in the police was an unpleasant idea; and yet, permit him to enjoy his cadaverous triumph over me,—this too I could not think of. What was to be done? or, if nothing could be done, was there anything further that I could *assume* in the matter? Yes, as before I had prospectively assumed that Bartleby would depart, so now I might retrospectively assume that departed he was. In the legitimate carrying out of this assumption, I might enter my office in a great hurry, and pretending not to see Bartleby at all, walk straight against him as if he were air. Such a proceeding would in a singular degree have the appearance of a home-thrust.[7] It was hardly possible that Bartleby could withstand such an application of the doctrine of assumptions. But upon second thoughts the success of the plan seemed rather dubious. I resolved to argue the matter over with him again.

"Bartleby," said I, entering the office, with a quietly severe expression, "I am seriously displeased. I am pained, Bartleby. I had thought better of you. I had imagined you of such a gentlemanly organization, that in any delicate dilemma a slight hint would suffice—in short, an assumption. But it appears I am deceived. Why," I added, unaffectedly starting, "you have not even touched that money yet," pointing to it, just where I had left it the evening previous.

He answered nothing.

"Will you, or will you not, quit me?" I now demanded in a sudden passion, advancing close to him.

"I would prefer *not* to quit you," he replied, gently emphasizing the *not*.

"What earthly right have you to stay here? Do you pay any rent? Do you pay my taxes? Or is this property yours?"

He answered nothing.

"Are you ready to go on and write now? Are your eyes recovered? Could you copy a small paper for me this morning? or help examine a few lines? or step round to the post office? In a word, will you do any-

7. Thrust that reaches its mark.

thing at all, to give a coloring to your refusal to depart the premises?"

He silently retired into his hermitage.

I was now in such a state of nervous resentment that I thought it but prudent to check myself at present from further demonstrations. Bartleby and I were alone. I remembered the tragedy of the unfortunate Adams and the still more unfortunate Colt in the solitary office of the latter; and how poor Colt, being dreadfully incensed by Adams, and imprudently permitting himself to get wildly excited, was at unawares hurried into his fatal act—an act which certainly no man could possibly deplore more than the actor himself. Often it had occurred to me in my ponderings upon the subject, that had that altercation taken place in the public street, or at a private residence, it would not have terminated as it did. It was the circumstance of being alone in a solitary office, up stairs, of a building entirely unhallowed by humanizing domestic associations—an uncarpeted office, doubtless, of a dusty, haggard sort of appearance;—this it must have been, which greatly helped to enhance the irritable desperation of the hapless Colt.[8]

But when this old Adam[9] of resentment rose in me and tempted me concerning Bartleby, I grappled him and threw him. How? Why, simply by recalling the divine injunction: "A new commandment[1] give I unto you, that ye love one another." Yes, this it was that saved me. Aside from higher considerations, charity often operates as a vastly wise and prudent principle—a great safeguard to its possessor. Men have committed murder for jealousy's sake, and anger's sake, and hatred's sake, and selfishness' sake, and spiritual pride's sake; but no man that ever I heard of, ever committed a diabolical murder for sweet charity's sake. Mere self-interest, then, if no better motive can be enlisted, should, especially with high-tempered men, prompt all beings to charity and philanthropy. At any rate, upon the occasion in question, I strove to drown my exasperated feelings towards the scrivener by benevolently construing his conduct. Poor fellow, poor fellow! thought I, he don't mean anything; and besides, he has seen hard times, and ought to be indulged.

I endeavored also immediately to occupy myself, and at the same time to comfort my despondency. I tried to fancy that in the course of the morning, at such time as might prove agreeable to him, Bartleby, of his own free accord, would emerge from his hermitage, and take up some decided line of march in the direction of the door. But no. Half-past twelve o'clock came; Turkey began to glow in the face, overturn his inkstand, and become generally obstreperous; Nippers abated down into quietude and courtesy; Ginger Nut munched his noon apple; and Bartleby remained standing at his window in one of his profoundest dead-wall reveries. Will it be credited? Ought I to acknowledge it? That afternoon I left the office without saying one further word to him.

Some days now passed, during which, at leisure intervals I looked a

8. In 1841, John C. Colt, brother of the famous gunmaker, unintentionally killed Samuel Adams, a printer, when he hit him on the head during a fight.

9. Sinful element in human nature; see, e.g., "Invocation of Blessing on the Child," in the *Book of Common Prayer*: "Grant that the old Adam in this child may be so buried, that the new man may be raised up in him." Christ is sometimes called the "new Adam."

1. In *John* 13:34, where, however, the phrasing is "I give unto . . ."

little into "Edwards on the Will," and "Priestley on Necessity."[2] Under the circumstances, those books induced a salutary feeling. Gradually I slid into the persuasion that these troubles of mine touching the scrivener, had been all predestinated from eternity, and Bartleby was billeted upon me for some mysterious purpose of an all-wise Providence, which it was not for a mere mortal like me to fathom. Yes, Bartleby, stay there behind your screen, thought I; I shall persecute you no more; you are harmless and noiseless as any of these old chairs; in short, I never feel so private as when I know you are here. At least I see it, I feel it; I penetrate to the predestinated purpose of my life. I am content. Others may have loftier parts to enact; but my mission in this world, Bartleby, is to furnish you with office-room for such period as you may see fit to remain.

I believe that this wise and blessed frame of mind would have continued with me, had it not been for the unsolicited and uncharitable remarks obtruded upon me by my professional friends who visited the rooms. But thus it often is, that the constant friction of illiberal minds wears out at last the best resolves of the more generous. Though to be sure, when I reflected upon it, it was not strange that people entering my office should be struck by the peculiar aspect of the unaccountable Bartleby, and so be tempted to throw out some sinister observations concerning him. Sometimes an attorney having business with me, and calling at my office, and finding no one but the scrivener there, would undertake to obtain some sort of precise information from him touching my whereabouts; but without heeding his idle talk, Bartleby would remain standing immovable in the middle of the room. So after contemplating him in that position for a time, the attorney would depart, no wiser than he came.

Also, when a Reference[3] was going on, and the room full of lawyers and witnesses and business was driving fast; some deeply occupied legal gentleman present, seeing Bartleby wholly unemployed, would request him to run round to his (the legal gentleman's) office and fetch some papers for him. Thereupon, Bartleby would tranquilly decline, and yet remain idle as before. Then the lawyer would give a great stare, and turn to me. And what could I say? At last I was made aware that all through the circle of my professional acquaintance, a whisper of wonder was running round, having reference to the strange creature I kept at my office. This worried me very much. And as the idea came upon me of his possibly turning out a long-lived man, and keep occupying my chambers, and denying my authority; and perplexing my visitors; and scandalizing my professional reputation; and casting a general gloom over the premises; keeping soul and body together to the last upon his savings (for doubtless he spent but half a dime a day), and in the end perhaps outlive me, and claim possession of my office by right of his perpetual occupancy: as all these dark anticipations crowded

2. Jonathan Edwards (1703–1758), New England Calvinist theologian and revivalist, in *The Freedom of the Will* (1754), argued that man is not in fact free, for though he chooses according to the way he sees things, that way is predetermined (by biography, environment, and character), and he acts out of personality rather than by will. Joseph Priestley (1733–1804), Dissenting preacher, scientist, grammarian, and philosopher, in *The Doctrine of Philosophical Necessity* (1777), argued that free will is theologically objectionable, metaphysically incomprehensible, and morally undesirable.

3. Consultation or committee meeting.

upon me more and more, and my friends continually intruded their relentless remarks upon the apparition in my room; a great change was wrought in me. I resolved to gather all my faculties together, and forever rid me of this intolerable incubus.

Ere revolving any complicated project, however, adapted to this end, I first simply suggested to Bartleby the propriety of his permanent departure. In a calm and serious tone, I commended the idea to his careful and mature consideration. But having taken three days to meditate upon it, he apprised me that his original determination remained the same; in short, that he still preferred to abide with me.

What shall I do? I now said to myself, buttoning up my coat to the last button. What shall I do? what ought I to do? what does conscience say I *should* do with this man, or rather ghost. Rid myself of him, I must; go, he shall. But how? You will not thrust him, the poor, pale, passive mortal,—you will not thrust such a helpless creature out of your door? you will not dishonor yourself by such cruelty? No, I will not, I cannot do that. Rather would I let him live and die here, and then mason up his remains in the wall. What then will you do? For all your coaxing, he will not budge. Bribes he leaves under your own paperweight on your table; in short, it is quite plain that he prefers to cling to you.

Then something severe, something unusual must be done. What! surely you will not have him collared by a constable, and commit his innocent pallor to the common jail? And upon what ground could you procure such a thing to be done?—a vagrant, is he? What! he a vagrant, a wanderer, who refuses to budge? It is because he will *not* be a vagrant, then, that you seek to count him *as* a vagrant. That is too absurd. No visible means of support: there I have him. Wrong again: for indubitably he *does* support himself, and that is the only unanswerable proof that any man can show of his possessing the means so to do. No more then. Since he will not quit me, I must quit him. I will change my offices; I will move elsewhere; and give him fair notice, that if I find him on my new premises I will then proceed against him as a common trespasser.

Acting accordingly, next day I thus addressed him: "I find these chambers too far from the City Hall; the air is unwholesome. In a word, I propose to remove my offices next week, and shall no longer require your services. I tell you this now, in order that you may seek another place."

He made no reply, and nothing more was said.

On the appointed day I engaged carts and men, proceeded to my chambers, and having but little furniture, everything was removed in a few hours. Throughout, the scrivener remained standing behind the screen, which I directed to be removed the last thing. It was withdrawn; and being folded up like a huge folio, left him the motionless occupant of a naked room. I stood in the entry watching him a moment, while something from within me upbraided me.

I re-entered, with my hand in my pocket—and—and my heart in my mouth.

"Good-bye, Bartleby; I am going—good-bye, and God some way bless you; and take that," slipping something in his hand. But it dropped upon the floor, and then,—strange to say—I tore myself from him whom I had so longed to be rid of.

Established in my new quarters, for a day or two I kept the door locked, and started at every footfall in the passages. When I returned to my rooms after any little absence, I would pause at the threshold for an instant, and attentively listen, ere applying my key. But these fears were needless. Bartleby never came nigh me.

I thought all was going well, when a perturbed-looking stranger visited me, inquiring whether I was the person who had recently occupied rooms at No. — Wall Street.

Full of forebodings, I replied that I was.

"Then sir," said the stranger, who proved a lawyer, "you are responsible for the man you left there. He refuses to do any copying; he refuses to do anything; he says he prefers not to; and he refuses to quit the premises."

"I am very sorry, sir," said I, with assumed tranquillity, but an inward tremor, "but, really, the man you allude to is nothing to me—he is no relation or apprentice of mine, that you should hold me responsible for him."

"In mercy's name, who is he?"

"I certainly cannot inform you. I know nothing about him. Formerly I employed him as a copyist; but he has done nothing for me now for some time past."

"I shall settle him then,—good morning, sir."

Several days passed, and I heard nothing more; and though I often felt a charitable prompting to call at the place and see poor Bartleby, yet a certain squeamishness of I know not what withheld me.

All is over with him, by this time, thought I at last, when through another week no further intelligence reached me. But coming to my room the day after, I found several persons waiting at my door in a high state of nervous excitement.

"That's the man—here he comes," cried the foremost one, whom I recognized as the lawyer who had previously called upon me alone.

"You must take him away, sir, at once," cried a portly person among them, advancing upon me, and whom I knew to be the landlord of No. — Wall Street. "These gentlemen, my tenants, cannot stand it any longer; Mr. B——" pointing to the lawyer, "has turned him out of his room, and he now persists in haunting the building generally, sitting upon the banisters of the stairs by day, and sleeping in the entry by night. Everybody is concerned; clients are leaving the offices; some fears are entertained of a mob; something you must do, and that without delay."

Aghast at this torrent, I fell back before it, and would fain have locked myself in my new quarters. In vain I persisted that Bartleby was nothing to me—no more than to anyone else. In vain:—I was the last person known to have anything to do with him, and they held me to the terrible account. Fearful then of being exposed in the papers (as one person present obscurely threatened) I considered the matter, and at length said, that if the lawyer would give me a confidential interview with the scrivener, in his (the lawyer's) own room, I would that afternoon strive my best to rid them of the nuisance they complained of.

Going upstairs to my old haunt, there was Bartleby silently sitting upon the banister at the landing.

"What are you doing here, Bartleby?" said I.

"Sitting upon the banister," he mildly replied.

I motioned him into the lawyer's room, who then left us.

"Bartleby," said I, "are you aware that you are the cause of great tribulation to me, by persisting in occupying the entry after being dismissed from the office?"

No answer.

"Now one of two things must take place. Either you must do something, or something must be done to you. Now what sort of business would you like to engage in? Would you like to re-engage in copying for someone?"

"No; I would prefer not to make any change."

"Would you like a clerkship in a drygoods store?"

"There is too much confinement about that. No, I would not like a clerkship; but I am not particular."

"Too much confinement," I cried, "why you keep yourself confined all the time!"

"I would prefer not to take a clerkship," he rejoined, as if to settle that little item at once.

"How would a bartender's business suit you? There is no trying of the eyesight in that."

"I would not like it at all; though, as I said before, I am not particular."

His unwonted wordiness inspirited me. I returned to the charge.

"Well then, would you like to travel through the country collecting bills for the merchants? That would improve your health."

"No, I would prefer to be doing something else."

"How then would going as a companion to Europe, to entertain some young gentleman with your conversation,—how would that suit you?"

"Not at all. It does not strike me that there is anything definite about that. I like to be stationary. But I am not particular."

"Stationary you shall be then," I cried, now losing all patience, and for the first time in all my exasperating connection with him fairly flying into a passion. "If you do not go away from these premises before night, I shall feel bound—indeed I *am* bound—to—to—to quit the premises myself!" I rather absurdly concluded, knowing not with what possible threat to try to frighten his immobility into compliance. Despairing of all further efforts, I was precipitately leaving him, when a final thought occurred to me—one which had not been wholly unindulged before.

"Bartleby," said I, in the kindest tone I could assume under such exciting circumstances, "will you go home with me now—not to my office, but my dwelling—and remain there till we can conclude upon some convenient arrangement for you at our leisure? Come, let us start now, right away."

"No: at present I would prefer not to make any change at all."

I answered nothing; but effectually dodging everyone by the suddenness and rapidity of my flight, rushed from the building, ran up Wall Street toward Broadway, and jumping into the first omnibus was soon removed from pursuit. As soon as tranquillity returned I distinctly perceived that I had now done all that I possibly could, both in respect to the demands of the landlord and his tenants, and with regard to my own desire and sense of duty, to benefit Bartleby, and shield him from rude persecution. I now strove to be entirely carefree and quiescent; and my conscience justified me in the attempt; though indeed it was not so successful as I could have wished. So fearful was I of being again hunted out by the incensed landlord and his exasperated tenants, that, surrendering my business to Nippers, for a few days I drove about the upper part of the town and through the suburbs, in my rockaway; crossed over to Jersey City and Hoboken, and paid fugitive visits to Manhattanville and Astoria. In fact I almost lived in my rockaway for the time.

When again I entered my office, lo, a note from the landlord lay upon the desk. I opened it with trembling hands. It informed me that the writer had sent to the police, and had Bartleby removed to the Tombs as a vagrant. Moreover, since I knew more about him than anyone else, he wished me to appear at that place, and make a suitable statement of the facts. These tidings had a conflicting effect upon me. At first I was indignant; but at last almost approved. The landlord's energetic, summary disposition had led him to adopt a procedure which I do not think I would have decided upon myself; and yet as a last resort, under such peculiar circumstances, it seemed the only plan.

As I afterwards learned, the poor scrivener, when told that he must be conducted to the Tombs, offered not the slightest obstacle, but in his pale unmoving way, silently acquiesced.

Some of the compassionate and curious bystanders joined the party; and headed by one of the constables arm in arm with Bartleby, the silent procession filed its way through all the noise, and heat, and joy of the roaring thoroughfares at noon.

The same day I received the note I went to the Tombs, or to speak more properly, the Halls of Justice. Seeking the right officer, I stated the purpose of my call, and was informed that the individual I described was indeed within. I then assured the functionary that Bartleby was a perfectly honest man, and greatly to be compassionated, however unaccountably eccentric. I narrated all I knew, and closed by suggesting the idea of letting him remain in as indulgent confinement as possible till something less harsh might be done—though indeed I hardly knew what. At all events, if nothing else could be decided upon, the alms-house must receive him. I then begged to have an interview.

Being under no disgraceful charge, and quite serene and harmless in all his ways, they had permitted him freely to wander about the prison, and especially in the inclosed grass-platted yards thereof. And so I found him there, standing all alone in the quietest of the yards, his face towards a high wall, while all around, from the narrow slits of the jail windows, I thought I saw peering out upon him the eyes of murderers and thieves.

"Bartleby!"

"I know you," he said, without looking round,—"and I want nothing to say to you."

"It was not I that brought you here, Bartleby," said I, keenly pained at his implied suspicion. "And to you, this should not be so vile a place. Nothing reproachful attaches to you by being here. And see, it is not so sad a place as one might think. Look, there is the sky, and here is the grass."

"I know where I am," he replied, but would say nothing more, and so I left him.

As I entered the corridor again, a broad meat-like man, in an apron, accosted me, and jerking his thumb over his shoulder said—"Is that your friend?"

"Yes."

"Does he want to starve? If he does, let him live on the prison fare, that's all."

"Who are you?" asked I, not knowing what to make of such an unofficially-speaking person in such a place.

"I am the grub-man. Such gentlemen as have friends here, hire me to provide them with something good to eat."

"Is this so?" said I, turning to the turnkey.

He said it was.

"Well then," said I, slipping some silver into the grub-man's hands (for so they called him). "I want you to give particular attention to my friend there; let him have the best dinner you can get. And you must be as polite to him as possible."

"Introduce me, will you?" said the grub-man, looking at me with an expression which seemed to say he was all impatience for an opportunity to give a specimen of his breeding.

Thinking it would prove of benefit to the scrivener, I acquiesced; and asking the grub-man his name, went up with him to Bartleby.

"Bartleby, this is Mr. Cutlets; you will find him very useful to you."

"Your sarvant, sir, your sarvant," said the grub-man, making a low salutation behind his apron. "Hope you find it pleasant here, sir;—spacious grounds—cool apartments, sir—hope you'll stay with us some time—try to make it agreeable. May Mrs. Cutlets and I have the pleasure of your company to dinner, sir, in Mrs. Cutlets' private room?"

"I prefer not to dine today," said Bartleby, turning away. "It would disagree with me; I am unused to dinners." So saying he slowly moved to the other side of the inclosure, and took up a position fronting the dead-wall.

"How's this?" said the grub-man, addressing me with a stare of astonishment. "He's odd, ain't he?"

"I think he is a little deranged," said I, sadly.

"Deranged? deranged is it? Well now, upon my word, I thought that friend of yourn was a gentleman forger; they are always pale and genteel-like, them forgers. I can't help pity 'em—can't help it, sir. Did you know Monroe Edwards?" he added touchingly, and paused. Then, laying his hand pityingly on my shoulder, sighed, "he died of consumption at Sing Sing. So you weren't acquainted with Monroe?"

"No, I was never socially aquainted with any forgers. But I cannot stop longer. Look to my friend yonder. You will not lose by it. I will see you again."

Some few days after this, I again obtained admission to the Tombs, and went through the corridors in quest of Bartleby; but without finding him.

"I saw him coming from his cell not long ago," said a turnkey, "may be he's gone to loiter in the yards."

So I went in that direction.

"Are you looking for the silent man?" said another turnkey passing me. "Yonder he lies—sleeping in the yard there. 'Tis not twenty minutes since I saw him lie down."

The yard was entirely quiet. It was not accessible to the common prisoners. The surrounding walls, of amazing thickness, kept off all sounds behind them. The Egyptian character of the masonry weighed upon me with its gloom. But a soft imprisoned turf grew under foot. The heart of the eternal pyramids, it seemed, wherein, by some strange magic, through the clefts, grass seed, dropped by birds, had sprung.

Strangely huddled at the base of the wall, his knees drawn up, and lying on his side, his head touching the cold stones, I saw the wasted Bartleby. But nothing stirred. I paused; then went close up to him; stooped over, and saw that his dim eyes were open; otherwise he seemed profoundly sleeping. Something prompted me to touch him. I felt his hand, when a tingling shiver ran up my arm and down my spine to my feet.

The round face of the grub-man peered upon me now. "His dinner is ready. Won't he dine today, either? Or does he live without dining?"

"Lives without dining," said I, and closed the eyes.

"Eh!—He's asleep, ain't he?"

"With kings and counsellors,"[4] murmured I.

There would seem little need for proceeding further in this history. Imagination will readily supply the meager recital of poor Bartleby's interment. But ere parting with the reader, let me say, that if this little narrative has sufficiently interested him, to awaken curiosity as to who Bartleby was, and what manner of life he led prior to the present narrator's making his acquaintance, I can only reply, that in such curiosity I fully share, but am wholly unable to gratify it. Yet here I hardly know whether I should divulge one little item of rumor, which came to my ear a few months after the scrivener's decease. Upon what basis it rested, I could never ascertain; and hence, how true it is I cannot now tell. But inasmuch as this vague report has not been without a certain strange suggestive interest to me, however sad, it may prove the same with some others; and so I will briefly mention it. The report was this: that Bartleby had been a subordinate clerk in the Dead Letter Office at Washington, from which he had been suddenly removed by a change in the administration. When I think over this rumor, I cannot adequately express the emotions which seize me. Dead letters! does it not sound like dead men? Conceive a man by nature and misfortune prone to a pallid hopelessness, can any business seem more fitted to heighten it than that of continually handling these dead letters, and assorting them for the flames? For by the cartload they are annually burned. Sometimes from out the folded paper the pale clerk takes a ring:—the finger it was meant for, perhaps, molders in the grave; a banknote sent in swiftest charity:—he whom it would relieve, nor eats nor hungers any more; pardon for those who died despairing; hope for those who died unhoping; good tidings for those who died stifled by unrelieved calamities. On errands of life, these letters speed to death.

Ah Bartleby! Ah humanity!

p. 1853

4. I.e., dead. See *Job* 3:13–14: ". . . then had I been at rest, With kings and counsellors of the earth, which built desolate places for themselves."

HENRY JAMES

The Tree of Knowledge

1

It was one of the secret opinions, such as we all have, of Peter Brench that his main success in life would have consisted in his never having committed himself about the work, as it was called, of his friend Morgan Mallow. This was a subject on which it was, to the best of his belief, impossible with veracity to quote him, and it was nowhere on record that he had, in the connection, on any occasion and in any embarrassment, either lied or spoken the truth. Such a triumph had its honor even for a man of other triumphs—a man who had reached fifty, who had escaped marriage, who had lived within his means, who had been in love with Mrs. Mallow for years without breathing it, and who, last not least, had judged himself once for all. He had so judged himself in fact that he felt an extreme and general humility to be his proper portion; yet there was nothing that made him think so well of his parts as the course he had steered so often through the shallows just mentioned. It became thus a real wonder that the friends in whom he had most confidence were just those with whom he had most reserves. He couldn't tell Mrs. Mallow—or at least he supposed, excellent man, he couldn't—that she was the one beautiful reason he had never married; any more than he could tell her husband that the sight of the multiplied marbles in that gentleman's studio was an affliction of which even time had never blunted the edge. His victory, however, as I have intimated, in regard to these productions, was not simply in his not having let it out that he deplored them; it was, remarkably, in his not having kept it in by anything else.

The whole situation, among these good people, was verily a marvel, and there was probably not such another for a long way from the spot that engages us—the point at which the soft declivity of Hampstead began at that time to confess in broken accents to Saint John's Wood.[1] He despised Mallow's status and adored Mallow's wife, and yet was distinctly fond of Mallow, to whom, in turn, he was equally dear. Mrs. Mallow rejoiced in the statues—though she preferred, when pressed, the busts; and if she was visibly attached to Peter Brench it was because of his affection for Morgan. Each loved the other moreover for the love borne in each case to Lancelot, whom the Mallows respectively cherished as their only child and whom the friend of their fireside identified as the third—but decidedly the handsomest—of his godsons. Already in the old years it had come to that—that no one, for such a relation, could possibly have occurred to any of them, even to the baby itself, but Peter. There was luckily a certain independence, of the pecuniary sort, all round: the Master could never otherwise have spent his solemn *Wanderjahre*[2] in Florence and Rome, and continued by the Thames as well as by the Arno and the Tiber to add unpurchased group to group and model, for what was too apt to prove

1. Sections of northwest London.
2. A journeyman's year of travel before settling to work; also the title of the second volume (1821–29) of the famous novel *Wilhelm Meister* by Johann Wolfgang von Goethe (1749–1832).

in the event mere love, fancy-heads of celebrities either too busy or too buried—too much of the age or too little of it—to sit. Neither could Peter, lounging in almost daily, have found time to keep the whole complicated tradition so alive by his presence. He was massive but mild, the depositary of these mysteries—large and loose and ruddy and curly, with deep tones, deep eyes, deep pockets, to say nothing of the habit of long pipes, soft hats and brownish grayish weather-faded clothes, apparently always the same.

He had "written," it was known, but had never spoken, never spoken in particular of that; and he had the air (since, as was believed, he continued to write) of keeping it up in order to have something more —as if he hadn't at the worst enough—to be silent about. Whatever his air, at any rate, Peter's occasional unmentioned prose and verse were quite truly the result of an impulse to maintain the purity of his taste by establishing still more firmly the right relation of fame to feebleness. The little green door of his domain was in a garden wall on which the discolored stucco made patches, and in the small detached villa behind it everything was old, the furniture, the servants, the books, the prints, the immemorial habits and the new improvements. The Mallows, at Carrara Lodge, were within ten minutes, and the studio there was on their little land, to which they had added, in their happy faith, for building it. This was the good fortune, if it was not the ill, of her having brought him in marriage a portion that put them in a manner at their ease and enabled them thus, on their side, to keep it up. And they did keep it up—they always had—the infatuated sculptor and his wife, for whom nature had refined on the impossible by relieving them of the sense of the difficult. Morgan had at all events everything of the sculptor but the spirit of Phidias—the brown velvet, the becoming *beretto*,[3] the "plastic" presence, the fine fingers, the beautiful accent in Italian and the old Italian factotum. He seemed to make up for everything when he addressed Egidio with the "tu"[4] and waved him to turn one of the rotary pedestals of which the place was full. They were tremendous Italians at Carrara Lodge, and the secret of the part played by this fact in Peter's life was in a large degree that it gave him, sturdy Briton as he was, just the amount of "going abroad" he could bear. The Mallows were all his Italy, but it was in a measure for Italy he liked them. His one worry was that Lance—to which they had shortened his godson—was, in spite of a public school,[5] perhaps a shade too Italian. Morgan meanwhile looked like somebody's flattering idea of somebody's own person as expressed in the great room provided at the Uffizzi Museum[6] for the general illustration of that idea by eminent hands. The Master's sole regret that he hadn't been born rather to the brush than to the chisel sprang from his wish that he might have contributed to that collection.

It appeared with time at any rate to be to the brush that Lance had been born; for Mrs. Mallow, one day when the boy was turning twenty, broke it to their friend, who shared, to the last delicate mor-

3. Cap with tassel, usually *berretto*.
4. The familiar form of the second-person pronoun, literally "thou," but roughly equivalent to first-naming someone in English.
5. English boarding-school, usually for the well-to-do.
6. Art Museum in Florence with world's finest collection of Italian Renaissance painting, the reference here being to artists' self-portraits.

sel, their problems and pains, that it seemed as if nothing would really do but that he should embrace the career. It had been impossible longer to remain blind to the fact that he was gaining no glory at Cambridge, where Brench's own college had for a year tempered its tone to him as for Brench's own sake. Therefore why renew the vain form of preparing him for the impossible? The impossible—it had become clear—was that he should be anything but an artist.

"Oh dear, dear!" said poor Peter.

"Don't you believe in it?" asked Mrs. Mallow, who still, at more than forty, had her violet velvet eyes, her creamy satin skin and her silken chestnut hair.

"Believe in what?"

"Why in Lance's passion."

"I don't know what you mean by 'believing in it.' I've never been unaware, certainly, of his disposition, from his earliest time, to daub and draw; but I confess I've hoped it would burn out."

"But why should it," she sweetly smiled, "with his wonderful heredity? Passion is passion—though of course indeed *you*, dear Peter, know nothing of that. Has the Master's ever burned out?"

Peter looked off a little and, in his familiar formless way, kept up for a moment a sound between a smothered whistle and a subdued hum. "Do you think he's going to be another Master?"

She seemed scarce prepared to go that length, yet she had on the whole a marvelous trust. "I know what you mean by that. Will it be a career to incur the jealousies and provoke the machinations that have been at times almost too much for his father? Well—say it may be, since nothing but claptrap, in these dreadful days, *can*, it would seem, make its way, and since, with the curse of refinement and distinction, one may easily find one's self begging one's bread. Put it at the worst —say he *has* the misfortune to wing his flight further than the vulgar taste of his stupid countrymen can follow. Think, all the same, of the happiness—the same the Master has had. He'll *know*."

Peter looked rueful. "Ah but *what* will he know?"

"Quiet joy!" cried Mrs. Mallow, quite impatient and turning away.

2

He had of course before long to meet the boy himself on it and to hear that practically everything was settled. Lance was not to go up again,[7] but to go instead to Paris where, since the die was cast, he would find the best advantages. Peter had always felt he must be taken as he was, but had never perhaps found him so much of that pattern as on this occasion. "You chuck Cambridge then altogether? Doesn't that seem rather a pity?"

Lance would have been like his father, to his friend's sense, had he had less humor, and like his mother had he had more beauty. Yet it was a good middle way for Peter that, in the modern manner, he was, to the eye, rather the young stockbroker than the young artist. The youth reasoned that it was a question of time—there was such a mill to go through, such an awful lot to learn. He had talked with

7. Not to return to the university.

fellows and had judged. "One has got, today," he said, "don't you see? to know."

His interlocutor, at this, gave a groan. "Oh hang it, *don't* know!"

Lance wondered. " 'Don't'? Then what's the use—?"

"The use of what?"

"Why of anything. Don't you think I've talent?"

Peter smoked away for a little in silence; then went on; "It isn't knowledge, it's ignorance that—as we've been beautifully told—is bliss."

"Don't you think I've talent," Lance repeated.

Peter, with his trick of queer kind demonstrations, passed his arm round his godson and held him a moment. "How do I know?"

"Oh," said the boy, "if it's your own ignorance you're defending?—"

Again, for a pause, on the sofa, his godfather smoked. "It isn't. I've the misfortune to be omniscient."

"Oh well," Lance laughed again, "if you know *too* much—!"

"That's what I do, and it's why I'm so wretched."

Lance's gaiety grew. "Wretched? Come, I say!"

"But I forgot," his companion went on—"you're not to know about that. It would indeed for you too make the too much. Only I'll tell you what I'll do." And Peter got up from the sofa. "If you'll go up again I'll pay your way at Cambridge."

Lance stared, a little rueful in spite of being still more amused. "Oh Peter! You disapprove so of Paris?"

"Well, I'm afraid of it."

"Ah I see!"

"No, you don't see—yet. But you will—that is you would. And you mustn't."

The young man thought more gravely. "But one's innocence, already—!"

"Is considerably damaged? Ah that won't matter," Peter persisted—"we'll patch it up here."

"Here? Then you want me to stay at home?"

Peter almost confessed to it. "Well, we're so right—we four together—just as we are. We're so safe. Come, don't spoil it."

The boy, who had turned to gravity, turned from this, on the real pressure in his friend's tone, to consternation. "Then what's a fellow to be?"

"My particular care. Come, old man"—and Peter now fairly pleaded—"*I'll* look out for you."

Lance, who had remained on the sofa with his legs out and his hands in his pockets, watched him with eyes that showed suspicion. Then he got up. "You think there's something the matter with me—that I can't make a success."

"Well, what do you call a success?"

Lance thought again. "Why the best sort, I suppose, is to please one's self. Isn't that the sort that, in spite of cabals and things, is—in his own peculiar line—the Master's?"

There were so much too many things in this question to be answered at once that they practically checked the discussion, which became particularly difficult in the light of such renewed proof that, though the young man's innocence might, in the course of his studies, as he contended, somewhat have shrunken, the finer essence of it still remained. That was indeed exactly what Peter had assumed and what above all he desired; yet perversely enough it gave him a chill. The boy believed in the cabals and things, believed in the peculiar line, believed, to be brief, in the Master. What happened a month or two later wasn't that he went up again at the expense of his godfather, but that a fortnight after he had got settled in Paris this personage sent him fifty pounds.

He had meanwhile at home, this personage, made up his mind to the worst; and what that might be had never yet grown quite so vivid to him as when, on his presenting himself one Sunday night, as he never failed to do, for supper, the mistress of Carrara Lodge met him with an appeal as to—of all things in the world—the wealth of the Canadians. She was earnest, she was even excited. "Are many of them *really* rich?"

He had to confess he knew nothing about them, but he often thought afterwards of that evening. The room in which they sat was adorned with sundry specimens of the Master's genius, which had the merit of being, as Mrs. Mallow herself frequently suggested, of an unusually convenient size. They were indeed of dimensions not customary in the products of the chisel, and they had the singularity that, if the objects and features intended to be small looked too large, the objects and features intended to be large looked too small. The Master's idea, either in respect to this matter or to any other, had in almost any case, even after years, remained undiscoverable to Peter Brench. The creations that so failed to reveal it stood about on pedestals and brackets, on tables and shelves, a little staring white population, heroic, idyllic, allegoric, mythic, symbolic, in which "scale" had so strayed and lost itself that the public square and the chimney piece seemed to have changed places, the monumental being all diminutive and the diminutive all monumental; branches at any rate, markedly, of a family in which stature was rather oddly irrespective of function, age, and sex. They formed, like the Mallows themselves, poor Brench's own family—having at least to such a degree the note of familiarity. The occasion was one of those he had long ago learned to know and to name—short flickers of the faint flame, soft gusts of a kinder air. Twice a year regularly the Master believed in his fortune, in addition to believing all the year round in his genius. This time it was to be made by a bereaved couple from Toronto, who had given him the handsomest order for a tomb to three lost children, each of whom they desired to see, in the composition, emblematically and characteristically represented.

Such was naturally the moral of Mrs. Mallow's question: if their wealth was to be assumed, it was clear, from the nature of their admiration, as well as from mysterious hints thrown out (they were a little odd!) as to other possibilities for the same mortuary sort, that their further patronage might be; and not less evident that should the Master become at all known in those climes nothing would be more inevitable than a run of Canadian custom. Peter had been present before at runs of custom, colonial and domestic—present at each of those of which the aggregation had left so few gaps in the marble company round him; but it was his habit never at these junctures to prick the bubble in advance. The fond illusion, while it lasted, eased the wound of elections never won, the long ache of medals and diplomas carried off, on every chance, by everyone but the Master; it moreover lighted the lamp that would glimmer through the next eclipse. They lived, however, after all—as it was always beautiful to see—at a height scarce susceptible of ups and downs. They strained a point at times charmingly, strained it to admit that the public was here and there not too bad to buy; but they would have been nowhere without their attitude that the Master was always too good to sell. They were at all events deliciously formed, Peter often said to himself, for their fate; the Master had a vanity, his wife had a loyalty, of which success, depriving these things of innocence, would have diminished the merit and the grace. Anyone could be charming under a charm, and as he looked about him at a world of prosperity more void of proportion even than the Master's museum he wondered if he knew another pair that so completely escaped vulgarity.

"What a pity Lance isn't with us to rejoice!" Mrs. Mallow on this occasion sighed at supper.

"We'll drink to the health of the absent," her husband replied, filling his friend's glass and his own and giving a drop to their companion; "but we must hope he's preparing himself for a happiness much less like this of ours this evening—excusable as I grant it to be!—than like the comfort we have always (whatever has happened or has not happened) been able to trust ourselves to enjoy. The comfort," the Master explained, leaning back in the pleasant lamplight and firelight, holding up his glass and looking round at his marble family, quartered more or less, a monstrous brood, in every room—"the comfort of art in itself!"

Peter looked a little shyly at his wine. "Well—I don't care what you may call it when a fellow doesn't—but Lance must learn to *sell*, you know. I drink to his acquisition of the secret of a base popularity!"

"Oh yes, *he* must sell," the boy's mother, who was still more, however, this seemed to give out, the Master's wife, rather artlessly allowed.

"Ah," the sculptor after a moment confidently pronounced, "Lance *will*. Don't be afraid. He'll have learned."

"Which is exactly what Peter," Mrs. Mallow gaily returned—"why in the world were you so perverse, Peter?—wouldn't when he told him hear of."

Peter, when this lady looked at him with accusatory affection—a grace on her part not infrequent—could never find a word; but the Master, who was always all amenity and tact, helped him out now as he had often helped him before. "That's his old idea, you know—on which we've so often differed: his theory that the artist should be all impulse and instinct. *I* go in of course for a certain amount of school. Not too much—but a due proportion. There's where his protest came in," he continued to explain to his wife, "as against what *might*, don't you see? be in question for Lance."

"Ah well"—and Mrs. Mallow turned the violet eyes across the table at the subject of this discourse—"he's sure to have meant of course nothing but good. Only that wouldn't have prevented him, if Lance *had* taken his advice, from being in effect horribly cruel."

They had a sociable way of talking of him to his face as if he had been in the clay or—at most—in the plaster, and the Master was unfailingly generous. He might have been waving Egidio to make him revolve. "Ah but poor Peter wasn't so wrong as to what it may after all come to that he *will* learn."

"Oh but nothing artistically bad," she urged—still, for poor Peter, arch and dewy.

"Why just the little French tricks," said the Master: on which their friend had to pretend to admit, when pressed by Mrs. Mallow, that these aestheic vices had been the objects of his dread.

3

"I know now," Lance said to him the next year, "why you were so much against it." He had come back supposedly for a mere interval and was looking about him at Carrara Lodge, where indeed he had already on two or three occasions since his expatriation briefly reappeared. This had the air of a longer holiday. "Something rather awful has happened to me. It *isn't* so very good to know."

"I'm bound to say high spirits don't show in your face," Peter was rather ruefully forced to confess. "Still, are you very sure you do know?"

"Well, I at least know about as much as I can bear." These remarks were exchanged in Peter's den, and the young man, smoking cigarettes, stood before the fire with his back against the mantel. Something of his bloom seemed really to have left him.

Poor Peter wondered. "You're clear then as to what in particular I wanted you not to go for?"

"In particular?" Lance thought. "It seems to me that in particular there can have been only one thing."

They stood for a little sounding each other. "Are you quite sure?"

"Quite sure I'm a beastly duffer? Quite—by this time."

"Oh!"—and Peter turned away as if almost with relief.

"It's *that* that isn't pleasant to find out."

"Oh I don't care for 'that,'" said Peter, presently coming round again. "I mean I personally don't."

"Yet I hope you can understand a little that I myself should!"

"Well, what do you mean by it?" Peter skeptically asked.

And on this Lance had to explain—how the upshot of his studies in Paris had inexorably proved a mere deep doubt of his means. These studies had so waked him up that a new light was in his eyes; but what the new light did was really to show him too much. "Do you know what's the matter with me? I'm too horribly intelligent. Paris was really the last place for me. I've learned what I can't do."

Poor Peter stared—it was a staggerer; but even after they had had, on the subject, a longish talk in which the boy brought out to the full the hard truth of his lesson, his friend betrayed less pleasure than usually breaks into a face to the happy tune of "I told you so!" Poor Peter himself made now indeed so little a point of having told him so that Lance broke ground in a different place a day or two after. "What was it then that—before I went—you were afraid I should find out?" This, however, Peter refused to tell him—on the ground that if he hadn't yet guessed perhaps he never would, and that in any case nothing at all for either of them was to be gained by giving the thing a name. Lance eyed him on this an instant with the bold curiosity of youth—with the air indeed of having in his mind two or three names, of which one or other would be right. Peter nevertheless, turning his back again, offered no encouragement, and when they parted afresh it was with some show of impatience on the side of the boy. Accordingly on their next encounter Peter saw at a glance that he had now, in the interval, divined and that, to sound his note, he was only waiting till they should find themselves alone. This he had soon arranged and he then broken straight out. "Do you know your conundrum has been keeping me awake? But in the watches of the night the answer came over me—so that, upon my honor, I quite laughed out. Had you been supposing I had to go to Paris to learn *that*?" Even now, to see him still so sublimely on his guard, Peter's young friend had to laugh afresh. "You won't give a sign till you're sure? Beautiful old Peter!" But Lance at last produced it. "Why, hang it, the truth about the Master."

It made between them for some minutes a lively passage, full of wonder for each at the wonder of the other. "Then how long have you understood—"

"The true value of his work? I understood it," Lance recalled, "as soon as I began to understand anything. But I didn't begin fully to do that, I admit, till I got *là-bas*."[8]

"Dear, dear!"—Peter gasped with retrospective dread.

"But for what have you taken me? I'm a hopeless muff[9]—that I *had* to have rubbed in. But I'm not such a muff as the Master!" Lance declared.

"Then why did you never tell me—?"

"That I hadn't, after all"—the boy took him up—"remained such an idiot? Just because I never dreamed *you* knew. But I beg your pardon. I only wanted to spare you. And what I don't now understand is how the deuce then for so long you've managed to keep bottled."

Peter produced his explanation, but only after some delay and with a gravity not void of embarrassment. "It was for your mother."

"Oh!" said Lance.

"And that's the great thing now—since the murder *is* out. I want a promise from you. I mean"—and Peter almost feverishly followed it up —"a vow from you, solemn and such as you owe me here on the spot, that you'll sacrifice anything rather than let her ever guess—"

"That *I've* guessed?"—Lance took it in. "I see." He evidently after a moment had taken in much. "But what is it you've in mind that I may have a chance to sacrifice?"

"Oh one has always something."

Lance looked at him hard. "Do you mean that *you've* had—?" The look he received back, however, so put the question by that he found soon enough another. "Are you really sure my mother doesn't know?"

Peter, after renewed reflection, was really sure. "If she does she's too wonderful."

"But aren't we all too wonderful?"

"Yes," Peter granted—"but in different ways. The thing's so desper-

8. Over there (that is, Paris).
9. Someone without skill or aptitude, a duffer.

ately important because your father's little public consists only, as you know then," Peter developed—"well, of how many?"

"First of all," the Master's son risked, "of himself. And last of all too. I don't quite see of whom else."

Peter had an approach to impatience. "Of your mother, I say—*always*."

Lance cast it all up. "You absolutely feel that?"

"Absolutely."

"Well then with yourself that makes three."

"Oh *me!*"—and Peter, with a wag of his kind old head, modestly excused himself. "The number's at any rate small enough for any individual dropping out to be too dreadfully missed. Therefore, to put it in a nutshell, take care, my boy—that's all—that *you're* not!"

"I've got to keep on humbugging?" Lance wailed.

"It's just to warn you of the danger of your failing of that that I've seized this opportunity."

"And what do you regard in particular," the young man asked, "as the danger?"

"Why this certainty: that the moment your mother, who feels so strongly, should suspect your secret—well," said Peter desperately, "the fat would be on the fire."

Lance for a moment seemed to stare at the blaze. "She'd throw me over?"

"She's throw *him* over."

"And come round to us?"

Peter, before he answered, turned away. "Come round to *you*." But he had said enough to indicate—and, as he evidently trusted, to avert—the horrid contingency.

4

Within six months again, none the less, his fear was on more occasions than one all before him. Lance had returned to Paris for another trial; then had reappeared at home and had had, with his father, for the first time in his life, one of the scenes that strike sparks. He described it with much expression to Peter, touching whom (since they had never done so before) it was the sign of a new reserve on the part of the pair at Carrara Lodge that they at present failed, on a matter of intimate interest, to open themselves—if not in joy then in sorrow—to their good friend. This produced perhaps practically between the parties a shade of alienation and a slight intermission of commerce—marked mainly indeed by the fact that to talk at his ease with his old playmate Lance had in general to come to see him. The closest if not quite the gayest relation they had yet known together was thus ushered in. The difficulty for poor Lance was a tension at home—begotten by the fact that his father wished him to be at least the sort of success he himself had been. He hadn't "chucked" Paris—though nothing appeared more vivid to him than that Paris had chucked him: he would go back again because of the fascination in trying, in seeing, in sounding the depths—in learning one's lesson, briefly, even if the lesson were simply that of one's impotence in the presence of one's larger vision. But what did the Master, all aloft in his senseless fluency, know of impotence, and what vision—to be called such—had he in all his blind life ever had? Lance, heated and indignant, frankly appealed to his godparent on this score.

His father, it appeared, had come down on him for having, after so long, nothing to show, and hoped that on his next return this deficiency would be repaired. *The* thing, the Master complacently set forth, was—for any artist, however inferior to himself—at least to "do" something. "What can you do? That's all I ask!" *He* had certainly done enough, and there was no mistake about what he had to show. Lance had tears in his eyes when it came thus to letting his old friend know how great the strain might be on the "sacrifice" asked of him. It wasn't so easy to continue humbugging—as from son to parent—after feeling one's self despised for not groveling in mediocrity. Yet a noble duplicity was what, as they intimately faced the situation, Peter went on requiring; and it was still for a time what his young friend, bitter and sore, managed loyally to comfort him with. Fifty pounds more than once again, it was true, rewarded both in London and in Paris the young friend's loyalty; none the less sensibly, doubtless, at the moment, that the money was a direct advance on a decent sum for which Peter had long since privately prearranged an ultimate function. Whether by these arts or others, at all events, Lance's just resentment was kept for a season—but only for a season—at bay. The day arrived when he warned his companion that he could hold out—or hold in—no longer. Carrara Lodge had had to listen to another lecture delivered from a great height—an infliction really heavier at last than, without striking back or in some way letting the Master have the truth, flesh and blood could bear.

"And what I don't see is," Lance observed with a certain irritated eye for what was after all, if it came to that, owing to himself too; "what I don't see is, upon my honor, how *you*, as things are going, can keep the game up."

"Oh the game for me is only to hold my tongue," said placid Peter. "And I have my reason."

"Still my mother?"

Peter showed a queer face as he had often shown it before—that is by turning it straight away. "What will you have? I haven't ceased to like her."

"She's beautiful—she's a dear of course," Lance allowed; "but what is she to you, after all, and what is it to you that, as to anything whatever, she should or she shouldn't?"

Peter, who had turned red, hung fire a little. "Well—it's all simply what I make of it."

There was now, however, in his young friend a strange, an adopted insistence. "What are you after all to *her?*"

"Oh nothing. But that's another matter."

"She cares only for my father," said Lance the Parisian.

"Naturally—and that's just why."

"Why you've wished to spare her?"

"Because she cares so tremendously much."

Lance took a turn about the room, but with his eyes still on his host. "How awfully—always—you must have liked her!"

"Awfully. Always," said Peter Brench.

The young man continued for a moment to muse—then stopped again in front of him. "Do you know how much she cares?" Their eyes met on it, but Peter, as if his own found something new in Lance's, appeared to hesitate, for the first time in an age, to say he did know. "*I've* only just found out," said Lance. "She came to my room last night, after being present, in silence and only with her eyes on me, at what I had had to take from him: she came—and she was with me an extraordinary hour."

He had paused again and they had again for a while sounded each other. Then something—and it made him suddenly turn pale—came to Peter. "She *does* know?"

"She does know. She let it all out to me—so as to demand of me no more than 'that,' as she said, of which she herself had been capable. She has always, always known," said Lance without pity.

Peter was silent a long time; during which his companion might have heard him gently breathe, and on touching him might have felt within him the vibration of a long low sound suppressed. By the time he spoke at last he had taken everything in. "Then I do see how tremendously much."

"Isn't it wonderful?" Lance asked.

"Wonderful," Peter mused.

"So that if your original effort to keep me from Paris was to keep me from knowledge—!" Lance exclaimed as if with a sufficient indication of this futility.

It might have been at the futility Peter appeared for a little to gaze. "I think it must have been—without my quite at the time knowing it—to keep *me!*" he replied at last as he turned away.

1900

SIR ARTHUR CONAN DOYLE

The Adventure of the Speckled Band

In glancing over my notes of the seventy odd cases in which I have during the last eight years studied the methods of my friend Sherlock Holmes, I find many tragic, some comic, a large number merely strange, but none commonplace; for, working as he did rather for the love of his art than for the acquirement of wealth, he refused to associate himself with any investigation which did not tend towards the unusual, and even the fantastic. Of all these varied cases, however, I cannot recall any which presented more singular features than that which was associated with the well-known Surrey[1] family of the Roylotts of Stoke Moran. The events in question occurred in the early days of my association with Holmes, when we were sharing rooms as bachelors, in Baker Street.[2] It is possible that I might have placed them upon record before, but a promise of secrecy was made at the time, from which I have only been freed during the last month by the untimely death of the lady to whom the pledge was given. It is perhaps as well that the facts should now come to light, for I have reasons to know there are widespread rumors as to the death of Dr. Grimesby Roylott which tend to make the matter even more terrible than the truth.

It was early in April, in the year '83, that I woke one morning to find Sherlock Holmes standing, fully dressed, by the side of my bed. He was a late riser as a rule, and, as the clock on the mantelpiece showed me that it was only a quarter past seven, I blinked up at him in some surprise, and perhaps just a little resentment, for I was myself regular in my habits.

"Very sorry to knock you up,[3] Watson," said he, "but it's the common lot this morning. Mrs. Hudson has been knocked up, she retorted upon me, and I on you."

"What is it, then? A fire?"

"No, a client. It seems that a young lady has arrived in a considerable state of excitement, who insists upon seeing me. She is waiting now in the sitting room. Now, when young ladies wander about the metropolis at this hour of the morning, and knock sleepy people up out of their beds, I presume that it is something very pressing which they have to communicate. Should it prove to be an interesting case, you would, I am sure, wish to follow it from the outset. I thought at any rate that I should call you, and give you the chance."

"My dear fellow, I would not miss it for anything."

I had no keener pleasure than in following Holmes in his professional investigations, and in admiring the rapid deductions, as swift as intuitions, and yet always founded on a logical basis, with which he unraveled the problems which were submitted to him. I rapidly threw on my clothes, and was ready in a few minutes to accompany my friend down to the sitting room. A lady dressed in black and heavily veiled, who had been sitting in the window, rose as we entered.

"Good morning, madam," said Holmes cheerily. "My name is Sherlock Holmes. This is my intimate friend and associate, Dr. Watson, before whom you can speak as freely as before myself. Ha, I am glad to see that Mrs. Hudson has had the good sense to light the fire. Pray draw up to it, and I shall order you a cup of hot coffee, for I observe that you are shivering."

"It is not cold which makes me shiver," said the woman in a low

1. A county just south of London, one of the "Home Counties" around London—Berkshire, Hampshire, and Middlesex, mentioned later are also Home Counties. Stoke Moran is apparently fictional, though there is a Stoke D'Abernon three miles from the west Surrey town of Leatherhead, mentioned below, which is some 18 miles from London.

2. Near Regent's Park in north central London, a street that Holmes made famous.

3. Wake you up.

voice, changing her seat as requested.

"What then?"

"It is fear, Mr. Holmes. It is terror." She raised her veil as she spoke, and we could see that she was indeed in a pitiable state of agitation, her face all drawn and gray, with restless, frightened eyes, like those of some hunted animal. Her features and figure were those of a woman of thirty, but her hair was shot with premature gray, and her expression was weary and haggard. Sherlock Holmes ran her over with one of his quick, all-comprehensive glances.

"You must not fear," said he soothingly, bending forward and patting her forearm. "We shall soon set matters right, I have no doubt. You have come in by train this morning, I see."

"You know me, then?"

"No, but I observe the second half of a return ticket in the palm of your left glove. You must have started early, and yet you had a good drive in a dog cart, along heavy roads, before you reached the station."

The lady gave a violent start, and stared in bewilderment at my companion.

"There is no mystery, my dear madam," said he, smiling. "The left arm of your jacket is spattered with mud in no less than seven places. The marks are perfectly fresh. There is no vehicle save a dog cart which throws up mud in that way, and then only when you sit on the left-hand side of the driver."[4]

"Whatever your reasons may be, you are perfectly correct," said she. "I started from home before six, reached Leatherhead at twenty past, and came in by the first train to Waterloo.[5] Sir, I can stand this strain no longer, I shall go mad if it continues. I have no one to turn to—none, save only one, who cares for me, and he, poor fellow, can be of little aid. I have heard of you, Mr. Holmes; I have heard of you from Mrs. Farintosh, whom you helped in the hour of her sore need. It was from her that I had your address. Oh, sir, do you not think you could help me too, and at least throw a little light through the dense darkness which surrounds me? At present it is out of my power to reward you for your services, but in a month or two I shall be married, with the control of my own income, and then at least you shall not find me ungrateful."

Holmes turned to his desk, and unlocking it, drew out a small case-book which he consulted.

"Farintosh," said he. "Ah, yes, I recall the case; it was concerned with an opal tiara. I think it was before your time, Watson. I can only say, madam, that I shall be happy to devote the same care to your case as I did to that of your friend. As to reward, my profession is its reward; but you are at liberty to defray whatever expenses I may be put to, at the time which suits you best. And now I beg that you will lay before us everything that may help us in forming an opinion upon the matter."

"Alas!" replied our visitor. "The very horror of my situation lies in

4. In Britain the driver sits on the right; a lady would normally sit behind the driver, perhaps in the middle of the seat. The seats of the two benches of the dogcart are, however, back to back, and since even class distinction would not insist that the lady sit facing the rear, she perforce would sit on the left.

5. A main London railway station serving south and west of the metropolis.

the fact that my fears are so vague, and my suspicions depend so entirely upon small points, which might seem trivial to another, that even he to whom of all others I have a right to look for help and advice looks upon all that I tell him about it as the fancies of a nervous woman. He does not say so, but I can read it from his soothing answers and averted eyes. But I have heard, Mr. Holmes, that you can see deeply into the manifold wickedness of the human heart. You may advise me how to walk amid the dangers which encompass me."

"I am all attention, madam."

"My name is Helen Stoner, and I am living with my stepfather, who is the last survivor of one of the oldest Saxon families in England, the Roylotts of Stoke Moran, on the Western border of Surrey."

Holmes nodded his head. "The name is familiar to me," said he.

"The family was at one time among the richest in England, and the estate extended over the borders into Berkshire in the north, and Hampshire in the west. In the last century, however, four successive heirs were of a dissolute and wasteful disposition, and the family ruin was eventually completed by a gambler, in the days of the Regency.[6] Nothing was left save a few acres of ground and the two-hundred-year-old house, which is itself crushed under a heavy mortgage. The last squire dragged out his existence there, living the horrible life of an aristocratic pauper; but his only son, my stepfather, seeing that he must adapt himself to the new conditions, obtained an advance from a relative, which enabled him to take a medical degree, and went out to Calcutta, where, by his professional skill and his force of character, he established a large practice. In a fit of anger, however, caused by some robberies which had been perpetrated in the house, he beat his native butler to death, and narrowly escaped a capital sentence. As it was, he suffered a long term of imprisonment, and afterwards returned to England a morose and disappointed man.

"When Dr. Roylott was in India he married my mother, Mrs. Stoner, the young widow of Major-General Stoner, of the Bengal Artillery. My sister Julia and I were twins, and we were only two years old at the time of my mother's remarriage. She had a considerable sum of money, not less than a thousand a year,[7] and this she bequeathed to Dr. Roylott entirely whilst we resided with him, with a provision that a certain annual sum should be allowed to each of us in the event of our marriage. Shortly after our return to England my mother died—she was killed eight years ago in a railway accident near Crewe. Dr. Roylott then abandoned his attempts to establish himself in practice in London, and took us to live with him in the ancestral house at Stoke Moran. The money which my mother had left was enough for all our wants, and there seemed no obstacle to our happiness.

6. In 1811–20, the Prince of Wales, later George IV, served as Prince Regent in place of George III, who had been declared insane. The period was noted for the dandyism and dissoluteness of the court and London society.

7. Though only $5,000, its purchasing power may better be gauged by the fact that as late as 1905, according to Baedecker's famous guide of London, if a visitor "lives in a first-class hotel, dines at the table-d'hôte, drinks wine, frequents the theater and other places of amusement, and drives about in cabs . . . he must be prepared to spend 30–40 shillings a day"—that is, as much as *two* pounds a day!

"But a terrible change came over our stepfather about this time. Instead of making friends and exchanging visits with our neighbors, who had at first been overjoyed to see a Roylott of Stoke Moran back in the old family seat, he shut himself up in his house, and seldom came out save to indulge in ferocious quarrels with whoever might cross his path. Violence of temper approaching to mania has been hereditary in the men of the family, and in my stepfather's case it had, I believe, been intensified by his long residence in the tropics. A series of disgraceful brawls took place, two of which ended in the police court, until at last he became the terror of the village, and the folks would fly at his approach, for he is a man of immense strength, and absolutely uncontrollable in his anger.

"Last week he hurled the local blacksmith over a parapet into a stream and it was only by paying over all the money that I could gather together that I was able to avert another public exposure. He had no friends at all save the wandering gypsies, and he would give these vagabonds leave to encamp upon the few acres of bramble-covered land which represent the family estate, and would accept in return the hospitality of their tents, wandering away with them sometimes for weeks on end. He has a passion also for Indian animals, which are sent over to him by a correspondent, and he has at this moment a cheetah and a baboon, which wander freely over his grounds, and are feared by the villagers almost as much as their master.

"You can imagine from what I say that my poor sister Julia and I had no great pleasure in our lives. No servant would stay with us, and for a long time we did all the work of the house. She was but thirty at the time of her death, and yet her hair had already begun to whiten, even as mine has."

"Your sister is dead, then?"

"She died just two years ago, and it is of her death that I wish to speak to you. You can understand that, living the life which I have described, we were little likely to see anyone of our own age and position. We had, however, an aunt, my mother's maiden sister, Miss Honoria Westphail, who lives near Harrow, and we were occasionally allowed to pay short visits at this lady's house. Julie went there at Christmas two years ago, and met there a half-pay[8] Major of Marines, to whom she became engaged. My stepfather learned of the engagement when my sister returned, and offered no objection to the marriage; but within a fortnight of the day which had been fixed for the wedding, the terrible event occurred which has deprived me of my only companion."

Sherlock Holmes had been leaning back in his chair with his eyes closed, and his head sunk in a cushion, but he half opened his lids now, and glanced across at his visitor.

"Pray be precise as to details," said he.

"It is easy for me to be so, for every event of that dreadul time is seared into my memory. The manor house is, as I have already said, very old, and only one wing is now inhabited. The bedrooms in this wing are on the ground floor, the sitting rooms being in the

8. Reduced pay for service officer when he is on inactive duty.

central block of the buildings. Of these bedrooms the first is Dr. Roylott's, the second my sister's, and the third my own. There is no communication between them, but they all open out into the same corridor. Do I make myself plain?"

"Perfectly so."

"The windows of the three rooms open out upon the lawn. That fatal night Dr. Roylott had gone to his room early, though we knew that he had not retired to rest, for my sister was troubled by the smell of the strong Indian cigars which it was his custom to smoke. She left her room, therefore, and came into mine, where she sat for some time, chatting about her approaching wedding. At eleven o'clock she rose to leave me, but she paused at the door and looked back.

" 'Tell me, Helen,' said she, 'have you ever heard anyone whistle in the dead of the night?'

" 'Never,' said I.

" 'I suppose that you could not possibly whistle yourself in your sleep?'

" 'Certainly not. But why?'

" 'Because during the last few nights I have always, about three in the morning, heard a low clear whistle. I am a light sleeper, and it has awakened me. I cannot tell where it came from—perhaps from the next room, perhaps from the lawn. I thought that I would just ask you whether you had heard it.'

" 'No, I have not. It must be those wretched gypsies in the plantation.'

" 'Very likely. And yet if it were on the lawn I wonder that you did not hear it also.'

" 'Ah, but I sleep more heavily than you.'

" 'Well, it is of no great consequence, at any rate,' she smiled back at me, closed my door, and a few moments later I heard her key turn in the lock."

"Indeed," said Holmes. "Was it your custom always to lock yourselves in at night?"

"Always."

"And why?"

"I think that I mentioned to you that the Doctor kept a cheetah and a baboon. We had no feeling of security unless our doors were locked."

"Quite so. Pray proceed with your statement."

"I could not sleep that night. A vague feeling of impending misfortune impressed me. My sister and I, you will recollect, were twins, and you know how subtle are the links which bind two souls which are so closely allied. It was a wild night. The wind was howling outside, and the rain was beating and splashing against the windows. Suddenly, amidst all the hubbub of the gale, there burst forth the wild scream of a terrified woman. I knew that it was my sister's voice. I sprang from my bed, wrapped a shawl round me, and rushed into the corridor. As I opened my door I seemed to hear a low whistle, such as my sister described, and a few moments later a clanging sound, as if a mass of metal had fallen. As I ran down the passage my sister's door was unlocked, and revolved slowly upon its hinges. I stared at it horror-stricken, not knowing what was about to issue from it. By the light of the corridor lamp I saw my sister appear at the opening, her face blanched with terror, her hands groping for help, her whole figure swaying to and fro like that of a drunkard. I ran to her and threw my arms round her, but at that moment her knees seemed to give way and she fell to the ground. She writhed as one who is in terrible pain, and her limbs were dreadfully convulsed. At first I thought that she had not recognized me, but as I bent over her she suddenly shrieked out in a voice which I shall never forget, 'Oh, my God! Helen! It was the band! The speckled band!' There was something else which she would fain have said, and she stabbed with her finger into the air in the direction of the Doctor's room, but a fresh convulsion seized her and choked her words. I rushed out, calling loudly for my stepfather, and I met him hastening from his room in his dressing gown. When he reached my sister's side she was unconscious, and though he poured brandy down her throat, and sent for medical aid from the village, all efforts were in vain, for she slowly sank and died without having recovered her consciousness. Such was the dreadful end of my beloved sister."

"One moment," said Holmes: "are you sure about this whistle and metallic sound? Could you swear to it?"

"That was what the county coroner asked me at the inquiry. It is my strong impression that I heard it, and yet among the crash of the gale, and the creaking of an old house, I may possibly have been deceived."

"Was your sister dressed?"

"No, she was in her nightdress. In her right hand was found the charred stump of a match, and in her left a matchbox."

"Showing that she had struck a light and looked about her when the alarm took place. That is important. And what conclusions did the coroner come to?"

"He investigated the case with great care, for Dr. Roylott's conduct had long been notorious in the county, but he was unable to find any satisfactory cause of death. My evidence showed that the door had been fastened upon the inner side, and the windows were blocked by old-fashioned shutters with broad iron bars, which were secured every night. The walls were carefully sounded, and were shown to be quite solid all round, and the flooring was also thoroughly examined, with the same result. The chimney is wide, but is barred up by four large staples. It is certain, therefore, that my sister was quite alone when she met her end. Besides, there were no marks of any violence upon her."

"How about poison?"

"The doctors examined her for it, but without success."

"What do you think that this unfortunate lady died of, then?"

"It is my belief that she died of pure fear and nervous shock, though what it was which frightened her I cannot imagine."

"Were there gypsies in the plantation at the time?"

"Yes, there are nearly always some there."

"Ah, and what did you gather from this allusion to a band—a speckled band?"

"Sometimes I have thought that it was merely the wild talk of delirium, sometimes that it may have referred to some band of people, perhaps to these very gypsies in the plantation. I do not know whether the spotted handkerchiefs which so many of them wear over their heads might have suggested the strange adjective which she used."

Holmes shook his head like a man who is far from being satisfied.

"These are very deep waters," said he; "pray go on with your narrative."

"Two years have passed since then, and my life has been until lately lonelier than ever. A month ago, however, a dear friend, whom I have known for many years, has done me the honor to ask my hand in marriage. His name is Armitage—Percy Armitage—the second son of Mr. Armitage, of Crane Water, near Reading.[9] My stepfather has offered no opposition to the match, and we are to be married in the course of the spring. Two days ago some repairs were started in the west wing of the building, and my bedroom wall has been pierced, so that I have had to move into the chamber in which my sister died, and to sleep in the very bed in which she slept. Imagine, then, my thrill of terror when last night, as I lay awake, thinking over her terrible fate, I suddenly heard in the silence of the night the low whistle which had been the herald of her own death. I sprang up and lit the lamp, but nothing was to be seen in the room. I was too shaken to go to bed again, however, so I dressed, and as soon as it was daylight I slipped down, got a dog cart at the Crown Inn, which is opposite, and drove to Leatherhead, from whence I have come on this morning, with the one object of seeing you and asking your advice."

"You have done wisely," said my friend. "But have you told me all?"

"Yes, all."

"Miss Stoner, you have not. You are screening your stepfather."

"Why, what do you mean?"

For answer Holmes pushed back the frill of black lace which fringed the hand that lay upon our visitor's knee. Five little livid spots, the marks of four fingers and a thumb, were printed upon the white wrist.

"You have been cruelly used," said Holmes.

The lady colored deeply, and covered over her injured wrist. "He is a hard man," she said, "and perhaps he hardly knows his own strength."

There was a long silence, during which Holmes leaned his chin upon his hands and stared into the crackling fire.

"This is very deep business," he said at last. "There are a thousand details which I should desire to know before I decide upon our course of action. Yet we have not a moment to lose. If we were to come to Stoke Moran today, would it be possible for us to see over these rooms without the knowledge of your stepfather?"

"As it happens, he spoke of coming into town today upon some most important business. It is probable that he will be away all day, and that there would be nothing to disturb you. We have a house-

9. Berkshire town about 35 miles from London.

keeper now, but she is old and foolish, and I could easily get her out of the way."

"Excellent. You are not averse to this trip, Watson?"

"By no means."

"Then we shall both come. What are you going to do yourself?"

"I have one or two things which I would wish to do now that I am in town. But I shall return by the twelve o'clock train, so as to be there in time for your coming."

"And you may expect us early in the afternoon. I have myself some small business matters to attend to. Will you not wait and breakfast?"

"No, I must go. My heart is lightened already since I have confided my trouble to you. I shall look forward to seeing you again this afternoon." She dropped her thick black veil over her face, and glided from the room.

"And what do you think of it all, Watson?" asked Sherlock Holmes, leaning back in his chair.

"It seems to me to be a most dark and sinister business."

"Dark enough and sinister enough."

"Yet if the lady is correct in saying that the flooring and walls are sound, and that the door, window, and chimney are impassable, then her sister must have been undoubtedly alone when she met her mysterious end."

"What becomes, then, of these nocturnal whistles, and what of the very peculiar words of the dying woman?"

"I cannot think."

"When you combine the ideas of whistles at night, the presence of a band of gypsies who are on intimate terms with this old doctor, the fact that we have every reason to believe that the doctor has an interest in preventing his stepdaughter's marriage, the dying allusion to a band, and finally, the fact that Miss Helen Stoner heard a metallic clang, which might have been caused by one of those metal bars which secured the shutters falling back into their place, I think there is good ground to think that the mystery may be cleared along those lines."

"But what, then, did the gypsies do?"

"I cannot imagine."

"I see many objections to any such a theory."

"And so do I. It is precisely for that reason that we are going to Stoke Moran this day. I want to see whether the objections are fatal, or if they may be explained away. But what, in the name of the devil!"

The ejaculation had been drawn from my companion by the fact that our door had been suddenly dashed open, and that a huge man framed himself in the aperture. His costume was a peculiar mixture of the professional and of the agricultural, having a black top hat, a long frock coat, and a pair of high gaiters, with a hunting-crop swinging in his hand. So tall was he that his hat actually brushed the crossbar of the doorway, and his breadth seemed to span it across from side to side. A large face, seared with a thousand wrinkles, burned yellow with the sun, and marked with every evil passion, was turned from one to the other of us, while his deep-set, bile-shot eyes, and the high thin fleshless nose, gave him somewhat the resemblance to a fierce old bird of prey.

"Which of you is Holmes?" asked this apparition.

"My name, sir, but you have the advantage of me," said my companion quietly.

"I am Dr. Grimesby Roylott, of Stoke Moran."

"Indeed, Doctor," said Holmes blandly. "Pray take a seat."

"I will do nothing of the kind. My stepdaughter has been here. I have traced her. What has she been saying to you?"

"It is a little cold for the time of the year," said Holmes.

"What has she been saying to you?" screamed the old man furiously.

"But I have heard that the crocuses promise well," continued my companion imperturbably.

"Ha! You put me off, do you?" said our new visitor, taking a step forward, and shaking his hunting-crop. "I know you, you scoundrel! I have heard of you before. You are Holmes the meddler."

My friend smiled.

"Holmes the busybody!"

His smile broadened.

"Holmes the Scotland Yard jack-in-office." [1]

Holmes chuckled heartily. "Your conversation is most entertaining," said he. "When you go out close the door, for there is a decided draught."

"I will go when I have had my say. Don't you dare to meddle with my affairs. I know that Miss Stoner has been here—I traced her! I am a dangerous man to fall foul of! See here." He stepped swiftly forward, seized the poker, and bent it into a curve with his huge brown hands.

"See that you keep yourself out of my grip," he snarled, and hurling the twisted poker into the fireplace, he strode out of the room.

"He seems a very amiable person," said Holmes, laughing. "I am not quite so bulky, but if he had remained I might have shown him that my grip was not much more feeble than his own." As he spoke he picked up the steel poker, and with a sudden effort straightened it out again.

"Fancy his having the insolence to confound me with the official detective force! This incident gives zest to our investigation, however, and I only trust that our little friend will not suffer from her imprudence in allowing this brute to trace her. And now, Watson, we shall order breakfast, and afterwards I shall walk down to Doctors' Commons,[2] where I hope to get some data which may help us in this matter."

It was nearly one o'clock when Sherlock Holmes returned from his excursion. He held in his hand a sheet of blue paper, scrawled over with notes and figures.

"I have seen the will of the deceased wife," said he. "To determine its exact meaning I have been obliged to work out the present prices of the investments with which it is concerned. The total income, which at the time of the wife's death was little short of £1,100, is now

1. Self-important petty official.
2. Office which had jurisdiction over marriage licenses, registration of wills, etc.

through the fall in agricultural prices not more than £750. Each daughter can claim an income of £250, in case of marriage. It is evident, therefore, that if both girls had married, this beauty would have had a mere pittance, while even one of them would cripple him to a serious extent. My morning's work has not been wasted, since it has proved that he has the very strongest motives for standing in the way of anything of the sort. And now, Watson, this is too serious for dawdling, especially as the old man is aware that we are interesting ourselves in his affairs, so if you are ready we shall call a cab and drive to Waterloo. I should be very much obliged if you would slip your revolver into your pocket. An Eley's No. 2 is an excellent argument with gentlemen who can twist steel pokers into knots. That and a toothbrush are, I think, all that we need."

At Waterloo we were fortunate in catching a train for Leatherhead, where we hired a trap at the station inn, and drove for four or five miles through the lovely Surrey lanes. It was a perfect day, with a bright sun and a few fleecy clouds in the heavens. The trees and wayside hedges were just throwing out their first green shoots, and the air was full of the pleasant smell of the moist earth. To me at least there was a strange contrast between the sweet promise of the spring and this sinister quest upon which we were engaged. My companion sat in front of the trap, his arms folded, his hat pulled down over his eyes, and his chin sunk upon his breast, buried in the deepest thought. Suddenly, however, he started, tapped me on the shoulder, and pointed over the meadows.

"Look there!" said he.

A heavily timbered park stretched up in a gentle slope, thickening into a grove at the highest point. From amidst the branches there jutted out the gray gables and high rooftree of a very old mansion.

"Stoke Moran?" said he.

"Yes, sir, that be the house of Dr. Grimesby Roylott," remarked the driver.

"There is some building going on there," said Holmes: "that is where we are going."

"There's the village," said the driver, pointing to a cluster of roofs some distance to the left; "but if you want to get to the house, you'll find it shorter to go over this stile, and so by the footpath over the fields. There it is, where the lady is walking."

"And the lady, I fancy, is Miss Stoner," observed Holmes, shading his eyes. "Yes, I think we had better do as you suggest."

We got off, paid our fare, and the trap rattled back on its way to Leatherhead.

"I thought it as well," said Holmes, as we climbed the stile, "that this fellow should think we had come here as architects, or on some definite business. It may stop his gossip. Good afternoon, Miss Stoner. You see that we have been as good as our word."

Our client of the morning had hurried forward to meet us with a face which spoke her joy. "I have been waiting so eagerly for you," she cried, shaking hands with us warmly. "All has turned out splendidly. Dr. Roylott has gone to town, and it is unlikely that he will be back before evening."

"We have had the pleasure of making the Doctor's acquaintance," said Holmes, and in a few words he sketched out what had occurred. Miss Stoner turned white to the lips as she listened.

"Good heavens!" she cried, "he has followed me, then."

"So it appears."

"He is so cunning that I never know when I am safe from him. What will he say when he returns?"

"He must guard himself, for he may find that there is someone more cunning than himself upon his track. You must lock yourself from him tonight. If he is violent, we shall take you away to your aunt's at Harrow. Now, we must make the best use of our time, so kindly take us at once to the rooms which we are to examine."

The building was of gray, lichen-blotched stone, with a high central portion, and two curving wings, like the claws of a crab, thrown out on each side. In one of these wings the windows were broken, and blocked with wooden boards, while the roof was partly caved in, a picture of ruin. The central portion was in little better repair, but the right-hand block was comparatively modern, and the blinds in the windows, with the blue smoke curling up from the chimneys, showed that this was where the family resided. Some scaffolding had been erected against the end wall, and the stonework had been broken into, but there were no signs of any workmen at the moment of our visit. Holmes walked slowly up and down the ill-trimmed lawn, and examined with deep attention the outsides of the windows.

"This, I take it, belongs to the room in which you used to sleep, the center one to your sister's, and the one next to the main building to Dr. Roylott's chamber?"

"Exactly so. But I am now sleeping in the middle one."

"Pending the alterations, as I understand. By the way, there does not seem to be any very pressing need for repairs at that end wall."

"There were none. I believe that it was an excuse to move me from my room."

"Ah! that is suggestive. Now, on the other side of this narrow wing runs the corridor from which these three rooms open. There are windows in it, of course?"

"Yes, but very small ones. Too narrow for anyone to pass through."

"As you both locked your doors at night, your rooms were unapproachable from that side. Now, would you have the kindness to go into your room, and to bar your shutters."

Miss Stoner did so, and Holmes, after a careful examination through the open window, endeavored in every way to force the shutter open, but without success. There was no slit through which a knife could be passed to raise the bar. Then with his lens he tested the hinges, but they were of solid iron, built firmly into the massive masonry. "Hum!" said he, scratching his chin in some perplexity, "my theory certainly presents some difficulties. No one could pass these shutters if they were bolted. Well, we shall see if the inside throws any light upon the matter."

A small side door led into the whitewashed corridor from which the three bedrooms opened. Holmes refused to examine the third chamber, so we passed at once to the second, that in which Miss

Stoner was now sleeping, and in which her sister had met her fate. It was a homely little room, with a low ceiling and a gaping fireplace, after the fashion of old country houses. A brown chest of drawers stood in one corner, a narrow white-counterpaned bed in another, and a dressing table on the left-hand side of the window. These articles, with two small wickerwork chairs, made up all the furniture in the room, save for a square of Wilton carpet in the center. The boards round and the paneling of the walls were brown, worm-eaten oak, so old and discolored that it may have dated from the original building of the house. Holmes drew one of the chairs into a corner and sat silent, while his eyes traveled round and round and up and down, taking in every detail of the apartment.

"Where does that bell communicate with?" he asked at last, pointing to a thick bell-rope which hung down beside the bed, the tassel actually lying upon the pillow.

"It goes to the housekeeper's room."

"It looks newer than the other things?"

"Yes, it was only put there a couple of years ago."

"Your sister asked for it, I suppose?"

"No, I never heard of her using it. We used always to get what we wanted for ourselves."

"Indeed, it seemed unnecessary to put so nice a bell-pull there. You will excuse me for a few minutes while I satisfy myself as to this floor." He threw himself down upon his face with his lens in his hand, and crawled swiftly backwards and forwards, examining minutely the cracks between the boards. Then he did the same with the woodwork with which the chamber was paneled. Finally he walked over to the bed and spent some time in staring at it, and in running his eye up and down the wall. Finally he took the bell-rope in his hand and gave it a brisk tug.

"Why, it's a dummy," said he.

"Won't it ring?"

"No, it is not even attached to a wire. This is very interesting. You can see now that it is fastened to a hook just above where the little opening of the ventilator is."

"How very absurd! I never noticed that before."

"Very strange!" muttered Holmes, pulling at the rope. "There are one or two very singular points about this room. For example, what a fool a builder must be to open a ventilator in another room, when, with the same trouble, he might have communicated with the outside air!"

"That is also quite modern," said the lady.

"Done about the same time as the bell-rope?" remarked Holmes.

"Yes, there were several little changes carried out about that time."

"They seem to have been of a most interesting character—dummy bell-ropes, and ventilators which do not ventilate. With your permission, Miss Stoner, we shall now carry our researches into the inner apartment."

Dr. Grimesby Roylott's chamber was larger than that of his step-daughter, but was as plainly furnished. A camp bed, a small wooden shelf full of books, mostly of a technical character, an armchair beside the bed, a plain wooden chair against the wall, a round table, and a large iron safe were the principal things which met the eye. Holmes walked slowly round and examined each and all of them with the keenest interest.

"What's in here?" he asked, tapping the safe.

"My stepfather's business papers."

"Oh! You have seen inside then?"

"Only once, some years ago. I remember that it was full of papers."

"There isn't a cat in it, for example?"

"No. What a strange idea!"

"Well, look at this!" He took up a small saucer of milk which stood on the top of it.

"No; we don't keep a cat. But there is a cheetah and a baboon."

"Ah, yes, of course! Well, a cheetah is just a big cat, and yet a saucer of milk does not go very far in satisfying its wants, I daresay. There is one point which I should wish to determine." He squatted down in front of the wooden chair, and examined the seat of it with the greatest attention.

"Thank you. That is quite settled," said he, rising and putting his lens in his pocket. "Hullo! here is something interesting!"

The object which had caught his eye was a small dog lash hung on one corner of the bed. The lash, however, was curled upon itself, and tied so as to make a loop of whipcord.

"What do you make of that, Watson?"

"It's a common enough lash. But I don't know why it should be tied."

"That is not quite so common, is it? Ah, me! it's a wicked world, and when a clever man turns his brain to crime it is the worst of all. I think that I have seen enough now, Miss Stoner, and, with your permission, we shall walk out upon the lawn."

I had never seen my friend's face so grim, or his brow so dark, as it was when we turned from the scene of his investigation. We had walked several times up and down the lawn, neither Miss Stoner nor myself liking to break in upon his thoughts before he roused himself from his reverie.

"It is very essential, Miss Stoner," said he, "that you should absolutely follow my advice in every respect."

"I shall most certainly do so."

"The matter is too serious for any hesitation. Your life may depend upon your compliance."

"I assure you that I am in your hands."

"In the first place, both my friend and I must spend the night in your room."

Both Miss Stoner and I gazed at him in astonishment.

"Yes, it must be so. Let me explain. I believe that that is the village inn over there?"

"Yes, that is the 'Crown.'"

"Very good. Your windows would be visible from there?"

"Certainly."

"You must confine yourself to your room, on pretense of a headache, when your stepfather comes back. Then when you hear him retire for the night, you must open the shutters of your window, undo the hasp, put your lamp there as a signal to us, and then withdraw with everything which you are likely to want into the room which you used to occupy. I have no doubt that, in spite of the repairs, you could manage there for one night."

"Oh, yes, easily."

"The rest you will leave in our hands."

"But what will you do?"

"We shall spend the night in your room, and we shall investigate the cause of this noise which has disturbed you."

"I believe, Mr. Holmes, that you have already made up your mind," said Miss Stoner, laying her hand upon my companion's sleeve.

"Perhaps I have."

"Then for pity's sake tell me what was the cause of my sister's death."

"I should prefer to have clearer proofs before I speak."

"You can at least tell me whether my own thought is correct, and if she died from some sudden fright."

"No, I do not think so. I think that there was probably some more tangible cause. And now, Miss Stoner, we must leave you, for if Dr. Roylott returned and saw us, our journey would be in vain. Goodbye, and be brave, for if you will do what I have told you, you may rest assured that we shall soon drive away the dangers that threaten you."

Sherlock Holmes and I had no difficulty in engaging a bedroom and sitting room at the Crown Inn. They were on the upper floor, and from our window we could command a view of the avenue gate, and of the inhabited wing of Stoke Moran Manor House. At dusk we saw Dr. Grimesby Roylott drive past, his huge form looming up beside the little figure of the lad who drove him. The boy had some slight difficulty in undoing the heavy iron gates, and we heard the hoarse roar of the Doctor's voice, and saw the fury with which he shook his clenched fists at him. The trap drove on, and a few minutes later we saw a sudden light spring up among the trees as the lamp was lit in one of the sitting rooms.

"Do you know, Watson," said Holmes, as we sat together in the gathering darkness, "I have really some scruples as to taking you tonight. There is a distinct element of danger."

"Can I be of assistance?"

"Your presence might be invaluable."

"Then I shall certainly come."

"It is very kind of you."

"You speak of danger. You have evidently seen more in these rooms than was visible to me."

"No, but I fancy that I may have deduced a little more. I imagine that you saw all that I did."

"I saw nothing remarkable save the bell-rope, and what purpose that could answer I confess is more than I can imagine."

"You saw the ventilator, too?"

"Yes, but I do not think that it is such a very unusual thing to have a small opening between two rooms. It was so small a rat could hardly pass through."

"I knew that we should find a ventilator before ever we came to Stoke Moran."

"My dear Holmes!"

"Oh, yes, I did. You remember in her statement she said that her sister could smell Dr. Roylott's cigar. Now, of course that suggests at once that there must be a communication between the two rooms. It could only be a small one, or it would have been remarked upon at the coroner's inquiry. I deduced a ventilator."

"But what harm can there be in that?"

"Well, there is at least a curious coincidence of dates. A ventilator is made, a cord is hung, and a lady who sleeps in the bed dies. Does not that strike you?"

"I cannot as yet see any connection."

"Did you observe anything very peculiar about that bed?"

"No."

"It was clamped to the floor. Did you ever see a bed fastened like that before?"

"I cannot say that I have."

"The lady could not move her bed. It must always be in the same relative position to the ventilator and to the rope—for so we may call it, since it was clearly never meant for a bell-pull."

"Holmes," I cried, "I seem to see dimly what you are hitting at. We are only just in time to prevent some subtle and horrible crime."

"Subtle enough and horrible enough. When a doctor does go wrong he is the first of criminals. He has nerve and he has knowledge. Palmer and Pritchard[3] were among the heads of their profession. This man strikes even deeper, but, I think, Watson, that we shall be able to strike deeper still. But we shall have horrors enough before the night is over: for goodness' sake let us have a quiet pipe, and turn our minds for a few hours to something more cheerful."

About nine o'clock the light among the trees was extinguished, and all was dark in the direction of the Manor House. Two hours passed slowly away, and then, suddenly, just at the stroke of eleven, a single bright light shone out right in front of us.

"That is our signal," said Holmes, springing to his feet; "it comes from the middle window."

As we passed out he exchanged a few words with the landlord, explaining that we were going on a late visit to an acquaintance, and that it was possible that we might spend the night there. A moment later we were out on the dark road, a chill wind blowing in our faces, and one yellow light twinkling in front of us through the gloom to guide us on our somber errand.

There was little difficulty in entering the grounds, for unrepaired breaches gaped in the old park wall. Making our way among the trees, we reached the lawn, crossed it, and were about to enter through the window, when out from a clump of laurel bushes there darted what seemed to be a hideous and distorted child, who threw

3. William Palmer was executed in 1856 for poisoning a friend, Edward William Pritchard in 1865 for poisoning his wife and her mother. Both were physicians.

itself on the grass with writhing limbs, and then ran swiftly across the lawn into the darkness.

"My God!" I whispered, "did you see it?"

Holmes was for the moment as startled as I. His hand closed like a vise upon my wrist in his agitation. Then he broke into a low laugh, and put his lips to my ear.

"It is a nice household," he murmured, "that is the baboon."

I had forgotten the strange pets which the doctor affected. There was a cheetah, too; perhaps we might find it upon our shoulders at any moment. I confess that I felt easier in my mind when, after following Holmes's example and slipping off my shoes, I found myself inside the bedroom. My companion noiselessly closed the shutters, moved the lamp onto the table, and cast his eyes round the room. All was as we had seen it in the daytime. Then creeping up to me and making a trumpet of his hand, he whispered into my ear again so gently that it was all that I could do to distinguish the words:

"The least sound would be fatal to our plans."

I nodded to show that I had heard.

"We must sit without a light. He would see it through the ventilator."

I nodded again.

"Do not go to sleep; your very life may depend upon it. Have your pistol ready in case we should need it. I will sit on the side of the bed, and you in that chair."

I took out my revolver and laid it on the corner of the table.

Holmes had brought up a long thin cane, and this he placed upon the bed beside him. By it he laid the box of matches and the stump of a candle. Then he turned down the lamp and we were left in darkness.

How shall I ever forget that dreadful vigil? I could not hear a sound, not even the drawing of a breath, and yet I knew that my companion sat open-eyed, within a few feet of me, in the same state of nervous tension in which I was myself. The shutters cut off the least ray of light, and we waited in absolute darkness. From outside came the occasional cry of a night-bird, and once at our very window a long drawn, cat-like whine, which told us that the cheetah was indeed at liberty. Far away we could hear the deep tones of the parish clock, which boomed out every quarter of an hour. How long they seemed, those quarters! Twelve o'clock, and one, and two, and three, and still we sat waiting silently for whatever might befall.

Suddenly there was the momentary gleam of a light up in the direction of the ventilator, which vanished immediately, but was succeeded by a strong smell of burning oil and heated metal. Someone in the next room had lit a dark lantern. I heard a gentle sound of movement, and then all was silent once more, though the smell grew stronger. For half an hour I sat with straining ears. Then suddenly another sound became audible—a very gentle, soothing sound, like that of a small jet of steam escaping continually from a kettle. The instant, that we heard it, Holmes sprang from the bed, struck a match, and lashed furiously with his cane at the bell-pull.

"You see it, Watson?" he yelled. "You see it?"

But I saw nothing. At the moment when Holmes struck the light I heard a low, clear whistle, but the sudden glare flashing into my weary eyes made it impossible for me to tell what it was at which my friend lashed so savagely. I could, however, see that his face was deadly pale, and filled with horror and loathing.

He had ceased to strike, and was gazing up at the ventilator, when suddenly there broke from the silence of the night the most horrible cry to which I have ever listened. It swelled up louder and louder, a hoarse yell of pain and fear and anger all mingled in the one dreadful shriek. They say that away down in the village, and even in the distant parsonage, that cry raised the sleepers from their beds. It struck cold to our hearts, and I stood gazing at Holmes, and he at me, until the last echoes of it had died away into the silence from which it rose.

"What can it mean?" I gasped.

"It means that it is all over," Holmes answered. "And perhaps, after all, it is for the best. Take your pistol, and we shall enter Dr. Roylott's room."

With a grave face he lit the lamp, and led the way down the corridor. Twice he struck at the chamber door without any reply from within. Then he turned the handle and entered, I at his heels, with the cocked pistol in my hand.

It was a singular sight which met our eyes. On the table stood a dark lantern with the shutter half open, throwing a brilliant beam of light upon the iron safe, the door of which was ajar. Beside this table, on the wooden chair, sat Dr. Grimesby Roylott, clad in a long gray dressing gown, his bare ankles protruding beneath, and his feet thrust into red heelless Turkish slippers.[4] Across his lap lay the short stock with the long lash which we had noticed during the day. His chin was cocked upwards, and his eyes were fixed in a dreadful rigid stare at the corner of the ceiling. Round his brow he had a peculiar yellow band, with brownish speckles, which seemed to be bound tight round his head. As we entered he made neither sound nor motion.

"The band! the speckled band!" whispered Holmes.

I took a step forward: in an instant his strange headgear began to move, and there reared itself from among his hair the squat diamond-shaped head and puffed neck of a loathsome serpent.

"It is a swamp adder!"[5] cried Holmes—"the deadliest snake in India. He has died within ten seconds of being bitten. Violence does, in truth, recoil upon the violent, and the schemer falls into the pit which he digs for another.[6] Let us thrust this creature back into its den, and we can then remove Miss Stoner to some place of shelter, and let the county police know what has happened."

As he spoke he drew the dog whip swiftly from the dead man's lap, and throwing the noose round the reptile's neck, he drew it from its horrid perch, and, carrying it at arm's length, threw it into the iron safe, which he closed upon it.

4. Flat slipper of fabric or leather with elongated pointed toe.

5. There is no known snake of this name. The description most nearly fits, it is agreed, a cobra called the *Naja naja*.

6. *Ecclesiastes* 1:2—"He that diggeth a pit shall fall into it; and whoso breaketh a hedge, a serpent shall bite him."

Such are the true facts of the death of Dr. Grimesby Roylott, of Stoke Moran. It is not necessary that I should prolong a narrative which has already run to too great a length, by telling how we broke the sad news to the terrified girl, how we conveyed her by the morning train to the care of her good aunt at Harrow, of how the slow process of official inquiry came to the conclusion that the Doctor met his fate while indiscreetly playing with a dangerous pet. The little which I had yet to learn of the case was told me by Sherlock Holmes as we traveled back next day.

"I had," said he, "come to an entirely erroneous conclusion, which shows, my dear Watson, how dangerous it always is to reason from insufficient data. The presence of the gypsies, and the use of the word "band," which was used by the poor girl, no doubt, to explain the appearance which she had caught a horrid glimpse of by the light of her match, were sufficient to put me upon an entirely wrong scent. I can only claim the merit that I instantly reconsidered my position when, however, it became clear to me that whatever danger threatened an occupant of the room could not come either from the window or the door. My attention was speedily drawn, as I have already remarked to you, to this ventilator, and to the bell-rope which hung down to the bed. The discovery that this was a dummy, and that the bed was clamped to the floor, instantly gave rise to the suspicion that the rope was there as a bridge for something passing through the hole, and coming to the bed. The idea of a snake instantly occurred to me, and when I coupled it with my knowledge that the Doctor was furnished with a supply of creatures from India, I felt that I was probably on the right track. The idea of using a form of poison which could not possibly be discovered by any chemical test was just such a one as would occur to a clever and ruthless man who had had an Eastern training. The rapidity with which such a poison would take effect would also, from his point of view, be an advantage. It would be a sharp-eyed coroner indeed who could distinguish the two little dark punctures which would show where the poison fangs had done their work. Then I thought of the whistle. Of course, he must recall the snake before the morning light revealed it to the victim. He had trained it, probably by the use of the milk which we saw, to return to him when summoned. He would put it through the ventilator at the hour that he thought best, with the certainty that it would crawl down the rope, and land on the bed. It might or might not bite the occupant, perhaps she might escape every night for a week, but sooner or later she must fall a victim.

"I had come to these conclusions before ever I had entered his room. An inspection of his chair showed me that he had been in the habit of standing on it, which, of course, would be necessary in order that he should reach the ventilator. The sight of the safe, the saucer of milk, and the loop of whipcord were enough to finally dispel any doubts which may have remained. The metallic clang heard by Miss Stoner was obviously caused by her father hastily closing the door of his safe upon its terrible occupant. Having once made up my mind, you know the steps which I took in order to put the matter to the proof. I heard the creature hiss, as I have no doubt that you did also, and I instantly lit the light and attacked it."

"With the result of driving it through the ventilator."

"And also with the result of causing it to turn upon its master at the other side. Some of the blows of my cane came home, and roused its snakish temper, so that it flew upon the first person it saw. In this way I am no doubt indirectly responsible for Dr. Grimesby Roylott's death, and I cannot say that it is likely to weigh very heavily upon my conscience."

1892

FRANZ KAFKA

A Hunger Artist *

During these last decades the interest in professional fasting has markedly diminished. It used to pay very well to stage such great performances under one's own management, but today that is quite impossible. We live in a different world now. At one time the whole town took a lively interest in the hunger artist; from day to day of his fast the excitement mounted; everybody wanted to see him at least once a day; there were people who bought season tickets for the last few days and sat from morning till night in front of his small barred cage; even in the nighttime there were visiting hours, when the whole effect was heightened by torch flares; on fine days the cage was set out in the open air, and then it was the children's special treat to see the hunger artist; for their elders he was often just a joke that happened to be in fashion, but the children stood open-mouthed, holding each other's hands for greater security, marveling at him as he sat there pallid in black tights, with his ribs sticking out so prominently, not even on a seat but down among straw on the ground, sometimes giving a courteous nod, answering questions with a constrained smile, or perhaps stretching an arm through the bars so that one might feel how thin it was, and then again withdrawing deep into himself, paying no attention to anyone or anything, not even to the all-important striking of the clock that was the only piece of furniture in his cage, but merely staring into vacancy with half-shut eyes, now and then taking a sip from a tiny glass of water to moisten his lips.

Besides casual onlookers there were also relays of permanent watchers selected by the public, usually butchers, strangely enough, and it was their task to watch the hunger artist day and night, three of them at a time, in case he should have some secret recourse to nourishment. This was nothing but a formality, instituted to reassure the masses, for the initiates knew well enough that during his fast the artist would never in any circumstances, not even under forcible com-

* Translated by Willa and Edwin Muir.

pulsion, swallow the smallest morsel of food; the honor of his profession forbade it. Not every watcher, of course, was capable of understanding this, there were often groups of night watchers who were very lax in carrying out their duties and deliberately huddled together in a retired corner to play cards with great absorption, obviously intending to give the hunger artist the chance of a little refreshment, which they supposed he could draw from some private hoard. Nothing annoyed the artist more than such watchers; they made him miserable; they made his fast seem unendurable; sometimes he mastered his feebleness sufficiently to sing during their watch for as long as he could keep going, to show them how unjust their suspicions were. But that was of little use; they only wondered at his cleverness in being able to fill his mouth even while singing. Much more to his taste were the watchers who sat close up to the bars, who were not content with the dim night lighting of the hall but focused him in the full glare of the electric pocket torch given them by the impresario. The harsh light did not trouble him at all. In any case he could never sleep properly, and he could always drowse a little, whatever the light, at any hour, even when the hall was thronged with noisy onlookers. He was quite happy at the prospect of spending a sleepless night with such watchers; he was ready to exchange jokes with them, to tell them stories out of his nomadic life, anything at all to keep them awake and demonstrate to them again that he had no eatables in his cage and that he was fasting as not one of them could fast. But his happiest moment was when the morning came and an enormous breakfast was brought them, at his expense, on which they flung themselves with the keen appetite of healthy men after a weary night of wakefulness. Of course there were people who argued that this breakfast was an unfair attempt to bribe the watchers, but that was going rather too far, and when they were invited to take on a night's vigil without a breakfast, merely for the sake of the cause, they made themselves scarce, although they stuck stubbornly to their suspicions.

Such suspicions, anyhow, were a necessary accompaniment to the profession of fasting. No one could possibly watch the hunger artist continuously, day and night, and so no one could produce first-hand evidence that the fast had really been rigorous and continuous; only the artist himself could know that; he was therefore bound to be the sole completely satisfied spectator of his own fast. Yet for other reasons he was never satisfied; it was not perhaps mere fasting that had brought him to such skeleton thinness that many people had regretfully to keep away from his exhibitions, because the sight of him was too much for them, perhaps it was dissatisfaction with himself that had worn him down. For he alone knew, what no other initiate knew, how easy it was to fast. It was the easiest thing in the world. He made no secret of this, yet people did not believe him; at the best they set him down as modest; most of them, however, thought he was out for publicity or else was some kind of cheat who found it easy to fast because he had discovered a way of making it easy, and then had the impudence to admit the fact, more or less. He had to put up with all that, and in the course of time had got used to it, but his inner dissatisfaction always rankled, and never yet, after any term of fasting—this must be granted to his credit—had he left the cage of his own free will. The longest period of fasting was fixed by his impresario at forty days, beyond that term he was not allowed to go, not even in great cities, and there was good reason for it, too. Experience had proved that for about forty days the interest of the public could be stimulated by a steadily increasing pressure of advertisement, but after that the town began to lose interest, sympathetic support began notably to fall off; there were of course local variations as between one town and another or one country and another, but as a general rule forty days marked the limit. So on the fortieth day the flower-bedecked cage was opened, enthusiastic spectators filled the hall, a military band played, two doctors entered the cage to measure the results of the fast, which were announced through a megaphone, and finally two young ladies appeared, blissful at having been selected for the honor, to help the hunger artist down the few steps leading to a small table on which was spread a carefully chosen invalid repast. And at this very moment the artist always turned stubborn. True, he would entrust his bony arms to the outstretched helping hands of the ladies bending over him, but stand up he would not. Why stop fasting at this particular moment, after forty days of it? He had held out for a long time, an illimitably long time; why stop now, when he was in his best fasting form, or rather, not yet quite in his best fasting form? Why should he be cheated of the fame he would get for fasting longer, for being not only the record hunger artist of all time, which presumably he was already, but for beating his own record by a performance beyond human imagination, since he felt that there were no limits to his capacity for fasting? His public pretended to admire him so much, why should it have so little patience with him; if he could endure fasting longer, why shouldn't the public endure it? Besides, he was tired, he was comfortable sitting in the straw, and now he was supposed to lift himself to his full height and go down to a meal the very thought of which gave him a nausea that only the presence of the ladies kept him from betraying, and even that with an effort. And he looked up into the eyes of the ladies who were apparently so friendly and in reality so cruel, and shook his head, which felt too heavy on its strengthless neck. But then there happened yet again what always happened. The impresario came forward, without a word—for the band made speech impossible—lifted his arms in the air above the artist, as if inviting Heaven to look down upon its creature here in the straw, this suffering martyr, which indeed he was, although in quite another sense; grasped him round the emaciated waist, with exaggerated caution, so that the frail condition he was in might be appreciated; and committed him to the care of the blenching ladies, not without secretly giving him a shaking so that his legs and body tottered and swayed. The artist now submitted completely; his head lolled on his breast as if it had landed there by chance; his body was hollowed out; his legs in a spasm of self-preservation clung close to each other at the knees, yet scraped on the ground as if it were not really solid ground, as if they were only trying to find solid ground; and the whole weight of his body, a featherweight after all, relapsed onto one of the ladies, who, looking round for help and panting a little —this post of honor was not at all what she had expected it to be— first stretched her neck as far as she could to keep her face at least free from contact with the artist, then finding this impossible, and her more fortunate companion not coming to her aid but merely holding extended on her own trembling hand the little bunch of knucklebones that was the artist's, to the great delight of the spectators burst into tears and had to be replaced by an attendant who had long been stationed in readiness. Then came the food, a little of which the impresario managed to get between the artist's lips, while he sat in a kind of half-fainting trance, to the accompaniment of cheerful patter designed to distract the public's attention from the artist's condition; after that, a toast was drunk to the public, supposedly prompted by a whisper from the artist in the impresario's ear; the band confirmed it with a mighty flourish, the spectators melted away, and no one had any cause to be dissatisfied with the proceedings, no one except the hunger artist himself, he only, as always.

So he lived for many years, with small regular intervals of recuperation, in visible glory, honored by the world, yet in spite of that troubled in spirit, and all the more troubled because no one would take his trouble seriously. What comfort could he possibly need? What more could he possibly wish for? And if some good-natured person, feeling sorry for him, tried to console him by pointing out that his melancholy was probably caused by fasting, it could happen, especially when he had been fasting for some time, that he reacted with an outburst of fury and to the general alarm began to shake the bars of his cage like a wild animal. Yet the impresario had a way of punishing these outbreaks which he rather enjoyed putting into operation. He would apologize publicly for the artist's behavior, which was only to be excused, he admitted, because of the irritability caused by fasting; a condition hardly to be understood by well-fed people; then by natural transition he went on to mention the artist's equally incomprehensible boast that he could fast for much longer than he was doing; he praised the high ambition, the good will, the great self-denial undoubtedly implicit in such a statement; and then quite simply countered it by bringing out photographs, which were also on sale to the public, showing the artist on the fortieth day of a fast lying in bed almost dead from exhaustion. This perversion of the truth, familiar to the artist though it was, always unnerved him afresh and proved too much for him. What was a consequence of the premature ending of his fast was here presented as the cause of it! To fight against this lack of understanding, against a whole world of non-understanding, was impossible. Time and again in good faith he stood by the bars listening to the impresario, but as soon as the photographs appeared he always let go and sank with a groan back on to his straw, and the reassured public could once more come close and gaze at him.

A few years later when the witnesses of such scenes called them to mind, they often failed to understand themselves at all. For meanwhile the aforementioned change in public interest had set in; it seemed to happen almost overnight; there may have been profound causes for it, but who was going to bother about that; at any rate the pampered hunger artist suddenly found himself deserted one fine day by the amusement seekers, who went streaming past him to other more favored attractions. For the last time the impresario hurried him over half Europe to discover whether the old interest might still survive here and there; all in vain; everywhere, as if by secret agreement, a positive revulsion from professional fasting was in evidence. Of course it could not really have sprung up so suddenly as all that, and many premonitory symptoms which had not been sufficiently remarked or suppressed during the rush and glitter of success now came retrospectively to mind, but it was now too late to take any countermeasures. Fasting would surely come into fashion again at some future date, yet that was no comfort for those living in the present. What, then, was the hunger artist to do? He had been applauded by thousands in his time and could hardly come down to showing himself in a street booth at village fairs, and as for adopting another profession, he was not only too old for that but too fanatically devoted to fasting. So he took leave of the impresario, his partner in an unparalleled career, and hired himself to a large circus; in order to spare his own feelings he avoided reading the conditions of his contract.

A large circus with its enormous traffic in replacing and recruiting men, animals and apparatus can always find a use for people at any time, even for a hunger artist, provided of course that he does not ask too much, and in this particular case anyhow it was not only the artist who was taken on but his famous and long-known name as well; indeed considering the peculiar nature of his performance, which was not impared by advancing age, it could not be objected that here was an artist past his prime, no longer at the height of his professional skill, seeking a refuge in some quiet corner of a circus; on the contrary, the hunger artist averred that he could fast as well as ever, which was entirely credible; he even alleged that if he were allowed to fast as he liked, and this was at once promised him without more ado, he could astound the world by establishing a record never yet achieved, a statement which certainly provoked a smile among the other professionals, since it left out of account the change in public opinion, which the hunger artist in his zeal conveniently forgot.

He had not, however, actually lost his sense of the real situation and took it as a matter of course that he and his cage should be stationed, not in the middle of the ring as a main attraction, but outside, near the animal cages, on a site that was after all easily accessible. Large and gaily painted placards made a frame for the cage and announced what was to be seen inside it. When the public came thronging out in the intervals to see the animals, they could hardly avoid passing the hunger artist's cage and stopping there for a moment; perhaps they might even have stayed longer had not those pressing behind them in the narrow gangway, who did not understand why they should be held up on their way towards the excitements of the menagerie, made it impossible for anyone to stand gazing quietly for any length of time. And that was the reason why the hunger artist, who had of course been looking forward to these visiting hours as the main achievement of his life, began instead to shrink from them. At first he could hardly wait for the intervals; it was exhilarating to watch the crowds come streaming his way, until only too soon—not even the most obstinate self-deception, clung to almost consciously, could hold out against the fact

—the conviction was borne in upon him that these people, most of them, to judge from their actions, again and again, without exception, were all on their way to the menagerie. And the first sight of them from the distance remained the best. For when they reached his cage he was at once deafened by the storm of shouting and abuse that arose from the two contending factions, which renewed themselves continuously, of those who wanted to stop and stare at him—he soon began to dislike them more than the others—not out of real interest but only out of obstinate self-assertiveness, and those who wanted to go straight on to the animals. When the first great rush was past, the stragglers came along, and these, whom nothing could have prevented from stopping to look at him as long as they had breath, raced past with long strides, hardly even glancing at him, in their haste to get to the menagerie in time. And all too rarely did it happen that he had a stroke of luck, when some father of a family fetched up before him with his children, pointed a finger at the hunger artist and explained at length what the phenomenon meant, telling stories of earlier years when he himself had watched similar but much more thrilling performances, and the children, still rather uncomprehending, since neither inside nor outside school had they been sufficiently prepared for this lesson—what did they care about fasting?—yet showed by the brightness of their intent eyes that new and better times might be coming. Perhaps, said the hunger artist to himself many a time, things would be a little better if his cage were set not quite so near the menagerie. That made it too easy for people to make their choice, to say nothing of what he suffered from the stench of the menagerie, the animals' restlessness by night, the carrying past of raw lumps of flesh for the beasts of prey, the roaring at feeding times, which depressed him continually. But he did not dare to lodge a complaint with the management; after all, he had the animals to thank for the troops of people who passed his cage, among whom there might always be one here and there to take an interest in him, and who could tell where they might seclude him if he called attention to his existence and thereby to the fact that, strictly speaking, he was only an impediment on the way to the menagerie.

A small impediment, to be sure, one that grew steadily less. People grew familiar with the strange idea that they could be expected, in times like these, to take an interest in a hunger artist, and with this familiarity the verdict went out against him He might fast as much as he could, and he did so; but nothing could save him now, people passed him by. Just try to explain to anyone the art of fasting! Anyone who has no feeling for it cannot be made to understand it. The fine placards grew dirty and illegible, they were torn down; the little notice board telling the number of fast days achieved, which at first was changed carefully every day, had long stayed at the same figure, for after the first few weeks even this small task seemed pointless to the staff; and so the artist simply fasted on and on, as he had once dreamed of doing, and it was no trouble to him, just as he had always foretold, but no one counted the days, no one, not even the artist himself, knew what records he was already breaking, and his heart grew heavy. And when once in a time some leisurely passer-by stopped, made merry over the old figure on the board and spoke of swindling, that was in its way the stupidest lie ever invented by indifference and inborn malice, since it was not the hunger artist who was cheating; he was working honestly, but the world was cheating him of his reward.

Many more days went by, however, and that too came to an end. An overseer's eye fell on the cage one day and he asked the attendants why this perfectly good cage should be left standing there unused with dirty straw inside it; nobody knew, until one man, helped out by the notice board, remembered about the hunger artist. They poked into the straw with sticks and found him in it. "Are you still fasting?" asked the overseer. "When on earth do you mean to stop?" "Forgive me, everybody," whispered the hunger artist; only the overseer, who had his ear to the bars, understood him. "Of course," said the overseer, and tapped his forehead with a finger to let the attendants know what state the man was in, "we forgive you." "I always wanted you to admire my fasting," said the hunger artist. "We do admire it," said the overseer, affably. "But you shouldn't admire it," said the hunger artist. "Well, then we don't admire it," said the overseer, "but why shouldn't we admire it?" "Because I have to fast, I can't help it," said the hunger artist. "What a fellow you are," said the overseer, "and why can't you help it?" "Because," said the hunger artist, lifting his head a little and speaking, with his lips pursed, as if for a kiss, right into the overseer's ear, so that no syllable might be lost, "because I couldn't find the food I liked. If I had found it, believe me, I should have made no fuss and stuffed myself like you or anyone else." These were his last words, but in his dimming eyes remained the firm though no longer proud persuasion that he was still continuing to fast.

"Well, clear this out now!" said the overseer, and they buried the hunger artist, straw and all. Into the cage they put a young panther. Even the most insensitive felt it refreshing to see this wild creature leaping around the cage that had so long been dreary. The panther was all right. The food he liked was brought him without hesitation by the attendants; he seemed not even to miss his freedom; his noble body, furnished almost to the bursting point with all that it needed, seemed to carry freedom around with it too; somewhere in his jaws it seemed to lurk; and the joy of life streamed with such ardent passion from his throat that for the onlookers it was not easy to stand the shock of it. But they braced themselves, crowded round the cage, and did not want ever to move away.

1924

ISAAC BASHEVIS SINGER

Tanhum

Tanhum Makover buttoned his gaberdine and twisted his earlocks into curls. He wiped his feet on the straw mat before the door, as he had been told to. His prospective father-in-law, Reb Bendit Waldman, often reminded him that one could study the Torah and serve the Almighty and still not behave like an idle dreamer. Reb Bendit Waldman offered himself as an example. He was everything at once—a scholar, a fervent Chassid of the Sadgora rabbi [1] as well as a successful lumber merchant, a chess player, and the proprietor of a water mill. There was time for everything if one wasn't lazy, Reb Bendit said—even to teach yourself Russian and Polish and glance into a newspaper. How his prospective father-in-law managed all this was beyond Tanhum. Reb Bendit never seemed to hurry. He had a friendly word for everyone, even an errand boy or servant girl. Women burdened down by a heavy spirit came to him for advice. Nor did he neglect to visit the sick or—God forbid—to escort a corpse. Tanhum often resolved to be like his prospective father-in-law, but he simply couldn't manage it. He would grow absorbed in some sacred book and before he knew it half the day had gone by. He tried to maintain a proper appearance, but a button would loosen and dangle by a thread until it dropped off and got lost. His boots were always muddied, his shirt collars frayed. As often as he knotted the band of his breeches it always came untied again. He resolved to commit two pages of the Gemara [2] to memory each day so that in three and a half years he might finish with the Talmud, but he couldn't manage even this. He would become preoccupied with some Talmudic controversy and linger over it for weeks on end. The questions and doubts wouldn't let him rest. Certainly there was mercy in Heaven, but why did little children or even dumb animals have to suffer? Why did man have to end up dying, and a steer under the slaughterer's knife? Why had the miracles ceased and God's chosen people been forced to suffer exile for two thousand years? Tanhum probed in the Chassidic lore, the cabala[3] volumes, the ancient philosophy books. The questions they raised in his mind plagued him like flies. There were mornings when Tanhum awoke with a weight in his limbs, a pain in his temples, and no urge at all to study, pray, or even perform his ablutions. Today was one of those days. He opened the Gemara and sat there for two hours without turning a page. At prayer, he couldn't seem to grasp the meaning of the words. While reciting the eighteen benedictions,[4] he transposed the blessings. And it just so happened that today he was invited for lunch at his prospective father-in-law's.

Reb Bendit Waldman's house was constructed in such a way that one had to pass through the kitchen to get to the dining room. The kitchen was aswarm with women—Tanhum's prospective mother-in-law, her daughters-in-law, her daughters, including Tanhum's bride-to-be, Mira Fridl. Even before entering the house he heard the racket and commotion inside. The women of the house were all noisy

1. A member of the Jewish mystic order that orginated in Poland in the eighteenth century, stressing the pure heart and devotion but not asceticism and, in Poland, learning. Sadgora, a small town in Bukovina (now U.S.S.R.), whose Jewish residents in the nineteenth century were mostly Chassidim.

2. The supplementary second part of the Talmud, commentary on the first part (Mishnah), together making up the Jewish civil and religious law.

3. Mystical interpretation of Scriptures.

4. The principal Jewish prayer, which includes blessings of praise, prayer requests (for understanding, redemption, etc.), and thanksgiving.

and inclined to laughter, and often there were neighbors present. The cooking, baking, knitting, and needlepoint went on with a vengeance, and games of checkers, knucklebones, hide-and-seek, and wolf-and-goat[5] were played. On Chanukkah they rendered chicken fat; after Sukkoth they made coleslaw and pickled cucumbers; in the summers they put up jam. A fire was always kept going in the stove and under a tripod. The kitchen smelled of chicken soup, braised meat, cinnamon, and saffron. Cakes and cookies were baked for the Sabbath and holidays, to go with the roast geese, chickens, and ducks. One day they prepared for a circumcision and another day for the ceremony of redeeming the firstborn son;[6] now one of the family was becoming engaged, and now they all trouped off to a wedding. Tailors fitted coats, cobblers measured feet for shoes. At Reb Bendit Waldman's there was ample occasion to have a drink of cherry or sweet brandy and to nibble at an almond cookie, a babka,[7] or a honey cake. If a guest from another town came to visit, half the town sent over a kugel.[8] Reb Bendit made fun of the women of the house and their exaggerated sense of hospitality, but apparently he, too, enjoyed having his house full of people. Each time he went to Warsaw or Krakow he brought back all kinds of trinkets for the women—embroidered headkerchiefs, rings, shawls, and pins—and for the boys, pocketknives, pens, gold embossed skullcaps, and ornate phylactery bags. Apart from the usual wedding gifts—a set of the Talmud, a gold watch, a wine goblet, a spice box, a prayer shawl with silver brocade—Tanhum had already received all kinds of other presents. It wasn't mere talk when Tanhum's former fellow-students at the Brisk Yeshiva[9] said that he had fallen into a gravy pot. His bride-to-be, Mira Fridl, was considered a beauty, but Tanhum had not yet had a good look at her. How could he? During the signing of the marriage contract the women's parlor was jammed, and in the kitchen Mira Fridl was always surrounded by her sisters and sisters-in-law.

The moment Tanhum crossed the threshhold he lowered his eyes. True, everyone had his destined mate; forty days before he, Tanhum, had been born it had already been decided that Mira Fridl would become his spouse.[1] Still, he fretted that he wasn't a suitable enough son-in-law for Reb Bendit Waldman. All the members of the family were jolly, while he was reticent. He wasn't good at business or quick of tongue, not playful, not good at games, unable to perform stunts or do swimming tricks in the river. At twelve he already had to take free board at the homes of strangers in the towns where he was sent to study at the various yeshivas. His father died when Tanhum was still a child. His mother had remarried. Tanhum's stepfather was a poor peddler and had six children from a previous marriage. From childhood on, Tanhum went around in rags and was

5. Unidentified: there are, however, a Russian children's game and a chess game called wolf-and-sheep.

6. Every firstborn of the womb, man or animal, belongs to the Lord; clean animals must be sacrificed and humans redeemed, usually by the payment of money or its equivalent to the rabbi thirty days after the birth of the firstborn son. See *Exodus* 13:11–16, *Leviticus* 27:26.

7. A cake marblized with soft chocolate.

8. Pudding of noodles or potatoes.

9. The seminary of Brest-Litovsk, Lithuania.

1. Not a contractual arrangement; legend has it that a child's mate is determined in heaven forty days before he or she is born.

neglected. He constantly berated himself for not praying fervently enough or devoting himself sufficiently to Jewishness, and he warred eternally with evil thoughts.

This day, the tumult in the kitchen was louder than ever. Someone had apparently just told a joke or performed some antic, for the women laughed and clapped their hands. Usually when Tanhum came in, a respectful path was cleared for him, but now he had to push his way through the throng. Who knows, maybe they were making fun of him? The back of his neck felt hot and damp. He must be late, for Reb Bendit was already seated at the table, with his sons and sons-in-law, waiting for him to appear. Reb Bendit, in a flowered robe, his silver-white beard combed into two points and a silk skullcap down over his forehead, lolled grandly in his armchair at the head of the table. The men had apparently had a drink, for a carafe and glasses stood on the table, along with wafers to crunch on. The company was in a joking mood. Reb Bendit's eldest son, Leibush Meir, a big, fleshy fellow with a huge potbelly and a round reddish beard circling his fat face, shook with laughter. Yoshe, a son-in-law—short and round as a barrel and with liquid black eyes and thick lips—giggled into a handkerchief. Another son-in-law, Shlomele, the wag, jokester, and mimic, impudently imitated someone's gestures.

Reb Bendit asked Tanhum amiably, "You have a gold watch. Why aren't you on time?"

"It stopped running."

"You probably didn't wind it."

"He needs an alarm clock," Schlomele jested.

"Well, go wash your hands," and Reb Bendit pointed to the washstand.

While washing his hands Tanhum wet his sleeves. There was a towel hanging on the rack, but he stood helplessly dripping water on the floor. He often tripped, caught his clothing, and bumped into things, and he constantly had to be told where to go and what to do. There was a mirror in the dining room and Tanhum caught a glimpse of himself—a stooped figure with sunken cheeks, dark eyes below dishevelled brows, a tiny beard on the tip of the chin, a pale nose, and a pointed Adam's apple. It took him a few seconds to realize that he was looking at his reflection. At the table, Reb Bendit praised the dish of groats and asked the woman who had prepared it what ingredients she had used. Leibush Meir demanded a second helping as usual. Shlomele complained that he had found only one mushroom in his portion. After the soup, the conversation turned serious. Reb Bendit had bought a tract of forest in partnership with a Zamosc merchant, Reb Nathan Vengrover. The two partners had fallen out, and Reb Nathan had summoned Reb Bendit to the rabbi's the following Saturday night for a hearing. Reb Bendit complained to the company at lunch that his partner was totally lacking in common sense, a dolt, a ninny, a dunderhead. The sons and sons-in-law agreed that he was a jackass. Tanhum sat in terror. This was evil talk, slander, and who knows what else! According to the Gemara, one lost the world to come for speaking so disrespectfully of another man. Had they forgotten this or did they only pretend to forget? Tanhum wanted to warn them that they were violating the law: Thou shalt not go up and down as a talebearer among thy people. According to the Gemara, he should have stuffed up his ears with the lobes so as not to hear, but he couldn't embarrass his prospective father-in-law this way. He sank even lower in his chair. Two women now brought in the main course—a platter of beef cutlets and a tray of roast chicken floating in sauce. Tanhum grimaced. How could one eat such a repast on a weekday? Didn't they remember the destruction of the Temple?[2]

"Tanhum, are you eating or sleeping?"

It was his intended, Mira Fridl, speaking. Tanhum came to with a start. He saw her now for the first time—of medium build, fair, with golden hair and blue eyes, wearing a red dress. She smiled at him mischievously and even winked.

"Which would you prefer—beef or chicken?"

Tanhum wanted to answer, but the words stuck in his throat. For some time already, he had felt an aversion to meat. No doubt everything here was strictly kosher, but it seemed to him that the meat smelled of blood and that he could hear the bellowing of the cow writhing beneath the slaughterer's knife.

Reb Bendit said, "Give him some of each."

Mira Fridl served a cutlet and then, with her serving spoon poised over the platter of chicken, asked, "Which would you like—the breast or a leg?"

Again Tanhum was unable to answer. Instead, Shlomele the wag said with a leer, "He lusts for both."

As Mira Fridl bent over Tanhum to put a chicken leg on his plate, her bosom touched his shoulder. She added potatoes and carrots and Tanhum shrank away from her. He heard Shlomele snicker, and he was overcome with shame. I don't belong among them, he thought. They're making a fool of me. . . . He had an urge to stand up and flee.

"Eat, Tanhum, don't dillydally," Reb Bendit said. "One must have strength for the Torah."

Tanhum put his fork into the sauce and dug out a sliver of meat, doused it in horseradish, and sprinkled it with salt to blot out the taste. He ate a slice of bread. He was intimidated by Mira Fridl. What would they talk about after the wedding? She was a rich man's daughter, accustomed to a life of luxury. Her mother had told him that a goldsmith from Lublin had fashioned jewelry for Mira Fridl. All kinds of fur coats, jackets, and capes were being sewn for her, and she would be provided with furniture, rugs, and porcelain. How could he, Tanhum, exercise control over such a pampered creature? And why would she want him for a husband? Her father had undoubtedly coerced her into it. He wanted a Talmudist for a son-in-law. Tanhum envisioned himself standing under the wedding canopy with Mira Fridl, eating the golden soup,[3] dancing the wedding dance,

2. 2 *Chronicles* 36:19. Because of the wickedness of Israel and its kings, the Lord allows the Chaldeans to kill young men in Solomon's temple, burn it down, and break down the walls of Jerusalem.

3. The Jewish wedding ceremony takes place under a canopy (*chuppah*). The bride and groom fast until after the ceremony, then immediately go into a separate room to eat, sometimes a more or less ceremonial food—here, apparently, chicken soup.

and then being led off to the marriage chamber. He felt a sense of panic. None of this seemed fitting for his oppressed spirit. He began to sway and to beg the Almighty to guard him from temptations, impure thoughts, Satan's net. *Father in Heaven, save me!*

Leibush Meir burst into laughter. "What are you swaying for? It's a chicken leg, not Rashi's commentary."[4]

Reb Nathan was expected to bring his arbitrator, Reb Feivel, to the hearing. Reb Bendit Waldman also had his own arbitrator, Reb Fishel, but nevertheless he invited Tanhum to attend the proceedings too. He said that it would do Tanhum good to learn something about practical matters. If he turned to the rabbinate, he would have to know a little about business. It was entirely feasible that that stubborn villain, Reb Nathan, wouldn't agree to a compromise and would insist on the strict letter of the law, and Reb Bendit asked Tanhum therefore to take down the books and go over the sections that dealt with the codes governing business partnerships. Tanhum agreed reluctantly. The entire Torah was holy, of course, but Tanhum wasn't drawn to those laws dealing with money, manipulation, interests, and swindle. In former years when he studied these subjects in the Gemara, it hadn't occurred to him that there really were Jews who reneged on written agreements, stole, swore falsely, and cheated. The idea of meeting in the flesh a person who would deny a debt, violate a trust, and grow rich from deception was too painful to contemplate. Tanhum wanted to tell Reb Bendit that he had no intention of becoming a rabbi, and that it would be hard for him now to lay aside the treatise in which he was absorbed and turn to matters that were alien to him. But how could he refuse Reb Bendit, who had raised him out of poverty, and given him his daughter for a bride, and provided him with overcoats, underwear, a sheepskin coat, a residence, holy books, a prayer shawl with silver brocade, and a thirteen-pointed fur hat besides? This would have enraged his future mother-in-law and turned Mira Fridl against him. It would have incited a feud and provoked evil gossip. It would have led to who knows what quarrels.

During the next few days, Tanhum didn't have enough time to get deeply into "The Breastplate of Judgment"[5] and its many commentaries. He quickly scanned the text of Rabbi Caro and the annotations of Rabbi Moshe Isserles. He hummed and bit his lips. Obviously even in the old days there had been no lack of frauds and of rascals. Was it any wonder? Even the generation that received the Torah had its Korah, its Dathan, its Abiram.[6] Still, how could theft be reconciled with faith? How could one whose soul had stood on Mount Sinai defile it with crime?

4. Solomon Yitzhaki Rashi (1040–1105), French rabbinical scholar, whose commentary on the whole Talmud helped to establish the text, and whose commentary on the Pentateuch has served as the basis for most later scholarship.

5. The Talmud. Joseph Caro (1488–1575) author of a commentary and its abridgement, *Shulhan Arukh* ("The Prepared Table," 1564–65), which, with Moses Isserles' (c.1525–72) critical strictures, *Ha Mappah* ("The Tablecloth") are still considered authoritative by Orthodox Jews.

6. Leaders of the revolt against Moses in the desert who were destroyed by fire and earthquake. *Numbers* 16 and 26:9–11.

The Din Torah, the hearing, began on Saturday evening, and it looked as though it would last a whole week. The rabbi, Reb Efraim Engel, a patriarch of seventy and author of a book of legal opinions, told his wife to send all those who came seeking advice about other matters to the assistant rabbi. He bolted the door of his study and ordered his beadle to let only the participants enter. On the table stood the candles that had ushered out the Sabbath. The room smelled of wine, wax, and the spice box. From the way the family had decribed Reb Nathan Vengrover as a tough man and a speculator, Tanhum expected him to be tall, dark, and with the wild gaze of a gypsy, but in came a thin, stooped little man with a sparse beard the color of pepper, with a milky-white cataract in his left eye, and wearing a faded gaberdine, a sheepskin hat, and coarse boots. Pouches of bluish flesh dangled beneath his eyes and he had warts on his nose. Being the plaintiff, he was the first to speak. He immediately began to shout in a hoarse voice, and he kept on shouting and grunting throughout the proceedings.

Reb Bendit smoked an aromatic blend of tobacco in a pipe with an amber cover; Reb Nathan rolled cigarettes of cheap, stinking tobacco. Reb Bendit spoke deliberately and graced his words with proverbs and quotations from the saints; Reb Nathan slammed the table with his fist, yanked hairs from his beard, and called Reb Bendit a thief. He wouldn't even let his own arbitrator, Reb Feivel—who was the size of a cheder boy,[7] with eyes green as gooseberries and a red beard that fell to his loins—get a word in edgewise. Reb Bendit recalled the details of the agreement from memory, but Reb Nathan consulted whole stackfuls of papers that were filled with row upon row of a clumsy scribble and stained with erasures and blots. He didn't sit in the chair provided for him but paced to and fro, coughed, and spat into a handkerchief. Reb Bendit was sent all kinds of refreshments and drinks from home, but Reb Nathan didn't even go near the tea that the rabbi's wife brought in. From day to day his face grew more drawn, and was gray as dust and wasted as if from consumption. From nervous tension, he chewed his fingernails and tore his own notes into tiny shreds.

For the first two days, Tanhum was completely bewildered by what went on. The rabbi again and again implored Reb Nathan to speak to the point, not to mix up dates or inject matters that had no bearing on the subject. But it all came gushing out of Reb Nathan like water fom a pump. Gradually Tanhum came to understand that his prospective father-in-law was being accused of holding back profits and falsifying accounts. Reb Nathan Vengrover maintained that Reb Bendit had bribed Prince Sapieha's steward to chop down more acres of timber than had been stipulated in the contract. Nor would Reb Bendit allow Reb Nathan and his associate near the Squire, or to get in contact with the merchants who purchased the timber, which was tied in rafts and floated down the Vistula to Danzig. Reb Bendit had allegedly announced one price to Reb Nathan, when he had in fact got a higher one from the merchants. Reb

7. Schoolboy.

Bendit had claimed to have paid the brokers, loggers, and sawyers more than he actually did. He employed every trick and device to oust Reb Nathan from the partnership and to seize all the profits for himself. Reb Nathan pointed out that Reb Bendit had already twice gone bankrupt and subsequently settled for a third of his debts.

Reb Bendit had kept silent most of the time, awaiting his turn to speak, but finally he lost his patience. "Savage!" he shouted. "Hothead! Lunatic!"

"Usurer! Swindler! Robber!" Reb Nathan responded.

On the third day, Reb Bendit calmly began to refute Reb Nathan's charges. He proved that Reb Nathan contradicted himself, exaggerated, and didn't know a pine from an oak. How could he be allowed near the Squire when his Polish was so broken? How could he lay claim to half the income when he, Reb Bendit, had to lay out hush money to the gentry, stave off unfavorable decrees, shower assessors and marshals with gifts out of his own pocket? The more glibly Reb Bendit spoke, the more apparent it became to Tanhum that his prospective father-in-law had broken his agreement and had indeed sought to rob Reb Nathan of the profits and even part of his original investment. But how could this be, Tanhum wondered. How could Reb Bendit, a man in his sixties, a scholar, and a Chassid, commit such iniquities? What was his justification? He knew all the laws. He knew that no repentance could excuse the sin of robbery and theft unless one paid back every penny. The Day of Atonement[8] didn't forgive such transgressions. Could a man who believed in the Creator, in reward and punishment and in immortality of the soul, risk the world to come for the sake of a few thousand gulden?[9] Or was Reb Bendit a secret heretic?

In the closing days, Reb Bendit, his arbitrator, Reb Fishel, and Tanhum didn't go home for dinner—the maid brought them meat and soup. But Tanhum didn't touch the food. There was a gnawing in his stomach. His tongue was dry. He had a bad taste in his mouth, and he felt like vomiting. Although he fasted, his belly was bloated. A lump formed in his throat that he could neither swallow nor disgorge. He didn't weep but his eyes kept tearing over, and he saw everything as if through a mist. Tanhum reminded himself that only that past Sukkoth, when Reb Bendit had gone to the Sadgora rabbi, he had brought the rabbi an ivory ethrog box that was decorated with silver and embossed in gold. Inside, couched in flax, lay an ethrog[10] from Corfu that was pocked and budding. The Chassidim knew that besides contributing generously to the community, of which he was an elder, Reb Bendit also gave the rabbi a tithe. But what was the sense of robbing one person to give to another? Did he do all this to be praised in the Sadgora study houses and be seated at the rabbi's table? Had the greed for money and honors so blinded him that he didn't know the wrongs he committed? Yes, so it seemed, for during evening prayers Reb Bendit piously washed

8. Yom Kippur, last of the ten days of Pentitence, upon which, by fasting and prayer one may be released from sins or promises made to God, but vows to other men, community, court, or political regime are not annulled.

9. Gold or silver coin of Austria and Germany in wide use through eastern Europe.

10. Citron fruit which, with palm branch (lulab) was used to celebrate—and still symbolizes—the festival of Sukkoth.

his fingers in the basin, girdled his loins with a sash, stationed himself to pray at the eastern wall, swayed, bowed, beat his breast, and sighed. From time to time he stretched his hands up to Heaven. Several times during the arbitration he had invoked God's name.

Thursday night, when it came time to pass judgment, Reb Nathan Vengrover demanded a clear-cut decision: "No compromises! If the law says that what my partner did was right, then I don't demand even a groschen." [1]

"According to law, Reb Bendit has to take an oath," Reb Nathan's arbitrator Reb Feivel, asserted.

"I wouldn't swear even for a sackful of gold," Reb Bendit countered.

"In that case, pay up!"

"Not on your life!"

Both arbitrators, Reb Feivel and Reb Fishel, began to dispute the law. The rabbi drew "The Breastplate of Judgment" down from the bookcase.

Reb Bendit cast a glance at Tanhum. "Tanhum, why don't you speak up?"

Tanhum wanted to say that to appropriate another's possession was as serious an offense as swearing falsely. He also wanted to ask, "Why did you do it?" But he merely mumbled, "Since Father-in-Law signed an agreement, he must honor it."

"So you, too, turn on me, eh?"

"God forbid, but—"

" 'Art thou for us or for our adversaries?' " Reb Bendit quoted from the Book of Joshua,[2] in a dry voice.

"We don't live forever," Tanhum said haltingly.

"You go home!" Reb Bendit ordered.

Tanhum left the rabbi's study and went straight to his room at the inn. He didn't recite the Shema,[3] or undress, but sat on the edge of his cot the whole night. When the light began to break, he packed his Sabbath gaberdine, a few shirts, socks, and books in a straw basket, and walked down Synagogue Street to the bridge that led out of town. Months went by without any news of him. They even dredged the river for his body. Reb Bendit Waldman and Reb Nathan Vengrover reached an agreement. The rabbi and the arbitrators wouldn't permit it to come to oath-taking. Mira Fridl became engaged to a youth from Lublin, the son of a sugar manufacturer. Tanhum had left all his presents behind at the inn, and the bridegroom from Lublin inherited them. One winter day, a shipping agent brought news of Tanhum: he had gone back to the Brisk Yeshiva, from which Reb Bendit originally brought him to his town. Tanhum had become a recluse. He ate no meat, drank no wine, put pebbles inside his shoes, and slept on a bench behind the stove at the study house. When a new match was proposed to him in Brisk, he responded, "My soul yearns for the Torah."

1975

1. I.e., not even a thin dime.
2. *Joshua* 5:13. Before Jericho, Joshua sees a man with drawn sword and asks him this question; the answer: "captain of the host of the Lord."
3. *Shema Yisrael,* "Hear O Israel," the Jewish confession of faith, proclaiming the unity of God, recited morning and evening and on certain special occasions.

JOHN CHEEVER

The Country Husband

To begin at the beginning, the airplane from Minneapolis in which Francis Weed was traveling East ran into heavy weather. The sky had been a hazy blue, with the clouds below the plane lying so close together that nothing could be seen of the earth. Then mist began to form outside the windows, and they flew into a white cloud of such density that it reflected the exhaust fires. The color of the cloud darkened to gray, and the plane began to rock. Francis had been in heavy weather before, but he had never been shaken up so much. The man in the seat beside him pulled a flask out of his pocket and took a drink. Francis smiled at his neighbor, but the man looked away; he wasn't sharing his painkiller with anyone. The plane had begun to drop and flounder wildly. A child was crying. The air in the cabin was overheated and stale, and Francis' left foot went to sleep. He read a little from a paper book that he had bought at the airport, but the violence of the storm divided his attention. It was black outside the ports. The exhaust fires blazed and shed sparks in the dark, and, inside, the shaded lights, the stuffiness, and the window curtains gave the cabin an atmosphere of intense and misplaced domesticity. Then the lights flickered and went out. "You know what I've always wanted to do?" the man beside Francis said suddenly. "I've always wanted to buy a farm in New Hampshire and raise beef cattle." The stewardess announced that they were going to make an emergency landing. All but the child saw in their minds the spreading wings of the Angel of Death. The pilot could be heard singing faintly, "I've got sixpence, jolly, jolly sixpence. I've got sixpence to last me all my life . . ."[1] There was no other sound.

The loud groaning of the hydraulic valves swallowed up the pilot's song, and there was a shrieking high in the air, like automobile brakes, and the plane hit flat on its belly in a cornfield and shook them so violently that an old man up forward howled, "Me kidneys! Me kidneys!" The stewardess flung open the door, and someone opened an emergency door at the back, letting in the sweet noise of their continuing mortality—the idle splash and smell of a heavy rain. Anxious for their lives, they filed out of the doors and scattered over the cornfield in all directions, praying that the thread would hold. It did. Nothing happened. When it was clear that the plane would not burn or explode, the crew and the stewardess gathered the passengers together and led them to the shelter of a barn. They were not far from Philadelphia, and in a little while a string of taxis took them into the city. "It's just like the Marne,"[2] someone said, but there was surprisingly little relaxation of that suspiciousness with which many Americans regard their fellow-travelers.

In Philadelphia, Francis Weed got a train to New York. At the end of that journey, he crossed the city and caught, just as it was about to pull out, the commuting train that he took five nights a week to his

1. Song popular with Allied troops in World War II.
2. On September 8, 1914, over 1000 Paris taxicabs were requisitioned to move troops to the Marne River to halt the encircling Germans in what turned out to be the first German defeat of World War I.

home in Shady Hill.

He sat with Trace Bearden. "You know, I was in that plane that just crashed outside Philadelphia," he said. "We came down in a field . . ." He had traveled faster than the newspapers or the train, and the weather in New York was sunny and mild. It was a day in late September, as fragrant and shapely as an apple. Trace listened to the story, but how could he get excited? Francis had no powers that would let him re-create a brush with death—particularly in the atmosphere of a commuting train, journeying through a sunny countryside where already, in the slum gardens, there were signs of harvest. Trace picked up his newspaper, and Francis was left alone with his thoughts. He said good night to Trace on the platform at Shady Hill and drove in his secondhand Volkswagen up to the Blenhollow neighborhood, where he lived.

The Weeds' Dutch Colonial house was larger than it appeared to be from the driveway. The living room was spacious and divided like Gaul into three parts.[3] Around an ell to the left as one entered from the vestibule was the long table, laid for six, with candles and a bowl of fruit in the center. The sounds and smells that came from the open kitchen door were appetizing, for Julia Weed was a good cook. The largest part of the living room centered around a fireplace. On the right were some bookshelves and a piano. The room was polished and tranquil, and from the windows that opened to the west there was some late-summer sunlight, brilliant and as clear as water. Nothing here was neglected; nothing had not been burnished. It was not the kind of household where, after prying open a stuck cigarette box, you would find an old shirt button and a tarnished nickel. The hearth was swept, the roses on the piano were reflected in the polish of the broad top, and there was an album of Schubert waltzes on the rack. Louisa Weed, a pretty girl of nine, was looking out the western windows. Her younger brother Henry was standing beside her. Her still younger brother, Toby, was studying the figures of some tonsured monks drinking beer on the polished brass of the wood box. Francis, taking off his hat and putting down his paper, was not consciously pleased with the scene; he was not that reflective. It was his element, his creation, and he returned to it with that sense of lightness and strength with which any creature returns to its home. "Hi, everybody," he said. "The plane from Minneapolis . . ."

Nine times out of ten, Francis would be greeted with affection, but tonight the children are absorbed in their own antagonisms. Francis has not finished his sentence about the plane crash before Henry plants a kick in Louisa's behind. Louisa swings around, saying, "*Damn* you!" Francis makes the mistake of scolding Louisa for bad language before he punishes Henry. Now Louisa turns on her father and accuses him of favoritism. Henry is always right; she is persecuted and lonely; her lot is hopeless. Francis turns to his son, but the boy has justification for the kick—she hit him first; she hit him on the ear, which is dangerous. Louisa agrees with this passionately. She hit him on the ear, and she *meant* to hit him on the ear, because he messed up her china collection. Henry says that this is a lie. Little Toby turns away from the

3. Ancient France (Gaul) is so described by Julius Caesar in *The Gallic War*.

wood box to throw in some evidence for Louisa. Henry claps his hand over little Toby's mouth. Francis separates the two boys but accidentally pushes Toby into the wood box. Toby begins to cry. Louisa is already crying. Just then, Julia Weed comes into that part of the room where the table is laid. She is a pretty, intelligent woman, and the white in her hair is premature. She does not seem to notice the fracas. "Hello, darling," she says serenely to Francis. "Wash your hands, everyone. Dinner is ready." She strikes a match and lights the six candles in this vale of tears.[4]

This simple announcement, like the war cries of the Scottish chieftains, only refreshes the ferocity of the combatants. Louisa gives Henry a blow on the shoulder. Henry, although he seldom cries, has pitched nine innings and is tired. He bursts into tears. Little Toby discovers a splinter in his hand and begins to howl. Francis says loudly that he has been in a plane crash and that he is tired. Julia appears again, from the kitchen, and, still ignoring the chaos, asks Francis to go upstairs and tell Helen that everything is ready. Francis is happy to go; it is like getting back to headquarters company.[5] He is planning to tell his oldest daughter about the airplane crash, but Helen is lying on her bed reading a *True Romance* magazine, and the first thing Francis does is to take the magazine from her hand and remind Helen that he has forbidden her to buy it. She did not buy it, Helen replies. It was given to her by her best friend, Bessie Black. Everybody reads *True Romance*. Bessie Black's father reads *True Romance*. There isn't a girl in Helen's class who doesn't read *True Romance*. Francis expresses his detestation of the magazine and then tells her that dinner is ready—although from the sounds downstairs it doesn't seem so. Helen follows him down the stairs. Julia has seated herself in the candlelight and spread a napkin over her lap. Neither Louisa nor Henry has come to the table. Little Toby is still howling, lying face down on the floor. Francis speaks to him gently: "Daddy was in a plane crash this afternoon, Toby. Don't you want to hear about it?" Toby goes on crying. "If you don't come to the table now, Toby," Francis says, "I'll have to send you to bed without any supper." The little boy rises, gives him a cutting look, flies up the stairs to his bedroom, and slams the door. "Oh dear," Julia says, and starts to go after him. Francis says that she will spoil him. Julia says that Toby is ten pounds underweight and has to be encouraged to eat. Winter is coming, and he will spend the cold months in bed unless he has his dinner. Julia goes upstairs. Francis sits down at the table with Helen. Helen is suffering from the dismal feeling of having read too intently on a fine day, and she gives her father and the room a jaded look. She doesn't understand about the plane crash, because there wasn't a drop of rain in Shady Hill.

Julia returns with Toby, and they all sit down and are served. "Do I have to look at that big, fat slob?" Henry says, of Louisa. Everybody but Toby enters into this skirmish, and it rages up and down the table for five minutes. Toward the end, Henry puts his napkin over his head and, trying to eat that way, spills spinach all over his shirt. Francis asks Julia if the children couldn't have their dinner earlier.

4. Common figurative reference to earthly life (vale is valley), though here the tears are literal.

5. That is, like escaping from combat to relative safety behind the lines.

Julia's guns are loaded for this. She can't cook two dinners and lay two tables. She paints with lightning strokes that panorama of drudgery in which her youth, her beauty, and her wit have been lost. Francis says that he must be understood; he was nearly killed in an airplane crash, and he doesn't like to come home every night to a battlefield. Now Julia is deeply committed. Her voice trembles. He doesn't come home every night to a battlefield. The accusation is stupid and mean. Everything was tranquil until he arrived. She stops speaking, puts down her knife and fork, and looks into her plate as if it is a gulf. She begins to cry. "Poor Mummy!" Toby says, and when Julia gets up from the table, drying her tears with a napkin, Toby goes to her side. "Poor Mummy," he says. "Poor Mummy!" And they climb the stairs together. The other children drift away from the battlefield, and Francis goes into the back garden for a cigarette and some air.

It was a pleasant garden, with walks and flower beds and places to sit. The sunset had nearly burned out, but there was still plenty of light. Put into a thoughtful mood by the crash and the battle, Francis listened to the evening sounds of Shady Hill. "Varmints! Rascals!" old Mr. Nixon shouted to the squirrels in his bird-feeding station. "Avaunt and quit my sight!" A door slammed. Someone was playing tennis on the Babcocks' court; someone was cutting grass. Then Donald Goslin, who lived at the corner, began to play the "Moonlight Sonata."[6] He did this nearly every night. He threw the tempo out the window and played it *rubato*[7] from beginning to end, like an outpouring of tearful petulance, lonesomeness, and self-pity—of everything it was Beethoven's greatness not to know. The music rang up and down the street beneath the trees like an appeal for love, for tenderness, aimed at some lonely housemaid—some fresh-faced, homesick girl from Galway, looking at old snapshots in her third-floor room. "Here, Jupiter, here, Jupiter," Francis called to the Mercers' retriever. Jupiter crashed through the tomato vines with the remains of a felt hat in his mouth.

Jupiter was an anomaly. His retrieving instincts and his high spirits were out of place in Shady Hill. He was as black as coal, with a long, alert, intelligent, rakehell face. His eyes gleamed with mischief, and he held his head high. It was the fierce, heavily collared dog's head that appears in heraldry, in tapestry, and that used to appear on umbrella handles and walking sticks. Jupiter went where he pleased, ransacking wastebaskets, clotheslines, garbage pails, and shoe bags. He broke up garden parties and tennis matches, and got mixed up in the processional at Christ Church on Sunday, barking at the men in red dresses.[8] He crashed through old Mr. Nixon's rose garden two or three times a day, cutting a wide swath through the Condesa de Sastagos,[9] and as soon as Donald Goslin lighted his barbecue fire on Thursday nights, Jupiter would get the scent. Nothing the Goslins did could drive him away. Sticks and stones and rude commands only moved him to the edge of the terrace, where he remained, with his gallant and heraldic muzzle, waiting for Donald Goslin to turn his back and reach for the

6. Common title of Beethoven's *Sonata Quasi una Fantasia* (1802), one of the most famous, frequently played, and sentimentalized piano compositions.
7. With intentional deviations from strict tempo.
8. Probably the choir.
9. Rather uncommon yellow and red roses difficult to grow.

salt. Then he would spring onto the terrace, lift the steak lightly off the fire, and run away with the Goslins' dinner. Jupiter's days were numbered. The Wrightsons' German gardener or the Farquarsons' cook would soon poison him. Even old Mr. Nixon might put some arsenic in the garbage that Jupiter loved. "Here, Jupiter, Jupiter!" Francis called, but the dog pranced off, shaking the hat in his white teeth. Looking in at the windows of his house, Francis saw that Julia had come down and was blowing out the candles.

Julia and Francis Weed went out a great deal. Julia was well liked and gregarious, and her love of parties sprang from a most natural dread of chaos and loneliness. She went through her morning mail with real anxiety, looking for invitations, and she usually found some, but she was insatiable, and if she had gone out seven nights a week, it would not have cured her of a reflective look—the look of someone who hears distant music—for she would always suppose that there was a more brilliant party somewhere else. Francis limited her to two weeknight parties, putting a flexible interpretation on Friday, and rode through the weekend like a dory in a gale. The day after the airplane crash, the Weeds were to have dinner with the Farquarsons.

Francis got home late from town, and Julia got the sitter while he dressed, and then hurried him out of the house. The party was small and pleasant, and Francis settled down to enjoy himself. A new maid passed the drinks. Her hair was dark, and her face was round and pale and seemed familiar to Francis. He had not developed his memory as a sentimental faculty. Wood smoke, lilac, and other such perfumes did not stir him, and his memory was something like his appendix—a vestigial repository. It was not his limitation at all to be unable to escape the past; it was perhaps his limitation that he had escaped it so successfully. He might have seen the maid at other parties, he might have seen her taking a walk on Sunday afternoons, but in either case he would not be searching his memory now. Her face was, in a wonderful way, a moon face—Norman or Irish—but it was not beautiful enough to account for his feeling that he had seen her before, in circumstances that he ought to be able to remember. He asked Nellie Farquarson who she was. Nellie said that the maid had come through an agency, and that her home was Trénon, in Normandy—a small place with a church and a restaurant that Nellie had once visited. While Nellie talked on about her travels abroad, Francis realized where he had seen the woman before. It had been at the end of the war. He had left a replacement depot with some other men and taken a three-day pass in Trénon. On their second day, they had walked out to a crossroads to see the public chastisement of a young woman who had lived with the German commandant during the Occupation.

It was a cool morning in the fall. The sky was overcast, and poured down onto the dirt crossroads a very discouraging light. They were on high land and could see how like one another the shapes of the clouds and the hills were as they stretched off toward the sea. The prisoner arrived sitting on a three-legged stool in a farm cart. She stood by the cart while the mayor read the accusation and the sentence. Her head was bent and her face was set in that empty half smile behind which the whipped soul is suspended. When the mayor was finished, she undid her hair and let it fall across her back. A little man with a gray mustache cut off her hair with shears and dropped it on the ground. Then, with a bowl of soapy water and a straight razor, he shaved her skull clean. A woman approached and began to undo the fastenings of her clothes, but the prisoner pushed her aside and undressed herself. When she pulled her chemise over her head and threw it on the ground, she was naked. The women jeered; the men were still. There was no change in the falseness or the plaintiveness of the prisoner's smile. The cold wind made her white skin rough and hardened the nipples of her breasts. The jeering ended gradually, put down by the recognition of their common humanity. One woman spat on her, but some inviolable grandeur in her nakedness lasted through the ordeal. When the crowd was quiet, she turned—she had begun to cry—and, with nothing on but a pair of worn black shoes and stockings, walked down the dirt road alone away from the village. The round white face had aged a little, but there was no question but that the maid who passed his cocktails and later served Francis his dinner was the woman who had been punished at the crossroads.

The war seemed now so distant and that world where the cost of partisanship had been death or torture so long ago. Francis had lost track of the men who had been with him in Vésey. He could not count on Julia's discretion. He could not tell anyone. And if he had told the story now, at the dinner table, it would have been a social as well as a human error. The people in the Farquarsons' living room seemed united in their tacit claim that there had been no past, no war—that there was no danger or trouble in the world. In the recorded history of human arrangements, this extraordinary meeting would have fallen into place, but the atmosphere of Shady Hill made the memory unseemly and impolite. The prisoner withdrew after passing the coffee, but the encounter left Francis feeling languid; it had opened his memory and his senses, and left them dilated. He and Julia drove home when the party ended, and Julia went into the house. Francis stayed in the car to take the sitter home.

Expecting to see Mrs. Henlein, the old lady who usually stayed with the children, he was surprised when a young girl opened the door and came out onto the lighted stoop. She stayed in the light to count her textbooks. She was frowning and beautiful. Now, the world is full of beautiful young girls, but Francis saw here the difference between beauty and perfection. All those endearing flaws, moles, birthmarks, and healed wounds were missing, and he experienced in his consciousness that moment when music breaks glass, and felt a pang of recognition as strange, deep, and wonderful as anything in his life. It hung from her frown, from an impalpable darkness in her face—a look that impressed him as a direct appeal for love. When she had counted her books, she came down the steps and opened the car door. In the light, he saw that her cheeks were wet. She got in and shut the door.

"You're new," Francis said.

"Yes. Mrs. Henlein is sick. I'm Anne Murchison."

"Did the children give you any trouble?"

"Oh, no, no." She turned and smiled at him unhappily in the dim dashboard light. Her light hair caught on the collar of her jacket, and she shook her head to set it loose.

"You've been crying."

"Yes."

"I hope it was nothing that happened in our house."

"No, no, it was nothing that happened in your house." Her voice was bleak. "It's no secret. Everybody in the village knows. Daddy's an alcoholic, and he just called me from some saloon and gave me a piece of his mind. He thinks I'm immoral. He called just before Mrs. Weed came back."

"I'm sorry."

"Oh, *Lord!*" She gasped and began to cry. She turned toward Francis, and he took her in his arms and let her cry on his shoulder. She shook in his embrace, and this movement accentuated his sense of the fineness of her flesh and bone. The layers of their clothing felt thin, and when her shuddering began to diminish, it was so much like a paroxysm of love that Francis lost his head and pulled her roughly against him. She drew away. "I live on Belleview Avenue," she said. "You go down Lansing Street to the railroad bridge."

"All right." He started the car.

"You turn left at that traffic light. . . . Now you turn right here and go straight on toward the tracks."

The road Francis took brought him out of his own neighborhood, across the tracks, and toward the river, to a street where the near-poor lived, in houses whose peaked gables and trimmings of wooden lace conveyed the purest feelings of pride and romance, although the houses themselves could not have offered much privacy or comfort, they were all so small. The street was dark, and, stirred by the grace and beauty of the troubled girl, he seemed, in turning in to it, to have come into the deepest part of some submerged memory. In the distance, he saw a porch light burning. It was the only one, and she said that the house with the light was where she lived. When he stopped the car, he could see beyond the porch light into a dimly lighted hallway with an old-fashioned clothes tree. "Well, here we are," he said, conscious that a young man would have said something different.

She did not move her hands from the books, where they were folded, and she turned and faced him. There were tears of lust in his eyes. Determinedly—not sadly—he opened the door on his side and walked around to open hers. He took her free hand, letting his fingers in between hers, climbed at her side the two concrete steps, and went up a narrow walk through a front garden where dahlias, marigolds, and roses—things that had withstood the light frosts—still bloomed, and made a bittersweet smell in the night air. At the steps, she freed her hand and then turned and kissed him swiftly. Then she crossed the porch and shut the door. The porch light went out, then the light in the hall. A second later, a light went on upstairs at the side of the house, shining into a tree that was still covered with leaves. It took her only a few minutes to undress and get into bed, and then the house was dark.

Julia was asleep when Francis got home. He opened a second window and got into bed to shut his eyes on that night, but as soon as they were shut—as soon as he had dropped off to sleep—the girl entered his mind, moving with perfect freedom through its shut doors and filling chamber after chamber with her light, her perfume, and the music of her voice. He was crossing the Atlantic with her on the old *Mauretania*[1] and, later, living with her in Paris. When he woke from his dream, he got up and smoked a cigarette at the open window. Getting back into bed, he cast around in his mind for something he desired to do that would injure no one, and he thought of skiing. Up through the dimness in his mind rose the image of a mountain deep in snow. It was late in the day. Wherever his eyes looked, he saw broad and heartening things. Over his shoulder, there was a snow-filled valley, rising into wooded hills where the trees dimmed the whiteness like a sparse coat of hair. The cold deadened all sound but the loud, iron clanking of the lift machinery. The light on the trails was blue, and it was harder than it had been a minute or two earlier to pick the turns, harder to judge—now that the snow was all deep blue—the crust, the ice, the bare spots, and the deep piles of dry powder. Down the mountain he swung, matching his speed against the contours of a slope that had been formed in the first ice age, seeking with ardor some simplicity of feeling and circumstance. Night fell then, and he drank a Martini with some old friend in a dirty country bar.

In the morning, Francis' snow-covered mountain was gone, and he was left with his vivid memories of Paris and the *Mauretania*. He had been bitten gravely. He washed his body, shaved his jaws, drank his coffee, and missed the seven-thirty-one. The train pulled out just as he brought his car to the station, and the longing he felt for the coaches as they drew stubbornly away from him reminded him of the humors of love. He waited for the eight-two, on what was now an empty platform. It was a clear morning; the morning seemed thrown like a gleaming bridge of light over his mixed affairs. His spirits were feverish and high. The image of the girl seemed to put him into a relationship to the world that was mysterious and enthralling. Cars were beginning to fill up the parking lot, and he noticed that those that had driven down from the high land above Shady Hill were white with hoarfrost. This first clear sign of autumn thrilled him. An express train—a night train from Buffalo or Albany—came down the tracks between the platforms, and he saw that the roofs of the foremost cars were covered with a skin of ice. Struck by the miraculous physicalness of everything, he smiled at the passengers in the dining car, who could be seen eating eggs and wiping their mouths with napkins as they traveled. The sleeping-car compartments, with their soiled bed linen, trailed through the fresh morning like a string of rooming-house windows. Then he saw an extraordinary thing; at one of the bedroom windows sat an unclothed woman of exceptional beauty, combining her golden hair. She passed like an apparition through Shady Hill, combing and combing her hair, and Francis followed her with his eyes until she was out of sight. Then old Mrs. Wrightson joined him on the platform and began to talk.

"Well, I guess you must be surprised to see me here the third morning in a row," she said, "but because of my window curtains I'm becoming a regular commuter. The curtains I bought on Monday I

1. The original *Mauretania* (1907–1935), sister ship of the *Lusitania*, which was sunk by the Germans in 1915, was the most famous transatlantic liner of its day and held speed records for more than 20 years.

returned on Tuesday, and the curtains I bought Tuesday I'm returning today. On Monday, I got exactly what I wanted—it's a wool tapestry with roses and birds—but when I got them home, I found they were the wrong length. Well, I exchanged them yesterday, and when I got them home, I found they were still the wrong length. Now I'm praying to high Heaven that the decorator will have them in the right length, because you know my house, you *know* my living-room windows, and you can imagine what a problem they present. I don't know what to do with them."

"I know what to do with them," Francis said.

"What?"

"Paint them black on the inside, and shut up."

There was a gasp from Mrs. Wrightson, and Francis looked down at her to be sure that she knew he meant to be rude. She turned and walked away from him, so damaged in spirit that she limped. A wonderful feeling enveloped him, as if light were being shaken about him, and he thought again of Venus combing and combing her hair as she drifted through the Bronx. The realization of how many years had passed since he had enjoyed being deliberately impolite sobered him. Among his friends and neighbors, there were brilliant and gifted people—he saw that—but many of them, also, were bores and fools, and he had made the mistake of listening to them all with equal attention. He had confused a lack of discrimination with Christian love, and the confusion seemed general and destructive. He was grateful to the girl for this bracing sensation of independence. Birds were singing—cardinals and the last of the robins. The sky shone like enamel. Even the smell of ink from his morning paper honed his appetite for life, and the world that was spread out around him was plainly a paradise.

If Francis had believed in some hierarchy of love—in spirits armed with hunting bows, in the capriciousness of Venus and Eros[2]—or even in magical potions, philters, and stews, in scapulae and quarters of the moon,[3] it might have explained his susceptibility and his feverish high spirits. The autumnal loves of middle age are well publicized, and he guessed that he was face to face with one of these, but there was not a trace of autumn in what he felt. He wanted to sport in the green woods, scratch where he itched, and drink from the same cup.

His secretary, Miss Rainey, was late that morning—she went to a psychiatrist three mornings a week—and when she came in, Francis wondered what advice a psychiatrist would have for him. But the girl promised to bring back into his life something like the sound of music. The realization that this music might lead him straight to a trial for statutory rape[4] at the county courthouse collapsed his happiness. The photograph of his four children laughing into the camera on the beach at Gay Head reproached him. On the letterhead of his firm there was a drawing of the Laocoön[5] and the figure of the priest and his sons in

2. The Roman name for the goddess of love (Greek Aphrodite) and the Greek name for her son (Roman Cupid).

3. Love-inducing and predictive magic; *scapulae* are shoulderblades or bones of the back.

4. Criminal charge involving sexual relations with someone below the legal age of consent.

5. Famous Greek statue, described here, now in the Vatican museum; the "meaning" for Weed seems to reside in the physical struggle, not in the legend (in which the priest and his sons were punished for warning the Trojans about the wooden horse).

the coils of the snake appeared to him to have the deepest meaning.

He had lunch with Pinky Trabert. At a conversational level, the mores of his friends were robust and elastic, but he knew that the moral card house would come down on them all—on Julia and the children as well—if he got caught taking advantage of a babysitter. Looking back over the recent history of Shady Hill for some precedent, he found there was none. There was no turpitude; there had not been a divorce since he lived there; there had not even been a breath of scandal. Things seemed arranged with more propriety even than in the Kingdom of Heaven. After leaving Pinky, Francis went to a jeweler's and bought the girl a bracelet. How happy this clandestine purchase made him, how stuffy and comical the jeweler's clerks seemed, how sweet the women who passed at his back smelled! On Fifth Avenue, passing Atlas with his shoulders bent under the weight of the world,[6] Francis thought of the strenuousness of containing his physicalness within the patterns he had chosen.

He did not know when he would see the girl next. He had the bracelet in his inside pocket when he got home. Opening the door of his house, he found her in the hall. Her back was to him, and she turned when she heard the door close. Her smile was open and loving. Her perfection stunned him like a fine day—a day after a thunderstorm. He seized her and covered her lips with his, and she struggled but she did not have to struggle for long, because just then little Gertrude Flannery appeared from somewhere and said, "Oh, Mr. Weed . . ."

Gertrude was a stray. She had been born with a taste for exploration, and she did not have it in her to center her life with her affectionate parents. People who did not know the Flannerys concluded from Gertrude's behavior that she was the child of a bitterly divided family, where drunken quarrels were the rule. This was not true. The fact that little Gertrude's clothing was ragged and thin was her own triumph over her mother's struggle to dress her warmly and neatly. Garrulous, skinny, and unwashed, she drifted from house to house around the Blenhollow neighborhood, forming and breaking alliances based on an attachment to babies, animals, children her own age, adolescents, and sometimes adults. Opening your front door in the morning, you would find Gertrude sitting on your stoop. Going into the bathroom to shave, you would find Gertrude using the toilet. Looking into your son's crib, you would find it empty, and, looking further, you would find that Gertrude had pushed him in his baby carriage into the next village. She was helpful, pervasive, honest, hungry, and loyal. She never went home of her own choice. When the time to go arrived, she was indifferent to all its signs: "Go home, Gertrude," people could be heard saying in one house or another, night after night. "Go home, Gertrude. It's time for you to go home now, Gertrude." "You had better go home and get your supper, Gertrude." "I told you to go home twenty minutes ago, Gertrude." "Your mother will be worrying about you, Gertrude." "Go home, Gertude, go home."

There are times when the lines around the human eye seem like shelves of eroded stone and when the staring eye itself strikes us with

6. In Greek legend the Titan Atlas supported the heavens on his shoulders but has come to be depicted as bearing the globe; the statue is at Rockefeller Center.

such a wilderness of animal feeling that we are at a loss. The look Francis gave the little girl was ugly and queer, and it frightened her. He reached into his pocket—his hands were shaking—and took out a quarter. "Go home, Gertrude, go home, and don't tell anyone, Gertrude. Don't—" He choked and ran into the living room as Julia called down to him from upstairs to hurry and dress.

The thought that he would drive Anne Murchison home later that night ran like a golden thread through the events of the party that Francis and Julia went to, and he laughed uproariously at dull jokes, dried a tear when Mabel Mercer told him about the death of her kitten, and stretched, yawned, sighed, and grunted like any other man with a rendezvous at the back of his mind. The bracelet was in his pocket. As he sat talking, the smell of grass was in his nose, and he was wondering where he would park the car. Nobody lived in the old Parker mansion, and the driveway was used as a lovers' lane. Townsend Street was a dead end, and he could park there, beyond the last house. The old lane that used to connect Elm Street to the riverbanks was overgrown, but he had walked there with his children, and he could drive his car deep enough into the brushwoods to be concealed.

The Weeds were the last to leave the party, and their host and hostess spoke of their own married happiness while they all four stood in the hallway saying good night. "She's my girl," their host said, squeezing his wife. "She's my blue sky. After sixteen years, I still bite her shoulders. She makes me feel like Hannibal crossing the Alps."[7]

The Weeds drove home in silence. Francis brought the car up the driveway and sat still, with the motor running. "You can put the car in the garage," Julia said as she got out. "I told the Murchison girl she could leave at eleven. Someone drove her home." She shut the door, and Francis sat in the dark. He would be spared nothing then, it seemed, that a fool was not spared: ravening lewdness, jealousy, this hurt to his feelings that put tears in his eyes, even scorn—for he could see clearly the image he now presented, his arms spread over the steering wheel and his head buried in them for love.

Francis had been a dedicated Boy Scout when he was young, and, remembering the precepts of his youth, he left his office early the next afternoon and played some round-robin squash, but, with his body toned up by exercise and a shower, he realized that he might better have stayed at his desk. It was a frosty night when he got home. The air smelled sharply of change. When he stepped into the house, he sensed an unusual stir. The children were in their best clothes, and when Julia came down, she was wearing a lavender dress and her diamond sunburst. She explained the stir: Mr. Hubber was coming at seven to take their photograph for the Christmas card. She had put out Francis' blue suit and a tie with some color in it, because the picture was going to be in color this year. Julia was lighthearted at the thought of being photographed for Christmas. It was the kind of ceremony she enjoyed.

Francis went upstairs to change his clothes. He was tired from the

7. The Carthaginian general (274–183 B.C.) attacked the Romans from the rear by crossing the Alps, considered impregnable, with the use of elephants.

day's work and tired with longing, and sitting on the edge of the bed had the effect of deepening his weariness. He thought of Anne Murchison, and the physical need to express himself, instead of being restrained by the pink lamps on Julia's dressing table, engulfed him. He went to Julia's desk, took a piece of writing paper, and began to write on it. "Dear Anne, I love you, I love you, I love you . . ." No one would see the letter, and he used no restraint. He used phrases like "heavenly bliss," and "love nest." He salivated, sighed, and trembled. When Julia called him to come down, the abyss between his fantasy and the practical world opened so wide that he felt it affect the muscles of his heart.

Julia and the children were on the stoop, and the photographer and his assistant had set up a double battery of floodlights to show the family and the architectural beauty of the entrance to their house. People who had come home on a late train slowed their cars to see the Weeds being photographed for their Christmas card. A few waved and called to the family. It took half an hour of smiling and wetting their lips before Mr. Hubber was satisfied. The heat of the lights made an unfresh smell in the frosty air, and when they were turned off, they lingered on the retina of Francis' eyes.

Later that night, while Francis and Julia were drinking their coffee in the living room, the doorbell rang. Julia answered the door and let in Clayton Thomas. He had come to pay her for some theater tickets that she had given his mother some time ago, and that Helen Thomas had scrupulously insisted on paying for, though Julia had asked her not to. Julia invited him in to have a cup of coffee. "I won't have any coffee," Clayton said, "but I will come in for a minute." He followed her into the living room, said good evening to Francis, and sat awkwardly in a chair.

Clayton's father had been killed in the war, and the young man's fatherlessness surrounded him like an element. This may have been conspicuous in Shady Hill because the Thomases were the only family that lacked a piece; all the other marriages were intact and productive. Clayton was in his second or third year of college, and he and his mother lived alone in a large house, which she hoped to sell. Clayton had once made some trouble. Years ago, he had stolen some money and run away; he had got to California before they caught up with him. He was tall and homely, wore horn-rimmed glasses, and spoke in a deep voice.

"When do you go back to college, Clayton?" Francis asked.

"I'm not going back," Clayton said. "Mother doesn't have the money, and there's no sense in all this pretense. I'm going to get a job, and if we sell the house, we'll take an apartment in New York."

"Won't you miss Shady Hill?" Julia asked.

"No," Clayton said. "I don't like it."

"Why not?" Francis asked.

"Well, there's a lot here I don't approve of," Clayton said gravely. "Things like the club dances. Last Saturday night, I looked in toward the end and saw Mr. Granner trying to put Mrs. Minot into the trophy case. They were both drunk. I disapprove of so much drinking."

"It was Saturday night," Francis said.

"And all the dovecotes are phony," Clayton said. "And the way people clutter up their lives. I've thought about it a lot, and what seems to me to be really wrong with Shady Hill is that it doesn't have any future. So much energy is spent in perpetuating the place—in keeping out undesirables, and so forth—that the only idea of the future anyone has is just more and more commuting trains and more parties. I don't think that's healthy. I think people ought to be able to dream big dreams about the future. I think people ought to be able to dream great dreams."

"It's too bad you couldn't continue with college," Julia said.

"I wanted to go to divinity school," Clayton said.

"What's your church?" Francis asked.

"Unitarian, Theosophist, Transcendentalist, Humanist,"[8] Clayton said.

"Wasn't Emerson a transcendentalist?" Julia asked.

"I mean the English transcendentalists," Clayton said. "All the American transcendentalists were goops."

"What kind of a job do you expect to get?" Francis asked.

"Well, I'd like to work for a publisher," Clayton said, "but everyone tells me there's nothing doing. But it's the kind of thing I'm interested in. I'm writing a long verse play about good and evil. Uncle Charlie might get me into a bank, and that would be good for me. I need the discipline. I have a long way to go in forming my character. I have some terrible habits. I talk too much. I think I ought to take vows of silence. I ought to try not to speak for a week, and discipline myself. I've thought of making a retreat at one of the Episcopalian monasteries, but I don't like the Trinitarianism."

"Do you have any girl friends?" Francis asked.

"I'm engaged to be married," Clayton said. "Of course, I'm not old enough or rich enough to have my engagement observed or respected or anything, but I bought a simulated emerald for Anne Murchison with the money I made cutting lawns this summer. We're going to be married as soon as she finishes school."

Francis recoiled at the mention of the girl's name. Then a dingy light seemed to emanate from his spirit, showing everything—Julia, the boy, the chairs—in their true colorlessness. It was like a bitter turn of the weather.

"We're going to have a large family," Clayton said. "Her father's a terrible rummy, and I've had my hard times, and we want to have lots of children. Oh, she's wonderful, Mr. and Mrs. Weed, and we have so much in common. We like all the same things. We sent out the same Christmas card last year without planning it, and we both have an allergy to tomatoes, and our eyebrows grow together in the middle. Well, good night."

Julia went to the door with him. When she returned, Francis said that Clayton was lazy, irresponsible, affected, and smelly. Julia said that Francis seemed to be getting intolerant; the Thomas boy was young and should be given a chance. Julia had noticed other cases where Francis had been short-tempered. "Mrs. Wrightson has asked

8. All are deviations from orthodox Christianity and tend to be more man- than God-oriented, though their differences hardly seem reconcilable; the American Transcendentalists (see below) tended to change the emphasis from the study of thought rather than of sense objects among the English Transcendentalists to belief in "intuition."

everyone in Shady Hill to her anniversary party but us," she said.

"I'm sorry, Julia."

"Do you know why they didn't ask us?"

"Why?"

"Because you insulted Mrs. Wrightson."

"Then you know about it?"

"June Masterson told me. She was standing behind you."

Julia walked in front of the sofa with a small step that expressed, Francis knew, a feeling of anger.

"I did insult Mrs. Wrightson, Julia, and I meant to. I've never liked her parties, and I'm glad she's dropped us."

"What about Helen?"

"How does Helen come into this?"

"Mrs. Wrightson's the one who decides who goes to the assemblies."

"You mean she can keep Helen from going to the dances?"

"Yes."

"I hadn't thought of that."

"Oh, I knew you hadn't thought of it," Julia cried, thrusting hilt-deep into this chink of his armor. "And it makes me furious to see this kind of stupid thoughtlessness wreck everyone's happiness."

"I don't think I've wrecked anyone's happiness."

"Mrs. Wrightson runs Shady Hill and has run it for the last forty years. I don't know what makes you think that in a community like this you can indulge every impulse you have to be insulting, vulgar, and offensive."

"I have very good manners," Francis said, trying to give the evening a turn toward the light.

"Damn you, Francis Weed!" Julia cried, and the spit of her words struck him in the face. "I've worked hard for the social position we enjoy in this place, and I won't stand by and see you wreck it. You must have understood when you settled here that you couldn't expect to live like a bear in a cave."

"I've got to express my likes and dislikes."

"You can conceal your dislikes. You don't have to meet everything head-on, like a child. Unless you're anxious to be a social leper. It's no accident that we get asked out a great deal. It's no accident that Helen has so many friends. How would you like to spend your Saturday nights at the movies? How would you like to spend your Sundays raking up dead leaves? How would you like it if your daughter spent the assembly nights sitting at her window, listening to the music from the club? How would you like it—" He did something then that was, after all, not so unaccountable, since her words seemed to raise up between them a wall so deadening that he gagged: He struck her full in the face. She staggered and then, a moment later, seemed composed. She went up the stairs to their room. She didn't slam the door. When Francis followed, a few minutes later, he found her packing a suitcase.

"Julia, I'm very sorry."

"It doesn't matter," she said. She was crying.

"Where do you think you're going?"

"I don't know. I just looked at a timetable. There's an eleven-sixteen into New York. I'll take that."

"You can't go, Julia."

"I can't stay. I know that."

"I'm sorry about Mrs. Wrightson, Julia, and I'm—"

"It doesn't matter about Mrs. Wrightson. That isn't the trouble."

"What is the trouble?"

"You don't love me."

"I do love you, Julia."

"No, you don't."

"Julia, I do love you, and I would like to be as we were—sweet and bawdy and dark—but now there are so many people."

"You hate me."

"I don't hate you, Julia."

"You have no idea of how much you hate me. I think it's subconscious. You don't realize the cruel things you've done."

"What cruel things, Julia?"

"The cruel acts your subconscious drives you to in order to express your hatred of me."

"What, Julia?"

"I've never complained."

"Tell me."

"You don't know what you're doing."

"Tell me."

"Your clothes."

"What do you mean?"

"I mean the way you leave your dirty clothes around in order to express your subconscious hatred of me."

"I don't understand."

"I mean your dirty socks and your dirty pajamas and your dirty underwear and your dirty shirts!" She rose from kneeling by the suitcase and faced him, her eyes blazing and her voice ringing with emotion. "I'm talking about the fact that you've never learned to hang up anything. You just leave your clothes all over the floor where they drop, in order to humiliate me. You do it on purpose!" She fell on the bed, sobbing.

"Julia, darling!" he said, but when she felt his hand on her shoulder she got up.

"Leave me alone," she said. "I have to go." She brushed past him to the closet and came back with a dress. "I'm not taking any of the things you've given me," she said. "I'm leaving my pearls and the fur jacket."

"Oh, Julia!" Her figure, so helpless in its self-deceptions, bent over the suitcase made him nearly sick with pity. She did not understand how desolate her life would be without him. She didn't understand the hours that working women have to keep. She didn't understand that most of her friendships existed within the framework of their marriage, and that without this she would find herself alone. She didn't understand about travel, about hotels, about money. "Julia, I can't let you go! What you don't understand, Julia, is that you've come to be dependent on me."

She tossed her head back and covered her face with her hands. "Did you say that *I* was dependent on *you?*" she asked. "Is that what you said? And who is it that tells you what time to get up in the morning and when to go to bed at night? Who is it that prepares your meals and picks up your dirty clothes and invites your friends to dinner? If it weren't for me, your neckties would be greasy and your clothing would be full of moth holes. You were alone when I met you, Francis Weed, and you'll be alone when I leave. When Mother asked you for a list to send out invitations to our wedding, how many names did you have to give her? Fourteen!"

"Cleveland wasn't my home, Julia."

"And how many of your friends came to the church? Two!"

"Cleveland wasn't my home, Julia."

"Since I'm not taking the fur jacket," she said quietly, "you'd better put it back into storage. There's an insurance policy on the pearls that comes due in January. The name of the laundry and the maid's telephone number—all those things are in my desk. I hope you won't drink too much, Francis. I hope that nothing bad will happen to you. If you do get into serious trouble, you can call me."

"Oh, my darling, I can't let you go!" Francis said. "I can't let you go, Julia!" He took her in his arms.

"I guess I'd better stay and take care of you for a little while longer," she said.

Riding to work in the morning, Francis saw the girl walk down the aisle of the coach. He was surprised; he hadn't realized that the school she went to was in the city, but she was carrying books, she seemed to be going to school. His surprise delayed his reaction, but then he got up clumsily and stepped into the aisle. Several people had come between them, but he could see her ahead of him, waiting for someone to open the car door, and then, as the train swerved, putting out her hand to support herself as she crossed the platform into the next car. He followed her through that car and halfway through another before calling her name—"Anne! Anne!"—but she didn't turn. He followed her into still another car, and she sat down in an aisle seat. Coming up to her, all his feelings warm and bent in her direction, he put his hand on the back of her seat—even this touch warmed him—and, leaning down to speak to her, he saw that it was not Anne. It was an older woman wearing glasses. He went on deliberately into another car, his face red with embarrassment and the much deeper feeling of having his good sense challenged; for if he couldn't tell one person from another, what evidence was there that his life with Julia and the children had as much reality as his dreams of iniquity in Paris or the litter, the grass smell, and the cave-shaped trees in Lovers' Lane.

Late that afternoon, Julia called to remind Francis that they were going out for dinner. A few minutes later, Trace Bearden called. "Look, fellar," Trace said. "I'm calling for Mrs. Thomas. You know? Clayton, that boy of hers, doesn't seem able to get a job, and I wondered if you could help. If you'd call Charlie Bell—I know he's indebted to you—and say a good word for the kid, I think Charlie would—"

"Trace, I hate to say this," Francis said, "but I don't feel that I can do anything for that boy. The kid's worthless. I know it's a harsh thing to say, but it's a fact. Any kindness done for him would backfire in everybody's face. He's just a worthless kid, Trace, and there's nothing to be done about it. Even if we got him a job, he wouldn't be able to keep it for a week. I know that to be a fact. It's an awful thing, Trace, and I know it is, but instead of recommending that kid, I'd feel obliged to warn people against him—people who knew his father and would naturally want to step in and do something. I'd feel obliged to warn them. He's a thief . . ."

The moment this conversation was finished. Miss Rainey came in and stood by his desk. "I'm not going to be able to work for you any more, Mr. Weed," she said. "I can stay until the seventeenth if you need me, but I've been offered a whirlwind of a job, and I'd like to leave as soon as possible."

She went out, leaving him to face alone the wickedness of what he had done to the Thomas boy. His children in their photograph laughed and laughed, glazed with all the bright colors of summer, and he remembered that they had met a bagpiper on the beach that day and he had paid the piper a dollar to play them a battle song of the Black Watch.[9] The girl would be at the house when he got home. He would spend another evening among his kind neighbors, picking and choosing dead-end streets, cart tracks, and the driveways of abandoned houses. There was nothing to mitigate his feeling—nothing that laughter or a game of softball with the children would change—and, thinking back over the plane crash, the Farquarsons' new maid, and Anne Murchison's difficulties with her drunken father, he wondered how he could have avoided arriving at just where he was. He was in trouble. He had been lost once in his life, coming back from a trout stream in the north woods, and he had now the same bleak realization that no amount of cheerfulness or hopefulness or valor or perseverance could help him find, in the gathering dark, the path that he'd lost. He smelled the forest. The feeling of bleakness was intolerable, and he saw clearly that he had reached the point where he would have to make a choice.

He could go to a psychiatrist, like Miss Rainey; he could go to church and confess his lusts; he could go to a Danish massage parlor[1] in the West Seventies that had been recommended by a salesman; he could rape the girl or trust that he would somehow be prevented from doing this; or he could get drunk. It was his life, his boat, and, like every other man, he was made to be the father of thousands, and what harm could there be in a tryst that would make them both feel more kindly toward the world? This was the wrong train of thought, and he came back to the first, the psychiatrist. He had the telephone number of Miss Rainey's doctor, and he called and asked for an immediate appointment. He was insistent with the doctor's secretary—it was his manner in business—and when she said that the doctor's schedule was full for the next few weeks, Francis demanded an appointment that day and was told to come at five.

The psychiatrist's office was in a building that was used mostly by doctors and dentists, and the hallways were filled with the candy smell of mouthwash and memories of pain. Francis' character had been formed upon a series of private resolves—resolves about cleanliness, about going off the high diving board or repeating any other feat that

9. Originally a British Highland regiment that became a line regiment and distinguished itself in battle, including World War II battles.

1. Sometimes "fronts" for houses of prostitution.

challenged his courage, about punctuality, honesty, and virtue. To abdicate the perfect loneliness in which he had made his most vital decisions shattered his concept of character and left him now in a condition that felt like shock. He was stupefied. The scene for his *miserere mei Deus*[2] was, like the waiting room of so many doctors' offices, a crude token gesture toward the sweets of domestic bliss: a place arranged with antiques, coffee tables, potted plants, and etchings of snow-covered bridges and geese in flight, although there were no children, no marriage bed, no stove, even, in this travesty of a house, where no one had ever spent the night and where the curtained windows looked straight onto a dark air shaft. Francis gave his name and address to a secretary and then saw, at the side of the room, a policeman moving toward him. "Hold it, hold it," the policeman said. "Don't move. Keep your hands where they are."

"I think it's all right, officer," the secretary began. "I think it will be—"

"Let's make sure," the policeman said, and he began to slap Francis' clothes, looking for what—pistols, knives, an icepick? Finding nothing, he went off, and the secretary began a nervous apology: "When you called on the telephone, Mr. Weed, you seemed very excited, and one of the doctor's patients has been threatening his life, and we have to be careful. If you want to go in now?" Francis pushed open a door connected to an electrical chime, and in the doctor's lair sat down heavily, blew his nose into a handkerchief, searched in his pockets for cigarettes, for matches, for something, and said hoarsely, with tears in his eyes, "I'm in love, Dr. Herzog."

It is a week or ten days later in Shady Hill. The seven-fourteen has come and gone, and here and there dinner is finished and the dishes are in the dish-washing machine. The village hangs, morally and economically, from a thread; but it hangs by its thread in the evening light. Donald Goslin has begun to worry the "Moonlight Sonata" again. *Marcato ma sempre pianissimo!*[3] He seems to be wringing out a wet bath towel, but the housemaid does not heed him. She is writing a letter to Arthur Godfrey.[4] In the cellar of his house, Francis Weed is building a coffee table. Dr. Herzog recommended woodwork as a therapy, and Francis finds some true consolation in the simple arithmetic involved and in the holy smell of new wood. Francis is happy. Upstairs, little Toby is crying, because he is tired. He puts off his cowboy hat, gloves, and fringed jacket, unbuckles the belt studded with gold and rubies, the silver bullets and holsters, slips off his suspenders, his checked shirt, and Levis, and sits on the edge of his bed to pull off his high boots. Leaving this equipment in a heap, he goes to the closet and takes his space suit off a nail. It is a struggle for him to get into the long tights, but he succeeds. He loops the magic cape over his shoulders and, climbing onto the footboard of his bed, he spreads his arms and flies the short distance to the floor, landing with a thump that is audible to everyone in the house but himself.

"Go home, Gertrude, go home," Mrs. Masterson says. "I told you to

2. "Have mercy upon me, O God"; first words of 51st Psalm.
3. Stressed but still very softly.
4. At the time of the story, host of a daytime radio program especially popular with housewives.

go home an hour ago, Gertrude. It's way past your suppertime, and your mother will be worried. Go home!" A door on the Babcocks' terrace flies open, and out comes Mrs. Babcock without any clothes on, pursued by her naked husband. (Their children are away at boarding school, and their terrace is screened by a hedge.) Over the terrace they go and in at the kitchen door, as passionate and handsome a nymph and satyr[5] as you will find on any wall in Venice. Cutting the last of the roses in her garden, Julia hears old Mr. Nixon shouting at the squirrels in his bird-feeding station. "Rapscallions! Varmints! Avaunt and quit my sight!" A miserable cat wanders into the garden, sunk in spiritual and physical discomfort. Tied to its head is a small straw hat—a doll's hat—and it is securely buttoned into a doll's dress, from the skirts of which protrudes its long, hairy tail. As it walks, it shakes its feet, as if it had fallen into water.

"Here, pussy, pussy, pussy!" Julia calls.

"Here, pussy, here, poor pussy!" But the cat gives her a skeptical look and stumbles away in its skirts. The last to come is Jupiter. He prances through the tomato vines, holding in his generous mouth the remains of an evening slipper. Then it is dark; it is a night where kings in golden suits ride elephants over the mountains.

1958

ALBERT MURRAY

Train Whistle Guitar

Lil' Buddy's color was that sky blue in which hens cackled; it was that smoke blue in which dogs barked and mosquito hawks lit on barbed-wire fences. It was the color above meadows. It was my color too because it was a boy's color. It was whistling blue and hunting blue, and it went with baseball, and that was old Lil' Buddy again, and that blue beyond outfields was exactly what we were singing about when we used to sing that old one about it ain't gonna rain no more no more.[1]

Steel blue was a man's color. That was the clean, oil-smelling color of rifle barrels and railroad iron. That was the color that went with Luzana Cholly, and he had a steel-blue 32–20 on a 44 frame.[2] His complexion was not steel blue but leather brown like dark rawhide, but steel blue was the color that went with what he was. His hands were just like rawhide, and when he was not dressed up he smelled like green oak steam. He had on slick starched blue denim overalls then, and when he was dressed up he wore a black broadcloth box-back coat with hickory-striped peg-top pants, and he smelled like the barber shop and new money.

Luzana Cholly was there in that time and place as far back as I can remember, even before Lil' Buddy was. Because I can remember

5. Minor nature goddesses and mythical woodland gods half man, half goat; the terms are often used to refer to beautiful young girls and to lecherous men.

1. Dance song with both mountaineer and Negro versions that moved west from Kentucky and other Southern states and dates at least from the 1870s: "It ain't gonna rain, it ain't gonna snow,/It ain't gonna rain no mo';/Come on ev'rybody now,/Ain't gonna rain no mo'."

2. A smaller caliber barrel (32–20) on a larger mounting, more common in 1920s.

when I didn't know Lil' Buddy at all. I can remember when that house they moved to was built (Lil' Buddy's papa and mama were still living together when they came to Gasoline Point from Choctaw County, which was near the Mississippi line), and I can also remember when that street (which was called Chattanooga Lookout Street) was pushed all the way through to the AT&N[3] cut. That was before I had ever even heard of Lil' Buddy, and my buddy then was old Willie Marlowe. Lil' Buddy didn't come until after Willie Marlowe had gone to Detroit, Michigan, and that was not until after Mister One-Arm Will had been dead and buried for about nine months.

I can remember him there in that wee time when I couldn't even follow the stories I knew later they were telling about him, when it was only just grown folks talking, and all I could make of it was *Luzana, they are talking something about old Luzana again, and I didn't know what, to say nothing of where Louisiana was.* But old Luze was there even then and I could see him very clearly when they said his name because I had already seen him coming up that road that came by that house with the chinaberry yard, coming from around the bend and down in the railroad bottom; and I had already heard whatever that was he was picking on his guitar and heard that holler too. That was always far away and long coming. It started low like it was going to be a song, and then it jumped all the way to the very top of his voice and broke off, and then it started again, and this time was already at the top, and then it gave some quick jerking squalls and died away in the woods, the water, and the darkness (you always heard it at night), and Mama always said he was whooping and hollering like somebody back in the rosin-woods country, and Papa said it was one of them old Luzana swamp hollers. I myself always thought it was like a train, like a bad train saying look out this is me, and here I come, and I'm coming through.

That was even before I was big enough to climb the chinaberry tree. That was when they used to talk about the war and the Kaiser,[4] and I can remember that there was a war book with Germans in it, and I used to see sure-enough soldiers marching in the Mardi Gras parades. Soldier Boy Crawford was still wearing his Army coat then, and he was the one who used to tell about how Luze used to play his guitar in France, telling about how they would be going through some French town like the ones called Nancy and Saint Die and old Luze would drop out of the company and go and play around in the underground wine shops until he got as much cognac and as many French Frogs[5] as he wanted and then he would turn up in the company again and Capt'n would put him out by himself on the worst outpost he could find in No Man's Land and old Luze would stay out there sometimes for three or four days and nights knocking off patrol after patrol, and one time in another place, which was the Hindenburg Line,[6] old Luze was out there again and there were a few shots late in the afternoon and then it was all quiet until about three o'clock the next morning and then all hell broke loose, and the Capt'n thought that a whole German battalion was about to move in, and he sent five patrols out to find out

3. Alabama, Tennessee, and Northern Railroad.

4. Wilhelm II (1859–1941), ruler of Germany during World War I, 1914–1918.

5. Derogatory term for French.

6. Strong defense line established by the Germans in 1916 and the scene of heavy fighting, especially in 1917.

what was happening, but when they got there all they found was old Luze all dug in and bristling with enough ammunition to blow up kingdom come; he had crawled around all during the afternoon collecting hand grenades and a mortar and two machine guns and even a light two-wheel cannon, and when they asked him what was going on he told them that he had fallen off to sleep and when he woke up he didn't know whether or not any Germans had snuck up so he thought he'd better lay himself down a little light barrage. The next morning they found out that old Luze had wiped out a whole German platoon but when the Capt'n sent for him to tell him he was going to give him a medal, old Luze had cut out and was off somewhere picking the guitar and drinking cognac and chasing the mademoiselles again. He went through the whole war like that and he came out of the Army without a single scratch, didn't even get flat feet.

I heard a lot of stories about the war and I used to draw pictures of them fighting with bayonets in the Argonne Forest,[7] and Soldier Boy Crawford used to look at them and shake his head and give me a nickel and say that some day I was going to be a soldier too.

I used to draw automobiles too, especially the Hudson Super-Six, like old Long George Nisby had; he said it would do sixty on a straightaway, and he had a heavy blasting cut-out on it that jarred the ground. Old Man Perc Stranahan had a Studebaker but he was a white man and he didn't have a cut-out, and he drove as slow as a hearse. Old Gander said Old Man Perc always drove like he was trying to sneak up on something but he never was going to catch it like that. The cars I didn't like then were the flat-engine Buick and the old humpbacked Hupmobile. I liked the Maxwell and the Willys Knight and the Pierce Arrow.

I was playing train then too, and the trains were there before the automobiles were (there were many more horses and buggies in that part of town than there were automobiles then). I couldn't sit up in my nest in the chinaberry tree and see the trains yet, because I could not climb it yet, but I saw them when Papa used to take me to the L&N[8] bottom to see them come by and I knew them all, and the Pan American was the fastest and Number Four was the fastest that ran in the daytime. Old Luzana could tell you all about the Southern Pacific and the Santa Fe, but that was later. But I already knew something about the Southern Pacific because Cousin Roberta had already gone all the way to Los Angeles, California, on the Sunset Limited.

I used to be in bed and hear the night trains coming by. The Crescent came by at nine-thirty and if you woke up way in the middle of the night you could hear Number Two. I was in my warm bed in that house, and I could hear the whistle coming even before it got to Chickasabogue Bridge and it had a bayou sound then, and then I could hear the engine batting it hell-for-leather on down the line bound for Mobile and New Orleans, and the next time the whistle came it was for Three Mile Creek. It was getting on into the beel[9] then. I played train by myself in the daytime then, looking out the window

7. Forest in northeast France near Belgian border where Allies, including Americans, launched an offensive, September–November 1918.

8. Louisville and Nashville Railroad.

9. *Beal,* mouth of creek or valley.

along the side of the house like an engineer looking down along the drivers.

I used to hear old Stagolee playing the piano over in Hot Water Shorty's jook[1] at night too, even then, especially on Saturday night. They rocked all night long, and I was lying in my warm quilted bed by the window. Uncle Jimmy's bed was by the window on the other side of the fireplace. When it was cold, you could wake up way in the night and still see the red embers in the ashes, and hear the wind whining outside, and sometimes you could hear the boat whistles too, and I could lie listening from where I was and tell you when it was a launch pulling a log raft or a tugboat pulling a barge or a riverboat like the *Nettie Queen*, and sometimes it was a big ship like the *Luchenback* called the Looking Back, which was all the way down at the city wharf at the foot of Government Street.

I knew a lot about the big ships because Uncle Jimmy worked on the wharf. That was before the state docks were built and the big Gulf-going and ocean-going ships didn't come on past Mobile then unless they were going up to Chickasaw to be overhauled, but I had already seen them and had been on ships from England and France and Holland and naturally there were always ships from the Caribbean and South America because that was where the fruit boats came from.

All I could do was see old Luzana Cholly and hear him coming. I didn't really know him then, but I knew that he was blue steel and that he was always going and coming and that he had the best walk in the world, because I had learned how to do that walk and was already doing the stew out of it[2] long before Lil' Buddy ever saw it. They were calling me Mister Man, and that was when somebody started calling me The Little Blister, because they said I was calling myself blister trying to say Mister. Aun Tee called me My Mister and Mama called me My Little Man, but she had to drop the little part off when Lil' Buddy came, and that was how everybody started calling me The Man, although I was still nothing but a boy, and I said to myself old Luzana is the man, old Luzana is the one I want to be like.

Then I was getting to be big enough to go everywhere by myself and I was going to school. That was when I knew about Dunkin's Hill and going up through Egerton Lane. That was the short way to school, because that was the way the bell sound came. Buddy Babe and Sister Babe and old double-jointed, ox-jawed Jack Johnson all went that way too, but when it rained you couldn't get across the bottom, and that was when everybody went the Shelton way, going through behind Stranahan's store and Good Hope Baptist to the old car line and then along that red clay road by the Hillside store.

Then Lil' Buddy was there and it was sky blue and we were blue hunters and every day was for whistling and going somewhere to do something you had to be rawhide to do, and some day we were going to live in times and places that were blue steel too. We found out a lot about old Luzana then, and then we not only knew him we knew how to talk to him.

The best time (except when he was just sitting somewhere strumming on his guitar) was when he was on his way to the Gambling

1. Roadhouse, juke-joint.

2. Doing it expertly.

Woods. (So far as anybody knew, gambling and guitar picking and grabbing freight trains were the only steady jobs he ever had or ever would have, except during the time he was in the Army and the times he was in jail—and he not only had been in jail, he had been in the penitentiary!) We were his good luck when he was headed for a skin game, and we always used to catch him late Saturday afternoon right out there where Gins Alley came into the oil-tank road, because he would be coming from Miss Pauline's cookshop then. The Gambling Woods trail started right out across from Sargin' Jeff's. Sometimes old Luze would have the guitar slung across his back even then, and naturally he had his famous 32-20 in the holster under his right arm.

"Say now hey Mister Luzana," I would holler at him.

"Mister Luzana Cholly one-time," Lil' Buddy always said, and he said that was what old Luze's swamp holler said too.

"Mister Luzana Cholly all night long," I would say then.

"Nobody else!" he would holler back at us then, "nobody else but."

"The one and only Mister Luzana Cholly from Booze Ana Bolly come Solly go Molly hit 'em with the fun folly."

"Talk to me, little ziggy,[3] talk to me."

"Got the world in a jug," I might say then.

"And the stopper in your hand,"[4] old Lil' Buddy would say.

"You tell 'em, little crust busters, 'cause I ain't got the heart."

"He's a man among men."

"And Lord God among women!"

"Well tell the dy ya,"[5] old Luze would say then, standing wide-legged, laughing, holding a wad of Brown's Mule chewing tobacco in with his tongue at the same time. Then he would skeet[6] a stream of amber juice to one side like a batter does when he steps up to the plate and then he would wipe the back of his leathery hand across his mouth and squint his eyes.

"Tell the dy-damn-ya!"

"Cain't tell no more," Lil' Buddy would say then, and old Luze would frown and wink at me.

"How come, little sooner,[7] how goddam come?"

" 'Cause money talks."

"Well shut my mouth and call me suitcase."

"Ain't nobody can do that."

"I knowed you could tell 'em little ziggabo, I knowed good and damn well you could tell 'em."

"But we ain't gonna tell 'em no more."

"We sure ain't."

"Talk ain't no good if you ain't got nothing to back it up with."

Old Luze would laugh again and we would stand waiting and then he would run his hands deep down into his pockets and come out with two quarters between his fingers. He would throw them into the air and catch them again, one in each hand, and then he would cross his hands and flip one to me and one to Lil' Buddy.

"Now talk," he would say then. "Now talk, but don't say too much

3. Prison slang variant of "jig," "jigaboo," derogatory name for a black.
4. The two lines of dialogue are a common blues line.
5. Possibly Gullah phrase with variants used in songs, e.g., "Kushie Dye-yo."
6. Squirt.
7. Mongrel or bastard.

and don't talk too loud, and handle your money like the white folks does."

We were going to be like him even before we were going to be like cowboys. And we knew that blue steel was also root hog or die poor,[8] which was what we were going to have to do whether we liked it or not. Lil' Buddy said it was not just how rough-and-ready old hard-cutting Luze was and how nobody, black or white, was going to do him any dirt and get away with it, and all that. It was that too, but it was also something else. It was also the way he could do whatever he was doing and make it look so easy that he didn't even seem to have to think about it, and once he did it, that seemed to be just about the only real way to do it.

Old Luze did everything his own way just like old Satch[9] played baseball his way. But we knew that we wanted to be like him for more reasons than that too. Somehow or other just as he always seemed to be thirty-five years old and blue steel because he had already been so many places and done so many things you'd never heard of before, he also always seemed to be absolutely alone and not needing anybody else, self-sufficient, independent, dead sure, and at the same time so unconcerned.

Mama said he was don't-carified, and that was it too (if you know the full meaning of the Negro meaning of that expression). He was living in blue steel and his way was don't-carified, because he was blue steel too. Lil' Buddy said hellfied, and he didn't mean hell-defying either, you couldn't say he was hell-defying all the time, and you couldn't say he went for bad either, not even when he was doing that holler he was so notorious for. That *was* hell-defying in a way, but it was really I don't give a damn if I *am* hell-defying, and he was not going for bad because he didn't need to, since everybody, black and white, who knew anything about him at all already knew that when he made a promise it meant if it's the last thing I do, if it's the last thing I do on this earth—and they knew that could mean I'll kill you and pay for you as much as it meant anything else. Because the idea of going to jail didn't scare him at all, and the idea of getting shot at didn't seem to scare him either. *Because all he ever said about that was if they shoot at me they sure better not miss me, they sure better get me the first time.*

He was a Negro who was an out and out Nigger in the very best meaning of the word as Negroes use it among themselves (who are the only ones who can), and nobody in that time and that place seemed to know what to make of him. White folks said he was crazy, but what they really meant or should have meant was that he was confusing to them, because if they knew him well enough to say he was crazy they also had to know enough about him to know that he wasn't even foolhardy, not even careless, not even what they wanted to mean by biggity. The funny thing, as I remember it now, was how their confusion made them respect him in spite of themselves. Somehow or other it was as if they respected him precisely because he didn't

8. Work hard or die poor.

9. Satchell Paige, famed, almost legendary Negro league baseball player who was already in his forties when the major leagues admitted Negroes.

care anything about them one way or the other. They certainly respected the fact that he wasn't going to take any foolishness off of them.

Negroes said he was crazy too, but they meant their own meaning. They did not know what to make of him, but when they said he was crazy they almost did, because when they said it they really meant something else. They were not talking so much about what he did, but how he was doing it. They were talking about something like poetic madness, and that was the way they had of saying that he was doing something unheard of, doing the hell out of it, and getting away with whatever it was. You could tell that was what they meant by the very way they said it, by the sound of it, and by the way they were shaking their heads and laughing when they said it.

The way he always operated as a lone wolf and the unconcerned-, not the Negro-ness as such, were the main things then. (Naturally Lil' Buddy and I knew about Negroes and white folks, and we knew that there was something generally wrong with white folks, but it didn't seem so very important then. We knew that if you hit a white boy he would turn red and call you nigger that did not sound like the Nigger the Negroes said and he would run and get as many other white boys as he could and come back at you, and we knew that a full-grown white had to get somebody to back him up too, but we didn't really think about it much, because there were so many other things we were doing then.)

Nobody ever said anything about old Luzana's papa and mama, and when you suddenly wondered about them you realized that he didn't seem to have or need any family at all, it really was as if he had come full-grown out of the swamp somewhere. And he didn't seem to need a wife either. But that was because he was not going to settle down yet. Because he had lived with more women from time to time and place to place than the average man could even shake a stick at.

We knew somehow or other that the Negro-ness had something to do with the way we felt about him too, but except for cowboys and the New York Yankees and one or two other things, almost everything was Negro then; that is, everything that mattered was. So the Negro part was only natural, although I can see something special about it too now.

When you boil it all down, I guess the main thing was how when you no more than just said his name, *Louisiana Charlie, old Luzana Cholly, old Luze,* that was enough to make you know not only him and how he looked and talked and walked that sporty limp walk, but his whole way of being, and how you knew right off the bat that he all alone and unconcerned in his sharp-edged and rough-backed steel had made it what it was himself.

That was what old Lil' Buddy and I were going to do too, make a name for ourselves. Because we knew even then (and I already knew it before he came) that doing that was exactly what made you the kind of man we wanted to be. Mama said I was her little man, and Aun Tee always called me her little mister, but I wasn't anybody's man and mister yet and I knew it, and when I heard the sound of the name that Mama taught me how to write I always felt funny, and I always jumped even when I didn't move. That was in school, and I wanted to hide, and I always said *they are looking for me, they are trying to see who I am,* and I had to answer because it would be the teacher calling the roll, and I said Present, and it sounded like somebody else.

And when I found out what I found out about me and Aun Tee and knew that she was my flesh and blood mama, I also found out that I didn't know my real name at all, because I didn't know who my true father was. So I said *My name is Reynard the Fox,* and Lil' Buddy said *My name is Jack the Rabbit and my home is in the briar patch.*[1] That was old Luzana too, and when you heard that holler coming suddenly out of nowhere just as old Luze himself always seemed to come, it was just like it was coming from the briar patch.

So when Mama said what she said about me and Aun Tee at that wake that time and I heard it and had to believe it, I wished that old Luzana had been my real papa, but I didn't tell anybody that, not even Lil' Buddy although Lil' Buddy was almost in the same fix because he didn't have a mama any more and he didn't really love his papa because it was his papa that ran his mama away.

But we were buddies and we both did old Luzana's famous walk and we were going to be like him, and the big thing that you had to do to really get like him was to grab yourself a fast armful of fast freight train and get long gone from here. That was the real way to learn about the world, and we wanted to learn everything about it that we could. That was when we started practicing on the switch engine. That was down in the oilyards. You had to be slick to do even that because naturally your folks didn't want you doing stuff like that, because there was old Peg Leg Nat. Old Peg Leg butt-headed Nat could hop a freight almost as good as old Luzana could. He called himself mister-some-big-shit-on-a-stick. He spent most of his time fishing and sometimes he would come around pushing a wheelbarrow selling fresh fish, shrimps, and crabs, but every now and then he would strike out for somewhere on a freight just like old Luze did. Mama used to try to scare us with old Nat, telling us that a peg leg was just what messing around with freight trains would get you, and for a while she did scare us, but not for long, because then we found out that it never would have happened to old Nat if he hadn't been drunk and showing off. And anybody could see that getting his leg cut off hadn't stopped old Nat himself anyway since he could still beat any two-legged man we knew doing it except old Luze himself. Naturally we had to think about it, and naturally it did slow us up for a while, but it didn't really stop us. Because there was still old Luze, and that was who we were anyway, not old Peg Leg Nat.

Then that time when I found out all about me and Aun Tee, I was going to run away, and Lil' Buddy was ready too. Then old Lil' Buddy found out that old Luze was getting ready to get moving again and we were all set and just waiting and then it was the day itself.

I will always remember that one.

I had on my brogan shoes and I had on my corduroy pants under my overalls with my jumper tucked in. I had on my blue baseball cap

1. Reynard and Jack are traditional names for the fox and rabbit: the briar patch episode appears in the Uncle Remus story, by Joel Chandler Harris (1848–1908) in which the shrewd Br'er Rabbit, caught by Br'er Fox, pleads not to be thrown into the briar patch; so of course the fox throws him in and the rabbit escapes crying, "Bred en bawn in a brier-patch, Br'er Fox, bred en bawn in a brier-patch."

too and my rawhide wristband and I had my pitching glove folded in my hip pocket. Lil' Buddy had on just about the same thing except that he was carrying his first-base pad instead of his catcher's mitt. We had our other things and something to eat rolled up in our blanket rolls so that we could sling them over our shoulders and have our arms free.

Lil' Buddy had gotten his papa's pearl-handled .38 Smith & Wesson, and we both had good jackknives. We had some hooks and twine to fish with too, just in case, and of course we had our trusty old slingshots for birds.

It was May and school was not out yet, and so not only were we running away, we were playing hooky too. It was hot, and with that many clothes on we were sweating, but you had to have them, and that was the best way to carry them.

There was a thin breeze that came across the railroad from the river, the marsh, and Pole Cat Bay, but the sun was hot and bright, and you could see the rails downright shimmering under the high and wide open sky. We had always said that we were going to wait until school was out, but this was our chance now, and we didn't care about school much any more anyhow. This was going to be school now anyway, except it was going to be much better.

We were waiting in the thicket under the hill. That was between where the Dodge mill road came down and where the oil spur started, and from where we were, we could see up and down the clearing as far as we needed to, to the south all the way across Three Mile Creek bridge to the roundhouse, and where Mobile was, and to the north all the way up past that mill to the Chickasabogue Bridge. We knew just about from where old Luzana was going to come running, because we had been watching him do it for a long time now. We had that part down pat.

I don't know how long we had been waiting because we didn't have a watch but it had been a long time, and there was nothing to do but wait then.

"I wish it would hurry up and come on," Lil' Buddy said.

"Me too," I said.

"Got to get to splitting."

We were squatting on the blanket rolls, and Lil' Buddy was smoking another Lucky Strike, smoking the way we both used to smoke them in those old days, letting it hang dangling in the corner of your mouth, and tilting your head to one side with one eye squinted up like a gambler.

"Goddam it, watch me nail that sapsucker," he said.

"Man, you watch me."

You could smell the May woods there then, the dogwood, the honeysuckle, and the warm smell of the undergrowth; and you could hear the birds too, the jays, the thrushes, and even a woodpecker somewhere on a dead tree. I felt how moist and cool the soft dark ground was there in the shade, and you could smell that smell too, and smell the river and the marsh too.

Lil' Buddy finished the cigarette and flipped it out into the sunshine, and then sat with his back against a sapling and sucked his teeth. I looked out across the railroad to where the gulls were circling over the marsh and the river.

"Goddam it, when I come back here to this burg, I'm goddam man and a half," Lil' Buddy said all of a sudden.

"And don't care who knows it," I said.

"Boy, Chicago."

"Man, Detroit."

"Man, Philadelphia."

"Man, New York."

"Boy, I kinda wish old Gander was going too."

"I kinda wish so too."

"Old cat-eyed Gander."

"Old big-toed Gander."

"Old Gander is all right."

"Man, who you telling."

"That son of a bitch know his natural stuff."

"That bastard can steal lightning if he have to."

"Boy, how about that time."

"Man, hell yeah."

"Boy, but old Luze though."

"That Luze takes the cake for everything."

"Hot damn, boy we going!"

"It won't be long now."

"Boy, Los Angeles."

"Boy, St. Louis."

"Man, you know we going."

"Boy, you just watch me swing the sapsucker."

"Boy, snag it."

"Goddam."

"I'm going to natural-born kick that son of a bitch."

"Kick the living guts out of it."

"Boy and when we get back!" I said that and I could see it, coming back on the Pan American I would be carrying two suitcases and have a money belt and an underarm holster, and I would be dressed fit to kill.

"How long you think it will take us to get fixed to come back?" I said.

"Man, I don't know and don't care."

"You coming back when old Luze come back?"

"I don't know."

I didn't say anything else then. Because I was trying to think about how it was really going to be then. Because what I had been thinking about before was how I wanted it to be. I didn't say anything because I was thinking about myself then, thinking: *I always said I was going but I don't really know whether I want to go or not now. I want to go and I don't want to go.* I tried to see what was really going to happen and I couldn't, and I tried to forget it and think about something else, but I couldn't do that either.

I looked over at Lil' Buddy again. Who was lying back against the tree with his hands behind his head and his eyes closed. Whose legs were crossed, and who was resting easy like a ballplayer rests before time for the game to start. I wondered what he was really thinking. Did he really mean it when he said he did not know and didn't care? You couldn't tell what he was thinking, but you could tell that he wasn't going to back out now, no matter how he was feeling about it.

So I said to myself goddam it if Lil' Buddy can make it I can too, and I had more reason to be going away than he did anyway. *I had forgotten about that. I had forgotten all about it. And then I knew that I still loved Papa and they had always loved me and they had always known about me and Aun Tee.*

But I couldn't back out then, because what I had found out wasn't the real reason for going anyway. Old Luze was really the reason, old Luze and blue steel, old Luze and rawhide, old Luze and ever-stretching India Rubber.

"Hey Lebud."

"Hey."

"Going to the big league."

"You said it."

"Skipping city."

"You tell 'em."

"Getting further."

"Ain't no lie."

"Long gone."

"No crap."

That was when Lil' Buddy said my home is in the briar patch. My name is Jack the Rabbit and my natural home is in the briar patch. And I said it too, and I said that was where I was bred and born.

"Goddam it to hell," Lil' Buddy said then, "why don't it come on?"

"Son of a bitch," I said.

Then I was leaning back against my tree looking out across the sandy clearing at the sky and there were clean white pieces of clouds that looked like balled-up sheets in a washtub, and the sky was blue like rinse water with bluing in it, and I was thinking about Mama again, and hoping that it was all a dream.

But then the train was really coming and it wasn't a dream at all, and Lil' Buddy jumped up.

"Come on."

"I'm here."

The engine went by, and we were running across the clearing. My ears were ringing and I was sweating, and my collar was hot and my pants felt as if the seat had been ripped away. There was nothing but the noise and we were running into it, and then we were climbing up the hill and running along the slag and cinders. We were trotting along in reach of it then. We remembered to let an empty boxcar go by, and when the next gondola came, Lil' Buddy grabbed the front end and I got the back. I hit the hotbox with my right foot and stepped onto the step and pulled up. The wind was in my ears then, but I knew about that from practicing. I climbed on up the ladder and got down on the inside, and there was Lil' Buddy coming back toward me.

"Man, what did I tell you!"

"Did you see me lam into that sucker?"

"Boy, we low more nailed it."

"I bet old Luze will be kicking it any minute now."

"Cool hanging it."

"Boy, yair," I said, but I was thinking I hope old Luze didn't change his mind. I hope we don't miss him. I hope we don't have to start out all by ourselves.

"Going boy."

"Yeah."

"*Going,*
don't know where I'm going
but I'm going
Say now I'm going
don't know when I'm going
but I'm going."

We crawled up into the left front corner out of the wind, and there was nothing to do but wait then. We knew that she was going to have to pull into the hole for Number Four when she got twelve miles out, and that was when we were going to get to the open boxcar.

We got the cigarettes out and lit up, and there was nothing but the rumbling noise that the wide-open car made then, and the faraway sound of the engine and the low-rolling smoke coming back. That was just sitting there, and after we got a little more used to the vibration, nothing at all was happening except being there. You couldn't even see the scenery going by.

It was just being there and being in that time, and you never really remember anything about things like that except the sameness and the way you felt, and all I can remember now about that part is this nothingness of doing nothing and the feeling not of going but of being taken.

All I could see after we went through the bridge was the sky and the bare floor and the sides of the gondola, and all I can remember about myself is how I wished that something would happen, because I definitely did not want to be going then, and I was lost even though I knew good and well that I was not even twelve miles from home yet. Because although we certainly had been many times farther away and stayed longer, this already seemed to be farther and longer than all the other times put together.

Then we could tell that it was beginning to slow down, and we stood up and started getting ready. And then it was stopping and we were ready, and we climbed over and got down and started running for it. That was still in the bayou country and beyond the train smell there was the sour-sweet smell of the swamp. We were running on hard pounded slag then, and with the train quiet and waiting for Number Four, you could hear the double running of our feet echoing through the cypresses and the marshland.

The wide roadbed was almost half as high as the telegraph wires, and along the low right-of-way where the black creosote poles went along, you could see the blue and white lilies floating on the slimy green water. We came hustling hot to get to where we knew the empty car was, and then there we were.

And there old Luzana himself was.

He stood looking down at us from the door with an unlighted cigarette in his hand. We stopped dead in our tracks. I knew exactly what was going to happen then. It was suddenly so quiet that you could hear your heart pounding inside your head, and I was so embarrassed I didn't know what to do and I thought *now he's going to call us a name. Now he's never going to have anything to do with us anymore.*

We were just standing there waiting and he just let us stand there and feel like two puppies with their tails tucked between their legs, and then he started talking.

"It ain't like that. It ain't like that. It just ain't like that, it just ain't."

And he was shaking his head not only as if we couldn't understand him but also as if we couldn't even hear him.

"It ain't. Oh, but it ain't."

We didn't move. Lil' Buddy didn't even dig his toe into the ground.

"So this is what y'all up to. Don't say a word, not a word. Don't open your mouth."

I could have sunk right on down into the ground.

"What the hell y'all think y'all doing? Tell me that. Tell me. Don't say a word. Don't say a goddam mumbling word to me."

We weren't even about to say anything.

"I got a good mind to whale the sawdust out of you both. That's just what I oughta do."

But he didn't move. He just stood looking down.

"Well, I'll be a son of a bitch."

That was all he had said then, and then he jumped down, walked us back to where the switch frog was, and then there was nothing but just shamefaced waiting. Then Number Four came by and then finally we heard the next freight coming south and when it got there and slowed down for the switch he was standing waiting for a gondola and when it came he picked me up and put me on and then he picked Lil' Buddy up and put him on and then he caught the next car and came to where we were.

So we came slowpoking it right on back and got back in Gasoline Point before the whistles even started blowing for one o'clock. Imagine that. All of that had happened and it wasn't really afternoon yet. I could hardly believe it.

We came on until the train all but stopped for Three Mile Creek bridge and then he hopped down and took us off. He led us down the hill and went to a place the hobos used under the bridge. He sat down and lit another cigarette and flipped the match into the water and watched it float away and then he was looking at us and then he motioned for us to sit down too.

That was when he really told us what hitting the road was, and what blue steel was. He was talking evenly then, not scolding, just telling us man to boys, saying he was talking for our own good because doing what we were trying to do was more than a notion. He was talking quietly and evenly but you still couldn't face him, I know I couldn't and Lil' Buddy naturally couldn't because he never looked anybody straight in the eye anyway.

We were back and sitting under Three Mile Creek bridge and he was not really angry and then we were all eating our something-to-eat and then we could talk too, but we didn't have much to say that day.

He was doing the talking and all we wanted to do was ask questions and listen.

That was when he told us all about the chain gang and the penitentiary and the white folks, and you could see everything he said and you were there too, but you were not really in it this time because it was happening to him, not you, and it was him and you were not him, you were you. You could be rawhide and you could be blue steel but you couldn't really be Luzana Cholly, because he himself was not going to let you.

Then he was talking about going to school and learning to use your head like the smart white folks. You had to be a rawhide but you had to be patent leather too, then you would really be nimble, then you would really be not only a man but a big man. He said we had a lot of spunk and that was good but it wasn't good enough, it wasn't nearly enough.

And then he was talking about Negroes and white folks again, and he said the young generation of Negroes were supposed to be like Negroes and be like white folks too and still be Negroes. He sat looking out across the water then, and then we heard another freight coming and he got up and got ready and he said we could watch him but we'd better not try to follow him.

Then we were back up on the hill again and the train was coming and he stood looking at us with the guitar slung over his shoulder and then he put his hands on our shoulders and looked straight at us, and we had to look at him then, and we knew that we were not to be ashamed in front of him any more.

"Make old Luze proud of you," he said then, and he was almost pleading. "Make old Luze glad to take his hat off to you some of these days. You going further than old Luze ever even dreamed of. Old Luze ain't been nowhere. Old Luze don't know from nothing."

And then the train was there and we watched him snag it and then he was waving good-bye.

p. 1953

GRACE PALEY

A Conversation with My Father

My father is eighty-six years old and in bed. His heart, that bloody motor, is equally old and will not do certain jobs any more. It still floods his head with brainy light. But it won't let his legs carry the weight of his body around the house. Despite my metaphors, this muscle failure is not due to his old heart, he says, but to a potassium shortage. Sitting on one pillow, leaning on three, he offers last-minute advice and makes a request.

"I would like you to write a simple story just once more," he says, "the kind de Maupassant wrote, or Chekhov,[1] the kind you used to write. Just recognizable people and then write down what happened to them next."

I say, "Yes, why not? That's possible." I want to please him, though I don't remember writing that way. I *would* like to try to tell such a story, if he means the kind that begins: "There was a woman . . ." followed by plot, the absolute line between two points which I've always despised. Not for literary reasons, but because it takes all hope away. Everyone, real or invented, deserves the open destiny of life.

Finally I thought of a story that had been happening for a couple of years right across the street. I wrote it down, then read it aloud. "Pa," I said, "how about this? Do you mean something like this?"

> Once in my time there was a woman and she had a son. They lived nicely, in a small apartment in Manhattan. This boy at about fifteen became a junkie, which is not unusual in our neighborhood. In order to maintain her close friendship with him, she became a junkie too. She said it was part of the youth culture, with which she felt very much at home. After a while, for a number of reasons, the boy gave it all up and left the city and his mother in disgust. Hopeless and alone, she grieved. We all visit her.

"O.K., Pa, that's it," I said, "an unadorned and miserable tale."

"But that's not what I mean," my father said. "You misunderstood me on purpose. You know there's a lot more to it. You know that. You left everything out. Turgenev[2] wouldn't do that. Chekhov wouldn't do that. There are in fact Russian writers you never heard of, you don't have an inkling of, as good as anyone, who can write a plain ordinary story, who would not leave out what you have left out. I object not to facts but to people sitting in trees talking senselessly, voices from who knows where . . ."

"Forget that one, Pa, what have I left out now? In this one?"

"Her looks, for instance."

"Oh. Quite handsome, I think. Yes."

"Her hair?"

"Dark, with heavy braids, as though she were a girl or a foreigner."

"What were her parents like, her stock? That she became such a person. It's interesting, you know."

"From out of town. Professional people. The first to be divorced in their county. How's that? Enough?" I asked.

"With you, it's all a joke," he said. "What about the boy's father? Why didn't you mention him? Who was he? Or was the boy born out of wedlock?"

"Yes," I said. "He was born out of wedlock."

"For Godsakes, doesn't anyone in your stories get married? Doesn't anyone have the time to run down to City Hall before they jump into bed?"

1. Guy de Maupassant (1850–93) wrote heavily plotted, ironic stories, Chekhov realistic stories that often had no resolution (see *Lady with the Dog*) and sometimes with little plot.

2. Ivan Sergevich Turgenev (1818–1883) wrote stories and novels deeply embedded in the culture of his time; his best-known novel, *Fathers and Sons*, deals with the conflict between generations.

"No," I said. "In real life, yes. But in my stories, no."

"Why do you answer me like that?"

"Oh, Pa, this is a simple story about a smart woman who came to N.Y.C. full of interest love trust excitement very up to date, and about her son, what a hard time she had in this world. Married or not, it's of small consequence."

"It is of great consequence," he said.

"O.K.," I said.

"O.K. O.K. yourself," he said, "but listen. I believe you that she's good-looking, but I don't think she was so smart."

"That's true," I said. "Actually that's the trouble with stories. People start out fantastic. You think they're extraordinary, but it turns out as the work goes along, they're just average with a good education. Sometimes the other way around, the person's a kind of dumb innocent, but he outwits you and you can't even think of an ending good enough."

"What do you do then?" he asked. He had been a doctor for a couple of decades and then an artist for a couple of decades and he's still interested in details, craft, technique.

"Well, you just have to let the story lie around till some agreement can be reached between you and the stubborn hero."

"Aren't you talking silly, now?" he asked. "Start again," he said. "It so happens I'm not going out this evening. Tell the story again. See what you can do this time."

"O.K.," I said. "But it's not a five-minute job." Second attempt:

> Once, across the street from us, there was a fine handsome woman, our neighbor. She had a son whom she loved because she'd known him since birth (in helpless chubby infancy, and in the wrestling, hugging ages, seven to ten, as well as earlier and later). This boy, when he fell into the fist of adolescence, became a junkie. He was not a hopeless one. He was in fact hopeful, an ideologue and successful converter. With his busy brilliance, he wrote persuasive articles for his high-school newspaper. Seeking a wider audience, using important connections, he drummed into Lower Manhattan newsstand distribution a periodical called *Oh! Golden Horse!*
>
> In order to keep him from feeling guilty (because guilt is the stony heart of nine tenths of all clinically diagnosed cancers in America today, she said), and because she had always believed in giving bad habits room at home where one could keep an eye on them, she too became a junkie. Her kitchen was famous for a while—a center for intellectual addicts who knew what they were doing. A few felt artistic like Coleridge and others were scientific and revolutionary like Leary.[3] Although she was often high herself, certain good mothering reflexes remained, and she saw to it that there was lots of orange juice around and honey and milk and vitamin pills. However, she never cooked anything but chili, and that no more than once a week. She explained, when we talked to her, seriously, with neighborly concern, that it was

3. Samuel Taylor Coleridge (1772–1834), English Romantic poet, says he wrote his allegedly unfinished poem *Kubla Khan* in an opium dream. Timothy Leary (b. 1920), American psychologist who promoted the use of psychedelic drugs.

her part in the youth culture and she would rather be with the young, it was an honor, than with her own generation.

One week, while nodding through an Antonioni[4] film, this boy was severely jabbed by the elbow of a stern and proselytizing girl, sitting beside him. She offered immediate apricots and nuts for his sugar level, spoke to him sharply, and took him home.

She had heard of him and his work and she herself published, edited, and wrote a competitive journal called *Man Does Live By Bread Alone.* In the organic heat of her continuous presence he could not help but become interested once more in his muscles, his arteries, and nerve connections. In fact he began to love them, treasure them, praise them with funny little songs in *Man does Live . . .*

the fingers of my flesh transcend
my transcendental soul
the tightness in my shoulders end
my teeth have made me whole

To the mouth of his head (that glory of will and determination) he brought hard apples, nuts, wheat germ, and soybean oil. He said to his old friends, From now on, I guess I'll keep my wits about me. I'm going on the natch. He said he was about to begin a spiritual deep-breathing journey. How about you too, Mom? he asked kindly.

His conversion was so radiant, splendid, that neighborhood kids his age began to say that he had never been a real addict at all, only a journalist along for the smell of the story. The mother tried several times to give up what had become without her son and his friends a lonely habit. This effort only brought it to supportable levels. The boy and his girl took their electronic mimeograph and moved to the bushy edge of another borough. They were very strict. They said they would not see her again until she had been off drugs for sixty days.

At home alone in the evening, weeping, the mother read and reread the seven issues of *Oh! Golden Horse!* They seemed to her as truthful as ever. We often crossed the street to visit and console. But if we mentioned any of our children who were at college or in the hospital or dropouts at home, she would cry out, My baby! My baby! and burst into terrible, face-scarring, time-consuming tears. The End.

First my father was silent, then he said, "Number One: You have a nice sense of humor. Number Two: I see you can't tell a plain story. So don't waste time." Then he said sadly, "Number Three: I suppose that means she was alone, she was left like that, his mother. Alone. Probably sick?"

I said, "Yes."

"Poor woman. Poor girl, to be born in a time of fools, to live among fools. The end. The end. You were right to put that down. The end."

I didn't want to argue, but I had to say, "Well, it is not necessarily the end, Pa."

4. Michelangelo Antonioni (b. 1912), Italian director (*Blow-Up, Zabriskie Point*), whose neo-realist, often slow-moving films investigate society.

"Yes," he said, "what a tragedy. The end of a person."

"No, Pa," I begged him. "It doesn't have to be. She's only about forty. She could be a hundred different things in this world as time goes on. A teacher or a social worker. An ex-junkie! Sometimes it's better than having a master's in education."

"Jokes," he said. "As a writer that's your main trouble. You don't want to recognize it. Tragedy! Plain tragedy! Historical tragedy! No hope. The end."

"Oh, Pa," I said. "She could change."

"In your own life, too, you have to look it in the face." He took a couple of nitroglycerin.[5] "Turn to five," he said, pointing to the dial on the oxygen tank. He inserted the tubes into his nostrils and breathed deep. He closed his eyes and said, "No."

I had promised the family to always let him have the last word when arguing, but in this case I had a different responsibility. That woman lives across the street. She's my knowledge and my invention. I'm sorry for her. I'm not going to leave her there in that house crying. (Actually neither would Life, which unlike me has no pity.)

Therefore: She did change. Of course her son never came home again. But right now, she's the receptionist in a storefront community clinic in the East Village. Most of the customers are young people, some old friends. The head doctor has said to her, "If we only had three people in this clinic with your experiences . . ."

"The doctor said that?" My father took the oxygen tubes out of his nostrils and said, "Jokes. Jokes again."

"No, Pa, it could really happen that way, it's a funny world nowadays."

"No," he said. "Truth first. She will slide back. A person must have character. She does not."

"No, Pa," I said. "That's it. She's got a job. Forget it. She's in that storefront working."

"How long will it be?" he asked. "Tragedy! You too. When will you look it in the face?"

1974

URSULA K. LE GUIN

The Ones Who Walk Away from Omelas[1]

With a clamor of bells that set the swallows soaring, the Festival of Summer came to the city Omelas, bright-towered by the sea. The rigging of the boats in harbor sparkled with flags. In the streets between houses with red roofs and painted walls, between old moss-grown

5. Medicine for certain heart conditions.

1. The author says the name comes from "a road sign: Salem (Oregon) backwards. . . . Salem equals schelomo equals salaam equals Peace. Melas. O melas. Omelas. Homme hélas." The last phrase equals "Man, alas."

gardens and under avenues of trees, past great parks and public buildings, processions moved. Some were decorous: old people in long stiff robes of mauve and gray, grave master workmen, quiet, merry women carrying their babies and chatting as they walked. In other streets the music beat faster, a shimmering of gong and tambourine, and the people went dancing, the procession was a dance. Children dodged in and out, their high calls rising like the swallows' crossing flights over the music and the singing. All the processions wound towards the north side of the city, where on the great water-meadow called the Green Fields boys and girls, naked in the bright air, with mud-stained feet and ankles and long, lithe arms, exercised their restive horses before the race. The horses wore no gear at all but a halter without bit. Their manes were braided with streamers of silver, gold, and green. They flared their nostrils and pranced and boasted to one another; they were vastly excited, the horse being the only animal who has adopted our ceremonies as his own. Far off to the north and west the mountains stood up half encircling Omelas on her bay. The air of morning was so clear that the snow still crowning the Eighteen Peaks burned with white-gold fire across the miles of sunlit air, under the dark blue of the sky. There was just enough wind to make the banners that marked the racecourse snap and flutter now and then. In the silence of the broad green meadows one could hear the music winding through the city streets, farther and nearer and ever approaching, a cheerful faint sweetness of the air that from time to time trembled and gathered together and broke out into the great joyous clanging of the bells.

Joyous! How is one to tell about joy? How describe the citizens of Omelas?

They were not simple folk, you see, though they were happy. But we do not say the words of cheer much any more. All smiles have become archaic. Given a description such as this one tends to make certain assumptions. Given a description such as this one tends to look next for the King, mounted on a splendid stallion and surrounded by his noble knights, or perhaps in a golden litter borne by great-muscled slaves. But there was no king. They did not use swords, or keep slaves. They were not barbarians, I do not know the rules and laws of their society, but I suspect that they were singularly few. As they did without monarchy and slavery, so they also got on without the stock exchange, the advertisement, the secret police, and the bomb. Yet I repeat that these were not simple folk, not dulcet shepherds, noble savages, bland utopians. They were not less complex than us. The trouble is that we have a bad habit, encouraged by pedants and sophisticates, of considering happiness as something rather stupid. Only pain is intellectual, only evil interesting. This is the treason of the artist: a refusal to admit the banality of evil and the terrible boredom of pain. If you can't lick 'em, join 'em. If it hurts, repeat it. But to praise despair is to condemn delight, to embrace violence is to lose hold of everything else. We have almost lost hold; we can no longer describe a happy man, nor make any celebration of joy. How can I tell you about the people of Omelas? They were not naïve and happy children—though their children were, in fact, happy. They were mature, intelligent, passionate adults whose lives were not wretched. O miracle! but I wish I could describe it better. I wish I could convince you. Omelas sounds in my words like a city in a fairy tale, long ago and far away, once upon a time. Perhaps it would be best if you imagined it as your own fancy bids, assuming it will rise to the occasion, for certainly I cannot suit you all. For instance, how about technology? I think that there would be no cars or helicopters in and above the streets; this follows from the fact that the people of Omelas are happy people. Happiness is based on a just discrimination of what is necessary, what is neither necessary nor destructive, and what is destructive. In the middle category, however—that of the unnecessary but undestructive, that of comfort, luxury, exuberance, etc. —they could perfectly well have central heating, subway trains, washing machines, and all kinds of marvelous devices not yet invented here, floating light-sources, fuelless power, a cure for the common cold. Or they could have none of that: it doesn't matter. As you like it. I incline to think that people from towns up and down the coast have been coming in to Omelas during the last days before the Festival on very fast little trains and double-decked trams, and that the train station of Omelas is actually the handsomest building in town, though plainer than the magnificent Farmers' Market. But even granted trains, I fear that Omelas so far strikes some of you as goody-goody. Smiles, bells, parades, horses, bleh. If so, please add an orgy. If an orgy would help, don't hesitate. Let us not, however, have temples from which issue beautiful nude priests and priestesses already half in ecstasy and ready to copulate with any man or woman, lover or stranger, who desires union with the deep godhead of the blood, although that was my first idea. But really it would be better not to have any temples in Omelas—at least, not manned temples. Religion yes, clergy no. Surely the beautiful nudes can just wander about, offering themselves like divine soufflés to the hunger of the needy and the rapture of the flesh. Let them join the processions. Let tambourines be struck above the copulations, and the glory of desire be proclaimed upon the gongs, and (a not unimportant point) let the offspring of these delightful rituals be beloved and looked after by all. One thing I know there is none of in Omelas is guilt. But what else should there be? I thought at first there were no drugs, but that is puritanical. For those who like it, the faint insistent sweetness of *drooz* may perfume the ways of the city, *drooz* which first brings a great lightness and brilliance to the mind and limbs, and then after some hours a dreamy languor, and wonderful visions at last of the very arcana and inmost secrets of the Universe, as well as exciting the pleasure of sex beyond all belief; and it is not habit-forming. For more modest tastes I think there ought to be beer. What else, what else belongs in the joyous city? The sense of victory, surely, the celebration of courage. But as we did without clergy, let us do without soldiers. The joy built upon successful slaughter is not the right kind of joy; it will not do; it is fearful and it is trivial. A boundless and generous contentment, a magnanimous triumph felt not against some outer enemy but in communion with the finest and fairest in the souls of all men everywhere and the splendor of the world's summer: this is what swells the hearts of the people of Omelas, and the victory they celebrate is that of life. I really don't think many of them need to take *drooz.*

Most of the processions have reached the Green Fields by now. A marvelous smell of cooking goes forth from the red and blue tents of the provisioners. The faces of small children are amiably sticky; in the benign gray beard of a man a couple of crumbs of rich pastry are entangled. The youths and girls have mounted their horses and are beginning to group around the starting line of the course. An old woman, small, fat, and laughing, is passing out flowers from a basket, and tall young men wear her flowers in their shining hair. A child of nine or ten sits at the edge of the crowd, alone, playing on a wooden flute. People pause to listen, and they smile, but they do not speak to him, for he never ceases playing and never sees them, his dark eyes wholly rapt in the sweet, thin magic of the tune.

He finishes, and slowly lowers his hands holding the wooden flute.

As if that little private silence were the signal, all at once a trumpet sounds from the pavilion near the starting line: imperious, melancholy, piercing. The horses rear on their slender legs, and some of them neigh in answer. Sober-faced, the young riders stroke the horses' necks and soothe them, whispering, "Quiet, quiet, there my beauty, my hope. . . ." They begin to form in rank along the starting line. The crowds along the racecourse are like a field of grass and flowers in the wind. The Festival of Summer has begun.

Do you believe? Do you accept the festival, the city, the joy? No? Then let me describe one more thing.

In a basement under one of the beautiful public buildings of Omelas, or perhaps in the cellar of one of its spacious private homes, there is a room. It has one locked door, and no window. A little light seeps in dustily between cracks in the boards, secondhand from a cobwebbed window somewhere across the cellar. In one corner of the little room a couple of mops, with stiff, clotted, foul-smelling heads, stand near a rusty bucket. The floor is dirt, a little damp to the touch, as cellar dirt usually is. The room is about three paces long and two wide: a mere broom closet or disused tool room. In the room a child is sitting. It could be a boy or a girl. It looks about six, but actually is nearly ten. It is feeble-minded. Perhaps it was born defective, or perhaps it has become imbecile through fear, malnutrition, and neglect. It picks its nose and occasionally fumbles vaguely with its toes or genitals, as it sits hunched in the corner farthest from the bucket and the two mops. It is afraid of the mops. It finds them horrible. It shuts its eyes, but it knows the mops are still standing there; and the door is locked; and nobody will come. The door is always locked; and nobody ever comes, except that sometimes—the child has no understanding of time or interval—sometimes the door rattles terribly and opens, and a person, or several people, are there. One of them may come in and kick the child to make it stand up. The others never come close, but peer in at it with frightened, disgusted eyes. The food bowl and the water jug are hastily filled, the door is locked, the eyes disappear. The people at the door never say anything, but the child, who has not always lived in the tool room, and can remember sunlight and its mother's voice, sometimes speaks. "I will be good," it says. "Please let me out. I will be good!" They never answer. The child used to scream for help at night, and cry a good deal, but now it only makes a kind of whining, "eh-haa, eh-haa," and it speaks less and less often. It is so thin there are no calves to its legs; its belly protrudes; it lives on a half-bowl of corn meal and grease a day. It is naked. Its buttocks and thighs are a mass of festered sores, as it sits in its own excrement continually.

They all know it is there, all the people of Omelas. Some of them have come to see it, others are content merely to know it is there. They all know that it has to be there. Some of them understand why, and some do not, but they all understand that their happiness, the beauty of their city, the tenderness of their friendships, the health of their children, the wisdom of their scholars, the skill of their makers, even the abundance of their harvest and the kindly weathers of their skies, depend wholly on this child's abominable misery.

This is usually explained to children when they are between eight and twelve, whenever they seem capable of understanding; and most of those who come to see the child are young people, though often enough an adult comes, or comes back, to see the child. No matter how well the matter has been explained to them, these young spectators are always shocked and sickened at the sight. They feel disgust, which they had thought themselves superior to. They feel anger, outrage, impotence, despite all the explanations. They would like to do something for the child. But there is nothing they can do. If the child were brought up into the sunlight out of that vile place, if it were cleaned and fed and comforted, that would be a good thing, indeed; but if it were done, in that day and hour all the prosperity and beauty and delight of Omelas would wither and be destroyed. Those are the terms. To exchange all the goodness and grace of every life in Omelas for that single, small improvement: to throw away the happiness of thousands for the chance of the happiness of one: that would be to let guilt within the walls indeed.

The terms are strict and absolute; there may not even be a kind word spoken to the child.

Often the young people go home in tears, or in a tearless rage, when they have seen the child and faced this terrible paradox. They may brood over it for weeks or years. But as time goes on they begin to realize that even if the child could be released, it would not get much good of its freedom: a little vague pleasure of warmth and food, no doubt, but little more. It is too degraded and imbecile to know any real joy. It has been afraid too long ever to be free of fear. Its habits are too uncouth for it to respond to humane treatment. Indeed, after so long it would probably be wretched without walls about it to protect it, and darkness for its eyes, and its own excrement to sit in. Their tears at the bitter injustice dry when they begin to perceive the terrible justice of reality, and to accept it. Yet it is their tears and anger, the trying of their generosity and the acceptance of their helplessness, which are perhaps the true source of the splendor of their lives. Theirs is no vapid, irresponsible happiness. They know that they, like the child, are not free. They know compassion. It is the existence of the child, and their knowledge of its existence, that makes possible the nobility of their architecture, the poignancy of their music, the profundity of their science. It is because of the child that they are so gentle with children. They know that if the wretched one were not there sniveling in the dark, the other one, the flute-player, could make no joyful music as the young riders line up in their beauty for the race in the sunlight of the first morning of summer.

Now do you believe in them? Are they not more credible? But there is one more thing to tell, and this is quite incredible.

At times one of the adolescent girls or boys who go to see the child does not go home to weep or rage, does not, in fact, go home at all. Sometimes also a man or woman much older falls silent for a day or two, and then leaves home. These people go out into the street, and walk down the street alone. They keep walking, and walk straight out of the city of Omelas, through the beautiful gates. They keep walking across the farmlands of Omelas. Each one goes alone, youth or girl, man or woman. Night falls; the traveler must pass down village streets, between the houses with yellow-lit windows, and on out into the darkness of the fields. Each alone, they go west or north, towards the mountains. They go on. They leave Omelas, they walk ahead into the darkness, and they do not come back. The place they go towards is a place even less imaginable to most of us than the city of happiness. I cannot describe it at all. It is possible that it does not exist. But they seem to know where they are going, the ones who walk away from Omelas.

1975

WOODY ALLEN

The Kugelmass Episode

Kugelmass, a professor of humanities at City College, was unhappily married for the second time. Daphne Kugelmass was an oaf. He also had two dull sons by his first wife, Flo, and was up to his neck in alimony and child support.

"Did I know it would turn out so badly?" Kugelmass whined to his analyst one day. "Daphne had promise. Who suspected she'd let herself go and swell up like a beach ball? Plus she had a few bucks, which is not in itself a healthy reason to marry a person, but it doesn't hurt, with the kind of operating nut[1] I have. You see my point?"

Kugelmass was bald and as hairy as a bear, but he had soul.

"I need to meet a new woman," he went on. "I need to have an affair. I may not look the part, but I'm a man who needs romance. I need softness, I need flirtation. I'm not getting younger, so before it's too late I want to make love in Venice, trade quips at '21,'[2] and exchange coy glances over red wine and candlelight. You see what I'm saying?"

1. Budget, expenses.

2. Celebrity nightclub and restaurant.

Dr. Mandel shifted in his chair and said, "An affair will solve nothing. You're so unrealistic. Your problems run much deeper."

"And also this affair must be discreet," Kugelmass continued. "I can't afford a second divorce. Daphne would really sock it to me."

"Mr. Kugelmass—"

"But it can't be anyone at City College, because Daphne also works there. Not that anyone on the faculty at C.C.N.Y. is any great shakes, but some of those coeds . . ."

"Mr. Kugelmass—"

"Help me. I had a dream last night. I was skipping through a meadow holding a picnic basket and the basket was marked 'Options.' And then I saw there was a hole in the basket."

"Mr. Kugelmass, the worst thing you could do is act out. You must simply express your feelings here, and together we'll analyze them. You have been in treatment long enough to know there is no overnight cure. After all, I'm an analyst, not a magician."

"Then perhaps what I need is a magician," Kugelmass said, rising from his chair. And with that he terminated his therapy.

A couple of weeks later, while Kugelmass and Daphne were moping around in their apartment one night like two pieces of old furniture, the phone rang.

"I'll get it," Kugelmass said. "Hello."

"Kugelmass?" a voice said. "Kugelmass, this is Persky."

"Who?"

"Persky. Or should I say The Great Persky?"

"Pardon me?"

"I hear you're looking all over town for a magician to bring a little exotica into your life? Yes or no?"

"Sh-h-h," Kugelmass whispered. "Don't hang up. Where are you calling from, Persky?"

Early the following afternoon, Kugelmass climbed three flights of stairs in a broken-down apartment house in the Bushwick section of Brooklyn. Peering through the darkness of the hall, he found the door he was looking for and pressed the bell. I'm going to regret this, he thought to himself.

Seconds later, he was greeted by a short, thin, waxy-looking man.

"*You're* Persky the Great?" Kugelmass said.

"The Great Persky. You want a tea?"

"No, I want romance. I want music. I want love and beauty."

"But not tea, eh? Amazing. O.K., sit down."

Persky went to the back room, and Kugelmass heard the sounds of boxes and furniture being moved around. Persky reappeared, pushing before him a large object on squeaky roller-skate wheels. He removed some old silk handkerchiefs that were lying on its top and blew away a bit of dust. It was a cheap-looking Chinese cabinet, badly lacquered.

"Persky," Kugelmass said, "what's your scam?"[3]

"Pay attention," Persky said. "This is some beautiful effect. I developed it for a Knights of Pythias[4] date last year, but the booking fell through. Get into the cabinet."

3. Scheme, confidence trick.

4. Secret fraternal society.

"Why, so you can stick it full of swords or something?"

"You see any swords?"

Kugelmass made a face and, grunting, climbed into the cabinet. He couldn't help noticing a couple of ugly rhinestones glues onto the raw plywood just in front of his face. "If this is a joke," he said.

"Some joke. Now, here's the point. If I throw any novel into this cabinet with you, shut the doors, and tap it three times, you will find yourself projected into that book."

Kugelmass made a grimace of disbelief.

"It's the emess,"[5] Persky said. "My hand to God. Not just a novel, either. A short story, a play, a poem. You can meet any of the women created by the world's best writers. Whoever you dreamed of. You could carry on all you like with a real winner. Then when you've had enough you give a yell, and I'll see you're back here in a split second."

"Persky, are you some kind of outpatient?"

"I'm telling you it's on the level," Persky said.

Kugelmass remained skeptical. "What are you telling me—that this cheesy homemade box can take me on a ride like you're describing?"

"For a double sawbuck."[6]

Kugelmass reached for his wallet. "I'll believe this when I see it," he said.

Persky tucked the bills in his pants pocket and turned toward his bookcase. "So who do you want to meet? Sister Carrie? Hester Prynne? Ophelia? Maybe someone by Saul Bellow? Hey, what about Temple Drake?[7] Although for a man your age she'd be a workout."

"French. I want to have an affair with a French lover."

"Nana?"[8]

"I don't want to have to pay for it."

"What about Natasha in 'War and Peace'?"[9]

"I said French. I know! What about Emma Bovary? That sounds to me perfect."

"You got it, Kugelmass. Give me a holler when you've had enough." Persky tossed in a paperback copy of Flaubert's novel.

"You sure this is safe?" Kugelmass asked as Persky began shutting the cabinet doors.

"Safe. Is anything safe in this crazy world?" Persky rapped three times on the cabinet and then flung open the doors.

Kugelmass was gone. At the same moment, he appeared in the bedroom of Charles and Emma Bovary's house at Yonville.[1] Before him was a beautiful woman, standing alone with her back turned to him as she folded some linen. I can't believe this, thought Kugelmass, staring at the doctor's ravishing wife. This is uncanny. I'm here. It's her.

Emma turned in surprise. "Goodness, you startled me," she said.

5. Truth.
6. Twenty dollars.
7. Respectively, the fallen heroine of Theodore Dreiser's *Sister Carrie* (1900); the adulterous heroine of Nathaniel Hawthorne's *The Scarlet Letter* (1850); Hamlet's fiancée, who drowns herself; Bellow's heroines are intensely neurotic, sexual, and vindictive; the victim of a bizarre rape in Faulkner's *Sanctuary* (1931), who is also the heroine of his *Requiem for a Nun* (1950).
8. Prostitute-heroine of Émile Zola's *Nana* (1880).
9. Saucy heroine of the novel (1865–1869) by Tolstoy.
1. Town in Normandy, France, where much of Flaubert's novel *Madame Bovary* (1857) is set.

"Who are you?" She spoke in the same fine English translation as the paperback.

It's simply devastating, he thought. Then, realizing that it was he whom she had addressed, he said, "Excuse me. I'm Sidney Kugelmass. I'm from City College. A professor of humanities. C.C.N.Y.? Uptown. I—oh, boy!"

Emma Bovary smiled flirtatiously and said, "Would you like a drink? A glass of wine, perhaps?"

She is beautiful, Kugelmass thought. What a contrast with the troglodyte who shared his bed! He felt a sudden impulse to take this vision into his arms and tell her she was the kind of woman he had dreamed of all his life.

"Yes, some wine," he said hoarsely. "White. No, red. No, white. Make it white."

"Charles is out for the day," Emma said, her voice full of playful implication.

After the wine, they went for a stroll in the lovely French countryside. "I've always dreamed that some mysterious stranger would appear and rescue me from the monotony of this crass rural existence," Emma said, clasping his hand. They passed a small church. "I love what you have on," she murmured. "I've never seen anything like it around here. It's so . . . so modern."

"It's called a leisure suit," he said romantically. "It was marked down." Suddenly he kissed her. For the next hour they reclined under a tree and whispered together and told each other deeply meaningful things with their eyes. Then Kugelmass sat up. He had just remembered he had to meet Daphne at Bloomingdale's.[2] "I must go," he told her. "But don't worry, I'll be back."

"I hope so," Emma said.

He embraced her passionately, and the two walked back to the house. He held Emma's face cupped in his palms, kissed her again, and yelled, "O.K., Persky! I got to be at Bloomingdale's by three-thirty."

There was an audible pop, and Kugelmass was back in Brooklyn.

"So? Did I lie?" Persky asked triumphantly.

"Look, Persky, I'm right now late to meet the ball and chain at Lexington Avenue, but when can I go again? Tomorrow?"

"My pleasure. Just bring a twenty. And don't mention this to anybody."

"Yeah. I'm going to call Rupert Murdoch."[3]

Kugelmass hailed a cab and sped off to the city. His heart danced on point. I am in love, he thought, I am the possessor of a wonderful secret. What he didn't realize was that at this very moment students in various classrooms across the country were saying to their teachers, "Who is this character on page 100? A bald Jew is kissing Madame Bovary?" A teacher in Sioux Falls, South Dakota, sighed and thought, Jesus, these kids, with their pot and acid. What goes through their minds!

2. Chic New York department store.

3. Australian newspaper baron, who, in addition to several British papers, owns the New York *Post*, the *Village Voice*, and *New York* magazine.

Daphne Kugelmass was in the bathroom-accessories department at Bloomingdale's when Kugelmass arrived breathlessly. "Where've you been?" she snapped. "It's four-thirty."

"I got held up in traffic," Kugelmass said.

Kugelmass visited Persky the next day, and in a few minutes was again passed magically to Yonville. Emma couldn't hide her excitement at seeing him. The two spent hours together, laughing and talking about their different backgrounds. Before Kugelmass left, they made love. "My God, I'm doing it with Madame Bovary!" Kugelmass whispered to himself. "Me, who failed freshman English."

As the months passed, Kugelmass saw Persky many times and developed a close and passionate relationship with Emma Bovary. "Make sure and always get me into the book before page 120," Kugelmass said to the magician one day. "I always have to meet her before she hooks up with this Rodolphe character."[4]

"Why?" Persky asked. "You can't beat his time?"

"Beat his time. He's landed gentry. Those guys have nothing better to do than flirt and ride horses. To me, he's one of those faces you see in the pages of *Women's Wear Daily*. With the Helmut Berger[5] hairdo. But to her he's hot stuff."

"And her husband suspects nothing?"

"He's out of his depth. He's a lackluster little paramedic who's thrown in his lot with a jitterbug. He's ready to go to sleep by ten, and she's putting on her dancing shoes. Oh, well . . . See you later."

And once again Kugelmass entered the cabinet and passed instantly to the Bovary estate at Yonville. "How you doing, cupcake?" he said to Emma.

"Oh, Kugelmass," Emma sighed. "What I have to put up with. Last night at dinner, Mr. Personality dropped off to sleep in the middle of the dessert course. I'm pouring my heart out about Maxim's[6] and the ballet, and out of the blue I hear snoring."

"It's O.K., darling. I'm here now," Kugelmass said, embracing her. I've earned this, he thought, smelling Emma's French perfume and burying his nose in her hair. I've suffered enough. I've paid enough analysts. I've searched till I'm weary. She's young and nubile, and I'm here a few pages after Léon and just before Rodolphe. By showing up during the correct chapters, I've got the situation knocked.

Emma, to be sure, was just as happy as Kugelmass. She had been starved for excitement, and his tales of Broadway night life, of fast cars and Hollywood and TV stars, enthralled the young French beauty.

"Tell me again about O.J. Simpson,"[7] she implored that evening, as she and Kugelmass strolled past Abbé Bournisien's church.

"What can I say? The man is great. He sets all kinds of rushing records. Such moves. They can't touch him."

4. The provincial aristocratic womanizer who seduces Emma, after she has a first romantic, idealistic flirtation with the mooning young Léon (who is mentioned below). The Abbé Bournisien and Binet, mentioned later, are minor characters in the novel.

5. Gossipy New York fashion newspaper; handsome German actor (b. 1942) who often plays decadent characters (*The Damned, Portrait of Dorian Gray*).

6. Fashionable Paris restaurant.

7. Famous football running back, recently retired, though he's still seen running through airports in TV commercials.

"And the Academy Awards?" Emma said wistfully. "I'd give anything to win one."

"First you've got to be nominated."

"I know. You explained it. But I'm convinced I can act. Of course, I'd want to take a class or two. With Strasberg[8] maybe. Then, if I had the right agent—"

"We'll see, we'll see. I'll speak to Persky."

That night, safely returned to Persky's flat, Kugelmass brought up the idea of having Emma visit him in the big city.

"Let me think about it," Persky said. "Maybe I could work it. Stranger things have happened." Of course, neither of them could think of one.

"Where the hell do you go all the time?" Daphne Kugelmass barked at her husband as he returned home late that evening. "You got a chippie stashed somewhere?"

"Yeah, sure, I'm just the type," Kugelmass said wearily. "I was with Leonard Popkin. We were discussing Socialist agriculture in Poland. You know Popkin. He's a freak on the subject."

"Well, you've been very odd lately," Daphne said. "Distant. Just don't forget about my father's birthday. On Saturday?"

"Oh, sure, sure," Kugelmass said, heading for the bathroom.

"My whole family will be there. We can see the twins. And Cousin Hamish. You should be more polite to Cousin Hamish—he likes you."

"Right, the twins," Kugelmass said, closing the bathroom door and shutting out the sound of his wife's voice. He leaned against it and took a deep breath. In a few hours, he told himself, he would be back in Yonville again, back with his beloved. And this time, if all went well, he would bring Emma back with him.

At three-fifteen the following afternoon, Persky worked his wizardry again. Kugelmass appeared before Emma, smiling and eager. The two spent a few hours at Yonville with Binet and then remounted the Bovary carriage. Following Persky's instructions, they held each other tightly, closed their eyes, and counted to ten. When they opened them, the carriage was just drawing up at the side door of the Plaza Hotel, where Kugelmass had optimistically reserved a suite earlier in the day.

"I love it! It's everything I dreamed it would be," Emma said as she swirled joyously around the bedroom, surveying the city from their window. "There's F.A.O. Schwarz.[9] And there's Central Park, and the Sherry[1] is which one? Oh, there—I see. It's too divine."

On the bed there were boxes from Halston and Saint Laurent.[2] Emma unwrapped a package and held up a pair of black velvet pants against her perfect body.

"The slacks suit is by Ralph Lauren," Kugelmass said. "You'll look like a million bucks in it. Come on, sugar, give us a kiss."

8. Lee Strasberg's acting school taught the natural acting style known as "The Method" to such stars as Marlon Brando.

9. Well-known toy store.

1. Sherry-Netherland Hotel, also in Central Park area.

2. Famous and expensive fashion designers and couturiers, as is Ralph Lauren, below.

"I've never been so happy!" Emma squealed as she stood before the mirror. "Let's go out on the town. I want to see 'Chorus Line' and the Guggenheim and this Jack Nicholson[3] character you always talk about. Are any of his flicks showing?"

"I cannot get my mind around this," a Stanford professor said. "First a strange character named Kugelmass, and now she's gone from the book. Well, I guess the mark of a classic is that you can reread it a thousand times and always find something new."

The lovers passed a blissful weekend. Kugelmass had told Daphne he would be away at a symposium in Boston and would return Monday. Savoring each moment, he and Emma went to the movies, had dinner in Chinatown, passed two hours at a discothèque, and went to bed with a TV movie. They slept till noon on Sunday, visited SoHo, and ogled celebrities at Elaine's.[4] They had caviar and champagne in their suite on Sunday night and talked until dawn. That morning, in the cab taking them to Persky's apartment, Kugelmass thought, It was hectic, but worth it. I can't bring her here too often, but now and then it will be a charming contrast with Yonville.

At Persky's, Emma climbed into the cabinet, arranged her new boxes of clothes neatly around her, and kissed Kugelmass fondly. "My place next time," she said with a wink. Persky rapped three times on the cabinet. Nothing happened.

"Hmm," Persky said, scratching his head. He rapped again, but still no magic. "Something must be wrong," he mumbled.

"Persky, you're joking!" Kugelmass cried. "How can it not work?"

"Relax, relax. Are you still in the box, Emma?"

"Yes."

Persky rapped again—harder this time.

"I'm still here, Persky."

"I know, darling. Sit tight."

"Persky, we *have* to get her back," Kugelmass whispered. "I'm a married man, and I have a class in three hours. I'm not prepared for anything more than a cautious affair at this point."

"I can't understand it," Persky muttered. "It's such a reliable little trick."

But he could do nothing. "It's going to take a little while," he said to Kugelmass. "I'm going to have to strip it down. I'll call you later."

Kugelmass bundled Emma into a cab and took her back to the Plaza. He barely made it to his class on time. He was on the phone all day, to Persky and to his mistress. The magician told him it might be several days before he got to the bottom of the trouble.

"How was the symposium?" Daphne asked him that night.

"Fine, fine," he said, lighting the filter end of a cigarette.

"What's wrong? You're as tense as a cat."

"Me? Ha, that's a laugh. I'm as calm as a summer night. I'm

3. A Broadway musical; the Solomon R. Guggenheim Museum; Nicholson starred in the films *Easy Rider, One Flew Over the Cuckoo's Nest, Five Easy Pieces.*

4. SoHo is the new center of the contemporary art scene south of Greenwich Village. Elaine's restaurant is frequented by publishing and newspaper notables.

just going to take a walk." He eased out the door, hailed a cab, and flew to the Plaza.

"This is no good," Emma said. "Charles will miss me."

"Bear with me, sugar," Kugelmass said. He was pale and sweaty. He kissed her again, raced to the elevators, yelled at Persky over a pay phone in the Plaza lobby, and just made it home before midnight.

"According to Popkin, barley prices in Kraków have not been this stable since 1971," he said to Daphne, and smiled wanly as he climbed into bed.

The whole week went by like that. On Friday night, Kugelmass told Daphne there was another symposium he had to catch, this one in Syracuse. He hurried back to the Plaza, but the second weekend there was nothing like the first. "Get me back into the novel or marry me," Emma told Kugelmass. "Meanwhile, I want to get a job or go to class, because watching TV all day is the pits."

"Fine. We can use the money," Kugelmass said. "You consume twice your weight in room service."

"I met an Off Broadway producer in Central Park yesterday, and he said I might be right for a project he's doing," Emma said.

"Who is this clown?" Kugelmass asked.

"He's not a clown. He's sensitive and kind and cute. His name's Jeff Something-or-Other, and he's up for a Tony."[5]

Later that afternoon, Kugelmass showed up at Persky's drunk.

"Relax," Persky told him. "You'll get a coronary."

"Relax. The man says relax. I've got a fictional character stashed in a hotel room, and I think my wife is having me tailed by a private shamus."[6]

"O.K., O.K. We know there's a problem." Persky crawled under the cabinet and started banging on something with a large wrench.

"I'm like a wild animal," Kugelmass went on. "I'm sneaking around town, and Emma and I have had it up to here with each other. Not to mention a hotel tab that reads like the defense budget."

"So what should I do? This is the world of magic," Persky said. "It's all nuance."

"Nuance, my foot. I'm pouring Dom Pérignon and black eggs[7] into this little mouse, plus her wardrobe, plus she's enrolled at the Neighborhood Playhouse[8] and suddenly needs professional photos. Also, Persky, Professor Fivish Kopkind, who teaches Comp Lit and who has always been jealous of me, has identified me as the sporadically appearing character in the Flaubert book. He's threatened to go to Daphne. I see ruin and alimony jail. For adultery with Madame Bovary, my wife will reduce me to beggary."

"What do you want me to say? I'm working on it night and day. As far as your personal anxiety goes, that I can't help you with. I'm a magician, not an analyst."

5. Broadway Drama Critics' Award comparable to Oscar.
6. Detective.
7. An especially fine champagne and caviar.
8. Founded in 1915 to bring drama to the lower East Side of New York City, its productions tended to have social implications or to be experimental. The theater closed in 1927, but its production company continues to perform.

By Sunday afternoon, Emma had locked herself in the bathroom and refused to respond to Kugelmass's entreaties. Kugelmass stared out the window at the Wollman Rink[9] and contemplated suicide. Too bad this is a low floor, he thought, or I'd do it right now. Maybe if I ran away to Europe and started life over . . . Maybe I could sell the *International Herald Tribune,* like those young girls used to.[1]

The phone rang. Kugelmass lifted it to his ear mechanically.

"Bring her over," Persky said. "I think I got the bugs out of it."

Kugelmass's heart leaped. "You're serious?" he said. "You got it licked?"

"It was something in the transmission. Go figure."

"Persky, you're a genius. We'll be there in a minute. Less than a minute."

Again the lovers hurried to the magician's apartment, and again Emma Bovary climbed into the cabinet with her boxes. This time there was no kiss. Persky shut the doors, took a deep breath, and tapped the box three times. There was the reassuring popping noise, and when Persky peered inside, the box was empty. Madame Bovary was back in her novel. Kugelmass heaved a great sigh of relief and pumped the magician's hand.

"It's over," he said. "I learned my lesson. I'll never cheat again, I swear it." He pumped Persky's hand again and made a mental note to send him a necktie.

Three weeks later, at the end of a beautiful spring afternoon, Persky answered his doorbell. It was Kugelmass, with a sheepish expression on his face.

"O.K., Kugelmass," the magician said. "Where to this time?"

"It's just this once," Kugelmass said. "The weather is so lovely, and I'm not getting any younger. Listen, you've read 'Portnoy's Complaint'? Remember The Monkey?"[2]

"The price is now twenty-five dollars, because the cost of living is up, but I'll start you off with one freebie, due to all the trouble I caused you."

"You're good people," Kugelmass said, combing his few remaining hairs as he climbed into the cabinet again. "This'll work all right?"

"I hope. But I haven't tried it much since all that unpleasantness."

"Sex and romance," Kugelmass said from inside the box. "What we go through for a pretty face."

Persky tossed in a copy of "Portnoy's Complaint" and rapped three times on the box. This time, instead of a popping noise there was a dull explosion, followed by a series of crackling noises and a shower of sparks. Persky leaped back, was seized by a heart attack, and dropped dead. The cabinet burst into flames, and eventually the entire house burned down.

Kugelmass, unaware of this catastrophe, had his own problems. He had not been thrust into "Portnoy's Complaint," or into any other

9. Skating rink in Central Park.

1. This was what some American drop-outs of the 1950s did; Jean Seberg portrayed one in the 1959 film *Breathless.*

2. The leading character in Philip Roth's 1969 novel, The Monkey is less romantic than Flaubert's Emma Bovary and sexually carefree and . . . experimental.

novel, for that matter. He had been projected into an old textbook, "Remedial Spanish," and was running for his life over a barren, rocky terrain as the word *"tener"* ("to have")—a large and hairy irregular verb—raced after him on its spindly legs.

p. 1977

JOYCE CAROL OATES

The Lady with the Pet Dog

1

Strangers parted as if to make way for him.

There he stood. He was there in the aisle, a few yards away, watching her.

She leaned forward at once in her seat, her hand jerked up to her face as if to ward off a blow—but then the crowd in the aisle hid him, he was gone. She pressed both hands against her cheeks. He was not there, she had imagined him.

"My God," she whispered.

She was alone. Her husband had gone out to the foyer to make a telephone call; it was intermission at the concert, a Thursday evening.

Now she saw him again, clearly. He was standing there. He was staring at her. Her blood rocked in her body, draining out of her head . . . she was going to faint. . . . They stared at each other. They gave no sign of recognition. Only when he took a step forward did she shake her head *no—no—keep away*. It was not possible.

When her husband returned, she was staring at the place in the aisle where her lover had been standing. Her husband leaned forward to interrupt that stare.

"What's wrong?" he said. "Are you sick?"

Panic rose in her in long shuddering waves. She tried to get to her feet, panicked at the thought of fainting here, and her husband took hold of her. She stood like an aged woman, clutching the seat before her.

At home he helped her up the stairs and she lay down. Her head was like a large piece of crockery that had to be held still, it was so heavy. She was still panicked. She felt it in the shallows of her face, behind her knees, in the pit of her stomach. It sickened her, it made her think of mucus, of something thick and gray congested inside her, stuck to her, that was herself and yet not herself—a poison.

She lay with her knees drawn up toward her chest, her eyes hotly open, while her husband spoke to her. She imagined that other man saying, *Why did you run away from me?* Her husband was saying other words. She tried to listen to them. He was going to call the doctor, he said, and she tried to sit up. "No, I'm all right now," she said quickly. The panic was like lead inside her, so thickly congested.

How slow love was to drain out of her, how fluid and sticky it was inside her head!

Her husband believed her. No doctor. No threat. Grateful, she drew her husband down to her. They embraced, not comfortably. For years now they had not been comfortable together, in their intimacy and at a distance, and now they struggled gently as if the paces of this dance were too rigorous for them. It was something they might have known once, but had now outgrown. The panic in her thickened at this double betrayal: she drew her husband to her, she caressed him wildly, she shut her eyes to think about that other man.

A crowd of men and women parting, unexpectedly, and there he stood—there he stood—she kept seeing him, and yet her vision blotched at the memory. It had been finished between them, six months before, but he had come out here . . . and she had escaped him, now she was lying in her husband's arms, in his embrace, her face pressed against his. It was a kind of sleep, this love-making. She felt herself falling asleep, her body falling from her. Her eyes shut.

"I love you," her husband said fiercely, angrily.

She shut her eyes and thought of that other man, as if betraying him would give her life a center.

"Did I hurt you? Are you—?" her husband whispered.

Always this hot flashing of shame between them, the shame of her husband's near failure, the clumsiness of his love—

"You didn't hurt me," she said.

2

They had said good-by six months before. He drove her from Nantucket, where they had met, to Albany, New York, where she visited her sister. The hours of intimacy in the car had sealed something between them, a vow of silence and impersonality: she recalled the movement of the highways, the passing of other cars, the natural rhythms of the day hypnotizing her toward sleep while he drove. She trusted him, she could sleep in his presence. Yet she could not really fall asleep in spite of her exhaustion, and she kept jerking awake, frightened, to discover that nothing had changed—still the stranger who was driving her to Albany, still the highway, the sky, the antiseptic odor of the rented car, the sense of a rhythm behind the rhythm of the air that might unleash itself at any second. Everywhere on this highway, at this moment, there were men and women driving together, bonded together—what did that mean, to be together? What did it mean to enter into a bond with another person?

No, she did not really trust him; she did not really trust men. He would glance at her with his small cautious smile and she felt a declaration of shame between them.

Shame.

In her head she rehearsed conversations. She said bitterly, "You'll be relieved when we get to Albany. Relieved to get rid of me." They had spent so many days talking, confessing too much, driven to a pitch of childish excitement, laughing together on the beach, breaking into that pose of laughter that seems to eradicate the soul, so many days of this that the silence of the trip was like the silence of a hospital—all these surface noises, these rattles and hums, but an interior silence, a befuddlement. She said to him in her imagination, "One of us should die." Then she leaned over to touch him. She caressed the back of his neck. She said, aloud, "Would you like me to drive for a while?"

They stopped at a picnic area where other cars were stopped—couples, families—and walked together, smiling at their good luck. He put his arm around her shoulders and she sensed how they were in a posture together, a man and a woman forming a posture, a figure, that someone might sketch and show to them. She said slowly, "I don't want to go back. . . ."

Silence. She looked up at him. His face was heavy with her words, as if she had pulled at his skin with her fingers. Children ran nearby and distracted him—yes, he was a father too, his children ran like that, they tugged at his skin with their light, busy fingers.

"Are you so unhappy?" he said.

"I'm not unhappy, back there. I'm nothing. There's nothing to me," she said.

They stared at each other. The sensation between them was intense, exhausting. She thought that this man was her savior, that he had come to her at a time in her life when her life demanded completion, an end, a permanent fixing of all that was troubled and shifting and deadly. And yet it was absurd to think this. No person could save another. So she drew back from him and released him.

A few hours later they stopped at a gas station in a small city. She went to the women's rest room, having to ask the attendant for a key, and when she came back her eye jumped nervously onto the rented car—why? did she think he might have driven off without her?—onto the man, her friend, standing in conversation with the young attendant. Her friend was as old as her husband, over forty, with lanky, sloping shoulders, a full body, his hair thick, a dark, burnished brown, a festive color that made her eye twitch a little—and his hands were always moving, always those rapid conversational circles, going nowhere, gestures that were at once a little aggressive and apologetic.

She put her hand on his arm, a claim. He turned to her and smiled and she felt that she loved him, that everything in her life had forced her to this moment and that she had no choice about it.

They sat in the car for two hours, in Albany, in the parking lot of a Howard Johnson's restaurant, talking, trying to figure out their past, There was no future. They concentrated on the past, the several days behind them, lit up with a hot, dazzling August sun, like explosions that already belonged to other people, to strangers. Her face was faintly reflected in the green-tinted curve of the windshield, but she could not have recognized that face. She began to cry; she told herself: *I am not here, this will pass, this is nothing*. Still, she could not stop crying. The muscles of her face were springy, like a child's, unpredictable muscles. He stroked her arms, her shoulders, trying to comfort her. "This is so hard . . . this is impossible . . ." he said. She felt panic for the world outside this car, all that was not herself and this man, and at the same time she understood that she was free of him, as people are free of other people, she would leave him soon, safely, and within a few days he would have fallen into the past, the impersonal past. . . .

"I'm so ashamed of myself!" she said finally.

She returned to her husband and saw that another woman, a shadow-woman, had taken her place—noiseless and convincing, like a dancer performing certain difficult steps. Her husband folded her in his arms and talked to her of his own loneliness, his worries about his business, his health, his mother, kept tranquilized and mute in a nursing home, and her spirit detached itself from her and drifted about the rooms of the large house she lived in with her husband, a shadow-woman delicate and imprecise. There was no boundary to her, no edge. Alone, she took hot baths and sat exhausted in the steaming water, wondering at her perpetual exhaustion. All that winter she noticed the limp, languid weight of her arms, her veins bulging slightly with the pressure of her extreme weariness. *This is fate,* she thought, to be here and not there, to be one person and not another, a certain man's wife and not the wife of another man. The long, slow pain of this certainty rose in her, but it never became clear, it was baffling and imprecise. She could not be serious about it; she kept congratulating herself on her own good luck, to have escaped so easily, to have freed herself. So much love had gone into the first several years of her marriage that there wasn't much left, now, for another man. . . . She was certain of that. But the bath water made her dizzy, all that perpetual heat, and one day in January she drew a razor blade lightly across the inside of her arm, near the elbow, to see what would happen.

Afterward she wrapped a small towel around it, to stop the bleeding. The towel soaked through. She wrapped a bath towel around that and walked through the empty rooms of her home, lightheaded, hardly aware of the stubborn seeping of blood. There was no boundary to her in this house, no precise limit. She could flow out like her own blood and come to no end.

She sat for a while on a blue love seat, her mind empty. Her husband telephoned her when he would be staying late at the plant. He talked to her always about his plans, his problems, his business friends, his future. It was obvious that he had a future. As he spoke she nodded to encourage him, and her heartbeat quickened with the memory of her own, personal shame, the shame of this man's particular, private wife. One evening at dinner he leaned forward and put his head in his arms and fell asleep, like a child. She sat at the table with him for a while, watching him. His hair had gone gray, almost white, at the temples—no one would guess that he was so quick, so careful a man, still fairly young about the eyes. She put her hand on his head, lightly, as if to prove to herself that he was real. He slept, exhausted.

One evening they went to a concert and she looked up to see her lover there, in the crowded aisle, in this city, watching her. He was standing there, with his overcoat on, watching her. She went cold. That morning the telephone had rung while her husband was still home, and she had heard him answer it, heard him hang up—it must have been a wrong number—and when the telephone rang again, at 9:30, she had been afraid to answer it. She had left home to be out of the range of that ringing, but now, in this public place, in this busy auditorium, she found herself staring at that man, unable to make any sign to him, any gesture of recognition. . . .

He would have come to her but she shook her head. *No. Stay away.*

Her husband helped her out of the row of seats, saying, "Excuse us, please. Excuse us," so that strangers got to their feet, quickly, alarmed, to let them pass. Was that woman about to faint? What was wrong?

At home she felt the blood drain slowly back into her head. Her husband embraced her hips, pressing his face against her, in that silence that belonged to the earliest days of their marriage. She thought, *He will drive it out of me.* He made love to her and she was back in the auditorium again, sitting alone, now that the concert was over. The stage was empty; the heavy velvet curtains had not been drawn; the musicians' chairs were empty, everything was silent and expectant; in the aisle her lover stood and smiled at her—Her husband was impatient. He was apart from her, working on her, operating on her; and then, stricken, he whispered, "Did I hurt you?"

The telephone rang the next morning. Dully, sluggishly, she answered it. She recognized his voice at once—that "Anna?" with its lifting of the second syllable, questioning and apologetic and making its claim—"Yes, what do you want?" she said.

"Just to see you. Please—"

"I can't."

"Anna, I'm sorry, I didn't mean to upset you—"

"I can't see you."

"Just for a few minutes—I have to talk to you—"

"But why, why now? Why now?" she said.

She heard her voice rising, but she could not stop it. He began to talk again, drowning her out. She remembered his rapid conversation. She remembered his gestures, the witty energetic circling of his hands.

"Please don't hang up!" he cried.

"I can't—I don't want to go through it again—"

"I'm not going to hurt you. Just tell me how you are."

"Everything is the same."

"Everything is the same with me."

She looked up at the ceiling, shyly. "Your wife? Your children?"

"The same."

"Your son?"

"He's fine—"

"I'm glad to hear that. I—"

"Is it still the same with you, your marriage? Tell me what you feel. What are you thinking?"

"I don't know. . . ."

She remembered his intense, eager words, the movement of his hands, that impatient precise fixing of the air by his hands, the jabbing of his fingers.

"Do you love me?" he said.

"No," she said.

She could not answer.

"I'll come over to see you," he said.

What will come next, what will happen?

Flesh hardening on his body, aging. Shrinking. He will grow old, but not soft like her husband. They are two different types: he is nervous, lean, energetic, wise. She will grow thinner, as the tension radiates out from her backbone, wearing down her flesh. Her collarbones will jut out of her skin. Her husband, caressing her in their bed, will discover that she is another woman—she is not there with him—instead she is rising in an elevator in a downtown hotel, carrying a book as a prop, or walking quickly away from that hotel, her head bent and filled with secrets. Love, what to do with it? . . . Useless as moths' wings, as moths fluttering. . . . She feels the flutterings of silky, crazy wings in her chest.

He flew out to visit her every several weeks, staying at a different hotel each time. He telephoned her, and she drove down to park in an underground garage at the very center of the city.

She lay in his arms while her husband talked to her, miles away, one body fading into another. He will grow old, his body will change, she thought, pressing her cheek against the back of one of these men. If it was her lover, they were in a hotel room: always the propped-up little booklet describing the hotel's many services, with color photographs of its cocktail lounge and dining room and coffee shop. Grow old, leave me, die, go back to your neurotic wife and your sad, ordinary children, she thought, but still her eyes closed gratefully against his skin and she felt how complete their silence was, how they had come to rest in each other.

"Tell me about your life here. The people who love you," he said, as he always did.

One afternoon they lay together for four hours. It was her birthday and she was intoxicated with her good fortune, this prize of the afternoon, this man in her arms! She was a little giddy, she talked too much. She told him about her parents, about her husband. . . . "They were all people I believed in, but it turned out wrong. Now, I believe in you. . . ." He laughed as if shocked by her words. She did not understand. Then she understood. "But I believe truly in you. I can't think of myself without you," she said. . . . He spoke of his wife, her ambitions, her intelligence, her use of the children against him, her use of his younger son's blindness, all of his words gentle and hypnotic and convincing in the late afternoon peace of this hotel room . . . and she felt the terror of laughter, threatening laughter. Their words, like their bodies, were aging.

She dressed quickly in the bathroom, drawing her long hair up around the back of her head, fixing it as always, anxious that everything be the same. Her face was slightly raw, from his face. The rubbing of his skin. Her eyes were too bright, wearily bright. Her hair was blond but not so blond as it had been that summer in the white Nantucket air.

She ran water and splashed it on her face. She blinked at the water. Blind. Drowning. She thought with satisfaction that soon, soon, he would be back home, in that house on Long Island she had never seen, with that woman she had never seen, sitting on the edge of another bed, putting on his shoes. She wanted nothing except to be free of him. Why not be free? *Oh,* she thought suddenly, *I will follow you back and kill you. You and her and the little boy. What is there to stop me?*

She left him. Everyone on the street pitied her, that look of absolute zero.

3

A man and a child, approaching her. The sharp acrid smell of fish. The crashing of waves. Anna pretended not to notice the father with his son—there was something strange about them. That frank, silent intimacy, too gentle, the man's bare feet in the water and the boy a few feet away, leaning away from his father. He was about nine years old and still his father held his hand.

A small yipping dog, a golden dog, bounded near them.

Anna turned shyly back to her reading; she did not want to have to speak to these neighbors. She saw the man's shadow falling over her legs, then over the pages of her book, and she had the idea that he wanted to see what she was reading. The dog nuzzled her; the man called him away.

She watched them walk down the beach. She was relieved that the man had not spoken to her.

She saw them in town later that day, the two of them brown-haired and patient, now wearing sandals, walking with that same look of care. The man's white shorts were soiled and a little baggy. His pullover shirt was a faded green. His face was broad, the cheekbones wide, spaced widely apart, the eyes stark in their sockets, as if they fastened onto objects for no reason, ponderous and edgy. The little boy's face was pale and sharp; his lips were perpetually parted.

Anna realized that the child was blind.

The next morning, early, she caught sight of them again. For some reason she went to the back door of her cottage. She faced the sea breeze eagerly. Her heart hammered. . . . She had been here, in her family's old house, for three days, alone, bitterly satisfied at being alone, and now it was a puzzle to her how her soul strained to fly outward, to meet with another person. She watched the man with his son, his cautious, rather stooped shoulders above the child's small shoulders.

The man was carrying something, it looked like a notebook. He sat on the sand, not far from Anna's spot of the day before, and the dog rushed up to them. The child approached the edge of the ocean, timidly. He moved in short jerky steps, his legs stiff. The dog ran around him. Anna heard the child crying out a word that sounded like "Ty"—it must have been the dog's name—and then the man joined in, his voice heavy and firm.

"Ty—"

Anna tied her hair back with a yellow scarf and went down to the beach.

The man glanced around at her. He smiled. She stared past him at the waves. To talk to him or not to talk—she had the freedom of that choice. For a moment she felt that she had made a mistake, that the child and the dog would not protect her, that behind the man's ordinary, friendly face there was a certain arrogant maleness—then she relented, she smiled shyly.

"A nice house you've got there," the man said.

She nodded her thanks.

The man pushed his sunglasses up on his forehead. Yes, she recognized the eyes of the day before—intelligent and nervous, the sockets pale, untanned.

"Is that your telephone ringing?" he said.

She did not bother to listen. "It's a wrong number," she said.

Her husband calling: she had left home for a few days, to be alone.

But the man, settling himself on the sand, seemed to misinterpret this. He smiled in surprise, one corner of his mouth higher than the other. He said nothing. Anna wondered: *What is he thinking?* The dog was leaping about her, panting against her legs, and she laughed in embarrassment. She bent to pet it, grateful for its busyness. "Don't let him jump up on you," the man said. "He's a nuisance."

The dog was a small golden retriever, a young dog. The blind child, standing now in the water, turned to call the dog to him. His voice was shrill and impatient.

"Our house is the third one down—the white one," the man said.

She turned, startled. "Oh, did you buy it from Dr. Patrick? Did he die?"

"Yes, finally. . . ."

Her eyes wandered nervously over the child and the dog. She felt the nervous beat of her heart out to the very tips of her fingers, the fleshy tips of her fingers: little hearts were there, pulsing. *What is he thinking?* The man had opened his notebook. He had a piece of charcoal and he began to sketch something.

Anna looked down at him. She saw the top of his head, his thick brown hair, the freckles on his shoulders, the quick, deft movement of his hand. Upside down, Anna herself being drawn. She smiled in surprise.

"Let me draw you. Sit down," he said.

She knelt awkwardly a few yards away. He turned the page of the sketch pad. The dog ran to her and she sat, straightening out her skirt beneath her, flinching from the dog's tongue. "Ty!" cried the child. Anna sat, and slowly the pleasure of the moment began to glow in her; her skin flushed with gratitude.

She sat there for nearly an hour. The man did not talk much. Back and forth the dog bounded, shaking itself. The child came to sit near them, in silence. Anna felt that she was drifting into a kind of trance while the man sketched her, half a dozen rapid sketches, the surface of her face given up to him. "Where are you from?" the man asked.

"Ohio. My husband lives in Ohio."

She wore no wedding band.

"Your wife—" Anna began.

"Yes?"

"Is she here?"

"Not right now."

She was silent, ashamed. She had asked an improper question. But the man did not seem to notice. He continued drawing her, bent over the sketch pad. When Anna said she had to go, he showed her the drawings—one after another of her, Anna, recognizably Anna, a woman in her early thirties, her hair smooth and flat across the top of her head, tied behind by a scarf. "Take the one you like best," he said, and she picked one of her with the dog in her lap, sitting very straight, her brows and eyes clearly defined, her lips girlishly pursed, the dog and her dress suggested by a few quick irregular lines.

"Lady with pet dog," the man said.

She spent the rest of that day reading, nearer her cottage. It was not really a cottage—it was a two-story house, large and ungainly and weathered. It was mixed up in her mind with her family, her own childhood, and she glanced up from her book, perplexed, as if waiting for one of her parents or her sister to come up to her. Then she thought of that man, the man with the blind child, the man with the dog, and she could not concentrate on her reading. Someone—probably her father—had marked a passage that must be important, but she kept reading and rereading it: *We try to discover in things, endeared to us on that account, the spiritual glamour which we ourselves have cast upon them; we are disillusioned, and learn that they are in themselves barren and devoid of the charm that they owed, in our minds, to the association of certain ideas. . . .*

She thought again of the man on the beach. She lay the book aside and thought of him: his eyes, his aloneness, his drawings of her.

They began seeing each other after that. He came to her front door in the evening, without the child; he drove her into town for dinner. She was shy and extremely pleased. The darkness of the expensive restaurant released her; she heard herself chatter; she leaned forward and seemed to be offering her face up to him, listening to him. He talked about his work on a Long Island newspaper and she seemed to be listening to him, as she stared at his face, arranging her own face into the expression she had seen in that charcoal drawing. Did he see her like that, then?—girlish and withdrawn and patrician? She felt the weight of his interest in her, a force that fell upon her like a blow. A repeated blow. Of course he was married, he had children—of course she was married, permanently married. This flight from her husband was not important. She had left him before, to be alone, it was not important. Everything in her was slender and delicate and not important.

They walked for hours after dinner, looking at the other strollers, the weekend visitors, the tourists, the couples like themselves. Surely they were mistaken for a couple, a married couple. *This is the hour in which everything is decided,* Anna thought. They had both had several drinks and they talked a great deal. Anna found herself saying too much, stopping and starting giddily. She put her hand to her forehead, feeling faint.

"It's from the sun—you've had too much sun—" he said.

At the door to her cottage, on the front porch, she heard herself asking him if he would like to come in. She allowed him to lead her inside, to close the door. *This is not important,* she thought clearly, *he doesn't mean it, he doesn't love me, nothing will come of it.* She was frightened, yet it seemed to her necessary to give in; she had to leave Nantucket with that act completed, an act of adultery, an accomplishment she would take back to Ohio and to her marriage.

Later, incredibly, she heard herself asking: "Do you . . . do you love me?"

"You're so beautiful!" he said, amazed.

She felt this beauty, shy and glowing and centered in her eyes. He stared at her. In this large, drafty house, alone together, they were like accomplices, conspirators. She could not think: how old was she? which year was this? They had done something unforgivable together, and the knowledge of it was tugging at their faces. A cloud seemed to pass over her. She felt herself smiling shrilly.

Afterward, a peculiar raspiness, a dryness of breath. He was silent. She felt a strange, idle fear, a sense of the danger outside this room and this old, comfortable bed—a danger that would not recognize her as the lady in that drawing, the lady with the pet dog. There was nothing to say to this man, this stranger. She felt the beauty draining out of her face, her eyes fading.

"I've got to be alone," she told him.

He left, and she understood that she would not see him again. She stood by the window of the room, watching the ocean. A sense of shame overpowered her: it was smeared everywhere on her body, the smell of it, the richness of it. She tried to recall him, and his face was confused in her memory: she would have to shout to him across a jumbled space, she would have to wave her arms wildly. *You love me! You must love me!* But she knew he did not love her, and she did not love him; he was a man who drew everything up into himself, like all men, walking away, free to walk away, free to have his own thoughts, free to envision her body, all the secrets of her body. . . . And she lay down again in the bed, feeling how heavy this body had become, her insides heavy with shame, the very backs of her eyelids coated with shame.

"This is the end of one part of my life," she thought.

But in the morning the telephone rang. She answered it. It was her lover: they talked brightly and happily. She could hear the eagerness in his voice, the love in his voice, that same still, sad amazement—she understood how simple life was, there were no problems.

They spent most of their time on the beach, with the child and the dog. He joked and was serious at the same time. He said, once, "You have defined my soul for me," and she laughed to hide her alarm. In a few days it was time for her to leave. He got a sitter for the boy and took the ferry with her to the mainland, then rented a car to drive her up to Albany. She kept thinking: *Now something will happen. It will come to an end.* But most of the drive was silent and hypnotic. She wanted him to joke with her, to say again that she had defined his soul for him, but he drove fast, he was serious, she distrusted the hawkish look of his profile—she did not know him at all. At a gas station she splashed her face with cold water. Alone in the grubby little rest room, shaky and very much alone. In such places are women totally alone with their bodies. The body grows heavier, more evil, in such silence. . . . On the beach everything had been noisy with sunlight and gulls and waves; here, as if run to earth, everything was cramped and silent and dead.

She went outside, squinting. There he was, talking with the station attendant. She could not think as she returned to him whether she wanted to live or not.

She stayed in Albany for a few days, then flew home to her husband. He met her at the airport, near the luggage counter, where her three pieces of pale-brown luggage were brought to him on a conveyor belt, to be claimed by him. He kissed her on the cheek. They shook hands, a little embarrassed. She had come home again.

"How will I live out the rest of my life?" she wondered.

In January her lover spied on her: she glanced up and saw him, in a public place, in the DeRoy Symphony Hall. She was paralyzed with fear. She nearly fainted. In this faint she felt her husband's body, loving her, working its love upon her, and she shut her eyes harder to keep out the certainty of his love—sometimes he failed at loving her, sometimes he succeeded, it had nothing to do with her or her pity or her ten years of love for him, it had nothing to do with a woman at all. It was a private act accomplished by a man, a husband or a lover, in communion with his own soul, his manhood.

Her husband was forty-two years old now, growing slowly into middle age, getting heavier, softer. Her lover was about the same age, narrower in the shoulders, with a full, solid chest, yet lean, nervous. She thought, in her paralysis, of men and how they love freely and eagerly so long as their bodies are capable of love, love for a woman; and then, as love fades in their bodies, it fades from their souls and they become immune and immortal and ready to die.

Her husband was a little rough with her, as if impatient with himself. "I love you," he said fiercely, angrily. And then, ashamed, he said, "Did I hurt you? . . ."

"You didn't hurt me," she said.

Her voice was too shrill for their embrace.

While he was in the bathroom she went to her closet and took out that drawing of the summer before. There she was, on the beach at Nantucket, a lady with a pet dog, her eyes large and defined, the dog in her lap hardly more than a few snarls, a few coarse soft lines of charcoal . . . her dress smeared, her arms oddly limp . . . her hands not well drawn at all. . . . She tried to think: did she love the man who had drawn this? did he love her? The fever in her husband's body had touched her and driven her temperature up, and now she stared at the drawing with a kind of lust, fearful of seeing an ugly soul in that woman's face, fearful of seeing the face suddenly through her lover's eyes. She breathed quickly and harshly, staring at the drawing.

And so, the next day, she went to him at his hotel. She wept, pressing against him, demanding of him. "What do you want? Why are you here? Why don't you let me alone?" He told her that he wanted nothing. He expected nothing. He would not cause trouble.

"I want to talk about last August," he said.

"Don't—" she said.

She was hypnotized by his gesturing hands, his nervousness, his obvious agitation. He kept saying, "I understand. I'm making no claims upon you."

They became lovers again.

He called room service for something to drink and they sat side by side on his bed, looking through a copy of *The New Yorker*, laughing at the cartoons. It was so peaceful in this room, so complete. They were on a holiday. It was a secret holiday. Four-thirty in the afternoon, on a Friday, an ordinary Friday: a secret holiday.

"I won't bother you again," he said.

He flew back to see her again in March, and in late April. He telephoned her from his hotel—a different hotel each time—and she came down to him at once. She rose to him in various elevators, she knocked on the doors of various rooms, she stepped into his embrace, breathless and guilty and already angry with him, pleading with him. One morning in May, when he telephoned, she pressed her forehead against the doorframe and could not speak. He kept saying, "What's wrong? Can't you talk? Aren't you alone?" She felt that she was going insane. Her head would burst. Why, why did he love her, why did he pursue her? Why did he want her to die?

She went to him in the hotel room. A familiar room: had they been here before? "Everything is repeating itself. Everything is stuck," she said. He framed her face in his hands and said that she looked thinner—was she sick?—what was wrong? She shook herself free. He, her lover, looked about the same. There was a small, angry pimple on his neck. He stared at her, eagerly and suspiciously. Did she bring bad news?

"So you love me? You love me?" she asked.

"Why are you so angry?"

"I want to be free of you. The two of us free of each other."

"That isn't true—you don't want that—"

He embraced her. She was wild with that old, familiar passion for him, her body clinging to his, her arms not strong enough to hold him. Ah, what despair!—what bitter hatred she felt!—she needed this man for her salvation, he was all she had to live for, and yet she could not believe in him. He embraced her thighs, her hips, kissing her, pressing his warm face against her, and yet she could not believe in him, not really. She needed him in order to live, but he was not worth her love, he was not worth her dying. . . . She promised herself this: when she got back home, when she was alone, she would draw the razor more deeply across her arm.

The telephone rang and he answered it: a wrong number.

"Jesus," he said.

They lay together, still. She imagined their posture like this, the two of them one figure, one substance; and outside this room and this bed there was a universe of disjointed, separate things, blank things, that had nothing to do with them. She would not be Anna out there, the lady in the drawing. He would not be her lover.

"I love you so much . . ." she whispered.

"Please don't cry! We have only a few hours, please. . . ."

It was absurd, their clinging together like this. She saw them as a single figure in a drawing, their arms and legs entwined, their heads pressing mutely together. Helpless substance, so heavy and warm and doomed. It was absurd that any human being should be so important to another human being. She wanted to laugh: a laugh might free them both.

She could not laugh.

Sometime later he said, as if they had been arguing, "Look. It's you. You're the one who doesn't want to get married. You lie to me—"

"Lie to you?"

"You love me but you won't marry me, because you want something left over—Something not finished—All your life you can attribute your misery to me, to our not being married—you are using me—"

"Stop it! You'll make me hate you!" she cried.

"You can say to yourself that you're miserable because of *me*. We will never be married, you will never be happy, neither one of us will ever be happy—"

"I don't want to hear this!" she said.

She pressed her hands flatly against her face.

She went to the bathroom to get dressed. She washed her face and part of her body, quickly. The fever was in her, in the pit of her belly. She would rush home and strike a razor across the inside of her arm and free that pressure, that fever.

The impatient bulging of the veins: an ordeal over.

The demand of the telephone's ringing: that ordeal over.

The nuisance of getting the car and driving home in all that five o'clock traffic: an ordeal too much for a woman.

The movement of this stranger's body in hers: over, finished.

Now, dressed, a little calmer, they held hands and talked. They had to talk swiftly, to get all their news in: he did not trust the people who worked for him, he had faith in no one, his wife had moved to a textbook publishing company and was doing well, she had inherited a Ben Shahn[1] painting from her father and wanted to "touch it up a little"—she was crazy!—his blind son was at another school, doing fairly well, in fact his children were all doing fairly well in spite of the stupid mistake of their parents' marriage—and what about her? What about her life? She told him in a rush the one thing he wanted to hear: that she lived with her husband lovelessly, the two of them polite strangers, sharing a bed, lying side by side in the night in that bed, bodies out of which souls had fled. There was no longer even any shame between them.

"And what about me? Do you feel shame with me still?" he asked.

She did not answer. She moved away from him and prepared to leave.

Then, a minute later, she happened to catch sight of his reflection in the bureau mirror—he was glancing down at himself, checking himself mechanically, impersonally, preparing also to leave. He too would leave this room: he too was headed somewhere else.

She stared at him. It seemed to her that in this instant he was breaking from her, the image of her lover fell free of her, breaking from her . . . and she realized that he existed in a dimension quite

1. Famous American painter (1898–1969) who specialized in scenes of social protest.

apart from her, a mysterious being. And suddenly, joyfully, she felt a miraculous calm. This man was her husband, truly—they were truly married, here in this room—they had been married haphazardly and accidentally for a long time. In another part of the city she had another husband, a "husband," but she had not betrayed that man, not really. This man, whom she loved above any other person in the world, above even her own self-pitying sorrow and her own life, was her truest lover, her destiny. And she did not hate him, she did not hate herself any longer; she did not wish to die; she was flooded with a strange certainty, a sense of gratitude, of pure selfless energy. It was obvious to her that she had, all along, been behaving correctly; out of instinct.

What triumph, to love like this in any room, anywhere, risking even the craziest of accidents!

"Why are you so happy? What's wrong?" he asked, startled. He stared at her. She felt the abrupt concentration in him, the focusing of his vision on her, almost a bitterness in his face, as if he feared her. What, was it beginning all over again? Their love beginning again, in spite of them? "How can you look so happy?" he asked. "We don't have any right to it. Is it because . . . ?"

"Yes," she said.

1972

The Novel

A PREFACE TO THE NOVEL

We've been reading short stories and a few other kinds of brief narrative, but this book is called an introduction to *fiction,* and there is a very important kind of fiction we've been ignoring—the **novel.** We've all read novels; indeed, some people think fiction is virtually another name for novel. It's so familiar a form we scarcely ever stop to ask ourselves just what the novel, as distinct from other fictional kinds, is. Let's look at some of its characteristics:

The novel is a long narrative. Though it is arbitrary to say just where the long short story becomes the short novel, and we would always do better judging individual works, we can expect that most fictional narratives of less than about 15,000 words (about 25 pages in this book) will display the characteristic development of the short story. Longer works than these will likely be **short novels** (also called **novellas** or **novelettes**). *The Short Happy Life of Francis Macomber,* at about 14,000 words, most readers consider a short story; *Bartleby,* at about 16,000 words, many call a short novel, and almost everyone would agree that *The Temptation of Jack Orkney,* which is very nearly twice that long, is a short novel. Somewhere around 50,000 words (over 80 pages in this book) we begin to speak simply of novels.

What differentiates the novel from the short story is not only length, but a combination as well of number of characters, scenes, and incidents; duration and scope of the action; and complexity of the whole work or of one or more of the elements. *Heart of Darkness* is an initiation story, like those in Chapter 6 or like *Young Goodman Brown.* Indeed, the central themes of the Conrad and Hawthorne stories—the fundamental and universal evil in man's nature—are strikingly similar. Yet *Young Goodman Brown* is a short story of about average length, and *Heart of Darkness* is a short novel. The distinction is partly one of length—*Heart of Darkness* is six or seven times as long as *Young Goodman Brown*—and partly a matter of the greater scope and complexity of the longer work. The Conrad novel has many more separate scenes and incidents, several more characters, and a journey that in time and space is many times longer than Brown's journey into the New England woods. While both narratives treat moral evil, *Heart of Darkness* treats political and economic evil as well, and at the same time raises other related but tangential themes such as questioning man's ability to transmit knowledge gained from experience. *The Temptation of Jack Orkney* is only three times as long as Chekhov's *The Lady with the Dog* (and if anyone could write a 7,000-word novel it would be that master of economy, Chekhov), yet, by virtue of length, scope, and complexity, *Orkney* is a short novel and *The Lady with the Dog* a short story. Both show a man coming to an awareness of the underlying mystery in existence; both do so through the consciousness of the protagonist; both frequently change scene and setting (indeed, the time and distance covered in the Chekhov story are greater than those in the Lessing). *Orkney,* however, has a considerably larger cast of characters, a larger variety of incidents, and, aside from the theme involving life's mystery, treats politics and political history, group dynamics, the relation of generations, the extent to which we are determined by heredity. We know more of Orkney's past and in more detail, and we know more facets of his life and character than we do of Gurov's. These quantitative factors do not necessarily lead to qualitative judgments: more may be —but is not necessarily—better, and essences may be more revealing, more profound, more moving at times than detail.

Though novels by virtue of their length are not necessarily better than short stories, sheer length does make a difference in the nature of the reading experience. There is more to take in as we read, more to evaluate or "process," more to select and to remember; there are therefore more details to make into patterns and more patterns to project in the way of anticipating what will happen next and what it all means. Reading the first part of *The Most Dangerous Game* we pieced together hints about superstition and the discovery of a Gothic castle in the middle of the jungle and anticipated that the story might have something to do with the supernatural or monstrous. We may also have stored the early conversation about hunting, so that when the Cossack colonel turns out to be a hunter and to know about Rainsford's hunting prowess, we may have related the two details and anticipated a pattern. In the early pages of *The Temptation of Jack Orkney,* the dying father, Orkney's sense of his own aging and mortality, the encounter with the young girl on the train, the opportunity of a job in Nigeria, and the title may lead us to anticipate one form of development. His identification with his father and his expecting a special message from him, his sense that his brother and sister are different from him (and perhaps not so intelligent, sophisticated, worthy), his surprising discovery that they are physically and spiritually closer together than he had thought, and the introduction of the younger generation, contribute to a different pattern and set of expectations. His socialist activism, his journalism, the rather different activism of the young, and the religious theme give us still more to digest, formulate, anticipate as the story grows in length and piles on incident, detail, characters.

Though the "guessing game" may be more complicated and difficult in the novel than in the short story, and the suspense or anticipation more intense (who, after all, bothers to turn to the end of a short story to see how it will come out?), at the end there is but one outcome, all the rest wrong and discarded like the Gothic expectations in *The Most Dangerous Game.* So what's the difference?

Well, there is first of all the difference in the experience, in duration as well as in complexity and intensity. Though we may be interrupted or we may put down a short story and pick it up again, most often we read it in a single sitting. Sometimes we read short novels that way, and once in a while we pick up a full-length novel some evening, as a contemporary did *Jane Eyre*, and read it through in a sitting, marrying Mr. Rochester at three o'clock in the morning. Most of the time, however, we live with a novel over a period of time, and during the day, while we are doing other things, characters, episodes, and scenes come back to us, or we see new shapes and possibilities or harden our expectations of what is to come. When we return to the novel, we re-enter its world, readjust our minds and imaginations to it, and give it what we might think of as stereo-imaginative depth or solidity. The novel is a different narrative kind from the short story in a sense not because of what *it* is but of what *we* become while we read it. Nor do our "wrong guesses," the false leads in the story, go away entirely, despite their ultimate irrelevance to the outcome. They are part of the novel, part of the experience of reading it, even when we read it again knowing how it will come out: the alternative possibilities are part of the texture of the work. *Heart of Darkness* differs from *Young Goodman Brown* not only in length, setting, characters, but in all that *might* have happened in it but didn't.

Even at the end of a story it is not always possible to "discard the irrelevant" and reduce the whole to a single pattern or meaning. The precise meaning of a haunting story like *The Lottery*, for example, is elusive. But after a few readings, several of them perhaps at a single sitting, we can hold almost all the details of the story in mind at once, so that it finally has a rather fixed shape or presence no matter how indefinable its ultimate significance. *Heart of Darkness* has a similar elusiveness, but the sheer weight of detail makes it all but impossible (at least for me) to hold in the mind at once and fit into a definitive pattern; we forget some detail or cannot fit others in, so that each reading is to a greater or lesser degree a partial one. The first-person narrator who is not Marlowe, the shelling of the African coast, the Russian sailor and his book, the helmsman and his death, the skulls, the Amazonian dancer, The Intended—what "minor" details are we forgetting this time? (And what details are minor in this reading?) We must go back and read the novel again, experience it again. And when we have finished it, we are not finished with it. The duration of the experience, the variety and complexity of mental and emotional activities as we read a novel each time, the fact that a novel hardly ever can be taken entirely into our minds, reconstructed and contemplated in its entirety and made our own —all of these qualities or potential qualities inhere in the rather obvious and trivial statement that "The novel is a long narrative."

The novel is a continuous narrative. There are long narratives that we don't call novels because they are not continuous. John Cheever's *The Housebreaker of Shady Hill*, for example (from which *The Country Husband* is taken), is a book-length work of fiction about people who live in a new, middle-class, commuter suburb of New York City just after World War II. But rather than one continuous narrative, the book is made up of a number of narratives, each about a different set of characters. This is clearly a collection of short stories, not a novel. *The Book of the Thousand Nights and a Night (The Arabian*

Nights) is a long narrative or series of narratives in prose, connected by a frame story: here Shahrazad seeks to stave off execution by keeping her husband enthralled from night to night by the stories she tells. Her stories make no continuous whole, involving different sets of characters, settings, actions, kinds of action, and even kinds of reality. The frame is insufficient to bind the work into a continuous narrative that could be called a novel. Dickens's *Pickwick Papers* begins with a comparable frame—the adventures of the members of the Pickwick Club—and is somewhat more fully bound together by the fact that most of the early episodes involve the club members and most of them follow, at least chronologically, one from the other. In the first half of the novel, however, there are a good many stories within the story, told by strangers, involving characters we have not heard of before and won't hear of again—some of the stories funny, some melodramatic, some realistic, some fantastic. But the frame does —even if at first just barely—hold the narrative together, and in the second half the "miscellany" becomes a novel, bound together by the continuing story of the famous Bardell v. Pickwick breach of promise suit and its consequences. The book emerges, as a result, as one of the looser and baggier of those loose, baggy monsters called Victorian novels, but a novel nevertheless. There are episodic novels in which a hero or heroine runs into one adventure after another without logical or necessary connection, and in some cases even without the change or development in the central character we find in such novels as Defoe's *Moll Flanders.*

If we chose, we could make these same distinctions about television programs. Continuous, with characters developing through the episodes, *Roots* and *Upstairs, Downstairs* would be novels, wouldn't they? But is *All in the Family,* for example, or *The Rockford Files* a novel or a collection of "short stories"?

Novels contain a number of characters and incidents, as we have mentioned earlier in connection with length. They vary greatly, however, not only in the number of characters and incidents, or the ratio of characters to incident, but also in the amount of emphasis on an individual character or characters and the tightness of the connection of the incidents. *Crime and Punishment* contains a fairly large number of characters and a rather large number of incidents, but it centers on a single character—the student Raskalnikov—and on a single action—his planning and carrying out a murder, and its consequences. Huckleberry Finn's numerous adventures as he travels down the Mississippi River are bound together not by a single action nor by any inherent logic in their sequence but by the river, by the central character and his language (unlike Raskalnikov, Huck tells his own story), and by the overall pattern of Huck's attempt to escape society and its attempt to trap him. *War and Peace* follows many characters both fictional and historical (including Napoleon) through many incidents before, during, and after the French invasion of Russia in 1812. The whole is woven together by the relationships of the characters, the story of the impact of the war and of Western culture on Russian society, and by the interconnected themes of private and public history, the individual's sense of free will and apparent historical necessity, chance and Divine will.

The novel is a temporal genre. I have already stressed the fact that a novel because of its length offers a reading experience of some duration: it is read over a fairly extended period of time. Because of its length it also can cover in sufficient detail a rather long period of fictional time. It typically covers years and it is not unusual for a novel to span the major portion of a character's life. Even in James Joyce's *Ulysses* (1922), where the action is carefully restricted to less than a day, through various kinds of exposition, especially characters' memories and associations, we learn a good deal about the three main characters' pasts (and a full earlier history of one, Stephen Dedalus, is available to us in another Joyce novel, *Portrait of the Artist as a Young Man*). Time is, indeed, one of the typical subjects of the novel. There are, for example, **historical novels**—novels set in the past that involve actual people or events of the past, that often investigate the nature of history or the effect of the past on the present or of historical forces on the individual—novels such as *War and Peace,* the novels of Sir Walter Scott, or *Gone With the Wind.* There are **fictional biographies** or **autobiographies** like *Sons and Lovers* and *David Copperfield,* which narrate the story of a character's life in third- or first-person respectively. There are even novels that quite directly treat time itself: Marcel Proust's *Remembrance of Things Past* (whose French title literally means *In Search of Lost Time*) or another, more recent multivolume novel, Anthony Powell's *A Dance to the Music of Time,* not to mention such time-ridden novels as Thomas Wolfe's *Of Time and the River.*

The dominant novel kind, the **Bildungsroman** or **apprentice novel**, exemplified by Goethe's *Wilhelm Meister* (1796–1829), demands a rather extensive period of fictional time, for it traces the protagonist from youth to maturity, usually from his rejection of his family, his society, and religion and his roving search for a new order, purpose, and meaning in life, to his discovery of or return to a new home, society, and world-view. If, as some would maintain, all short stories are initiation stories, it may as readily be claimed that all novels are *Bildungsromanen.* Initiation, the sudden insight or illumination (what Joyce called an *epiphany*) is indeed eminently suited to the compact form of the short story, and so too the narrative of growth and change, of quest and development, is suited to the broader, more inclusive form and more leisurely pace of the novel.

The novel is a long continuous narrative in prose, with a number of characters and incidents, and informed by time. Like the short story, it is a *written, original form* (see Chapter 8). We cannot confidently go beyond this simple and somewhat superficial definition, for *the novel genre is a form in flux.*

Indeed, it is not a genre in being but a genre-becoming; an evolutionary, adaptive, ever-changing form, like biological species seen in time-lapse photography. The novel was born about the time when an old order of the world—hierarchical and static, in which everything (serf, knight, king; all literary genres) had a fixed or ideal nature and a predetermined and proper place in a *vertical* Great Chain of Being—was toppling, and a new world view was arising—*horizontal,* dominated by time, history, process, evolution. It is no wonder that the characteristic and dominant genre of that world is dynamic and without an ideal or fixed form.

Though there were long narrative prose works in the classical periods which some would now call novels, there were no definitions of the novel as a genre then, as there were of comedy, tragedy, epic, pastoral, and other established forms, nor was there anything called the novel for centuries to come. During the Middle Ages in Italy there were brief, more or less realistic tales like those in Boccaccio's *Decameron* that were called **novelle** (singular, *novella*), and there was in Europe a still older form known as the **romance** (because it was chiefly written in the Romance languages) that in the Middle Ages recounted the high-flown, fanciful adventures of knights and princesses and other wondrous tales. In France, from about the middle of the seventeenth century to the middle of the eighteenth the two streams merged into what we would at some point call novels: perhaps Mlle. de Scudéry's romances at the beginning of this period; perhaps the *Princesse de Clèves* (1678) and other relatively realistic works by Marguerite de la Vergne (Mme. de la Fayette); certainly Prévost's *Manon Lescaut* and Marivaux's *Marianne* in 1731. The narrative traditions of the Continent were fed in England by local narratives and traditions from the Arthurian legends through the moral allegories of John Bunyan (whose *Pilgrim's Progress* was published in 1678). Early in the eighteenth century Daniel Defoe conflated journalistic narrative, spiritual autobiography, and travel literature into works such as *Robinson Crusoe* (1719) and *Moll Flanders* (1722) that many consider the first "true" novels in English. Others, however, call Samuel Richardson's *Pamela; or, Virtue Rewarded* (1740–41) the first English novel. *Pamela* stimulated—or irritated—Henry Fielding into writing the story of Pamela's "virtuous brother," Joseph Andrews (1742), to be followed in 1749 by *Tom Jones.* By the middle of the eighteenth century, then, the English novel was well under way.

A century or so later it seemed quite reasonable to identify the novel genre with **verisimilitude** or **realism** in its many aspects. Looking back from the 1850s or '60s, the best fiction seemed to be that which had contributed to "the rise of realism," as with Defoe's use of concrete physical detail; Charlotte Brontë's unbeautiful heroines and unhandsome heroes; George Eliot's imperfect "heroes" and her villains more weak than evil (to use only English examples). The history of the novel seemed one of "progress" from the errantly romantic, the exaggerated and incredible, to increasingly broad, deep, and skillful representations of everyday life. Even Victor Hugo (*Les Misérables*) and Dickens could be excused for their melodrama because of their social realism. The demonic *Wuthering Heights* and *Moby-Dick* might be grudgingly admitted to have a certain amount of power, but they were so overblown, so awkward that they were not admitted into the best critical company.

The century that followed the 1850s and '60s seemed to confirm the graph of rising and widening realism. The "lower classes" were now admitted into the novel as other than rogues or clowns. **Naturalism** portrayed people and their actions as largely determined by their biological natures. Following Émile Zola, Stephen Crane found nature merely indifferent and valueless. Humanity's lofty ideals and values, for Thomas Hardy, were out of step with nature's law, having outstripped God's plan, if there was a God, if there was a plan. For Conrad, natural man or man in nature was corrupt; all values were artificial, like rules of a game, but it was man's necessity, role, and glory to make and live by such rules, no matter that they were inevitably fictions. The dark and desperate view of humanity and nature, and even the phoniness of civilization itself, seemed confirmed by the First World War, and this view manifested itself in the novels of Hemingway and Fitzgerald and the entire "Lost Generation."

Meanwhile, the whole conception of human reality—our perception of our inner selves and the relationship between our perceptions and the reality of the outside world—was undergoing the same kind of questioning and revision that was giving birth to the newest of the sciences, psychology. From the mid-nineteenth to the mid-twentieth century the common assumption was that truth—about our motives, our "real selves"—lay deep within. If we could only strip away the outer layers of artificiality or pretense or hypocrisy, in look and language, and peer inside the human consciousness, we would really know truth. Over the years, George Eliot, Henry James, Marcel Proust analyzed the workings of their characters' minds and motives with increasing subtlety. Analysis is logical, and conventional language and narrative are satisfactory tools. Consciousness, however, is not essentially logical, and to reflect or represent its workings more unconventional methods are required. James Joyce, Virginia Woolf, and William Faulkner presented the mind at work not as a logical or systematic processor of stimuli and thoughts, but as a **stream of consciousness**—a rapid and ceaseless flow of perceptions, images, memories, and desires just on and just below the surface of the mind. Joyce represented this stream in *Ulysses* not only without logical analysis but in broken sentence fragments and somewhat bewildering sequences and recurrences of images.

Ulysses seems child's play, however, compared to Joyce's next (and last) novel, *Finnegan's Wake* (1939), which explores the nighttime world, the unconscious. One may analyze such a world in conventional, logical language, but to represent it accurately, Joyce felt obliged to reject analytical connectives, conventional syntax, and punctuation—the preconscious mind probably doesn't contain commas and subordinating conjunctions. He even had to dissolve and re-form words into something like perpetual puns, syllables suggesting simultaneously several words (sometimes in various languages). In such a world mere narrative sequence was of course the first thing to go.

For many readers—and writers—*Finnegan's Wake* marked a dead end. Just as a half-century earlier Dostoevsky showed in *Notes from the Underground* that the interior workings of the mind were as contradictory, confusing, and deceptive as spoken or social language, so Joyce's last novel seemed to suggest that to plumb the depths of consciousness was to reveal not some portable truth but chaos. There was quite soon in writers such as Alain Robbe-Grillet and other creators of **le nouveau roman** (the "new novel") a return from the depths of consciousness to the surface of experience. But the discouraging failure to reach truth by psychological analysis now extended to other structures—away with the artificiality of plot, which with its simple cause-effect assumptions did not represent but analyzed and thus distorted reality, and of character, which was a similar analytical distortion, presuming consistency, essence, unity in that bundle of contradictions known as a person. For an increasing number of novelists, the pretense that fiction somehow represented reality gave way.

I've already suggested in Chapter 7, "A Mode: Fantasy," the intellectual forces I see at work undermining our assumptions about the nature of reality and our faith in our ability to perceive and represent it in mathematics or literature. There is no way that this revolution could not have affected that genre most sensitive to social and perceptual change, the novel. The novel tradition no longer looks like the story of the rise of realism. There is new interest in and respect for the romance, the Gothic, the grotesque, the fantastic. We admire Joyce less nowadays for his dear, dirty Dublin than for the music and mystery of his words and his vision, and Lawrence's sexual scenarios as much for their mystical implications as for their physical explicitness. We no longer seek to explain (or explain away) what seemed fantastic in Kafka, Dostoyevsky, Dickens, but seek in them instead a kind of profound perception of human and cosmic irrationality.

The novel of our time has given us this new perspective and made us review its roots. John Fowles in *The Magus*, and Robert Coover in *The Universal Baseball Association*, for example, by the interpenetration of "reality" and fantasy, of fictions or games that may be real and reality that may be false, blur the borders of the regions of fact and fiction. Gabriel García Márquez so shifts time-schemes and juxtaposes people and events from different eras, and introduces the fantastic, the unnatural, the legendary and interweaves it so casually with the everyday, the borders are once more blurred. And it is now common in fiction for the author to intervene "in person" or as narrator, not merely to comment but to point out that you are reading fiction, an arbitrary and artificial world, and that he or she as maker of that fiction can change or "erase" events or characters and make it all otherwise.

We can, then, no longer assume that verisimilitude is a necessary characteristic of the novel, or that the history of the novel is a history of increasingly full and successful representation of everyday reality. Unless we want to say, as some have, that the novel in our time is in decline, or as others have been saying for some time, that the novel as a form is dead and is to be replaced by some other form of prose narrative.

The novel, in its relatively brief history, has already taken for its own subject matter ghosts and governesses, gold and gods; all continents and classes; packing plants and Providence; baseball and Beelzebub. It has absorbed into itself the disciplines of history, sociology, anthropology, journalism, and psychology, among others; it has taken in when needed the forms of the sermon, travel literature, autobiography spiritual and confessional, biography and history complete with footnotes, essays familiar and formal, analyses and processes from the causes of Napoleon's invasion of Russia, determinism and free will, to extracting sperm from a whale. It has been lyric and dramatic, comic and tragic, satiric and epic. Its very lack of generic definition has permitted it to adapt to the needs of each generation and decade for more than two centuries. It is probably doing so even now.

JOSEPH CONRAD

Heart of Darkness

1

The *Nellie,* a cruising yawl, swung to her anchor without a flutter of the sails, and was at rest. The flood had made, the wind was nearly calm, and being bound down the river, the only thing for it was to come to and wait for the turn of the tide.

The sea-reach[1] of the Thames stretched before us like the beginning of an interminable waterway. In the offing the sea and the sky were welded together without a joint, and in the luminous space the tanned sails of the barges drifting up with the tide seemed to stand still in red clusters of canvas sharply peaked, with gleams of varnished sprits. A haze rested on the low shores that ran out to sea in vanishing flatness. The air was dark above Gravesend,[2] and farther back still seemed condensed into a mournful gloom, brooding motionless over the biggest, and the greatest, town on earth.

The Director of Companies was our captain and our host. We four affectionately watched his back as he stood in the bows looking to seaward. On the whole river there was nothing that looked half so nautical. He resembled a pilot, which to a seaman is trustworthiness personified. It was difficult to realize his work was not out there in the luminous estuary, but behind him, within the brooding gloom.

Between us there was, as I have already said somewhere, the bond of the sea. Besides holding our hearts together through long periods of separation, it had the effect of making us tolerant of each other's yarns—and even convictions. The Lawyer—the best of old fellows—had, because of his many years and many virtues, the only cushion on deck, and was lying on the only rug. The Accountant had brought out already a box of dominoes, and was toying architecturally with the bones. Marlow sat cross-legged right aft, leaning against the mizzen-mast. He had sunken cheeks, a yellow complexion, a straight back, an ascetic aspect, and, with his arms dropped, the palms of hands outwards, resembled an idol. The Director, satisfied the anchor had good hold, made his way aft and sat down amongst us. We exchanged a few words lazily. Afterwards there was silence on board the yacht. For some reason

1. Straight course of an otherwise winding river as it approaches the sea.
2. Easternmost large town on the Thames before it reaches the sea, 26 miles from London.

or other we did not begin that game of dominoes. We felt meditative, and fit for nothing but placid staring. The day was ending in a serenity of still and exquisite brilliance. The water shone pacifically; the sky, without a speck, was a benign immensity of unstained light; the very mist on the Essex marshes was like a gauzy and radiant fabric, hung from the wooded rises inland, and draping the low shores in diaphanous folds. Only the gloom to the west, brooding over the upper reaches, became more somber every minute, as if angered by the approach of the sun.

And at last, in its curved and imperceptible fall, the sun sank low, and from glowing white changed to a dull red without rays and without heat, as if about to go out suddenly, stricken to death by the touch of that gloom brooding over a crowd of men.

Forthwith a change came over the waters, and the serenity became less brilliant but more profound. The old river in its broad reach rested unruffled at the decline of day, after ages of good service done to the race that peopled its banks, spread out in the tranquil dignity of a waterway leading to the uttermost ends of the earth. We looked at the venerable stream not in the vivid flush of a short day that comes and departs forever, but in the august light of abiding memories. And indeed nothing is easier for a man who has, as the phrase goes, "followed the sea" with reverence and affection, than to evoke the great spirit of the past upon the lower reaches of the Thames. The tidal current runs to and fro in its unceasing service, crowded with memories of men and ships it has borne to the rest of home or to the battles of the sea. It had known and served all the men of whom the nation is proud, from Sir Francis Drake to Sir John Franklin,[3] knights all, titled and untitled—the great knights-errant of the sea. It had borne all the ships whose names are like jewels flashing in the night of time, from the *Golden Hind* returning with her round flanks full of treasure, to be visited by the Queen's Highness and thus pass out of the gigantic tale, to the *Erebus* and *Terror*, bound on other conquests—and that never returned. It had known the ships and the men. They had sailed from Deptford, from Greenwich, from Erith—the adventurers and the settlers; kings' ships and the ships of men on 'Change; captains, admirals, the dark "interlopers" of the Eastern trade, and the commissioned "generals" of East India fleets. Hunters for gold or pursuers of fame, they all had gone out on that stream, bearing the sword, and often the torch, messengers of the might within the land, bearers of a spark from the sacred fire. What greatness had not floated on the ebb of that river into the mystery of an unknown earth! . . . The dreams of men, the seed of commonwealths, the germs of empires.

The sun set; the dusk fell on the stream, and lights began to appear along the shore. The Chapman lighthouse, a three-legged thing erect on a mud-flat, shone strongly. Lights of ships moved in the fairway—a great stir of lights going up and going down. And farther west on the upper reaches the place of the monstrous town was still marked om-

3. Drake (1545?–1596), admiral under Elizabeth I and first Englishman to sail around the world, sailed the *Golden Hind;* Franklin (1786–1847) led a party in the *Erebus* and *Terror* on an ill-fated search for the Northwest Passage which none survived.

inously on the sky, a brooding gloom in sunshine, a lurid glare under the stars.

"And this also," said Marlow suddenly, "has been one of the dark places of the earth."

He was the only man of us who still "followed the sea." The worst that could be said of him was that he did not represent his class. He was a seaman, but he was a wanderer too, while most seamen lead, if one may so express it, a sedentary life. Their minds are of the stay-at-home order, and their home is always with them—the ship; and so is their country—the sea. One ship is very much like another, and the sea is always the same. In the immutability of their surroundings the foreign shores, the foreign faces, the changing immensity of life, glide past, veiled not by a sense of mystery but by a slightly disdainful ignorance; for there is nothing mysterious to a seaman unless it be the sea itself, which is the mistress of his existence and as inscrutable as Destiny. For the rest, after his hours of work, a casual stroll or a casual spree on shore suffices to unfold for him the secret of a whole continent, and generally he finds the secret not worth knowing. The yarns of seamen have a direct simplicity, the whole meaning of which lies within the shell of a cracked nut. But Marlow was not typical (if his propensity to spin yarns be excepted), and to him the meaning of an episode was not inside like a kernel but outside, enveloping the tale which brought it out only as a glow brings out a haze, in the likeness of one of these misty halos that sometimes are made visible by the spectral illumination of moonshine.

His remark did not seem at all surprising. It was just like Marlow. It was accepted in silence. No one took the trouble to grunt even; and presently he said, very slow:

"I was thinking of very old times, when the Romans first came here, nineteen hundred years ago—the other day. . . . Light came out of this river since—you say Knights? Yes; but it is like a running blaze on a plain, like a flash of lightning in the clouds. We live in the flicker—may it last as long as the old earth keeps rolling! But darkness was here yesterday. Imagine the feelings of a commander of a fine—what d'ye call 'em?—trireme in the Mediterranean, ordered suddenly to the north; run overland across the Gauls in a hurry; put in charge of one of these craft the legionaries—a wonderful lot of handy men they must have been too—used to build, apparently by the hundred, in a month or two, if we may believe what we read. Imagine him here—the very end of the world, a sea the color of lead, a sky the color of smoke, a kind of ship about as rigid as a concertina—and going up this river with stores, or orders, or what you like. Sandbanks, marshes, forests, savages—precious little to eat fit for a civilized man, nothing but Thames water to drink. No Falernian wine[4] here, no going ashore. Here and there a military camp lost in a wilderness, like a needle in a bundle of hay—cold, fog, tempests, disease, exile, and death—death skulking in the air, in the water, in the bush. They must have been dying like flies here. Oh yes—he did it. Did it very well, too, no doubt, and without thinking much about it either, except afterwards to brag of what he

4. Famous ancient wine from the region of Naples.

had gone through in his time, perhaps. They were men enough to face the darkness. And perhaps he was cheered by keeping his eye on a chance of promotion to the fleet at Ravenna[5] by and by, if he had good friends in Rome and survived the awful climate. Or think of a decent young citizen in a toga—perhaps too much dice, you know—coming out here in the train of some prefect, or tax-gatherer, or trader, even, to mend his fortunes. Land in a swamp, march through the woods, and in some inland post feel the savagery, the utter savagery, had closed round him—all that mysterious life of the wilderness that stirs in the forest, in the jungles, in the hearts of wild men. There's no initiation either into such mysteries. He has to live in the midst of the incomprehensible, which is also detestable. And it has a fascination, too, that goes to work upon him. The fascination of the abomination—you know. Imagine the growing regrets, the longing to escape, the powerless disgust, the surrender, the hate."

He paused.

"Mind," he began again, lifting one arm from the elbow, the palm of the hand outwards, so that, with his legs folded before him, he had the pose of a Buddha preaching in European clothes and without a lotus-flower[6]—"Mind, none of us would feel exactly like this. What saves us is efficiency—the devotion to efficiency. But these chaps were not much account, really. They were no colonists; their administration was merely a squeeze, and nothing more, I suspect. They were conquerors, and for that you want only brute force—nothing to boast of, when you have it, since your strength is just an accident arising from the weakness of others. They grabbed what they could get for the sake of what was to be got. It was just robbery with violence, aggravated murder on a great scale, and men going at it blind—as is very proper for those who tackle a darkness. The conquest of the earth, which mostly means the taking it away from those who have a different complexion or slightly flatter noses than ourselves, is not a pretty thing when you look into it too much. What redeems it is the idea only. An idea at the back of it; not a sentimental pretense but an idea; and an unselfish belief in the idea—something you can set up, and bow down before, and offer a sacrifice to. . . ."

He broke off. Flames glided in the river, small green flames, red flames, white flames, pursuing, overtaking, joining, crossing each other —then separating slowly or hastily. The traffic of the great city went on in the deepening night upon the sleepless river. We looked on, waiting patiently—there was nothing else to do till the end of the flood; but it was only after a long silence, when he said, in a hesitating voice, "I suppose you fellows remember I did once turn fresh-water sailor for a bit," that we knew we were fated, before the ebb began to run, to hear about one of Marlow's inconclusive experiences.

"I don't want to bother you much with what happened to me personally," he began, showing in this remark the weakness of many tellers of tales who seem so often unaware of what their audience would best

5. Roman naval base on the Adriatic (though now inland).

6. Buddha is often depicted sitting on a lotus seat or standing on a lotus pedestal, the lotus flower representing spirituality, perfection, immortality, divine birth, and regeneration.

like to hear; "yet to understand the effect of it on me you ought to know how I got out there, what I saw, how I went up that river to the place where I first met the poor chap. It was the farthest point of navigation and the culminating point of my experience. It seemed somehow to throw a kind of light on everything about me—and into my thoughts. It was somber enough too—and pitiful—not extraordinary in any way—not very clear either. No, not very clear. And yet it seemed to throw a kind of light.

"I had then, as you remember, just returned to London after a lot of Indian Ocean, Pacific, China Seas—a regular dose of the East—six years or so, and I was loafing about, hindering you fellows in your work and invading your homes, just as though I had got a heavenly mission to civilize you. It was very fine for a time, but after a bit I did get tired of resting. Then I began to look for a ship—I should think the hardest work on earth. But the ships wouldn't even look at me. And I got tired of that game too.

"Now when I was a little chap I had a passion for maps. I would look for hours at South America, or Africa, or Australia, and lose myself in all the glories of exploration. At that time there were many blank spaces on the earth, and when I saw one that looked particularly inviting on a map (but they all look that) I would put my finger on it and say, When I grow up I will go there. The North Pole was one of these places, I remember. Well, I haven't been there yet, and shall not try now. The glamour's off. Other places were scattered about the Equator, and in every sort of latitude all over the two hemispheres. I have been in some of them, and . . . well, we won't talk about that. But there was one yet—the biggest, the most blank, so to speak—that I had a hankering after.

"True, by this time it was not a blank space any more. It had got filled since my boyhood with rivers and lakes and names. It had ceased to be a blank space of delightful mystery—a white patch for a boy to dream gloriously over. It had become a place of darkness. But there was in it one river especially, a mighty big river, that you could see on the map, resembling an immense snake uncoiled, with its head in the sea, its body at rest curving afar over a vast country, and its tail lost in the depths of the land. And as I looked at the map of it in a shop-window, it fascinated me as a snake would a bird—a silly little bird. Then I remembered there was a big concern, a Company for trade on that river. Dash it all! I thought to myself, they can't trade without using some kind of craft on that lot of fresh water—steamboats! Why shouldn't I try to get charge of one? I went on along Fleet Street, but could not shake off the idea. The snake had charmed me.

"You understand it was a Continental concern, that Trading Society; but I have a lot of relations living on the Continent, because it's cheap and not so nasty as it looks, they say.

"I am sorry to own I began to worry them. This was already a fresh departure for me. I was not used to get things that way, you know. I always went my own road and on my own legs where I had a mind to go. I wouldn't have believed it of myself; but, then—you see—I felt somehow I must get there by hook or by crook. So I worried them. The men said, 'My dear fellow,' and did nothing. Then—would you believe it?—I tried the women. I, Charlie Marlow, set the women to work—to get a job. Heavens! Well, you see, the notion drove me. I had an aunt, a dear enthusiastic soul. She wrote: 'It will be delightful. I am ready to do anything, anything for you. It is a glorious idea. I know the wife of a very high personage in the Administration, and also a man who has lots of influence with,' etc. etc. She was determined to make no end of fuss to get me appointed skipper of a river steamboat, if such was my fancy.

"I got my appointment—of course; and I got it very quick. It appears the Company had received news that one of their captains had been killed in a scuffle with the natives. This was my chance, and it made me the more anxious to go. It was only months and months afterwards, when I made the attempt to recover what was left of the body, that I heard the original quarrel arose from a misunderstanding about some hens. Yes, two black hens. Fresleven—that was the fellow's name, a Dane—thought himself wronged somehow in the bargain, so he went ashore and started to hammer the chief of the village with a stick. Oh, it didn't surprise me in the least to hear this, and at the same time to be told that Fresleven was the gentlest, quietest creature that ever walked on two legs. No doubt he was; but he had been a couple of years already out there engaged in the noble cause, you know, and he probably felt the need at last of asserting his self-respect in some way. Therefore he whacked the old nigger mercilessly, while a big crowd of his people watched him, thunderstruck, till some man—I was told the chief's son—in desperation at hearing the old chap yell, made a tentative jab with a spear at the white man—and of course it went quite easy between the shoulder-blades. Then the whole population cleared into the forest, expecting all kinds of calamities to happen, while, on the other hand, the steamer Fresleven commanded left also in a bad panic, in charge of the engineer, I believe. Afterwards nobody seemed to trouble much about Fresleven's remains, till I got out and stepped into his shoes. I couldn't let it rest, though; but when an opportunity offered at last to meet my predecessor, the grass growing through his ribs was tall enough to hide his bones. They were all there. The supernatural being had not been touched after he fell. And the village was deserted, the huts gaped black, rotting, all askew within the fallen enclosures. A calamity had come to it, sure enough. The people had vanished. Mad terror had scattered them, men, women, and children, through the bush, and they had never returned. What became of the hens I don't know either. I should think the cause of progress got them, anyhow. However, through this glorious affair I got my appointment, before I had fairly begun to hope for it.

"I flew around like mad to get ready, and before forty-eight hours I was crossing the Channel to show myself to my employers, and sign the contract. In a very few hours I arrived in a city that always makes me think of a whited sepulchre. Prejudice no doubt. I had no difficulty in finding the Company's offices. It was the biggest thing in the town, and everybody I met was full of it. They were going to run an oversea empire, and make no end of coin by trade.

"A narrow and deserted street in deep shadow, high houses, innumerable windows with venetian blinds, a dead silence, grass sprouting between the stones, imposing carriage archways right and left, immense double doors standing ponderously ajar. I slipped through one of these cracks, went up a swept and ungarnished staircase, as arid as a desert, and opened the first door I came to. Two women, one fat and the other slim, sat on straw-bottomed chairs, knitting black wool. The slim one got up and walked straight at me—still knitting with downcast eyes—and only just as I began to think of getting out of her way, as you would for a somnambulist, stood still, and looked up. Her dress was as plain as an umbrella-cover, and she turned round without a word and preceded me into a waiting-room. I gave my name, and looked about. Deal table in the middle, plain chairs all round the walls, on one end a large shining map, marked with all the colors of a rainbow. There was a vast amount of red—good to see at any time, because one knows that some real work is done in there, a deuce of a lot of blue, a little green, smears of orange, and, on the East Coast, a purple patch, to show where the jolly pioneers of progress drink the jolly lager-beer.[7] However, I wasn't going into any of these. I was going into the yellow. Dead in the center. And the river was there—fascinating—deadly—like a snake. Ough! A door opened, a white-haired secretarial head, but wearing a compassionate expression, appeared, and a skinny forefinger beckoned me into the sanctuary. Its light was dim, and a heavy writing-desk squatted in the middle. From behind that structure came out an impression of pale plumpness in a frock-coat. The great man himself. He was five feet six, I should judge, and had his grip on the handle-end of ever so many millions. He shook hands, I fancy, murmured vaguely, was satisfied with my French. *Bon voyage.*

"In about forty-five seconds I found myself again in the waiting-room with the compassionate secretary, who, full of desolation and sympathy, made me sign some document. I believe I undertook amongst other things not to disclose any trade secrets. Well, I am not going to.

"I began to feel slightly uneasy. You know I am not used to such ceremonies, and there was something ominous in the atmosphere. It was just as though I had been let into some conspiracy—I don't know—something not quite right; and I was glad to get out. In the outer room the two women knitted black wool feverishly. People were arriving, and the younger one was walking back and forth introducing them. The old one sat on her chair. Her flat cloth slippers were propped up on a foot-warmer, and a cat reposed on her lap. She wore a starched white affair on her head, had a wart on one check, and silver-rimmed spectacles hung on the tip of her nose. She glanced at me above the glasses. The swift and indifferent placidity of that look troubled me. Two youths with foolish and cheery countenances were being piloted over, and she threw at them the same quick glance of unconcerned wisdom. She seemed to know all about them and about me too. An eerie feeling came over me. She seemed uncanny and fateful. Often far away there I thought of these two, guarding the door of Darkness, knitting black wool as for a warm pall, one introducing, introducing continuously to

7. Though British territories or colonies are almost universally shown as red, there seems to be no fixed color system now or in the 19th century for indicating national holdings. Here the blue seems to be French; green, Portuguese; orange, German; purple, Dutch; yellow, the Congo Free State.

the unknown, the other scrutinizing the cheery and foolish faces with unconcerned old eyes. *Ave!* Old knitter of black wool. *Morituri te salutant.*[8] Not many of those she looked at ever saw her again—not half, by a long way.

"There was yet a visit to the doctor. 'A simple formality,' assured me the secretary, with an air of taking an immense part in all my sorrows. Accordingly a young chap wearing his hat over the left eyebrow, some clerk I suppose—there must have been clerks in the business, though the house was as still as a house in a city of the dead—came from somewhere upstairs, and led me forth. He was shabby and careless, with inkstains on the sleeves of his jacket, and his cravat was large and billowy, under a chin shaped like the toe of an old boot. It was a little too early for the doctor, so I proposed a drink, and hereupon he developed a vein of joviality. As we sat over our vermouths he glorified the Company's business, and by and by I expressed casually my surprise at him not going out there. He became very cool and collected all at once. 'I am not such a fool as I look, quoth Plato to his disciples,' he said sententiously, emptied his glass with great resolution, and we rose.

"The old doctor felt my pulse, evidently thinking of something else the while. 'Good, good for there,' he mumbled, and then with a certain eagerness asked me whether I would let him measure my head. Rather surprised, I said Yes, when he produced a thing like callipers and got the dimensions back and front and every way, taking notes carefully. He was an unshaven little man in a threadbare coat like a gaberdine, with his feet in slippers, and I thought him a harmless fool. 'I always ask leave, in the interests of science, to measure the crania of those going out there,' he said. 'And when they come back too?' I asked. 'Oh, I never see them,' he remarked; 'and, moreover, the changes take place inside, you know.' He smiled, as if at some quiet joke. 'So you are going out there. Famous.[9] Interesting too.' He gave me a searching glance, and made another note. 'Ever any madness in your family?' he asked, in a matter-of-fact tone. I felt very annoyed. 'Is that question in the interests of science too?' 'It would be,' he said, without taking notice of my irritation, 'interesting for science to watch the mental changes of individuals, on the spot, but . . .' 'Are you an alienist?'[1] I interrupted. 'Every doctor should be—a little,' answered that original imperturbably. 'I have a little theory which you Messieurs who go out there must help me to prove. This is my share in the advantages my country shall reap from the possession of such a magnificent dependency. The mere wealth I leave to others. Pardon my questions, but you are the first Englishman coming under my observation . . .' I hastened to assure him I was not in the least typical. 'If I were,' said I, 'I wouldn't be talking like this with you.' 'What you say is rather profound, and probably erroneous,' he said, with a laugh. 'Avoid irritation more than exposure to the sun. Adieu. How do you English say, eh? Good-bye. Ah! Good-bye. Adieu. In the tropics one must before everything keep calm.' . . . He lifted a warning forefinger. . . . *'Du calme, du calme. Adieu.'*

"One thing more remained to do—say good-bye to my excellent

8. Gladiators' salutation to the Roman emperor: "Hail! . . . Those who are about to die salute you."

9. Excellent, splendid.

1. Psychiatrist.

aunt. I found her triumphant. I had a cup of tea—the last decent cup of tea for many days—and in a room that most soothingly looked just as you would expect a lady's drawing room to look, we had a long quiet chat by the fireside. In the course of these confidences it became quite plain to me I had been represented to the wife of the high dignitary, and goodness knows to how many more people besides, as an exceptional and gifted creature—a piece of good fortune for the Company—a man you don't get hold of every day. Good Heavens! and I was going to take charge of a two-penny-halfpenny river-steamboat with a penny whistle attached! It appeared, however, I was also one of the Workers, with a capital—you know. Something like an emissary of light, something like a lower sort of apostle. There had been a lot of such rot let loose in print and talk just about that time, and the excellent woman, living right in the rush of all that humbug, got carried off her feet. She talked about 'weaning those ignorant millions from their horrid ways,' till, upon my word, she made me quite uncomfortable. I ventured to hint that the Company was run for profit.

" 'You forget, dear Charlie, that the laborer is worthy of his hire,'[2] she said brightly. It's queer how out of touch with truth women are. They live in a world of their own, and there had never been anything like it, and never can be. It is too beautiful altogether, and if they were to set it up it would go to pieces before the first sunset. Some confounded fact we men have been living contentedly with ever since the day of creation would start up and knock the whole thing over.

"After this I got embraced, told to wear flannel, be sure to write often, and so on—and I left. In the street—I don't know why—a queer feeling came to me that I was an imposter. Odd thing that I, who used to clear out for any part of the world at twenty-four hours' notice, with less thought than most men give to the crossing of a street, had a moment—I won't say of hesitation, but of startled pause, before this commonplace affair. The best way I can explain it to you is by saying that, for a second or two, I felt as though, instead of going to the center of a continent, I were about to set off for the center of the earth.

"I left in a French steamer, and she called in every blamed port they have out there, for, as far as I could see, the sole purpose of landing soldiers and custom-house officers. I watched the coast. Watching a coast as it slips by the ship is like thinking about an enigma. There it is before you—smiling, frowning, inviting, grand, mean, insipid, or savage, and always mute with an air of whispering, Come and find out. This one was almost featureless, as if still in the making, with an aspect of monotonous grimness. The edge of a colossal jungle, so dark green as to be almost black, fringed with white surf, ran straight, like a ruled line, far, far away along a blue sea whose glitter was blurred by a creeping mist. The sun was fierce, the land seemed to glisten and drip with steam. Here and there grayish-whitish specks showed up clustered inside the white surf, with a flag flying above them perhaps—settlements some centuries old, and still no bigger than pinheads on the untouched expanse of their background. We pounded along, stopped, landed soldiers; went on, landed custom-house clerks to levy toll in

2. Words of Jesus in *Luke* 10:7.

what looked like a God-forsaken wilderness, with a tin shed and a flag-pole lost in it; landed more soldiers—to take care of the custom-house clerks presumably. Some, I heard, got drowned in the surf; but whether they did or not, nobody seemed particularly to care. They were just flung out there, and on we went. Every day the coast looked the same, as though we had not moved; but we passed various places—trading places—with names like Gran' Bassam, Little Popo; names that seemed to belong to some sordid farce acted in front of a sinister back-cloth. The idleness of a passenger, my isolation amongst all these men with whom I had no point of contact, the oily and languid sea, the uniform somberness of the coast, seemed to keep me away from the truth of things, within the toil of a mournful and senseless delusion. The voice of the surf heard now and then was a positive pleasure, like the speech of a brother. It was something natural, that had its reason, that had a meaning. Now and then a boat from the shore gave one a momentary contact with reality. It was paddled by black fellows. You could see from afar the white of their eyeballs glistening. They shouted, sang; their bodies streamed with perspiration; they had faces like grotesque masks—these chaps; but they had bone, muscle, a wild vitality, an intense energy of movement, that was as natural and true as the surf along their coast. They wanted no excuse for being there. They were a great comfort to look at. For a time I would feel I belonged still to a world of straightforward facts; but the feeling would not last long. Something would turn up to scare it away. Once, I remember, we came upon a man-of-war anchored off the coast. There wasn't even a shed there, and she was shelling the bush. It appears the French had one of their wars going on thereabouts. Her ensign dropped limp like a rag; the muzzles of the long six-inch guns stuck out all over the low hull; the greasy, slimy swell swung her up lazily and let her down, swaying her thin masts. In the empty immensity of earth, sky, and water, there she was, incomprehensible, firing into a continent. Pop, would go one of the six-inch guns; a small flame would dart and vanish, a little white smoke would disappear, a tiny projectile would give a feeble screech—and nothing happened. Nothing could happen. There was a touch of insanity in the proceeding, a sense of lugubrious drollery in the sight; and it was not dissipated by somebody on board assuring me earnestly there was a camp of natives—he called them enemies!—hidden out of sight somewhere.

"We gave her her letters (I heard the men in that lonely ship were dying of fever at the rate of three a day) and went on. We called at some more places with farcical names, where the merry dance of death and trade goes on in a still and earthy atmosphere as of an overheated catacomb; all along the formless coast bordered by dangerous surf, as if Nature herself had tried to ward off intruders; in and out of rivers, streams of death in life, whose banks were rotting into mud, whose waters, thickened into slime, invaded the contorted mangroves, that seemed to writhe at us in the extremity of an impotent despair. Nowhere did we stop long enough to get a particularized impression, but the general sense of vague and oppressive wonder grew upon me. It was like a weary pilgrimage amongst hints for nightmares.

"It was upward of thirty days before I saw the mouth of the big river.

We anchored off the seat of the government. But my work would not begin till some two hundred miles farther on. So as soon as I could I made a start for a place thirty miles higher up.

"I had my passage on a little sea-going steamer. Her captain was a Swede, and knowing me for a seaman, invited me on the bridge. He was a young man, lean, fair, and morose, with lanky hair and a shuffling gait. As we left the miserable little wharf, he tossed his head contemptuously at the shore. 'Been living there?' he asked. I said, 'Yes.' 'Fine lot these government chaps—are they not?' he went on, speaking English with great precision and considerable bitterness. 'It is funny what some people will do for a few francs a month. I wonder what becomes of that kind when it goes up country?' I said to him I expected to see that soon. 'So-o-o!' he exclaimed. He shuffled athwart, keeping one eye ahead vigilantly. 'Don't be too sure,' he continued. 'The other day I took up a man who hanged himself on the road. He was a Swede, too.' 'Hanged himself! Why, in God's name?' I cried. He kept on looking out watchfully. 'Who knows? The sun too much for him, or the country perhaps.'

"At last we opened a reach. A rocky cliff appeared, mounds of turned-up earth by the shore, houses on a hill, others with iron roofs, amongst a waste of excavations, or hanging to the declivity. A continuous noise of the rapids above hovered over this scene of inhabited devastation. A lot of people, mostly black and naked, moved about like ants. A jetty projected into the river. A blinding sunlight drowned all this at times in a sudden recrudescence of glare. 'There's your Company's station,' said the Swede, pointing to three wooden barrack-like structures on the rocky slope. 'I will send your things up. Four boxes did you say? So. Farewell.'

"I came upon a boiler wallowing in the grass, then found a path leading up the hill. It turned aside for the boulders, and also for an undersized railway truck lying there on its back with its wheels in the air. One was off. The thing looked as dead as the carcass of some animal. I came upon more pieces of decaying machinery, a stack of rusty rails. To the left a clump of trees made a shady spot, where dark things seemed to stir feebly. I blinked, the path was steep. A horn tooted to the right, and I saw the black people run. A heavy and dull detonation shook the ground, a puff of smoke came out of the cliff, and that was all. No change appeared on the face of the rock. They were building a railway. The cliff was not in the way or anything; but this objectless blasting was all the work going on.

"A slight clinking behind me made me turn my head. Six black men advanced in a file, toiling up the path. They walked erect and slow, balancing small baskets full of earth on their heads, and the clink kept time with their footsteps. Black rags were wound round their loins, and the short ends behind waggled to and fro like tails. I could see every rib, the joints of their limbs were like knots in a rope; each had an iron collar on his neck, and all were connected together with a chain whose bights swung between them, rhythmically clinking. Another report from the cliff made me think suddenly of that ship of war I had seen firing into a continent. It was the same kind of ominous voice; but these men could by no stretch of imagination be called enemies. They were called criminals, and the outraged law, like the bursting shells, had come to them, an insoluble mystery from the sea. All their meager breasts panted together, the violently dilated nostrils quivered, the eyes stared stonily uphill. They passed me within six inches, without a glance, with that complete, deathlike indifference of unhappy savages. Behind this raw matter one of the reclaimed, the product of the new forces at work, strolled despondently, carrying a rifle by its middle. He had a uniform jacket with one button off, and seeing a white man on the path, hoisted his weapon to his shoulder with alacrity. This was simple prudence, white men being so much alike at a distance that he could not tell who I might be. He was speedily reassured, and with a large, white, rascally grin, and a glance at his charge, seemed to take me into partnership in his exalted trust. After all, I also was a part of the great cause of these high and just proceedings.

"Instead of going up, I turned and descended to the left. My idea was to let that chain-gang get out of sight before I climbed the hill. You know I am not particularly tender; I've had to strike and to fend off. I've had to resist and to attack sometimes—that's only one way of resisting—without counting the exact cost, according to the demands of such sort of life as I had blundered into. I've seen the devil of violence, and the devil of greed, and the devil of hot desire; but, by all the stars! these were strong, lusty, red-eyed devils, that swayed and drove men—men, I tell you. But as I stood on this hillside, I foresaw that in the blinding sunshine of that land I would become acquainted with a flabby, pretending, weak-eyed devil of a rapacious and pitiless folly. How insidious he could be, too, I was only to find out several months later and a thousand miles farther. For a moment I stood appalled, as though by a warning. Finally I descended the hill, obliquely, towards the trees I had seen.

"I avoided a vast artificial hole somebody had been digging on the slope, the purpose of which I found it impossible to divine. It wasn't a quarry or a sandpit, anyhow. It was just a hole. It might have been connected with the philanthropic desire of giving the criminals something to do. I don't know. Then I nearly fell into a very narrow ravine, almost no more than a scar in the hillside. I discovered that a lot of imported drainage-pipes for the settlement had been tumbled in there. There wasn't one that was not broken. It was a wanton smash-up. At last I got under the trees. My purpose was to stroll into the shade for a moment; but no sooner within than it seemed to me I had stepped into the gloomy circle of some Inferno. The rapids were near, and an uninterrupted, uniform, headlong, rushing noise filled the mournful stillness of the grove, where not a breath stirred, not a leaf moved, with a mysterious sound—as though the tearing pace of the launched earth had suddenly become audible.

"Black shapes crouched, lay, sat between the trees, leaning against the trunks, clinging to the earth, half coming out, half effaced within the dim light, in all the attitudes of pain, abandonment, and despair. Another mine on the cliff went off, followed by a slight shudder of the soil under my feet. The work was going on. The work! And this was the place where some of the helpers had withdrawn to die.

"They were dying slowly—it was very clear. They were not enemies, they were not criminals, they were nothing earthly now—nothing but black shadows of disease and starvation, lying confusedly in the greenish gloom. Brought from all the recesses of the coast in all the legality of time contracts, lost in uncongenial surroundings, fed on unfamiliar food, they sickened, became inefficient, and were then allowed to crawl away and rest. These moribund shapes were free as air—and nearly as thin. I began to distinguish the gleam of the eyes under the trees. Then, glancing down, I saw a face near my hand. The black bones reclined at full length with one shoulder against the tree, and slowly the eyelids rose and the sunken eyes looked up at me, enormous and vacant, a kind of blind, white flicker in the depths of the orbs, which died out slowly. The man seemed young—almost a boy—but you know with them it's hard to tell. I found nothing else to do but to offer him one of my good Swede's ship's biscuits I had in my pocket. The fingers closed slowly on it and held—there was no other movement and no other glance. He had tied a bit of white worsted round his neck—Why? Where did he get it? Was it a badge—an ornament—a charm—a propitiatory act? Was there any idea at all connected with it? It looked startling round his black neck, this bit of white thread from beyond the seas.

"Near the same tree two more bundles of acute angles sat with their legs drawn up. One, with his chin propped on his knees, stared at nothing, in an intolerable and appalling manner: his brother phantom rested its forehead, as if overcome with a great weariness; and all about others were scattered in every pose of contorted collapse, as in some picture of a massacre or a pestilence. While I stood horror-struck, one of these creatures rose to his hands and knees, and went off on all-fours towards the river to drink. He lapped out of his hand, then sat up in the sunlight, crossing his shins in front of him, and after a time let his woolly head fall on his breastbone.

"I didn't want any more loitering in the shade, and I made haste towards the station. When near the buildings I met a white man, in such an unexpected elegance of get-up that in the first moment I took him for a sort of vision. I saw a high starched collar, white cuffs, a light alpaca jacket, snowy trousers, a clean necktie, and varnished boots. No hat. Hair parted, brushed, oiled, under a green-lined parasol held in a big white hand. He was amazing, and had a pen-holder behind his ear.

"I shook hands with this miracle, and I learned he was the Company's chief accountant, and that all the bookkeeping was done at this station. He had come out for a moment, he said, 'to get a breath of fresh air.' The expression sounded wonderfully odd, with its suggestion of sedentary desk-life. I wouldn't have mentioned the fellow to you at all, only it was from his lips that I first heard the name of the man who is so indissolubly connected with the memories of that time. Moreover, I respected the fellow. Yes; I respected his collars, his vast cuffs, his brushed hair. His appearance was certainly that of a hairdresser's dummy; but in the great demoralization of the land he kept up his appearance. That's backbone. His starched collars and got-up shirt-fronts were achievements of character. He had been out nearly three years; and, later, I could not help asking him how he managed to sport such linen. He had just the faintest blush, and said modestly, 'I've been teaching one of the native women about the station. It was difficult. She had a distaste for the work.' Thus this man had verily accomplished something. And he was devoted to his books, which were in apple-pie order.

"Everything else in the station was in a muddle,—heads, things, buildings. Strings of dusty niggers with splay feet arrived and departed; a stream of manufactured goods, rubbishy cottons, beads, and brass-wire sent into the depths of darkness, and in return came a precious trickle of ivory.

"I had to wait in the station for ten days—an eternity. I lived in a hut in the yard, but to be out of the chaos I would sometimes get into the accountant's office. It was built of horizontal planks, and so badly put together that, as he bent over his high desk, he was barred from neck to heels with narrow strips of sunlight. There was no need to open the big shutter to see. It was hot there too; big flies buzzed fiendishly, and did not sting, but stabbed. I sat generally on the floor, while, of faultless appearance (and even slightly scented), perching on a high stool, he wrote, he wrote. Sometimes he stood up for exercise. When a truckle-bed with a sick man (some invalided agent from up-country) was put in there, he exhibited a gentle annoyance. 'The groans of this sick person,' he said, 'distract my attention. And without that it is extremely difficult to guard against clerical errors in this climate.'

"One day he remarked, without lifting his head, 'In the interior you will no doubt meet Mr. Kurtz.' On my asking who Mr. Kurtz was, he said he was a first-class agent; and seeing my disappointment at this information, he added slowly, laying down his pen, 'He is a very remarkable person.' Further questions elicited from him that Mr. Kurtz was at present in charge of a trading-post, a very important one, in the true ivory-country, at 'the very bottom of there. Sends in as much ivory as all the others put together . . .' He began to write again. The sick man was too ill to groan. The flies buzzed in a great peace.

"Suddenly there was a growing murmur of voices and a great tramping of feet. A caravan had come in. A violent babble of uncouth sounds burst out on the other side of the planks. All the carriers were speaking together, and in the midst of the uproar the lamentable voice of the chief agent was heard 'giving it up'[3] tearfully for the twentieth time that day. . . . He rose slowly. 'What a frightful row,' he said. He crossed the room gently to look at the sick man, and returning, said to me, 'He does not hear.' 'What! Dead?' I asked, startled. 'No, not yet,' he answered, with great composure. Then, alluding with a toss of the head to the tumult in the station-yard, 'When one has got to make correct entries, one comes to hate those savages—hate them to the death.' He remained thoughtful for a moment. 'When you see Mr. Kurtz,' he went on, 'tell him from me that everything here'—he glanced at the desk—'is very satisfactory. I don't like to write to him—with those messengers of ours you never know who may get hold of your letter—at that Central Station.' He stared at me for a moment with his mild, bulging eyes. 'Oh, he will go far, very far,' he began again. 'He will be a somebody in

3. Uttering a cry.

the Administration before long. They, above—the Council in Europe, you know—mean him to be.'

"He turned to his work. The noise outside had ceased, and presently in going out I stopped at the door. In the steady buzz of flies the homeward-bound agent was lying flushed and insensible; the other, bent over his books, was making correct entries of perfectly correct transactions; and fifty feet below the doorstep I could see the still treetops of the grove of death.

"Next day I left that station at last, with a caravan of sixty men, for a two-hundred-mile tramp.

"No use telling you much about that. Paths, paths, everywhere; a stamped-in network of paths spreading over the empty land, through long grass, through burnt grass, through thickets, down and up chilly ravines, up and down stony hills ablaze with heat; and a solitude, a solitude, nobody, not a hut. The population had cleared out a long time ago. Well, if a lot of mysterious niggers armed with all kinds of fearful weapons suddenly took to traveling on the road between Deal[4] and Gravesend, catching the yokels right and left to carry heavy loads for them, I fancy every farm and cottage thereabouts would get empty very soon. Only here the dwellings were gone too. Still, I passed through several abandoned villages. There's something pathetically childish in the ruins of grass walls. Day after day, with the stamp and shuffle of sixty pair of bare feet behind me, each pair under a 60-lb. load. Camp, cook, sleep; strike camp, march. Now and then a carrier dead in harness, at rest in the long grass near the path, with an empty water-gourd and his long staff lying by his side. A great silence around and above. Perhaps on some quiet night the tremor of far-off drums, sinking, swelling, a tremor vast, faint; a sound weird, appealing, suggestive, and wild—and perhaps with as profound a meaning as the sound of bells in a Christian country. Once a white man in an unbuttoned uniform, camping on the path with an armed escort of lank Zanzibaris,[5] very hospitable and festive—not to say drunk. Was looking after the upkeep of the road, he declared. Can't say I saw any road or any upkeep, unless the body of a middle-aged negro, with a bullet-hole in the forehead, upon which I absolutely stumbled three miles farther on, may be considered as a permanent improvement. I had a white companion too, not a bad chap, but rather too fleshy and with the exasperating habit of fainting on the hot hillsides, miles away from the least bit of shade and water. Annoying, you know, to hold your own coat like a parasol over a man's head while he is coming to. I couldn't help asking him once what he meant by coming there at all. 'To make money, of course. What do you think?' he said scornfully. Then he got fever, and had to be carried in a hammock slung under a pole. As he weighed sixteen stone[6] I had no end of rows with the carriers. They jibbed, ran away, sneaked off with their loads in the night—quite a mutiny. So, one evening, I made a speech in English with gestures, not one of which was lost to the sixty pairs of eyes before me, and the

4. Port near Dover.

5. Zanzibar, a British-controlled island off the *East* Coast of Africa, supplied mercenaries for service throughout the continent.

6. I.e., 224 pounds; a stone, 14 pounds, is a standard British measure.

next morning I started the hammock off in front all right. An hour afterwards I came upon the whole concern wrecked in a bush—man, hammock, groans, blankets, horrors. The heavy pole had skinned his poor nose. He was very anxious for me to kill somebody, but there wasn't the shadow of a carrier near. I remembered the old doctor—'It would be interesting for science to watch the mental changes of individuals, on the spot.' I felt I was becoming scientifically interesting. However, all that is to no purpose. On the fifteenth day I came in sight of the big river again, and hobbled into the Central Station. It was on a backwater surrounded by scrub and forest, with a pretty border of smelly mud on one side, and on the three others enclosed by a crazy[7] fence of rushes. A neglected gap was all the gate it had, and the first glance at the place was enough to let you see the flabby devil was running that show. White men with long staves in their hands appeared languidly from amongst the buildings, strolling up to take a look and me, and then retired out of sight somewhere. One of them, a stout, excitable chap with black moustaches, informed me with great volubility and many digressions, as soon as I told him who I was, that my steamer was at the bottom of the river. I was thunderstruck. What, how, why? Oh, it was 'all right.' The 'manager himself' was there. All quite correct. 'Everybody had behaved splendidly! splendidly!'—'You must,' he said in agitation, 'go and see the general manager at once. He is waiting.'

"I did not see the real significance of that wreck at once. I fancy I see it now, but I am not sure—not at all. Certainly the affair was too stupid—when I think of it—to be altogether natural. Still . . . But at the moment it presented itself simply as a confounded nuisance. The steamer was sunk. They had started two days before in a sudden hurry up the river with the manager on board, in charge of some volunteer skipper, and before they had been out three hours they tore the bottom out of her on stones, and she sank near the south bank. I asked myself what I was to do there, now my boat was lost. As a matter of fact, I had plenty to do in fishing my command out of the river. I had to set about it the very next day. That, and the repairs when I brought the pieces to the station, took some months.

"My first interview with the manager was curious. He did not ask me to sit down after my twenty-mile walk that morning. He was commonplace in complexion, in feature, in manners, and in voice. He was of middle size and of ordinary build. His eyes, of the usual blue, were perhaps remarkably cold, and he certainly could make his glance fall on one as trenchant and heavy as an axe. But even at these times the rest of his person seemed to disclaim the intention. Otherwise there was only an indefinable, faint expression of his lips, something stealthy—a smile—not a smile—I remember it, but I can't explain. It was unconscious, this smile was, though just after he had said something it got intensified for an instant. It came at the end of his speeches like a seal applied on the words to make the meaning of the commonest phrase appear absolutely inscrutable. He was a common trader,

7. Irregular and/or shaky.

from his youth up employed in these parts—nothing more. He was obeyed, yet he inspired neither love nor fear, nor even respect. He inspired uneasiness. That was it! Uneasiness. Not a definite mistrust—just uneasiness—nothing more. You have no idea how effective such a . . . a . . . faculty can be. He had no genius for organizing, for initiative, or for order even. That was evident in such things as the deplorable state of the station. He had no learning, and no intelligence. His position had come to him—why? Perhaps because he was never ill . . . He had served three terms of three years out there. . . . Because triumphant health in the general rout of constitutions is a kind of power in itself. When he went home on leave he rioted on a large scale—pompously. Jack[8] ashore—with a difference—in externals only. This one could gather from his casual talk. He originated nothing, he could keep the routine going—that's all. But he was great. He was great by this little thing that it was impossible to tell what could control such a man. He never gave that secret away. Perhaps there was nothing within him. Such a suspicion made one pause—for out there there were no external checks. Once when various tropical diseases had laid low almost every 'agent' in the station, he was heard to say, 'Men who come out here should have no entrails.' He sealed the utterance with that smile of his, as though it had been a door opening into a darkness he had in his keeping. You fancied you had seen things—but the seal was on. When annoyed at mealtimes by the constant quarrels of the white men about precedence, he ordered an immense round table to be made, for which a special house had to be built. This was the station's mess-room. Where he sat was the first place—the rest were nowhere. One felt this to be his unalterable conviction. He was neither civil nor uncivil. He was quiet. He allowed his 'boy'—an overfed young negro from the coast—to treat the white men, under his very eyes, with provoking insolence.

"He began to speak as soon as he saw me. I had been very long on the road. He could not wait. Had to start without me. The up-river stations had to be relieved. There had been so many delays already that he did not know who was dead and who was alive, and how they got on—and so on, and so on. He paid no attention to my explanations, and, playing with a stick of sealing wax, repeated several times that the situation was 'very grave, very grave.' There were rumors that a very important station was in jeopardy, and its chief, Mr. Kurtz, was ill. Hoped it was not true. Mr. Kurtz was . . . I felt weary and irritable. Hang Kurtz, I thought. I interrupted him by saying I had heard of Mr. Kurtz on the coast. 'Ah! So they talk of him down there,' he murmured to himself. Then he began again, assuring me Mr. Kurtz was the best agent he had, an exceptional man, of the greatest importance to the Company; therefore I could understand his anxiety. He was, he said, 'very, very uneasy.' Certainly he fidgeted on his chair a good deal, exclaimed, 'Ah, Mr. Kurtz!' broke the stick of sealing wax and seemed dumbfounded by the accident. Next thing he wanted to know 'how long it would take to' . . . I interrupted him again. Being hungry, you know, and kept on my feet too, I was getting savage.

8. Sailor.

'How can I tell?' I said. 'I haven't even seen the wreck yet—some months, no doubt.' All this talk seemed to me so futile. 'Some months,' he said. 'Well, let us say three months before we can make a start. Yes. That ought to do the affair.' I flung out of his hut (he lived all alone in a clay hut with a sort of verandah) muttering to myself my opinion of him. He was a chattering idiot. Afterwards I took it back when it was borne in upon me startingly with what extreme nicety he had estimated the time requisite for the 'affair.'

"I went to work the next day, turning, so to speak, my back on that station. In that way only it seemed to me I could keep my hold on the redeeming facts of life. Still, one must look about sometimes; and then I saw this station, these men strolling aimlessly about in the sunshine of the yard. I asked myself sometimes what it all meant. They wandered here and there with their absurd long staves in their hands, like a lot of faithless pilgrims bewitched inside a rotten fence. The word 'ivory' rang in the air, was whispered, was sighed. You would think they were praying to it. A taint of imbecile rapacity blew through it all, like a whiff from some corpse. By Jove! I've never seen anything so unreal in my life. And outside, the silent wilderness surrounding this cleared speck on the earth struck me as something great and invincible, like evil or truth, waiting patiently for the passing away of this fantastic invasion.

"Oh, those months! Well, never mind. Various things happened. One evening a grass shed full of calico, cotton prints, beads, and I don't know what else, burst into a blaze so suddenly that you would have thought the earth had opened to let an avenging fire consume all that trash. I was smoking my pipe quietly by my dismantled steamer, and saw them all cutting capers in the light, with their arms lifted high, when the stout man with moustaches came tearing down to the river, a tin pail in his hand, assured me that everybody was 'behaving splendidly, splendidly,' dipped about a quart of water and tore back again. I noticed there was a hole in the bottom of his pail.

"I strolled up. There was no hurry. You see the thing had gone off like a box of matches. It had been hopeless from the very first. The flame had leaped high, driven everybody back, lighted up everything—and collapsed. The shed was already a heap of embers glowing fiercely. A nigger was being beaten near by. They said he had caused the fire in some way; be that as it may, he was screeching most horribly. I saw him, later, for several days, sitting in a bit of shade looking very sick and trying to recover himself: afterwards he arose and went out—and the wilderness without a sound took him into its bosom again. As I approached the glow from the dark I found myself at the back of two men, talking. I heard the name of Kurtz pronounced, then the words, 'take advantage of this unfortunate accident.' One of the men was the manager. I wished him a good evening. 'Did you ever see anything like it—eh? it is incredible,' he said, and walked off. The other man remained. He was a first-class agent, young, gentlemanly, a bit reserved, with a forked little beard and a hooked nose. He was standoffish with the other agents, and they on their side said he was the manager's spy upon them. As to me, I had hardly ever spoken to him before. We got into talk, and by and by we strolled away from the hissing ruins. Then he asked me to his room, which was in the main building of the station. He struck a match, and I perceived that this young aristocrat had not only a silver-mounted dressing-case but also a whole candle all to himself. Just at that time the manager was the only man supposed to have any right to candles. Native mats covered the clay walls; a collection of spears, assegais, shields, knives, was hung up in trophies. The business entrusted to this fellow was the making of bricks—so I had been informed; but there wasn't a fragment of a brick anywhere in the station, and he had been there more than a year—waiting. It seems he could not make bricks without something, I don't know what—straw[9] maybe. Anyway, it could not be found there, and as it was not likely to be sent from Europe, it did not appear clear to me what he was waiting for. An act of special creation perhaps. However, they were all waiting—all the sixteen or twenty pilgrims of them—for something; and upon my word it did not seem an uncongenial occupation, from the way they took it, though the only thing that ever came to them was disease—as far as I could see. They beguiled the time by backbiting and intriguing against each other in a foolish kind of way. There was an air of plotting about that station, but nothing came of it, of course. It was as unreal as everything else—as the philanthropic pretense of the whole concern, as their talk, as their government, as their show of work. The only real feeling was a desire to get appointed to a trading-post where ivory was to be had, so that they could earn percentages. They intrigued and slandered and hated each other only on that account—but as to effectually lifting a little finger—oh no. By Heavens! there is something after all in the world allowing one man to steal a horse while another must not look at a halter. Steal a horse straight out. Very well. He has done it. Perhaps he can ride. But there is a way of looking at a halter that would provoke the most charitable of saints into a kick.

"I had no idea why he wanted to be sociable, but as we chatted in there it suddenly occurred to me the fellow was trying to get at something—in fact, pumping me. He alluded constantly to Europe, to the people I was supposed to know there—putting leading questions as to my acquaintances in the sepulchral city, and so on. His little eyes glittered like mica discs—with curiosity—though he tried to keep up a bit of superciliousness. At first I was astonished, but very soon I became awfully curious to see what he would find out from me. I couldn't possibly imagine what I had in me to make it worth his while. It was very pretty to see how he baffled himself, for in truth my body was full only of chills, and my head had nothing in it but that wretched steamboat business. It was evident he took me for a perfectly shameless prevaricator. At last he got angry, and, to conceal a movement of furious annoyance, he yawned. I rose. Then I noticed a small sketch in oils, on a panel, representing a woman, draped and blindfolded,

9. In *Exodus* 5, the Hebrews, slaves of the Egyptians, had to make a certain number of bricks daily, the straw for the process supplied by the Egyptians, but the Pharaoh ordered the supplying of straw stopped while keeping the daily quota the same; not only was a good deal of time lost searching for straw, but little else than stubble could be found.

carrying a lighted torch. The background was somber—almost black. The movement of the woman was stately, and the effect of the torch-light on the face was sinister.

"It arrested me, and he stood by civilly, holding an empty half-pint champagne bottle (medical comforts) with the candle stuck in it. To my question he said Mr. Kurtz had painted this—in this very station more than a year ago—while waiting for means to go to his trading-post. 'Tell me, pray,' said I, 'who is this Mr. Kurtz?'

" 'The chief of the Inner Station,' he answered in a short tone, looking away. 'Much obliged,' I said, laughing. 'And you are the brick-maker of the Central Station. Everyone knows that.' He was silent for a while. 'He is a prodigy,' he said at last. 'He is an emissary of pity, and science, and progress, and devil knows what else. We want,' he began to declaim suddenly, 'for the guidance of the cause entrusted to us by Europe, so to speak, higher intelligence, wide sympathies, a singleness of purpose.' 'Who says that?' I asked. 'Lots of them,' he replied. 'Some even write that; and so *he* comes here, a special being, as you ought to know.' 'Why ought I to know?' I interrupted, really surprised. He paid no attention. 'Yes. Today he is chief of the best station, next year he will be assistant-manager, two years more and . . . but I daresay you know what he will be in two years' time. You are of the new gang—the gang of virtue. The same people who sent him specially also recommended you. Oh, don't say no. I've my own eyes to trust.' Light dawned upon me. My dear aunt's influential acquaintances were producing an unexpected effect upon that young man. I nearly burst into a laugh. 'Do you read the Company's confidential correspondence?' I asked. He hadn't a word to say. It was great fun. 'When Mr. Kurtz,' I continued severely, 'is General Manager, you won't have the opportunity.'

"He blew the candle out suddenly, and we went outside. The moon had risen. Black figures strolled about listlessly, pouring water on the glow, whence proceeded a sound of hissing; steam ascended in the moonlight; the beaten nigger groaned somewhere. 'What a row the brute makes!' said the indefatigable man with the moustaches, appearing near us. 'Serve him right. Transgression—punishment—bang! Pitiless, pitiless. That's the only way. This will prevent all conflagrations for the future. I was just telling the manager . . .' He noticed my companion, and became crestfallen all at once. 'Not in bed yet,' he said, with a kind of servile heartiness; 'it's so natural. Ha! Danger—agitation.' He vanished. I went on to the river-side, and the other followed me. I heard a scathing murmur at my ear, 'Heaps of muffs—go to.' The pilgrims could be seen in knots gesticulating, discussing. Several had still their staves in their hands. I verily believe they took these sticks to bed with them. Beyond the fence the forest stood up spectrally in the moonlight, and through the dim stir, through the faint sounds of that lamentable courtyard, the silence of the land went home to one's very heart—its mystery, its greatness, the amazing reality of its concealed life. The hurt nigger moaned feebly somewhere near by, and then fetched a deep sigh that made me mend my pace away from there. I felt a hand introducing itself under my arm. 'My dear sir,' said the fellow, 'I don't want to be misunderstood, and especially by you, who will see Mr. Kurtz long before I can have that pleasure. I wouldn't like him to get a false idea of my disposition. . . .'

"I let him run on, this papier-mâché Mephistopheles, and it seemed to me that if I tried I could poke my forefinger through him, and would find nothing inside but a little loose dirt, maybe. He, don't you see, had been planning to be assistant-manager by and by under the present man, and I could see that the coming of that Kurtz had upset them both not a little. He talked precipitately, and I did not try to stop him. I had my shoulders against the wreck of my steamer, hauled up on the slope like a carcass of some big river animal. The smell of mud, of primeval mud, by Jove! was in my nostrils, the high stillness of primeval forest was before my eyes; there were shiny patches on the black creek. The moon had spread over everything a thin layer of silver—over the rank grass, over the mud, upon the wall of matted vegetation standing higher than the wall of a temple, over the great river I could see through a somber gap glittering, glittering, as it flowed broadly by without a murmur. All this was great, expectant, mute, while the man jabbered about himself. I wondered whether the stillness on the face of the immensity looking at us two were meant as an appeal or as a menace. What were we who had strayed in here? Could we handle that dumb thing, or would it handle us? I felt how big, how confoundedly big, was that thing that couldn't talk and perhaps was deaf as well. What was in there? I could see a little ivory coming out from there, and I had heard Mr. Kurtz was in there. I had heard enough about it too—God knows! Yet somehow it didn't bring any image with it—no more than if I had been told an angel or a fiend was in there. I believed it in the same way one of you might believe there are inhabitants in the planet Mars. I knew once a Scotch sailmaker who was certain, dead sure, there were people in Mars. If you asked him for some idea how they looked and behaved, he would get shy and mutter something about 'walking on all-fours.' If you as much as smiled, he would—though a man of sixty—offer to fight you. I would not have gone so far as to fight for Kurtz, but I went for him near enough to a lie. You know I hate, detest, and can't bear a lie, not because I am straighter than the rest of us, but simply because it appals me. There is a taint of death, a flavor of mortality in lies—which is exactly what I hate and detest in the world—what I want to forget. It makes me miserable and sick, like biting something rotten would do. Temperament, I suppose. Well, I went near enough to it by letting the young fool there believe anything he liked to imagine as to my influence in Europe. I became in an instant as much of a pretense as the rest of the bewitched pilgrims. This simply because I had a notion it somehow would be of help to that Kurtz whom at the time I did not see—you understand. He was just a word for me. I did not see the man in the name any more than you do. Do you see him? Do you see the story? Do you see anything? It seems to me I am trying to tell you a dream—making a vain attempt, because no relation of a dream can convey the dream-sensation, that commingling of absurdity, surprise, and bewilderment in a tremor of struggling revolt, that notion of being captured by the incredible which is of the very essence of dreams. . . ."

He was silent for a while.

". . . No, it is impossible; it is impossible to convey the life-sensation of any given epoch of one's existence—that which makes its truth, its meaning—its subtle and pentrating essence. It is impossible. We live, as we dream—alone. . . ."

He paused again as if reflecting, then added:

"Of course in this you fellows see more than I could then. You see me, whom you know. . . ."

It had become so pitch dark that we listeners could hardly see one another. For a long time already he, sitting apart, had been no more to us than a voice. There was not a word from anybody. The others might have been asleep, but I was awake. I listened, I listened on the watch for the sentence, for the word, that would give me the clue to the faint uneasiness inspired by this narrative that seemed to shape itself without human lips in the heavy night-air of the river.

". . . Yes—I let him run on," Marlow began again, "and think what he pleased about the powers that were behind me. I did! And there was nothing behind me! There was nothing but that wretched, old, mangled steamboat I was leaning against, while he talked fluently about 'the necessity for every man to get on.' 'And when one comes out here, you conceive, it is not to gaze at the moon.' Mr. Kurtz was a 'universal genius,' but even a genius would find it easier to work with 'adequate tools—intelligent men.' He did not make bricks—why, there was a physical impossibility in the way—as I was well aware; and if he did secretarial work for the manager, it was because 'no sensible man rejects wantonly the confidence of his superiors.' Did I see it? I saw it. What more did I want? What I really wanted was rivets, by Heaven! Rivets. To get on with the work—to stop the hole. Rivets I wanted. There were cases of them down at the coast—cases—piled up—burst—split! You kicked a loose rivet at every second step in that station yard on the hillside. Rivets had rolled into the grove of death. You could fill your pockets with rivets for the trouble of stooping down—and there wasn't one rivet to be found where it was wanted. We had plates that would do, but nothing to fasten them with. And every week the messenger, a lone negro, letter-bag on shoulder and staff in hand, left our station for the coast. And several times a week a coast caravan came in with trade goods—ghastly glazed calico that made you shudder only to look at it, glass beads value about a penny a quart, confounded spotted cotton handkerchiefs. And no rivets. Three carriers could have brought all that was wanted to set that steamboat afloat.

"He was becoming confidential now, but I fancy my unresponsive attitude must have exasperated him at last, for he judged it necessary to inform me he feared neither God nor devil, let alone any mere man. I said I could see that very well, but what I wanted was a certain quantity of rivets—and rivets were what really Mr. Kurtz wanted, if he had only known it. Now letters went to the coast every week. . . . 'My dear sir,' he cried, 'I write from dictation.' I demanded rivets. There was a way—for an intelligent man. He changed his manner;

became very cold, and suddenly began to talk about a hippopotamus; wondered whether sleeping on board the steamer (I stuck to my salvage night and day) I wasn't disturbed. There was an old hippo that had the bad habit of getting out on the bank and roaming at night over the station grounds. The pilgrims used to turn out in a body and empty every rifle they could lay hands on at him. Some even had sat up o' nights for him. All this energy was wasted, though. 'That animal has a charmed life,' he said; 'but you can say this only of brutes in this country. No man—you apprehend me?—no man here bears a charmed life.' He stood there for a moment in the moonlight with his delicate hooked nose set a little askew, and his mica eyes glittering without a wink, then, with a curt Good-night, he strode off. I could see he was disturbed and considerably puzzled, which made me feel more hopeful than I had been for days. It was a great comfort to turn from that chap to my influential friend, the battered, twisted, ruined, tin-pot steamboat. I clambered on board. She rang under my feet like an empty Huntley & Palmer biscuit-tin kicked along a gutter; she was nothing so solid in make, and rather less pretty in shape, but I had expended enough hard work on her to make me love her. No influential friend would have served me better. She had given me a chance to come out a bit—to find out what I could do. No, I don't like work. I had rather laze about and think of all the fine things that can be done. I don't like work—no man does—but I like what is in the work—the chance to find yourself. Your own reality—for yourself, not for others—what no other man can ever know. They can only see the mere show, and never can tell what it really means.

"I was not surprised to see somebody sitting aft, on the deck, with his legs dangling over the mud. You see I rather chummed with the few mechanics there were in that station, whom the other pilgrims naturally despised—on account of their imperfect manners, I suppose. This was the foreman—a boiler-maker by trade—a good worker. He was a lank, bony, yellow-faced man, with big intense eyes. His aspect was worried, and his head was as bald as the palm of my hand; but his hair in falling seemed to have stuck to his chin, and had prospered in the new locality, for his beard hung down to his waist. He was a widower with six young children (he had left them in charge of a sister of his to come out there), and the passion of his life was pigeon-flying. He was an enthusiast and a connoisseur. He would rave about pigeons. After work hours he used sometimes to come over from his hut for a talk about his children and his pigeons; at work, when he had to crawl in the mud under the bottom of the steamboat, he would tie up that beard of his in a kind of white serviette he brought for the purpose. It had loops to go over his ears. In the evening he could be seen squatted on the banks rinsing that wrapper in the creek with great care, then spreading it solemly on a bush to dry.

"I slapped him on the back and shouted 'We shall have rivets!' He scrambled to his feet exclaiming 'No! Rivets!' as though he couldn't believe his ears. Then in a low voice, 'You . . . eh?' I don't know why we behaved like lunatics. I put my finger to the side of my nose and nodded mysteriously. 'Good for you!' he cried, snapped his fingers above his head, lifting one foot. I tried a jig. We capered on the iron deck. A frightful clatter came out of that hulk, and the virgin forest on the other bank of the creek sent it back in a thundering roll upon the sleeping station. It must have made some of the pilgrims sit up in their hovels. A dark figure obscured the lighted doorway of the manager's hut, vanished, then, a second or so after, the doorway itself vanished too. We stopped, and the silence driven away by the stamping of our feet flowed back again from the recesses of the land. The great wall of vegetation, an exuberant and entangled mass of trunks, branches, leaves, boughs, festoons, motionless in the moonlight, was like a rioting invasion of soundless life, a rolling wave of plants, piled up, crested, ready to topple over the creek, to sweep every little man of us out of his little existence. And it moved not. A deadened burst of mighty splashes and snorts reached us from afar, as though an ichthyosaurus had been taking a bath of glitter in the great river. 'After all,' said the boiler-maker in a reasonable tone, 'why shouldn't we get the rivets?' Why not, indeed! I did not know of any reason why we shouldn't. 'They'll come in three weeks,' I said confidently.

"But they didn't. Instead of rivets there came an invasion, an infliction, a visitation. It came in sections during the next three weeks, each section headed by a donkey carrying a white man in new clothes and tan shoes, bowing from that elevation right and left to the impressed pilgrims. A quarrelsome band of footsore sulky niggers trod on the heels of the donkey; a lot of tents, camp-stools, tin boxes, white cases, brown bales would be shot down in the courtyard, and the air of mystery would deepen a little over the muddle of the station. Five such instalments came, with their absurd air of disorderly flight with the loot of innumerable outfit shops and provision stores, that, one would think, they were lugging, after a raid, into the wilderness for equitable division. It was an inextricable mess of things decent in themselves but that human folly made look like the spoils of thieving.

"This devoted band called itself the Eldorado Exploring Expedition, and I believe they were sworn to secrecy. Their talk, however, was the talk of sordid buccaneers: it was reckless without hardihood, greedy without audacity, and cruel without courage; there was not an atom of foresight or of serious intention in the whole batch of them, and they did not seem aware these things are wanted for the work of the world. To tear treasure out of the bowels of the land was their desire, with no more moral purpose at the back of it than there is in burglars breaking into a safe. Who paid the expenses of the noble enterprise I don't know; but the uncle of our manager was leader of that lot.

"In exterior he resembled a butcher in a poor neighborhood, and his eyes had a look of sleepy cunning. He carried his fat paunch with ostentation on his short legs, and during the time his gang infested the station spoke to no one but his nephew. You could see these two roaming about all day long with their heads close together in an everlasting confab.

"I had given up worrying myself about the rivets. One's capacity for that kind of folly is more limited than you would suppose. I said Hang!—and let things slide. I had plenty of time for meditation, and now and then I would give some thought to Kurtz. I wasn't very interested in him. No. Still, I was curious to see whether this man, who had come out equipped with moral ideas of some sort, would climb to the top after all, and how he would set about his work when there."

2

"One evening as I was lying flat on the deck of my steamboat, I heard voices approaching—and there were the nephew and the uncle strolling along the bank. I laid my head on my arm again, and had nearly lost myself in a doze, when somebody said in my ear, as it were: 'I am as harmless as a little child, but I don't like to be dictated to. Am I the manager—or am I not? I was ordered to send him there. It's incredible.' . . . I became aware that the two were standing on the shore alongside the forepart of the steamboat, just below my head. I did not move; it did not occur to me to move; I was sleepy. 'It *is* unpleasant,' grunted the uncle. 'He has asked the Administration to be sent there,' said the other, 'with the idea of showing what he could do; and I was instructed accordingly. Look at the influence that man must have. Is it not frightful?' They both agreed it was frightful, then made several bizarre remarks: 'Make rain and fine weather—one man—the Council—by the nose'—bits of absurd sentences that got the better of my drowsiness, so that I had pretty near the whole of my wits about me when the uncle said, 'The climate may do away with this difficulty for you. Is he alone there?' 'Yes,' answered the manager; 'he sent his assistant down the river with a note to me in these terms: "Clear this poor devil out of the country, and don't bother sending more of that sort. I had rather be alone than have the kind of men you can dispose of with me." It was more than a year ago. Can you imagine such impudence?' 'Anything since then?' asked the other hoarsely. 'Ivory,' jerked the nephew; 'lots of it—prime sort—lots—most annoying, from him.' 'And with that?' questioned the heavy rumble. 'Invoice,' was the reply fired out, so to speak. Then silence. They had been talking about Kurtz.

"I was broad awake by this time, but, lying perfectly at ease, remained still, having no inducement to change my position. 'How did that ivory come all this way?' growled the elder man, who seemed very vexed. The other explained that it had come with a fleet of canoes in charge of an English half-caste clerk Kurtz had with him; that Kurtz had apparently intended to return himself, the station being by that time bare of goods and stores, but after coming three hundred miles, had suddenly decided to go back, which he started to do alone in a small dugout with four paddlers, leaving the half-caste to continue down the river with the ivory. The two fellows there seemed astounded at anybody attempting such a thing. They were at a loss for an adequate motive. As for me, I seemed to see Kurtz for the first time. It was a distinct glimpse: the dugout, four paddling savages, and the lone white man turning his back suddenly on the headquarters, on relief, on thoughts of home—perhaps; setting his face towards the depths of the wilderness, towards his empty and desolate station. I did not know the motive. Perhaps he was just simply a fine fellow who stuck to his work for its own sake. His name, you understand, had not been pronounced once. He was 'that man.' The half-caste, who, as far as I could see, had conducted a difficult trip with great prudence and pluck, was invariably alluded to as 'that scoundrel.' The 'scoundrel' had reported that the 'man' had been very ill—had recovered imperfectly. . . . The two below me moved away then a few paces, and strolled back and forth at some little distance. I heard: 'Military post—doctor—two hundred miles—quite alone now—unavoidable delays—nine months—no news—strange rumors.' They approached again, just as the manager was saying, 'No one, as far as I know, unless a species of wandering trader—a pestilential fellow, snapping ivory from the natives.' Who was it they were talking about now? I gathered in snatches that this was some man supposed to be in Kurtz's district, and of whom the manager did not approve. 'We will not be free from unfair competition till one of these fellows is hanged for an example,' he said, 'Certainly,' grunted the other; 'get him hanged! Why not? Anything—anything can be done in this country. That's what I say; nobody here, you understand, *here,* can endanger your position. And why? You stand the climate—you outlast them all. The danger is in Europe; but there before I left I took care to—' They moved off and whispered, then their voices rose again. 'The extraordinary series of delays is not my fault. I did my possible.' The fat man sighed, 'Very sad.' 'And the pestiferous absurdity of his talk,' continued the other; 'he bothered me enough when he was here. "Each station should be like a beacon on the road towards better things, a center for trade of course, but also for humanizing, improving, instructing." Conceive you—that ass! And he wants to be manager! No, it's—' Here he got choked by excessive indignation, and I lifted my head the least bit. I was surprised to see how near they were—right under me. I could have spat upon their hats. They were looking on the ground, absorbed in thought. The manager was switching his leg with a slender twig: his sagacious relative lifted his head. 'You have been well since you came out this time?' he asked. The other gave a start. 'Who? I? Oh! Like a charm—like a charm. But the rest—oh, my goodness! All sick. They die so quick, too, that I haven't the time to send them out of the country—it's incredible!' 'H'm. Just so,' grunted the uncle. 'Ah! my boy, trust to this—I say, trust to this.' I saw him extend his short flipper of an arm for a gesture that took in the forest, the creek, the mud, the river—seemed to beckon with a dishonoring flourish before the sunlit face of the land a treacherous appeal to the lurking death, to the hidden evil, to the profound darkness of its heart. It was so startling that I leaped to my feet and looked back at the edge of the forest, as though I had expected an answer of some sort to that black display of confidence. You know the foolish notions that come to one sometimes. The high stillness confronted these two figures with its ominous patience, waiting for the passing away of a fantastic invasion.

"They swore aloud together—out of sheer fright, I believe—then, pretending not to know anything of my existence, turned back to the station. The sun was low; and leaning forward side by side, they seemed to be tugging painfully uphill their two ridiculous shadows of unequal length, that trailed behind them slowly over the tall grass without bending a single blade.

"In a few days the Eldorado Expedition went into the patient wilderness, that closed upon it as the sea closes over a diver. Long afterwards the news came that all the donkeys were dead. I know nothing as to the fate of the less valuable animals. They, no doubt, like the rest of us, found what they deserved. I did not inquire. I was then rather excited at the prospect of meeting Kurtz very soon. When I say very soon I mean it comparatively. It was just two months from the day we left the creek when we came to the bank below Kurtz's station.

"Going up that river was like traveling back to the earliest beginnings of the world, when vegetation rioted on the earth and the big trees were kings. An empty stream, a great silence, an impenetrable forest. The air was warm, thick, heavy, sluggish. There was no joy in the brilliance of sunshine. The long stretches of the waterway ran on, deserted, into the gloom of overshadowed distances. On silvery sandbanks hippos and alligators sunned themselves side by side. The broadening waters flowed through a mob of wooded islands; you lost your way on that river as you would in a desert, and butted all day long against shoals, trying to find the channel, till you thought yourself bewitched and cut off forever from everything you had known once—somewhere—far away—in another existence perhaps. There were moments when one's past came back to one, as it will sometimes when you have not a moment to spare to yourself; but it came in the shape of an unrestful and noisy dream, remembered with wonder amongst the overwhelming realities of this strange world of plants, and water, and silence. And this stillness of life did not in the least resemble a peace. It was the stillness of an implacable force brooding over an inscrutable intention. It looked at you with a vengeful aspect. I got used to it afterwards; I did not see it any more; I had no time. I had to keep guessing at the channel; I had to discern, mostly by inspiration, the signs of hidden banks; I watched for sunken stones; I was learning to clap my teeth smartly before my heart flew out, when I shaved by a fluke some infernal sly old snag that would have ripped the life out of the tin-pot steamboat and drowned all the pilgrims; I had to keep a look-out for the signs of dead wood we could cut up in the night for next day's steaming. When you have to attend to things of that sort, to the mere incidents of the surface, the reality—the reality, I tell you—fades. The inner truth is hidden—luckily, luckily. But I felt it all the same; I felt often its mysterious stillness watching me at my monkey tricks, just as it watches you fellows performing on your respective tight-ropes for—what is it? half a crown a tumble—"

"Try to be civil, Marlow," growled a voice, and I knew there was at least one listener awake besides myself.

"I beg your pardon. I forgot the heartache which makes up the rest of the price. And indeed what does the price matter, if the trick be well done? You do your tricks very well. And I didn't do badly either, since I managed not to sink that steamboat on my first trip. It's a wonder to me yet. Imagine a blindfolded man set to drive a van over a bad road.

I sweated and shivered over that business considerably, I can tell you. After all, for a seaman, to scrape the bottom of the thing that's supposed to float all the time under his care is the unpardonable sin. No one may know of it, but you never forget the thump—eh? A blow on the very heart. You remember it, you dream of it, you wake up at night and think of it—years after—and go hot and cold all over. I don't pretend to say that steamboat floated all the time. More than once she had to wade for a bit, with twenty cannibals splashing around and pushing. We had enlisted some of these chaps on the way for a crew. Fine fellows—cannibals—in their place. They were men one could work with, and I am grateful to them. And, after all, they did not eat each other before my face: they had brought along a provision of hippo-meat which went rotten, and made the mystery of the wilderness stink in my nostrils. Phoo! I can sniff it now. I had the manager on board and three or four pilgrims with their staves—all complete. Sometimes we came upon a station close by the bank, clinging to the skirts of the unknown, and the white men rushing out of a tumble-down hovel, with great gestures of joy and surprise and welcome, seemed very strange—had the appearance of being held there captive by a spell. The word 'ivory' would ring in the air for a while—and on we went again into the silence, along empty reaches, round the still bends, between the high walls of our winding way, reverberating in hollow claps the ponderous beat of the stern-wheel. Trees, trees, millions of trees, massive, immense, running up high; and at their foot, hugging the bank against the stream, crept the little begrimed steamboat, like a sluggish beetle crawling on the floor of a lofty portico. It made you feel very small, very lost, and yet it was not altogether depressing, that feeling. After all, if you were small, the grimy beetle crawled on—which was just what you wanted it to do. Where the pilgrims imagined it crawled to I don't know. To some place where they expected to get something, I bet! For me it crawled towards Kurtz—exclusively; but when the steam-pipes started leaking we crawled very slow. The reaches opened before us and closed behind, as if the forest had stepped leisurely across the water to bar the way for our return. We penetrated deeper and deeper into the heart of darkness. It was very quiet there. At night sometimes the roll of drums behind the curtain of trees would run up the river and remain sustained faintly, as if hovering in the air high over our heads, till the first break of day. Whether it meant war, peace, or prayer we could not tell. The dawns were heralded by the descent of a chill stillness; the woodcutters slept, their fires burned low; the snapping of a twig would make you start. We were wanderers on a prehistoric earth, on an earth that wore the aspect of an unknown planet. We could have fancied ourselves the first of men taking possession of an accursed inheritance, to be subdued at the cost of profound anguish and of excessive toil. But suddenly, as we struggled round a bend, there would be a glimpse of rush walls, of peaked grass-roofs, a burst of yells, a whirl of black limbs, a mass of hands clapping, of feet stamping, of bodies swaying, of eyes rolling, under the droop of heavy and motionless foliage. The steamer toiled along slowly on the edge of a black and incomprehensible frenzy. The prehistoric man was cursing us, praying to us, welcoming us—who could tell? We were cut off from the comprehension of our surroundings; we glided past like phantoms, wondering and secretly appalled, as sane men would be before an enthusiastic outbreak in a madhouse. We could not understand because we were too far and could not remember, because we were traveling in the night of first ages, of those ages that are gone, leaving hardly a sign—and no memories.

"The earth seemed unearthly. We are accustomed to look upon the shackled form of a conquered monster, but there—there you could look at a thing monstrous and free. It was unearthly, and the men were— No, they were not inhuman. Well, you know, that was the worst of it—this suspicion of their not being inhuman. It would come slowly to one. They howled and leaped, and spun, and made horrid faces; but what thrilled you was just the thought of their humanity—like yours—the thought of your remote kinship with this wild and passionate uproar. Ugly. Yes, it was ugly enough; but if you were man enough you would admit to yourself that there was in you just the faintest trace of a response to the terrible frankness of that noise, a dim suspicion of there being a meaning in it which you—you so remote from the night of first ages—could comprehend. And why not? The mind of man is capable of anything—because everything is in it, all the past as well as all the future. What was there after all? Joy, fear, sorrow, devotion, valor, rage—who can tell?—but truth—truth stripped of its cloak of time. Let the fool gape and shudder—the man knows, and can look on without a wink. But he must at least be as much of a man as these on the shore. He must meet that truth with his own true stuff—with his own inborn strength. Principles? Principles won't do. Acquisitions, clothes, pretty rags—rags that would fly off at the first good shake. No; you want a deliberate belief. An appeal to me in this fiendish row—is there? Very well; I hear; I admit, but I have a voice too, and for good or evil mine is the speech that cannot be silenced. Of course, a fool, what with sheer fright and fine sentiments, is always safe. Who's that grunting? You wonder I didn't go ashore for a howl and a dance? Well, no—I didn't. Fine sentiments, you say? Fine sentiments be hanged! I had no time. I had to mess about with white-lead[1] and strips of woollen blanket helping to put bandages on those leaky steam-pipes—I tell you. I had to watch the steering, and circumvent those snags, and get the tin-pot along by hook or by crook. There was surface-truth enough in these things to save a wiser man. And between whiles I had to look after the savage who was fireman. He was an improved specimen; he could fire up a vertical boiler.[2] He was there below me, and, upon my word, to look at him was as edifying as seeing a dog in a parody of breeches and a feather hat, walking on his hind legs. A few months of training had done for that really fine chap. He squinted at the steam-gauge and at the water-gauge with an evident effort of intrepidity—and he had filed teeth too, the poor devil, and the wool of his pate shaved into queer patterns, and three ornamental scars on each of his cheeks. He ought to have been clapping his hands and

1. Putty.

2. An upright, simple, easily fired boiler.

stamping his feet on the bank, instead of which he was hard at work, a thrall to strange witchcraft, full of improving knowledge. He was useful because he had been instructed; and what he knew was this—that should the water in that transparent thing disappear, the evil spirit inside the boiler would get angry through the greatness of his thirst, and take a terrible vengeance. So he sweated and fired up and watched the glass fearfully (with an impromptu charm, made of rags, tied to his arm, and a piece of polished bone, as big as a watch, stuck flatways through his lower lip), while the wooded banks slipped past us slowly, the short noise was left behind, the interminable miles of silence—and we crept on, towards Kurtz. But the snags were thick, the water was treacherous and shallow, the boiler seemed indeed to have a sulky devil in it, and thus neither that fireman nor I had any time to peer into our creepy thoughts.

"Some fifty miles below the Inner Station we came upon a hut of reeds, an inclined and melancholy pole, with the unrecognizable tatters of what had been a flag of some sort flying from it, and a neatly stacked woodpile. This was unexpected. We came to the bank, and on the stack of firewood found a flat piece of board with some faded pencil-writing on it. When deciphered it said: 'Wood for you. Hurry up. Approach cautiously.' There was a signature, but it was illegible—not Kurtz—a much longer word. 'Hurry up.' Where? Up the river? 'Approach cautiously.' We had not done so. But the warning could not have been meant for the place where it could be only found after approach. Something was wrong above. But what—and how much? That was the question. We commented adversely upon the imbecility of that telegraphic style. The bush around said nothing, and would not let us look very far, either. A torn curtain of red twill hung in the doorway of the hut, and flapped sadly in our faces. The dwelling was dismantled; but we could see a white man had lived there not very long ago. There remained a rude table—a plank on two posts; a heap of rubbish reposed in a dark corner, and by the door I picked up a book. It had lost its covers, and the pages had been thumbed into a state of extremely dirty softness; but the back had been lovingly stitched afresh with white cotton thread, which looked clean yet. It was an extraordinary find. Its title was *An Inquiry into Some Points of Seamanship*, by a man Towser, Towson—some such name—Master in His Majesty's Navy. The matter looked dreary reading enough, with illustrative diagrams and repulsive tables of figures, and the copy was sixty years old. I handled this amazing antiquity with the greatest possible tenderness, lest it should dissolve in my hands. Within, Towson or Towser was inquiring earnestly into the breaking strain of ships' chains and tackle, and other such matters. Not a very enthralling book; but at the first glance you could see there a singleness of intention, an honest concern for the right way of going to work, which made these humble pages, thought out so many years ago, luminous with another than a professional light. The simple old sailor, with his talk of chains and purchases,[3] made me forget the jungle and the pilgrims in a delicious sensation of having come upon

3. Levers, or system of pulleys.

something unmistakably real. Such a book being there was wonderful enough; but still more astounding were the notes penciled in the margin, and plainly referring to the text. I couldn't believe my eyes! They were in cipher! Yes, it looked like cipher. Fancy a man lugging with him a book of that description into this nowhere and studying it—and making notes—in cipher at that! It was an extravagant mystery.

"I had been dimly aware for some time of a worrying noise, and when I lifted my eyes I saw the woodpile was gone, and the manager, aided by all the pilgrims, was shouting at me from the riverside. I slipped the book into my pocket. I assure you to leave off reading was like tearing myself away from the shelter of an old and solid friendship.

"I started the lame engine ahead. 'It must be this miserable trader—this intruder,' exclaimed the manager, looking back malevolently at the place we had left. 'He must be English,' I said. 'It will not save him from getting into trouble if he is not careful,' muttered the manager darkly. I observed with assumed innocence that no man was safe from trouble in this world.

"The current was more rapid now, the steamer seemed at her last gasp, the stern-wheel flopped languidly, and I caught myself listening on tiptoe for the next beat of the float,[4] for in sober truth I expected the wretched thing to give up every moment. It was like watching the last flickers of a life. But still we crawled. Sometimes I would pick out a tree a little way ahead to measure our progress towards Kurtz by, but I lost it invariably before we got abreast. To keep the eyes so long on one thing was too much for human patience. The manager displayed a beautiful resignation. I fretted and fumed and took to arguing with myself whether or no I would talk openly with Kurtz; but before I could come to any conclusion it occurred to me that my speech or my silence, indeed any action of mine, would be a mere futility. What did it matter what anyone knew or ignored? What did it matter who was manager? One gets sometimes such a flash of insight. The essentials of this affair lay deep under the surface, beyond my reach, and beyond my power of meddling.

"Towards the evening of the second day we judged ourselves about eight miles from Kurtz's station. I wanted to push on; but the manager looked grave, and told me the navigation up there was so dangerous that it would be advisable, the sun being very low already, to wait where we were till next morning. Moreover, he pointed out that if the warning to approach cautiously were to be followed, we must approach in daylight—not at dusk, or in the dark. This was sensible enough. Eight miles meant nearly three hours' steaming for us, and I could also see suspicious ripples at the upper end of the reach. Nevertheless, I was annoyed beyond expression at the delay, and most unreasonably too, since one night more could not matter much after so many months. As we had plenty of wood, and caution was the word, I brought up in the middle of the stream. The reach was narrow, straight, with high sides like a railway cutting. The dusk came gliding into it long before the sun had set. The current ran smooth and swift, but a dumb im-

4. Blade on paddle-wheel.

mobility sat on the banks. The living trees, lashed together by the creepers and every living bush of the undergrowth, might have been changed into stone, even to the slenderest twig, to the lightest leaf. It was not sleep—it seemed unnatural, like a state of trance. Not the faintest sound of any kind could be heard. You looked on amazed, and began to suspect yourself of being deaf—then the night came suddenly, and struck you blind as well. About three in the morning some large fish leaped, and the loud splash made me jump as though a gun had been fired. When the sun rose there was a white fog, very warm and clammy, and more blinding than the night. It did not shift or drive; it was just there, standing all round you like something solid. At eight or nine, perhaps, it lifted as a shutter lifts. We had a glimpse of the towering multitude of trees, of the immense matted jungle, with the blazing little ball of the sun hanging over it—all perfectly still—and then the white shutter came down again, smoothly, as if sliding in greased grooves. I ordered the chain, which we had begun to heave in, to be paid out again. Before it stopped running with a muffled rattle, a cry, a very loud cry, as of infinite desolation, soared slowly in the opaque air. It ceased. A complaining clamor, modulated in savage discords, filled our ears. The sheer unexpectedness of it made my hair stir under my cap. I don't know how it struck the others: to me it seemed as though the mist itself had screamed, so suddenly, and apparently from all sides at once, did this tumultuous and mournful uproar arise. It culminated in a hurried outbreak of almost intolerably excessive shrieking, which stopped short, leaving us stiffened in a variety of silly attitudes, and obstinately listening to the nearly as appalling and excessive silence. 'Good God! What is the meaning—?' stammered at my elbow one of the pilgrims—a little fat man, with sandy hair and red whiskers, who wore side-spring boots, and pink pajamas tucked into his socks. Two others remained openmouthed a whole minute, then dashed into the little cabin, to rush out incontinently and stand darting scared glances, with Winchesters at 'ready' in their hands. What we could see was just the steamer we were on, her outlines blurred as though she had been on the point of dissolving, and a misty strip of water, perhaps two feet broad, around her—and that was all. The rest of the world was nowhere, as far as our eyes and ears were concerned. Just nowhere. Gone, disappeared; swept off without leaving a whisper or a shadow behind.

"I went forward, and ordered the chain to be hauled in short, so as to be ready to trip the anchor and move the steamboat at once if necessary. 'Will they attack?' whispered an awed voice. 'We will all be butchered in this fog,' murmured another. The faces twitched with the strain, the hands trembled slightly, the eyes forgot to wink. It was very curious to see the contrast of expressions of the white men and of the black fellows of our crew, who were as much strangers to that part of the river as we, though their homes were only eight hundred miles away. The whites, of course greatly discomposed, had besides a curious look of being painfully shocked by such an outrageous row. The others had an alert, naturally interested expression; but their faces were essentially quiet, even those of the one or two who grinned as they hauled at the chain. Several exchanged short, grunting phrases, which seemed to settle the matter to their satisfaction. Their head-man, a young, broad-chested black, severely draped in dark-blue fringed cloths, with fierce nostrils and his hair all done up artfully in oily ringlets, stood near me. 'Aha!' I said, just for good fellowship's sake. 'Catch 'im,' he snapped, with a bloodshot widening of his eyes and a flash of sharp teeth—'catch 'im. Give 'im to us.' 'To you, eh?' I asked; 'what would you do with them?' 'Eat 'im!' he said curtly, and, leaning his elbow on the rail, looked out into the fog in a dignified and profoundly pensive attitude. I would no doubt have been properly horrified, had it not occurred to me that he and his chaps must be very hungry: that they must have been growing increasingly hungry for at least this month past. They had been engaged for six months (I don't think a single one of them had any clear idea of time, as we at the end of countless ages have. They still belonged to the beginnings of time—had no inherited experience to teach them, as it were), and of course, as long as there was a piece of paper written over in accordance with some farcical law or other made down the river, it didn't enter anybody's head to trouble how they would live. Certainly they had brought with them some rotten hippo-meat, which couldn't have lasted very long, anyway, even if the pilgrims hadn't, in the midst of a shocking hullabaloo, thrown a considerable quantity of it overboard. It looked like a high-handed proceeding; but it was really a case of legitimate self-defense. You can't breathe dead hippo waking, sleeping, and eating, and at the same time keep your precarious grip on existence. Besides that, they had given them every week three pieces of brass wire, each about nine inches long; and the theory was they were to buy their provisions with that currency in riverside villages. You can see how *that* worked. There were either no villages, or the people were hostile, or the director, who like the rest of us fed out of tins, with an occasional old he-goat thrown in, didn't want to stop the steamer for some more or less recondite reason. So, unless they swallowed the wire itself, or made loops of it to snare the fishes with, I don't see what good their extravagant salary could be to them. I must say it was paid with a regularity worthy of a large and honorable trading company. For the rest, the only thing to eat—though it didn't look eatable in the least—I saw in their possession was a few lumps of some stuff like half-cooked dough, of a dirty lavender color, they kept wrapped in leaves, and now and then swallowed a piece of, but so small that it seemed done more for the look of the thing than for any serious purpose of sustenance. Why in the name of all the gnawing devils of hunger they didn't go for us—they were thirty to five—and have a good tuck-in[5] for once, amazes me now when I think of it. They were big powerful men, with not much capacity to weigh the consequences, with courage, with strength, even yet, though their skins were no longer glossy and their muscles no longer hard. And I saw that something restraining, one of those human secrets that baffle probability, had come into play there. I looked at them with a swift quickening of interest—not because it occurred to me I might be eaten by them before very long, though I own to you that just then I per-

5. Meal.

ceived—in a new light, as it were—how unwholesome the pilgrims looked, and I hoped, yes, I positively hoped, that my aspect was not so—what shall I say?—so—unappetizing: a touch of fantastic vanity which fitted well with the dream-sensation that pervaded all my days at that time. Perhaps I had a little fever too. One can't live with one's finger everlastingly on one's pulse. I had often 'a little fever,' or a little touch of other things—the playful paw-strokes of the wilderness, the preliminary trifling before the more serious onslaught which came in due course. Yes; I looked at them as you would on any human being, with a curiosity of their impulses, motives, capacities, weaknesses, when brought to the test of an inexorable physical necessity. Restraint! What possible restraint? Was it superstition, disgust, patience, fear—or some kind of primitive honor? No fear can stand up to hunger, no patience can wear it out, disgust simply does not exist where hunger is; and as to superstition, beliefs, and what you may call principles, they are less than chaff in a breeze. Don't you know the devilry of lingering starvation, its exasperating torment, its black thoughts, its somber and brooding ferocity? Well, I do. It takes a man all his inborn strength to fight hunger properly. It's really easier to face bereavement, dishonor, and the perdition of one's soul—than this kind of prolonged hunger. Sad, but true. And these chaps too had no early reason for any kind of scruple. Restraint! I would just as soon have expected restraint from a hyena prowling amongst the corpses of a battlefield. But there was the fact facing me—the fact dazzling, to be seen, like the foam on the depths of the sea, like a ripple on an unfathomable enigma, a mystery greater—when I thought of it—than the curious, inexplicable note of desperate grief in this savage clamor that had swept by us on the river-bank, behind the blind whiteness of the fog.

"Two pilgrims were quarreling in hurried whispers as to which bank. 'Left.' 'No, no; how can you? Right, right, of course.' 'It is very serious,' said the manager's voice behind me; 'I would be desolated if anything should happen to Mr. Kurtz before we came up.' I looked at him, and had not the slightest doubt he was sincere. He was just the kind of man who would wish to preserve appearances. That was his restraint. But when he muttered something about going on at once, I did not even take the trouble to answer him. I knew, and he knew, that it was impossible. Were we to let go our hold of the bottom, we would be absolutely in the air—in space. We wouldn't be able to tell where we were going to—whether up or down stream, or across—till we fetched against one bank or the other—and then we wouldn't know at first which it was. Of course I made no move. I had no mind for a smash-up. You couldn't imagine a more deadly place for a shipwreck. Whether drowned at once or not, we were sure to perish speedily in one way or another. 'I authorize you to take all the risks,' he said, after a short silence. 'I refuse to take any,' I said shortly; which was just the answer he expected, though its tone might have surprised him. 'Well, I must defer to your judgment. You are captain,' he said, with marked civility. I turned my shoulder to him in sign of my appreciation, and looked into the fog. How long would it last? It was the most hopeless look-out. The approach to this Kurtz grubbing for ivory in the wretched bush was beset by as many dangers as though he had been an enchanted princess sleeping in a fabulous castle. 'Will they attack, do you think?' asked the manager, in a confidential tone.

"I did not think they would attack, for several obvious reasons. The thick fog was one. If they left the bank in their canoes they would get lost in it, as we would be if we attempted to move. Still, I had also judged the jungle of both banks quite impenetrable—and yet eyes were in it, eyes that had seen us. The river-side bushes were certainly very thick; but the undergrowth behind was evidently penetrable. However, during the short lift I had seen no canoes anywhere in the reach—certainly not abreast of the steamer. But what made the idea of attack inconceivable to me was the nature of the noise—of the cries we had heard. They had not the fierce character boding of immediate hostile intention. Unexpected, wild, and violent as they had been, they had given me an irresistible impression of sorrow. The glimpse of the steam-boat had for some reason filled those savages with unrestrained grief. The danger, if any, I expounded, was from our proximity to a great human passion let loose. Even extreme grief may ultimately vent itself in violence—but more generally takes the form of apathy. . . .

"You should have seen the pilgrims stare! They had no heart to grin, or even to revile me; but I believe they thought me gone mad—with fright, maybe. I delivered a regular lecture. My dear boys, it was no good bothering. Keep a look-out? Well, you may guess I watched the fog for the signs of lifting as a cat watches a mouse; but for anything else our eyes were of no more use to us than if we had been buried miles deep in a heap of cotton-wool. It felt like it too—choking, warm, stifling. Besides, all I said, though it sounded extravagant, was absolutely true to fact. What we afterwards alluded to as an attack was really an attempt at repulse. The action was very far from being aggressive—it was not even defensive, in the usual sense: it was undertaken under the stress of desperation, and in its essence was purely protective.

"It developed itself, I should say, two hours after the fog lifted, and its commencement was at a spot, roughly speaking, about a mile and a half below Kurtz's station. We had just floundered and flopped round a bend, when I saw an islet, a mere grassy hummock of bright green, in the middle of the stream. It was the only thing of the kind; but as we opened the reach more, I perceived it was the head of a long sandbank, or rather of a chain of shallow patches stretching down the middle of the river. They were discolored, just awash, and the whole lot was seen just under the water, exactly as a man's backbone is seen running down the middle of his back under the skin. Now, as far as I did see, I could go to the right or to the left of this. I didn't know either channel, of course. The banks looked pretty well alike, the depth appeared the same; but as I had been informed the station was on the west side, I naturally headed for the western passage.

"No sooner had we fairly entered it than I became aware it was much narrower than I had supposed. To the left of us there was the long uninterrupted shoal, and to the right a high steep bank heavily overgrown with bushes. Above the bush the trees stood in serried ranks. The twigs overhung the current thickly, and from distance to distance a large limb of some tree projected rigidly over the stream. It was then well on in the afternoon, the face of the forest was gloomy, and a broad strip of shadow had already fallen on the water. In this shadow we steamed up—very slowly, as you may imagine. I sheered her well inshore—the water being deepest near the bank, as the sounding-pole informed me.

"One of my hungry and forbearing friends was sounding in the bows just below me. This steamboat was exactly like a decked scow. On the deck there were two little teak-wood houses, with doors and windows. The boiler was in the fore-end, and the machinery right astern. Over the whole there was a light roof, supported on stanchions. The funnel projected through that roof, and in front of the funnel a small cabin built of light planks served for a pilot-house. It contained a couch, two camp-stools, a loaded Martini-Henry[6] leaning in one corner, a tiny table, and the steering wheel. It had a wide door in front and a broad shutter at each side. All these were always thrown open, of course. I spent my days perched up there on the extreme fore-end of that roof, before the door. At night I slept, or tried to, on the couch. An athletic black belonging to some coast tribe, and educated by my poor predecessor, was the helmsman. He sported a pair of brass earrings, wore a blue cloth wrapper from the waist to the ankles, and thought all the world of himself. He was the most unstable kind of fool I had ever seen. He steered with no end of a swagger while you were by; but if he lost sight of you, he became instantly the prey of an abject funk, and would let that cripple of a steamboat get the upper hand of him in a minute.

"I was looking down at the sounding-pole, and feeling much annoyed to see at each try a little more of it stick out of that river, when I saw my poleman give up the business suddenly, and stretch himself flat on the deck, without even taking the trouble to haul his pole in. He kept hold on it though, and it trailed in the water. At the same time the fireman, whom I could also see below me, sat down abruptly before his furnace and ducked his head. I was amazed. Then I had to look at the river mighty quick, because there was a snag in the fairway. Sticks, little sticks, were flying about—thick: they were whizzing before my nose, dropping below me, striking behind me against my pilot-house. All this time the river, the shore, the woods, were very quiet—perfectly quiet. I could only hear the heavy splashing thump of the stern-wheel and the patter of these things. We cleared the snag clumsily. Arrows, by Jove! We were being shot at! I stepped in quickly to close the shutter on the land-side. That fool-helmsman, his hands on the spokes, was lifting his knees high, stamping his feet, champing his mouth, like a reined-in horse. Confound him! And we were staggering within ten feet of the bank. I had to lean right out to swing the heavy shutter, and I saw a face amongst the leaves on the level with my own, looking at me very fierce and steady; and then suddenly, as though a veil had been removed from my eyes, I made out, deep in the tangled gloom, naked breasts, arms, legs, glaring eyes—the bush was swarming with human limbs in movement, glistening, of bronze color. The twigs shook,

6. Breech-action rifle.

swayed, and rustled, the arrows flew out of them, and then the shutter came to. 'Steer her straight,' I said to the helmsman. He held his head rigid, face forward; but his eyes rolled, he kept on lifting and setting down his feet gently, his mouth foamed a little. 'Keep quiet!' I said in a fury. I might just as well have ordered a tree not to sway in the wind. I darted out. Below me there was a great scuffle of feet on the iron deck; confused exclamations; a voice screamed, 'Can you turn back?' I caught sight of a V-shaped ripple on the water ahead. What? Another snag! A fusillade burst out under my feet. The pilgrims had opened with their Winchesters, and were simply squirting lead into that bush. A deuce of a lot of smoke came up and drove slowly forward. I swore at it. Now I couldn't see the ripple or the snag either. I stood in the doorway, peering, and the arrows came in swarms. They might have been poisoned, but they looked as though they wouldn't kill a cat. The bush began to howl. Our wood-cutters raised a warlike whoop; the report of a rifle just at my back deafened me. I glanced over my shoulder, and the pilot-house was yet full of noise and smoke when I made a dash at the wheel. The fool-nigger had dropped everything, to throw the shutter open and let off that Martini-Henry. He stood before the wide opening, glaring, and I yelled at him to come back, while I straightened the sudden twist out of that steamboat. There was no room to turn even if I had wanted to, the snag was somewhere very near ahead in that confounded smoke, there was no time to lose, so I just crowded her into the bank—right into the bank, where I knew the water was deep.

"We tore slowly along the overhanging bushes in a whirl of broken twigs and flying leaves. The fusillade below stopped short, as I had foreseen it would when the squirts got empty. I threw my head back to a glinting whiz that traversed the pilot-house, in at one shutter-hole and out at the other. Looking past that mad helmsman, who was shaking the empty rifle and yelling at the shore, I saw vague forms of men running bent double, leaping, gliding, distinct, incomplete, evanescent. Something big appeared in the air before the shutter, the rifle went overboard, and the man stepped back swiftly, looked at me over his shoulder in an extraordinary, profound, familiar manner, and fell upon my feet. The side of his head hit the wheel twice, and the end of what appeared a long cane clattered round and knocked over a little camp-stool. It looked as though after wrenching that thing from somebody ashore he had lost his balance in the effort. The thin smoke had blown away, we were clear of the snag, and looking ahead I could see that in another hundred yards or so I would be free to sheer off, away from the bank; but my feet felt so very warm and wet that I had to look down. The man had rolled on his back and stared straight up at me; both his hands clutched that cane. It was the shaft of a spear that, either thrown or lunged through the opening, had caught him in the side just below the ribs; the blade had gone in out of sight, after making a frightful gash; my shoes were full; a pool of blood lay very still, gleaming dark-red under the wheel; his eyes shone with an amazing luster. The fusillade burst out again. He looked at me anxiously, gripping the spear like something precious, with an air of being afraid

I would try to take it away from him. I had to make an effort to free my eyes from his gaze and attend to the steering. With one hand I felt above my head for the line of the steam whistle, and jerked out screech after screech hurriedly. The tumult of angry and warlike yells was checked instantly, and then from the depths of the woods went out such a tremulous and prolonged wail of mournful fear and utter despair as may be imagined to follow the flight of the last hope from the earth. There was a great commotion in the bush; the shower of arrows stopped, a few dropping shots rang out sharply—then silence, in which the languid beat of the stern-wheel came plainly to my ears. I put the helm hard a-starboard at the moment when the pilgrim in pink pajamas, very hot and agitated, appeared in the doorway. 'The manager sends me—' he began in an official tone, and stopped short. 'Good God!' he said, glaring at the wounded man.

"We two whites stood over him, and his lustrous and inquiring glance enveloped us both. I declare it looked as though he would presently put to us some question in an understandable language; but he died without uttering a sound, without moving a limb, without twitching a muscle. Only in the very last moment, as though in response to some sign we could not see, to some whisper we could not hear, he frowned heavily, and that frown gave to his black death-mask an inconceivably somber, brooding, and menacing expression. The luster of inquiring glance faded swiftly into vacant glassiness. 'Can you steer?' I asked the agent eagerly. He looked very dubious; but I made a grab at his arm, and he understood at once I meant him to steer whether or no. To tell you the truth, I was morbidly anxious to change my shoes and socks. 'He is dead,' murmured the fellow, immensely impressed. 'No doubt about it,' said I, tugging like mad at the shoe-laces. 'And by the way, I suppose Mr. Kurtz is dead as well by this time.'

"For the moment that was the dominant thought. There was a sense of extreme disappointment, as though I had found out I had been striving after something altogether without a substance. I couldn't have been more disgusted if I had traveled all this way for the sole purpose of talking with Mr. Kurtz. Talking with . . . I flung one shoe overboard, and became aware that that was exactly what I had been looking forward to—a talk with Kurtz. I made the strange discovery that I had never imagined him as doing, you know, but as discoursing. I didn't say to myself, 'Now I will never see him,' or 'Now I will never shake him by the hand,' but, 'Now I will never hear him.' The man presented himself as a voice. Not of course that I did not connect him with some sort of action. Hadn't I been told in all the tones of jealousy and admiration that he had collected, bartered, swindled, or stolen more ivory than all the other agents together? That was not the point. The point was in his being a gifted creature, and that of all his gifts the one that stood out pre-eminently, that carried with it a sense of real presence, was his ability to talk, his words—the gift of expression, the bewildering, the illuminating, the most exalted and the most contemptible, the pulsating stream of light, or the deceitful flow from the heart of an impenetrable darkness.

"The other shoe went flying unto the devil-god of that river. I thought, By Jove! it's all over. We are too late; he has vanished—the gift has vanished, by means of some spear, arrow, or club. I will never hear that chap speak after all—and my sorrow had a startling extravagance of emotion, even such as I had noticed in the howling sorrow of these savages in the bush. I couldn't have felt more of lonely desolation somehow, had I been robbed of a belief or had missed my destiny in life. . . . Why do you sigh in this beastly way, somebody? Absurd? Well, absurd. Good Lord! mustn't a man ever— Here, give me some tobacco."

There was a pause of profound stillness, then a match flared, and Marlow's lean face appeared, worn, hollow, with downward folds and dropped eyelids, with an aspect of concentrated attention; and as he took vigorous draws at his pipe, it seemed to retreat and advance out of the night in the regular flicker of the tiny flame. The match went out.

"Absurd!" he cried. "This is the worst of trying to tell . . . Here you all are, each moored with two good addresses, like a hulk with two anchors, a butcher round one corner, a policeman round another, excellent appetites, and temperature normal—you hear—normal from year's end to year's end. And you say, Absurd! Absurd be—exploded! Absurd! My dear boys, what can you expect from a man who out of sheer nervousness had just flung overboard a pair of new shoes? Now I think of it, it is amazing I did not shed tears. I am, upon the whole, proud of my fortitude. I was cut to the quick at the idea of having lost the inestimable privilege of listening to the gifted Kurtz. Of course I was wrong. The privilege was waiting for me. Oh yes, I heard more than enough. And I was right, too. A voice. He was very little more than a voice. And I heard—him—it—this voice—other voices—all of them were so little more than voices—and the memory of that time itself lingers around me, impalpable, like a dying vibration of one immense jabber, silly, atrocious, sordid, savage, or simply mean, without any kind of sense. Voices, voices—even the girl herself—now—"

He was silent for a long time.

"I laid the ghost of his gifts at last with a lie," he began suddenly. "Girl! What? Did I mention a girl? Oh, she is out of it—completely. They—the women I mean—are out of it—should be out of it. We must help them to stay in that beautiful world of their own, lest ours gets worse. Oh, she had to be out of it. You should have heard the disinterred body of Mr. Kurtz saying, 'My Intended.' You would have perceived directly then how completely she was out of it. And the lofty frontal bone of Mr. Kurtz! They say the hair goes on growing sometimes, but this—ah—specimen was impressively bald. The wilderness had patted him on the head, and, behold, it was like a ball—an ivory ball; it had caressed him, and—lo!—he had withered; it had taken him, loved him, embraced him, got into his veins, consumed his flesh, and sealed his soul to its own by the inconceivable ceremonies of some devilish initation. He was its spoiled and pampered favorite. Ivory? I should think so. Heaps of it, stacks of it. The old mud shanty was bursting with it. You would think there was not a single tusk left either above or below the ground in the whole country. 'Mostly fossil,' the manager had remarked disparagingly. It was no more fossil than I am; but they call it fossil when it is dug up. It appears these niggers do bury the tusks sometimes—but evidently they couldn't bury this parcel deep enough to save the gifted Mr. Kurtz from his fate. We filled the steamboat with it, and had to pile a lot on the deck. Thus he could see and enjoy as long as he could see, because the appreciation of this favor had remained with him to the last. You should have heard him say, 'My ivory.' Oh yes, I heard him. 'My Intended, my ivory, my station, my river, my—' everything belonged to him. It made me hold my breath in expectation of hearing the wilderness burst into a prodigious peal of laughter that would shake the fixed stars in their places. Everything belonged to him—but that was a trifle. The thing was to know what he belonged to, how many powers of darkness claimed him for their own. That was the reflection that made you creepy all over. It was impossible—it was not good for one either—trying to imagine. He had taken a high seat amongst the devils of the land—I mean literally. You can't understand. How could you?—with solid pavement under your feet, surrounded by kind neighbors ready to cheer you or to fall on you, stepping delicately between the butcher and the policeman, in the holy terror of scandal and gallows and lunatic asylums—how can you imagine what particular region of the first ages a man's untrammeled feet may take him into by the way of solitude—utter solitude without a policeman—by the way of silence—utter silence, where no warning voice of a kind neighbor can be heard whispering of public opinion? These little things make all the great difference. When they are gone you must fall back upon your own innate strength, upon your own capacity for faithfulness. Of course you may be too much of a fool to go wrong—too dull even to know you are being assaulted by the powers of darkness. I take it, no fool ever made a bargain for his soul with the devil: the fool is too much of a fool, or the devil too much of a devil—I don't know which. Or you may be such a thunderingly exalted creature as to be altogether deaf and blind to anything but heavenly sights and sounds. Then the earth for you is only a standing place—and whether to be like this is your loss or your gain I won't pretend to say. But most of us are neither one nor the other. The earth for us is a place to live in, where we must put up with sights, with sounds, with smells, too, by Jove!—breathe dead hippo, so to speak, and not be contaminated. And there, don't you see? your strength comes in, the faith in your ability for the digging of unostentatious holes to bury the stuff in—your power of devotion, not to yourself, but to an obscure, back-breaking business. And that's difficult enough. Mind, I am not trying to excuse or even explain—I am trying to account to myself for—for—Mr. Kurtz—for the shade of Mr. Kurtz. This initiated wraith from the back of Nowhere honored me with its amazing confidence before it vanished altogether. This was because it could speak English to me. The original Kurtz had been educated partly in England, and—as he was good enough to say himself—his sympathies were in the right place. His mother was half-English, his father was half-French. All Europe contributed to the making of Kurtz; and by and by I learned that, most appropriately, the International Society for the Suppression of Savage Customs had entrusted him with the making of a report, for its future guidance. And he had written it too. I've seen it. I've read it. It was eloquent, vibrating with eloquence, but too high-strung, I think. Seventeen pages of close writing he had found time for! But this must have been before his—let us say—nerves went wrong, and caused him to preside at certain midnight dances ending with unspeakable rites, which—as far as I reluctantly gathered from what I heard at various times—were offered up to him—do you understand?—to Mr. Kurtz himself. But it was a beautiful piece of writing. The opening paragraph, however, in the light of later information, strikes me now as ominous. He began with the argument that we whites, from the point of development we had arrived at, 'must necessarily appear to them [savages] in the nature of supernatural beings—we approach them with the might as of a deity,' and so on, and so on. 'By the simple exercise of our will we can exert a power for good practically unbounded,' etc. etc. From that point he soared and took me with him. The peroration was magnificent, though difficult to remember, you know. It gave me the notion of an exotic Immensity ruled by an august Benevolence. It made me tingle with enthusiasm. This was the unbounded power of eloquence—of words—of burning noble words. There were no practical hints to interrupt the magic current of phrases, unless a kind of note at the foot of the last page, scrawled evidently much later, in an unsteady hand, may be regarded as the exposition of a method. It was very simple, and at the end of that moving appeal to every altruistic sentiment it blazed at you, luminous and terrifying, like a flash of lightning in a serene sky: 'Exterminate all the brutes!' The curious part was that he had apparently forgotten all about that valuable postscriptum, because, later on, when he in a sense came to himself, he repeatedly entreated me to take good care of 'my pamphlet' (he called it), as it was sure to have in the future a good influence upon his career. I had full information about all these things, and, besides, as it turned out, I was to have the care of his memory. I've done enough for it to give me the indisputable right to lay it, if I choose, for an everlasting rest in the dust-bin of progress, amongst all the sweepings and, figuratively speaking, all the dead cats of civilization. But then, you see, I can't choose. He won't be forgotten. Whatever he was, he was not common. He had the power to charm or frighten rudimentary souls into an aggravated witch-dance in his honor; he could also fill the small souls of the pilgrims with bitter misgivings: he had one devoted friend at least, and he had conquered one soul in the world that was neither rudimentary nor tainted with self-seeking. No; I can't forget him, though I am not prepared to affirm the fellow was exactly worth the life we lost in getting to him. I missed my late helmsman awfully—I missed him even while his body was still lying in the pilot-house. Perhaps you will think it passing strange this regret for a savage who was no more account than a grain of sand in a black Sahara. Well, don't you see, he had done something, he had steered; for months I had him at my back—a help—an instrument. It was a kind of partnership. He steered for me—I had to look after him, I worried about his deficiencies, and thus a subtle bond had been created, of which I only became aware when it was suddenly broken. And the intimate profundity of that look he gave me when he received his hurt remains to this day in my memory—like a claim of distant kinship affirmed in a supreme moment.

"Poor fool! If he had only left that shutter alone. He had no restraint, no restraint—just like Kurtz—a tree swayed by the wind. As soon as I had put on a dry pair of slippers, I dragged him out, after first jerking the spear out of his side, which operation I confess I performed with my eyes shut tight. His heels leaped together over the little door-step; his shoulders were pressed to my breast; I hugged him from behind desperately. Oh! he was heavy, heavy; heavier than any man on earth, I should imagine. Then without more ado I tipped him overboard. The current snatched him as though he had been a wisp of grass, and I saw the body roll over twice before I lost sight of it for ever. All the pilgrims and the manager were then congregated on the awning-deck about the pilot-house, chattering at each other like a flock of excited magpies, and there was a scandalized murmur at my heartless promptitude. What they wanted to keep that body hanging about for I can't guess. Embalm it, maybe. But I had also heard another, and a very ominous, murmur on the deck below. My friends the wood-cutters were likewise scandalized, and with a better show of reason—though I admit that the reason itself was quite inadmissible. Oh, quite! I had made up my mind that if my late helmsman was to be eaten, the fishes alone should have him. He had been a very second-rate helmsman while alive, but now he was dead he might have become a first-class temptation, and possibly cause some startling trouble. Besides, I was anxious to take the wheel, the man in pink pajamas showing himself a hopeless duffer at the business.

"This I did directly the simple funeral was over. We were going half-speed, keeping right in the middle of the stream, and I listened to the talk about me. They had given up Kurtz, they had given up the station; Kurtz was dead, and the station had been burnt—and so on, and so on. The red-haired pilgrim was beside himself with the thought that at least this poor Kurtz had been properly revenged. 'Say! We must have made a glorious slaughter of them in the bush. Eh? What do you think? Say?' He positively danced, the bloodthirsty little gingery beggar.[7] And he had nearly fainted when he saw the wounded man! I could not help saying, 'You made a glorious lot of smoke, anyhow.' I had seen, from the way the tops of the bushes rustled and flew, that almost all the shots had gone too high. You can't hit anything unless you take aim and fire from the shoulder; but these chaps fired from the hip with their eyes shut. The retreat, I maintained—and I was right—was caused by the screeching of the steam-whistle. Upon this they forgot Kurtz, and began to howl at me with indignant protests.

"The manager stood by the wheel murmuring confidentially about the necessity of getting well away down the river before dark at all events, when I saw in the distance a clearing on the riverside and the outlines of some sort of building. 'What's this?' I asked. He clapped his

7. Red-haired scoundrel.

hands in wonder. 'The station!' he cried. I edged in at once, still going half-speed.

"Through my glasses I saw the slope of a hill interspersed with rare trees and perfectly free from undergrowth. A long decaying building on the summit was half buried in the high grass; the large holes in the peaked roof gaped black from afar; the jungle and the woods made a background. There was no enclosure or fence of any kind; but there had been one apparently, for near the house half a dozen slim posts remained in a row, roughly trimmed, and with their upper ends ornamented with round carved balls. The rails, or whatever there had been between, had disappeared. Of course the forest surrounded all that. The river-bank was clear, and on the water side I saw a white man under a hat like a cart-wheel beckoning persistently with his whole arm. Examining the edge of the forest above and below, I was almost certain I could see movements—human forms gliding here and there. I steamed past prudently, then stopped the engines and let her drift down. The man on the shore began to shout, urging us to land. 'We have been attacked,' screamed the manager. 'I know—I know. It's all right,' yelled back the other, as cheerful as you please. 'Come along. It's all right. I am glad.'

"His aspect reminded me of something I had seen—something funny I had seen somewhere. As I maneuvered to get alongside, I was asking myself, 'What does this fellow look like?' Suddenly I got it. He looked like a harlequin. His clothes had been made of some stuff that was brown holland probably, but it was covered with patches all over, with bright patches, blue, red, and yellow—patches on the back, patches on the front, patches on elbows, on knees; colored binding round his jacket, scarlet edging at the bottom of his trousers; and the sunshine made him look extremely gay and wonderfully neat withal, because you could see how beautifully all this patching had been done. A beardless, boyish face, very fair, no features to speak of, nose peeling, little blue eyes, smiles and frowns chasing each other over that open countenance like sunshine and shadow on a wind-swept plain. 'Look out, captain!' he cried; 'there's a snag lodged in here last night.' What! Another snag? I confess I swore shamefully. I had nearly holed my cripple, to finish off that charming trip. The harlequin on the bank turned his little pug-nose up to me. 'You English?' he asked, all smiles. 'Are you?' I shouted from the wheel. The smiles vanished, and he shook his head as if sorry for my disappointment. Then he brightened up. 'Never mind!' he cried encouragingly. 'Are we in time?' I asked. 'He is up there,' he replied, with a toss of the head up the hill, and becoming gloomy all of a sudden. His face was like the autumn sky, overcast one moment and bright the next.

"When the manager, escorted by the pilgrims, all of them armed to the teeth, had gone to the house, this chap came on board. 'I say, I don't like this. These natives are in the bush,' I said. He assured me earnestly it was all right. 'They are simple people,' he added; 'well, I am glad you came. It took me all my time to keep them off.' 'But you said it was all right,' I cried. 'Oh, they meant no harm,' he said; and as I stared he corrected himself, 'Not exactly.' Then vivaciously, 'My faith, your pilot-house wants a clean up!' In the next breath he advised me to keep enough steam on the boiler to blow the whistle in case of any trouble. 'One good screech will do more for you than all your rifles. They are simple people,' he repeated. He rattled away at such a rate he quite overwhelmed me. He seemed to be trying to make up for lots of silence, and actually hinted, laughing, that such was the case. 'Don't you talk with Mr. Kurtz?' I said. 'You don't talk with that man—you listen to him,' he exclaimed with severe exaltation. 'But now—' He waved his arm, and in the twinkling of an eye was in the uttermost depths of despondency. In a moment he came up again with a jump, possessed himself of both my hands, shook them continuously, while he gabbled: 'Brother sailor . . . honor . . . pleasure . . . delight . . . introduce myself . . . Russian . . . son of an arch-priest . . . Government of Tambov . . . What? Tobacco! English tobacco; the excellent English tobacco! Now, that's brotherly. Smoke? Where's a sailor that does not smoke?'

"The pipe soothed him, and gradually I made out he had run away from school, had gone to sea in a Russian ship; ran away again; served some time in English ships; was now reconciled with the arch-priest. He made a point of that. 'But when one is young one must see things, gather experience, ideas; enlarge the mind.' 'Here!' I interrupted. 'You can never tell! Here I met Mr. Kurtz,' he said, youthfully solemn and reproachful. I held my tongue after that. It appears he had persuaded a Dutch trading-house on the coast to fit him out with stores and goods, and had started for the interior with a light heart, and no more idea of what would happen to him than a baby. He had been wandering about that river for nearly two years alone, cut off from everybody and everything. 'I am not so young as I look. I am twenty-five,' he said. 'At first old Van Shuyten would tell me to go to the devil,' he narrated with keen enjoyment; 'but I stuck to him, and talked and talked, till at last he got afraid I would talk the hind-leg off his favorite dog, so he gave me some cheap things and a few guns, and told me he hoped he would never see my face again. Good old Dutchman, Van Shuyten. I sent him one small lot of ivory a year ago, so that he can't call me a little thief when I get back. I hope he got it. And for the rest, I don't care. I had some wood stacked for you. That was my old house. Did you see?'

"I gave him Towson's book. He made as though he would kiss me, but restrained himself. 'The only book I had left, and I thought I had lost it,' he said, looking at it ecstatically. 'So many accidents happen to a man going about alone, you know. Canoes get upset sometimes—and sometimes you've got to clear out so quick when the people get angry.' He thumbed the pages. 'You made notes in Russian?' I asked. He nodded. 'I thought they were written in cipher,' I said. He laughed, then became serious. 'I had lots of trouble to keep these people off,' he said. 'Did they want to kill you?' I asked. 'Oh no!' he cried, and checked himself. 'Why did they attack us?' I pursued. He hesitated, then said shamefacedly, "They don't want him to go.' 'Don't they?' I said curiously. He nodded a nod full of mystery and wisdom. 'I tell you,' he cried, 'this man has enlarged my mind.' He opened his arms wide, staring at me with his little blue eyes that were perfectly round."

3

"I looked at him, lost in astonishment. There he was before me, in motley, as though he had absconded from a troupe of mimes, enthusiastic, famulous.[8] His very existence was improbable, inexplicable, and altogether bewildering. He was an insoluble problem. It was inconceivable how he had existed, how he had succeeded in getting so far, how he had managed to remain—why he did not instantly disappear. 'I went a little farther,' he said, 'then still a little farther—till I had gone so far that I don't know how I'll ever get back. Never mind. Plenty time. I can manage. You take Kurtz away quick—quick—I tell you.' The glamour of youth enveloped his parti-colored rags, his destitution, his loneliness, the essential desolation of his futile wanderings. For months—for years—his life hadn't been worth a day's purchase; and there he was gallantly, thoughtlessly alive, to all appearance indestructible solely by the virtue of his few years and of his unreflecting audacity. I was seduced into something like admiration—like envy. Glamour urged him on, glamour kept him unscathed. He surely wanted nothing from the wilderness but space to breathe in and to push on through. His need was to exist, and to move onwards at the greatest possible risk, and with a maximum of privation. If the absolutely pure, uncalculating, unpractical spirit of adventure had ever ruled a human being, it ruled this be-patched youth. I almost envied him the possession of this modest and clear flame. It seemed to have consumed all thought of self so completely, that, even while he was talking to you, you forgot that it was he—the man before your eyes—who had gone through these things. I did not envy him his devotion to Kurtz, though. He had not meditated over it. It came to him, and he accepted it with a sort of eager fatalism. I must say that to me it appeared about the most dangerous thing in every way he had come upon so far.

"They had come together unavoidably, like two ships becalmed near each other, and lay rubbing sides at last. I suppose Kurtz wanted an audience, because on a certain occasion, when encamped in the forest, they had talked all night, or more probably Kurtz had talked. 'We talked of everything,' he said, quite transported at the recollection. 'I forgot there was such a thing as sleep. The night did not seem to last an hour. Everything! Everything! . . . Of love too.' 'Ah, he talked to you of love!' I said, much amused. 'It isn't what you think,' he cried, almost passionately. 'It was in general. He made me see things—things.'

"He threw his arms up. We were on deck at the time, and the headman of my wood-cutters, lounging near by, turned upon him his heavy and glittering eyes. I looked around, and I don't know why, but I assure you that never, never before, did this land, this river, this jungle, the very arch of this blazing sky, appear to me so hopeless and so dark, so impenetrable to human thought, so pitiless to human weakness. 'And, ever since, you have been with him, of course?' I said.

"On the contrary. It appears their intercourse had been very much broken by various causes. He had, as he informed me proudly, man-

8. Like a famulus, a sorcerer's assistant.

aged to nurse Kurtz through two illnesses (he alluded to it as you would to some risky feat), but as a rule Kurtz wandered alone, far in the depths of the forest. 'Very often coming to this station, I had to wait days and days before he would turn up,' he said. 'Ah, it was worth waiting for!—sometimes.' 'What was he doing? exploring or what?' I asked. 'Oh yes, of course'; he had discovered lots of villages, a lake too—he did not know exactly in what direction; it was dangerous to inquire too much—but mostly his expeditions had been for ivory. 'But he had no goods to trade with by that time,' I objected. 'There's a good lot of cartridges left even yet,' he answered, looking away. 'To speak plainly, he raided the country,' I said. He nodded. 'Not alone, surely!' He muttered something about the villages round that lake. 'Kurtz got the tribe to follow him, did he?' I suggested. He fidgeted a little. 'They adored him,' he said. The tone of these words was so extraordinary that I looked at him searchingly. It was curious to see his mingled eagerness and reluctance to speak of Kurtz. The man filled his life, occupied his thoughts, swayed his emotions. 'What can you expect?' he burst out; 'he came to them with thunder and lightning, you know—and they had never seen anything like it—and very terrible. He could be very terrible. You can't judge Mr. Kurtz as you would an ordinary man. No, no, no! Now—just to give you an idea—I don't mind telling you, he wanted to shoot me too one day—but I don't judge him.' 'Shoot you!' I cried. 'What for?' 'Well, I had a small lot of ivory the chief of that village near my house gave me. You see I used to shoot game for them. Well, he wanted it, and wouldn't hear reason. He declared he would shoot me unless I gave him the ivory and then cleared out of the country, because he could do so, and had a fancy for it, and there was nothing on earth to prevent him killing whom he jolly well pleased. And it was true too. I gave him the ivory. What did I care! But I didn't clear out. No, no. I couldn't leave him. I had to be careful, of course, till we got friendly again for a time. He had his second illness then. Afterwards I had to keep out of the way; but I didn't mind. He was living for the most part in those villages on the lake. When he came down to the river, sometimes he would take to me, and sometimes it was better for me to be careful. This man suffered too much. He hated all this, and somehow he couldn't get away. When I had a chance I begged him to try and leave while there was time; I offered to go back with him. And he would say yes, and then he would remain; go off on another ivory hunt; disappear for weeks; forget himself amongst these people—forget himself—you know.' 'Why! he's mad,' I said. He protested indignantly. Mr. Kurtz couldn't be mad. If I had heard him talk, only two days ago, I wouldn't dare hint at such a thing. . . . I had taken up my binoculars while we talked, and was looking at the shore, sweeping the limit of the forest at each side and at the back of the house. The consciousness of there being people in that bush, so silent, so quiet—as silent and quiet as the ruined house on the hill—made me uneasy. There was no sign on the face of nature of this amazing tale that was not so much told as suggested to me in desolate exclamations, completed by shrugs, in interrupted phrases, in hints ending in deep sighs. The woods were unmoved, like a mask—

heavy, like the closed door of a prison—they looked with their air of hidden knowledge, of patient expectation, of unapproachable silence. The Russian was explaining to me that it was only lately that Mr. Kurtz had come down to the river, bringing along with him all the fighting men of that lake tribe. He had been absent for several months—getting himself adored, I suppose—and had come down unexpectedly, with the intention to all appearance of making a raid either across the river or down stream. Evidently the appetite for more ivory had got the better of the—what shall I say?—less material aspirations. However, he had got much worse suddenly. 'I heard he was lying helpless, and so I came up—took my chance,' said the Russian. 'Oh, he is bad, very bad.' I directed my glass to the house. There were no signs of life, but there were the ruined roof, the long mud wall peeping above the grass, with three little square window-holes, no two of the same size; all this brought within reach of my hand, as it were. And then I made a brusque movement, and one of the remaining posts of that vanished fence leaped up in the field of my glass. You remember I told you I had been struck at the distance by certain attempts at ornamentation, rather remarkable in the ruinous aspect of the place. Now I had suddenly a nearer view, and its first result was to make me throw my head back as if before a blow. Then I went carefully from post to post with my glass, and I saw my mistake. These round knobs were not ornamental but symbolic; they were expressive and puzzling, striking and disturbing—food for thought and also for vultures if there had been any looking down from the sky; but at all events for such ants as were industrious enough to ascend the pole. They would have been even more impressive, those heads on the stakes, if their faces had not been turned to the house. Only one, the first I had made out, was facing my way. I was not so shocked as you may think. The start back I had given was really nothing but a movement of surprise. I had expected to see a knob of wood there, you know. I returned deliberately to the first I had seen—and there it was, black, dried, sunken, with closed eyelids—a head that seemed to sleep at the top of that pole, and, with the shrunken dry lips showing a narrow white line of the teeth, was smiling too, smiling continuously at some endless and jocose dream of that eternal slumber.

"I am not disclosing any trade secrets. In fact the manager said afterwards that Mr. Kurtz's methods had ruined the district. I have no opinion on that point, but I want you clearly to understand that there was nothing exactly profitable in these heads being there. They only showed that Mr. Kurtz lacked restraint in the gratification of his various lusts, that there was something wanting in him—some small matter which, when the pressing need arose, could not be found under his magnificent eloquence. Whether he knew of this deficiency himself I can't say. I think the knowledge came to him at last—only at the very last. But the wilderness had found him out early, and had taken on him a terrible vengeance for the fantastic invasion. I think it had whispered to him things about himself which he did not know, things of which he had no conception till he took counsel with this great solitude—and the whisper had proved irresistibly fascinating. It echoed loudly within him because he was hollow at the core. . . . I put down the glass, and the head that had appeared near enough to be spoken to seemed at once to have leaped away from me into inaccessible distance.

"The admirer of Mr. Kurtz was a bit crestfallen. In a hurried, indistinct voice he began to assure me he had not dared to take these—say, symbols—down. He was not afraid of the natives; they would not stir till Mr. Kurtz gave the word. His ascendancy was extraordinary. The camps of these people surrounded the place, and the chiefs came every day to see him. They would crawl . . . 'I don't want to know anything of the ceremonies used when approaching Mr. Kurtz,' I shouted. Curious, this feeling that came over me that such details would be more intolerable than those heads drying on the stakes under Mr. Kurtz's windows. After all, that was only a savage sight, while I seemed at one bound to have been transported into some lightless region of subtle horrors, where pure, uncomplicated savagery was a positive relief, being something that had a right to exist—obviously—in the sunshine. The young man looked at me with surprise. I suppose it did not occur to him that Mr. Kurtz was no idol of mine. He forgot I hadn't heard any of these splendid monologues on, what was it? on love, justice, conduct of life—or what not. If it had come to crawling before Mr. Kurtz, he crawled as much as the veriest savage of them all. I had no idea of the conditions, he said: these heads were the heads of rebels. I shocked him excessively by laughing. Rebels! What would be the next definition I was to hear? There had been enemies, criminals, workers—and these were rebels. Those rebellious heads looked very subdued to me on their sticks. 'You don't know how such a life tries a man like Kurtz,' cried Kurtz's last disciple. 'Well, and you?' I said. 'I! I! I am a simple man. I have no great thoughts. I want nothing from anybody. How can you compare me to . . . ?' His feelings were too much for speech, and suddenly he broke down. 'I don't understand,' he groaned. 'I've been doing my best to keep him alive, and that's enough. I had no hand in all this. I have no abilities. There hasn't been a drop of medicine or a mouthful of invalid food for months here. He was shamefully abandoned. A man like this, with such ideas. Shamefully! Shamefully! I—I—haven't slept for the last ten nights. . . .'

"His voice lost itself in the calm of the evening. The long shadows of the forest had slipped downhill while we talked, had gone far beyond the ruined hovel, beyond the symbolic row of stakes. All this was in the gloom, while we down there were yet in the sunshine, and the stretch of the river abreast of the clearing glittered in a still and dazzling splendor, with a murky and overshadowed bend above and below. Not a living soul was seen on the shore. The bushes did not rustle.

"Suddenly round the corner of the house a group of men appeared, as though they had come up from the ground. They waded waist-deep in the grass, in a compact body, bearing an improvised stretcher in their midst. Instantly, in the emptiness of the landscape, a cry arose whose shrillness pierced the still air like a sharp arrow flying straight to the very heart of the land; and, as if by enchantment, streams of human beings—of naked human beings—with spears in their hands, with bows, with shields, with wild glances and savage movements, were poured into the clearing by the dark-faced and pensive forest. The bushes shook, the grass swayed for a time, and then everything stood still in attentive immobility.

" 'Now, if he does not say the right thing to them we are all done for,' said the Russian at my elbow. The knot of men with the stretcher had stopped too, half-way to the steamer, as if petrified. I saw the man on the stretcher sit up, lank and with an uplifted arm, above the shoulders of the bearers. 'Let us hope that the man who can talk so well of love in general will find some particular reason to spare us this time,' I said. I resented bitterly the absurd danger of our situation, as if to be at the mercy of that atrocious phantom had been a dishonoring necessity. I could not hear a sound, but through my glasses I saw the thin arm extended commandingly, the lower jaw moving, the eyes of that apparition shining darkly far in its bony head that nodded with grotesque jerks. Kurtz—Kurtz—that means 'short' in German—don't it? Well, the name was as true as everything else in his life—and death. He looked at least seven feet long. His covering had fallen off, and his body emerged from it pitiful and appalling as from a winding-sheet. I could see the cage of his ribs all astir, the bones of his arm waving. It was as though an animated image of death carved out of old ivory had been shaking its hand with menaces at a motionless crowd of men made of dark and glittering bronze. I saw him open his mouth wide—it gave him a weirdly voracious aspect, as though he had wanted to swallow all the air, all the earth, all the men before him. A deep voice reached me faintly. He must have been shouting. He fell back suddenly. The stretcher shook as the bearers staggered forward again, and almost at the same time I noticed that the crowd of savages was vanishing without any perceptible movement of retreat, as if the forest that had ejected these beings so suddenly had drawn them in again as the breath is drawn in a long aspiration.

"Some of the pilgrims behind the stretcher carried his arms—two shotguns, a heavy rifle, and a light revolver-carbine—the thunderbolts of that pitiful Jupiter. The manager bent over him murmuring as he walked beside his head. They laid him down in one of the little cabins—just a room for a bed-place and a camp-stool or two, you know. We had brought his belated correspondence, and a lot of torn envelopes and open letters littered his bed. His hand roamed feebly amongst these papers. I was struck by the fire of his eyes and the composed languor of his expression. It was not so much the exhaustion of disease. He did not seem in pain. This shadow looked satiated and calm, as though for the moment it had had its fill of all the emotions.

"He rustled one of the letters, and looking straight in my face said, 'I am glad.' Somebody had been writing to him about me. These special recommendations were turning up again. The volume of tone he emitted without effort, almost without the trouble of moving his lips, amazed me. A voice! a voice! It was grave, profound, vibrating, while the man did not seem capable of a whisper. However, he had enough strength in him—factitious no doubt—to very nearly make an end of us, as you shall hear directly.

"The manager appeared silently in the doorway; I stepped out at once and he drew the curtain after me. The Russian, eyed curiously by the pilgrims, was staring at the shore. I followed the direction of his glance.

"Dark human shapes could be made out in the distance, flitting indistinctly against the gloomy border of the forest, and near the river two bronze figures, leaning on tall spears, stood in the sunlight under fantastic headdresses of spotted skins, warlike and still in statuesque repose. And from right to left along the lighted shore moved a wild and gorgeous apparition of a woman.

"She walked with measured steps, draped in striped and fringed cloths, treading the earth proudly, with a slight jingle and flash of barbarous ornaments. She carried her head high; her hair was done in the shape of a helmet; she had brass leggings to the knees, brass wire gauntlets to the elbow, a crimson spot on her tawny cheek, innumerable necklaces of glass beads on her neck; bizarre things, charms, gifts of witch-men, that hung about her, glittered and trembled at every step. She must have had the value of several elephant tusks upon her. She was savage and superb, wild-eyed and magnificent; there was something ominous and stately in her deliberate progress. And in the hush that had fallen suddenly upon the whole sorrowful land, the immense wilderness, the colossal body of the fecund and mysterious life seemed to look at her, pensive, as though it had been looking at the image of its own tenebrous and passionate soul.

"She came abreast of the steamer, stood still, and faced us. Her long shadow fell to the water's edge. Her face had a tragic and fierce aspect of wild sorrow and of dumb pain mingled with the fear of some struggling, half-shaped resolve. She stood looking at us without a stir, and like the wilderness itself, with an air of brooding over an inscrutable purpose. A whole minute passed, and then she made a step forward. There was a low jingle, a glint of yellow metal, a sway of fringed draperies, and she stopped as if her heart had failed her. The young fellow by my side growled. The pilgrims murmured at my back. She looked at us all as if her life had depended upon the unswerving steadiness of her glance. Suddenly she opened her bared arms and threw them up rigid above her head, as though in an uncontrollable desire to touch the sky, and at the same time the swift shadows darted out on the earth, swept around on the river, gathering the steamer in a shadowy embrace. A formidable silence hung over the scene.

"She turned away slowly, walked on, following the bank, and passed into the bushes to the left. Once only her eyes gleamed back at us in the dusk of the thickets before she disappeared.

" 'If she had offered to come aboard I really think I would have tried to shoot her,' said the man of patches nervously. 'I had been risking my life every day for the last fortnight to keep her out of the house. She got in one day and kicked up a row about those miserable rags I picked up in the storeroom to mend my clothes with. I wasn't decent. At least it must have been that, for she talked like a fury to Kurtz for an hour, pointing at me now and then. I don't understand the dialect of this tribe. Luckily for me, I fancy Kurtz felt too ill that day to care, or there would have been mischief. I don't understand. . . . No—it's too much for me. Ah, well, it's all over now.'

"At this moment I heard Kurtz's deep voice behind the curtain: 'Save me!—save the ivory, you mean. Don't tell me. Save *me!* Why, I've had to save you. You are interrupting my plans now. Sick! Sick! Not so sick as you would like to believe. Never mind. I'll carry my ideas out yet—I will return. I'll show you what can be done. You with your little peddling notions—you are interfering with me. I will return. I . . .'

"The manager came out. He did me the honor to take me under the arm and lead me aside. 'He is very low, very low,' he said. He considered it necessary to sigh, but neglected to be consistently sorrowful. 'We have done all we could for him—haven't we? But there is no disguising the fact, Mr. Kurtz has done more harm than good to the Company. He did not see the time was not ripe for vigorous action. Cautiously, cautiously—that's my principle. We must be cautious yet. The district is closed to us for a time. Deplorable! Upon the whole, the trade will suffer. I don't deny there is a remarkable quantity of ivory —mostly fossil. We must save it, at all events—but look how precarious the position is—and why? Because the method is unsound.' 'Do you,' said I, looking at the shore, 'call it "unsound method"?' 'Without doubt,' he exclaimed hotly. 'Don't you?' . . . 'No method at all,' I murmured after a while. 'Exactly,' he exulted. 'I anticipated this. Shows a complete want of judgment. It is my duty to point it out in the proper quarter.' 'Oh,' said I, 'that fellow—what's his name?—the brickmaker, will make a readable report for you.' He appeared confounded for a moment. It seemed to me I had never breathed an atmosphere so vile, and I turned mentally to Kurtz for relief—positively for relief. 'Nevertheless, I think Mr. Kurtz is a remarkable man,' I said with emphasis. He started, dropped on me a cold heavy glance, said very quietly, 'He *was*,' and turned his back on me. My hour of favor was over; I found myself lumped along with Kurtz as a partisan of methods for which the time was not ripe: I was unsound! Ah! but it was something to have at least a choice of nightmares.

"I had turned to the wilderness really, not to Mr. Kurtz, who, I was ready to admit, was as good as buried. And for a moment it seemed to me as if I also were buried in a vast grave full of unspeakable secrets. I felt an intolerable weight oppressing my breast, the smell of the damp earth, the unseen presence of victorious corruption, the darkness of an impenetrable night. . . . The Russian tapped me on the shoulder. I heard him mumbling and stammering something about 'brother seaman—couldn't conceal—knowledge of matters that would affect Mr. Kurtz's reputation.' I waited. For him evidently Mr. Kurtz was not in his grave; I suspect that for him Mr. Kurtz was one of the immortals. 'Well!' said I at last, 'speak out. As it happens, I am Mr. Kurtz's friend —in a way.'

"He stated with a good deal of formality that had we not been 'of the same profession,' he would have kept the matter to himself without regard to consequences. He suspected 'there was an active ill-will towards him on the part of these white men that—' 'You are right,'

I said, remembering a certain conversation I had overheard. 'The manager thinks you ought to be hanged.' He showed a concern at this intelligence which amused me at first. 'I had better get out of the way quietly,' he said earnestly. 'I can do no more for Kurtz now, and they would soon find some excuse. What's to stop them? There's a military post three hundred miles from here.' 'Well, upon my word,' said I, 'perhaps you had better go if you have any friends amongst the savages near by.' 'Plenty,' he said. 'They are simple people—and I want nothing, you know.' He stood biting his lip, then: 'I don't want any harm to happen to these whites here, but of course I was thinking of Mr. Kurtz's reputation—but you are a brother seaman—' 'All right,' said I, after a time. 'Mr. Kurtz's reputation is safe with me.' I did not know how truly I spoke.

"He informed me, lowering his voice, that it was Kurtz who had ordered the attack to be made on the steamer. 'He hated sometimes the idea of being taken away—and then again . . . But I don't understand these matters. I am a simple man. He thought it would scare you away—that you would give it up, thinking him dead. I could not stop him. Oh. I had an awful time of it this last month.' 'Very well,' I said. 'He is all right now.' 'Ye-e-es,' he muttered, not very convinced apparently. 'Thanks,' said I; 'I shall keep my eyes open.' 'But quiet—eh?' he urged anxiously. 'It would be awful for his reputation if anybody here—' I promised a complete discretion with great gravity. 'I have a canoe and three black fellows waiting not very far. I am off. Could you give me a few Martini-Henry cartridges?' I could, and did, with proper secrecy. He helped himself, with a wink at me, to a handful of my tobacco. 'Between sailors—you know—good English tobacco.' At the door of the pilot-house he turned round—'I say, haven't you a pair of shoes you could spare?' He raised one leg. 'Look.' The soles were tied with knotted strings sandal-wise under his bare feet. I rooted out an old pair, at which he looked with admiration before tucking it under his left arm. One of his pockets (bright red) was bulging with cartridges, from the other (dark blue) peeped 'Towson's Inquiry,' etc. etc. He seemed to think himself excellently well equipped for a renewed encounter with the wilderness. 'Ah! I'll never, never meet such a man again. You ought to have heard him recite poetry—his own too it was, he told me. Poetry!' He rolled his eyes at the recollection of these delights. 'Oh, he enlarged my mind!' 'Good-bye,' said I. He shook hands and vanished in the night. Sometimes I ask myself whether I had ever really seen him—whether it was possible to meet such a phenomenon! . . .

"When I woke up shortly after midnight his warning came to my mind with its hint of danger that seemed, in the starred darkness, real enough to make me get up for the purpose of having a look round. On the hill a big fire burned, illuminating fitfully a crooked corner of the station-house. One of the agents with a picket of a few of our blacks, armed for the purpose, was keeping guard over the ivory; but deep within the forest, red gleams that wavered, that seemed to sink and rise from the ground amongst confused columnar shapes of intense blackness, showed the exact position of the camp where Mr. Kurtz's adorers were keeping their uneasy vigil. The monotonous beating of a big drum filled the air with muffled shocks and a lingering vibration. A steady droning sound of many men chanting each to himself some weird incantation came out from the black, flat wall of the woods as the humming of bees comes out of a hive, and had a strange narcotic effect upon my half-awake senses. I believe I dozed off leaning over the rail, till an abrupt burst of yells, an overwhelming outbreak of a pent-up and mysterious frenzy, woke me up in a bewildered wonder. It was cut short all at once, and the low droning went on with an effect of audible and soothing silence. I glanced casually into the little cabin. A light was burning within, but Mr. Kurtz was not there.

"I think I would have raised an outcry if I had believed my eyes. But I didn't believe them at first—the thing seemed so impossible. The fact is, I was completely unnerved by a sheer blank fright, pure abstract terror, unconnected with any distinct shape of physical danger. What made this emotion so overpowering was—how shall I define it?—the moral shock I received, as if something altogether monstrous, intolerable to thought and odious to the soul, had been thrust upon me unexpectedly. This lasted of course the merest fraction of a second, and then the usual sense of commonplace, deadly danger, the possibility of a sudden onslaught and massacre, or something of the kind, which I saw impending, was positively welcome and composing. It pacified me, in fact, so much, that I did not raise an alarm.

"There was an agent buttoned up inside an ulster and sleeping on a chair on deck within three feet of me. The yells had not awakened him; he snored very slightly; I left him to his slumbers and leaped ashore. I did not betray Mr. Kurtz—it was ordered I should never betray him—it was written I should be loyal to the nightmare of my choice. I was anxious to deal with this shadow by myself alone—and to this day I don't know why I was so jealous of sharing with anyone the peculiar blackness of that experience.

"As soon as I got on the bank I saw a trail—a broad trail through the grass. I remember the exultation with which I said to myself, 'He can't walk—he is crawling on all-fours—I've got him.' The grass was wet with dew. I strode rapidly with clenched fists. I fancy I had some vague notion of falling upon him and giving him a drubbing. I don't know. I had some imbecile thoughts. The knitting old woman with the cat obtruded herself upon my memory as a most improper person to be sitting at the other end of such an affair. I saw a row of pilgrims squirting lead in the air out of Winchesters held to the hip. I thought I would never get back to the steamer, and imagined myself living alone and unarmed in the woods to an advanced age. Such silly things—you know. And I remember I confounded the beat of the drum with the beating of my heart, and was pleased at its calm regularity.

"I kept to the track though—then stopped to listen. The night was very clear; a dark blue space, sparkling with dew and starlight, in which black things stood very still. I thought I could see a kind of motion ahead of me. I was strangely cocksure of everything that night. I actually left the track and ran in a wide semicircle (I verily believe chuckling to myself) so as to get in front of that stir, of that motion I had seen—if indeed I had seen aything. I was circumventing Kurtz as though it had been a boyish game.

"I came upon him, and, if he had not heard me coming, I would have fallen over him too, but he got up in time. He rose, unsteady, long, pale, indistinct, like a vapor exhaled by the earth, and swayed slightly, misty and silent before me; while at my back the fires loomed between the trees, and the murmur of many voices issued from the forest. I had cut him off cleverly; but when actually confronting him I seemed to come to my senses, I saw the danger in its right proportion. It was by no means over yet. Suppose he began to shout? Though he could hardly stand, there was still plenty of vigor in his voice. 'Go away —hide yourself,' he said, in that profound tone. It was very awful. I glanced back. We were within thirty yards of the nearest fire. A black figure stood up, strode on long black legs, waving long black arms, across the glow. It had horns—antelope horns, I think—on its head. Some sorcerer, some witch-man, no doubt: it looked fiend-like enough. 'Do you know what you are doing?' I whispered. 'Perfectly,' he answered, raising his voice for that single word: it sounded to me far off and yet loud, like a hail through a speaking-trumpet. If he makes a row we are lost, I thought to myself. This clearly was not a case for fisticuffs, even apart from the very natural aversion I had to beat that Shadow—this wandering and tormented thing. 'You will be lost,' I said —'utterly lost.' One gets sometimes such a flash of inspiration, you know. I did say the right thing, though indeed he could not have been more irretrievably lost than he was at this very moment, when the foundations of our intimacy were being laid—to endure—to endure—even to the end—even beyond.

" 'I had immense plans,' he muttered irresolutely. 'Yes,' said I; 'but if you try to shout I'll smash your head with—' There was not a stick or a stone near. 'I will throttle you for good,' I corrected myself. 'I was on the threshold of great things,' he pleaded, in a voice of longing, with a wistfulness of tone that made my blood run cold. 'And now for this stupid scoundrel—' 'Your success in Europe is assured in any case,' I affirmed steadily. I did not want to have the throttling of him, you understand—and indeed it would have been very little use for any practical purpose. I tried to break the spell—the heavy, mute spell of the wilderness—that seemed to draw him to its pitiless breast by the awakening of forgotten and brutal instincts, by the memory of gratified and monstrous passions. This alone, I was convinced, had driven him out to the edge of the forest, to the bush, towards the gleam of fires, the throb of drums, the drone of weird incantations; this alone had beguiled his unlawful soul beyond the bounds of permitted aspirations. And, don't you see, the terror of the position was not in being knocked on the head—though I had a very lively sense of that danger too—but in this, that I had to deal with a being to whom I could not appeal in the name of anything high or low. I had, even like the niggers, to invoke him—himself—his own exalted and incredible degradation. There was nothing either above or below him, and I knew it. He had kicked himself loose of the earth. Confound the man! he had kicked the very earth to pieces. He was alone, and I before him did not know whether I stood on the ground or floated in the air. I've been telling you what we said—repeating the phrases we pronounced—but what's the good? They were common everyday words—the familiar, vague sounds exchanged on every waking day of life. But what of that? They had behind them, to my mind, the terrific suggestiveness of words heard in dreams, of phrases spoken in nightmares. Soul! If anybody had ever struggled with a soul, I am the man. And I wasn't arguing with a lunatic either. Believe me or not, his intelligence was perfectly clear—concentrated, it is true, upon himself with horrible intensity, yet clear; and therein was my only chance—barring, of course, the killing him there and then, which wasn't so good, on account of unavoidable noise. But his soul was mad. Being alone in the wilderness, it had looked within itself, and, by Heavens! I tell you, it had gone mad. I had—for my sins, I suppose, to go through the ordeal of looking into it myself. No eloquence could have been so withering to one's belief in mankind as his final burst of sincerity. He struggled with himself too. I saw it—I heard it. I saw the inconceivable mystery of a soul that knew no restraint, no faith, and no fear, yet struggling blindly with itself. I kept my head pretty well; but when I had him at last stretched on the couch, I wiped my forehead, while my legs shook under me as though I had carried half a ton on my back down that hill. And yet I had only supported him, his bony arm clasped round my neck—and he was not much heavier than a child.

"When next day we left at noon, the crowd, of whose presence behind the curtain of trees I had been acutely conscious all the time, flowed out of the woods again, filled the clearing, covered the slope with a mass of naked, breathing, quivering, bronze bodies. I steamed up a bit, then swung downstream, and two thousand eyes followed the evolutions of the splashing, thumping, fierce river-demon beating the water with its terrible tail and breathing black smoke into the air. In front of the first rank, along the river, three men, plastered with bright red earth from head to foot, strutted to and fro restlessly. When we came abreast again, they faced the river, stamped their feet, nodded their horned heads, swayed their scarlet bodies; they shook towards the fierce river-demon a bunch of black feathers, a mangy skin with a pendent tail—something that looked like a dried gourd; they shouted periodically together strings of amazing words that resembled no sounds of human language; and the deep murmurs of the crowd, interrupted suddenly, were like the responses of some satanic litany.

"We had carried Kurtz into the pilot-house: there was more air there. Lying on the couch, he stared through the open shutter. There was an eddy in the mass of human bodies, and the woman with helmeted head and tawny cheeks rushed out to the very brink of the stream. She put out her hands, shouted something, and all that wild mob took up the shout in a roaring chorus of articulated, rapid, breathless utterance.

" 'Do you understand this?' I asked.

"He kept on looking out past me with fiery, longing eyes, with a mingled expression of wistfulness and hate. He made no answer, but

I saw a smile, a smile of indefinable meaning, appear on his colorless lips that a moment after twitched convulsively. 'Do I not?' he said slowly, gasping, as if the words had been torn out of him by a supernatural power.

"I pulled the string of the whistle, and I did this because I saw the pilgrims on deck getting out their rifles with an air of anticipating a jolly lark. At the sudden screech there was a movement of abject terror through that wedged mass of bodies. 'Don't! don't you frighten them away,' cried someone on deck disconsolately. I pulled the string time after time. They broke and ran, they leaped, they crouched, they swerved, dodged the flying terror of the sound. The three red chaps had fallen flat, face down on the shore, as though they had been shot dead. Only the barbarous and superb woman did not so much as flinch, and stretched tragically her bare arms after us over the somber and glittering river.

"And then that imbecile crowd down on the deck started their little fun, and I could see nothing more for smoke.

"The brown current ran swiftly out of the heart of darkness, bearing us down towards the sea with twice the speed of our upward progress; and Kurtz's life was running swiftly too, ebbing, ebbing out of his heart into the sea of inexorable time. The manager was very placid, he had no vital anxieties now, he took us both in with a comprehensive and satisfied glance: the 'affair' had come off as well as could be wished. I saw the time approaching when I would be left alone of the party of 'unsound method.' The pilgrims looked upon me with disfavor. I was, so to speak, numbered with the dead. It is strange how I accepted this unforeseen partnership, this choice of nightmares forced upon me in the tenebrous land invaded by these mean and greedy phantoms.

"Kurtz discoursed. A voice! a voice! It rang deep to the very last. It survived his strength to hide in the magnificent folds of eloquence the barren darkness of his heart. Oh, he struggled! he struggled! The wastes of his weary brain were haunted by shadowy images now—images of wealth and fame revolving obsequiously round his unextinguishable gift of noble and lofty expression. My Intended, my station, my career, my ideas—these were the subjects for the occasional utterances of elevated sentiments. The shade of the original Kurtz frequented the bedside of the hollow sham, whose fate it was to be buried presently in the mold of primeval earth. But both the diabolic love and the unearthly hate of the mysteries it had penetrated fought for the possession of that soul satiated with primitive emotions, avid of lying fame, of sham distinction, of all the appearances of success and power.

"Sometimes he was contemptibly childish. He desired to have kings meet him at railway stations on his return from some ghastly Nowhere, where he intended to accomplish great things. 'You show them you have in you something that is really profitable, and then there will be no limits to the recognition of your ability,' he would say. 'Of course you must take care of the motives—right motives—always.' The long reaches that were like one and the same reach, monotonous bends that were exactly alike, slipped past the steamer with their multitude of secular[9] trees looking patiently after this grimy fragment of another world, the forerunner of change, of conquest, of trade, of massacres, of blessings. I looked ahead—piloting. 'Close the shutter,' said Kurtz suddenly one day; 'I can't bear to look at this.' I did so. There was a silence. 'Oh, but I will wring your heart yet!' he cried at the invisible wilderness.

"We broke down—as I had expected—and had to lie up for repairs at the head of an island. This delay was the first thing that shook Kurtz's confidence. One morning he gave me a packet of papers and a photograph—the lot tied together with a shoestring. 'Keep this for me,' he said. 'This noxious fool' (meaning the manager) 'is capable of prying into my boxes when I am not looking.' In the afternoon I saw him. He was lying on his back with closed eyes, and I withdrew quietly, but I heard him mutter, 'Live rightly, die, die . . .' I listened. There was nothing more. Was he rehearsing some speech in his sleep, or was it a fragment of a phrase from some newspaper article? He had been writing for the papers and meant to do so again, 'for the furthering of my ideas. It's a duty.'

"His was an impenetrable darkness. I looked at him as you peer down at a man who is lying at the bottom of a precipice where the sun never shines. But I had not much time to give him, because I was helping the engine-driver to take to pieces the leaky cylinders, to straighten a bent connecting-rod, and in other such matters. I lived in an infernal mess of rust, filings, nuts, bolts, spanners, hammers, ratchet-drills—things I abominate, because I don't get on with them. I tended the little forge we fortunately had aboard; I toiled wearily in a wretched scrap-heap—unless I had the shakes too bad to stand.

"One evening coming in with a candle I was startled to hear him say a little tremulously, 'I am lying here in the dark waiting for death.' The light was within a foot of his eyes. I forced myself to murmur, 'Oh, nonsense!' and stood over him as if transfixed.

"Anything approaching the change that came over his features I have never seen before, and hope never to see again. Oh, I wasn't touched. I was fascinated. It was as though a veil had been rent. I saw on that ivory face the expression of somber pride, of ruthless power, of craven terror—of an intense and hopeless despair. Did he live his life again in every detail of desire, temptation, and surrender during that supreme moment of complete knowledge? He cried in a whisper at some image, at some vision—he cried out twice, a cry that was no more than a breath:

" 'The horror! The horror!'

"I blew the candle out and left the cabin. The pilgrims were dining in the mess-room, and I took my place opposite the manager, who lifted his eyes to give me a questioning glance, which I successfully ignored. He leaned back, serene, with that peculiar smile of his sealing the unexpressed depths of his meanness. A continuous shower of small flies streamed upon the lamp, upon the cloth, upon our hands and faces. Suddenly the manager's boy put his insolent black head in the doorway, and said in a tone of scathing contempt:

9. Ancient.

" 'Mistah Kurtz—he dead.'

"All the pilgrims rushed out to see. I remained, and went on with my dinner. I believe I was considered brutally callous. However, I did not eat much. There was a lamp in there—light, don't you know—and outside it was so beastly, beastly dark. I went no more near the remarkable man who had pronounced a judgment upon the adventures of his soul on this earth. The voice was gone. What else had been there? But I am of course aware that next day the pilgrims buried something in a muddy hole.

"And then they very nearly buried me.

"However, as you see, I did not go to join Kurtz there and then. I did not. I remained to dream the nightmare out to the end, and to show my loyalty to Kurtz once more. Destiny. My destiny! Droll thing life is—that mysterious arrangement of merciless logic for a futile purpose. The most you can hope from it is some knowledge of yourself—that comes too late—a crop of unextinguishable regrets. I have wrestled with death. It is the most unexciting contest you can imagine. It takes place in an impalpable grayness, with nothing underfoot, with nothing around, without spectators, without clamor, without glory, without the great desire of victory, without the great fear of defeat, in a sickly atmosphere of tepid skepticism, without much belief in your own right, and still less in that of your adversary. If such is the form of ultimate wisdom, then life is a greater riddle than some of us think it to be. I was within a hair's-breadth of the last opportunity for pronouncement, and I found with humiliation that probably I would have nothing to say. This is the reason why I affirm that Kurtz was a remarkable man. He had something to say. He said it. Since I had peeped over the edge myself, I understand better the meaning of his stare, that could not see the flame of the candle, but was wide enough to embrace the whole universe, piercing enough to penetrate all the hearts that beat in the darkness. He had summed up—he had judged. 'The horror!' He was a remarkable man. After all, this was the expression of some sort of belief; it had candor, it had conviction, it had a vibrating note of revolt in its whisper, it had the appalling face of a glimpsed truth—the strange commingling of desire and hate. And it is not my own extremity I remember best—a vision of grayness without form filled with physical pain, and a careless contempt for the evanescence of all things—even of this pain itself. No! It is his extremity that I seem to have lived through. True, he had made that last stride, he had stepped over the edge, while I had been permitted to draw back my hesitating foot. And perhaps in this is the whole difference; perhaps all the wisdom, and all truth, and all sincerity, are just compressed into that inappreciable moment of time in which we step over the threshold of the invisible. Perhaps! I like to think my summing-up would not have been a word of careless contempt. Better his cry—much better. It was an affirmation, a moral victory paid for by innumerable defeats, by abominable terrors, by abominable satisfactions. But it was a victory! That is why I have remained loyal to Kurtz to the last, and even beyond, when a long time after I heard once more, not his own voice, but the echo of his magnificent eloquence thrown to me from a soul as translucently pure as a cliff of crystal.

"No, they did not bury me, though there is a period of time which I remember mistily, with a shuddering wonder, like a passage through some inconceivable world that had no hope in it and no desire. I found myself back in the sepulchral city resenting the sight of people hurrying through the streets to filch a little money from each other, to devour their infamous cookery, to gulp their unwholesome beer, to dream their insignificant and silly dreams. They trespassed upon my thoughts. They were intruders whose knowledge of life was to me an irritating pretense, because I felt so sure they could not possibly know the things I knew. Their bearing, which was simply the bearing of commonplace individuals going about their business in the assurance of perfect safety, was offensive to me like the outrageous flauntings of folly in the face of a danger it is unable to comprehend. I had no particular desire to enlighten them, but I had some difficulty in restraining myself from laughing in their faces, so full of stupid importance. I daresay I was not very well at that time. I tottered about the streets—there were various affairs to settle—grinning bitterly at perfectly respectable persons. I admit my behavior was inexcusable, but then my temperature was seldom normal in these days. My dear aunt's endeavors to 'nurse up my strength' seemed altogether beside the mark. It was not my strength that wanted nursing, it was my imagination that wanted soothing. I kept the bundle of papers given me by Kurtz, not knowing exactly what to do with it. His mother had died lately, watched over, as I was told, by his Intended. A clean-shaved man, with an official manner and wearing gold-rimmed spectacles, called on me one day and made inquiries, at first circuitous, afterwards suavely pressing, about what he was pleased to denominate certain 'documents.' I was not surprised, because I had had two rows with the manager on the subject out there. I had refused to give up the smallest scrap out of that package, and I took the same attitude with the spectacled man. He became darkly menacing at last, and with much heat argued that the Company had the right to every bit of information about its 'territories.' And, said he, 'Mr. Kurtz's knowledge of unexplored regions must have been necessarily extensive and peculiar—owing to his great abilities and to the deplorable circumstances in which he had been placed: therefore—' I assured him Mr. Kurtz's knowledge, however extensive, did not bear upon the problems of commerce or administration. He invoked then the name of science. 'It would be an incalculable loss if,' etc. etc. I offered him the report on the 'Suppression of Savage Customs,' with the postscriptum torn off. He took it up eagerly, but ended by sniffing at it with an air of contempt. 'This is not what we had a right to expect,' he remarked. 'Expect nothing else,' I said. 'There are only private letters.' He withdrew upon some threat of legal proceedings, and I saw him no more; but another fellow, calling himself Kurtz's cousin, appeared two days later, and was anxious to hear all the details about his dear relative's last moments. Incidentally he gave me to understand that Kurtz had been essentially a great musician. 'There was the making of an immense success,' said the man, who was an organist, I believe, with lank gray hair flowing over a greasy coat-collar. I had no reason to doubt his statement; and to this day I am unable to say what was Kurtz's profession, whether he ever had any—which was the greatest of his talents. I had taken him for a painter who wrote for the papers, or else for a journalist who could paint—but even the cousin (who took snuff during the interview) could not tell me what he had been—exactly. He was a universal genius—on that point I agreed with the old chap, who thereupon blew his nose noisily into a large cotton handkerchief and withdrew in senile agitation, bearing off some family letters and memoranda without importance. Ultimately a journalist anxious to know something of the fate of his 'dear colleague' turned up. This visitor informed me Kurtz's proper sphere ought to have been politics 'on the popular side.' He had furry straight eyebrows, bristly hair cropped short, an eyeglass on a broad ribbon, and, becoming expansive, confessed his opinion that Kurtz really couldn't write a bit—'but Heavens! how that man could talk! He electrified large meetings. He had faith—don't you see?—he had the faith. He could get himself to believe anything—anything. He would have been a splendid leader of an extreme party.' 'What party?' I asked. 'Any party,' answered the other. 'He was an—an—extremist.' Did I not think so? I assented. Did I know, he asked, with a sudden flash of curiosity, 'what it was that had induced him to go out there?' 'Yes,' said I, and forthwith handed him the famous Report for publication, if he thought fit. He glanced through it hurriedly, mumbling all the time, judged 'it would do,' and took himself off with this plunder.

"Thus I was left at last with a slim packet of letters and the girl's portrait. She struck me as beautiful—I mean she had a beautiful expression. I know that the sunlight can be made to lie too, yet one felt that no manipulation of light and pose could have conveyed the delicate shade of truthfulness upon those features. She seemed ready to listen without mental reservation, without suspicion, without a thought for herself. I concluded I would go and give her back her portrait and those letters myself. Curiosity? Yes; and also some other feeling perhaps. All that had been Kurtz's had passed out of my hands: his soul, his body, his station, his plans, his ivory, his career. There remained only his memory and his Intended—and I wanted to give that up too to the past, in a way—to surrender personally all that remained of him with me to that oblivion which is the last word of our common fate. I don't defend myself. I had no clear perception of what it was I really wanted. Perhaps it was an impulse of unconscious loyalty, or the fulfillment of one of those ironic necessities that lurk in the facts of human existence. I don't know. I can't tell. But I went.

"I thought his memory was like the other memories of the dead that accumulate in every man's life—a vague impress on the brain of shadows that had fallen on it in their swift and final passage; but before the high and ponderous door, between the tall houses of a street as still and decorous as a well-kept alley in a cemetery, I had a vision of him on the stretcher, opening his mouth voraciously, as if to devour all the earth with all its mankind. He lived then before me; he lived as much as he had ever lived—a shadow insatiable of splendid appearances, of frightful realities; a shadow darker than the shadow of the night, and draped nobly in the folds of a gorgeous eloquence. The vision seemed to enter the house with me—the stretcher, the phantom-bearers, the wild crowd of obedient worshippers, the gloom of the forests, the glitter of the reach between the murky bends, the beat of the drum, regular and muffled like the beating of a heart—the heart of a conquering darkness. It was a moment of triumph for the wilderness, an invading and vengeful rush which, it seemed to me, I would have to keep back alone for the salvation of another soul. And the memory of what I had heard him say afar there, with the horned shapes stirring at my back, in the glow of fires, within the patient woods, those broken phrases came back to me, were heard again in their ominous and terrifying simplicity. I remembered his abject pleading, his abject threats, the colossal scale of his vile desires, the meanness, the torment, the tempestuous anguish of his soul. And later on I seemed to see his collected languid manner, when he said one day, 'This lot of ivory now is really mine. The Company did not pay for it. I collected it myself at a very great personal risk. I am afraid they will try to claim it as theirs though. H'm. It is a difficult case. What do you think I ought to do—resist? Eh? I want no more than justice.' . . . He wanted no more than justice—no more than justice. I rang the bell before a mahogany door on the first floor, and while I waited he seemed to stare at me out of the glassy panel—stare with that wide and immense stare embracing, condemning, loathing all the universe. I seemed to hear the whispered cry, 'The horror! The horror!'

"The dusk was falling. I had to wait in a lofty drawing room with three long windows from floor to ceiling that were like three luminous and bedraped columns. The bent gilt legs and backs of the furniture shone in indistinct curves. The tall marble fireplace had a cold and monumental whiteness. A grand piano stood massively in a corner; with dark gleams on the flat surfaces like a somber and polished sarcophagus. A high door opened—closed. I rose.

"She came forward, all in black, with a pale head, floating towards me in the dusk. She was in mourning. It was more than a year since his death, more than a year since the news came; she seemed as though she would remember and mourn forever. She took both my hands in hers and murmured, 'I had heard you were coming.' I noticed she was not very young—I mean not girlish. She had a mature capacity for fidelity, for belief, for suffering. The room seemed to have grown darker, as if all the sad light of the cloudy evening had taken refuge on her forehead. This fair hair, this pale visage, this pure brow, seemed surrounded by an ashy halo from which the dark eyes looked out at me. Their glance was guileless, profound, confident, and trustful. She carried her sorrowful head as though she were proud of that sorrow, as though she would say, I—I alone know how to mourn for him as he deserves. But while we were still shaking hands, such a look of awful desolation came upon her face that I perceived she was one of those creatures that are not the playthings of Time. For her he had died only yesterday. And, by Jove! the impression was so powerful that for me too he seemed to have died only yesterday—nay, this very minute. I saw her and him in the same instant of time—his death and her sorrow—I saw her sorrow in the very moment of his death. Do you understand? I saw them together—I heard them together. She had said, with a deep catch of the breath, 'I have survived'; while my strained ears seemed to hear distinctly, mingled with her tone of despairing regret, the summing-up whisper of his eternal condemnation. I asked myself what I was doing there, with a sensation of panic in my heart as though I had blundered into a place of cruel and absurd mysteries not fit for a human being to behold. She motioned me to a chair. We sat down. I laid the packet gently on the little table, and she put her hand over it. . . . 'You knew him well,' she murmured, after a moment of mourning silence.

" 'Intimacy grows quickly out there,' I said. 'I knew him as well as it is possible for one man to know another.'

" 'And you admired him,' she said. 'It was impossible to know him and not to admire him. Was it?'

" 'He was a remarkable man,' I said unsteadily. Then before the appealing fixity of her gaze, that seemed to watch for more words on my lips, I went on, 'It was impossible not to—'

" 'Love him,' she finished eagerly, silencing me into an appalled dumbness. 'How true! how true! But when you think that no one knew him so well as I! I had all his noble confidence. I knew him best.'

" 'You knew him best,' I repeated. And perhaps she did. But with every word spoken the room was growing darker, and only her forehead, smooth and white, remained illumined by the unextinguishable light of belief and love.

" 'You were his friend,' she went on. 'His friend,' she repeated, a little louder. 'You must have been, if he had given you this, and sent you to me. I feel I can speak to you—and oh! I must speak. I want you —you who have heard his last words—to know I have been worthy of him. . . . It is not pride. . . . Yes! I am proud to know I understood him better than anyone on earth—he told me so himself. And since his mother died I have had no one—no one—to—to—'

"I listened. The darkness deepened. I was not even sure whether he had given me the right bundle. I rather suspect he wanted me to take care of another batch of his papers which, after his death, I saw the manager examining under the lamp. And the girl talked, easing her pain in the certitude of my sympathy; she talked as thirsty men drink. I had heard that her engagement with Kurtz had been disapproved by her people. He wasn't rich enough or something. And indeed I don't know whether he had not been a pauper all his life. He had given me some reason to infer that it was his impatience of comparative poverty that drove him out there.

" '. . . Who was not his friend who had heard him speak once?' she was saying. 'He drew men towards him by what was best in them.' She looked at me with intensity. 'It is the gift of the great,' she went on, and the sound of her low voice seemed to have the accompaniment of all the other sounds, full of mystery, desolation, and sorrow, I had ever heard—the ripple of the river, the soughing of the trees swayed by the wind, the murmurs of the crowds, the faint ring of incomprehensible words cried from afar, the whisper of a voice speaking from beyond the threshold of an eternal darkness. 'But you have heard him! You know!' she cried.

" 'Yes, I know,' I said with something like despair in my heart, but bowing my head before the faith that was in her, before that great and saving illusion that shone with an unearthly glow in the darkness, in the triumphant darkness from which I could not have defended her—from which I could not even defend myself.

" 'What a loss to me—to us!'—she corrected herself with beautiful generosity; then added in a murmur, 'To the world.' By the last gleams of twilight I could see the glitter of her eyes, full of tears—of tears that would not fall.

" 'I have been very happy—very fortunate—very proud,' she went on. 'Too fortunate. Too happy for a little while. And now I am unhappy for—for life.'

"She stood up; her fair hair seemed to catch all the remaining light in a glimmer of gold. I rose too.

" 'And of all this,' she went on mournfully, 'of all his promise, and of all his greatness, of his generous mind, of his noble heart, nothing remains—nothing but a memory. You and I—'

" 'We shall always remember him,' I said hastily.

" 'No!' she cried. 'It is impossible that all this should be lost—that such a life should be sacrificed to leave nothing—but sorrow. You know what vast plans he had. I knew of them too—I could not perhaps understand—but others knew of them. Something must remain. His words, at least, have not died.'

" 'His words will remain,' I said.

" 'And his example,' she whispered to herself. 'Men looked up to him—his goodness shone in every act. His example—'

" 'True,' I said; 'his example too. Yes, his example. I forgot that.'

" 'But I do not. I cannot—I cannot believe—not yet. I cannot believe that I shall never see him again, that nobody will see him again, never, never, never.'

"She put out her arms as if after a retreating figure, stretching them back and with clasped pale hands across the fading and narrow sheen of the window. Never see him! I saw him clearly enough then. I shall see this eloquent phantom as long as I live, and I shall see her too, a tragic and familiar Shade, resembling in this gesture another one, tragic also, and bedecked with powerless charms, stretching bare brown arms over the glitter of the infernal stream, the stream of darkness. She said suddenly very low, 'He died as he lived.'

" 'His end,' said I, with dull anger stirring in me, 'was in every way worthy of his life.'

" 'And I was not with him,' she murmured. My anger subsided before a feeling of infinite pity.

" 'Everything that could be done—' I mumbled.

" 'Ah, but I believed in him more than anyone on earth—more than his own mother, more than—himself. He needed me! Me! I would have treasured every sigh, every word, every sign, every glance.'

"I felt like a chill grip on my chest. 'Don't,' I said, in a muffled voice.

" 'Forgive me. I—I—have mourned so long in silence—in silence. . . . You were with him—to the last? I think of his loneliness. Nobody near to understand him as I would have understood. Perhaps no one to hear . . .'

" 'To the very end,' I said shakily. 'I heard his very last words. . . .' I stopped in a fright.

" 'Repeat them,' she murmured in a heart-broken tone. 'I want—

I want—something—something—to—to live with.'

"I was on the point of crying at her, 'Don't you hear them?' The dusk was repeating them in a persistent whisper all around us, in a whisper that seemed to swell menacingly like the first whisper of a rising wind. 'The horror! The horror!'

" 'His last word—to live with,' she insisted. 'Don't you understand I loved him—I loved him—I loved him!'

"I pulled myself together and spoke slowly.

" 'The last word he pronounced was—your name.'

"I heard a light sigh and then my heart stood still, stopped dead short by an exulting and terrible cry, by the cry of inconceivable triumph and of unspeakable pain. 'I knew it—I was sure!' . . . She knew. She was sure. I heard her weeping; she had hidden her face in her hands. It seemed to me that the house would collapse before I could escape, that the heavens would fall upon my head. But nothing happened. The heavens do not fall for such a trifle. Would they have fallen, I wonder, if I had rendered Kurtz that justice which was his due? Hadn't he said he wanted only justice? But I couldn't. I could not tell her. It would have been too dark—too dark altogether. . . ."

Marlow ceased, and sat apart, indistinct and silent, in the pose of a meditating Buddha. Nobody moved for a time. "We have lost the first of the ebb," said the Director suddenly. I raised my head. The offing was barred by a black bank of clouds, and the tranquil waterway leading to the uttermost ends of the earth flowed somber under an overcast sky—seemed to lead into the heart of an immense darkness.

1902

DORIS LESSING

The Temptation of Jack Orkney

His father was dying. It was a telegram, saying also: *you unobtainable telephone.* He had been on the telephone since seven that morning. It was the housekeeper who had sent the telegram. Did Mrs. Markham not know that she could have asked the telephone authorities to interrupt his conversations for an urgent message? The irritation of the organizer who is manipulating intractable people and events now focused on Mrs. Markham, but he tried to alleviate it by reminding himself that Mrs. Markham was housekeeper not only to his father but to a dozen other old people.

It had been a long time since he had actually organized something political; others had been happy to organize *him*—his name, his presence, his approval. But an emotional telephone call from an old friend, Walter Kenting, before seven that morning, appealing that they "all" should make a demonstration of some sort about the refugees—the nine million refugees of Bangladesh,[1] this time—and the information

1. Religious and political tensions precipitated a civil war between East and West Pakistan, bringing disease and famine throughout the spring and summer of 1971. India intervened and brought an end to the war in December 1971, with West Pakistan becoming simply Pakistan and East Pakistan becoming the independent nation of Bangladesh.

that he was the only person available to do the organizing, had returned him to a politically active past. Telephoning, he soon discovered that even the small demonstration they envisaged would be circumscribed, because people were saying they could see no point in a demonstration when television, the radio and every newspaper did little else but tell the world about these millions of sufferers. What was the point of a dozen or twenty people "sitting down" or "marching" or even being hungry for twenty-four hours in some prominent place? Surely the point of these actions in the past had been to draw public attention to a wrong?

Now the strength of his reaction to Mrs. Markham's inadequacy made him understand that his enthusiastic response to Walter so early that morning had been mostly because of weeks, months, of inactivity. He could not be so exaggerating details if he were not underemployed. He had been making occupation for himself, calling it stocktaking. He had been reading old diaries, articles of his own twenty or more years old, letters of people he had not seen, sometimes for as long. Immersing himself in his own past had of course been uncomfortable; this is what it had been really like in Korea, Israel, Pretoria,[2] during such-and-such an event: memory had falsified. One knew that it did, but he had believed himself exempt from this law. Every new day of this deliberate evocation of the past had made his own part in it seem less worthwhile, had diminished his purposes and strengths. It was not that he now lacked offers to work, but that he could not make himself respond with the enthusiastic willingness which he believed every job of work needed. Of his many possibilities the one that attracted him most was to teach journalism in a small college in Nigeria, but he could not make up his mind to accept: his wife didn't want to go. Did he want to leave her in England for two years? No; but at one time this certainly would not have been his reaction!

Nor did he want to write another adventure book; in such empty times in the past he had written, under noms de plume, novels whose attraction was the descriptions of the countries he had set them in. He had traveled a great deal in his life, often dangerously, in the course of this war or that, as a soldier and as a journalist.

He might also write a serious book of social or political analysis: he had several to his credit.

He could do television work, or return to active journalism.

The thing was that now the three children were through university he did not need to earn so much money.

"Leisure, leisure at last!" he had cried, as so many of his friends were doing, finding themselves similarly placed.

But half a morning's energetic organizing was enough to tell him—exactly as his mother had been used to tell him when he was adolescent: "Your trouble is, you haven't got enough to do!"

He sent a telegram to Mrs. Markham: *Arriving train early evening.* Flying would save him an hour; proper feeling would no doubt choose the air, but he needed the train's pace to adjust him for what

2. The capital city of the Union of South Africa; scene of racial tension and sporadic violence.

was ahead. He rang Walter Kenting to say that with the organizing still undone, urgent family matters were claiming him. Walter was silent at this, so he said: "Actually, my old man is going to die in the next couple of days. It has been on the cards for some time."

"I am sorry," said Walter. "I'll try Bill or Mona. I've got to go to Dublin in fifteen minutes. Are you going to be back by Saturday—oh of course you don't know." Realizing that he was sounding careless or callous, he said, "I do hope things will be all right." This was worse and he gave up: "You think that a twenty-four-hour fast meets the bill better than the other possibilities? Is that what most people feel, do you think?"

"Yes. But I don't think they are as keen as usual."

"Well, of course not, there's too much of bloody everything, that's why. You could be demonstrating twenty-four hours a day. Anyway, I've got to get to my plane."

While Jack packed, which he knew so well how to do, in ten minutes, he remembered that he had a family. Should everyone be at the deathbed? Oh surely not! He looked for his wife; she was out. Of course! The children off her hands, she too had made many exclamations about the attractions of leisure, but almost at once she signed up for a Psychology Course as part of a plan to become a Family Counselor. She had left a note for him: "Darling, there's some cold lamb and salad." He now left a note for her: "Old man on his way out. See you whenever. Tell girls and Joseph. All my love. Jack."

On that train he thought of what he was in for. A family reunion, no less. His brother wasn't so bad, but the last time he had seen Ellen, she had called him a Boy Scout, and he had called her a Daughter of the British Empire.[3] Considering it a compliment, she had been left with the advantage. A really dreadful woman, and as for her husband—surely he wouldn't be there too? He would have to be, as a man? Where would they all fit in? Certainly not in that tiny flat. He should have put in his note to Rosemary that she should telephone hotels in S——. Would the other grandchildren be there? Well, Cedric and Ellen would be certain to do the right thing, whatever that was: as for himself, he could telephone home when he had found what the protocol was. But good God, surely it was bad enough that three of them, grownup and intelligent people—grownup, anyway, were going to have to sit about waiting, in a deathbed scene, because of—superstition. Yes, that was what it was. Certainly no more than outdated social custom. And it all might go on for days. But perhaps the old man would be pleased? At the approach of a phrase similar to those suitable for deaths and funerals, he felt irritation again; this would lead, unless he watched himself, to self-mockery, the spirit of farce. Farce was implicit, anyway, in a situation which had himself, Ellen, and Cedric in one room.

Probably the old man wasn't even conscious. He should have telephoned Mrs. Markham before rushing off like—well, like a journalist, with two pairs of socks, a spare shirt, and a sweater. He should have bought a black tie? Would the old man have wished it? Jack

3. Primarily colonial organizations of women descended from British subjects. The official functions of the organization are charitable and educational, but it is characterized by conservative, class-conscious, and nationalistic and imperialistic values.

noted the arrival of an indubitably "suitable" phrase, and feared worse for the immediate future.

The old man had not worn black or altered his cheerfulness when his wife died.

His wife, Jack's mother.

The depression that he had suspected was in wait for him now descended. He understood that he had been depressed for some time; this was like dark coming down into a fog. He had not admitted that he was depressed, but he ought to have known it by the fact that what he had woken up to each morning was not his own expectation of usefulness or accomplishment, but his wife's.

Now, if Rosemary died . . . but he would not think about that; it would be morbid.

When his mother died, his father had made the simplest of funerals for her—religious, of course. All the family, the grandchildren too, had stayed in the old house, together for the first time in years. The old man had behaved like a man who knew that his grief ought not to be inflicted on others. Jack had not been close to his mother; he had not liked her. He was close to no member of the family. He now knew that he loved his wife, but that had not been true until recently. There were his beautiful daughters. There was his son Joseph, who was a chip off the old block—so everyone insisted on saying, though it infuriated Joseph. But they could not meet without quarreling. That was closeness of a kind?

He ought to have been more attentive, when the mother died, to the old man, who had probably been concealing a good deal behind his mild dignity. Of course! And, looking back ten years, Jack knew that he had known what his father was feeling, had been sympathetic, but had also been embarrassed and unable to give anything of himself —out of fear that more would be asked?—had pretended obtuseness.

The old house was Church property, divided into units for old people who had been good parishioners. None had been friends before going to live there, but now it seemed that they were all close friends, or at least kept each other company in a variety of ways under the eyes of Mrs. Markham, who also lived there, looked after the house, after them. She put flowers in the church and mended surplices and garments of that sort—she was fifty, poor old thing. Jack now told himself that he was over fifty, although "the baby of the family," and that his sister Ellen, with whom he was to spend an unknown number of days, was fifty-five, while his boring brother Cedric was older still.

This train was not full and moved pleasantly through England's green and pleasant land. There were two other people in the compartment. Secondclass. Jack traveled secondclass when he could: this was one of the ways he used to check up on himself that he was not getting soft with success—if you could call what he had success. His brother and sister did, but that was the way they looked at life.

One fellow passenger was a middleaged woman, and one a girl of about twenty-three or twenty-four who leaned an elbow on the window ledge and stared at Buckinghamshire, then Berkshire, then Wiltshire,[4] all green and soft on this summery day. Her face was hidden

4. English counties westward from London.

behind glittering yellow hair. Jack classed her as a London secretary on her way home for a family visit, and as the kind of young person he would get on with—that is, like his daughters rather than his son.

He was finding the company of his girls all pleasure and healing. It seemed to him that everything he had looked for in women now flowed generously towards him from Carrie and Elizabeth. It was not that they always approved him, far from it; it was the quality of their beauty that caressed and dandled him. The silk of their hair flattered, their smiles, even when for somebody else, gave him answers to questions that he had been asking of women—so it seemed to him now—all his life.

Though of course he did not see much of them; while living in the same house, upstairs, they led their own lives.

The woman, whom he disliked because she was not young and beautiful—he was aware that he should be ashamed of this reaction, but put this shame onto an agenda for the future—got off the train, and now the girl at the window turned towards him and the rest of the journey was bound to be delightful. He had been right—of course, he was always right about people. She worked in an office in Great Portland Street,[5] and she was going for a visit to her parents—no, she "got on" with them all right, but she was always pleased to be back in her flat with her friends. She was not a stranger to Jack's world; that is, she was familiar with the names of people whose lives expressed concern for public affairs, public wrong and suffering, and she used the names of his friends with a proprietary air—she had, as it were, eaten them up to form herself, as he, Jack, had in his time swallowed Keir Hardie, Marx, Freud, Morris[6] and the rest. She, those like her, now possessed "the Old Guard," their history, their opinions, their claims. To her, Walter Kenting, Bill, Mona, were like statues on plinths, each representing a degree of opinion. When the time came to give her his own name, he said it was Jack Sebastian, not Jack Orkney, for he knew he would join the pantheon of people who were her parents-in-opinion and, as he had understood, were to be criticized, like parents.

The last time he had been Jack Sebastian was to get him out of a tight spot in Ecuador, during a small revolution; he had escaped prison and possible death by this means.

If he told this girl about that, he knew that as he sat opposite her, she would gaze in judiciously measured admiration at a man retreating from her into history. He listened to her talk about herself, and knew that if things had been otherwise—he meant not his father's dying, but his recently good relations with his wife—he could easily have got off the train with the girl, and persuaded her to spend the rest of her holiday with him, having made excuses to her family. Or he could have met her in London. But all he wanted now was to hear her voice, and to let himself be stimulated by the light from her eyes and her hair.

She got off the train, with a small laughing look that made his

5. Street in central London where British Broadcasting Services and other offices are located.

6. James Keir Hardie (1856–1915), miner, journalist, labor union leader, helped to politicize the British labor unions. William Morris (1834–1896), poet, artist, manufacturer, helped organize the Socialist League in England.

heart beat, and she strode off across the platform with her banners of yellow hair streaming behind her, leaving him alone in the brown compartment full of brown air.

At the station he was looking for a taxi when he saw his brother Cedric. A brown suit that discreetly confined a small stomach came towards him. That suit could only clothe a member of the professional classes; it had to be taken into account before the face, which was, as it happened, a mild pale face that had a look on it of duty willingly performed.

Cedric said, in his way of dealing all at once with every possible contingency: "Mrs. Markham said it had to be this train. I came because Ellen has only just come herself; I arrived first."

He had a Rover,[7] dark blue, not new. He and Jack, defined by this car and particularly accurately in this country town, drove through soothingly ancient streets.

The brothers drove more or less in silence to the church precincts. As they passed in under a thirteenth-century stone archway, Cedric said: "Ellen booked a room for you. It is the Royal Arms, and she and I are there too. It is only five minutes from Father."

They walked in silence over grass to the back door of this solid brick house which the Church devoted to the old. Not as a charity of course. These were the old whose own saved money or whose children could pay for their rooms and for Mrs. Markham. The poor old were elsewhere.

Mrs. Markham came forward from her sittingroom and said: "How do you do, Mr. Orkney?" to Jack, smiling like a hostess at Cedric. "I am sure you would like some tea now," she directed. "I'll bring you some up." She was like the woman on the train. And like Ellen.

He followed his brother up old wooden stairs that gleamed, and smelled of lavender and wax polish. As always happened, the age of the town, and of the habits of the people who lived in it, the smell of tradition, enveloped Jack in well-being; he had to remind himself that he was here for an unpleasant occasion. At the top of the stairs various unmarked doors were the entrances to the lives of four old people. Cedric opened one without knocking, and Jack followed him into a room he had been in twice before on duty visits. It was a smallish but pleasant room with windows overlooking the lawns that surrounded the church.

Sister Ellen, in thick gray tweed, sat knitting. She said: "Oh Jack, there you are, we are all here at last."

Jack sat. Cedric sat. They had to arrange their feet so as not to entangle in the middle of the small floor. They all exchanged news. The main thing that had happened to the three of them was that the children had all grown up.

The grandchildren, eight of them, knew each other, and had complicated relationships: they were a family, unlike their parents.

Mrs. Markham brought tea, of the kind appropriate to this room, this town: scones, butter, jam, comb honey, fruit buns, cherry cake, fruit cake. Also cream. She left giving the three a glance that said: At last it is all as it should be.

7. Expensive "middle-class" car, roughly equivalent to Buick.

Jack asked: "Have you seen him?"

"No," said Cedric, a fraction of a second before Ellen did. It was clear that here was competition for the perfect disposition of his death. Jack was remembering how these two had fought for domination over each other, and over, of course, himself.

"That is to say," said Ellen, "we have seen him, but he was not conscious."

"Another stroke?" asked Jack.

"He had another before Christmas," said Cedric, "but he didn't tell us, he didn't want to worry us."

"I heard about it through Jilly," said Ellen. Jilly was her daughter.

"And I through Ann," said Cedric. Ann was his.

Jack had now to remind himself that these names represented persons, not samples of pretty infancy.

"He is very close to Ann," said Cedric.

"He is fond of Jilly too," said Ellen.

"I suppose there is a nurse in there?" asked Jack. "Oh, of course, there must be."

"There is a day nurse and a night nurse, and they change places at dawn and dusk," said Ellen. "I must say I am glad of this tea. There was no restaurant on the train."

"I wonder if I could see him?" asked Jack, and then corrected it: "I shall go in to see him." He knew, as he spoke, that all the way on the train he had in fact been waiting for the moment when he could walk into the little bedroom, and his father would smile at him and say—he had not been able to imagine what, but it must be something that he had been waiting to hear from him, or from somebody, for years. This surely was the real purpose of coming here? That what he had in fact been expecting was something like a "deathbed scene," with vital advice and mutual comfort, embarrassed him, and he felt that he was stupid. Now he understood that embarrassment was the air of this room: the combat between elder brother and sister was nominal; they skirmished from habit to cover what they felt. Which was that they were in a position not allowed for by their habits of living. Jack had a vision of rapidly running trains—their lives; but they had had to stop the trains, had had to pull the emergency cords, and at great inconvenience to everyone, because of this ill-timed death. Death had to be ill-timed? It was its nature? Why was it felt to be? There was something ridiculous about this scene in which he was trapped: three middleaged children sitting about in one room, idle, thinking of their real lives which stagnated, while in another room an old man lay dying, attended by a strange woman.

"I'm going in," he said, and this time got up, instinctively careful of his head: he was tall in this lowceilinged room.

"Go in without knocking," said Ellen.

"Yes," Cedric confirmed.

Jack stooped under the doorframe. An inappropriate picture had come into his mind. It was of his sister, in a scarlet pinafore and bright blue checkered sleeves, tugging a wooden horse which was held by a pale plump boy. Jack had been scared that when Ellen got the horse a real fight would start. But Cedric held on, lips tight, being jerked by Ellen's tugs as a dog is tugged by the other dog who has fastened his teeth into the bit of meat or the stick. This scene had taken place in the old garden, for it had been enclosed by pink hydrangeas, while gravel had crunched underfoot. They must all have been very young, because Ellen had still been the classic golden-haired beauty; later she became large and ordinary.

What he was really seeing was his father sitting up against high pillows. A young woman in white sat with her hands folded watching the dying man. But he looked asleep. It was only when he saw the healthy young woman that Jack understood that his father had become a small old man: he had definitely shrunk. The room was dark, and it was not until Jack stood immediately above his father that he saw the mouth was open. But what was unexpected was that the eyelids had swelled and were blue, as if decomposition had set in there already. Those bruised lids affected Jack like something in bad taste, like a fart at a formal meal, or when making love of a romantic sort. He looked in appeal at the nurse who said in a normal voice which she did not lower at all: "He did stir a moment ago, but he didn't really come to himself."

Jack nodded, not wanting to break the hush of time that surrounded the bed, and bent lower, trying not to see the dying lids, but remembering what he could of his father's cool, shrewd, judging look. It seemed to him as if the bruised puffs of flesh were trembling, might lift. But his stare did not have the power to rouse his father, and soon Jack straightened himself—cautiously. Where did the Church put its tall old people, he wondered, and backed out of the room, keeping his eyes on the small old man in his striped pajamas, which showed very clean under a dark gray cardigan that was fastened under the collar with a gold tiepin, giving him a formal, dressed-up look.

"How does he seem?" asked Ellen. She had resumed her knitting.

"Asleep."

"Unconscious," said Cedric.

Jack asserted himself—quite easily, he saw with relief. "He doesn't look unconscious to me. On the contrary, I thought he nearly woke up."

They knew the evening was wearing on: their watches told them so. It remained light; an interminable summer evening filled the sky above the church tower. A young woman came through the room, a coat over her white uniform, and in a moment the other nurse came past them, on her way out.

"I think we might as well have dinner," said Ellen, already folding her knitting.

"Should one of us stay perhaps?" corrected Cedric. He stayed, and Jack had hotel dinner and a bottle of wine with his sister; he didn't dislike being with her as much as he had expected. He was even remembering times when he had been fond of Ellen.

They returned to keep watch, while Cedric took his turn for dinner. At about eleven the doctor came in, disappeared for five minutes into the bedroom, and came out saying that he had given Mr. Orkney an injection. By the time they had thought to ask what the injection was, he had said that his advice was they should all get a good night's sleep, and had gone. Each hesitated before saying that they intended to take the doctor's advice: This situation, traditionally productive of guilt, was doing its work well.

Before they had reached the bottom of the stairs, the nurse came after them: "Mr. Orkney, Mr. Orkney . . ." Both men turned, but she said: "Jack? He was asking for Jack?"

Jack ran up the stairs, through one room, into the other. But it seemed as if the old man had not moved since he had last seen him. The nurse had drawn the curtains, shutting out the sky so full of light, of summer, and had arranged the lamp so that it made a bright space in the dark room. In this was a wooden chair with a green cushion on it, and on the cushion a magazine. The lit space was like the detail of a picture much magnified. The nurse said: "Really, with that injection, he ought not to wake now." She took her place again with the magazine on her lap, inside the circle of light.

Yet he had woken, he had asked for himself, Jack, and for nobody else. Jack was alert, vibrating with his nearness to what his father might say. But he stood helpless, trying to make out the bruises above the eyes, which the shadows were hiding. "I'll stay here the night," he declared, all energy, and strode out, only just remembering to lower his head in time, to tell his sister and his brother, who had come back up the stairs.

"The nurse thinks he is unlikely to wake, but I am sure it would be what he would wish if one of us were to stay."

That he had used another of the obligatory phrases struck Jack with more than amusement: now it was with relief as well. Now the fact that the prescribed phrases made their appearance one after the other was like a guarantee that he was behaving appropriately, that everything would go smoothly and without embarrassment, and that he could expect his father's eyes to appear from behind the corrupted lids—that he would speak the words Jack needed to hear. Cedric and Ellen quite understood, but demanded to be called at once if . . . They went off together across the bright grass towards the hotel.

Jack sat up all night; but there was no night, midsummer swallowed the dark; at midnight the church was still glimmering and people strolled, talking softly, over the lawns. He had skimmed through Trollope's *The Small House at Allington,*[8] and had dipped into a book of his own called *With the Guerrillas in Guatemala.* The name on the spine was Jack Henge, and now he wondered if he had ever told his father that this was one of his noms de plume, and he thought that if so, it showed a touching interest on his father's part, but if not, that there must have been some special hidden sympathy shown in the choice or chance that led to its sitting here on the old man's shelves side by side with the complete works of Trollope and George Eliot and Walter Scott. But of course, it was unlikely now that he would ever know. . . . His father had not woken, had not stirred, all night. Once he had tiptoed in, and the nurse had lifted her head and smiled; clearly, though the old man had gone past the divisions of day and night, the living must still adhere to them, for the day nurse had spoken aloud, but now it was night, the nurse whispered: "The injection is working well. You try to rest, Mr. Ork-

8. Novel (1864) by Anthony Trollope (1815–1882).

ney." Her solicitude for him, beaming out from the bright cave hollowed from the dark of the room, enclosed them together in the night's vigil, and when the day nurse came, and the night nurse went yawning, looking pale, and tucking dark strands of hair as if tidying up after a night's sleep, her smile at Jack was that of a comrade after a shared ordeal.

Almost at once the day nurse came back into the livingroom and said: "Is there someone called Ann?"

"Yes, a granddaughter; he was asking for her?"

"Yes. Now, he was awake for a moment."

Jack suppressed: "He didn't ask for me?"—and ran back into the bedroom, which was now filled with a stuffy light that presented the bruised lids to the nurse and to Jack.

"I'll tell my brother that Ann has been asked for."

Jack walked through fresh morning air that had already brought a few people onto the grass around the church, to the hotel, where he found Cedric and Ellen at breakfast.

He said that no, he had not been wanted, but that Ann was wanted now. Ellen and Cedric conferred and agreed that Ann "could reasonably be expected" never to forgive them if she was not called. Jack saw that these words soothed them both; they were comforting himself. He was now suddenly tired. He drank coffee, refused breakfast, and decided on an hour's sleep. Ellen went to telephone greetings and the news that nothing had changed to her family; Cedric to summon Ann, while Jack wondered if he should telephone Rosemary. But there was nothing to say. He fell on his bed and dreamed, woke, dreamed again, woke, forced himself back to sleep but was driven up out of it to stand in the middle of his hotel room, full of horror. His dreams had been landscapes of dark menacing shapes that were of man's making—metallic, like machines, steeped in a cold gray light, and scattered about on a plain where cold water lay spilled about, gleaming. This water reflected, he knew, death, or news, or information about death, but he stood too far away on the plain to see what pictures lay on its surfaces.

Now, Jack was one of those who do not dream. He prided himself on never dreaming. Of course he had read the "new" information that everyone dreamed every night, but he distrusted this information. For one thing, he shared in the general distrust of science, of its emphatic pronouncements; for another, traveling around the world as he had, he had long ago come to terms with the fact that certain cultures were close to aspects of life which he, Jack, had quite simply forbidden. He had locked a door on them. He knew that some people claimed to see ghosts, feared their dead ancestors, consulted witchdoctors, dreamed dreams. How could he not know? He had lived with them. But he, Jack, was of that part of mankind delivered from all that; he, Jack, did not consult the bones or allow himself to be afraid of the dark. Or dream. He did not dream.

He felt groggy, more than tired: the cold of the dream was undermining him, making him shiver. He got back into bed, for he had slept only an hour, and continued with the same dream. Now he and Walter Kenting were interlopers on that death-filled plain, and they were to be shot, one bullet each, on account of nonspecified crimes.

He woke again: it was ten minutes later. He decided to stay awake. He bathed, changed his shirt and his socks, washed the shirt and socks he had taken off, and hung them over the bath to drip. Restored by these small ritual acts which he had performed in so many hotel rooms and in so many countries, he ordered fresh coffee, drank it in the spirit of one drinking a tonic or prescribed medicine, and walked back across sunlit grass to the old people's house.

He entered on the scene he had left. Ellen and Cedric sat with their feet almost touching, one knitting and one reading the *Daily Telegraph.* Ellen said: "You haven't slept long." Cedric said: "He asked for you again."

"*What!*" While he had slept, his energies draining into that debilitating dream, he might have heard, at last, what his father wanted to say. "I think I'll sit with him a little."

"That might not be a bad idea," said his sister. Was she annoyed that she had not been "asked for"? If so, she showed no sign of it.

The little sitting room was full of light; sunshine lay on the old wood sills. But the bedroom was dark, warm, and smelled of many drugs.

The nurse had the only chair—today just a piece of furniture among many. He made her keep it, and sat down slowly on the bed, as if this slow subsidence could make his weight less.

He kept his eyes on his father's face. Since yesterday the bruises had spread beyond the lids: the flesh all around the eyes and as far down as the cheekbones was stained.

"He has been restless," said the nurse, "but the doctor should be here soon." She spoke as if the doctor could answer any question that could possibly ever be asked; and Jack, directed by her as he had been by his sister and his brother, now listened for the doctor's coming. The morning went past. His sister came to ask if he would go with her to luncheon. She was hungry, but Cedric was not. Jack said he would stay, and while she was gone the doctor came.

He sat on the bed—Jack had risen from it, retreating to the window. The doctor took the old man's wrist in his hand and seemed to commune with the darkened eyelids. "I rather think that perhaps. . . ." He took out a plastic box from his case that held the ingredients of miracle-making: syringes, capsules, methylated spirits.

Jack asked: "What effect does that have?" He wanted to ask: Are you keeping him alive when he should be dead?

The doctor said: "Sedative and painkiller."

"A heart stimulant?"

Now the doctor said: "I have known your father for thirty years." He was saying: I have more right than you have to say what he would have wanted.

Jack had to agree; he had no idea if his father would want to be allowed to die, as nature directed, or whether he would like to be kept alive as long as possible.

The doctor administered an injection, as light and as swift as the strike of a snake, rubbed the puncture with one gentle finger, and said, "Your father looked after himself. He has plenty of life in him yet."

He went out. Jack looked in protest at the nurse: what on earth had been meant? Was his father not dying? The nurse smiled, timidly, and from that smile Jack gathered that the words had been spoken for his father's sake, in case he was able to hear them, understand them, and be fortified by them.

He saw the nurse's face change; she bent over the old man, and Jack took a long step and was beside her. In the bruised flesh the eyes were open and stared straight up. This was not the human gaze he had been wanting to meet, but a dull glare from chinks in damaged flesh.

"Ann," said the old man. "Is Ann here?"

From the owner of those sullen eyes Jack might expect nothing; as an excuse to leave the room, he said to the nurse, "I'll tell Ann's father."

In the livingroom sunlight had left the sills. Cedric was not there. "It's Ann he wants," Jack said. "He has asked again."

"She is coming. She has to come from Edinburgh. She is with Maureen."

Ellen said this as if he was bound to know who Maureen was. She was probably one of Cedric's ghastly wife's ghastly relations. Thinking of the awfulness of Cedric's wife made him feel kindly towards Ellen. Ellen wasn't really so bad. There she sat, knitting, tired and sad but not showing it. When you came down to it she didn't look all that different from Rosemary—unbelievably also a middleaged woman. But at this thought Jack's loyalty to the past rebelled. Rosemary, though a large, fresh-faced, graying woman, would never wear a suit which looked as if its edges might cut, or hair set in a helmet of ridges and frills. She wore soft and pretty clothes, and her hair was combed straight and long, as she had always worn it: he had begged her to keep it like that. But if you came to think of it, probably the lives the two women led were similar. Probably they were all more alike than any one of them would care to admit. Including Cedric's awful wife.

He looked at Ellen's lids, lowered while she counted stitches. They were her father's eyes and lids. When she lay dying probably her lids would bruise and puff.

Cedric came in. He was very like the old man—more like him than any of them. He, Jack, was more like their mother, but when he was dying perhaps his own lids. . . . Ellen looked up, smiled at Cedric, then at Jack. They were all smiling at each other. Ellen laid down her knitting, and lit herself a cigarette. The brothers could see that this was the point when she might cry. But Mrs. Markham came in, followed by a well-brushed man all white cuffs and collar and pink fresh skin.

"The Dean," she breathed, with the smile of a girl.

The Dean said: "No, don't get up. I dropped in. I am an old friend of your father's, you know. Many and many a game of chess have we played in this room. . . ." and he had followed Mrs. Markham into the bedroom.

"He had Extreme Unction[9] yesterday," said Ellen.

"Oh," said Jack. "I didn't realize that Extreme Unction was part of his. . . ." He stopped, not wanting to hurt feelings. He believed both Ellen and Cedric to be religious.

9. Last rite in Catholic churches including Anglo-Catholic or "High" Anglican.

"He got very High in the end," said Cedric.

Ellen giggled. Jack and Cedric looked inquiry. "It sounded funny," she said. "You know, the young ones talk about getting high."

Cedric's smile was wry; and Jack remembered there had been talk about his elder son, who had threatened to become addicted. What to? Jack could not remember; he would have to ask the girls.

"I suppose he wants a church service and to be buried?" asked Jack.

"Oh yes," said Cedric. "I have got his will."

"Of course, you would have."

"Well, we'll have to get through it all," said Ellen. It occurred to Jack that this was what she probably said, or thought, about her own life: Well, I've just got to get through it. The thought surprised him; Ellen was pleasantly surprising him. Now he heard her say: "Well, I suppose some people have to have religion."

And now Jack looked at her in disbelief.

"Yes," said Cedric, equally improbably, "it must be a comfort for them, one can see that." He laid small strong hands around his crossed knees and made the knuckles crack.

"Oh, Cedric," complained Ellen, as she had as a girl: this knuckle-cracking had been Cedric's way of expressing tension since he had been a small boy.

"Sorry," said Cedric. He went on, letting his hands fall to his sides, and swing there, in a conscious effort towards relaxing himself, "From time to time I take my pulse—as it were. Now that I am getting on for sixty one can expect the symptoms. Am I getting God? Am I still myself? Yes, no, doubtful? But so far, I can report an even keel, I am happy to say."

"Oh one can understand it," said Ellen. "God knows, one can understand it only too well. But I really would be ashamed. . . ."

Both Ellen and Cedric were looking to him, to add his agreement of which they were sure, of course. But he could not speak. He had made precisely the same joke a month ago, in a group of "the Old Guard" about taking his pulse to find out if he had caught religion. And everyone had confessed to the same practice. To get God, after a lifetime of enlightened rationalism, would be the most shameful of capitulations.

Now his feelings were the same as those of members of a particularly exclusive Club on being forced to admit the lower classes; or the same as the Victorian Bishop who, traveling to some cannibal-land to baptize the converted, had been heard to say that he could wish that his Church admitted degrees of excellence in its material: he could not believe that his lifetime of impeccable service would weigh the same as those of these so recently benighted ones.

Besides, Jack was shocked: to hear these ideas from Ellen, looking as she did, leading the life she did—she had no right to them! She sounded vulgar.

She was saying: "Of course I do go to church sometimes to please Freddy." Her husband. "But he seems to be losing fervor rather than gaining it, I am glad to say."

"Yes," said Cedric. "I am afraid I have rather the same thing with Muriel. We have compromised on Christmas and Easter. She says it is bad for my image not to be a church-goer. Petersbank is a small place you know, and the good people do like their lawyers and doctors to be pillars of society. But I find that sort of trimming[1] repulsive and I tell her so."

Again they waited for Jack; again he had to be silent. But surely by now they would take his opinions for granted? Why should they? If they could become atheist, then what might he not become? The next thing, they'll turn out to be socialists, he thought. Surely all this godlessness must be a new development? He could have sworn that Ellen had been devout and Cedric correct towards a Church which—as far as Jack had been concerned—had been irritation, humiliation, tedium, throughout his childhood. Even now he could not think of the meaningless services, the Sunday school, the fatuity of the parsons, the social conformity that was associated with the Church, without feeling as if he had escaped from a sticky trap.

Ellen was saying: "As for me, I am afraid I find it harder to believe as I get older. I mean, God, in this terrible world, with new horrors every minute. No, I am afraid it is all too much."

"I quite agree," said Cedric. "The devil's more like it."

"Yes," said Jack, able to speak at last. "Yes, that's about it, I'm afraid." It was the best he could do. The room was now full of good feeling, and they would have begun to talk about their childhood if the bedroom door had not opened, and the Dean come out. The smile he had shed on the nurse was still on his healthy lips, and he now let it benefit the three, while he raised his hand in what looked like a benediction. "No, don't get up!" He was almost at once out of the other door, followed close by Mrs. Markham.

The look the three now shared repudiated the Dean and all his works. Ellen smiled at her brother exactly as—he realized in capitulation to a totally unforeseen situation—his own wife would have done. Cedric nodded private comment on the stupidities of mankind.

Soon Cedric went to the bedroom, to return with the report that the old man looked pretty deep in. Then Ellen went and came back saying that she didn't know how the nurse could bear it in that dark room. But as she sat down, she said: "In the old days, one of us would have been in there all the time?"

"Yes" said Cedric. "All of us."

"Not just a nurse," said Ellen. "Not a stranger."

Jack was thinking that if he had stuck it out, then he would have been there when his father called for him, but he said: "I'm glad it is a nurse. I don't think there is very much left of *him*."

Ann arrived. What Jack saw first was a decided, neat little face, and that she wore a green jacket and trousers that were not jeans but "good" as her Aunt Ellen used the word. Ellen always had "good" clothes that lasted a long time. Ann's style was not, for instance, like Jack's daughters', who wore rags and rubbish and cast-offs and who looked enchanting, like princesses in disguise. She kissed her father, because he was waiting for her to do this. She stood examining them with care. Her father could be seen in her during that leisurely, unembarrassed examination: it was both her right and her duty to do this. Now Jack saw that she was small, with a white skin that looked

1. Compromise.

greenish where it was shaded, and hair as pale as her father's had been. Her eyes, like her father's, were green.

She said: "Is he still alive?"

The voice was her father's, and it took her aunt and her uncle back, back—she did not know the reason for their strained, reluctant smiles as they gazed at her.

They were suffering that diminution, that assault on individuality which is the worst of families: some invisible dealer had shuffled noses, hands, shoulders, hair and reassembled them to make—little Ann, for instance. The dealer made out of parts a unit that the owner would feed, maintain, wash, medicate for a lifetime, thinking of it as "mine," except at moments like these, when knowledge was forced home that everyone was put together out of stock.

"Well," said Ann, "you all look dismal enough. Why do you?"

She went into the bedroom, leaving the door open. Jack understood that Ann had principles about attitudes towards death: like his own daughters.

The three crowded into the room.

Ann sat on the bed, high up near the pillow, in a way that hid the old man's face from them. She was leaning forward, the nurse—whom Ann had ignored—ready to intervene.

"Grandad!" she said. "Grandad! It's me!"

Silence. Then it came home to them that the improbable had happened, that she had called up Lazarus. They heard the old man's voice, quite as they remembered it: "It's you, is it? It is little Ann?"

"Yes, Grandad, it's Ann."

They crowded forward, to see over her shoulder. They saw their father, smiling normally. He looked like a tired old man, that was all. His eyes, surrounded by the puffy bruises, had light in them.

"Who are these people?" he asked. "Who are all these tall people?"

The three retreated, leaving the door open.

Silence from the bedroom, then singing. Ann was singing in a small clear voice: All Things Bright and Beautiful.[2]

Jack looked at Cedric, Ellen looked at Cedric. He deprecated: "Yes, I am afraid that she is. That's the bond, you see."

"Oh," said Ellen, "I see, that explains it."

The singing went on:

All things bright and beautiful,
All creatures great and small,
All things wise and wonderful,
The Lord God made them all.

The singing went on, verse after verse, like a lullaby.

"She came to stay with him," said Cedric. "At Easter, I think it was. She slept here, on the floor."

Jack said: "My girls are religious. But not my son of course."

They looked blankly sympathetic; it occurred to Jack that his son's fame was after all circumscribed to a pretty small circle.

"He takes after me," said Jack.

"Ah," said Cedric.

"A lot of them are religious," said Ellen, brisk.

2. Hymn published in 1848 by Cecil Alexander on an article from the Anglican Creed.

"It's the *kind* of religion that sticks in one's craw," said Jack. "Simple faith and Celtic crosses."

"I agree," said Cedric. "Pretty low-level stuff."

"Does the level matter?" asked Ellen. "Surely *c'est le premier pas qui coûte?*"[3]

At which Jack looked at his sister in a disbelief that was meant to be noticed. Cedric, however, did not seem surprised: of course, he saw Ellen more often. He said mildly: "I don't agree. One wouldn't mind if they went on to something a bit more elevated. It's this servants'-hall village-green mother's-meeting sort of thing. You spend a fortune trying to educate them decently and then it ends up in . . . My eldest was a Jesus freak for a few months, for example. After Winchester, Balliol,[4] the lot."

"What is a Jesus freak?" inquired Ellen.

"What it sounds like."

Normally Jack would have cut out emotionally and mentally at the words "servants' hall," but he was still with them. He said: "What gets me is that they spout it all out, so pat and pretty, you know, and you get the feeling it might be anything, anything they had picked up or lay to hand—*pour épater le bourgeois,*[5] you know." At this he had to think that the other two must be thinking, but were too polite to say, that his own socialism, a degree or two off full communism, when he was in his teens, had had no deeper cause. This unspoken comment brought the conversation to a stop.

The singing had stopped too. It was getting dark.

"Well," said Ellen, "I tell you what I am going to do, I am going to have a bath and then dinner and then a good night's sleep. I think Ann is meeting Father's requirements better than we could."

"Yes," said Cedric.

He went to the door, and communicated this news to his daughter, who said she would be fine, she would be super, she would stay with her grandad, and if she got tired she could sleep on the floor.

Over the dinner table at the hotel, it was a reunion of people who had not met for a long time. They drank some wine, and were sentimental.

But the little time of warmth died with the coffee, served in the hall, which let in drafts from the street every time somebody came in.

Jack said: "I'll turn in, I didn't sleep last night."

"Nor I."

"Nor I."

They nodded at each other; to kiss would have been exaggerated. Jack went upstairs, while Cedric and Ellen went to telephone their families.

In the bedroom he stood by the window and watched how the light filled the lime outside. Breaths of tree-air came to his face. He was full of variegated emotions, none, he was afraid, to do with his father: they were about his brother and his sister, his childhood, that past of his which everything that happened to him these days seemed to evoke, seemed to present to him, sharp, clear, and for the most part painful; he did not feel he could sleep, he was over-stimulated.

3. "It's the first step that counts."

4. Winchester is a prestigious English "public" or prep school; Balliol an Oxford University college.

5. "To shock the conventional (middle class)."

He would lie on his bed for a rest. Waking much later, to a silence that said the night had deepened all around him, with the heaviness of everybody's sleeping, he started up into a welter of feeling that he could not face, and so burrowed back into sleep again, there to be met by—but it was hard to say what.

Terror was not the word. Nor fear. Yet there were no other words that he knew for the state he found himself in. It was more like a state of acute attention, as if his whole being—memory, body, present and past chemistries—had been assaulted by a warning, so that he had to attend to it. He was standing, as it were, at the alert, listening to something which said: Time is passing, be quick, listen, attend.

It was the knowledge of passing time that was associated with the terror, so that he found himself standing upright in the dark room crying out: "Oh, no, no, I understand, I am sorry, I . . ." He was whimpering like a puppy. The dark was solid around him, and he didn't know where he was. He believed himself to be in a grave, and he rushed to the window, throwing it open as if he were heaving a weight off himself. The window was hard to open. At last he forced it, leaning out to let the tree-air come to his face, but it was not air that came in, but a stench, and this smell was confirmation of a failure which had taken place long ago, in some choice of his, that he had now forgotten. The feeling of urgency woke him: he was lying on his bed. Now he really did shoot into the center of the room, while the smell that had been the air of the dream was fading around him. He was terrified. But that was not the word. . . . He feared that the terror would fade, he would forget what he had dreamed; the knowledge that there was something that had to be done, done soon, would fade, and he would forget even that he had dreamed.

What *had* he dreamed? Something of immense importance.

But as he stood there, with the feeling of urgency draining away and his daytime self coming back, even while he knew, as powerfully as he had ever known anything, that the dream was the most important statement ever made to him, the other half of him was asserting old patterns of thought, which said that to dream was neurotic and to think of death morbid.

He turned on the light, out of habit, a child chasing away night-fears, and then at once switched it off again, since the light was doing its job too well: the dream was dwindling into a small feeling that remarked in a tiny nagging voice that he should be attending to something. And Jack was chasing after the dream: No, no, don't go. . . .

But the feeling of the dream had gone, and he was standing near the window, telling himself—but it was an intellectual statement now, without force—that he had had a warning. A warning? Was it that? By whom? To whom? He must do something . . . but what? *He had been terrified of dying:* he had been forced to be afraid of that. For the first time in his life he had been made to feel the fear of death. He knew that this is what he would feel when he was in his father's position, lying propped on pillows, with people around him waiting for him to die. (If the state of the world would allow his death such a degree of civilization!)

All his life he had said lightly: Oh, death, I'm not afraid of death; it will be like a candle going out, that's all. On these occasions when, just like his brother Cedric, he checked up on himself for internal weakness, he had said to himself: I shall die, just like a cat or a dog, and too bad, when I die, that's that. He had known the fear of fear of course: he had been a soldier in two wars. He had known what it was to rehearse in his mind all the possible deaths that were available to him, removing pain and horror by making them familiar, and choosing suitable ways of responding—words, postures, silences, stoicisms—that would be a credit to him, to humanity. He knew very well the thought that to be hit over the head like an ox, stunned before the throat was cut, was the highest that he could hope for: annihilation was what he had elected.

But his dream had been horror of annihilation, the threat of nothingness. . . . It already seemed far away. He stretched his arms up behind his head, feeling the strength of his body. *His* body, that was made of fragments of his mother and his father, and of their mothers and their fathers, and shared with little Ann, with his daughters, and of course with his son—exactly like him, his copy. Yes, his, his body, strong, and pulsing with energy—he pushed away the warning from the dream, and switched on the light again, feeling that *that* was over. It was one in the morning, hardly the hour, in an English country hotel, to ask for tea, for coffee. He knew he would not dare to lie again on that bed, so he went down to let himself out. He was going to his father.

Ann was wrapped in blankets, lying on the floor of the livingroom. He knelt by her and gazed at the young face, the perfect eyelids that sealed her eyes shut like a baby's, incisive but delicate, shining, whole.

He sat on his father's bed where Ann had sat, and saw that the old man was slipping away. Jack could not have said why he knew, but he did know the death would be this day: it occurred to him that if he had not had that dream, he would not have known; he would not have been equipped to know, without the dream.

He walked the rest of the night away, standing to watch the bulk of the old church dwindling down under a sky lightening with dawn. When the birds began, he returned to the hotel, bathed, and with confidence woke his sister and brother, saying that yes, they could have breakfast but should not take too much time over it.

At eight-thirty they arrived to find Ann again crouched up on the bed near the old man, crooning to him bits of hymn, old tunes, nursery rhymes. He died without opening his eyes again.

Cedric said he would deal with all the arrangements, and that he would notify them of the funeral, which would probably be on Monday. The three children of the old man separated in good feeling and with kisses, saying that they really ought to see more of each other. And Jack said to Ann that she must come and visit. She said yes, it would be super, she could see Elizabeth and Carrie again, how about next weekend? There was to be a Pray-in for Bangladesh.

Jack returned to his home, or rather, to his wife. She was out. He suppressed grievance that there was no note from her; after all, he had not telephoned. She was at another class, he supposed.

He went to see if anybody was in the girls' flat. Carrie and Elizabeth had made rooms for themselves on the top floor, and paid rent for them. They both had good jobs. There was an attic room used occasionally by Joseph.

Hearing sounds, he knocked, with a sense of intruding, and was bidden to come in by Carrie, who seemed in conflict at the sight of him. This was because she, like the others, had been waiting for his coming, waiting for the news of the death. She had prepared the appropriate responses, but had just finished cooking a meal, and was putting dishes on the table. A young man whose face he did not know was coming towards the table, ready to eat.

Carrie was flushed, her long dark hair fell about, and she was wearing something like a white sack, bordered with deep white lace.

"My father died," he said.

"Oh poor you," said Carrie.

"I don't know," said Jack.

"This is Bob," said Carrie. "My father. Dad, would you like to eat with us? It is a business lunch, actually."

"No, no," said Jack. "I'll see you later." She called after him: "Dad, Dad, I'm sorry about Grandad."

"Oh, he was due to go," Jack called back.

He cut himself bread and cheese, and rang Walter's office. Walter was back from Dublin, but had to fly to Glasgow that afternoon: he was to appear on television in a debate on the Common Market. He would be back by midday Saturday: the Twenty-four-Hour Fast would start at two o'clock Saturday. Thirty people were expected to take part. It was a good thing Jack was back: he could take over again.

But what was there to be done?

Nothing much, really; he should keep a tag on the names; some might decide to drop out again. Considering the scale of the horror at that moment taking place in India, the mass misery, it would be a surprisingly small turn-out—he was sorry, he had to leave, a car was waiting.

It is normal to feel, on returning to the place one lives in, after having been away, that one has not left at all: this is not what Jack was feeling now. Whether it was because he was so tired, or because he was more upset by his father's death than he knew, he felt at a distance from his commonplace self, and particularly at a distance from the Jack Orkney who knew so well how to organize a sit-down, or a march, or how to produce such occasions properly for the Press or television.

Walter's contrasting the numbers of the people involved in the Bangladesh tragedy with the numbers who were prepared not to eat, publicly, for twenty-four hours in London, had struck him as bathos, as absurdity, but he knew that normally that was how he would be reacting himself.

Now he tried to restore himself by summoning well-tried thoughts. Every time the radio or television was turned on, every time you saw a newspaper, the figure *nine million* was used, with the information that these refugees had no future, or none of the normal kind. (India's short, sharp, efficient war that reprieved these same nine million was of course months in the future.) But there was nothing to be done; this catastrophe had the same feeling as the last, which had been Nigeria:[6]

6. Political tensions stemming from tribal differences caused the Ibo in eastern

a large number of people would die of starvation or would be murdered, but there was no power strong enough to stop this.

It was this feeling of helplessness that seemed to be the new factor; each time there was something of this kind, the numbers of people grew larger, and the general helplessness augmented. Yet all that had happened was that great catastrophes were being brought to general attention more forcefully than in the past. Not long ago, as recently as thirty years ago, it had been a commonplace for small paragraphs in newspapers to say that six, seven, eight million people had died, were dying of starvation, in China; communism had put an end to famine, or to the world's hearing about it. A very short time ago, a decade, several million might die in a bad season in India; the green revolution[7] had (possibly temporarily) checked that. In Russia millions had died in the course of some great scheme or other: the collectivization of the peasants, for instance.

The most shocking thing that had happened to his generation was the event summed up by the phrase "six million Jews." Although so many millions of people had been killed or had died in that war, and in a thousand awful ways, it was that one thing, the *six million,* which seemed worst. Because, of course, as everyone knew, it had been willed and deliberate murder. . . . Was it really any more deliberate than the *nine million* of Stalin's forcible collectivization? And how about that *nine,* or *ninety million,* the figure for the deaths of black men in Africa caused by white men in the course of bringing civilization to that continent? (This figure, whatever it was, never could accumulate about it the quality of senseless horror that had the figure for the death camps and gas chambers under Hitler. Why not?) During the next twelve months, between *twelve* and *twenty-four* million would die of starvation in the world (the figure depended on the source of calculation). The twelve months after, this figure would double—by the end of a decade, the numbers of people expected to die annually of hunger was beyond calculation. . . . These figures, and many more, clicked through his well-stocked journalist's head, and against them he heard Walter's voice, rather tetchy, critical, saying that there would only be thirty people for the Twenty-four-Hour Fast.

Yes, of course it was ridiculous to think on these lines and particularly when you were tired; he had been thrown off balance worse than he knew. He would sleep for a little—no, no, better not, he would rather not; he would not go to his bed unless Rosemary could be with him. Well, there were things that he ought to be doing, he was sure: for one thing, he had not read the newspapers for three days, nor listened to the news. He regarded it as his responsibility to read all the newspapers every day as if knowing what was bad could prevent worse. He did not want to read the papers; he wanted to sit down and wait quietly for his wife. This made him guilty, and he was associating his reluctance to plunge into the misery and threat of the newspapers with the brutalizing of everybody, everyone's acceptance of horror as normal—well, it was, when had storms of blood and destruction *not* swept continuously over the globe?

Nigeria to try to form their own country, Biafra. The resulting civil war and massive starvation forced Biafra to fall in January 1970.

7. Descriptive term for improved quick-growing varieties of rice and wheat which have high yields.

His will was being attacked: he had no will. This was why he needed to see Rosemary. This thought, he knew, had put a small whimsical grimace onto his face; the grimace was for the benefit of an observer. The observer was himself; it was there for the sake of his pride—a very odd thing had happened between him and his wife. For a long time, in fact for most of the marriage, they would have said that they were unhappily married. It had been a war marriage of course, like those of most of their contemporaries. It had begun in passion, separation, dislocation. They had felt, on beginning to live together for the first time, when they had been married for nearly six years, that their good times had been stolen from them. Then three children: they had turned Rosemary into an obsessed complaining woman; so he had seen her, and so she now saw herself during that period. He was most often out of England, and had many affairs, some of them serious. He knew she had been in love with someone else; she, like himself, had refused to consider a divorce because of the effect on the children. There was of course nothing remarkable in this history; but some of the men he knew had divorced, leaving first wives to bring up children. He knew that many of his friends' wives, like Rosemary, had been obsessed with grievance at their lot, yet had been dutiful mothers.

Various unhappy balances had been achieved by himself and Rosemary, always regarded as secondbest. Best was in fantasy, or what other people had. Then the children grew up, and were no longer there to be cooked for, worried about, shopped for, nursed—suddenly these two people who had been married thirty years discovered they were enjoying each other. They could not use the words "a second honeymoon" because they had never had a first. Jack remembered that at the other end of what now seemed like a long tunnel of responsibility, worry, guilt—relieved by frequent exile, whose enjoyability caused more guilt—had been a young woman with whom he had been more in love than with anybody since. He relaxed into the pleasures of his home, pleasure with Rosemary, who, appreciated at last, took on energy and poise, lost her listlessness, her reproach, her patience under neglect.

It had been the completeness of her revival that was the only thing disturbing about their being in love again: Jack lived marveling that so little a thing as his own attention should be enough to nourish this creature, to burnish her with joy. He could not help being guilty anew that so little an effort towards self-discipline would have produced the kindness which could have made this woman's life happy, instead of a martyrdom. Yet he knew he had not been capable of even so small an effort: he had found her intolerable, and the marriage a burden, and that was the truth. But the thought he could not come to terms with was this: what sort of a creature was she, to be fed and made happy by the love of a creature like himself?

And Rosemary was not the only woman he observed enjoying a new lease on life. At parties of "the Old Guard" it was enough simply to look around at the wives of the same age as his own wife, the women recently released from nursery and kitchen, to see many in the same condition, without having to ask if a second honeymoon was in progress—and here was another source of unease. He was not able to ask, to discuss frankly, or even to raise the matter at all, and yet these were friends, he had been with them, worked with them, faced a hundred emergencies with them—but they did not have with each other the friendship of the kind that would enable them to talk about their relationships with each other, with their wives, their wives with them. Yet this was friendship, or at least it was as close to friendship as he was likely to get. Intimacy he had known, but with women with whom he was having affairs. Intimacy, frankness, trust, had, as it were, been carried inside him, to be bestowed on loved women, and withdrawn when that love had ended because he was married. So it was not that he had not known perfect intimacy; it was that he had known it with several people, one after another. What was left now of these relationships was a simplicity of understanding when he met these women again—those that he did meet, for after all, many of these affairs had taken place in other countries. But even now he had to admit that this state had never been achieved with his wife, as good as their relation now was; for what he could not share with her was a feeling he could not control that he had to value her less for being so satisfied—more, fulfilled—with so little. Himself.

Yet, for all these reservations, the last two years had been better than anything he had expected with a woman, except in the expectations of his dreams about marriage so long ago. They went for holidays together, for weekends to old friends, to the theater, for special meals at restaurants, and for long walks. They made little treats for each other, gave each other presents, had developed the private language of lovers. And all the time her gaiety and energy grew, while she could not prevent herself watching him—not knowing that she did it, and this humbled him and made him wretched—for the return of the old tyrant, the boor. Always he was aware that their happiness lacked a foundation.

But what foundation ought there to be?

Now he wanted to tell his wife the dream he had had about death. This is why he had been longing to see her. But he had not allowed himself to understand the truth, which was that he couldn't tell her. She dreaded change in him; she would feel the dream as a threat. And it was. For another thing, this new easy affection they had would not admit the words he would have to use. What words? None he knew could convey the quality of the dream. The habits of their life together made it inevitable that if he said: Rosemary, I had a terrible dream; well, no, that was not it, its terribleness is not the point, wait, I must tell you—she would reply: Oh, Jack, you must have eaten something. Are you well?—And she would run off to get him a glass of medicine of some sort. Her smile at him, while she handed it to him, would say that she knew, they both knew, that he didn't really need it, but she enjoyed looking after him when at last he was enjoying being looked after.

Tea time came. Jack watched the young man from upstairs walk away under the summer's load of leaf. The telephone rang twice, both times for Rosemary. He took messages. He saw Elizabeth come up the path to the side door, nearly called to her, but decided not. He sat on into the summer afternoon, feeling that it was appropriate to be melancholy: it was what was expected of him. But that was not it! It was as if he had no substance at all, there was nothing to him, no purpose, no worth. . . . Something was draining quietly away from him, had been, for a long time.

Elizabeth came running in, saying: "Oh, Father, I am so sorry, you must be feeling low." Caroline came after her. Carrie was now dressed in a purple shawl over tight red cotton trousers. Elizabeth, still in what she had worn to work, had on a dark green trouser suit, but her own personality had been asserted since she came home: she had tied her hair back with an exotic-looking piece of red material, and it was making a froth of gold curls around her face. His cold heart began to stir and to warm, and they sat themselves down opposite ready to share his grief.

Rosemary now came in, a large, tall woman, smiling and shedding energy everywhere.

"Oh, darling," said she, "you didn't telephone. I am so sorry. You have had tea, I hope?"

"He's dead," said Elizabeth to her mother.

"He died this morning," said Jack, not believing that it had been that morning.

Rosemary slowed her movements about the room, and when she turned to him, her face, like the faces of her daughters, was not smiling.

"When is the funeral?"

"I don't know yet."

"I'll come with you," said Elizabeth.

"I won't," said Carrie. "I don't like funerals. Not our kind of funeral."

"And I won't either, if you don't mind," said Rosemary. "That is, not unless you want me there." A glass and decanter had appeared beside him, and Rosemary was causing whiskey to descend into the glass in a gold stream.

The whiskey was not the point, the women's serious faces not the point, the funeral and who was at it, not the point.

"There is no need for any of you to come," he said. And added, as he had been afraid he might: "It wouldn't be expected of you."

All three showed relief, even Elizabeth.

Rosemary hated funerals: they were morbid. Carrie, being sort of Buddhist, believed, apparently, in putting corpses out for the vultures. Elizabeth's Christianity, like Ann's, was without benefit of church services.

"Oh no, I want to come with you," said Elizabeth.

"Well, we'll see."

He told them about the death—a mild and well-ordered affair. He said that Ellen and Cedric had been there, and watched for his wife's humorous glance so that he could return it: she wanted to convey sympathy for having to be with his family even for two days. Then he began speaking about the Twenty-four-Hour Fast. He did not ask if they would join him, but he was hoping they would.

Now, while Rosemary had early on been inculcated with his left-wing opinions, during all the years of their unhappiness his activities had been seen by her as being in some subtle way directed against her, or, at any rate, as depriving her of something. But recently she had several times gone with him to a meeting or a demonstration. Looking guilty, she said that she couldn't join the Fast, because she had a lecture on Saturday night on Stress in the Family. She made it sound funny, in her way of appearing like an intelligent child submitting to official pedantry; but there was no doubt she would be at the lecture. Carrie said nothing: she thought any kind of politics silly. Elizabeth said she would have joined the Fast, but she had a demonstration of her own on Saturday.

Jack now remembered Ann's program, said that Ann was coming down at the weekend for a Pray-in. It turned out that this was the same as Elizabeth's. Both girls were pleased that Ann was coming, and starting talking about her and her relations with her parents. These were not very good: Ann found them materialistic, conventional, bourgeois. Jack was not able to be much amused; he found himself in sympathy with Cedric, possibly even with his sister-in-law. Probably Elizabeth and Carrie said to their friends that their parents were materialistic and bourgeois. He knew that his son Joseph did.

The girls had been going out for the evening, but because of the death, and wanting to cheer their father up, they stayed in to supper. Rosemary's new practice, now that the decades of compulsive cooking, buying, fussing, were done with, was to keep food to its simplest. She offered them soup, toast, and fruit. The girls protested: the parents could see that this was because they needed to do some thing to show their sympathy. Rosemary and Jack sat hand in hand on the sofa, while the girls made a long and delicious meal for them all.

They went to bed early: it was still not quite dark outside. But he needed to make love with his wife, feeling that here at least the cold which threatened him would be held at bay.

But the shell of himself loved, the shell of himself held Rosemary while she fell asleep and turned away from him. He was awake, listening to the tides of blood moving in his body.

He crept downstairs again. He read the newspapers—making himself do so, like a penance for callousness. He listened to the radio, avoiding news bulletins. He did not go to bed again until it was fully light, and was woken an hour later by Cedric: practical reasons had set the funeral for tomorrow, Saturday, at eleven.

Friday he spent in the activities that the journalist was so good at. Saturday was not a good day for train and air services: to reach S—— in time for the funeral, and to be back by two, would need luck and ingenuity. He checked the weather forecast: rain and mist were expected. Having made the arrangements, he rang Mona, since Walter was still in Glasgow. Mona was not only a wife of an "Old Guard," but one in her own right. It had been agreed that he, Jack, would be on the steps of the church at ten, to welcome the fasters as they arrived, and to see that the posters proclaiming the event were in place. He now asked Mona to do all this, explaining why.

"Oh dear," she said, "I am so sorry about your father. Yes, luckily I can do it. Who is coming?—wait, I'll get a pencil."

He gave her the names over the telephone, while she wrote them down.

They were the names of people with whom he had been associated in a dozen different ways, ever since the war ended; it seemed now as if the war had been an instrument to shake out patterns of people who would work and act together—or against each other—for the rest of their lives. They had not known about this process while it was happening, but that was when "the Old Guard" had been formed. The phrase was a joke of course, and for family use: he certainly would never use it to Walter, Bill, Mona, and the rest—they would be hurt by it. Carrie had said one day, reporting a telephone call, "I didn't get his name, but it sounded like one of the Old Guard."

These names appeared constantly together on dozens, hundreds, of letterheads, appeals, protests, petitions; if you saw one name, you could assume the others. Yet their backgrounds had been very different, of all classes, countries, even races. Some had been communists, some had fought communism. They were Labor and Liberal, vegetarian and pacifist, feeders of orphaned children, builders of villages in Africa and India, rescuers of refugees and survivors of natural and manmade calamities. They were journalists and editors, actors and writers, film makers and trade unionists. They wrote books on subjects like Unemployment in the Highlands and The Future of Technology. They sat on councils and committees and the boards of semi-charitable organizations; they were Town Councilors, members of Parliament, creators of documentary film programs. They had taken the same stands on Korea and Kenya, on Cyprus and Suez, on Hungary and the Congo, on Nigeria, the Deep South and Brazil, on South Africa and Rhodesia and Ireland and Vietnam and . . . and now they were sharing opinions and emotions on the nine million refugees from Bangladesh.

Once, when they had come together to express a view, it had been a minority view, and to get what they believed publicized had sometimes been difficult or impossible. Now something had happened which not all of them had understood: when they expressed themselves about this or that, it was happening more and more often that their views were identical with conventional views put forward freely by majorities everywhere. Once they had been armed with aggressive optimistic views about society, about how to change it; now they were on the defensive. Once they had forecast utopias; now they forecast calamity, failed to prevent calamity, and then worked to minimize calamity.

This view of the Old Guard had been presented to Jack by his son, the chip off the old block.

When Jack had finished the list of names, Mona said: "Surely we can do better than that?" and he said, apologetically (why, when it was not his fault?): "I think a lot of people are feeling that the media are doing it for us."

Then he decided to ring his son, who had not yet heard about his grandfather. To reach Joseph was not easy, since he worked for a variety of "underground" organizations, slept in many places, might even be out of the country.

At last Jack rang Elizabeth, who was already at her place of work, heard where Joseph was likely to be, and finally reached his son. On hearing that his grandfather was dead, Joseph said: "Oh that's bad, I am sorry." On being asked if he and his friends "with nothing better to do" would like to join the Twenty-four-Hour Fast, he said: "But haven't you been reading the newspapers?" Jack did not want to say that he had not read them enough to know what his son's program was likely to be, but it turned out that "all of us" were organizing a Protest March for that Sunday.

In his son's briskness, modified because of the death, Jack heard his own youth speaking, and a sense of justice made him sound apologetic towards his son. He felt, too, the start of exhaustion. This was because his effort to be fair made it necessary to resurrect his own youth as he talked to Joseph, and it took the energy that in fantasy he would be using to bring Joseph around to see his point of view. He had recently been indulging fantasies of confronting Joseph with: Look, I have something of great importance to say, can you let me have an hour or two? He was on the point of saying this now, but Joseph said: "I have to rush off, I'm sorry, see you, give my love to everyone."

He knew exactly what he wanted to say, not only to his son—to his own youthful self—but to the entire generation, or rather, to that part of it which was political, the political youth. What he felt was, he knew, paradoxical: it was because his son was so much like him that he felt he had no son, no heir. What he wanted was for his son to carry on from himself, from where he, Jack, stood now: to be his continuation.

It was not that his youthful self had been, was, conceited, crude, inexperienced, intolerant: he knew very well that his own middleaged capacities of tact and the rest were not much more than the oil these same qualities—not much changed—used to get their own way; he wasn't one to admire middle-aged blandness, expertise.

What he could not endure was that his son, all of them, would have to make the identical journey he and his contemporaries had made, to learn lessons exactly as if they had never been learned before.

Here, at precisely this point, was the famous "generation gap"; here it had always been. It was not that the young were unlike their parents, that they blazed new trails, thought new thoughts, displayed new forms of courage. On the contrary, they behaved exactly like their parents, thought as they had—and, exactly like their parents, could not listen to this simple message: that it had all been done before.

It was this that was so depressing, and which caused the dryness of only just achieved tolerance on the part of the middleaged towards "the youth"—who, as they themselves had done, behaved as if youth and the freedom they had to "experiment" was the only good they had, or could expect in their lives.

But this time the "gap" was much worse because a new kind of despair had entered into the conciousness of mankind; things were too desperate, the future of humanity depended on humanity being able to achieve new forms of intelligence, of being able to learn from experience. That humanity was unable to learn from experience was written there for everyone to see, since the new generation of the intelligent and consciously active youth behaved identically with every generation before them.

This endless cycle, of young people able to come to maturity only in making themselves into a caste which had to despise and dismiss their parents, insisting pointlessly on making their own discoveries—it was, quite simply, uneconomic. The world could not afford it.

Every middleaged person (exactly as his or her parents had done) swallowed the disappointment of looking at all the intelligence and bravery of his or her children being absorbed in—repetition, which would end, inevitably in them turning into the Old Guard. Would, that is, if Calamity did not strike first. Which everybody knew now it was going to.

Watching his son and his friends was like watching laboratory animals unable to behave in any way other than that to which they had been trained—as he had done, as the Old Guard had done. . . . At this point in the fantasy, his son having accepted or at least listened to all this, Jack went on to what was really his main point. What was worst of all was that "the youth" had not learned, were repeating, the old story of socialist recrimination and division. Looking back over his time—and after all recently he had had plenty of time to do just this, and was not that important, that a man had reached quiet water after such a buffeting and a racing and could think and reflect?—he could see one main message. This was that the reason for the failure of socialism to achieve what it could was obvious: that some process, some mechanism was at work which made it inevitable that every political movement had to splinter and divide, then divide again and again, into smaller groups, sects, parties, each one dominated, at least temporarily, by some strong figure, some hero, or father, or guru figure, each abusing and insulting the others. If there had been a united socialist movement, not only in his time—which he saw as that since the Second World War—but in the time before that, and the epoch before that, and before that, there would have been a socialist Britain long ago.

But as night followed day, the same automatic process went on . . . but if it *was* automatic, he imagined his son saying, then why talk to me like this?—Ah, Jack would reply, but you have to be better, don't you see? You have to, otherwise it's all at an end, it's finished, can't you see that? Can't you see that this process where one generation springs, virginal and guiltless—or so it sees itself—out of its debased predecessors, with everything new to learn, makes it inevitable that there must soon be division, and self-righteousness and vituperation? Can't you see that that has happened to your lot? There are a dozen small newspapers, a dozen because of their differences. But suppose there had been one or two? There are a dozen little groups, each jealously defending their differences of dogma on policy, sex, history. Suppose there had been just one?

But of course there could not be only one; history showed there could not—history showed this, clearly, to those who were prepared to study history. But the young did not study history, because history began with them. Exactly as history had begun with Jack and his friends.

But the world could no longer afford this. . . . The fantasy did not culminate in satisfactory emotion, in an embrace, for instance, between father and son; it ended in a muddle of dull thoughts. Because the fantasy had become increasingly painful, Jack had recently developed it in a way which was less personal—less challenging, less real? He had been thinking that he could discuss all these thoughts with the Old Guard and afterwards there could perhaps be a conference? Yes, there might be a confrontation, or something of that kind, between the Old Guard and the New Young. Things could be said publicly which never seemed to get themselves said privately? It could all be thrashed out and then . . . Meanwhile there was the funeral to get through.

That night, Friday, the one before the funeral, no sooner had he gone to sleep than he dreamed. It was not the same dream, that of the night in the hotel room, but it came as it were out of the same area. A corridor, long, dark, narrow, led to the place of the first dream, but at its entrance stood a female figure which at first he believed was his mother as a young woman. He believed this because of what he felt, which was an angry shame and inadequacy: these emotions were associated for him with some childhood experience which he supposed he must have suppressed; sometimes he thought he was on the point of remembering it. The figure wore a straight white dress with loose lacy sleeves. It had been his mother's dress, but both Elizabeth and Carrie had worn it "for fun." This monitor was at the same time his mother and his daughters, and she was directing him forward into the darkness of the tunnel.

His wife was switching on lights and looking at him with concern. He soothed her back to sleep and, for the second night running, left his bed soon after he had got into it to read the night away and to listen to radio stations from all over the world.

Next morning he traveled to the airport in light fog, to find the flight delayed. He had left himself half an hour's free play, and in half an hour the flight was called and he was airborne, floating west inside gray cloud that was his inner state. He who had flown unmoved through the skies of most countries of the world, and in every kind of weather, was feeling claustrophobic, and had to suppress wanting to batter his way out of the plane and run away across the mists and fogs of this upper country. He made himself think of something else: returned to the fantasy about the Conference. He imagined the scene, the hall packed to the doors, the platform manned by the well known among the various generations of socialists. He saw himself there, with Walter on one side, and his son on the other. He imagined how he or Walter would speak, explaining to the young that the survival of the world depended on them, that they had the chance to break this cycle of having to repeat and repeat experience: they could be the first generation to consciously take a decision to look at history, to absorb it, and in one bound to transcend it. It would be like a willed mutation.

He imagined the enthusiasm of the Conference—a sober and intelligent enthusiasm, of course. He imagined the ending of the Conference when . . . and here his experience took hold of him, and told him what would happen. In the first place, only some of the various socialist groups would be at the Conference. Rare people indeed would be prepared to give up the hegemony of their little groups to something designed to end little groups. The Conference would throw up some strong personalities, who would energize and lead; but very soon these would disagree and become enemies and form rival movements. In no time at all, this movement to end schism would have added to it. As always happened. So, if this was what Jack knew was bound to happen, why did he . . . They were descending through heavy cloud. There was heavy rain in S——. The taxi crawled through slow traffic. By now he knew he would not be in time to reach the cemetery. If he had really wanted to make sure of being at the funeral, he would have come down last night. Why hadn't he? He might as well go back now for all the good he was doing; but he went on. At the cemetery the funeral was over. Two young men were shoveling earth into the hole at the bottom of which lay his father: like the men in the street who continually dig up and rebury drains and pipes and wires. He took the same taxi back to the house in the church precincts where he found Mrs. Markham tidying the rooms ready to hold the last years of another man or woman, and his brother Cedric sorting out the old man's papers. Cedric was crisp: he quite understood the delay; he too would have been late for the funeral if he had not taken the precaution of booking rooms in the Royal Arms. But both he and Ellen had been there, with his wife and Ellen's husband. Also Ann. It would have been nice if Jack had been there, but it didn't matter.

It was now a warm day, all fog forgotten. Jack found a suitable flight back to London. High in sunlight, he wondered if his father had felt as if he had no heir? He had been a lawyer: Cedric had succeeded him. In his youth he had defended labor agitators, conscientious objectors, taken on that kind of case: from religious conviction, not from social feeling. Well, did it make any difference why a thing was done if it was done? This thought, seditious of everything Jack believed, lodged in his head—and did not show signs of leaving. It occurred to Jack that perhaps the old man had seen himself as his heir, and not Cedric, who had always been so cautious and respectable? Well, he would not now know what his father had thought; he had missed his chance to find out.

Perhaps he could talk to Ann and find out what the old man had been thinking? The feebleness of this deepened the inadequacy which was undermining him—an inadequacy which seemed to come from the dream of the female in a white dress? Why had that dream fitted his two lovely daughters into that stern unforgiving figure? He dozed, but kept waking himself for fear of dreaming. That he was now in brilliant sunshine over a floor of shining white cloud so soon after the flight through fog dislocated his sense of time, of continuity even more: it was four days ago that he had had the telegram from Mrs. Markham?

They ran into fog again above Heathrow,[8] and had to crawl around in the air for half an hour before they could land. It was now four, and the Twenty-four-Hour Fast had begun at two. He decided he would not join them, but he would drop in and explain why not.

He took the underground to Trafalgar Square.[9]

Twenty people, all well known to him and to the public, were grouped on the steps and porch of St. Martin's. Some sat on cushions, some on stools. A large professionally made banner said: THIS IS A

8. The major London airport.
9. The underground is the London subway system; Trafalgar Square a large central London area, frequently the site of demonstrations; St. Martin's in the Fields a nearby church.

TWENTY-FOUR-HOUR FAST FOR THE STARVING MILLIONS OF BANGLADESH. Each faster had flasks of water, blankets and coats for the night ahead. Meanwhile it was a warm misty afternoon. Walter had a thick black sweater tied around his neck by the sleeves. Walter was the center of the thing; the others related to him. Jack stood on the other side of the road thinking that his idea of talking with these his old friends about a joint conference with "the youth" was absurd, impractical; now that he was again in the atmosphere of ordinary partisan politics, he could see that it was.

He was longing to join them, but this was because he wanted to be enclosed in a group of like-minded people, to be supported by them, to be safe and shielded from doubts and fears. And dreams.

By Walter was his wife, Norah, a small pretty woman whom he had always thought of as Walter's doormat. He had done, that is, until he had understood how afraid Rosemary had been of himself. Norah had once said to him after a meeting: "If Walter had been an ordinary man, I might have resented giving up my career, but when you are married to someone like Walter, then of course you are glad to submerge yourself. I feel as if this has been my contribution to the Movement." Norah had been a journalist.

Walter's face, usually a fist of intention and power, was beaming, expansive: they all looked as if they were at a picnic, Jack thought. Smug, too. That he should think this astounded him, for he knew that he loved and admired them. Yet now, looking at Walter's handsome face, so well known to everyone from newspaper and television, it had over it a mask of vanity. This was so extraordinary a metamorphosis of Jack's view of his friend that he felt as if an alien was inhabiting him: a film had come over his eyes, distorting the faces of everyone he looked at. He was looking at masks of vanity, complacency, stupidity or, in the case of Walter's Norah, a foolish admiration. Then Jack's sense of what was happening changed; it was not that he was looking through distorting film, but that a film had been stripped off what he looked at. He was staring at faces that horrified him because of their naked self-centeredness: he searched faces that must be like his own, for something he could admire, or need. And hastily he wiped his hand down over his own face, for he knew that on it was fastened a mask of vanity; he could feel it there. Under it, under an integument that was growing inwards into his flesh, he could feel something small, formless, blind—something pitiful and unborn.

Now, disgusted with his treachery, but still unable to take his hand down from his face, unable to prevent himself from trying to tug off that mask fastened there, he walked over to his friends who, seeing him come, smiled and looked about them for a place where he could sit. He said: "I can't join you, I am afraid. Transport trouble," he added ridiculously, as first surprise, then incomprehension showed on their faces. Now he saw that Walter had already registered: *His father!* and saw that this born commander was framing the words he would use as soon as Jack turned his back: "His father has died, he has just come from the funeral." But this was no reason why he shouldn't be with them: he agreed, absolutely. Now he moved away, but glanced back with a wave and a smile; they were all gazing after the small drama embodied in: His father has just died. They looked as if they were hungry for the sensation of it—he was disliking himself for criticizing people whom he knew to be decent and courageous, who, ever since he had known them, had taken risks, given up opportunities, devoted themselves to what they believed to be right. To what *he* believed was right. . . . He was also a bit frightened. Thoughts that he would never have believed he was capable of accommodating were taking root in him; he felt as if armies of others waited to invade.

He decided to walk down to the river, perhaps even to take a trip to Greenwich,[1] if he could get on to a boat at all on a warm Saturday afternoon. He saw coming towards him a little procession under banners of: JESUS IS YOUR SAVIOR and JESUS LIVES! All the faces under the banners were young; these young people were in no way distinguished by their clothes from the young ones he had watched marching, with whom he had marched, for the last fifteen years or more. Their clothes were gay and imaginative, their hair long, their faces all promise. He was smiling at Ann, who carried a square of cardboard that said JESUS CARES ABOUT BANGLADESH. A voice said, "Hello, Dad!" and he saw his Elizabeth, her golden hair in heavy pigtails over either shoulder. Hands, Ann's and Elizabeth's, pulled him in beside them. In this way one of the most prominent members of the Old Guard found himself marching under a poster which said: CHRIST CAME TO FEED THE HUNGRY. REMEMBER BANGLADESH! Ann's little face beamed with happiness and the results of the exercise. "It was a nice funeral," she said. "I was telling Liz about it. It had a good feeling. Grandad liked it, I am sure."

To this Jack found himself unable to reply, but he smiled and with a couple of hundred Jesus-lovers, negotiated the Square, aided by some indulgent policemen. In a few moments he would pass his friends on the steps of the church.

"I shouldn't be here," he said. "False pretenses."

"Oh why?" inquired his daughter, really disappointed in him. "I don't see that at all!"

Ann's look was affectionate and forgiving.

Around him they were singing Onward, Christian Soldiers. They sang and marched or, rather, shuffled and ambled, and he modified his pace to theirs, and allowed his depression to think for him that whether the banners were secular and atheist on principle, or under the aegis of Jesus, twenty-four million people would die in the world this year of starvation, and that he would not give a new penny for the chances of anybody in this Square living another ten years without encountering disaster.

He was now aware that Mona was staring at him: in her decisive face, in her unequivocal eyes, was not a trace of what he usually saw there—the reminder of their brief but pleasurable affair. She turned to tug at Walter's sleeve, in a way that betrayed panic—more than ordinary shock, anyway. Now they all turned to look at him; they were all blank, they could not take it in. He had a need to wave his arms and shout: Nonsense, can't you see that I am with my daughter and my niece? He felt he should apologize. He could not stand being

1. Several miles down the river Thames from the center of London.

condemned by them, his side, his family, but even as he nodded and smiled embarrassed greeting, he saw that Walter, whose mouth at first had really dropped open, had seen Elizabeth, whom of course he had known all her life. All was explainable! For the second time in half an hour Jack watched Walter framing words with which to exculpate him: Jack was with his daughter, that was it! After all, Jack was not the only one among them whose offspring had caught God in various extraordinary forms!

Jack entered the Square with the children, was informed that they would come to visit him later, and he left them singing energetic hymns by a fountain.

He took buses home. He was looking forward to letting the false positions of the day dissolve themselves into unimportance while he laughed over them with his wife; but now he remembered that she would not be there, nor expect him to be.

There was a note, not to him but to Carrie, saying: "Please feed the cat, shall be very late, might stay at Judy Miller's, please lock all doors much love."

It was seven: it seemed like midafternoon. He drew the curtains to make a night, and sat in it with a glass of whiskey. Later Ann came in to tell him about the funeral, about Jesus. He moved his position in his chair so that he could look at her shining eyelids. Carrie came in, and he looked at her, but her eyes were a woman's. He knew about her love life, because she talked freely to her parents about it, but if she had never said a word he would have known from her knowledgeable breasts, from the way the flesh was molded to her eyeballs by kisses. She breathed tenderness, and care for him; he was happy she was there, but it was Ann he wanted to look at.

They discussed their respective faiths. Ann did not need to join a church because she had a direct relationship with Jesus, who loved her as she loved Him. Carrie defined her religion as "sort of Eastern, she supposed." No, she didn't think it was Buddhist so much as Hindu. She believed in reincarnation but could not see the point of cow-worship, though anything that made people be nice to animals was worth it, she thought. Had Ann read the Upanishads? That was what she believed in. She was taking it for granted that her father had not, and would not. She would like to be a vegetarian, but after all she shared a kitchen with Elizabeth, who would object. . . . Here Elizabeth came in, having bathed and put on an ancient peacock-blue lace dinner dress that had holes in the sleeves; Jack remembered Rosemary in it, twenty years before. Elizabeth was indignant, and said she would not at all mind Carrie turning vegetarian, she was ready to be one herself. But what would they feed the cat on? Were human beings going to kill all the cats and dogs in the world because they weren't vegetarian? Carrie got angry at this, and said: There you are; I told you, I knew you didn't want to be vegetarian! Ann restored good feeling by laughing at them both.

They went on discussing the exact nuances of their beliefs, *I* believe that, no, I don't agree with that, no I think it is more that . . . surely not, oh no, how can you believe that? An hour or so went by. Jack lifted the drawn curtain: there was a heavy golden light everywhere, thunder in the evening sky, the trees had damp yellow aureoles. He dropped the curtain, and they were in a small low lamplight, and the three girls were discussing Women's Liberation. Jack hated women talking about this, not because he disagreed with any of it, but because he had never been able to cope with it; it was all too much for him. He felt increasingly that he had reason to feel guilty about practically every relationship he ever had with a woman except for two or three special love affairs, which were outside ordinary categorization, but did not know how to change himself—if, indeed, he wanted to. These three young women had different, but precisely defined, opinions about the roles of women, with Carrie representing an extreme of femininity, and Ann, surprisingly, militant. Elizabeth talked about the lot of working women and had no time for what she called "futile psychologizing." This phrase made them quarrel, and for the first time Jack saw Ann strident. The quarrel went on, and then they saw that Jack was silent, and they remembered that his father was just dead, and they cooked for him, handing him many dishes, each as if it were a poultice for some wound he had suffered. Then, with an effort towards being reasonable, they went on discussing their ideological positions about Women's Liberation. Jack was again in the condition he had been in in the Square, when he had looked across traffic at his old friends. All he had been able to see there was a variety of discreditable emotions; all he could see in these charming faces was self-importance. What mattered to them was the moment when they said: I think so-and-so; no, I don't think that. He knew that what they believed was not as important to them as that they had come to an opinion and the reasons why they had reached that opinion. They possessed their beliefs or opinions; they owned them.

Now they were back to religion again: the other two attacked Ann for being Christian when Christianity's history in relation to women was so retrogressive. To which Ann said to Carrie: "You can talk, how about women in India?"

"Yes," and Carrie, "but then I don't believe in women being the same as men."

This started the quarrel again, and their voices rose.

He had to stop himself saying that they sounded like a Conference of World Churches debating doctrinal differences, because he knew that if it came to dogmas, and disagreements about historical personalities, then his faith, socialism, beat them all. He looked at, listened to, his daughters, his brother's daughter, and knew that in two, three, ten years (if they were all allowed to live so long) they would be laying claim, with exactly the same possessiveness, to other creeds, faiths, attitudes.

Again he felt like a threatened building, the demolition teams at work on its base. He was seeing, like a nightmare, the world like a little ball covered over the minuscule creatures all vociferously and viciously arguing and killing each other over beliefs which they had come to hold by accident of environment, of geography.

He told the girls he had not been sleeping well, must go to bed: he could no longer stand listening while they staked precise claims in fields of doctrine. They went off, kissing him fondly: he knew from the warmth of the kisses that they had talked about his reactions to Grandad's death; everything was bound to be much worse for him of course because he was an atheist and did not believe in survival after death.

They each had a different version of their futures. Ann for instance believed that she would sit up after her death, exactly as she was now, but better, and would recognize her friends and family, and Jesus would be there too.

Jack was thinking that his own attitude to life after death had been collected quite casually: when he was young and forming (or acquiring) his opinions, the people and writers he admired wore atheism like a robe of honor. Not to believe in an after-life was like a certificate of bravery and, above all, clarity of thinking. If he had been young now, he might have collected, according to the chances of his experience, and just as lightly, any one of a variety of opinions. Reincarnation? Why not? After all, as Carrie said, it was an optimistic and forward-looking creed. But when he was young he couldn't have taken to a belief in reincarnation, if for no other reason than that he never met anyone who had it. He had known that a few cranks believed in it, and people in India, but that was about it.

Now he made a ritual of going to bed. The sky was still full of light, so he made the room black. He drank hot milk. He wooed sleep, which he had never done in his life, and soon lay awake, hands behind his head. But he could not spend a third night reading and listening to the radio. Then lights crashed on and his wife was in the room. She was apologetic, and quite understood that he hadn't felt like joining the Fast. Her mind, he could see, was on her lecture and the friends she had met afterwards. He watched her dimming her vitality, damping her good mood, because she was afraid of it disturbing him. She lay in bed smiling, bright-eyed. She asked about the funeral, was sorry he had not reached it. Poor Jack! Smiling, she offered her arms, and grateful, he went into them. He would have gone on making love all night, but she went to sleep. In the close protective dark he lay beside his wife and in imagination saw the sky fill with dawn.

He fell asleep, he fell into a dream. In the dream he was thinking of what he had kept out of his consciousness all day, for to think of it was morbid. His father lay in a tight box under feet of wet soil. He, Jack, lay with him. He stifled and panicked, and the weight on him was as if he had been buried alive, in wet cement. He woke, and finding that although a cool damp light lay everywhere, and birds were at work on the lawn, it was only half past four; he went downstairs, turned on the radio, and made pictures in his head of the towns the stations were in, and lists of the people he had known in these towns, and then divided these into friends and enemies, and then, by a different classification, into the dead and the living, and so he returned in memory to the wars he had fought in or had reported, and relived, in a half-sleep, crisis-points, moments of danger, when he might have been killed, that now made him sweat and tremble but which he had simply lived through. When it seemed to him as if hours of a new day had already passed, he went back upstairs and got into bed beside his wife.

But at breakfast she betrayed that she had known he had not been beside her: she started to talk about the job in Nigeria. He knew that she did not want to go away for two years, leaving all her new interests, new friends, new freedom. There she would be back inside duties she had escaped from. There would be much social life. Yet it sounded as if she was trying to bring herself to believe she wanted to go if he did: she was worried about him.

He said, instead of replying about Nigeria, that he would like to go to church, just to see what it was like these days. She took in a puzzled but patient breath, let it sigh out of her, and looked at him with loving and respectful eyes—just like, he thought, the way Norah looked at Walter. She said: "Oh, I can understand why. You mean, you missed the funeral service?"

Perhaps it was because he had missed the funeral service. He put on a suit and she a dress, and they went to church together, for the first time, except for weddings. Carrie and Elizabeth went with them, Carrie because God was everywhere, Elizabeth because He was particularly in churches. Ann would not come; she had Jesus by the hand as she sat on the floor reading the Sunday newspapers.

He sat through the service in a rage; perhaps it was a retrospective rage; certainly this was what he had felt throughout years of compulsory attendance at Evensong and Matins, and Services Early and Late, at his public school. He did not mind that it was mumbo jumbo: it was bound to be! What he minded was that people voluntarily submitted themselves to the ministry of men palpably no better than themselves, men whose characters were written on their faces. This was perhaps what had first directed him towards socialism? He had not been able to stand that people submitted to being lied to, cheated, dominated by their equals? He was again afflicted by yesterday's disability: a film had rolled away from what he looked at. That man, wearing black and white lace and embroidery, and dangling strips of this and that color—the sort of attractive nonsense that Carrie and Liz might wear—that man intoning and dancing and posturing through the service, had a face like Walter's. They were both public men, performers. Their features were permanently twisted by vanity and self-importance. Jack kept passing his hand across his own face, feeling the ugliness of the love of power on it. And Rosemary put her arm in his, asking if he felt well, if he had toothache? He replied with violence that he must have been mad to want to come; he apologized for inflicting it on her.

"Oh it doesn't matter for once," she said, with mildness, but glanced over her shoulder to see if Carrie and Elizabeth had heard: it was extraordinary how they all kowtowed to their children, as if they feared to offend them.

After the midday meal he felt as if he could sleep at last, and did so.

The dream pulled him down into itself as he rolled onto his bed in the sultry yellow afternoon light—and passed out. This time, as he sank down beside his father, who was very cold—he could feel the cold coming out and claiming him—the weight pressed them both down, right through the earth that was below the tight box. His father disappeared and he, Jack, quite alone, was rocking on a light blue sea. This too dissolved into air, but not before he had been pierced through and through with an extraordinary pain that was also a sweetness. He had not known anything like this before; in the dream he was saying to himself: That's a new thing, this sweetness. It was quickly gone, but astonishing, so that he woke up, pleased to wake up, as if out of a nightmare, yet what he had been happy to wake from was that high, piercing sweetness. Unhealthy, he judged it. It was not yet tea time; he had slept an hour and not been refreshed. He went down to be told as a joke by his wife that a journalist had rung that morning to find out his views on the Twenty-four-Hour Fast; did his not having been there mean that he was against it? Ann had answered, and had said that Mr. Orkney was at church. The journalist had seemed surprised, Ann said. She had had to repeat it more than once. Had she meant that Jack Orkney was at a wedding? At a christening? No, no, at church, at Sunday morning service.

Jack knew the journalist; they had been in several foreign fields together. Jack was now seriously worried, as a man is when faced with the loss of reputation. He said to himself: I was not worried what people thought of me when I was young. He was answered: You mean, you were not worried by what people said who were not *your side*. He said: Well, but now it is not a personal thing, criticism of me is a criticism of my side; surely it is right to worry about letting my own side down?

There was no answer to this, except a knowledge he was dishonest.

Rosemary suggested a long walk. He could see she had been thinking how to make him whole again—how to protect her own happiness, he could not prevent himself thinking. He was more than ready to walk as many miles away as they could before dark; when they had first met, before they married, one of their things had been to walk miles, sometimes for days on end. Now they walked until it was dark, at eleven o'clock; they worked out it was over fifteen miles, and were pleased that this was still so easy for them, at their age, and in the middle of their undemanding life. But the night now confronted Jack, a narrow tunnel at the end of which waited a white-robed figure, pointing him into annihilation. That night he did not sleep. The windows were open, the curtains drawn back, the room full of light from the sky. He pretended to sleep, so as to protect his wife from anxiety, but she lay alert beside him, also pretending sleep.

Next morning it was a week since Mrs. Markham's wire, and he became concerned for his health. He knew that not to sleep for night after night, as he was doing, was simply not possible. During the following days he went further into this heightened, over-sensitized state, like a country of which he had heard rumors, but had not believed in. On its edges his wife and daughters smiled and were worried about him. He slept little, and when he did he was monitored by the female figure in white, now a composite of his mother, his wife, and his daughters, but quite impersonal; she used their features but was an imposter. This figure had become like an angel on a wedding cake, or on a tomb, full of false sentiment; its appearance was accompanied, like a strain of particularly nauseating and banal music, by the sweetly piercing emotion, only it was much worse now; it was the essence of banality, of mawkishness, like being rolled in powdered sugar and swallowed into an insipid smile. The horror of this clinging sickliness was worse even than the nightmare—he could no longer remember the quality of that, only that it had occurred—of the night in the hotel. His bed, the bedroom, soon the entire house, was tainted by this emotion, which was more a sensation, even like nausea, as if he could never rid himself of the taste of a concentration of saccharin which he had accidentally swallowed. He was all day in a state of astonishment, and self-distrust; he made excuses not to go to bed.

Walter came to see him. Unannounced. As soon as Jack saw him getting out of his car, he remembered something which told him why Walter had come. About four years before, Mona had reviewed a religious book, the memoirs of some sort of mystic, in a way which surprised them all. They would have expected a certain tone—light, carefully non-solemn, for it did not do to give importance to something which did not deserve it—not mocking, of course, which would have had the same result, but the tone you use to indicate to children that while you may be talking about, let's say, ghosts, or telling a story about a witch, the subject is not one to be taken seriously. But Mona had not used this subtly denigrating tone. Various of the Old Guard had commented on this. Then she had reviewed a book of religious poetry, which of course could not be dismissed in the light disinfecting tone, since poetry was obviously in a different category—but the point was that none of them would have reviewed it at all. For one thing no editor would think of asking them to. It was all very upsetting. There had been a party at Bill's house and Mona was not there. She had been discussed: she was at the age when women "get" religion. Jack, fond of Mona, offered to go and see her. His visit was to find out, as he put it to himself, if she was "still with us." He had found her amiable, and her usual self, helping to organize a conference for the coming week. He had probed—oh tactfully, of course. He mentioned an article in one of the Sundays about a certain well-known religious figure, and said he found the man a nauseating self-seeker. Mona had said that she was inclined to agree. He had said casually, "Of course I am only too ready to forgive somebody who can't face old age and all that without being cushioned by God." Mona had remarked that for her part she could not believe in personal survival after death. Well, of course not, but for years that she could not would have been taken for granted. He remembered feeling protective affection for her, as if he were helping to save her from a danger. Seeing Walter at a meeting to do with the Crisis in Our Communications a week later, he had said that he had made a point of visiting Mona and that she had seemed quite sound to him.

He knew now what to expect from Walter.

Walter was looking furtive. Of course Jack knew that his furtiveness was not anything he would have noticed normally: this state he was in exaggerated every emotion on other people's faces into caricatures. But Walter was playing a double part, almost that of a spy (as he had with Mona, of course, now he came to think of it), and Furtiveness was written large on him.

Walter mentioned the Fast—a success—and then made a clumsy sort of transition which Jack missed, and was talking about Lourdes.[2]

2. Town in southwestern France where in 1858 a French peasant girl, now Saint

Jack wondered why Lourdes? And then he laughed: it was a short laugh, of astonishment, and Walter did not notice it. Or rather, had not expected a laugh in this place, found it discordant, and therefore discounted it, as if it had not happened. Walter was trying to find out if Jack's religious conversion—the rumor had spread that he went to church on Sundays—included a belief in miracles, such as took place, they said, at Lourdes. Jack said he had been to Lourdes once for the *Daily* . . . over some so-called miracles some years ago. Walter nodded, as if to say: That's right. He was already feeling relieved, because Jack had used the right tone. But he was still showing the anxiety of a priest who knew his beliefs to be the correct ones and was afraid of a lamb straying from the flock. He mentioned that Mona was suspected of having become a Roman Catholic. "Good God, no," said Jack, "she can't have." He sounded shocked. This was because his reaction was that she had been deceiving him, had lied. He sat silent, trying to remember the exact tones of her voice, how she had looked. If she was a Catholic, could she have said she did not believe in a personal survival? But he knew nothing at all of what Catholics thought, except that they did not believe in birth control, but did believe in the Pope.

Remembering that Walter was still there, and silent, he looked up to see him smiling with relief. The smile seemed to him extraordinary in its vulgarity, yet he knew that what he was seeing was the pleasure of a good comrade: Walter was happy that nothing was going to spoil their long friendship. The spontaneity of his reply over Mona had reassured him; now, mission accomplished, Walter was already thinking about the various obligations he had to get back to. But he stayed a little, to discuss some committee on pollution he was helping to set up.

He talked: Jack listened, wondering if this was the right time to raise the question of "the young." Walter's two sons were both classic revolutionaries and they despised their father for his success, his position in the socialist world, for "his compromises with the ruling class." Jack was thinking that of all the people in the world it was Walter, so like himself in experience, position and—he was afraid—character, with whom he should be able to talk about his preoccupation. But he was beginning to realize that there was a difference, and it was obviously an important one, between them. Jack was more on the outskirts of politics. He was more of a freelance, but Walter was always in the thick of every political struggle, always involved with the actual details of organization. He never did anything else. And this was why he was so far from Jack's present vision of things, which saw them all—the people like them—continually planning and arranging and organizing towards great goals, but fated to see these plans fail, or becoming so diluted by pressures of necessity that the results resembled nothing of what had been envisaged at the start. Sitting there, looking at his old friend's forceful and energetic face, it was in a double vision. On the one hand he thought that this was the one man he knew whom he would trust to see them all through

Bernadette, claimed to have seen visions of the Virgin Mary in a grotto. A shrine built on the site annually attracts nearly 3 million people hoping to be cured by the waters of the grotto's spring.

any public or private tight spot; but at the same time he wanted to howl out, in a protest of agonized laughter, that if the skies fell (as they might very well do), if the seas rolled in, if all the water became undrinkable and the air poisoned and the food so short everyone was scratching for it in the dust like animals, Walter, Bill, Mona, himself, and all those like them, would be organizing Committees, Conferences, Sitdowns, Fasts, Marches, Protests and Petitions, and writing to the authorities about the undemocratic behavior of the police.

Walter was talking about some negotiation with the Conservatives. Normally, Jack would be listening to an admirably concise and intelligent account of human beings in conflict. Now Jack could see only that on his friend's face was a look which said: *I am Power.* Jack suddenly got up, with a gesture of repulsion. Walter rose automatically, still talking, not noticing Jack's condition. Jack reminded himself that in criticizing Walter he had forgotten that he must be careful about himself: he had again, and suddenly, become conscious of the expressions that were fitting themselves down over his face, reflecting from Walter's, horrifying him in their complacency or their cruelty. And his limbs, his body, kept falling into postures of self-esteem and self-approval.

Walter was moving to the door, still talking. Jack, trying to keep his face blank, to prevent his limbs from expressing emotions which seemed to him appropriate for a monster, moved cautiously after him. Walter stood in the door—talking. Jack wanted him to go. It tired him, this self-observation he could not stop: there was his image at the door oblivious to anything in the world but his own analysis of events. Yet at last, as Walter said goodbye and he saw Jack again—which he had not done for some minutes, being too self-absorbed—a worried look came into his face, and because of this look Jack knew that what Walter saw was a man standing in a rigid unnatural position who had his hands at his lower cheeks, fretfully fingering the jawbone, as if it were out of place.

Walter said, in a simple and awkward voice: "It's a bit of a shock when your old man goes. I know when mine died it took me quite a time to get back to normal."

He left, like a health visitor, and Jack thought that Walter had had to get back to normal when his father died. He was thinking, too, that the cure for his condition was activity. Walter was more sensible than himself: he filled every moment of his time.

He decided to go to the family doctor for sleeping pills. This was a house that self-consciously did not go in for pills of any kind. Or did not now: Rosemary, during what she now called "my silly time" —which after all had gone on for some years—had taken sleeping pills a lot. But that, even while she did it, had seemed to her a betrayal of her real nature. The girls went in for health in various ways—diets, yoga, homemade bread. His son was too strong—of course!—to need medicine. He smoked pot, Jack believed, and on principle —well, so would Jack have done at his age; the law on marijuana was absurd.

He told the doctor he was not sleeping well. The doctor asked for how long. He had to think. Well, for about a month, perhaps six weeks.

The doctor said: "That's not going to kill you, Jack!"

"All right, but before I get into the habit of not sleeping I'd like something—and *not* a placebo, please." The glance the doctor gave him at this told him that he had in fact been deciding to prescribe a placebo, but there had been something in Jack's voice to make him change his mind.

"Is there anything else worrying you?"

"Nothing. Or everything."

"I see," said the doctor, and prescribed sleeping pills and anti-depressants.

Jack had the prescriptions made up, then changed his mind; if he started taking these pills, it would be some sort of capitulation. To what, he did not know. Besides, he was thinking: Perhaps they might make it worse? "It" was not only the sweet mawkishness which threatened him at every turn, in a jingle of a tune for an advertisement on television, a shaft of light from behind a cloud at sunrise, a kitten playing in the next garden, but the feeling, getting worse, that he was transparent, an automaton of unlikable and predictable reactions. He was like a spy in his own home, noticing the slightest reactions of thought or emotion in his wife and daughters, seeing them as robots. If they knew how he was seeing them, how loathsome they were in their predictability, their banality, they would turn and kill him. And quite rightly. For he was not human. He was outside humanity. He even found himself walking abruptly out of rooms where he was sitting with Rosemary, or one or other of the girls; he could not stand his own horror and pity because of them, himself, everybody.

Yet they were treating him with perfect kindness. He knew that this was what it really was: even if he had to see it all as falsity, mere habits of kindness, sympathy, consideration, tact, which none of them really felt, wanting him to get back to normal, so that life could go on without stress. His wife particularly longed for this. While he took care that he did not betray the horror he was immersed in, she knew well enough their time was over—the gaiety and charm of it, the irresponsibility. Probably for good. Being what she was, thoughtful, considerate (taught by society to show thoughtfulness and sympathy when she wasn't really feeling it, he could not stop himself thinking), she was trying to decide what to do for the best. Sometimes she asked if he didn't think he should write another book—even if he would like to make a trip abroad without her; she talked about Nigeria. Each time Nigeria was mentioned his response to it was strong: it was the idea of forgetting himself entirely in an active and tightly planned life.

But he did not want to commit himself. He felt he would be losing an opportunity—but of what? And besides, how could he? He believed he was seriously ill, in some inconceivable, unprecedented way; how could he take a job when his energies had to go into presenting a bland and harmless surface to those around him, into preventing his hand rising furtively up to his face, to see if the masks of greed or power were fastened there, into watching the postures his body assumed, which must betray his vices to anyone looking his way—or would betray them, if everybody wasn't blind and deaf, absorbed in their kindness, their awful, automatic, meaningless "sympathy."

One night his son arrived upstairs. Joseph used sometimes to come, unannounced, and went up through the girls' room to the attic to sleep. He took food from his sisters' kitchen. Sometimes he brought friends.

About a year ago there had been a row over the friends. Feeling one evening as if the top part of his house had been invaded by a stealthy army, Jack had gone up and found a dozen or so young men, and a couple of girls, all lying about on sleeping bags and blankets under the rafters. They had moved in. A girl was cooking sausages in a frying pan that was on a camping stove; about a foot away was a drum that had written on it: PARAFFIN. INFLAMMABLE. The flame from the stove was turned too high, and showed around the edges of the frying pan. Jack jumped forward, turned it down, removed the pan, and stood up, facing them, the pan in his hand. His usual responses to his son—apology, or the exhaustion due to the effort to be fair, had been cut, and he asked: "What's the matter with you lot? What's wrong? You aren't stupid!"

Coming up the stairs he had been preparing a "humorous" remark —which he was afraid would sound pompous, to the effect: "How about introducing me to my guests?" Now he stared at them, and the young faces stared back. There was a half-scared smile on the face of the girl who had been cooking, but no one said anything. "I think you had better get out," said Jack at last, and went downstairs. Soon after he had watched the whole lot cross the garden like a tribe on the move, with their stove, their cartons, their paper-carriers, their guitars, their sleeping bags.

Now he came to think of it, this incident had been the beginning of his inadmissible depression. He had spent days, weeks, months, thinking about it. He felt there was a contempt there, in the carelessness, that went beyond anything he knew how to cope with; he did not understand it, them—his son. Who, meanwhile, had resumed his habits, and continued to drop in for a night or two when he had nowhere better to sleep. So it was not, Jack reasoned, that Joseph despised a roof over his head, as such? They had all been so stoned they had not known what they were doing? No, it hadn't seemed like it. They had not bothered to look at the drum, had not known it was full? But that was scarcely an excuse—no, it was all too much, not understandable. . . . He had not talked to his son since, only seen him go past.

The telephone rang from upstairs: Carrie said that Joseph would be down to see him in a few moments, if Jack "had nothing better to do."

Instantly Jack was on the defensive: he knew that Joseph criticized him for having been away so much when the three children were growing up. This message was a reference to that—*again?* If it was simply careless, what had come into his head, then that made it even worse, in a way. . . . Joseph came running lightly down the stairs and into the livingroom. A muscular young man, he wore skin-tight blue jeans, a tight blue sweatshirt, and a small red scarf at his throat tied like a pirate's. The clothes were old, but as much care had gone into their choosing, preparation and presentation as a model getting ready for a photograph. . . . While Jack knew he had already begun the process of comparison that always left him exhausted, he could not stop, and he was wondering: Was it that we were as obsessed with what we wore but I've forgotten it? No, it's not that: our convention was that it was bourgeois to spend time and money on clothes, that was it, but their convention is different; that's all it is and it is not important.

Joseph had a strong blue gaze, and a strong straight mouth. The mouth was hidden under a wiry golden beard. A mane of wiry yellow hair fell to his shoulders. Jack thought that the beard and the long hair were there because they were fashionable, and would be dropped the moment they were not. . . . *Well, why not? He wished very much he could have swaggered about in beard and mane—that was the truth.*

This aggressively vivid young man sat on a chair opposite Jack, put his palms down on his thighs with his fingers pointing towards each other, and the elbows out. In this considering, alert position he looked at his father.

Jack, a faded, larger, softer version of what he was seeing, waited.

Joseph said: "I hear you have got religion."

"The opium," said Jack, in a formal considering way, "of the people: Yes. If that's what it is, I have got it."

Jack felt particularly transparent, because of his son's forceful presence. He knew that his posture, the smile on his face, were expressing apology. He already knew the meeting was doomed to end unpleasantly. Yet he was looking for the words to appeal to his son, to begin the "real" talk that they should be having. Joseph said: "Well, that's your business." He sounded impatient; having raised the subject, or at least used it as an opener, now he was saying that his father's processes were of no interest or importance.

"You've been following the Robinson affair?"

Jack could not remember for a moment which affair that was, but did not like to say no.

"We have to pay the defense lawyer. And there's the bail. We need at least three thousand pounds."[3]

Jack did not say anything. It was not from policy, but inadequacy, yet he saw his son beginning to make the irritable movements of power, of confidence, checked and thwarted. It crossed his mind that of course his son saw him as powerful and confident, and this it was that accounted for the aggression, the hostility, the callousness. Into Jack's mind now came sets of words framed rhetorically; since this was not how he was feeling, he was surprised. "Why does it have to be like this, that more hate is used on people of the same side, thus preventing us ever from uniting in a common front, preventing us from bringing down the enemy?" These were words from the imaginary conversation with Joseph that he so often indulged in: only now did it strike him that he never had fantasies of a personal relationship—of their going for a holiday together, for instance, or just spending an evening, or walking for an hour or so. "Can't you see?" —the inner rhetoric-maker was continuing, "that the vigor of your criticism, your iconoclasm, your need to condemn the past without

3. At the time of the story, roughly six or seven thousand dollars.

learning from it, will take you relentlessly to stand exactly where your despised elders stand now?"

It suddenly occurred to Jack, and for the first time, that he had repudiated his past. This so frightened him, leaving him, as it must, by himself out in the air somewhere, without comrades and allies—*without a family*—that he almost forgot Joseph's presence. He was thinking: For weeks now, ever since the old man's death—before, even?—I've been thinking as if I have abandoned socialism.

Joseph was saying: "I don't have to tell you what the conditions are like in that prison, how they are being treated."

Jack saw that the "I don't have to tell you" was in fact an admission that in spite of everything he said, Joseph saw him as an ally. "You've come to me for money?" he asked, as if there could be another reason.

"Yeah. Yeah. That's about it, I suppose."

"Why do you have to be American?" Jack asked in sudden real irritation. "You're not American. Why do you all have to?"

Joseph said, with a conscious smile: "It's a mannerism, that's all." Then he looked stern again, in command.

Jack said: "I'm one of the old rich lefties you were publicly despising not long ago. You didn't want to have anything to do with us, you said."

Joseph frowned and made irritable movements which said that he felt that the sort of polemic which abused people not standing exactly where he stood was rather like breathing, a tradition, and he genuinely felt his father was being unreasonable in taking such remarks personally. Then he said, as if nothing better could be expected: "Then I take it it is no?"

"No," said Jack, "I am sorry."

Joseph got up; but he looked hesitant, and even now could sit down—if Jack said the right things. If he could push aside the rhetorical sentences that kept coming to his tongue: how should they not?—he had spent many hours of fantasy insuring that they would!

Jack suddenly heard himself saying, in a low, shaking, emotional voice: "I am so sick of it all. It all goes on and on. Over and over again."

"Well," said Joseph, "they say it is what always happens, so I suppose that ought to make us feel better." His smile was his own, not forced, or arranged.

Jack saw that Joseph had taken what he had said as an appeal for understanding between them personally: he had believed that his father was saying he was sick of their bad relations.

Had that been what he was saying? He had imagined he was talking about the political cycle. Jack now understood that if in fact he made enough effort, Joseph would respond, and then . . . He heard himself saying: "Like bloody automatons. Over and over again. Can't you see that it is going to take something like twenty years for you lot to become old rich lefties?"

"Or would if we aren't all dead first," said Joseph, ending the thing as Jack would, and with a calm, almost jolly smile. He left, saying: "The Robinson brothers are likely to get fifteen years if we don't do something."

Jack, as if a button had been pushed, was filled with guilt about the Robinson brothers and almost got up to write a check there and then. But he did not: it had been an entirely automatic reaction.

He spent a few days apparently in the state he had been in for weeks; but he knew himself to have reached the end of some long inner process that had proved too much for him. This interview with his son had been its end, as, very likely, the scene in the attic had been its beginning? Who knew? Who could know! Not Jack. He was worn out, as at the end of a long vigil. He found himself one morning standing in the middle of his livingroom saying over and over again: "I can't stand any more of this. I can't. I won't."

He found the pills and took them with the same miserable determination that he would have had to use to kill something that had to be killed. Almost at once he began to sleep, and the tension eased. He no longer felt as if he was carrying around, embodied in himself, a question as urgent as a wound that needed dressing, but that he had no idea what the language was in which he might find an answer. He ceased to experience the cloying sweetness that caused a mental nausea a hundred times worse than the physical. In a few days he had already stopped seeing his wife and daughters as great dolls who supplied warmth, charm, sympathy, when the buttons of duty or habit were pressed. Above all, he did not have to be on guard against his own abhorrence: his fingers did not explore masks on his face, nor was he always conscious of the statements made by his body and his limbs.

He was thinking that he was probably already known throughout the Left as a renegade; yet, examining the furniture in his mind, he found it not much changed.

It occurred to him, and he went on to consider it in a brisk judicious way, that it was an extraordinary thing that whereas he could have sat for an examination at a moment's notice on the history, the ideas, and the contemporary situation of socialism, communism, and associated movements, with confidence that he would know the answers even to questions on the details of some unimportant sect in some remote country, he was so ignorant of religious history and thought that he could not have answered any questions at all. His condition in relation to religious questions was like that of a person hearing of socialism for the first time and saying: "Oh yes, I've often thought it wasn't fair that some people should have more than others. You agree, do you?"

He decided to go to the British Museum Reading Room.[4] He had written many of his books there. His wife was delighted, knowing that this meant he was over the crisis.

He sent in his card for books on the history of the religions, on comparative religion, and on the relation of religion to anthropology.

For the first few days it seemed that he was still under the spell of his recent experience: he could not keep his attention from wandering from the page, and the men and women all around him bending over books seemed to him insane; this habit of solving all questions by imbibing information through the eyes off the printed page was

4. The British Museum Library is the British equivalent of the Library of Congress.

a form of self-hypnotism. He was seeing them and himself as a species that could not function unless it took in information in this way.

But this soon passed and he was able to apply himself.

As he read, he conscientiously examined what he thought; was this changing at all? No, his distaste for the whole business could be summed up by an old idea of his, which was that if he had been bred, let us say, in Pakistan, that would have been enough for him to kill other people in the name of Mohammed, and if he had been born in India, to kill Moslems without a qualm. That had he been born in Italy, he would have been one brand of Christian, and if he had stuck with his family's faith he would be bound to suspect Roman Catholicism. But above all what he felt was that this was an outdated situation. What was he doing sitting here surrounded by histories and concordances and expositions and exegetics? He would be better occupied doing almost anything else—a hundred years ago, yes, well, that had been different. The struggle for a Victorian inside the Church had meant something; for a man or a woman then to say: "If I had been born an Arab I would be praying five times a day looking at Mecca, but had I been a Tibetan I would have believed in the Dalai Lama"—that kind of statement had needed courage then, and the effort to make it had been worthwhile.

There were, of course, the mystics. But the word was associated for him with the tainted sweetness that had so recently afflicted him, with self-indulgence, and posturing, and exaggerated behavior. He read, however, Simone Weil and Teilhard de Chardin;[5] these were the names he knew.

He sat, carefully checking his responses: he was more in sympathy with Simone Weil, because of her relations with the poor, less with Teilhard de Chardin, who seemed to him not very different from any sort of intellectual: he could have been a useful sort of politician, for instance? It occurred to him that he was in the process of choosing a degree or class of belief, like a pipe from a display of pipes, or a jacket in a shop, that would be on easy terms with the ideas he was already committed to and, above all, would not disturb his associates. He could imagine himself saying to Walter: "Well, yes, it is true that I am religious in a way—I can see the point of Simone Weil, she took poverty into account. She was a socialist of a kind, really."

He bought more books by both Simone Weil and Teilhard de Chardin, and took them home, but did not read them; he had lost interest, and besides an old mechanism had come into force. He realized that sitting in the Reading Room he had been thinking of writing a book describing, but entirely as a tourist, the varieties of religious behavior he had actually witnessed: a festival in Ceylon involving sacred elephants, for instance. The shape of this book was easy to find: he would describe what he had seen. The tone of it, the style—well, there might be a difficulty. There should not of course

5. Simone Weil (1909–43), French mystic and social philosopher who believed that everything in the world can be raised only by grace; Pierre Teilhard de Chardin (1881–1955), French philosopher, paleontologist and Jesuit who believed that man is evolving toward a final spiritual unity.

be the slightest tone of contempt; a light affectionate amusement would be appropriate. He found himself thinking that when the Old Guard read it they would be relieved as to the health of his state of mind.

Abandoning the Reading Room, he found that Carrie was becoming seriously interested in a young man met through her brother. He was one of the best of the new young revolutionaries, brave, forthright, everything a young revolutionary should be. Carrie was in the process of marrying her father? A difficulty was that this young man and Joseph had recently quarreled. They had disagreed so violently over some policy that Joseph had left his particular group, and had formed another. Rosemary thought the real reason for the quarrel was that Joseph resented his sister loving his friend but did not realize it. Jack took his wife to task over this, saying that to discredit socialist action because it had, or might have, psychological springs was one of the oldest of reaction's tricks. But, said Rosemary, every action had a psychological base, didn't it, so why shouldn't one describe what it was? Jack surprised himself by his vehemence in this discussion—it was, in fact, a quarrel. For he believed, with Rosemary, that probably Joseph was reacting emotionally: he had always been jealous of his sisters. Whatever the truth of it was, Carrie was certainly forgetting her "Eastern thing." She was already talking about it as of a youthful and outgrown phase. Rosemary, in telling Jack this, kept glancing apologetically at him; the last thing she wanted to do, she said, was to disparage any experience which he might be going through himself. Or had gone through.

Had gone through.

There was a Conference on the theme of Saving Earth from Man, and he had been afraid he wasn't going to be asked. He was, and Mona rang up to say she would like to go with him. She made some remarks that could be openings to his joining her in a position that combined belief in God with progressive action; he could see that she was willing to lay before him this position, which she had verbalized in detail. He closed that door, hoping it did not sound like a snub. He was again thinking of something called "religion" as an area colored pink or green on a map and in terms of belief in an after-life like a sweetened dummy[6] for adults. In addition to this, he had two sets of ideas, or feelings, in his mind: one, those he had always held, or held since his early maturity; the other, not so much a set of ideas as a feeling of unease, disquiet, guilt, which amounted to a recognition that he had missed an opportunity of some sort, but that the failure had taken place long before his recent experience. Which he now summarized to himself in Walter's words as: It's a shock when your old man dies. His life had been set in one current, long ago; a fresh current, or at least, a different one, had run into it from another source; but, unlike the springs and rivers of myth and fairy tale, it had been muddied and unclear.

He could see that his old friends were particularly delighted to see him at the Conference, ready to take an active part. He was on the

6. Baby's pacifier.

platform, and he spoke several times, rather well. By the time the Conference was over, there was no doubt he was again confirmed as one of the Old Guard, trusted and reliable.

Because of the attention the Conference got, he was offered a good job on television, and he nearly took it. But what he needed was to get out of England for a bit. Again Rosemary mentioned Nigeria. Her case was a good one. He would enjoy it, it was work he would do well, he would be contributing valuably. She would enjoy it too, she added loyally. As of course she would, in many ways. After all, it was only for two years, and when she came back it would be easy for her to pick up what she had dropped. And Family Counselors would still be needed after all! Something that had seemed difficult now seemed easy, not much more than a long trip to Europe. They were making it easy, of course, because of that refusal to look at the consequences of a thing that comes from wanting to leave options open. Spending two years in Africa would change them both, and they did not want to admit that they had become reluctant to change.

On the night after he had formally agreed to go to Nigeria he had the dream again, the worst. If worst was the word?—in this region of himself different laws applied. He was dropping into nothingness, the void: he was fighting his way to a window and there he battered on panes to let in air, and as he hit with his fists and shouted for help the air around him thinned and became exhausted—and he ceased to exist.

He had forgotten how terrible—or how powerful—that dream had been.

He paced his house, wearing the night away. It was too late: he was going to Nigeria because he had not known what else it was he could do.

During that night he could feel his face falling into the lines and folds of his father's face—at the time, that is, when his father had been an elderly, rather than an old man. His father's old man's face had been open and sweet, but before achieving that goodness—like the inn at the end of a road which you have no alternative but to use?—he had had the face of a Roman, heavy-lidded, skeptical, obdurate, facing into the dark: the man whose pride and strength has to come from a conscious ability to suffer, in silence, the journey into negation.

During the days that followed, when the household was all plans and packing and arranging and people running in and out, Jack was thinking that there was only one difference between himself now and himself as he had been before "the bit of a shock." He had once been a man whose sleep had been—nothing, nonexistent, he had slept like a small child. Now, in spite of everything, although he knew that fear could lie in wait there, his sleep had become another country, lying just behind his daytime one. Into that country he went nightly, with an alert, even if ironical interest—the irony was due to his habits of obedience to his past—for a gift had been made to him. Behind the face of the skeptical world was another, which no conscious decision of his could stop him exploring.

1972